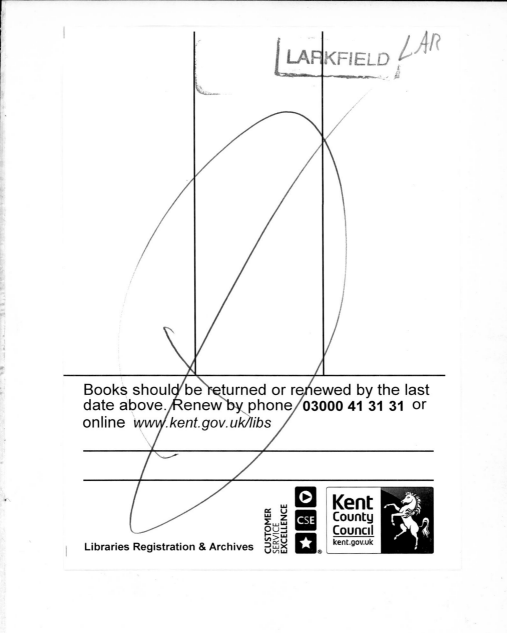

THE EXTINCTION FILES

PANDEMIC

A.G.
RIDDLE

HEAD
of ZEUS

First published in the US in 2017 by Riddle Inc.

First published in the UK in 2017 by Head of Zeus, Ltd

9 7 5 3 1 2 4 6 8

A catalogue record for this book is available from
the British Library.

ISBN (TPBO): 9781788541282

Typeset by Adrian McLaughlin

Printed and bound in Great Britain by
CPI Group (UK) Ltd, Croydon CRO 4YY

Head of Zeus Ltd
First Floor East
5–8 Hardwick Street
London EC1R 4RG

WWW.HEADOFZEUS.COM

This novel is dedicated to a group of heroes we rarely hear about. After hurricanes and other natural disasters, they are among the first to arrive and the last to leave. Around the world, they operate in war-torn regions, though they carry no weapons to protect themselves. Right now, these individuals are putting their lives at risk to protect us from threats that pose a danger to every human, in every nation on Earth.

They live among us; they are our neighbors and our friends and our family members. They are the men and women working in public health in the US and abroad. Researching their exploits was a source of great inspiration while writing this novel. They are the true heroes of a story like *Pandemic*.

A NOTE ABOUT
FACT AND FICTION

Pandemic is a work of both fact and fiction. I have attempted to depict the CDC and WHO responses to a deadly outbreak in Africa as accurately as fiction allows. Several experts in the field contributed to this work. Any errors, however, are mine alone.

Much of the science included in *Pandemic* is real. In particular, research regarding the M13 phage and GP3 protein is 100% factual. Therapies developed from M13 and GP3 are currently in clinical trials, where they show great promise in curing Alzheimer's, Parkinson's, and amyloid disorders.

My website includes a fact vs. fiction section and other bonus content for *Pandemic*.

Thanks for reading.

GERRY
A.G. RIDDLE

PROLOGUE

THE US COAST GUARD cutter had been searching the Arctic Ocean for three months, though none of the crew knew exactly what they were searching for. At their last port, the icebreaker had taken on a team of thirty scientists and a dozen crates filled with some very strange instruments. The crew was told nothing about their guests or the mysterious equipment. Day after day, ice broke and crumbled at the *Healy*'s bow, and the men and women aboard carried on with their duties, operating in radio silence as instructed.

The secrecy and monotony of the crew's daily routine inspired an endless flow of rumors. They speculated while they took their meals and in their off-hours, while playing chess, cards, and video games. Their best guess was that they were searching for a submarine or sunken military ship—likely of American or perhaps Russian origin—or perhaps a cargo vessel carrying dangerous material. A few of the crew believed they were searching for nuclear warheads, fired decades ago during the Cold War but aborted over the Arctic Ocean.

At four a.m. Anchorage time, the phone on the wall by the captain's bunk buzzed. The man grabbed it without turning on the light.

"Miller."

"Stop the ship, Captain. We've found it." The mission's chief scientist, Dr. Hans Emmerich, hung up without another word.

After calling the bridge and ordering a full stop, Captain Walter Miller dressed quickly and made his way to the ship's main research bay. Like the rest of the crew, he was curious about what *it* was. But most of all he wanted to know if what lay beneath them was a threat to the 117 men and women serving aboard his ship.

Miller nodded at the guards by the hatch and ducked inside. A dozen scientists were arguing by a bank of screens. He marched toward them, squinting at the images that showed the rocky sea floor bathed in a green hue. In the middle of the images lay a dark, oblong object.

"Captain." Dr. Emmerich's voice was like a clothesline, stopping Miller in his tracks. "I'm afraid we're exceptionally busy at the moment." Emmerich stepped in front of the Coast Guard officer and tried to corral him away from the screens, but Miller stood his ground.

"I came to see if we can provide any assistance," Miller said.

"We're quite capable, Captain. Please maintain your current position—and radio silence."

Miller motioned toward the screens. "So you've been looking for a sub."

Emmerich said nothing.

"Is it American? Russian?"

"We believe it's a vessel of... multi-national sponsorship."

Miller squinted, wondering what that meant.

"Now, Captain, you really must excuse me. We have a lot of work to do. We'll be launching the submersible soon."

Miller nodded. "Understood. Good luck, Doctor."

When the captain was gone, Emmerich instructed two of the younger researchers to stand by the door. "Nobody else gets in."

At his computer terminal, Emmerich sent an encrypted email.

> Have located wreck believed to be RSV *Beagle*.
> Commencing search. Coordinates and initial
> imagery attached.

Thirty minutes later, Dr. Emmerich and three other scientists sat in the submersible, making their way to the ocean floor.

☣

On the other side of the world, the cargo ship *Kentaro Maru* was moving through the Indian Ocean just off the coast of Somalia.

In a conference room adjacent to the ship's bridge, two men had been arguing all afternoon, their shouts causing the crew to wince periodically.

A bridge officer knocked on the door and waited nervously. They ignored him and continued yelling at each other.

He knocked again.

Silence.

He swallowed hard and pushed the door open.

A tall man named Conner McClain stood behind the long conference table. His angry expression made his badly scarred face look even more hideous. He spoke quickly, with an Australian accent, his volume just below a yell.

"For your sake, this better blow my mind, Lieutenant."

"Sir, the Americans have found the *Beagle*."

"How?"

"They're using a new seafloor mapping tech—"

"Are they on a plane, submarine, or ship?"

"A ship. The *Healy*. It's a US Coast Guard icebreaker. They're launching a submersible though."

"Do they know what's on the *Beagle* yet?"

"We don't know. We don't think so."

"Good. Sink the icebreaker."

The other man in the conference room spoke for the first time. "Don't do this, Conner."

"We have no choice."

"We do. This is an opportunity."

"Opportunity for what?"

"To show the world what's aboard the *Beagle*."

Conner turned to the young officer. "You have your orders, Lieutenant. Dismissed."

When the door closed, Conner spoke quietly to the other man in the conference room. "We're on the verge of the most important event in human history. We're not going to let the barbarian hordes *vote* on it."

☣

Dr. Hans Emmerich held his breath when the submarine's outer hatch opened.

Behind him, Dr. Peter Finch studied a laptop screen. "Clear. Seal's good."

"Radiation?" Emmerich asked.

"Negligible."

Emmerich and the three scientists descended the ladder into the vessel. The LED lights from their suit helmets cast white beams through the dark tomb as they moved slowly through the cramped corridors, careful not to let anything catch on their suits. A tear could be deadly.

When they reached the vessel's bridge, Emmerich aimed his helmet lamps at a bronze plaque on the wall. "Prometheus, Alpha One. Are you receiving this?"

A scientist on the *Healy* responded instantly. "Copy, Alpha One, receiving audio and video."

The plaque on the wall read:

RSV BEAGLE

HONG KONG

1 MAY 1965

ORDO AB CHAO

Emmerich exited the bridge and began searching for the captain's stateroom. If he was lucky, the logs would be stored there, and they would finally reveal where the *Beagle* had been and what the crew had discovered. If he was right, the vessel held evidence of a scientific revelation that would forever change the course of human history.

Dr. Finch's voice crackled in Emmerich's earpiece. "Alpha One, Alpha Two, do you copy?"

"Copy, Alpha Two."

"We've reached the lab level. Should we enter?"

"Affirmative, Alpha Two. Proceed with caution."

In the dark corridor, Emmerich waited.

"Alpha One, we're seeing two exam rooms with metal tables, maybe ten feet long. Rooms are sealed for bio-containment. The rest of the area is filled with long rows of storage bins, like large deposit boxes in a vault. Should we open one?"

"Negative, Alpha Two," Emmerich said quickly. "Are they numbered?"

"Affirmative," Finch said.

"We'll have to find the inventory."

"Hold on. There's a metal disc on each bin." A pause. "The disc covers a viewport like a peephole. There are bones in this one. Human. No, wait. They can't be."

Another researcher spoke. "There's a mammal in this one, feline. Species unknown. It must have been frozen alive. It's still in ice."

Emmerich heard the clicks of metal discs sliding back and forth like the shutter of a camera.

"Alpha One, you should get down here. It's like Noah's Ark." Emmerich began shuffling through the cramped corridor, still being careful not to let anything puncture his suit. "Prometheus, Alpha One. Are you recording video and audio from Alpha Two, Three, and Four?"

When no response came, Emmerich stopped in his tracks. "Prometheus, this is Alpha One, do you copy?"

He called a second time, and a third. Then he heard a loud boom, and the floor beneath him shook.

"Prometheus?"

DAY 1

320 infected
0 dead

CHAPTER 1

DR. ELIM KIBET sat in his white-walled office, watching the sun rise over the rocky landscape of northeastern Kenya. The Mandera Referral Hospital was a run-down facility in one of the most impoverished corners of the world, and it had recently become his responsibility. Some in his shoes would consider that a burden. He considered it an honor.

Beyond his closed door, screams pierced the silence. Footsteps pounded the hallway and a nurse yelled, "Doctor, come quick!"

There was no question which doctor they were calling for: Elim Kibet was the only physician left. The others had departed after the terror attacks. Many of the nurses had followed. The government had denied requests for armed guards at the rural hospital. They had also defaulted on an agreement to pay the health workers fairly and on time. That had sent another wave of workers fleeing the crumbling facility. The hospital operated with a skeleton staff now. The remaining members either had no place to go or were too dedicated to leave. Or, in the case of Elim Kibet, both.

He donned his white coat and hurried down the hall, toward the cries for help.

Mandera was one of Kenya's poorest counties. Per capita income was 267 US dollars—less than 75 cents per day. The dusty, dirt road town lay at the crossroads of three nations: Kenya, Somalia, and Ethiopia. People in Mandera lived off the land, often barely scraping by, and found joy where they could. It was a place of breathtaking beauty and unspeakable brutality.

The world's deadliest diseases were endemic to the region, but they were far from the most dangerous elements in the area. Al-Shabaab, an Islamic terror group and affiliate of al-Qaeda, attacked the villages and government facilities frequently. Their ruthlessness was staggering. Less than a year ago, al-Shabaab militants stopped a bus outside Mandera and ordered all the Muslim passengers to get off. They refused and instead crowded around the Christian passengers. Al-Shabaab dragged everyone from the bus—both Muslim and Christian—lined them up, and shot them. Thirty-seven people died.

As Elim raced down the dingy hall, that was his first thought—another al-Shabaab attack.

To his surprise, he found two young white men in the exam room, their dark brown hair long and shaggy, their thick beards dripping with sweat. One man stood by the door, holding a video camera. The other lay on the exam table, rolling side to side, his eyes closed. The stench of diarrhea and vomit was overwhelming.

Two nurses were leaning over the man, performing an intake exam. One drew a thermometer from the man's mouth and turned to Elim. "A hundred and four, Doctor."

The young man with the video camera let it fall to the side and caught Elim by the upper arm. "You've gotta help him!"

Elim pulled free and extended his arm to push the man into the corner, away from the exam table.

"I will. Back away, please."

Elim's initial diagnosis was malaria. The disease was rampant in tropical and subtropical regions, especially impoverished areas like Mandera, which was only about two hundred and fifty miles from the equator. Worldwide, over two hundred million people were infected with malaria each year, and nearly half a million died from the disease. Ninety percent of those deaths took place in Africa, where a child died of malaria every minute. Westerners visiting Kenya frequently came down with malaria as well. It was treatable, and that gave Elim some hope as he snapped on a pair of rubber gloves and began his exam.

The patient was barely conscious. His head tossed from side to side as he mumbled. When Elim pulled the man's shirt up, his diagnosis changed immediately. A rash ran from his abdomen to his chest.

Typhoid fit these symptoms better. It was also endemic to the region, and was caused by bacteria—*Salmonella typhi*—that bred in open pools of water. Typhoid was manageable. Curable. Fluoroquinolones—one of the few antibiotics they had on hand—would treat it.

Elim's hope vanished when the man's eyelids parted. Yellow, jaundiced eyes stared up at him. Blood pooled at the corner of his left eye, then trickled down his face.

"Get back," Elim said, spreading his arms out, sweeping the nurses with him.

"What's the matter with him?" the man's friend asked.

"Clear the room," Elim said.

The nurses evacuated immediately, but the young man stood his ground. "I'm not leaving him."

"You must."

"I won't."

Elim studied the young man. There was something off here. The camera, his demeanor, showing up here of all places.

"What's your name?"

"Lucas. Turner."

"Why are you here, Mr. Turner?"

"He's sick—"

"No, why are you in Kenya? What are you doing here in Mandera?"

"Starting a business."

"What?"

"CityForge. It's like crowdfunding for startup city governments," Lucas said, sounding rehearsed.

Elim shook his head. *What's he talking about?*

"You know what's wrong with him?" Lucas asked.

"Perhaps. You need to leave the room."

"No way."

"Listen to me. Your friend has a very dangerous disease. It is likely contagious. You are at great risk."

"What's he got?"

"I don't—"

"You have to have an idea," Lucas insisted.

Elim glanced around, confirming that the nurses had left the room. "Marburg," he said quietly. When Lucas showed no reaction, he added, "Possibly Ebola."

Color drained from Lucas's sweaty face, making his dark, shaggy hair contrast even more with his pale skin. He looked at his friend on the table, then trudged out of the room.

Elim walked over to the exam table and said, "I'm going to call for help. I will do everything I can for you, sir."

He removed his gloves, tossed them in the waste bin, and drew out his smartphone. He took a photo of the rash, asked the man to open his eyes, and snapped another photo, then sent the images to the Kenyan Ministry of Health.

At the door, he instructed the nurse waiting outside to keep anyone but him from entering the room. He returned a few moments later wearing a protective gown, facemask, boot covers, and goggles. He carried the only treatment he could provide his patient.

On a narrow wooden table in the dingy room, he lined up three plastic buckets. Each bucket had a piece of brown tape with a single word written on it: vomit, feces, urine. In the man's condition, Elim wasn't optimistic that he could segregate his exiting bodily fluids, but that was the standard protocol for Ebola and similar diseases, and Elim intended to follow it. Despite having few supplies and little staff, the African doctor was determined to provide the best care he possibly could. It was his duty.

He handed the man a small paper cup filled with pills—antibiotics, to treat any secondary infections—and a bottle labeled ORS: oral rehydration salts.

"Swallow these, please."

With a shaky hand, the man downed the pills and took a small sip from the bottle. He winced at the taste of the mixture.

"I know. It tastes bad, but you must. You must stay hydrated."

On average, Ebola killed half of those it infected. Even when the body's immune system defeated the disease itself, the diarrhea during its acute phase was often fatal due to dehydration.

"I will return soon," Elim said.

Outside the room, Elim carefully removed his PPE—personal protective equipment. He knew they didn't have enough PPE in the hospital to protect all the staff who would need to care for the man. They desperately needed more equipment—and help. In the meantime, Elim would have to isolate the sick man and quarantine Lucas long enough to determine if he was infected too.

The middle-aged physician was weighing his next move when the nurse called out once again.

He raced to the hospital's triage room, where he found yet another westerner, a tall white man leaning against the door frame. He was older than the other two, but like the other sick man he was pale, sweaty, and smelled of diarrhea and vomit.

"Is he with the others?" Elim asked.

"I don't know," the nurse answered. "They sent him from the airport."

"Sir, please lift your shirt up."

He lifted his shirt up revealing a wide rash.

Elim took a photo to email to the Ministry of Health. To the triage nurse he said, "Escort him to Exam Two. Do not touch him. Keep your distance. Leave the room. No one enters."

He dialed the Kenya Ministry of Health's Emergency Operation Center. When the line connected, he said, "I'm calling from Mandera Referral Hospital. We have a problem here."

CHAPTER 2

HE HAD BEEN beaten up. That was his first thought upon waking. His ribs radiated pain. His legs ached. He reached up and touched the tender knot on the left side of his head and quickly drew his hand away.

He was sprawled out on a king size bed. The morning sun shone through sheer curtains, blinding him and sparking even more pain in his throbbing head.

He shut his eyes and turned away.

When he slowly opened his eyes again, he saw the nightstand held a silver lamp and a small writing pad. The letterhead read: *Concord Hotel, Berlin.*

He tried to remember checking in, but he couldn't. And more: he didn't know what day it was. Or why he was in Berlin. Or his own name, for that matter. *What happened to me?*

He rose and hobbled to the bathroom. His ribs ached with every step. He separated the blue button-up shirt tangled with his khaki pants. A bruise covered his left side; it was dark blue and black in the center, rimmed with red edges.

He examined himself in the mirror. His face was fit and trim, with high cheekbones. Thick blond hair fell to his eyebrows, curling slightly at the ends. He had a faint tan, but from his complexion and smooth hands, it was clear that he worked inside in a white-collar profession. He searched for the knot on his head. It was large, but the blow hadn't broken the skin.

He reached in his pockets and found only a thin piece of paper the size of a business card. He drew it out and examined it: a 20% off coupon from Quality Dry Cleaning for Less.

On the back, he—or perhaps someone else—had scribbled three lines of text.

The first:

ZDUQ KHU

The second:

7379623618

And the third line was simply three diamonds inside parentheses.

(◇◇◇)

A code of some sort.

His head hurt too much for codes.

He laid the card on the vanity, and walked through the bedroom into the living area where he stopped cold. A man lay on the floor. His face was pale and ashy. He wasn't breathing.

A single white page lay near the dead man in front of the door to the suite. It was a bill for the stay, which apparently had begun a week before and included several deliveries from room service.

Most importantly, the guest name was printed at the top. *Desmond Hughes.* He knew at once that this was his name, but seeing it brought no flood of memories, only recognition.

The man on the floor was tall and slender. His hair was gray, thinning, and closely cropped. He wore a dark suit, a white dress shirt, and no tie. A ring of bruises circled his muscular neck.

Desmond knelt next to the body and began to reach into the man's pants pockets—then stopped, his instincts kicking in. He grabbed the small wastebasket under the desk, pulled out the plastic liner, and covered his hand, ensuring he didn't leave any fingerprints or DNA.

The man's pocket held a wallet and a hard plastic employee ID card for Rapture Therapeutics. There was no job title listed on the ID card, just a name: Gunter Thorne. The picture matched the pale face lying sideways on the thin carpet. His German ID card and credit cards all showed the same name.

Desmond slid the items back into the man's pocket and gently pulled the lapel of his suit back, revealing a black handgun in a holster.

Desmond sat back on his haunches, which made his legs ache. He stood, trying to stretch them, and scanned the room. It was pristine. Cleaned recently, no doubt. He searched it, but it was utterly devoid of any clues. There was no luggage, nothing hanging in the closet. The small safe was open and empty. There weren't even any toiletries.

He checked the bill again. No calls.

What did it all mean? It was as if he had only come here to eat. Or to hide. Did he live in Berlin? If not for Gunter Thorne's dead body in the living room, Desmond would have already called the front desk to find a reputable urgent care facility. He couldn't now, not without knowing more. And he had only one clue.

He walked back to the bathroom and picked up the coupon with the sequence of letters and numbers on the back. As he stared at it, he realized something about the parentheses. In financial statements, they indicated a negative number—a loss. A deduction from a running balance.

How did he know that? Was he in finance?

He sat on the bed and took the pad from the side table. What was the key here? Deduction. A loss. Negative.

Three diamonds inside the parentheses. So negative three— subtract three. Yes—the bottom line had to be the key, the first two lines the message. The name of the code popped into his mind: a simple substitution cipher. And more, it was a Caesar shift cipher, used famously by Julius Caesar for his secret correspondence.

Desmond took each of the letters and subtracted three—so Z became W, and D became A. He did the same with the numbers. That yielded:

WARN HER
4046390385

He placed dashes after the third and sixth numbers, producing:

404-639-0385

Warn her. And a phone number. Warn her of what? Through the opening between the bedroom and living room, he eyed Gunter Thorne's dead body. Maybe Rapture Therapeutics or whomever had sent Gunter to the hotel room was after "her" as well. Or maybe it was all unrelated. Or *maybe*, Desmond had set all of this up to trap Gunter here. She could be an accomplice of his somehow. Either way, she might have answers.

Desmond picked up the phone and dialed.

On the third ring, a woman answered, sounding groggy. "Shaw."

"Hi. It's… Desmond. Hughes."

She sounded more alert when she spoke again. "Hi."

"Hi." He had no clue where to begin. "Are you… expecting my call?"

She sighed into the receiver. He heard her rustling, sitting up perhaps. "What is this, Desmond?"

"Do we know each other?"

Her tone was sad now. "This isn't funny, Des."

"Look, I just, can you tell me who you are? Where you work? Please." A pause.

"Peyton Shaw."

When he said nothing, she added, "I work at the CDC now. I'm an epidemiologist."

A knock at the suite's door rang out—three raps, firm—from the living room.

Desmond waited, thinking. The clock on the table read 7:34 a.m. Too early for maid service.

"Hello?" Peyton said.

Three more knocks, louder this time, followed by a man's deep voice: "*Polizei.*"

"Listen to me, Peyton. I think you're in danger."

"What? What're you talking about?"

Three more knocks, insistent, loud enough to wake anyone in the neighboring room. "*Polizei! Herr Hughes, bitte öffnen Sie die Tür.*"

"I'll call you back."

He hung up and sprinted to the door, ignoring the pain in his legs. Through the peephole he saw two uniformed police officers, along with a man in a dark suit—likely hotel security.

The hotel employee was moving a key card toward the door lock.

CHAPTER 3

IN ATLANTA, DR. PEYTON SHAW sat up in bed with the cord-less phone to her ear. "Desmond?"

The line was dead.

She hung up and waited, expecting Desmond to call back.

It was 1:34 a.m. on Saturday night, and she had been home alone, asleep for over three hours. She was wide awake now, though. And unnerved.

She felt the urge to take a look around the two-bedroom condo and make sure there wasn't someone else inside. She had lived alone since moving to Atlanta in her twenties, and with a few exceptions, she had always felt safe.

She grabbed her cell phone, rose from the platform bed, and paced cautiously out of her bedroom. Every few seconds her bare feet squeaked against the cold hardwood floors. The front door was shut and the deadbolt locked. The door to the second bedroom, which she used as a home office, was also closed, hiding it from the open-concept living room and kitchen. She'd found that pictures of pandemics around the world were a real mood-killer for company and gentleman callers, so she always kept her office door shut.

At the floor-to-ceiling windows in the living room, she peered down at Peachtree Street, which was mostly deserted at this hour. She felt a chill through the glass; it was colder than usual outside for late November.

She waited, still hoping the home phone would ring. She had

considered canceling the landline a dozen times, but a few people still had the number, and for reasons she couldn't fathom, the cable and internet bill actually came out cheaper with the home phone.

She ran a hand through her shoulder-length brown hair. Her mother was half-Chinese, half-German, and they shared the same porcelain skin. She wasn't quite sure what she'd gotten from her father, who was English, and had died when she was six.

She plopped down on the gray fabric couch and tucked her freezing feet under her bottom, trying to warm them. On her cell phone, she did something she hadn't done in a long time—something she had sworn she would stop doing: she opened Google and searched for Desmond Hughes. Hearing Desmond's voice had rattled her. His last words—*You're in danger*—still lingered in her mind.

The first hit was the website for Icarus Capital, a venture capital firm. Desmond was listed first on the *Our People* page as the founder and managing partner. His smile was confident, maybe even bordering on arrogant.

She clicked the *Investments* page and read the introduction:

> It is said that there's no time like the present. At Icarus Capital, we disagree. We think there's no time like the future. That's what we invest in: the future. More specifically, we invest in people who are inventing the future. Here's a sampling of those people and their companies. If you're inventing the future, get in touch. We want to help.

Peyton scanned the companies listed: Rapture Therapeutics, Phaethon Genetics, Rendition Games, Cedar Creek Entertainment, Rook Quantum Sciences, Extinction Parks, Labyrinth Reality, CityForge, and Charter Antarctica.

She didn't recognize any of them.

She clicked the next link in the web search results, which was a video of Desmond at a conference. An interviewer off-camera asked a question: "Icarus has invested in a really eclectic mix of startups, everything from pharma, biotech, virtual reality, grid computing, and even extreme vacationing in places like Antarctica. What's the thread that ties it all together? For the entrepreneurs out there in the audience, can you tell them what you're looking for in a startup?"

Sitting in a club chair on stage, Desmond held up the mic and spoke calmly, but with infectious enthusiasm. A slight grin curled at the edges of his mouth. His eyes were focused, unblinking.

"Well, as you say, it's hard to categorize exactly what kind of company Icarus is looking for. What I can tell you is that each of our investments is part of a larger, coordinated experiment."

The interviewer raised his eyebrows. "Interesting. What kind of experiment?"

"It's a scientific experiment—one meant to answer a very important question."

"Which is?"

"Why do we exist?"

The moderator feigned shock and turned to the crowd. "Is that all?"

The audience laughed, and Desmond joined in.

Desmond leaned forward in the club chair, glanced at the moderator, then focused on the camera. "Okay, I think it's fair to say that many of you out there—in the audience and watching this video—would say the answer to that question is simple: we exist because the physical properties of this planet support the emergence of biological life, that we are biologically inevitable because of Earth's environment. That's true, but the real question is *why*? *Why* does the universe support biological life? To what end? What is humanity's destiny? I believe there is an answer."

"Wow. You almost sound like a person of faith."

"I am. I have absolute faith. I believe there's a great process at work all around us, a larger picture of which we have only seen a very small sliver."

"And you think the technology Icarus is funding will deliver this ultimate truth?"

"I'd bet my life on it."

☣

Peyton had just fallen asleep again when a noise from the bedside table woke her. She froze, listening, but it stopped suddenly.

It came again: something brushing up against the table.

A vibration.

A glow emanated from beyond the lamp, throwing light up at the ceiling.

She exhaled, grabbed her buzzing cell phone, and checked the time—3:35 a.m. She didn't recognize the number, but she knew the country code. 41. Switzerland.

She answered immediately.

"Peyton, I'm sorry to wake you," Dr. Jonas Becker said.

The German epidemiologist led a rapid outbreak response team for the World Health Organization. Peyton held a similar job at the Centers for Disease Control. The two epidemiologists had worked together a dozen times in hot zones around the world, and over that time, they had developed a special bond.

"It's okay," she said. "What's happened?"

"I just emailed you."

"Hang on."

Peyton's bare feet again slapped against the hardwood floor as she raced to the second bedroom. She sat at the cheap Ikea desk, woke her laptop, and activated her secure VPN software, opening a remote link to her terminal at the CDC.

She studied the pictures in the email, taking in every detail.

"I see it," she said.

"The Kenyan Ministry of Health sent us this a few hours ago. A doctor at a regional hospital in Mandera took the photos."

Peyton had never heard of Mandera. She opened Google Maps and studied the location. It sat on the far northeast of Kenya, right at the borders with Somalia and Ethiopia – the worst possible place for an outbreak.

"It's obviously some kind of hemorrhagic fever," Jonas said. "Rift Valley is endemic to the region. So are Ebola and Marburg. After the Ebola outbreak in West Africa, everybody here is taking this very seriously. I've already had a call from the director-general's office."

"Are these the only known cases?"

"At the moment."

"What do we know about them?" Peyton asked.

"Not much. All three men claim to be westerners visiting the country."

That got Peyton's attention.

"The two younger males are Americans. They're recent college graduates from UNC-Chapel Hill. They went to Kenya as part of some kind of startup. The other man is from London. He works for a British company installing radar systems."

"What kind of radar systems?"

"For air traffic control. He was working at the Mandera airport when he became ill."

"They have an airport?"

"Not much of one. It was a dirt airstrip until a few months ago. The government has been upgrading it: paved runway, better equipment. It opened last week."

Peyton massaged her temple. A functioning airport in a hot zone was a nightmare scenario.

"We're inquiring about the airport—traffic, who was at the opening ceremony, other foreigners who might have worked on the project. We've also contacted Public Health England, and they're already working on it. It's eight-forty in the morning there, so they'll be in touch with the British man's family and co-workers soon. When we know how long he's been in Kenya, we'll make a call on quarantining them."

Peyton scanned the email's text, noting the names of the two younger men. "We'll start tracing contacts for the Americans, see if we can build a timeline of where they've been, how long they've been in the country. What else can we do?"

"That's about it for now. The Kenyans haven't asked yet, but if things go the way they did in West Africa, it's safe to assume they're going to need a lot of help."

Help meant money and supplies. During the Ebola outbreak

in West Africa, the CDC had deployed hundreds of people and supplied equipment including PPE, thousands of body bags, and countless field test kits.

"I'll talk to Elliott," Peyton said. "We'll loop in State and USAID."

"There's something else. We've just had our security briefing here. Mandera County is a very dangerous place. There's a terrorist group in the region called al-Shabaab. They're as brutal as ISIS, not fans of Americans, and when they hear you're in the region, it could get even more dangerous. We'll be in Nairobi late tonight, but I was thinking we would wait for your team. We can link up with a Kenyan military escort and head north together."

"It'll probably be Saturday before we get there."

"That's okay, we'll wait. There's a lot we can do in Nairobi."

"Great. Thank you, Jonas."

"Safe travels."

Peyton placed the phone on the desk, stood, and studied the world map that covered the wall. Colored pushpins dotted every continent. Each pin corresponded to an outbreak, except for one. In eastern Uganda, along the border with Kenya, deep inside Mount Elgon National Park, hung a silver lapel pin. It featured a rod with a serpent wrapped around it—the traditional symbol of medicine known as the Rod of Asclepius, most frequently seen inside the six-pointed Star of Life on ambulances. The pin had belonged to Peyton's brother, Andrew. It was Andrew who had inspired her to pursue a career in epidemiology, and she always took his pin with her when she went into the field. It was all she had left of him.

She took the silver keepsake off the map, placed it in her pocket, and pushed a red pin into the map where Kenya, Ethiopia, and Somalia met, marking it as an outbreak of a viral hemorrhagic fever.

She always kept two duffel bags packed: a first world bag and a third world bag. She grabbed the third world bag and added the appropriate AC adapters for Kenya.

As soon as things slowed down, she'd have to call her mother and sister to let them know she was deploying. Thanksgiving was in four days, and Peyton had a feeling she was going to miss it.

She hated to admit it, but in a way Peyton was relieved. Her sister, Madison, was Peyton's only remaining sibling. The death of their brother had brought them closer, but recently every conversation with Madison had ended with her sister asking Peyton why she wasn't dating and insisting that her chance for a family was rapidly slipping away. At thirty-eight, Peyton had to concede the point, but she wasn't entirely sure she *wanted* a family. In fact, she wasn't at all sure what she wanted from her life outside of work. Her work had become her life, and she believed what she was doing was important. She liked getting the calls in the middle of the night. The mystery every outbreak brought, knowing her hard work saved lives, that every second mattered.

And as of right now, the clock was ticking.

☣

On the street below, a man sitting in a car watched Peyton pull out of the underground parking deck.

He spoke into the open comm line as he cranked the car. "Subject is on the move. No visitors. No text messages. Only one phone call—from her contact at the WHO."

CHAPTER 4

DESMOND STARED THROUGH the peephole, watching the security guard bring the key card toward the door lock. Two uniformed Berlin police officers stood beside him, hands on their hips.

Desmond flipped the privacy latch, preventing the door from opening. "Just a minute, please," he said in English, trying his best to sound annoyed. "I'm not dressed."

"Please hurry, Mr. Hughes," the security guard said. Desmond studied the dead man lying on the floor. His mind rifled through options.

Option one: go out the window. He walked to the tall glass and examined it. He was at least ten stories up, and there was no fire escape or any other means to get to the ground in one, non-splattered piece. Besides, it looked like the window didn't open.

Option two: make a run for it. He gave that zero chance of success. He was in no shape to push past three men, much less beat them in a foot race.

That left option three: hiding the body and seeing it through.

But where?

The living room was furnished with a desk and office chair, a couch, a side chair, and an entertainment center. A heating unit sat under the tall windows and floor-to-ceiling drapes. A wide opening with double pocket doors led to the bedroom, which held a king size bed with two nightstands, another window with a heating unit under it, and a closet. The narrow bathroom opened only from the bedroom.

Quickly, Desmond made his decision.

Lifting the dead man sent pain through his body. His ribs radiated sharp spikes that overwhelmed him, nearly gagging him at one point. The man was tall, about Desmond's height at nearly six feet, but lean. He was likely only 150 pounds, but he felt more like 300. Rigor mortis had set in. Gunter Thorne had been dead for hours.

As he dragged the body, Desmond wondered how he knew how long it took rigor mortis to set in. But what concerned him the most was that he had never really considered just opening the door, letting the police in, and explaining his situation. It was as if somewhere in the recesses of his mind, he knew he was someone who needed to avoid the police—that he had something to hide. That if all the facts came to light, it wouldn't be good for him. He needed his freedom right now. He needed to find out what had happened to him.

He was sweaty and panting when they knocked again. He dried his face, raced to the door, and cracked it, peering out suspiciously.

"Yes?"

The security guard spoke. "May we come in, Mr. Hughes?"

Saying no would arouse suspicion, and Desmond couldn't keep them out. Without a word, he swung the door wider.

The three men strode in, their eyes scanning the room, hands near their waists. One of the officers wandered into the bedroom, nearing the closet and the bathroom. The doors to both were closed.

"What's this about?" Desmond asked.

"We had a call about a disturbance," the police officer in the living room said, without making eye contact. He glanced behind the couch, then over at the entertainment center. He seemed to be in charge.

Through the opening to the bedroom, Desmond saw the other officer eyeing the closed wardrobe doors. He reached out, opened them, then froze. His eyes moved from the floor to the ceiling. He turned to look at Desmond.

"No luggage?"

"I sent it down already," he said quickly, trying to seem as if they were wasting his time. He needed to turn the tide, go on the offensive to get them out of the room. "What sort of disturbance? Are you sure you have the right room?"

The officer in the living room seemed to have finished his search. He turned his attention to Desmond.

"Are you in town for business or pleasure, Mr. Hughes?"

"Bit of both."

"What sort of work do you do?"

"Technology," he said dismissively. "Listen, am I in danger here? Should I call the American embassy?" He let his voice rise with each line, sounding more frantic. "Can you at least tell me what's going on?"

The policeman pressed on. "How long are you in town for, Mr. Hughes?"

"A week. What does it matter?"

The police officer was unshaken. It wasn't working.

Out of the corner of his eye, he saw the other officer approaching the bathroom door, one hand on his gun, the other reaching for the doorknob.

Desmond changed tacks. He focused on the security guard and spoke rapidly. "You know this is going in my online review."

The guard's eyes grew wide.

"Yeah, it is," Desmond pressed on. "I think an apt title would be: Stay here for Gestapo-style police interrogation and crappy wifi."

The guard looked at the officer. "Are you finished?"

Desmond heard the bathroom door creak open. A second later the lights flipped on. The police officer looked back at his partner and the security guard. Standing his ground, his hand still on his sidearm, he shook his head quickly.

"Yes. We are done here," the other officer said. "Very sorry to have disturbed you, Mr. Hughes. Please enjoy your stay in Berlin."

The three men gathered at the door. The security guard had just gripped the handle when a sound erupted in the room: skin sliding across glass. The squealing noise ceased, and all three men paused, then turned back to face Desmond. Behind him, gravity had taken over, pulling Gunter Thorne's dead body down toward the floor. Desmond had propped the dead man against the window in the corner and covered him with the drapes—but he was free now. His face rubbed across the glass a second more before his body hit the heating unit and tumbled to the floor with a thud.

Desmond didn't hesitate. He lunged forward, covering the distance to the three men in less than a second. He swung his right hand with all the force he could muster. It collided with the rightmost police officer's face, on the cheekbone below his left eye. The man's head flew back and hit the metal door casing. He was knocked out instantly.

Desmond rolled and pressed his body into the security guard, who was standing between the two officers, keeping the man from extending his arms. The remaining police officer drew his gun and was raising it, but Desmond quickly completed a 180-degree spin and rammed his elbow into the officer's forehead. The man slammed back against the wooden door, then tumbled forward, unconscious, his gun flying. Desmond leapt to it, picked it up, and pointed it at the security guard.

"Hands where I can see them. Step away from the door." The guard's hands trembled as he raised them.

"I don't want to hurt you, but if you yell out, I will. Do you understand?"

The man nodded.

"Why were they here?"

"It is as they said—a call."

"Who called them?"

He shook his head. "I do not know—"

"Who?"

"They said it was an anonymous tip."

"Are there more downstairs?"

"I don't—"

"Don't lie to me!" Desmond said, raising the weapon.

The man closed his eyes. "Two cars arrived. I don't know if they stayed or not."

"Turn around."

The man didn't move. "Do it."

Slowly, the security guard turned, his hands shaking violently now. Desmond drew the butt of the gun back and clocked the man on the head, sending him to the floor.

He dragged the guard's body back from the door, then ejected the gun's magazine and verified that there was no bullet in the chamber and the safety was on. He pulled his shirttail out and tucked the gun into his waistband, then collected the spare magazines from both police officers. He took the younger officer's police ID and the radio from the security guard. He tucked the clear earpiece in and listened to the chatter for a moment. It was sparse and in German, but he understood it for the most part.

He had to decide: stairs or elevator. Front door or back.

Each route had pros and cons. Racing down the stairway would only raise the suspicion of anyone monitoring the security cameras, as would going out the back. So: elevator, front door.

He collected all the cash the three men carried—312 euros in total. He needed the money to get away, and as he was already on the hook for resisting arrest, assaulting a police officer, and possibly murder, he figured robbery wouldn't complicate his situation that much.

In the hall, he marched casually to the elevator and punched the button. It opened after a few seconds, revealing a white-haired woman who didn't acknowledge him.

There was no chatter on the security channel as he rode down. When the door opened to the lobby, Desmond stood aside, allowing the woman to exit first.

On the radio, a voice in German asked, "Gerhardt, are you still in 1207?"

Desmond fell in behind the woman. "Gerhardt, come in."

By the revolving glass door, two uniformed police officers stood chatting and smiling. They were twenty feet away. When they saw Desmond, they fell silent and stared at him.

CHAPTER 5

PEYTON ARRIVED AT CDC headquarters shortly before four a.m. The campus, though typically associated with Atlanta, was actually located just outside the city limits to the northeast, in the affluent Druid Hills community in unincorporated DeKalb County. The CDC's precursor organization had been founded in Atlanta for one simple reason: to combat malaria. At the time, in July 1946, the disease was America's greatest public health concern, especially in the hot, humid southeast. Being centrally positioned in America's malaria hotbed had been a significant advantage.

When Peyton first began working at the CDC, getting into the building had been as easy as swiping her card. Now the process was much more stringent and included an x-ray and pat-down. She knew security was important, but she was still anxious to get in and get started. Every second mattered.

Once security checked her in, she made her way directly to the CDC's Emergency Operations Center—the organization's command center for outbreak responses. The EOC's main room looked like mission control for a NASA launch, with rows of connected desks filling the floor, all with flat-screen monitors. A wall-to-wall screen showed a map of the world and tallied statistics related to current operations. The EOC could seat 230 people for eight-hour shifts, and soon the center would be buzzing with activity. Even at this early hour, more than a dozen EOC staff members sat at their desks, fielding phone calls and typing away.

Peyton said hello to the staffers she knew and asked if there were any updates. The EOC's large conference room was dark, but a sign on the door announced an all-hands meeting for the Mandera Outbreak at eight a.m.

A color-coded marker on the wall indicated the CDC's current Emergency Response Activation Level. There were three possible levels: red meant level one—the highest, most critical level. Yellow was level two, and green was for level three. The marker on the wall was yellow, which meant that the EOC and CDC's Division of Emergency Operations would be calling in staff and offering significant support to the outbreak response. Peyton was glad to see that.

At her office, she began prepping for the deployment. Her duffel bag contained the essentials for any outbreak investigation: clothes, toiletries, a satellite GPS, sunblock, gowns, gloves, goggles, a portable projector, and MREs—meals ready-to-eat. The MREs were particularly essential for outbreaks in the third world; often the local food and water harbored the very pathogen they were fighting.

Peyton put in rush orders for the other things the team would need in Mandera, including location-specific medications, mosquito netting, insect repellent, and satsleeves—sleeves that slid onto smartphones to give them satellite phone capability with data access. The satphone sleeves would enable team members to keep their regular phone numbers and contacts as well as access their email and other data. Being able to take a picture in the field and instantly upload it could well change the course of an outbreak response—and save lives.

Next, she began preparing packets for the team. She printed maps of Mandera and surrounding areas, and made lists of contacts at the CDC's Kenya office, the US embassy, the EOC, WHO Kenya, and the Kenyan Ministry of Health and Public Sanitation. She pulled up a questionnaire she had used in the field during the Ebola outbreak in West Africa and made a few modifications, adapting it to the region. She printed hundreds of copies. Some epidemiologists were pushing to go paperless in the field, but Peyton still preferred good old printed forms: they never crashed, their batteries never died, and roadside bandits were infinitely less interested in file folders than tablets. Paper worked.

That left one major decision: personnel.

Someone knocked softly on the open door to her office, and she turned to find her supervisor Elliott Shapiro leaning against the door frame.

"Hi," she said.

"How do you always get here so fast?"

"I sleep with one eye open."

He smiled. "Right. What're you working on?"

"Personnel."

"Good. You see the pictures?"

"Yeah."

"Looks bad."

"Very. We really need to be there right now," Peyton said. "If it gets to Nairobi, we'll be in trouble."

"I agree. I'll make some calls, see if I can get you there any sooner."

"Thanks."

"Call me if you need me," he said, stepping out of her office.

"Will do."

Peyton looked up a number on the CDC's intranet directory for a colleague she'd never met: Joseph Ruto. Ruto led the CDC's country operations in Kenya. They had 172 people in Kenya, a mix of US assignees and Kenyans working for the agency. Most were concentrated at the CDC office in Nairobi, where they worked closely with the Kenyan Ministry of Health.

Peyton took some time to read Ruto's internal status reports. She was about to call him when she had an idea—one that might well save one or both of the Americans' lives. A few quick searches told her it was possible. It might also prevent the pathogen from spreading to Nairobi.

Elliott once again appeared in her doorway. "Caught a break. Air Force is going to give you a ride to Nairobi."

"That's great," Peyton said.

"Won't be first-class accommodations. It's a troop and cargo transport, but it'll get you there. They'll pick you up at Dobbins Air Reserve Base at one-thirty. It's in Marietta. Just take I-75/85, stay on 75 at the split, and get off at exit 261. You can't miss it."

Elliott always gave her directions, even in the age of smartphone navigation, and even to places he likely knew Peyton had visited before, such as Dobbins. She never stopped him; she just nodded and scribbled a note. She figured it was a generational thing, a product of not growing up with a cell phone glued to his hand or Google Maps a click away. It was one of Elliott's many idiosyncrasies that Peyton had come to tolerate and then to like.

"Speaking of planes," she said, "I want to get your take on something. One of the Americans, Lucas Turner, was asymptomatic when he arrived at Mandera. Assuming he's been in close contact with the other man, and assuming this is a viral hemorrhagic fever, I think we should expect him to break with the disease."

"That's fair."

"I want to develop a plan of care for him now. If he breaks with the infection, we can't treat him in Mandera. Dani Beach Hospital and Kenyatta National in Nairobi are both candidates, but I don't favor either—we risk spreading the infection to the staff there and the region."

"You want to bring him back here."

"I do."

Elliott bunched his eyebrows up. "What're you thinking?"

"I want the air ambulance to accompany us to Nairobi, then fly to Mandera and be on standby. If Turner even has a high fever, I want to bring him back to Emory."

Emory University Hospital was next to the CDC on Clifton Road—close enough for CDC staff to walk there. Emory had a special isolation unit capable of dealing with patients infected with Ebola and other bio-safety level four pathogens; it was one of only four such facilities in the US. It had been used, with great success, to treat Americans who had been infected with Ebola during the 2014 outbreak.

"I don't know, Peyton. Bringing a patient with an unidentified, deadly, infectious disease back to the US? If word gets out, the press will scare the daylights out of everybody."

"It could also save his life. And we could bring back blood, saliva, and tissue samples from anyone else who's infected. We could test them here, in our BSL-4. It keeps the samples and testing out of Nairobi, and it enables the Kenyans to keep the outbreak quiet—which I know they'll want to do. We get to potentially save a life and get a huge head start on figuring out what we're dealing with."

Elliott nodded and exhaled deeply. "All right, but I'll have to get the director's approval—he'll have to deal with the fallout and the press if it goes wrong. But I'll give it my full support."

"Thanks."

"What about the other American?" Elliott asked.

"That's a tougher case. He was already in critical condition when he arrived in Mandera, and I don't favor flying him back to the US—we're talking roughly eighteen hours in the air, maybe more. He could die in transit. Beating the infection may be his only chance. I want to take some ZMapp with us."

ZMapp was the only available treatment for Ebola; it had been successful in treating several physicians who contracted the disease in 2014, but had yet to undergo human clinical trials. Its effects were largely unknown.

Elliott nodded. "You want me to get the legal guardians' consent to treat?"

"Please. The patients may be in no shape to give informed consent."

"I'll work on it." Elliott glanced at the papers strewn about her desk. "You selected your team yet?"

"Just about," Peyton said. "You ready for the conference?"

"No amount of coffee could make me ready for that."

CHAPTER 6

AS HE WALKED across the marble-floored lobby, Desmond realized why the police officers were looking at him: because he was looking at them. The natural human reaction was to look back at someone staring at you, and the instinct seemed more honed in those drawn to law enforcement. Such individuals had almost a sixth sense about predators and threats.

Despite her stoic demeanor in the elevator, the white-haired woman was quite frail. She shuffled slowly across the lobby, breathing heavily.

Desmond averted his eyes from the police, stepped aside, and power-walked past her. She was moving away from the revolving glass door, toward a swinging door with a silver bar straight across it. The bellhop was scanning the board of keys, oblivious to his oncoming guest.

Desmond swung the door open and stood in the cool November air, holding it for the lady, facing away, as she slowly approached.

"*Vielen dank*," she whispered as she passed.

He opened the door to a cab for her, then slid into the next one in line.

The police were still inside, but the radio chatter on the security channel was feverish now; they would send someone to look for Gerhardt soon. When they did, they would find the four bodies, only three of which were alive.

In German, the driver asked for a destination, which told Desmond that the hotel was not the haunt of foreign tourists or business travelers, but rather of native Germans. It was yet another clue, another piece that might reveal who he was and why he was in Berlin.

Desmond almost answered, *Bahnhof*—train station—but stopped himself. When the fallen police officers and dead man were found, a citywide search would ensue. Security would be intensified at the train stations and airports, and possibly along the highways and rivers as well.

He needed to think. He needed to know more about what was happening. The answers might still be in Berlin.

In German, he told the man to just drive.

The car didn't move. In the rear-view mirror, the middle-aged man scrutinized his passenger. In English, he said, "I need a destination."

"Please, just drive. I've had a fight with my girlfriend, and I need to get out for a while. I want to see the city."

Desmond exhaled when the driver punched the meter and pulled away from the hotel.

Now the question became where to go. His first priority was clear: to get off the streets of Berlin. The police clearly didn't have his description when they were sent to the hotel—the officers in the lobby didn't recognize him. Apparently it was just as the security guard had said: an anonymous tip about a disturbance in his hotel room. But who had called it in? Had they wanted to check on Gunter Thorne—the dead man? Or had his death been loud enough to alarm a nearby guest who called the police instead of hotel security?

As he rode through the streets of Berlin, a memory came to Desmond, of walking in a warehouse, his footsteps echoing on the concrete floor. Metal rafters hung high above, and the aisle was lined with cubicles enclosed in milky-white sheet plastic. He could hear the faint, rhythmic beeping of EKGs and could just make out hospital beds inside the isolated cubes. Plastic bags filled with clear liquid hung beside the patients, who appeared to be of all races, genders, and ages. Why were they here, in this makeshift hospital?

Workers in containment suits shuffled in and out of the patient cubicles. Up ahead a cart was stacked with black body bags. Two workers carried another bag out of a cubicle and tossed it on the heap.

Desmond was wearing one of the suits too. It was warm inside. He hated the sensation of being enclosed; he couldn't wait to rip it off.

The memory shifted, and he was standing in an office with plate glass windows that looked down on the rows of plastic-wrapped cubicles. The room was crowded with people, their backs turned to him, all facing a large screen with a world map. Red dots marked major cities. Arced lines spread across the screen, connecting the dots, representing flights between the cities. A man with scars on his face and long blond hair stood before them, speaking slowly.

"Soon, the world will change. Stay the course. The coming days will be the most difficult of your life. But when this is finished, the world will know the truth: we saved the entire human race from extinction."

As quickly as it had come, the memory ended, and Desmond was back in the taxi in Berlin, the city flying by in a blur.

Desmond desperately needed to figure out his next move. He needed information, especially about the local area. He drew a twenty-euro note from his pocket and slipped it past the clear plastic security barrier.

"I wonder if you'd be willing to tell me a bit about Berlin. It's my first time here."

The driver seemed hesitant at first, but finally began to speak. Weaving through the crowded streets, the driver spoke with great pride, describing a city that had played a pivotal role in European history for almost a thousand years.

Desmond asked him to discuss the city's layout, anything remarkable about getting in and out, and the major districts and neighborhoods. The man was wound up now, talking almost without pause, and didn't seem to mind the direction.

Berlin was a sprawling city that covered over 340 square miles—

larger than New York City and nine times the size of Paris. It was also one of the German Republic's sixteen federal states. Berlin had twelve boroughs, or districts. Each was governed by a council of five and a mayor.

Desmond counted it all as good news. Berlin was a big city—which made it a good place to hide.

The driver told him that Berlin's new *hauptbahnhof* was now the largest train station in Europe and that the city also had several rivers and over seventeen hundred bridges—more than Venice. Boat tours were common, and many places in the city could be accessed by boat.

Desmond asked about tourism. The driver, who had lived in East Berlin until the wall fell in 1989, was happy to report that Berlin was currently the most popular tourist destination in Germany and one of the top three in Europe. During the previous year, nearly thirty million people had visited Berlin, which had only three and a half million permanent residents. The influx of tourists had put a strain on the city's housing market, making it tough for Berliners to find a decent apartment to rent. Many estate agents and other enterprising individuals were now signing annual leases on apartments simply to sublet them to tourists on sites like Airbnb. In fact, the city's senate had recently passed a law requiring renters to notify their landlord if they were subletting. Still, nearly two-thirds of the twelve thousand apartments for sublet were unregistered and operated illegally.

Desmond turned the facts over in his mind, a plan forming.

From his pocket, he took out the only clue he had about who he was: the coupon for the dry cleaner. He considered asking the driver to take him there, but he knew it was only a matter of time before the police found the driver and learned where he had dropped Desmond off. He needed to make his trail disappear.

"What's Berlin's busiest tourist attraction?"

"The Brandenburg Gate," the driver said. "Or perhaps the Reichstag. They are next to each other, so it makes no matter."

"Drop me there, would you?"

Fifteen minutes later, Desmond paid the driver and exited the cab.

"Be careful," the man said before welcoming a new fare and driving away.

From the Brandenburg Gate, Desmond strolled quickly into the Tiergarten, Berlin's oldest park and, at 520 acres, one of the largest urban parks in Germany. It had once been the private hunting reserve for Berlin's elite, and it retained much of that untouched character. Desmond moved along its walking trails before exiting the park on Tiergartenstraße, where he hailed a rickshaw. He rode for twenty minutes, until he saw another rickshaw unloading its passenger. He stopped the driver, who seemed to never tire, paid him, and hopped into the other rickshaw. He did the change once more, then got in a cab and showed the driver the coupon from Quality Dry Cleaning for Less.

"Do you know where this address is?"

The driver nodded. "It's in Wedding, in Mitte."

"Where's that?"

"In the center of the city."

"Perfect. Let's go there."

Twenty minutes later, Desmond stood outside the dry cleaner, which was a narrow store with a plate glass façade. The buildings along the street were run-down, but the area was bustling; the sidewalks swarmed with younger people and immigrants from around the world. A cloud of cigarette smoke hung in the air above them, and farther up, satellite dishes lined the roofs. Through open second-story windows, Desmond could hear radio and TV shows in foreign languages—Arabic and Turkish, he thought.

Behind the counter in the dry cleaner, he found a short, bald Asian man with round glasses sewing a shirt. The shopkeeper set down his needle and thread, got off his stool, and nodded once at Desmond.

"I need to pick up."

"Tag?"

"I don't have a tag."

The man slid over to a keyboard and monitor on the counter. "Name?"

"Desmond Hughes." He spelled it.

As he typed, the shopkeeper said, "ID?"

Desmond stood silently, contemplating what to do.

The shopkeeper eyed him. "No ID, no pickup."

Desmond held up the police ID he'd taken from the officer in his hotel room. "This is a police investigation. We're looking for Desmond Hughes."

The Asian man raised his hands slightly. "Okay, okay."

The shopkeeper repeated the name, spelling out each letter deliberately as he finished typing the name. He shook his head.

"There's nothing. No Desmond Hughes."

Desmond wondered if he had misread the clue. Maybe he was supposed to meet someone here—not pick up his dry cleaning. "How many people work here?"

That seemed to scare the man. "No one. Only me."

"Look, this has nothing to do with your business or employees. Is there someone else in the back I can talk to?"

"No. No one."

Desmond glanced behind him out the large front window, just in time to see a police patrol car roll by. He turned, waiting for it to pass.

He wouldn't get anything else from the dry cleaner. Maybe it was just a random coupon and had nothing to do with who he was or what was going on. Finally, he said, "Okay, thank you. You've been very helpful."

On the street, he moved with the throngs of people, trying to stay out of the line of sight of cars passing by. Two blocks from the dry cleaner, he spotted a mobile phone store, where he bought a disposable smartphone. They were common in Europe; tourists and temporary workers often used them to avoid roaming charges for calls and data. The phone and a prepaid GSM SIM card severely depleted his cash supply. Money would become a real problem soon. He made a note to only use the mobile data in an emergency until he solved his cash problem.

He bought a doner kebab from a street vendor, wolfed it down, and slipped into a crowded coffee shop with free wifi. He locked himself in the single toilet bathroom, ensuring no security cameras could see his actions or record his conversations. His first instinct was to search the internet for himself, to dig into the mystery of who he was—and to look up Peyton Shaw. But he had to cover the bases of survival first. He needed to get off the street as soon as possible.

The cab driver was right. There were tons of flats and rooms for rent on a nightly basis in Berlin, but many of the listing sites, like Airbnb, required him to register and pay with a credit card in order to rent. That wouldn't work. He found a site that required landlords to pay-to-list, and began bookmarking suitable accommodations. Luckily there were quite a few studio flats available in Wedding. Most were run-down, but they were cheap.

He dialed the number listed for a promising flat nearby. Without thinking about it, he spoke excitedly, with a New England accent far different from his neutral, Midwestern accent.

"Oh, hi, do you have the flat for rent on Amsterdamer Straße?"

"Yes, that is correct." The woman's voice held little emotion.

"Is it available for the next three days?"

"Yes."

"Wonderful, wonderful. Listen, I'm in Berlin for business, and I could really use some help. I took the train in and when I woke up it was all gone—I mean everything: my luggage, laptop, wallet, passport, money, credit cards, you name it, gone. The rascals even slipped my wedding ring off!"

"Oh, that's terrible," the woman said with a little more sympathy.

"My wife wired me some money, and I'm looking for a place to rent. Can we meet? You'll see I've got an honest face!" Desmond let out a goofy, nervous laugh that matched the fake exasperated accent he had affected.

"Ah, well, okay." The woman said it would be three hours before she could get to the flat. Desmond agreed and ended the call. Assuming it worked out, he'd be off the street soon.

He opened a web browser and scanned the top German news sources. *Bild* carried no news about him, but a breaking news banner at the top of *Spiegel Online* read: *Berlin police launch citywide manhunt for American man wanted for murder and assaulting two police officers.*

Desmond clicked the link and scanned the article. The hunt was being run by the *Landeskriminalamt*—the LKA—the police division charged with investigating major crimes and conducting special manhunts. The LKA would be coordinating a number of units. Reading the list gave Desmond pause about staying in the city.

The *Spezialeinsatzkommando*—the state police's SWAT teams— were on standby for locations to raid. *Mobiles Einsatzkommando* —the special operative agents of the LKA—were being deployed to every borough to conduct a manhunt. *Wasserschutzpolizei*— the river police—were monitoring all the city's waterways. *Zentraler Verkehrsdienst*—the traffic police—had engaged local and highway patrol units (*Autobahnpolizei*) to search for him. They even had *Diensthundführer*—K9 units—at the Concord, picking up his scent.

They were about to turn the city upside down looking for him. Despite naming him, the article didn't have any details about who he was or his background. This was both a relief and a disappointment. It would make it harder for them to find him— but it told him nothing about who he was.

Desmond opened the phone's map application and found what he needed. Despite the citywide manhunt launching, Wedding looked like it would be a perfect place to hide. But Desmond still had the sense that he was missing something—and that the dry cleaner was somehow part of the puzzle.

☣

Three blocks away, Desmond sat in the changing room of a secondhand thrift shop. Two outfits hung on the inside of the door, both Turkish-made and more casual than his button-up shirt and khakis.

When he slipped his pants off, what he saw took his breath away. Burn scars spread from his feet to his knees. The mottled flesh looked like creamy-white tree roots growing across his body. They were old scars, remnants of a horrible event. The feeling was unnerving—not being able to remember the fire that had torched his legs. He searched the rest of his body. Above his pelvis on the right side, he found a puckered, rounded scar below his ribs. *A healed gunshot wound?* Scattered about his torso and arms were smaller, straight scars where knife wounds had likely healed. In the hotel room, he had been so focused on the aching black and blue bruise on his left side that he hadn't noticed anything else. Now he longed to know where he'd come from, what sort of life he'd led—what sort of person he was. Or, at least, had been.

As he stared at the floor, something inside the crumpled-up khaki pants caught his eye: a pink tag stapled to the garment's care instructions. He had seen similar tags before, only hours ago, attached to clear plastic bags hanging in rows... in the dry cleaner.

He had found the claim tag.

He detached it, then carefully searched both the shirt and pants, finding nothing else of interest. He sold the shirt and pants to the thrift shop—he needed the money, and police across the city likely had pictures of him wearing them by now. A sign on the wall claimed all items were thoroughly cleaned before being offered for sale, and he hoped it was true; if not, the police dogs might pick up the scent in the store. With some of his extra money he purchased a ball cap, sunglasses, and a backpack. In the changing room, he put the extra clothes and the spare magazines for the policeman's gun inside.

Ten minutes later, he once again stood outside the dry cleaner. The older Asian man was gone; a younger man, also Asian, now sat at the counter, hunched over a textbook, a pencil in his hand, scribbling notes.

Desmond walked in and slid him the tag without a word.

The teenager searched the rows of hanging clothes, checking the tag several times. After a few minutes he shook his head and returned to the counter.

"You're picking up late. There's a fee."

"How much?"

"Three euros per day."

"How late am I?"

Desmond was already dangerously low on cash; he had just enough to pay the rent at the crummy flat for three days, and he was due to meet the landlord in less than an hour.

The teen worked the computer, searching the tag number. "Fourteen days late. Forty-two euros plus the cleaning. Fifty-five total with tax."

If he paid, Desmond wouldn't have enough for rent for all three nights. He considered pulling the police ID again, but that would only invite problems. So he forked the cash over and waited while the teen thrashed around in the back for what felt like an hour. Desmond hoped it would be worth it—that whatever he, or someone, had stashed here contained something to get him out of the fix he was in.

The boy emerged with a plastic hanging bag covering an expensive-looking navy suit. Desmond could barely resist the urge to tear it open and examine it right there. His appointment with the landlord, however, was fast approaching, so with the suit hanging over his shoulder, he made his way to the meeting spot.

He found a young woman in her mid-twenties, a cigarette in her hand, standing in front of a run-down three-story building. Four Middle Eastern teenagers sat on the steps outside the front door, arguing in a language Desmond didn't recognize.

"Are you Ingrid?" he asked in the same New England accent he had used before.

"Ja." She put the cigarette out and accepted Desmond's hand when he extended it eagerly.

"I'm Peter Wilkinson. We spoke earlier. Thank you so much for meeting me on such short notice."

She led him inside, up a winding, narrow staircase, and into the tiny, but clean flat.

"It's perfect," Desmond said. "Now listen, this suit is literally all they left me with. Guess they didn't know it was mine!" He smiled sheepishly. "I need it for my meeting tomorrow, and," he sighed, "I'm running low on cash."

The woman shook her head. "If you can't pay, you simply cannot stay here."

"I've got enough for one night." He handed her the folded-up euros. "I'll get you the rest."

Ingrid hesitated.

"Look, if I can't pay tomorrow, I'll leave. Promise. My wife is going to wire me some more money. I promise. Okay?"

Ingrid glanced away from him. "All right. I'll come back tomorrow with my boyfriend. Please pay or be gone."

"No problem. Thank you again."

The moment the door closed, Desmond ripped into the plastic dry cleaning bag and searched the suit. The patch inside the jacket listed the maker as Richard Anderson, 13 Savile Row. He wondered if it was another clue. He ran his fingers over the embroidery—and felt a lump.

His heart beat faster. There was something sewn inside the suit.

CHAPTER 7

AT CDC HEADQUARTERS in Atlanta, Peyton was working on the central mystery in the outbreak in Mandera: the patients. She believed she had just made a breakthrough.

The two young Americans had started a nonprofit organization called CityForge. Its mission was to help villages grow by giving them funding for infrastructure and mentoring from city leaders in the developed world. CityForge's funding came from individuals, who donated via the CityForge website. The investments were treated as municipal bonds, which meant the donors would benefit financially if the villages thrived. Villages used the money to bring electricity, education, better roads, health care, internet, public sanitation, police enforcement, and other vital services to their citizens.

As part of the CityForge model, local leaders were trained to film the village's gradual transformation. The videos gave the mentors in the developed world a way to follow the progress of the villages. In almost real time, city council leaders, mayors, police chiefs, and others could see the villages change, and could offer guidance. Individual donors could also follow the villages' progress, like a reality show, seeing how the money they provided was improving the lives of the current residents and laying the groundwork for generations to come.

The CityForge founders had come up with the idea while they were undergraduates at UNC-Chapel Hill, and after graduating this past May, they had set out to make their concept a reality.

They had spent the summer promoting their startup and raising money from friends, family, and passionate supporters. They used the funds for their trip to Kenya, where they planned to document every stop along the way—and identify their first "CityForge villages." And, for reasons that remained unclear to Peyton, the two boys had made a pact not to shave or cut their hair during the trip.

She clicked the *Supporters* page and read the names. Icarus Capital was among the corporate sponsors. She had seen the name before—hours ago, in her apartment. It was Desmond Hughes' investment firm. Was he involved in some way? She thought it was an odd coincidence, but she couldn't think of a way to act on the connection.

Even thinking about Desmond rattled her. She fought to stay focused. Another tab on the CityForge site featured a map with every stop the two young men had made. Most included one or more videos of the two Americans touring the village and doing interviews with residents. Mostly, they highlighted how infrastructure could change the villagers' lives. For a few of the villages, the videos continued after the two Americans had left. The more recent films had been uploaded by village leaders hoping to attract financial supporters.

The trip log was a dream for an epidemiologist. Peyton wondered if one of the videos would show the origin of the outbreak. She might even be able to track its spread.

The key to stopping an outbreak was containment. The first step in containment was to isolate anyone who was infected, and the second step was to interview all the infected patients and develop a list of every person they had come into contact with— a process called contact tracing. From those contacts, Peyton and her team would begin a repeating process. They would search for contacts. If the contact was sick, they would isolate them and trace anyone *they* had come into contact with; if the contact was asymptomatic, they would test them for the disease and typically quarantine them until Peyton and her team could be sure the person was infection-free. For Ebola, that quarantine period was twenty-one days. Eventually, when they had no new contacts to trace, they would end up with two groups: infected and quarantined.

But contact lists grew quickly. With each passing hour, a pathogen would reach more and more people. Time was of the essence; in most cases, the first few days of an outbreak determined everything after.

On a pad, Peyton had written the names of the two Americans, Steven Cobb and Lucas Turner, as well as the British patient, Andrew Blair. Between them, she had drawn a large X. The X was the variable, the unknown—what she needed to find. At some point, the British man had interacted with one or both of the Americans. Either that, or all three had a common contact—someone still out there, continuing to spread the disease. It was imperative that she find out where each of them had been and whom they had interacted with. The travel log could be the key to doing that.

If Peyton and her team did their job correctly, they'd end up with a contact tree that eventually had a root contact: the first person to contract the disease, often called patient zero or the index case.

That was the on-the-ground detective work: tracing the pathogen to its origin, containing every person it had touched, and either treating the patients or simply waiting for the outbreak to burn itself out.

But even with the video travel log, Peyton and her team were going to need a lot of help in Kenya.

She picked up her office phone and called Joseph Ruto, head of the CDC's office in Kenya. Ruto was just finishing a late lunch in Nairobi, which was eight hours ahead of Atlanta.

She briefed him on their plans, with the caveat that they might change after the morning conference. The man struck her as competent and focused, and she counted that as a very good sign.

It was just before six a.m. when she hung up. She had been waiting to make the next call; she wanted her people to get as much rest as possible. Sleep might be hard to come by in the coming days.

She dialed the EOC's head of watch and requested they contact all of the Epidemiology Intelligence Service agents.

"All of them?" the watch officer asked.

"Everyone assigned to CDC HQ. Instruct them to be in the building by seven a.m. for a pre-conference briefing. They need to come packed and prepared to leave in a few hours. If they're deployed, they'll be working either in Nairobi or in the field in rural Kenya. Instruct them to plan accordingly."

"Understood, Dr. Shaw."

The EIS program was a two-year fellowship established at the CDC in 1951. It had begun as a Cold War initiative focused on bioterror. Today, it was one of the most prestigious and sought-after fellowships in applied epidemiology, known for producing the world's best disease detectives. Candidates applying to the program needed to be either a physician with at least a year of clinical experience, a veterinarian, a PhD-level scientist with a background in public health, or a health care professional with at least a masters degree. There were currently 160 EIS officers, seventy percent of whom were women.

During their fellowship, EIS officers often worked in the field, on the front lines of outbreaks. During the 2014 Ebola outbreak, every one of the 158 EIS officers deployed. They served in seventeen countries, eight states, Washington, DC, and the CDC's Emergency Operations Center. During that time, they collectively contributed 6,903 days of service—almost nineteen years combined. Peyton hoped for everyone's sake that the current outbreak would be concluded much quicker.

Peyton was the CDC's leading field epidemiologist, and she was also an EIS instructor. She took both jobs very seriously. The EIS officers she was training could well be making the calls during the next major outbreak or leading the first response at the state level or overseas. Alumni from the program included the current CDC director, past and current acting surgeon generals, branch and division leaders across the CDC, and state and local epidemiologists across the country.

She hadn't had a chance to work with every fellow in the

current class, and this might be a good opportunity. She began browsing through the personnel files, assembling her team.

☣

At seven a.m., Peyton stood at the podium in Auditorium A of Building 19 on the CDC campus. A fourth of the EIS officers were deployed at local and state health offices; they had dialed in to the presentation. The officers who worked at CDC HQ were assembled in the room. One hundred and twenty faces stared down at Peyton.

"Good morning. I'm about to brief you on an outbreak of what we believe is a viral hemorrhagic fever in a small town in Kenya. Pay close attention. Some of you will be deployed today; we'll fly to Kenya this afternoon. Others will support our field operations from CDC HQ for now. Depending on how things go, some of you may end up deployed to the field at a later date. Take notes, ask questions, and learn all you can. Your lives may depend on it. And so could someone else's.

"Okay. Here's what we know so far…"

CHAPTER 8

AT EIGHT A.M., the EOC's conference room was overflowing. Employees from several CDC divisions as well as representatives from the State Department and the US Agency for International Development (USAID) were on hand.

Peyton sat at the table next to Elliott Shapiro. The EIS agents she'd selected for the deployment were in Auditorium A, watching the conference on a projection screen.

After introductions, Elliott led a briefing on the current situation. The State Department representative, Derek Richards, spoke next.

"From our perspective, this is an outbreak in the worst possible place at the worst possible time. Let's start with some background."

Richards clicked his mouse, and an image of a badly burned building appeared.

"August, 1998. Truck bombs exploded outside the US embassies in Nairobi, Kenya, and Dar es Salaam, Tanzania. In Nairobi, 213 people died. Four thousand were injured. The attack was linked to al-Qaeda. In fact, it's what caused the FBI to put bin Laden on the ten-most-wanted list for the first time. Less than two weeks later, the Clinton administration launched cruise missiles at Sudan and Afghanistan in Operation Infinite Reach. The hit on bin Laden failed. In response, the Taliban renewed their commitment to harbor him, and the rest is history.

"State decided not to rebuild the embassy that was bombed in Nairobi. We built a new embassy directly across the street from the UN for security purposes.

46

"In the years since the Nairobi bombing, the security situation in Kenya has gotten worse. Crime rates are high across the country. It's particularly bad in the larger cities: Nairobi, Mombasa, Kisumu, and the coastal resorts. In Nairobi alone, there are ten carjackings every day. In May 2014, the US, UK, France and Australia began issuing travel warnings to their citizens in Kenya. The US went further, reducing our staff at the Nairobi embassy. The UK closed their consulate in Mombasa. The effects of the travel advisories were devastating to the Kenyan tourism industry. European travel to the country ground to a halt.

"Our main concern, however, is al-Shabaab. They're an Islamic terror group based in Somalia, with cells and operatives throughout Kenya. They want to turn Somalia into a fundamentalist Islamic state. They're essentially ISIS in East Africa. They're brutal, organized, and relentless. The African Union has deployed twenty-two thousand troops to Somalia to try to contain them. They're losing."

Richards clicked the mouse again, and a map of Somalia and Kenya appeared. Areas with terrorist activity were highlighted.

"In March 2016, we received intel that al-Shabaab was planning a large-scale attack on US and African Union forces in the region. The Air Force launched a strike in which manned aircraft and unmanned MQ-9 reaper drones hit an al-Shabaab training camp in northern Somalia. We killed about 150 of their fighters, including their number two. You can have no doubt that al-Shabaab is looking for any opportunity to retaliate. American personnel, of any kind, operating in Kenya will be pursued. For that reason, US embassy personnel must get express permission when traveling outside Nairobi, and in some neighborhoods in the city.

"Your status as non-combatants is likely to have no effect on al-Shabaab. In April 2015 they attacked students at Garissa University. They singled out Christians and shot them. They killed 147 people.

"Finally, I would like to present the recent decisions of medical and humanitarian organizations I know you respect."

Richards flipped through his papers; he apparently hadn't memorized this part of his presentation.

"In May 2015, Doctors Without Borders evacuated personnel from the Dadaab refugee camp because of security concerns. In total, they evacuated forty-two staff members to Nairobi and closed two of their four health posts.

"In July 2014, the Peace Corps suspended all activities in Kenya and evacuated all of its personnel because of the security situation."

Richards looked up from the papers and focused on Elliott. His tone was firm, bordering on aggressive.

"At State, we realize this is a serious outbreak with the potential to spread. Our official recommendation is that American personnel remain in Nairobi, offering support and coordination from there. The Kenyans and WHO personnel will be at far less risk in the field, and, in fact, the presence of American personnel may endanger them.

"If you decide to venture outside Nairobi, we recommend only doing so with Kenyan military forces that include units with combat experience and heavy artillery at their disposal. We would also advise you to wait until the NRO can position a satellite in geosynchronous orbit with the area you'll be operating in. And we strongly recommend you wait until the Navy can position a vessel with a rapid deployment force within striking distance of your theater of operations."

Peyton chewed her lip. She knew the recommendations were prudent but also that they would take time—especially the request to the National Reconnaissance Office, where bureaucratic red tape was a fact of life.

"How long would all that take?" Elliott asked.

"Unknown. DOD would have to advise on the RDF and vessel alignment; we're not privy to their fleet positioning, but it's safe to assume there are suitable vessels in the Gulf of Aden, Arabian Sea, and Indian Ocean. NRO would have to feed in on the sat requisition."

"Can you guess?"

"Maybe seventy-two hours," Richards said, "but I would again urge you not to go to Mandera at all, and if you do, to wait. Somalia is a failed state. We haven't had an embassy there since '91. It closed two years before the Battle of Mogadishu—that's when the Black Hawk Down incidents took place. Frankly, that's what you'll be looking at if al-Shabaab militants find you and engage the Kenyan army. We've got a couple hundred US troops at the Mogadishu airport, but I can't comment on whether they'd be able to assist in an emergency. I know CIA has special operators in Somalia. Also status unknown."

Elliott looked over at Peyton. They had worked together so long, knew each other so well, that she could sense what he was thinking. She confirmed it with a short nod that silently said, *We both know what we have to do.*

"All right," Elliott said, "we'd like to put in the requests to the NRO and DOD and expedite them as much as possible. I'll have the director make calls."

"You're going to wait?" Richards asked.

"No. We're going to deploy to Mandera with all possible haste." Richards shook his head in disbelief.

Elliott held up his hands. "Look, if we don't stop this outbreak in Mandera, we'll be fighting it in Nairobi and Mombasa and then in Cairo and Johannesburg and Casablanca. If we can't stop it in Africa, we'll be dealing with it here at home, in Atlanta, Chicago, New York, and San Francisco. Seventy-two hours could mean the difference between a local outbreak and a global pandemic, between a dozen deaths and millions. Right now, infected individuals could be boarding buses, trains, and aeroplanes. We don't know who they are or where they're going. They may well be on their way to infect cities anywhere in the world—cities that aren't on alert, that have no idea that a deadly pathogen has just touched down within its borders. Our only chance of stopping this outbreak is containing it. That has to happen now, not three days from now. Our people are among the best trained in the world. They need to be there—right now. We're the Centers for Disease Control and Prevention. We can't control this disease over the phone."

When the conference broke, Peyton spoke privately to the EIS officers she'd selected for deployment.

"You heard the security situation. If any of you feel uncomfortable, I need to know now. I'm not going to put anything on your file. I'll select an alternate and never say a word about it."

At one p.m., Peyton made her way downstairs and walked nervously through the lobby, unsure how many of the officers she'd find waiting for her.

Outside, it took her eyes a few seconds to adjust to the sun.

When the scene came into focus, she saw every one of the EIS officers she had selected standing in front of the vans, their duffel bags beside them. She nodded at them, and they loaded up and drove to Dobbins Air Reserve Base.

Less than an hour later, they were on their way to Nairobi.

From a chain link fence that ringed Dobbins ARB, the man who had been following Peyton watched the Air Force transport lift off. When it was out of sight, he typed a message to his superiors:

Subject is en route to target zone.

CHAPTER 9

IN THE SMALL flat in Berlin's Wedding neighborhood, Desmond carefully cut the stitches that held the patch inside the suit jacket. The Savile Row label fell away, revealing the contents of the secret pocket: two pre-paid Visa credit cards.

The cards were timely but he had hoped for more. In particular, he had hoped for some clue about who he was, why he was in Berlin, and most of all, what had happened to him before he'd woken up that morning in the Concord hotel with no memories.

Something about the cards struck him as odd: each had a small vertical scratch after the tenth number. To the common eye, it might look random, but the fact that both cards were marked raised his suspicion. Beside the mark on the first card were four smaller scratches. The second card had two small scratches to the right of the vertical line, just above the card numbers.

Was it another code? If so, it likely followed the pattern on the dry cleaning coupon—a simple substitution cipher. Add four to each of the first ten digits on the first card and two to the first ten digits on the second card. Ten numbers formed an American phone number.

Desmond drew out the prepaid smartphone and dialed, doing the math for each digit in his head. He listened anxiously as the first droning beep sounded. Another. A third. Then voicemail picked up. To his surprise, he heard his own voice.

"If you've reached this number, you know what to do. If you don't, you'd better figure it out fast."

When the beep sounded, Desmond paused, his mind racing. Was the voicemail box a sort of digital dead drop for messages to someone else? Or was he supposed to try to access the voicemail? He decided to do both.

"It's Desmond. I need help." He almost said his phone number, but stopped. The voicemail could have been hacked by whoever had sent Gunter Thorne to his hotel room, or the police could have found it by now. Revealing his new number might paint a target on his back; the police could trace the number to the nearest cell tower and triangulate his approximate location. He needed a digital dead drop of his own—something public and easy to access.

Thinking quickly, he said, "Leave a message on the Berlin Craigslist under Help Wanted—an ad for a tour guide. Use the words 'highway man' in your ad. Hurry."

The call had left him with more questions than answers. Hoping for those answers, he dialed the phone number from the second credit card, and again heard his own voice.

"You've reached Labyrinth Reality. If you know us, you know we think talking is the least interesting thing to do with your phone. I mean, come on, you're holding a location-aware computer in your hand. Do something cool with it."

At the beep, Desmond ignored his own words, leaving the same message he'd left on the first number.

Labyrinth Reality. He did an internet search for the name and found a website for a startup. The contact page listed an address in San Francisco and a number that was different from the one he had just called. He clicked the *Team* page, but he didn't recognize any of the dozen faces. They were all in their twenties or early thirties, several wearing Warby Parker glasses, a few with tattoos. All the pictures were candids: taken during a Ping-Pong game, at their desks, partially covering their faces in the hall. The titles were quirky, and so were the bios.

Desmond clicked the *Investors* page and read the firms listed: Seven Bridges Investments, Icarus Capital, Pax-Humana Fund, Invisible Sun Securities, and Singularity Consortium. The names seemed familiar, but no concrete memories emerged.

Labyrinth Reality's product was a mobile app that was location-aware and could be used for augmented reality. Users held their phones up at certain locations, and the app would reveal a digital layer with pictures and virtual items not visible to the naked eye. The app would also supplement the experience with videos and text related to the location. It was used for corporate scavenger hunts and games as well as geocaching. City tour groups were using it in Chicago and San Francisco. The app was positioned as a platform, enabling game developers, corporations, conference organizers, and individuals to create Labyrinth Realities to enhance whatever they were doing.

A banner at the top of the web page urged him to download the Labyrinth Reality app. He clicked the link and waited while the app downloaded. When he launched it, a dialog asked if he wanted to join a private labyrinth or the public space. He clicked private, and it prompted him for a passcode. He thought for a moment, then typed in the second phone number he had called— the one that referenced Labyrinth Reality.

A message flashed on the screen: *Welcome to the Hall of Shadows Private Labyrinth.* Two icons appeared. To the left was a beast with the head of a bull and the body of a man; to the right was a warrior wearing armor and holding a shield and a sword. The text under it asked:

Declare yourself: Minotaur or Hero

Desmond pondered the question. In some form it had haunted him since he had woken up: what was he? Was he a monster who had killed in that hotel room? He had assaulted the police officers and hotel security guard without hesitation. And he had been good at it; it probably wasn't the first time he had fought for his life and freedom. His scar-ridden body supported that idea. And in the recesses of his mind, somewhere, he knew that he had done bad things, though he couldn't remember them.

Yet deep down he still felt that he was a good person. Or maybe that was just what he wanted to be.

The thought brought clarity: he would enter the labyrinth as he *wanted* himself to be, not as he was or had been.

He clicked the hero icon. The screen faded, and a box popped up:

Searching for entrance...

A minute later, the text turned to red and flashed a new message:

No entrance found. Continue searching, Theseus
Never give up.

Desmond wondered what it all meant. He did a series of web searches, trying to connect the dots. The labyrinth had first appeared in Greek mythology. Daedalus and his son Icarus had built the labyrinth to hold the half-man, half-beast Minotaur that dwelled at its center. Daedalus was a brilliant craftsman and artist, and his design was so ingenious that he himself had almost gotten trapped within his own labyrinth.

At that moment, Desmond realized what he had suspected ever since he'd heard his own voice on the voicemail recording: like Daedalus, he was trapped in a labyrinth that he himself had constructed. But why? Did he have a proverbial Minotaur—a beast or secret he wished to hide from the world, or to protect the world from? Was he the monster he feared?

And he realized something else. If he had built this labyrinth, he must have known that at some point he would enter it, that he would lose his memories—either by his own choosing or by someone else's actions. Was the labyrinth an elaborate backup plan? Would it lead him to whatever it was he needed? Would it somehow allow him to get his memories back?

He eased himself up and folded the Murphy bed into the wall. That gave him room to pace in the tiny flat, no larger than twelve by twenty feet. The wall opposite the bed held a simple kitchen: a counter with a sink, small refrigerator, stove, microwave, and a TV. The bathroom was a wet room without a single square inch to spare.

Desmond walked to the window and looked down. It was six p.m., and the streets were packed. A layer of cigarette smoke mixed with car, bus, and motorcycle exhaust. The toxic brew drifted up, casting the scene in haze. The sun was low in the late November sky, and it would set soon.

He turned around. The flat's owner had attached a large mirror to the underside of the bed frame, and with the Murphy bed folded into the wall, the mirror made the space seem larger. Desmond stared at himself: at his toned, muscular face, at his blond, eyebrow-length hair, at the image of a man who was a complete mystery to him. His appearance wasn't overly remarkable in Berlin—as a fugitive, he would have been far more noticeable in Shanghai or Egypt—but still, he would have to alter his appearance. When night fell that would be his first task.

But at that moment, he had to unravel what was happening. He couldn't shake the feeling that there was something he needed to be doing.

He focused on what he knew: he had set up the phone numbers and left the voicemail greeting, knowing, or perhaps merely hoping, he would find them. The second voicemail greeting had led him to his own private labyrinth. What did the first phone number lead to? His words in the message had taunted him, saying he'd know what to do. What did he know?

He figured he must have purchased the prepaid credit cards first, then set up the phone numbers to match the credit card numbers. He did a series of internet searches and discovered that the first three digits of the phone numbers corresponded to Google Voice lines. The service was free and included an online control panel where users could access voicemail, forward the number to other phone lines, and more.

That was it: he could access the voicemail from the Google Voice app. He downloaded it to his cell and tried a few password combinations with no luck.

What am I missing?

He searched the suit again, but there were no other hidden pockets, nothing of note. He sat on a small wooden chair by the window to think. The plastic dry cleaning bag lay wadded up in the corner of the room. Through the clear layers, Desmond spotted a pink piece of paper stapled to the top.

He jumped up, ripped the plastic apart, and examined the small slip. It was a carbon copy of the dry-cleaning receipt. The name on the tag was Jacob Lawrence.

Desmond grabbed his phone and entered the name as the password on the Google Voice app. It worked.

The application opened and displayed the voicemail mailbox, which contained three messages, all from the same phone number. The first was dated two days before. He clicked it and read the transcript:

> I think someone's following me. Not sure. Don't call back. Meet me where we met the first time. Tomorrow. 10 a.m.

Desmond clicked the second message, which had been left yesterday at noon.

> Where were you? They searched my flat. I'm sure of it. I'm going to the police if you don't call me.

The last message was from today at eleven a.m.

> You're all over the news. Did you kill him? Call me or I'm going to the police—I'm serious. I'll tell them everything you told me and everything I know about you. I've given a colleague a folder with all my notes. If something happens to me, it will be in the police's hands within an hour.

Desmond's mind raced. Was the person who left these messages an ally or an enemy? One thing was certain: that person knew who he was.

He set his phone up to use the Google Voice number and verified that he was connected to the flat's wifi; he wanted his next call to be routed through Google's servers. The number that had left the voicemails had a Berlin extension. He clicked it from the app and listened as it rang.

A man's voice answered, speaking in German-accented English. "What happened?"

"We need to meet," Desmond said.

"No. I want answers—right now. Did you kill that man?"

"No," Desmond said automatically, still unsure if it was true or not.

"Is this connected to the Looking Glass?"

The Looking Glass. The words instantly struck a chord. The Looking Glass—it meant something to him, but he couldn't remember what.

"Are you still there?"

"Yes," Desmond said. "I'll explain when we meet."

Silence for a long moment, then, "Someone's following me. I'm staying with a friend, and I've told her everything. She's got the recordings of our previous conversations. If it's you—if you searched my flat and if something happens to me, she's going to the authorities."

"I understand. Believe me, I'm not going to hurt you. I'm a victim too."

A pause. Then he spoke with hesitation. "Where? When?"

Desmond considered a few options. He was exhausted, and he needed to prepare for the meeting. "Tomorrow at noon. The Brandenburg Gate. Stand in the tourist area, holding a sign that says Looking Glass Tours, prices negotiable. Wear a navy peacoat, blue jeans, and a black hat with nothing on it."

"You want to meet in public?"

"It's safer that way. Leave your phone at home. Come alone. Unarmed."

He snorted, sounding disgusted. "Says the man wanted for murder."

"Being wanted for murder doesn't mean I'm guilty of murder. You want answers, meet me tomorrow."

"Fine."

When the line went dead, Desmond began planning the meeting: every aspect, every possible contingency. If he played his cards right, he might soon know what was going on.

CHAPTER 10

THAT NIGHT, DR. Elim Kibet made his rounds at Mandera Referral Hospital, then retreated to his office, where he took off his worn white coat and began writing an email to the Kenyan Ministry of Public Health:

To whom it may concern:

The situation here has deteriorated. I again implore you to send help with all possible haste.

The American male, who arrived here this morning and presented with symptoms of an as-yet-unidentified hemorrhagic fever, has died. We are ill equipped to perform an autopsy or handle his remains. I have sealed his room and barred anyone from entering.

His passing distressed his companion greatly. More concerning, the young man, who is named Lucas Turner, has developed a fever, most recently recorded at 102. I fear it will continue to climb and that he will soon develop symptoms similar to his now-deceased companion. If so, his fate may well be the same.

I have endeavored to keep detailed notes on his progression and have instructed the staff to take pictures on the hour. Frankly, documenting the disease is perhaps the only useful thing I can do. I have also dedicated much of my time to recording the details of the two Americans' travel, including where they visited and whom they talked to. Additionally, I have asked Lucas about his friend's history of symptoms. I believe it will prove quite helpful to epidemiologists investigating this outbreak. I will forward my notes as I have time.

The British patient, who was brought in from the airport, remains in critical condition. I'm not optimistic that he will survive the night.

Lastly, we face a new crisis here at MCRH: personnel. I arrived this morning to find that over half of the hospital's staff did not report for work. I cannot blame them. As I have said, we are ill equipped to deal with these patients. I have instructed nurses to wear gowns, boot covers, facemasks, goggles, and double gloves, but I fear these measures may prove inadequate, and our supplies of protective equipment will very soon run out.

I ask you again:

Outside his office, a nurse yelled, "Dr. Kibet!"

Seconds later, the door swung open. The man was bent forward, his hands on his knees, catching his breath. "More infected," he said between pants.

Elim grabbed his coat, and the two men raced down the corridor to triage. Elim stopped in his tracks, taking in the horror.

Ten people, all local villagers, all very sick. Sweat and vomit stains covered their clothes. A few stared with yellowed, blood-shot eyes.

A nurse drew a thermometer from a man's mouth and turned to Elim. "A hundred and five."

It had spread to the villages. Elim wondered if help would be too late—for all of them.

CHAPTER 11

WHEN THE AIR Force transport reached cruising altitude, Peyton stretched out across several chairs, strapped herself in, and slept.

She had gotten only four hours of sleep the night before and had been going as hard as she could all day. Still, she set her alarm for thirty minutes later. She wanted to be fresh but not groggy for what came next.

Perhaps the most valuable skill she'd acquired while working at the CDC was the ability to sleep nearly anywhere. It had taken her years to master the practice. For her, thinking was the greatest enemy of sleep. When she was battling an outbreak, her mind never stopped working; thinking became a compulsion. But during her second year of fieldwork, she had learned a sleep technique she'd used ever since. When she needed to rest, she closed her eyes, refused to let her mind think, and instead focused on her breathing. She first forced herself to draw her breaths into her belly, allowing her abdomen to expand, not her chest. With each exhalation, she focused on the tip of her nose, where the breath touched as it flowed out of her, and counted the breaths. She rarely got past forty.

When her phone alarm buzzed in her pocket, she rose, stretched, and did a few light exercises.

She had been given the option of flying on the air ambulance instead of the Air Force transport. She would have been more comfortable there, but she'd wanted to remain with her team.

To Peyton, it was a matter of principle. Besides, they had work to do. She had insisted that three of the older CDC employees take the seats on the air ambulance. They would be working in Nairobi, in support positions, and all three had thanked her for the more comfortable accommodations.

Elliott had chosen the Air Force transport as well. It had a large compartment for cargo and a separate area for passengers. The passenger section had twelve rows, each with five seats in the center, plus a single row of seats lining each of the right and left walls. At the head of the compartment were two narrow openings beside a wide wall that held a whiteboard.

Peyton imagined that the whiteboard was routinely used to brief military personnel and hammer out mission details. She was about to do the same. In fact, to an outside observer, the scene reminiscent of a US Navy mission briefing.

Her audience included men and women dressed in tan service khakis identical to the uniforms worn by the US Navy, with similar rank insignias. Her troops, however, were not naval officers. They were officers in another uniformed service, one every bit as important.

Peyton was a CDC employee, but she was also a Commissioned Corps officer of the US Public Health Service. The Commissioned Corps was an elite team of highly skilled health professionals and one of the United States' seven uniformed services (the other six being the Army, Navy, Air Force, Marines, Coast Guard, and National Oceanic and Atmospheric Administration Commissioned Corps). Over six thousand men and women served in the Public Health Service Commissioned Corps, and they wore uniforms similar to the US Navy's: service dress blues, summer whites, and service khakis. Commissioned Corps officers held the same ranks as the Navy and Coast Guard: ensign to admiral.

Commissioned Corps officers served at the EPA, FDA, DOD, NIH, USDA, Coast Guard, CDC, and many other organizations. They were often the first responders during national disasters, and had deployed in response to hurricanes, earthquakes, and outbreaks. In 2001, over one thousand PHS officers deployed to New York City after the 9/11 attacks. In 2005, in the aftermath of three hurricanes—Katrina, Rita, and Wilma—more than two thousand PHS officers deployed to set up field hospitals and assist victims.

Over eight hundred Commissioned Corps officers worked full-time at the CDC. Visitors often mistook them for Navy officers.

Peyton held the rank of full commander in the Commissioned Corps; Elliott was rear admiral. Of the 160 EIS officers, 102 were Commissioned Corps officers.

The Corps was also well represented in the group sitting before Peyton: of the 63 men and women present, 51 were Commissioned Corps officers. Like Peyton, they dressed in service khakis, the PHSCC insignia on their left lapel, their rank insignia on their right.

Peyton pulled her shoulder-length black hair into a ponytail and smoothed out her rumpled uniform. She straightened the silver oak leaf that designated her rank and walked to the whiteboard.

Sixty-three faces focused on her. She saw nervousness and excitement and, above all else, trust—absolute trust in her ability to guide them through the coming deployment, to keep them safe, and to teach them what they needed to know. She felt the weight of their trust and the burden of her duty. She was an epidemiologist, but she considered her most important job to be that of a teacher. As an EIS instructor, it was her job to prepare her students for whatever they might encounter after their fellowship. The men and women who sat before her were the next generation of public health leaders. And one day, one of them would likely be standing where she was: leading a future CDC mission, or a state or city health department, or conducting vital research for the National Institutes of Health.

Being a teacher was a role she relished because along her own career path she herself had been lucky enough to have good teachers who cared. Fifteen years ago, Peyton had been sitting in a crowd like this one. She had been one of these faces, and it had been Elliott standing before them, giving a similar talk. She remembered how nervous she was during her first deployment. She still felt a hint of those nerves. Sometimes she wondered if there was a little excitement mixed in—the thrill of the mission, the stakes, the chase to find the origin of the outbreak and stop it before a catastrophe occurred. She had come to live for days like these. Being in the middle of a crisis almost felt more natural to her than the downtime she spent in Atlanta.

Since it was a long flight Peyton had decided to divide her briefing into two parts. The first would be background—information many of the full-time, seasoned CDC personnel knew by heart. Many of the EIS officers did too, but a refresher was prudent, and it was a great way to break the ice. This was the first foreign deployment for many of the officers, and Peyton knew they were nervous. Going over what they already knew would give them a boost of confidence.

She grabbed a blue marker from the whiteboard's tray. "Okay, let's get started. As you know from the preliminary briefing, we'll be splitting up in Nairobi. Eleven of you will be assisting with operations there; the remainder will join me in Mandera and will likely travel to the surrounding areas. However, I want each of you to be versed on our PPE protocol for the deployment, and I want to share some basic background information. We'll cover mission-specific directives once we get closer to landing." She quickly covered their PPE, which included gowns, coveralls, hoods, goggles, boot covers, gloves, and other items used to protect against infectious material.

"There's a chance that each of you will come into contact with the pathogen in some way. Those of you in Nairobi may be called into the field. First, know that it will be hot inside the suits. Kenya is located in a tropical zone. Nairobi is just eighty-eight miles from the equator. Even though it's November, the midday sun in Kenya will cook you. You'll be sweating before you put your suit on, and you'll sweat even more while wearing it.

"Second, you'll likely be unnerved by what you see. Some of us never get used to the human suffering we encounter during these deployments. There's nothing wrong with that. You're going to witness people living in poverty and circumstances you may have never seen before. If you feel overwhelmed, it's okay to excuse yourself. Just let a team member know, then walk away and take deep breaths. Whatever you do, *do not take your suit off*. Inspecting and donning your suit is important, but being careful while wearing it is even more important. After you've had contact with patients, you may have virus particles and bacteria on the outside of your suit, hood, goggles, gloves, and boots. Even a rip in your PPE will put your life at risk. When it comes to removing your suit: *take—your—time*. It won't be easy; one hour is about all anyone can stand in the suits in this kind of heat, and by the end of that hour, you'll be dying to get free. But again, take your time. Your life depends on it.

"Okay, what's our deployment goal here? Anybody?"

The EIS agents, most in their late twenties or early thirties, sat near the front. The permanent CDC staff on the mission were a bit older, and most had deployed for a dozen outbreaks before. They sat toward the back and kept quiet during the Q&A, giving the EIS officers the opportunity to answer and learn.

In the second row, a woman named Hannah Watson answered. Her strawberry-blond hair was tied in a ponytail, and like Peyton, she wore Commissioned Corps service khakis.

"Containment and treatment."

"Good." Peyton wrote the words in large block letters on the whiteboard. "What else?"

"Identification," Millen Thomas called out. He was a veterinarian of Indian descent, sitting several rows behind Hannah.

Peyton nodded as she wrote the word on the board. "Yes, it would be nice, at some point, to know exactly what we're dealing with here. What else?"

An EIS officer in plain clothes called out, "Capacity building."

"Very good. We are here to identify, treat, and contain this disease, but we're also here to help the Kenyans develop their own capacity to stop outbreaks. The CDC has poured millions of dollars into Kenya with the hope of developing a disease detection and surveillance system as well as native capability to respond to outbreaks.

"In the battle against pandemics," Peyton continued, "we have only one hope, and that's to stop outbreaks where they start. To do that, we need to enable the Kenyans. For those of us in the field, it means training the Kenyan field epidemiologists. In Nairobi, that means giving the staff in the Ministry of Health and their EOC the support and training they need.

"Okay." Peyton turned back to the board and circled the word *Identification*. "How do we identify?"

"Lab tests," a black-haired girl called out.

"Yes. We have a field test for Ebola: the ReEBOV Antigen Rapid Test Kit. ReEBOV will give us a result in about fifteen minutes. Accuracy is 92% for those infected and about 85% for those negative. What else?"

"Symptoms. Disease progression," a black man in the front row said.

"Correct. If we can establish a consistent pattern of symptoms, we can make a pretty good guess about what we're dealing with. We'll be taking patient histories from multiple locations. In Nairobi, your job will be to take all those data points and establish a clear pattern. We're looking for trends and commonalities. Now— assuming this is Ebola, what are the symptoms?"

Voices across the group called out:

"High fever."

"Severe headache."

"Diarrhea."

"Vomiting."

"Stomach pain."

"Fatigue and weakness."

"Bleeding."

"Bruising."

Peyton wrote quickly. "Good. The patients at Mandera presented with most of these symptoms. The physician there also reported seeing a rash. So we may or may not be dealing with Ebola. It may be a completely new filovirus or arenavirus. We know the disease we're facing is deadly and that it has sickened people in what we believe are two different locations. It takes a human anywhere from two to twenty days to develop Ebola symptoms.

On average, infected individuals develop symptoms eight to ten days after contact with the virus. All right. Again, if this is Ebola, how do we treat it?"

"We don't," said a white physician in the third row.

"ZMapp," a redheaded girl said.

"You're actually both right. There is no FDA-approved treatment for Ebola. There is no vaccine. If a patient breaks with the disease, we simply give them fluids, electrolytes, and treat any secondary infections. In short, the patient is on their own. The hope is that their immune system fights and defeats the virus. About half do; the average Ebola case fatality rate is fifty percent.

"It's also important to note that there are five known strains of Ebola: Zaire, Ivory Coast, Sudan, Bundibugyo, and Reston. Reston ebolavirus is the only strain that's airborne. It's named Reston because it was discovered in Reston, Virginia, only miles from the White House. It is quite possibly the greatest piece of luck in human history that the Reston strain only causes disease in non-human primates. In fact, during the Reston outbreak— which occurred at a primate facility—several researchers were infected. Luckily, all remained asymptomatic. If Ebola Reston had been deadly for humans, there would be a whole lot fewer of us around today. The other four strains of Ebola are among the most deadly pathogens on the planet. Zaire ebolavirus is the worst, killing up to ninety percent of those it infects.

"ZMapp is the only therapy that has proven effective in treating Ebola. It did very well in primate trials. During the 2014 West African Ebola outbreak, we treated seven Americans with ZMapp and an RNA interference drug called TKM-Ebola. Unfortunately, two of those patients died, but five survivors out of seven is still beating the usual odds. We have some ZMapp with us in the cargo hold, but it's a very small quantity, and I want to stress again that it is *not* FDA-approved and has had mixed results in humans.

"Can anybody tell me what type of therapy ZMapp is?"

A voice called out, "A monoclonal antibody."

"Correct. A monoclonal antibody or mab. In fact, it has three mabs. They're grown in tobacco plants, strangely enough, and they bind the Ebola protein as if they were antibodies made by the patient's own immune system. So, how might that impact future treatments? Anybody?"

Peyton paused and looked around the group. When no one answered, she continued. "Survivors. The antibodies that survivors produce could offer clues about new therapies and ways to fight the virus. So it's incredibly important that we document those survivors. In fact, there's research in progress right now that's doing just that: studying the immune systems of people who survived a Marburg outbreak years ago. In a worst-case scenario, we could also try using convalescent blood or plasma from survivors to treat critical personnel in Kenya.

"Survivors could also offer clues that would help in the development of a vaccine. In fact, Merck already has trials underway for an Ebola vaccine. Thus far, it appears to be incredibly effective, but we don't think it offers lifetime immunity. It hasn't received regulatory approval yet, and it doesn't protect against every strain of Ebola, so identification will be key here. Nevertheless, *if* this is Ebola, the Merck vaccine could get fast-track approval and end up saving a lot of lives in uninfected populations.

"Bonus question: can anyone name the other type of therapy in trials to treat Marburg and Ebola?"

Peyton scanned the group. When, once again, no response came, she said, "Small interfering RNA. Shows great promise, but it's a long way from the market.

"All right, let's discuss containment. What's the key?"

"Contact tracing," Hannah said.

"Exactly. Our goal is to find patient zero and build a tree of everyone they had contact with and everyone *those* people had contact with. It can be overwhelming. Some days you'll go out and it'll feel like the contact list is exploding—you'll be adding hundreds of people each day. But have faith and keep working at it. Eventually the list will start shrinking—if we're winning.

"Okay. What do we know about Ebola's transmission?"

"It's spread by bodily fluids," said a physician in the second row.

"Good. What else?"

"It's zoonotic," Millen said.

"Very good. Ebola and other filoviruses are all zoonotic—they jump from animals to humans and back. Zoonotic infections are a huge issue in central Africa. In fact, seventy-five percent of all the emerging infectious diseases here are zoonotic in nature. We can't just focus on human-to-human transmission to stop the spread.

"Now, raise your hand if you're a veterinarian."

Four hands went up. Three were Commissioned Corps members in tan khakis; the fourth wore civilian attire.

"Each of you will be assigned to one of the teams in the field doing contact tracing. What are you looking for?"

"Bats," they all said in unison.

"Correct. And what are bats?"

"Mammals," said one vet.

"Reservoir hosts," said another.

"Correct on both counts. The natural reservoir host for Ebola remains unknown, but we're almost certain that African fruit bats harbor the virus without symptoms. When it jumps from bats to humans, it wreaks havoc. So we're looking for anyone who may have come into contact with bats or bat droppings. Maybe they went into a cave or ate bush meat that contained bat, or maybe they consumed another animal that came into contact with a fruit bat. It's likely that when we find our index case, they'll have contracted the virus from a bat."

To the entire group, Peyton asked, "What do we do with people showing symptoms of the disease?"

"Isolation," they said in unison.

"And people they've had contact with but who show no symptoms?"

"Quarantine."

"That's right. In this instance, the quarantine period is twenty-one days from the time they first had contact with the virus. If they are symptom-free after twenty-one days, we turn them loose."

She looked over the assemblage. "Any questions?"

When no one spoke, she placed the marker pen back in the whiteboard's tray. "Good. Let's split up into groups. We've still got a lot to do before we arrive."

CHAPTER 12

IN BERLIN, DESMOND was preparing for the next day's meeting.

He had gone out just after sunset, when the streets were filled with people. Wearing the hat and secondhand clothes he'd purchased earlier in the day, he moved quickly, never making eye contact. At a drogerie, he bought the items he most desperately needed.

He stood now in the tiny, white-tiled wet room of the flat, watching his blond hair fall into the sink as the clippers buzzed. He left only about a quarter of an inch all over. He applied the dark hair dye and sat on the Murphy bed.

As he waited for the dye to soak in, he took out the disposable smartphone and did an internet search for himself—something he'd been wanting to do ever since he'd acquired the device.

The first hit was for a news article from *Spiegel Online*. The police had found the taxi driver. And more: American authorities had raided his home outside San Francisco. So he was an American—or at least had a home there.

The second search result was for Icarus Capital, where he was listed as the founder and managing partner. He quickly read his bio, but it was all about his career: investment successes, public speeches given, and a smattering of community commitments. He was a patron of the California Symphony, apparently. None of the organizations listed rang a bell.

He clicked the *Investments* page and read the names: Rapture Therapeutics, Phaethon Genetics, Rendition Games, Cedar Creek

Entertainment, Rook Quantum Sciences, Extinction Parks, Labyrinth Reality, CityForge, and Charter Antarctica.

Rapture Therapeutics. He had seen that name earlier that morning—on the employee ID card from the dead man in his hotel room.

He navigated to the Rapture Therapeutics website.

It was a biotech company focused on neurological therapies. Rapture had initially focused on helping patients manage depression, schizophrenia, bipolar, and other psychological conditions. Their most recent offering, Rapture Transcend, targeted brain plaques and eliminated them using a genetically engineered protein.

Desmond wondered if their work could be connected to what had happened to him. His firm was an investor in Rapture Therapeutics. Had he discovered something they didn't want him to know? Could he be part of a clinical trial gone bad?

He continued reading, intrigued by what he learned. The company seemed to be on the cusp of a major breakthrough. Two years ago, Rapture had licensed a therapy that might well hold the key to curing Parkinson's, Alzheimer's, Huntington's, amyloid disorders, and a host of other neurodegenerative diseases.

The key to this potential cure was reportedly discovered by accident. In 2004, an Israeli researcher named Beka Solomon was conducting Alzheimer's trials when she stumbled onto a new therapy that reduced the brain plaques associated with Alzheimer's by an astounding eighty percent. That made it far more effective than any treatment on the market.

But Solomon had actually begun her trials with a focus on a completely different therapy. She had genetically engineered mice to develop Alzheimer's and was treating the mice with a human-derived antibody, which she administered via their nasal passages. The problem was, her therapy didn't effectively cross the blood-brain barrier and reach the plaques in the parts of the brain affected by Alzheimer's. In what might go down as one of the greatest twists of scientific luck, Solomon decided to attach her antibody to a virus called M13 to transport it across the blood-brain barrier.

M13 was a special type of virus called a bacteriophage—a virus that infected only bacteria. And M13 infected only one *type* of bacteria: *Escherichia coli*, or *E. coli*. To Solomon's surprise, the antibody, when attached to M13, showed great success in her trials. But what was truly surprising was that the group of mice treated with the M13 virus alone—without Solomon's antibody therapy—*also* showed incredible improvement. The positive outcomes from the trials were due entirely to M13, not to Solomon's actual antibody therapy.

After a year of treatment, the mice that received M13 had, on average, less than a fourth of the plaques of those in the control group. Subsequent experiments showed that M13 could also dissolve other amyloid aggregates—the tau tangles found in Alzheimer's and the amyloid plaques associated with other diseases, including Parkinson's, Huntington's disease, and amyotrophic lateral sclerosis. The M13 phage even worked against the amyloids in prion diseases, a class that included Creutzfeldt-Jakob disease. The discovery was startling and represented a potentially huge breakthrough in the fight against neurodegenerative diseases.

After years of research, scientists discovered M13 was actually a set of proteins—called GP3—on the tip of the virus that was the key to its incredible ability. The GP3 proteins essentially enabled M13 to attach to *E. coli* and unzip the bacteria, allowing M13 to inject its own DNA inside for replication. And by a stroke of sheer luck, the GP3 proteins also unlocked clumps of misfolded proteins found in Alzheimer's, Parkinson's, Huntington's, and other diseases.

Desmond turned this information over in his mind. He had no doubt that Rapture Therapeutics was a large part of the puzzle. It was, after all, their employee—Gunter Thorne—he'd found dead in his hotel room.

Maybe the answers would come tomorrow at the meeting.

He closed the Rapture Therapeutics site and returned to the web search he'd done on himself. But the remaining links were of no help. He had no social media presence, and the other links were just articles about companies he was involved in or videos of him speaking at conferences or appearing in video interviews. His entire life seemed to be limited to his professional involvement in high-tech startups.

Next he did an internet search for Peyton Shaw. When he had called her that morning, she had known who he was. If he could find out who *she* was, and how she knew him, it might give him a clue to his own identity.

He learned that she was a leading field epidemiologist for the CDC. That was interesting. Was she somehow involved with Rapture Therapeutics? It seemed unlikely; her focus was infectious diseases.

He pulled up a video of Peyton Shaw giving a speech at the American Public Health Summit a few months before. She appeared on his screen, standing on a wide stage with a white background. Her white skin was silky smooth, her hair dark and shoulder length. She was clearly of European descent, but Desmond guessed there was an East Asian somewhere in her immediate family tree. She was thin and moved about the stage easily, with the grace of a dancer.

It was her eyes that Desmond focused on, however. They were large and bright and radiated an indescribable quality that he found captivating. She wasn't gorgeous, not a woman who would turn heads, but as he watched her, he was drawn to her. She possessed that certain charm that comes from confidence and being comfortable in one's own skin. And as she spoke, it was clear she was incredibly intelligent. Desmond didn't know what type of woman he had dated before, but if he were to choose at that moment, it would be someone like Peyton Shaw.

On the projection screen behind her, an image appeared of a field hospital in a rural, tropical area—likely somewhere in the third world.

"Humanity is fighting a war," she said to an unseen audience. "It is a global war—a war that has raged since our ancestors took their first steps. It may never end. This war has no borders, no treaties, no ceasefire. Our enemy lives among us. It is invisible, immortal, always adapting—and testing our defenses for weakness.

"It strikes when we least expect it. It kills and maims indiscriminately. It will attack any person, of any nation, race, or religion. Our immortal enemy is in this room. It is inside you. And me. That enemy is the pathogens that each and every one of us carries.

"For the most part, we live in an uncomfortable equilibrium with bacteria and viruses, both those inside of us and those outside, in the natural world. But every now and then, the war reignites. An old pathogen, long dormant, returns. A new mutation emerges. Those events are the epidemics and pandemics we confront. They are the battles we fight.

"Success for humanity means winning *every* battle. The stakes are high. Around the world, disease is the one enemy that unites every person of every race and nationality. When a pandemic occurs, we come together in a single, species-wide cause.

"In the history of our battle against pandemics, there have been lulls and wildfires, peaks and valleys. It is the wildfires we know well; they are committed to history. They are the times when we lost the battle. They are the dark years when the human race died en masse. When our population shrank. When we cowered and waited."

The screen changed to a painting of Europeans with bumps covering their bodies.

"In the third century, the Antonine Plague wiped out a third of Europe's population. And just when population levels were recovering, the Plague of Justinian in the sixth century killed almost half of all Europeans; up to fifty million people died from what we believe was bubonic plague.

"In the 1340s, the Plague once again remade Europe, forever changing the course of world history. At that time, we believe the world population was around 450 million. The Black Death killed at least 75 million. Some estimates go as high as 200 million. Imagine, in the span of four years between twenty and fifty percent of the world population dying.

"Europe, because of its large cities, population density, and advanced trade routes, has repeatedly been a hotbed for pandemics. But it is not alone."

The image switched to a picture of Spanish conquistadors meeting indigenous tribes at a shoreline, their wooden ships anchored in a bay behind them.

"Consider the New World when Europeans arrived. We've heard so much about the plight of native peoples in the present-day United States, but consider the populations of New Spain, present-day Mexico. In 1520, smallpox killed nearly eight million. Twenty-five years later, a mysterious viral hemorrhagic fever killed fifteen million—roughly eighty percent of their population at the time. Imagine that: a mysterious illness killing eight out of every ten people. In America, that would be over 240 million people. It's unthinkable, but it happened, right here in North America, less than five hundred years ago. We still haven't identified the pathogen that decimated Mexico in the sixteenth century, but we do know it returned twenty years later, in 1576, following two years of drought. It killed another two million from the already decimated population. To this day, we still have very few clues about what caused that pandemic. Most importantly, we don't know if or when it will return."

The image changed to a black-and-white photo of a field hospital with rows of iron single beds holding patients covered by wool blankets.

"1918. The Spanish Flu. Or, as it's more recently known, the 1918 Flu Epidemic. Less than one hundred years ago. Estimates are that one in every three people around the world contracted the pathogen. It killed one in five people who fell ill with the disease. As many as fifty million died. We think twenty-five million died in the first six months of the outbreak.

"So. Human history has a repeating theme: we battle pandemics, we lose, we die, it burns itself out, and we rebuild. We always come out the other side stronger. Humanity marches on.

"But today, we are more connected than ever before. Our population is four times larger than it was at the time of the last major global pandemic in 1918. We're more urbanized. We're disturbing more animal habitats. Most concerning, we are disturbing habitats where reservoir hosts for extremely deadly diseases reside. Fruit bats, rats, squirrels, fowl, and other hosts for zoonotic diseases are coming into contact with humans with greater frequency.

"If you ask any epidemiologist, they will tell you it's not a matter of *if*, but *when* the next global pandemic begins. That's why the work you're doing is so important. You're on the front lines of the battle against infectious diseases. Your actions may determine when the next pandemic occurs. At the local and state levels, your decisions will determine whether the next outbreak remains contained or goes global. At the risk of sounding hyperbolic, I believe that one or more of you, at some point in your career, may determine the fate of millions, and possibly billions, of lives. No pressure."

The crowd laughed, and Peyton smiled as the video ended.

Desmond considered Peyton's words as he washed the hair dye down the sink and applied bronzer to his face, neck, and ears, making his complexion turn darker. How did she fit with his situation?

He needed to talk to Peyton again. She might hold a clue he had missed. It was a risk, but he thought it was one worth taking.

He opened the Google Voice app and called her number in Atlanta. After three rings, her voicemail picked up. He decided to leave a message.

"Hi. It's Desmond. I called earlier. Sorry if I alarmed you. I'd very much like to speak with you, Peyton. Give me a call." He left his number, and wondered if she would call.

Once the bronzer dried, Desmond left the small flat. He needed cash for tomorrow. At an electronics store, he purchased two iPads with his Visa prepaid cards, then sold them at a pawn shop. With his cash problems solved gave him the funds he needed to execute his plan for the meeting.

At a sporting goods store, he bought five items he would need in case things went wrong. The purchases might raise suspicion, especially since he had paid cash, but he intended to be out of Berlin before it became a problem.

Back at the flat, he collapsed on the Murphy bed. It had been a long day, and the next day might be even longer.

He bundled up under the covers and stared at the peeling plaster ceiling. The decrepit radiator rumbled to life, the old iron monster grunting and breathing hot air into the freezing flat. Its heat was no match for the chill that beat past the poorly sealed windows. Slowly, it filled the room, and no matter how many blankets Desmond wrapped himself in, he got colder.

To his surprise, falling asleep in the cold brought to mind a memory. He saw himself trudging through the snow. The freezing powder was ankle deep. A small home sat in the distance. A wispy column of smoke rose from it, dissolving as it reached toward the full moon, a gray rope fraying in the sky. The snow fell faster with each step, whiting out the column of smoke and the cabin below.

Soon the snow was knee deep, slowing him almost to a halt. His legs burned with exhaustion as he lifted them, planted them, and pushed forward. His lungs ached from the cold. He just wanted to lie down and rest. But he resisted. He knew it would be his end. He had to keep going. Tears welled in his eyes, oozed onto his cheeks, and froze there. He carried something in his hands. It was heavy and cold, but he dared not drop it. His life depended on it.

Amid the wall of white snow, an orange beacon of light shined through: the glow from the windows of the home. Safety was in sight. Seeing the warm house gave Desmond the energy to push on, even though he wanted to simply collapse in the snow and give up.

At the porch, he grabbed a timber column, panting, willing himself to cross to the door. He imagined it opening, the man inside seeing him, picking him up, and carrying him to the warmth of the fire. But Desmond knew that wouldn't happen; the demon within the cabin wasn't that kind of man. He was likely warming himself by the fire, hoping the boy he had never wanted was dead, buried in the snow-covered fields, gone for good.

That thought steeled Desmond's will to live. He pushed forward, threw the door open, dropped the object he had carried, and stared at the man sitting by the large stone fire, a bottle of amber liquid at his side.

Without looking back, the monster called in a gruff, English accent, "Shut the bloody door, boy."

Desmond slammed the door, stripped his snow-coated jacket off, and rushed to the fire. The heat scorched him at first, and he drew back, collapsing on the wood floor as he pulled more of the frozen and soaked clothes off. Shivering, he stared at the man, silently asking, *Why didn't you come looking for me? Don't you care at all?*

The man snorted dismissively, looked back at the fire, and gripped the bottle by the neck. He took a long pull, then handed it to Desmond.

"Drink. It's the only thing for it."

Desmond hesitated, then took the bottle and sipped from it. The liquid was like fire on the back of his throat, burning at first, then numbing as it went down. Despite the wretched taste, he felt warmer. And less pain. A second later, he took another sip of the whiskey.

The memory faded, leaving the taste of liquor in his mouth.

Lying in the flat in Berlin, freezing, Desmond realized exactly what he wanted at that moment: a tall bottle of whiskey. He imagined himself leaving the flat, descending the stairs, and buying the bottle. He imagined the first drink hitting his lips, how warm he'd feel then, how much more relaxed he'd be, how much better he'd sleep, how much better things would go tomorrow.

But just as he was about to rise from the bed, his mind reminded him of something: drinking was something he didn't do anymore. And he also recalled why: drinking had already taken too much from him. Though he couldn't specifically remember it, he knew that years ago he had made a promise to himself not to let alcohol take anything else from him.

He was the kind of person who kept his promises, especially the ones he made to himself. He wouldn't seek warmth in a bottle that night—or any other night. He would bear the cold, and the pain in his body, and the painful memories. He would bear them all alone. He had done it before.

DAY 2

900 infected
13 dead

CHAPTER 13

AFTER HIS MORNING ritual, Dr. Elim Kibet donned an impermeable gown, boot covers, a facemask, goggles, and two pairs of gloves. As he walked the corridor, he barely recognized the sleepy, rural hospital. It was bustling with activity now. Everyone who had stayed was pitching in.

He opened a door and greeted his patient, the American named Lucas Turner. The young man had broken with the disease during the night. Despite his discomfort and ill health, Lucas was extremely polite. Elim knew the smell of chlorine emanating from his suit was overpowering, yet Lucas did not complain. He took the bottle of ORS Elim handed him and drank some, wincing as he swallowed.

"I know," Elim said. "It's bad. But it will keep you alive."

Lucas only nodded.

"I've sent another request for help. I'm optimistic that someone will come soon."

Lucas's cheeks were flushed, and red rings had begun forming around his eyes. He spoke with a scratchy voice. "I was wondering if you would send an email to my parents. My phone's dead." He took a sheet of paper off the side table and held it up. It contained an email address and a short, handwritten message.

Elim reached for it, but Lucas drew it back.

"I didn't know if you wanted to, like, put it in a plastic bag or... take a cell phone picture of it or something."

"Yes, that's a very wise idea, Mr. Turner."

Elim stripped the outer glove off his right hand, drew his phone out of his pocket, and snapped a photo.

Back at his desk, he composed an email to Lucas's parents.

Subject: A message from your son Lucas

Dear Sir and Madam,
I am a physician at Mandera Referral Hospital currently caring for your son. He asked me to pass this message along.
   Sincerely,
   Dr. Elim Kibet

** Message from Lucas**

Dear Mom and Dad,
Please don't worry about me. I know you worry yourselves sick as it is.
   Since my last email, I've begun running a fever. They don't know if I have what Steven had, but the doctors and nurses here are doing everything they can for me. I am in no pain.
   I want you to know that I love you and I appreciate all the opportunities you've given me. I feel very lucky. I've had the chance to work on a cause I believe in and see a part of the world few ever experience.
   I feel that my life has had purpose and meaning. I don't want to be grim or worry you. I'll see you soon.
   I love you both. Please don't worry.
   Lucas

Elim sent the email, then started making calls—to the Mandera County Commissioner, the County Health Director, National Disaster Operations Centre, and anyone else who would pick up.

When he was done, he sat back in his chair and paused: he was running a fever. He pulled his shirt up and froze. The bumps were small but unmistakable. The beginnings of a rash. He was infected with whatever had sickened and killed the American.

The hospital administrator appeared in his door, and Elim quickly jerked his shirt down.

"We've got company, Elim."

They walked to the main entrance and held their hands up to shade their eyes. Three large trucks had pulled up outside. They had just arrived—a cloud of brown dust they had kicked up was now engulfing the vehicles, preventing Elim from seeing any markings or identification.

Figures emerged from the dust cloud. They were dressed in protective suits, but carried military rifles. They formed up around the hospital and waited. Ten seconds later, a second wave of figures in PPE stepped out of the cloud and walked directly toward Elim.

☣

Off the Horn of Africa, the cargo vessel *Kentaro Maru* was slowly making its way down the coast of Somalia toward Kenya. It kept its distance from the shore, and out of the reach of pirates, though it was well equipped to repel such attacks.

In his cabin, Conner McClain sat at a desk, watching the drone footage of the trucks rolling up to Mandera Referral Hospital.

Behind him, the door opened and footsteps echoed on the floor.

He didn't turn to see his guest, who stood and watched the video for a moment.

"You think they'll take the boy back to America?"

"Yes. I do."

"We've located Desmond Hughes. He's still in Berlin. We'll have him within a few hours."

"Be very careful. Underestimating him will be the last thing you ever do."

When the door closed, Conner opened his email. It was time to begin phase two.

On another screen, a map and statistics showed infection rates around the world.

As expected, they were climbing.

CHAPTER 14

SPIEGEL ONLINE

Breaking News Alert

The Berlin Police are asking for help in finding Desmond Hughes, an American man wanted for murder as well as assaulting two police officers. Hughes, pictured above, was last seen near the Brandenburg Gate. If you have any information, call a special police hotline immediately at (030) 4664-8.

At around 7:30 a.m. yesterday morning two uniformed police officers and a hotel security guard were sent to investigate a disturbance at Hughes' hotel room. Shortly after entering the suite, Hughes assaulted the uniformed officers and held the hotel employee at gunpoint. He proceeded to rob all three men, steal a police handgun and ID card, and flee the scene in a taxi, which police have now located. The driver described Hughes as a quiet man who claimed to be a tourist interested in the city's layout and routes in and out. Authorities believe Hughes is still in Berlin and is considered armed and extremely dangerous.

Hours ago, law enforcement in America launched a raid on Hughes' lavish home outside San Francisco, California. They've told the press only that the home had been recently burglarized and ransacked.

CHAPTER 15

DESMOND HAD BARELY slept. The anticipation of talking to the source—and the hope that he might finally learn what had happened to him—had consumed his thoughts.

At first light, he took out his phone to do some research in preparation for the day. He wondered if whoever had sent Gunter Thorne to his hotel room would be prowling the streets, looking for him. He knew the Berlin police were. One or both groups might already know about his meeting with the mysterious man he had called—the person who had been corresponding with him via the Google Voice line. That meant that today would be a battle of intelligence—and, if they found him, physical might. Desmond wanted to be prepared. It took him hours to put the pieces in place, but by noon he was finished and on his way to the heart of Berlin, where his elaborate game would unfold.

He wore dark sunglasses and a baseball cap pulled down nearly to his eyebrows. Among the tourists and locals, he blended in well. He walked along the tree-lined thoroughfare of Unter Den Linden, his pace casual, his gaze straight ahead. Behind the dark glasses his eyes scanned everyone who passed him, every vehicle.

At the end of Unter Den Linden lay Pariser Platz, an open-air pedestrian square closed off to traffic, and beyond that was the Tiergarten, a lush green park crisscrossed with walking trails. The US and French embassies lined the square, and the UK embassy was close by. If Desmond was cornered by the police or the group who had sent Gunter Thorne to his hotel room, he would retreat to one of the embassies—but only as a last resort.

Desmond stood for a minute, looking across the square at Berlin's most visited and recognizable monument, the pre-eminent symbol of German history: Brandenburg Gate. His research last night had been fascinating. The gate had been constructed in the 1780s by Frederick William II, the King of Prussia, Germany's predecessor state. Conceived as the entrance to Unter den Linden—which led at the time to the Prussian palace at the end of the street—the sandstone monument had been modeled after the Propylaea in Athens. It featured twelve carved columns—six on the front side, six on the rear—and was massive: 66 feet tall, 213 feet wide.

During World War II, the buildings in Pariser Platz had been leveled, and the Brandenburg Gate was significantly damaged. It sat unrepaired until 1957, and even after its restoration it was rarely visited, as it was enclosed by the Berlin Wall, preventing residents of both the east and west from reaching it. Second only to the wall itself, the gate came to stand as a symbol of a divided country and capital.

It was before this gate's towering pillars that President Ronald Reagan stood in 1987 and said, "Mr. Gorbachev, tear down this wall." But it was the Germans themselves who tore it down—on November 9, 1989, after East Germany announced that its citizens could visit West Germany. And a month and a half later, on December 22, 1989, West German Chancellor Helmut Kohl walked through Brandenburg Gate to meet East German Prime Minister Hans Modrow, formalizing the unification of Germany after almost forty-five years of division.

As Desmond watched the midday sun shine down on the monument, casting shadows on the crowds bustling through Pariser Platz, he hoped the gate's history was a good omen—and that the day's events would set him on his own course to freedom.

A few hundred feet away, a man named Garin Meyer stepped out of a taxi and made his way to the center of Pariser Platz. He wore a navy peacoat, jeans, a ball cap, and aviator sunglasses. He took a spiral-bound notebook from his backpack, flipped it open, and held it to his chest, revealing a page with block letters:

LOOKING GLASS TOURS

He stood looking around and growing increasingly nervous.

In a white cargo van parked near Pariser Platz, two men wearing headphones hunched over a bank of computer screens, watching video feeds of the man holding the sign.

"Units One and Two, subject looks antsy. Be prepared to pursue and capture if he takes flight."

Clicks echoed over the open comm line, acknowledging the directive.

"Unit Three, confirm you've attached the tracking dot to the subject."

Another click echoed on the line.

They would know exactly where Garin Meyer went, and if they were successful, he would soon lead them to Desmond Hughes.

A runner in fluorescent spandex stopped in front of Garin, tied his shoe, then handed him a business card and darted off.

Garin read the card, stuffed the notebook into his backpack, and jogged across the square. He ducked inside a canvas-covered rickshaw, which took off, racing along Pariser Platz and onto the pedestrian trails in the Tiergarten.

"Subject is on the move," Unit Two announced over the open comm line.

A second later, he added, "He's switched. Subject is now in a rickshaw with a blue top."

The men in the cargo van could hear the field agents panting as they ran.

"I've lost him," Unit Two said.

"Units Three and Four, report."

"Unit Three. I've got him. He switched again outside the rose garden."

A long pause, then, "He's pulling away."

"Unit Six," a woman said. "I've got him. Passing the Bismarck Memorial."

She panted as her footfalls grew faster, then stopped. "Subject has exited the rickshaw. Be advised, a similarly dressed man has jumped into the rickshaw: peacoat and jeans. The shoes, sunglasses, and hat are different. Our subject is moving on foot."

One of the men in the van spoke over the open line, "Confirmed, tracking dot is moving on foot."

The woman's breathing slowed. "He's entering the English Garden, moving toward the teahouse. Please advise."

"Observe and follow, Unit Six," the agent in the van said. "Units Five and Seven, converge on the teahouse. Be advised meeting may be taking place there. Be on the lookout for Hughes and prepare to apprehend."

☣

The teahouse inside the Teirgarten's English Garden was packed with tourists. Garin squeezed past them and entered the men's restroom. The last rickshaw driver had given him another card:

In the restroom, seek the Looking Glass and await instructions.

Garin wasn't sure what it meant, but inside the bathroom, he found a paper sign taped to the second stall:

Out of Order
Looking Glass Sanitation

He slowly pushed the door open.

☣

Outside the teahouse, Unit Six watched Garin Meyer exit and race to a cab. She moved quickly, speaking into her mic. "Subject has exited the building, entering a cab with plate number B WT 393."

The lead agent in the van said, "Tracking confirmed. Units Five and Seven, pursue. Air One, do you have eyes on the cab?"

"Affirmative, Alpha Leader, target is painted. We're following."

As the cab pulled away from the curb, Units Five and Seven put their motorcycles in gear and followed a few cars behind, careful not to attract attention. Twenty minutes later, the subject exited the cab and entered a small cafe on Reichsstraße, a few blocks from the Olympic stadium built for the 1936 games. He sat at a small table in the back and took out his cell phone.

☣

Outside, the two units on motorcycles waited, as did the helicopter unit. Thirty minutes later, one of the agents in the van said, "You think Hughes got spooked?"

"Maybe."

"You want to make the call?"

"No. Let's wait a few more minutes."

They were both dreading the call—and the consequences. Conner McClain would not be happy.

The subject rose and walked to the bathroom. When he didn't emerge after five minutes, the lead agent said, "Units Five and Seven, take the subject into custody. Repeat, enter the cafe and take the subject into custody. Ground Two, bring the van around for extract."

The two agents entered the cafe, marched to the bathroom, and burst in, handguns drawn.

The bathroom was empty.

☣

In the van off Pariser Platz, the two agents shared a nervous glance. The lead agent took out his mobile phone and dialed.

Off the Horn of Africa, on board the *Kentaro Maru*, Conner McClain answered with a single word. "Report."

"We lost him."

Conner sighed and leaned back from the long desk. He stared at the screen on the wall. It showed a map, with red clouds spreading out from major cities across the world.

"Listen to me very carefully," he said. "Desmond Hughes is smarter than you are. He's smarter than I am. He's smarter than anyone I've ever met. Our only chance of catching him is to do something he's not willing to do—something he would never consider. Now tell me how you're going to find him. Quickly."

"Stand by." The agent in the van muted his headset to converse with his colleague.

He unmuted the line and said, "Okay, we could review cam footage from our field units of the cafe off Reichsstraße and the teahouse, look for any individuals in disguise—"

"Hughes would have thought of that. Remember, he's smarter than you are. Think outside the box. What's the one thing you have?"

The team leader muted his mic again. A minute later, he reactivated it and said, "Sorry, we've got nothing here."

"You know the identity of someone meeting with Hughes as we speak."

"We use our contacts to trace Meyer's mobile—"

"Hughes would have thought of that too: Meyer won't have his phone with him. Think about what you know."

"Uhmm…"

"You know that Meyer is scared. He will have another phone,

probably a disposable, and he will have given someone he loves and trusts the number—just in case. You find that person, you get to Garin Meyer. You get to him fast enough, you get Desmond Hughes—and we all live through this. I suggest you hurry, for all of our sakes."

☣

In the teahouse bathroom, Garin Meyer had expected to see Desmond Hughes waiting in the stall, but it was empty.

Garin entered, latched the door, and waited.

Someone in the next stall slipped a package wrapped in brown paper under the divider. A note on top read:

Put these on. Pass your clothes under. Wait twenty minutes. Then exit the teahouse and get in the taxi with license plate B FK 281.

In the package, Garin found a change of clothes, including shoes. He changed quickly in the cramped stall and shoved his own clothes under the partition.

A moment later, he heard the door to the next stall open. Voices whispered, though he couldn't make out the words, and the door to the bathroom swung open.

Twenty minutes later, he rose, exited the teahouse, and got in the taxi. The driver pulled away without asking for a destination.

☣

At Cafe Einstein in Unter Den Linden, a few blocks from Pariser Platz and the Brandenburg Gate, Desmond Hughes sat at an outside table, flipping through a print copy of *Die Welt*. He still wore the dark sunglasses and the ball cap pulled down to his eyebrows, blending in with the throngs of tourists bustling past. His calm demeanor hid the anticipation swelling inside him.

As he flipped the pages, a picture caught his eye: a photo of sick Africans stretched out on mats in a large room. Personnel in Tyvek containment suits leaned over them. The headline read:

Ebola Again?

93

He scanned the article. It featured several quotes from a Jonas Becker, a German physician working for the World Health Organization, who had recently been dispatched to Kenya to respond to what looked like an Ebola outbreak. But the name that jumped out at Desmond wasn't Becker's—it was Dr. Peyton Shaw. Becker was joining forces with Shaw, whom he had worked with during the 2014 Ebola outbreak. It quoted him as saying, "Peyton Shaw is the best disease detective in the world. I'm honored to be working with her and the Kenyan Ministry of Health to stop this outbreak. I'm confident we'll be successful—just as we were in West Africa."

Peyton Shaw—she's the key to all of this, Desmond thought.

But how? The message in his hotel room had said, *Warn Her*. Was the outbreak what he was supposed to warn her about? The memory he'd recalled yesterday morning replayed in his mind: the scene where he had walked through a warehouse filled with plastic-wrapped isolation rooms. It was all connected; he was sure of it. The pieces all fit together in some way.

At that moment, a man wearing a knit cap and large sunglasses stopped before Desmond, towering over him.

"That was very clever, Desmond."

CHAPTER 16

BERLIN'S UNTER DEN Linden boulevard was crammed with passersby. They weaved around the tables outside Cafe Einstein as they rushed to the Brandenburg Gate and the attractions in Pariser Platz, taking little note of Desmond and the man standing before him.

The visitor sat, though he kept his hands out of sight, one under the table, the other in his jacket pocket.

"Did you kill him?" he asked.

Desmond slowly lowered the paper copy of *Die Welt* to the table and leaned back. "What did I tell you on the phone?"

"I asked you a question."

"I have a gun pointed at you under this table," Desmond said. "If you're not the man I spoke with on the phone, I will shoot you, then I will figure out who sent you, and I will find them and get my answers from them."

The man grew very still. "You said to wear a navy peacoat, jeans, sunglasses, and a hat. To hold up a sign that said 'Looking Glass Tours' in Pariser Platz."

"Where are the clothes?"

The man swallowed, still visibly nervous. "I slipped them under a bathroom stall in the teahouse."

"What's your name?"

Confusion crossed the man's face.

"Humor me," Desmond said.

"Garin Meyer."

The night before, and all that morning, Desmond had considered very carefully what he would say to this man. And he had decided to lay it all on the line. He needed answers, and he sensed that time was running out.

"Garin, yesterday morning, when I woke up in the Concord Hotel, that man was dead in my living room. I had a big bruise on my ribs and a knot on my head, and I don't remember anything prior to that—who I am, what happened to me, or how he died."

Garin shook his head, clearly skeptical. "You're lying."

"I'm not. I found a note in my pocket. It led me to your phone number."

Garin squinted and glanced away from Desmond, as if contemplating whether he believed him.

"What do you want from me?"

"Answers. I'm trying to figure out what happened to me."

Garin looked incredulous. "*You* want answers from *me*?"

"What's wrong with that?"

"Because you owe *me* some answers." Garin glanced around. "Forget it. I'm done."

He began to stand, but Desmond leaned forward and grabbed his forearm. "You said someone was following you. What if it's the same person who killed Gunter Thorne?"

That got Garin's attention.

"You really want to walk away without hearing what I have to say?"

Garin exhaled and settled back into the chair.

"Okay. Good. Let's start over. How do we know each other? What do you do?"

"I'm an investigative journalist writing for *Der Spiegel*. You contacted me a few weeks ago."

"Why?"

"To discuss a story I'd written. It was about multi-national corporations that were possibly colluding with each other on everything from bid-fixing to currency manipulation and unauthorized clinical trials. You said I'd stumbled upon something much bigger, that I'd only seen the tip of the iceberg. You wanted to meet. You promised me the biggest story of my career, 'possibly the biggest story of all time.'"

"A story about what?"

"The Looking Glass."

The three words struck fear into Desmond. But try as he might, he couldn't remember why.

"What is the Looking Glass?" he asked.

"According to you, it's a project that has been going on for over two thousand years. A scientific endeavor on a scale the world has never seen before. You said the greatest scientific minds in history, across generations, had been working on the Looking Glass, and that it was near completion. Your words to me were that it would make the Manhattan Project and the creation of the nuclear bomb look like a middle school science fair exhibit."

"The Looking Glass is a weapon?"

"I don't know; you never told me. We were supposed to meet four days ago. You were going to tell me everything then, and I was going to write up the story and publish it online. You said it was the only way to stop what was going to happen. You said they had penetrated all levels of governments around the world, and that exposing them was the only way to stop them."

"Stop whom?"

"Again, I don't know."

"And you have no idea what the Looking Glass is, or does?"

"I wish I did. You wouldn't tell me over the phone, only that very soon the scientists building it would use it to take control of the human race, and that it would permanently alter humanity's future."

Desmond couldn't hide his disappointment. He had woken up this morning expecting to get answers. And so, it seemed, had Garin Meyer. The man had as many questions as Desmond did.

"Can you tell me anything else? Anything I said, even if you think it might be irrelevant."

"Just one other thing. You said there were three components of the Looking Glass: Rook, Rendition, and Rapture."

Rapture Therapeutics, Desmond thought. The dead man in his hotel room had been a security worker there. As for *Rook* and *Rendition*… he was sure he had seen those words somewhere too, but he couldn't place them.

Garin reached into his pocket and drew out a flip phone.

"I said no phones."

"You're also wanted for murder. This is a disposable I bought just in case there was trouble. Only my fiancée has the number."

Garin opened the phone, held it to his ear, and listened a moment, his body growing tense. He spoke in German, quickly, whispering, and Desmond had to focus in order to translate the words in his mind. "Don't worry, it's okay. Everything will be okay. I love you. I'll see you soon."

Something was wrong. Desmond glanced around, taking in every face, every car, every motorcycle, his focus sharpened, like an animal on the open prairie that had sensed a predator entering its territory.

Garin tapped a few keys on the phone.

"Hand me the phone, Garin."

The German reporter swallowed but kept his head down, typing more quickly.

Desmond reached across the table and grabbed the phone out of Garin's hands, drawing the attention of several people at nearby tables. The screen was open to the text messages window, where Garin had written a single line:

Cafe Einstein

"I'm sorry," Garin said. "They have my fiancée. They said they'd kill her if I didn't tell them where we were and keep you here."

Over Garin's shoulder, just down the street, Desmond saw a white cargo van pull away from the curb, its tires screeching, with two motorcycles close behind. All three vehicles were barreling toward the cafe.

"I'm sorry too, Garin."

Below the table, Desmond pulled the ring igniters on three tactical smoke grenades. Smoke billowed from under the table, pouring into the street. He took the remaining two canisters from his backpack, stood, pulled the ring igniters, and tossed them in opposite directions into the street. The smoke pulled a curtain across the thoroughfare. People shouted and shoved, scrambling to get off the street.

Desmond tossed Garin's phone onto the table and ran, covering his mouth with his arm, the handgun held straight down at his side in case they caught up to him. He moved quickly, turning off Unter den Linden, putting distance between himself and the scene.

Behind him, he heard tires lock and slide against pavement. Cars collided. The roar of the motorcycles ceased.

A block over from Unter den Linden, on Mittelstraße, he slipped into the cab he had paid to wait for this very contingency. The Arabic man behind the wheel began driving, whisking him away to the destination Desmond had given him, glancing in the mirror suspiciously.

Desmond knew he had to get off the streets. If he could make it to the Tränenpalast and onto the boat docked along the River Spree, he might have a chance.

The taxi turned.

Desmond never saw the black parcel van that crashed into the driver side, slamming his head into the window.

His vision went black, and he fought to stay conscious. He pulled the handle on his door and stumbled out. His eyes wouldn't focus. He reached in his pocket for the gun. He'd have to fight them.

Boots pounded the pavement: three figures in black body armor carrying assault rifles. They rushed toward him. He raised the gun, but a hand caught his arm. Another reached around him and covered his mouth with a cloth.

Slowly, the blackness became complete.

CHAPTER 17

THE WORLD HEALTH Organization and Health Canada operate an early warning system for pandemics. The system is called the Global Public Health Information Network, or GPHIN for short, and it has saved millions of lives.

In 2003, GPHIN identified SARS in Hong Kong long before local health agencies knew what was going on. SARS remained a largely regional epidemic instead of a global pandemic thanks to GPHIN and the prescient actions of several health workers, including a doctor who ordered the slaughter of 1.5 million chickens and birds who were likely infected with the virus.

In 2012, GPHIN again detected warning signs of an outbreak—this time of a respiratory illness in Jordan. The system was again correct, predicting the Middle East Respiratory Syndrome Coronavirus—MERS-CoV—before it went global.

In a sense, GPHIN is to global pandemics what the seismometer and Richter scale are to earthquakes. Every day, GPHIN collects data from local, state, regional, and national health departments. It also crawls social media and blogs, looking for signs of a new outbreak.

Hours after Peyton's team arrived in Kenya, GPHIN identified what could be called a tremor. The data supporting the alert was broad-based, with signals from official and informal sources around the world. The pattern of symptoms was consistent. Around the world, people were getting sick with a mysterious respiratory illness.

Within minutes, an analyst at Health Canada reviewed the alert and wrote the following memo:

> Respiratory alert Nov-22-A93 is a strong, broad-based signal consistent with an infectious disease being transmitted across continents in a short time span. Pathogen is unknown at this time but is most likely a flu strain, perhaps a new variant. Recommend further monitoring and investigation by local health departments.

Staff at the WHO's Global Outbreak and Alert Response Network (GOARN) filed the alert along with others they received from around the world that day.

CHAPTER 18

FROM HIS OFFICE, Elim watched the soldiers patrol the perimeter. Inside, figures dressed in protective suits roamed the halls. They had spent hours interrogating him, his staff, and his young American patient, Lucas Turner.

The British patient had died four hours ago. His death was quite messy. The man had been barely conscious since arriving, his fever and fatigue rendering him listless. In his final hours, however, he'd tried to rise from the bed and escape his room, shouting, confused, inconsolable. Elim had begun to suit up to enter the room, but they had stopped him. Instead, the suited team entered the patient's room. They placed a camcorder on a table in the corner and left without offering help, sealing the room again until the patient fell quiet for the last time. Then they marched to their trucks, returned with a body bag, and placed the man unceremoniously inside.

When the group had first arrived, Elim had thought the hospital was saved. Now he suspected they were all prisoners here, and they would leave the same way the British patient had.

CHAPTER 19

WHEN THE AIR Force transport plane was two hours away from Nairobi, Peyton walked to the whiteboard again.

"Listen up. We'll be landing soon, so let's go through a couple of procedural guidelines. We still don't know what this pathogen is. We may not know for another five days, maybe more. We're going to proceed as if we're dealing with Ebola.

"For those working in Nairobi, be in your hotel room at least one hour before sunset. I suggest you eat your meals together, do a head count, and retire to your rooms. Lock the door and wedge something under it. If somebody is missing or late getting back, call them immediately. If they don't answer, or if anything sounds amiss, call the US embassy and the EOC. Kidnapping and ransom is a possibility in Kenya.

"The security situation in the field may be fluid; consult the deployment briefing handout for SOPs and observe any updates from me. A word on food for those in the field: only eat your MREs. The people you'll encounter are often very hospitable and will likely be extremely grateful for our help. They may offer you food. It may be the only thing they have to offer. And it may well be safe to eat—but you are ordered to decline. Tell them that your supervisor requires you to eat only the government-issued food and that you're sorry.

"Any questions?"

Silence fell over the group for a few seconds, then one woman asked, "Are we doing anything organized for Thanksgiving?"

The question caught Peyton off guard. She had already forgotten about Thanksgiving.

"Uh, yeah," she said. "For those of you in Nairobi, there's probably something at the US embassy and/or CDC Kenya. I'll check into details and relay that to your team leaders. We'll need to arrange security. For the teams in the field with me, we'll figure something out. Other questions?"

A Commissioned Corps officer and physician named Phil Stevens spoke up. "Does that mean we're relaxing the bush meat policy to dine with the natives on Thursday?"

"Yes, but only for you, Dr. Stevens. The featured dish will be Fruit Bat Meatloaf. I've heard it's to die for."

When the laughs subsided, Peyton continued in a more serious tone. "Two pieces of personal advice. If this is one of your first deployments, I would strongly encourage you to call your loved ones when you land. Whoever that is—your spouse, mother, father, siblings—they will be worried about you, no matter what they tell you. Let them know you're all right and that things aren't as bad as the movies. Second, a note on entertainment."

This line always had the same effect: a majority of the men in the group perked up and began paying attention.

"Find a good book to read."

The rapt attention from the men faded visibly.

"I'm serious. The days ahead will be long and intense. It's great to have an outlet, a way to step out of this world and just relax and not have to worry about anything. Some days, you'll just want to go back to your hotel room or tent and have a stiff drink. I encourage you not to do so. Staying hydrated out there is tough enough. For your own safety, keeping a clear head is imperative. If you want to have that stiff drink, do it when you get home. If you didn't bring an e-reader with you, you can download a reading app for your smartphone. And if you're too tired to read, download an audiobook on your phone. I can't tell you how many nights in the field I've fallen asleep listening to a good book. But please download books *only* when you're connected to wifi. And do not, I repeat, do *not* watch Netflix, Amazon Prime, YouTube, or any video of any kind with the satellite sleeve attached. It costs us a fortune. I don't know exactly how much, but two years ago an EIS officer binge-watched some TV show and consumed tons of data. When the bill came in, someone from finance flipped out. They actually walked over to Elliott's office and threatened to limit our satphone access or set a data cutoff. It became kind of a big deal. Elliott talked him out of it, but we're still on probation. Remember: you watch Netflix, we lose satellite access, kids in Africa die. Got it? If you're connected to wifi, knock yourself out, just not over the satlink.

"One last thing. We're going to Kenya to stop this outbreak, and part of the reason we've been invited to help is because a lot of brave, hard-working Americans went to Kenya before us and built alliances and relationships. Some of them still work for the CDC in Kenya, building those partnerships each day. We should all keep that in mind.

"This is a particularly critical time for CDC relations in the region. I spoke with Joe Ruto, the head of our office in Kenya. In early 2015, we discovered that millions in funds the CDC had donated to the Kenya Medical Research Institute, or KEMRI, had gone missing. An audit uncovered mismanagement and fraud by officials at many levels at KEMRI. With the money gone, thousands of good people were laid off. There were protests outside KEMRI for days. And even though the CDC had no financial oversight, many of the protesters and laid-off employees blamed us. This deployment could be a big step toward rebuilding relationships.

"Every one of us is a representative of the CDC and the United States of America. Our actions could impact our relationships in the region. That could have consequences for us—and for the people just like you who will be on the next Air Force transport for future outbreaks. I'm not telling you to walk on eggshells or to be afraid to take decisive action. But if we can, we ought to do our best to leave our relationships there better than we found them."

When the pilot announced that they were on approach for Jomo Kenyatta Airport, half the CDC team had surrendered to sleep for one last nap. The lights were dark in the passenger compartment except for a few glowing laptop screens at the back and several reading lights. Duffel bags and wadded-up clothes lay under the heads of those sleeping. Wool blankets covered the floor and were draped across team members.

Peyton had fallen asleep on a row of five seats. When she awoke, she realized her legs were intertwined with the person sharing the row with her. She looked up and found Phil staring back at her. He sat up quickly, held his hand out, and pulled her up. They looked at each other a moment, then set about collecting their things and getting ready for the landing, which was surprisingly painless.

She smoothed out her uniform, threw her duffel bag over her shoulder, and marched down the ramp off the plane.

It was night in Nairobi, and beyond the airport tower, the city lights twinkled. A gust of warm wind blew a few strands of her shiny black hair into her face.

Ahead, twelve Japanese SUVs waited on the tarmac. The front passenger door of the second vehicle opened, and Jonas stepped out. The look on his face stopped Peyton in her tracks.

Something was wrong.

CHAPTER 20

THE BLACK SUVS rolled through Nairobi, bunching up at stoplights and stretching out in between, like a black snake stalking through a field of skyscrapers.

In the second car, Peyton rode in the back seat with Jonas Becker, her counterpart at the WHO. On the tarmac, he had told her only that he had urgent news to share. Whatever it was, he didn't want to share it in the presence of others.

"How was the flight?" he asked.

"Good. Long."

"You sleep?"

"A little."

"Sorry I woke you so early yesterday."

"Don't be. I needed the head start."

At the hotel, Jonas offered to carry Peyton's duffel, as he had a dozen times before. As always, she declined.

The hotel wasn't fancy, but it was in a safe part of town, near the American embassy. Kenyan troops stood guard in the parking lot, and Nairobi PD had several cars along the street.

The moment the door to Peyton's room closed, Jonas said, "It's reached the villages."

He spread a map out on one of the queen size beds and pointed to three highlighted areas outside Mandera.

Peyton got out her laptop, connected to wifi, and pulled up the travel log from CityForge. "The two Americans videoed and posted their travel route," she said. "We should cross-reference to see if they visited these villages."

Jonas ran a hand through his short brown hair and looked away, as if dreading something. Peyton was five foot six, and Jonas was only a few inches taller, putting their eyes on a near equal plane. He leaned against the brown wooden dresser, searching for the right words.

"What?" Peyton asked.

"The American who first reported symptoms, Steven Collins, died while you were en route. The British employee of the aviation company is also dead." Jonas paused. "And the other American, Lucas Turner, has now broken with the disease."

It was Peyton's worst fear. It took her a moment to realize he had said *the disease* instead of Ebola or Marburg or Yellow Fever.

"The Kenyan Ministry of Health sent a team yesterday. They've set up an Ebola treatment unit at Mandera," Jonas added.

"Have they tested anyone?"

"They've tested everyone: the Americans, the British man, and most of the villagers. No one has tested positive for Ebola."

"What did they use?"

"ReEBOV. It's confirmed: we're dealing with a new pathogen."

The ReEBOV Antigen Rapid Test could show a false positive or false negative in about one in ten patients tested for Ebola, but across a large sample group, it was likely to be correct. The fact that they had all tested negative sealed the case. This was a novel infectious agent.

Which meant Peyton's entire plan had to be thrown out the window. It was impossible to know whether ZMapp would be effective against the pathogen. Flying Lucas Turner back to Emory also presented a much greater risk if they didn't even know what they were bringing to the US.

Jonas helped her bounce a few ideas around. They worked out a tactical approach for after they landed in Mandera, assigning teams to contact trace at the airport and others to venture into the countryside to survey the villages. When they had a general plan together, they called the security advisors into the hotel room to get their input.

Their Kenyan military liaison, Colonel Magoro, informed them that a Kenyan army brigade had departed yesterday morning for Mandera County and was already set up. The Kenyan government was prepared to quarantine the entire county if needed.

The UN security officer reported that the African Union troops in southern Somalia had been alerted to the situation and were establishing checkpoints along the roads into Somalia. The Ethiopians were also in the loop and were taking similar measures.

There were two men from the American embassy in the room. One was a State Department official who listened to the security preparations, asked a lot of questions, and encouraged Colonel Magoro to bulk up the units that would be guarding Peyton's teams outside Mandera. The colonel granted the request without complaint.

The other American introduced himself only as embassy security, and despite listening intently to the briefing, he said nothing. Peyton assumed he was CIA. As the men filed out of the room, he handed her a card with a number in Nairobi. "Call us immediately if you run into any trouble. We'll do everything we can."

When they were gone, Jonas folded up the map and packed his things. Peyton thought he would leave, but he lingered, his demeanor changing, becoming a little more nervous.

"You're going to miss Thanksgiving, huh?" he said.

"Yeah."

"Parents disappointed?"

"Not really. They know I wouldn't be out here if it wasn't important."

"I know what you mean. You... have a sister, right?"

"Yeah. Older sister, Madison."

"And a nephew, niece?"

"Both now. Madison had her second child last year, a girl this time. Olivia."

He nodded, still seeming uncomfortable. Peyton was surprised by his sudden personal interest. Jonas had been a great partner over the years, but their relationship had remained strictly professional.

"What about you?" she asked, unsure what to say.

"No one missing me back in Geneva. Or Heidelberg. Parents passed away a few years ago. I have a sister in London, but she's got her career and family; keeps her pretty busy." He fidgeted with his bag a moment, then said, "So no strapping young man counting the hours until you return to Atlanta?"

"No, not for a while." Peyton looked around, wondering if he would say something else. Finally, she said, "What about you?"

"No, me neither. Kind of tough with the job."

"I know what you mean."

Jonas's mood seemed a little lighter, his nervousness gone. He put the backpack over his shoulders and walked to the door. "All right then. Lock up tight. See you in a few."

"Will do," Peyton said, watching him leave, a puzzled expression still on her face.

She took a triangular wooden block from her duffel and wedged it under the door. Just in case, she also moved a wood-framed chair from the desk and placed it against the door handle. She set a can of mace by her bed and hid a sheathed boot knife under the pillow beside her.

She assumed that the hotel washed the sheets regularly but figured the comforters were rarely cleaned, just wiped off and left to collect all manner of germs and bugs from hundreds of guests each year. So she took the comforter off the bed and placed it on the dresser. She definitely didn't want it near her face. In her line of work being germ-conscious sort of came with the territory.

For the first few years of her career, she had done exactly what she'd advised her EIS agents to do: she had called her mother whenever she landed for a deployment. As she'd grown older, she had gotten out of the habit, but that night in Nairobi, sitting on the stripped bed in her hotel room, Peyton dialed her mother.

Lin Shaw answered on the second ring, and Peyton got the impression that she had been crying.

"Everything all right?" Peyton asked.

"Yes, dear. Where are you?"

Peyton told her, and they made small talk, about the flight, and her sister, and her mother's quilting. After Peyton's father passed away, Lin had raised her son and two daughters alone. Peyton had always been close to her mother, but that night, for the first time in years, her mother ended the call by saying, "I love you very much."

When she hung up, Peyton wondered if her mother was sick. She got the distinct feeling there was a secret of some sort her mother wasn't telling her.

For some reason, her mind wandered to her brother, Andrew. He had died in Uganda, in 1991, while working on an AIDS awareness campaign for the WHO and Ugandan government. On a hot summer day in August, he was working in a village in the eastern part of the country, inside Mount Elgon National Park, when a forest fire consumed the village, killing Andrew, his Ugandan liaison, and all the residents. They had to verify his identity based on dental records and personal effects. At the funeral, on an overcast day in San Francisco, there was very little left to bury.

Peyton was thirteen then, and when the service was over, a woman with wavy blond hair walked over and introduced herself, speaking in an Australian accent. She had been a friend and colleague of Andrew, and Peyton sensed that perhaps they had been more. The woman reached into her pocket and brought out an item Peyton knew well: the silver pin Andrew had received a few years before at his medical school graduation—a gift from their father. The woman handed it to Peyton and said, "I believe your brother would have wanted you to have this."

Peyton had turned it over in her hand, examining the serpent that wrapped around the staff. She was surprised that it wasn't charred.

"I thought it burned."

"I had it cleaned and refinished. I wanted you to have it in the same condition it was in when your brother carried it. All things can be repaired, Peyton. Some simply require more time than others."

On that shadowy day in August, holding Andrew's pin as the wind blew through her hair, Peyton knew for sure that she wanted to be a physician—and that she wanted to work in the field, helping people. Maybe it was because she wanted to continue Andrew's work—he had been both her hero and her father figure—or maybe it was because she thought being an epidemiologist would somehow help her understand him or bring her closer to him. But she was certain being a doctor was what she wanted to do. And she had never regretted her career choice since. She knew the risks, and they were worth it to her.

She rose and set about getting ready for bed. She brushed her teeth, turned the shower on, and stripped off her tan service khakis. She sat naked on the closed toilet while she waited for the water to warm up. Her mind focused on her upcoming decision: Lucas Turner, the twenty-two-year-old American. Peyton wondered if he would be alive when she reached him. If so, what sort of shape would he be in? Would ZMapp be effective against the unknown viral hemorrhagic fever? Could it possibly make him sicker? And with or without ZMapp, would Lucas survive the trip to America? That was, *if* she followed the original plan she'd discussed with Elliott—the plan the director of the CDC had approved. That plan had been based on certain assumptions, and in the past hour, those assumptions had changed. The pathogen wasn't Ebola.

Emory had the advanced medical assistance Lucas needed—but if they flew him to Atlanta, she would be bringing an unknown, deadly pathogen into the United States, putting three hundred million lives at risk. All to save one young man. But if she left Lucas in Africa, he was, for all intents and purposes, on his own, left to fight off the infection or die, and that didn't sit right with Peyton.

In the steam-filled bathroom, a plan began to take shape in her mind.

DAY 3

32,000 infected
41 dead

CHAPTER 21

REUTERS NEWS ALERT

Authorities in Hong Kong and Singapore have issued an entry ban on anyone arriving with symptoms of an unidentified respiratory disease. Members of each government, speaking on the condition of anonymity, said that the disease in question is not another outbreak of SARS, but instead a contagion believed to be more flu-like and persistent in nature. It is unknown how many people are infected in either city at this time.

CHAPTER 22

AT FIVE A.M., Peyton, Jonas, and their teams loaded onto the Air Force transport and departed Nairobi for Mandera. The air ambulance and a Kenyan air force transport followed along.

The passenger compartment in the US Air Force transport was cramped. In total, seventy-eight members of the combined teams sat in chairs, on the floor, and against the walls. Some of the young men took turns standing and sitting while Peyton and Jonas carried out the briefing, giving the integrated teams their assignments.

When they landed, the sun was rising over the rocky, barren hills surrounding the airport. A convoy of military trucks with canvas backs sat waiting for them. Dr. Phil Stevens led the team that would be interviewing the airport's employees, building a timeline and contact tree for the British radar technician.

After Colonel Magoro had joined them, Kenyan army troops offloaded their gear and drove Peyton, Jonas, and their team quickly through Mandera. The ride across the streets of hard-packed dirt was bumpy and dusty. Through the red clouds billowing at the back of the truck, Peyton got a hazy view of the rural town.

She saw mostly single-story buildings arranged in a haphazard grid. They spread out from Mandera Road, the main thoroughfare that ran through the center of town. Livestock wandered the streets—cattle, camels, and goats driven by ranchers bringing them to market. Residents pushed single-wheeled carts loaded with produce. Kids stood on every block, gawking at them as they passed, many pausing soccer games to watch.

Their local guide shared some background on Mandera. It was the poorest of Kenya's forty-seven counties. Education was ranked at the bottom; there were a hundred students for every teacher. Health care facilities were the worst in the country. Mandera's residents were largely subsistence farmers and ranchers. The economic situation was dire.

In 2013, the Kenyan government had begun a process of devolution, handing much of the governing power in Mandera down to the county government. With the help of non-governmental organizations like the Red Cross and the UN, as well as support from the Kenyan government, the county had started turning its situation around. They had embarked on several large public works projects, including upgrading the airport and building a new government complex, a stadium, and an international livestock market. The convoy passed several of these projects, which were still in progress. The airport and the new governor's mansion seemed to be the only completed facilities.

The government had also updated and repaired Mandera Referral Hospital. The improvements had bolstered patient safety immensely, although the local terror attacks and recent payment problems had set their progress back. The county had also acquired its first ambulance and had contracted seven more with the Red Cross. But on the whole, the hospital was still a far cry from what administrators wanted for their county and their people.

Peyton listened intently to the story of a county that was making its best effort to improve the situation for its people. The outbreak had come at the worst time.

The convoy stopped at Mandera Referral Hospital, which was centrally located. Two bus stops were nearby, as were the town hall and post office. The facility itself was a collection of run-down single-story buildings connected by breezeways. A wooden sign painted blue with white letters hung over the courtyard entrance.

The Kenyan Ministry of Health had sent in a team shortly after the outbreak was reported, and they had brought with them a military escort to protect their team from al-Shabaab terrorists and to prevent local residents from entering the hot zone. From the looks of it, the Kenyans had done an excellent job: army troops in PPE patrolled the perimeter, assault rifles at their sides. To Peyton, the place looked more like a prison than a hospital, but she knew this was for the best, as it would keep the uninfected far away.

Peyton and Jonas made their way to a tent complex outside the hospital set up by the Kenyans. At a long folding table, the head of the Kenyan Ministry of Health's mission, Nia Okeke, gave her report. She was a little older than Peyton, her black hair slightly graying at her temples. She spoke without emotion, describing the situation succinctly.

Peyton was impressed with how much the Kenyans had done in such a short amount of time. On whiteboards that lined the walls of the tent, contact trees spread out in blue and red ink. Maps were marked. Numbers were tallied with times beside them.

When Nia finished her briefing, Peyton asked to see Lucas Turner.

"Of course. And there is someone else I believe you should also speak with," Nia said.

Peyton suited up, doused her PPE with chlorine, and headed toward the hospital. Jonas was close behind her, as was Hannah Watson, the physician and first-year EIS agent. Peyton had never worked with Hannah during a deployment, but in reviewing her file, she had learned that the young physician hoped to work as a field epidemiologist for the CDC after her EIS fellowship.

Peyton didn't envy what Hannah was about to go through. She could remember her first deployment similar to Mandera; she figured every field epidemiologist did. But it had to be done: Hannah had to learn, and reading and classroom instruction could only take her so far. She needed field experience, and Mandera was the perfect opportunity.

Peyton allowed Jonas to enter the hospital ahead of them.

"You clear on what you're doing?" Peyton asked Hannah, who held a refrigerated box at her right side.

The young physician nodded. Through the clear plastic goggles, Peyton could already see the drops of sweat forming on her strawberry-blond eyebrows.

"If you get too hot or need a second, just walk outside and breathe. If you need to take a break, don't hesitate. There's nothing wrong with stepping back for a minute."

Hannah nodded again, and Peyton thought she saw some of the tension drain out of the young physician. She hoped so.

☣

Inside the suit, Hannah could feel her entire body starting to sweat. It felt twice as hot inside the hospital as it had outside.

Nia led the three of them—Peyton, Jonas, and Hannah—to a large room where at least forty patients lay on mats, blankets, and pillows on the floor. Hannah felt her pulse accelerate. She had seen pictures of Ebola treatment units, but they hadn't prepared her for this moment. Time seemed to stand still as every detail leapt out at her. Plastic buckets labeled for vomit, feces, and urine lined the narrow walkways between the makeshift beds. Empty bottles of ORS were strewn across the floor. The buzzing ceiling fans fought a futile battle with the heat that seeped through the closed windows and rose from the bodies on the floor. Jaundiced eyes turned to stare at the newcomers.

With each step the thin rubber suit seemed to collapse in upon Hannah like a plastic bag whose air was being sucked out. The sensation of the PPE clinging to her sweaty forearms and thighs only reminded her that the thin layer was all that separated her from the pathogen that was killing these people. Any break, even the smallest tear, could let the pathogen in. She could be infected, relegated to fighting for her life in this place.

She could hear her own breathing inside the suit. Outside, she heard the moans and crying of the patients. But amid the sounds of agony, a beautiful sound cut through: singing. Groups in clumps performed church hymns and folk songs. The contrast of pain and beauty was inspiring—and unnerving.

The box Hannah carried had seemed light at first. Now it felt like an anvil. She set it down next to a young woman lying in the corner.

"I'm Dr. Hannah Watson. I'm with the CDC. I need to take a small sample of your blood for testing."

The woman slowly opened her yellow, bloodshot eyes but said nothing. A black fly landed on her face, causing her to turn her head, sending the insect back into the air.

Hannah drew out the ReEBOV test kit, took a drop of blood from the woman's finger, and placed a small bandage over the place she had pricked. She slipped the sample in the cooler and lifted the bottle of ORS by the woman's side. It was half full.

"How many bottles have you been drinking per day?" Hannah asked.

The woman just shook her head.

"You need to stay hydrated. Can I get you anything else?"

After a labored breath, the woman said, "No, Doctor. Thank you."

Glancing around, Hannah noticed on one wall someone had written the letters A through F to mark the rows, and along another wall, the numbers one through twelve marked the columns. She made a mental note that A1 was not taking enough fluids and that she had no other requests.

She took out another test kit, lifted the cooler, and moved to A2. Twenty minutes later, Hannah exited the hospital. She was so hot she felt like clawing the PPE off. It clung to her sweaty skin, a hot plastic film that felt like it was melting onto her. But Dr. Shaw's warning was fresh in her mind. She took her time doffing the suit, then hurried into the tent where an EIS agent was testing her samples from row A.

The agent looked up. "All negative for Ebola."

Hannah nodded. Dr. Shaw had told her to expect that. But even though the Kenyans had already tested the patients and found them negative for Ebola, the prudent course of action had been to run their own tests with kits from another manufacturing batch, just to be sure.

Hannah also knew that Dr. Shaw had likely planned this as part of her training. Hannah would be testing more patients in the field soon, in the villages around Mandera. She'd be on her own. And she was thankful for the opportunity to learn the procedure here, where she had help close by.

☣

Nia led Jonas and Peyton to the back corner of the large treatment room, where a middle-aged man was propped against the yellowing plaster wall. His eyes were closed, and he wore a sweat-soaked tank top. A folded white coat lay by his side.

"Doctors Shaw and Becker, this is Dr. Elim Kibet, Chief of Physicians here at Mandera."

Dr. Kibet opened his eyes, looked up at his visitors, and wiped the sweat from his forehead. He smiled weakly. "In the interest of full disclosure, I was the *only* physician here at Mandera." He focused on Peyton. "We did everything we could for the young Americans. I'm sorry. It was not much."

Peyton squatted down, bringing herself close to eye level with the doctor.

"We all appreciate your efforts, Dr. Kibet. The CDC, the American government, and especially those boys' parents."

Dr. Kibet reached under the white coat and brought out a spiral-bound notebook. He handed it to Peyton.

"Before the ministry arrived, I talked at length with Mr. Turner."

Peyton ensured her gloves were dry, then flipped through the notebook, scanning the ruled pages filled with neat handwriting. Dr. Kibet had been extremely thorough. Peyton hoped his notes might contain a clue that would lead them to the index case.

"Thank you, Doctor," she said. She looked up at Nia, who was studying her intently. Peyton got the impression there was something more going on here, but she wasn't sure what.

"Are you ready to see Mr. Turner?" the Kenyan woman asked.

Inside the orange Tyvek suit, Peyton felt as though the temperature had suddenly increased five degrees. She was aware of her breath, and of the weight of the decision she would soon have to make. It was a call that could determine the fate of the young man—and possibly millions of others.

CHAPTER 23

LUCAS TURNER FELT like he had been in the hospital room in Mandera for years. He knew it had only been a few days, but those days had been the longest of his life.

The disease had started with a pain in his neck, and a fever. He had felt fine otherwise. But a few hours later, his body was turning itself inside out. He vomited nearly everything he ate. The diarrhea emptied his bowels the moment any morsel reached them, then reached for more, like a hose sucking his insides out.

He was weak and constantly tired. It was impossible to concentrate. He drifted in and out of sleep, never knowing if it would be night or day when he awoke. He drank the rehydration salts, which grew more heinous with each bottle. He had no appetite, but at Dr. Kibet's insistence, he forced himself to eat. He dreaded it; he knew his body would reject the nourishment. He felt like he was fighting a losing battle, his own body now set against him.

The smell of chlorine in the small room was overpowering. Dr. Kibet had left several paperback novels and a Bible by his bed, but he couldn't muster the energy to read them, despite his boredom. His thoughts were of his parents and his sister. They would be devastated. At one point he wished he had never come to Africa; he cursed himself for being so naive. *Dreamers die foolish deaths.* He was instantly ashamed of the thought. He refused to live his life that way—with regret, second-guessing himself. He had followed his dream, it had led here, and that was that.

Life is uncertain; in the end we control only a single thing: our own thoughts. He set his mind to controlling those thoughts. He would stay positive, even if it was his fate to die here in this place.

At some point, when exactly he didn't know, Dr. Kibet stopped coming to his room. There were new personnel, in better containment suits. They were extremely cautious with him. Unlike Dr. Kibet, they asked him no questions and never stayed in the room a second longer than they had to. Dr. Kibet had treated him like a human being. These people treated him with clinical detachment.

The sun was setting. Through the narrow window, Lucas saw a group of the new personnel gathered around a bonfire, tossing their suits upon the blaze. The fire belched heavy black smoke, releasing plumes as more rubber shells were piled onto the inferno. He turned to the small mirror on the wall, which reflected bloodshot, watering eyes and pale skin. It was the face of a stranger. A monster.

☣

With Jonas close behind her, Peyton followed Nia into Lucas' room. He was asleep, and Peyton hated to wake him, but it had to be done. The clock was ticking—and they needed answers if they were to have any chance of stopping the pathogen's spread.

Nia reached out to shake the young man, but Peyton placed her hand on the woman's shoulder and moved in front of her. She sat on the edge of the bed, clasped Lucas's hand, and gently shook his forearm and said his name until he opened his eyes. Peyton forced a smile. Seeing this young American in the prime of his life so sick broke her heart. He had come here to try to make the world a better place. And that path had led him here—to this room, where he was dying.

Lucas looked down at her hand holding his, seeming surprised that she was touching him. Peyton knew he was scared and had probably been treated with an abundance of caution—and rightly so. Still, it always amazed her how humanizing a touch could be. Seeing the hope that formed in his eyes at that moment made her proud of the work that she did—and more sure than ever that she was exactly where she was supposed to be, doing what she was meant to do.

She leaned closer and spoke softly.

"Lucas, can you hear me?"

He nodded.

"My name is Peyton Shaw. I'm a doctor with the CDC. We're going to do everything we can to help you, okay?"

"Thank you," Lucas said. The words were barely audible.

Peyton picked up the bottle of ORS from the side table. "Drink a little. I know it tastes bad." She held it to his mouth, and Lucas drank, wincing slightly.

She set the bottle back on the table and waited for him to swallow.

"I read in Dr. Kibet's notes that Steven got sick about seven days ago. Can you tell me where you all were then?"

Lucas closed his eyes, trying to think. He shook his head. "I'm sorry. The days run together."

"That's okay. Can you remember the last time you two were healthy? Maybe a time when you were happy?"

A moment later, he said, "Mount Kenya. In the park."

"What happened there? Did you come into contact with any animals? A bat? Maybe a monkey?"

"No." He paused. "No, definitely not. It was our last stop before going to the villages." He smiled. "We had barbecue. And beer."

Peyton bunched her eyebrows up. "A local barbecue? What kind of meat was it?"

"No. North Carolina barbecue. From home. And local beer. Brewed in Raleigh."

"How?"

"A package from a sponsor."

"A sponsor?"

"Icarus Capital. Desmond Hughes. He's on our board."

Peyton stopped cold. The idea that Desmond could be involved both shocked and scared her. She was reminded of his words from the call. *I think you're in danger.*

She tried to keep her voice even. "Was anything else in the package?"

"Yeah, the food was just an extra. Mainly he was shipping us our video cameras. We had decided not to bring them in our airport luggage in case they got stolen along the way—plus we didn't want to have to lug them around until we were ready to go into the villages. We weren't even sure how many we needed. Desmond offered to ship them to us when we reached Mount Kenya. He sent the package to the lodge where we were camping. The barbecue and beer was unexpected. Desmond's note said good luck, and here's a taste of home."

"That was it?" Peyton asked. "Cameras, barbecue, and beer?"

"Yeah."

Lucas held a shaky hand up and massaged his throat. Peyton again brought the ORS bottle to his lips and let him drink a bit.

"How was Desmond Hughes involved in your company?"

"He's an investor," Lucas said, his voice a little clearer. "We only met him a few times. He's a technology investor and philanthropist. Kind of intense. Really smart. Into some crazy stuff."

"Like what?"

"Change-the-world type projects. Everything from AI to medical research to quantum physics. He said the only thing humanity hasn't upgraded is itself. He thinks it's time. He said the next version would be a quantum leap forward. He was even using himself as a guinea pig."

"Why was he interested in CityForge?"

"He said building better cities was the third world's only chance."

"Chance of what?"

"Surviving."

That got Peyton's attention. "Surviving?"

"His words, not mine. He believes if the third world doesn't catch up to the rest of the world, there will be a major catastrophe—an extinction-level event. He said that's why our work is so important."

"Interesting," Peyton said. "Why does he think that?"

"The absence of space junk."

"Space junk?"

"Probes from other civilizations. This was over dinner, so maybe he was drunk." Lucas thought for a moment. "Actually, I don't think he was drinking. Anyway, he said that the most disturbing revelation in human history is the existence of two seemingly impossible facts: one, that the universe is billions of years old; and two, that the moon is not covered with wrecked space probes from other advanced civilizations that came before us."

Peyton was confused. "How is any of that related to an impending extinction-level event?"

"I don't know. He said he and a small group of people knew the real truth about why there's no space junk. He said they would soon test their theory. He was pretty cryptic about the whole thing, to be honest, and I guess we were sort of blown away by him, so we weren't really asking a lot of questions. He's kind of larger than life. And his check for $150,000 cleared, so, you know, we listened and nodded." He paused. "Why all the questions about Desmond? Is he somehow connected to this? Is he sick?"

"Not that we're aware of," Peyton said, deep in thought.

"Was the food contaminated? Are people back in North Carolina infected?"

"No," Peyton said. "We still believe this is an isolated outbreak. I'm just covering all the bases. Listen, you've been very helpful, Lucas. I'll be right back, okay?"

☣

Outside the hospital, Peyton, Jonas, and Nia washed off their suits and carefully doffed them. They entered the next tent, where Peyton pulled off her soaking T-shirt and toweled the sweat from her body. When she looked up, she saw Nia, standing naked as well, her body still coated in sweat, staring at her. Jonas was turned away, avoiding looking at the two women as he slipped on dry clothes.

"Are you going to administer ZMapp to Mr. Turner?" Nia asked. She stared at Peyton without blinking.

Peyton returned her stare. "Maybe."

"I'd like doses for Dr. Kibet."

In that moment, Peyton realized why the Kenyan Ministry of Health official had insisted she meet Dr. Kibet. It was already difficult to deny treatment to a person in need, and even harder when you had met the person.

"I can't—"

"I will give him the dose myself. I ask only for the medication that might save his life. If we cannot save him, or at least do everything we can for him, it will be difficult to ask others to put themselves in harm's way. It is also the right thing to do for a man who has put himself at risk long before your fellow Americans appeared at his door."

Peyton pulled on a dry T-shirt. "I'll have to make a call."

She walked away before Nia could speak again.

Inside the main tent, she found Hannah sitting on a long table typing on a laptop. The young physician stood when she saw Peyton.

"Do you have the results?" Peyton asked.

Hannah nodded. "All negative for Ebola. I took blood and saliva samples as requested."

"Good. I'll be right back. Get the samples ready for transport."

It was 8:37 a.m. in Mandera; 12:37 a.m. in Atlanta. Peyton slid the satsleeve onto her phone and dialed Elliott Shapiro. She hated to call him so late, but it had to be done.

"Yeah," Elliott said, half-asleep.

"Sorry to wake you."

Peyton heard him rustling out of bed, his feet pacing across the floor, a door closing.

"It's okay. What's up?" His voice was still low.

"It's not Ebola. The Kenyans tested everybody. So did we."

"Symptoms?" he asked.

"All the classic symptoms of a filovirus. If I didn't have the results, I'd say it's Ebola or Marburg. But this thing moves faster than Ebola. Mortality rate looks to be high; no one has survived yet."

Elliott waited.

Peyton tried to keep her voice even, professional. "Steven Cole is dead. Lucas Turner is infected. His condition is critical." The steadiness seeped from her voice with the last words, and she took a breath. "This kid is dying, Elliott."

"What do you want to do?"

"I want to give him ZMapp and fly him back to Emory. It's what I would do if he were my son. But… it's not Ebola. We don't know if ZMapp will even help him, and we could be putting the entire continental US at risk."

"And?"

"And we might save his life—and figure out what this pathogen is, and help find a vaccine or treatment."

"Exactly," Elliott said.

"It's a bureaucratic nightmare."

"You put him on a plane and focus on your job out there. I'll deal with the bureaucrats. That's my job now."

"All right. There's one more thing. The Kenyans have asked for doses of ZMapp to administer to a physician here in Mandera."

"How many doses do you have?"

"Enough for twelve patients."

"That's tough," Elliott said. "I want to say yes, but we may need the drug for our people if they get sick. We can't make this stuff overnight."

"I agree."

"On the other hand, if we end up flying out of there with one dose left, we may have sentenced a man to death needlessly."

"Yeah. It's almost a no-win."

"Do what you think is right, Peyton. I'll back you either way."

"God, you're no help. I was hoping you'd make the call."

"Making big decisions is part of your job, young lady. And those decisions are going to get bigger soon. I'm not going to be around forever. You're going to have to run this place when I'm gone."

"I don't want your job."

"Too bad. I'm going to insist they give it to you."

"Then I'm going to retire."

"That's the emptiest threat I've ever heard. You're doing exactly what you were meant to do. Text me when you put the kid in the air. I'll work on getting more ZMapp."

☣

Back in the main tent complex, Peyton found Nia talking to three Kenyan government employees, pointing to the map and arguing. The tall black woman fell silent and straightened as Peyton approached.

"We'll give you doses for one patient," Peyton said. "On the condition that the Ministry of Health provides us with a waiver that says the medication is for research purposes only and will be used at the Kenyan government's sole discretion. The CDC has no knowledge of what will happen to the doses, and we make no commitment to provide further doses."

Nia shook her head. "We don't have time for paperwork."

"Then I suggest you make the call now. I doubt you'll have any issues. I've found you to be very persuasive."

☣

Peyton retrieved a dose of ZMapp from their supply crates, suited up again, and returned to Lucas's room. She knelt beside him. "Hi, Lucas. I'm going to give you a medication that we hope will help you fight the infection. I'll stay here for a bit to make sure you don't have a reaction, okay?"

He nodded.

"If everything goes well, we're going to put you into a special stretcher and transport you to the airport. You'll be flown back to Atlanta where they can give you the best care possible. We're going to do everything we can for you, Lucas."

A tear rolled from his bloodshot right eye onto his cheek. He cleared his throat, looked her in the eye, and said, "Thank you."

Peyton placed a hand on his shoulder. "You're welcome."

☣

Lucas had drifted off to sleep when they came to transport him to the aeroplane. As Dr. Shaw helped him from the bed and into the isolation stretcher, he wanted to stand and hug her. Before she had arrived, he had been sure he would die here. Now he was filled with hope. For the first time since the fever had set in, he believed he had a chance at living.

He felt like the luckiest person in the world.

☣

At the airport, Peyton watched the air ambulance personnel load Lucas onto the plane, along with the samples Hannah had taken.

"You think he'll make it?" Hannah asked.

"I hope so," Peyton said. She glanced at the younger physician. "You did great today. Seeing the treatment units firsthand is unnerving. You never get used to it, but it gets a little easier."

CHAPTER 24

ELIM KIBET WAS trying his best to read when Nia Okeke entered the room and marched past the rows of dying villagers. Behind her, a man pushed an empty wheelchair.

They stopped before Elim, and Nia squatted down and made eye contact through her clear plastic goggles.

"We're moving you, Elim."

He closed the paperback. "To where?"

"A patient room has opened up."

Elim's heart sank. It was the answer he had dreaded. If a patient room had opened up, it meant that Lucas had passed away.

He tried to stand, but his weakened legs failed him. Hands grabbed him and pulled him into the wheelchair. As he was wheeled out of the room, helpless eyes peered up at him from the floor, but everything passed in a haze, as if he were having a nightmare.

As he suspected, the wheelchair stopped at the exam room where he had last seen Lucas.

"When did he pass?"

"He's not dead. The Americans are flying him home."

Elim looked up, surprised. "That's good."

"Yes. It is. Now let's get you into bed."

Nia and the other man helped Elim up, got him settled, and walked out, leaving a cloud of chlorine in their wake.

Lying there in silence, Elim thought about how quickly a person's fate could change, how precious life and health are. He had walked into this very room two days ago as a practicing physician, a man in control, with the power to heal, looking down on the sick American on the same bed where he himself now lay. He had never known just how different the world looked from the other side.

He vowed that if he became well, he would cherish every day. And although he had never wished ill health on another person, there and then he wondered if every physician might benefit from being sick—*really* sick—just once. He wondered if it would make them all care a little more, or work a little harder, to have been on the other side for a while—to have placed their life and livelihood in the hands of a stranger, even if for only a short period. He had considered himself a very conscientious physician before this, but he imagined that if he lived, he would be even more dedicated to his patients.

Staring at the ceiling, he was reminded of an old Indian proverb: *A healthy person has a hundred wishes, but a sick person has only one.*

The door opened, and Nia reentered. She was carrying the three buckets Elim knew so well, some bottles of ORS, and a case labeled *CDC.*

She moved to his IV and began attaching something.

"What is that?"

"A gift from our American friends."

"What kind of gift?"

"ZMapp."

Elim sat up. "Don't give it to me."

She put a hand on his shoulder, forced him back onto the bed, and sat down. "For your sake, it's a good thing you are no longer the physician in charge here, Dr. Kibet."

"Give it to someone younger, with their life ahead of them."

Nia smiled at him for the first time. "I like to think you've still got some life ahead of you, Elim. Look, we don't even know if it will help. This is just a trial. We're not dealing with Ebola, so we need a guinea pig to tell us if ZMapp will even work. Someone who understands informed consent. Someone worth saving."

"There are lots of people worth saving."

"True. We chose you. Now, I've got work to do. Call me if you need me."

Before Elim could respond, she was gone.

As he closed his eyes, he realized that if he survived, he would be immune to whatever the terrible pathogen was. He could help others. He could go back to work without worry. That was something to look forward to. That was something to live for.

CHAPTER 25

TWENTY MILES FROM the Kenyan border, at a training camp in southern Somalia, a member of the al-Shabaab terror network turned his smartphone on and opened *Daily Nation*, Kenya's largest news site. He scoured the stories, looking for opportunities to advance his group's cause. The top headline immediately caught his eye:

Outbreak in Mandera

He sat bolt upright when he read the article's subheading:

Health Workers from the WHO and CDC Investigate Possible Ebola Outbreak in Mandera County

He rushed to the barracks and began waking the members of his cell. They had work to do.

☣

Peyton and Jonas sat in the back seat of an SUV, bouncing along the hardpacked red-dirt road. The engine roared as they plowed through a cloud of orange dust. There were six SUVs in the convoy, plus two armored troop carriers—one leading the procession, the other just behind the SUVs—and a Nora B-52 self-propelled artillery vehicle bringing up the rear.

Peyton and Jonas had used Dr. Kibet's notes and the CityForge website to trace Lucas and Steven's travel route. Based on their interviews with the sick villagers at Mandera Referral Hospital, as well as what they'd learned from the videos posted online, they had identified a village they believed to be ground zero in the outbreak. They were en route to that village now.

"What was that about in the hospital?" Jonas asked.

"What?"

"All the talk about Desmond Hughes. Is he connected to this somehow?"

"I don't know," Peyton said. She considered telling Jonas about the call from Desmond but decided against it.

"Do you know him? Hughes?"

Peyton hesitated. "I used to."

Jonas scrutinized her, as if trying to read through her words.

"I think we're missing something here," Peyton said.

"Such as?"

"I don't know yet. Something just doesn't... feel right."

"You think..."

"I think someone is responsible for this outbreak."

"Bioterror? Here?"

"I know. There's no strategic, political, or symbolic importance."

"Unless..." Jonas thought for a moment. "Unless you wanted to test a pathogen before wider release."

Peyton wanted to continue their conversation, but the car slowed, and the noise from the engine died down. And as the convoy's cloud of dust dissipated, Peyton got her first look at the village.

Her mouth ran dry. "Back up," she said, struggling to speak. "Tell the other units to keep their distance."

CHAPTER 26

CNN *Situation Room* Segment

Good morning, and thank you for joining us. Our top story this hour is a deadly outbreak in Kenya. It has already killed dozens, including one American and one British citizen, and anonymous sources at the CDC and State Department say the symptoms are similar to Ebola—though they've cautioned that tests to identify the disease are not yet in.

Most alarmingly, CNN has just learned that an infected patient is being transported to the United States as we speak. Authorities at the CDC say that Lucas Turner, a recent graduate of the University of North Carolina, contracted the disease while traveling in northeast Kenya.

We'll be updating this story as details unfold, but we want to hear what you think. Should the CDC be bringing patients with an unidentified, deadly disease back to the US? Let us know on Twitter, using hashtag *OutbreakInAfrica*.

CHAPTER 27

WHEN DESMOND CAME to, he was zip-tied to a chair in an aeroplane. The plane was level—apparently at cruising altitude—but it was encountering a fair amount of turbulence.

His hands were bound to the armrests, his legs tied below. He opened his eyes just slightly. Across from him, a muscle-bound man with a buzz cut sat gazing at a tablet, white earbuds plugged into his ears.

An escape plan took form in Desmond's mind. Keeping his eyes just barely cracked, he began rolling his head around, mumbling. The man pulled out his earbuds and set the tablet aside. His hulking form leaned over Desmond, straining to make out the words.

Desmond jerked his head forward, slamming the highest part of his forehead into his captor's face. The soldier fell to the floor in an unconscious heap.

Desmond bent forward and bit into the right armrest, trying to tear it open. If he could take a big enough bite, he could slide his hand free, take the man's gun, and—

A hand grabbed him by the back of his neck, pulled his head up, and covered his mouth with a cloth. A sweet aroma filled his nose and mouth, and his vision faded to black.

CHAPTER 28

HER FIRST GLIMPSE of the village had spooked Peyton. It was too quiet, too deserted. Something was wrong here, and she feared the worst.

She, Jonas, and their team trudged toward the village, all wearing PPE, several members carrying cases with sample collection kits, bottles of ORS, and medications. A white tent complex stood behind them. With the sun setting across the barren red landscape, they looked like space explorers walking on the surface of Mars.

Ahead, two dozen round huts baked in the last rays of sunlight, their mud-packed walls and thatched roofs weathering the heat. Goats wandered down the village's central road, weaving in and out of dust clouds drifting in the wind.

The first hut was empty. But at the second, Peyton found what she'd expected: dead bodies. Two adults, likely a man and his wife, lay on their backs. Caked blood covered their faces and chests. Flies swarmed them. Three children lay beside them—two sons and a daughter.

Peyton motioned to Hannah, who advanced into the home, set down her cooler, and began taking samples. Peyton knelt by the two adults, swatted away the flies, and searched for clues that might establish a rough time of death. From the looks of it, these bodies had been dead for several days at least. Not good.

They found more bodies in the other huts, and several outside. Some of the villagers had probably wanted to die with the sun on their faces or the stars above them. Peyton didn't blame them.

Just as she was turning to head back to the tent complex, she caught movement out of the corner of her eye. She froze, waited. Yes—there was someone, or something, just beyond the village, crouched, watching them.

Over the comm, Peyton said, "Jonas, did you see that?"

The German epidemiologist was already walking back to the tents. He stopped. "See what?"

Peyton set down her sample case and got ready to run. It wouldn't be easy in the suit, but taking it off wasn't an option. She spoke quickly on the comm line. "Colonel Magoro, do you copy?"

"Yes, Dr. Shaw."

"We need a team of your men at my location immediately. Do not transit the village—proceed around it, and use caution. Try to stay out of sight and stay quiet. Have your men take up a concealed position a hundred meters north of me."

"Understood," the Kenyan officer said.

"Hannah, take your team back to the tents and take off your suits. Get in the vehicles and prepare to leave."

Jonas returned to Peyton's side and glanced over at her, silently questioning what was going on. Peyton nodded subtly toward the bushes. Jonas took a step toward them, but she caught his arm, urging him to wait.

A moment later, Colonel Magoro said, "We're in position."

"Spread your men out and begin walking toward the village," Peyton said.

The Kenyan troops rose, assault rifles held in front of them, and stalked forward quietly, like big game hunters approaching a kill. Peyton wanted to run, but she focused on the group of yellow-green shrubs. If she was wrong about what she had seen, the mistake might be deadly. Sweat poured down her forehead. She desperately wanted to rip the helmet off, wipe her face, and pour cold water in the suit.

Suddenly, the bushes between the Kenyan troops and Peyton shook as three figures sprang forward. A woman, likely in her forties, a young boy, and a teenage girl, all emaciated. Surviving villagers, Peyton assumed. Their eyes were wild as they barreled toward Peyton and Jonas, away from the soldiers. They stumbled, trying to get their feet under them as they ran. Colonel Magoro and his men were close behind them, yelling in Swahili.

"Don't harm them!" Peyton said. "And keep your distance. They may be infected."

Fifteen minutes later, Peyton's team was back at the tent complex. Peyton had placed the three villagers in a field isolation tent just in case they were infectious.

She sat on the other side of a sheet plastic wall, watching the three Kenyans devour the MREs she had given them from her duffel. Though the sun had set, she was still sweating excessively.

Colonel Magoro sat beside her, ready to translate.

The teenage girl breathed heavily after finishing the meal in the plastic carton. She looked up at Peyton and, to the physician's surprise, spoke in English. "Thank you."

"You're welcome," Peyton said. "What's your name?"

"Halima."

"Halima, can you tell me what happened here?"

The teen glanced toward the village. "They got sick. Coughing, sneezing. Like a cold. Then it passed, but everyone got sicker. Started dying. It happened fast."

"Who was coughing and sneezing? Just a few people?"

Halima shook her head. "Everybody. All of us. All the others."

Peyton pondered her account. If it was true, it would rewrite the pathogenesis of the disease. Whatever the Mandera strain was, it began as a respiratory disease, then progressed into a hemorrhagic fever. It was the ultimate killer—a virus that was highly infectious in the days after contraction, then extremely deadly shortly thereafter.

In the distance, she saw a figure suited in PPE advancing toward the village. She rose to find out what was going on, but Jonas was there, leaning against a tent pole, his hand held up. "It's Hannah. She thought she saw something in one of the huts. She's going to check it out."

Peyton turned to Magoro. "Send some men to follow her. Tell them to stay outside the perimeter of the village and to bring night vision goggles."

"Yes, Doctor."

Magoro rose and spoke quickly into a handheld radio. Seconds later, ten men raced from the tent complex toward the village.

Peyton held a tablet up to the plastic divider. "Halima, have you seen any of these three men?"

On the screen were pictures of the two American college graduates and the British man.

The teenager shook her head.

"Can you ask the others?"

Halima spoke in a language Peyton couldn't place. It wasn't Swahili; perhaps it was a local dialect.

"No. They haven't seen them."

"Thank you. Can you remember when people began getting sick? When did they die?"

Halima consulted the other two villagers. "Three or four days ago, maybe."

"And the coughing and sneezing. How long ago did that begin?" Inside the isolation tent, the three spoke hurriedly, arguing. "We're not sure. Maybe a week. Maybe more."

Peyton nodded. "Thank you. You've been very helpful, Halima. The information you've given us may save many lives."

Ten minutes later, Hannah marched back into the tent complex, carrying a dark object Peyton couldn't make out. Whatever it was, she was taking great care with it. She bagged it before she entered the field decontamination chamber.

A short time later, Hannah placed the plastic bag on the conference table. Peyton, Jonas, Millen Thomas, and several members from the Kenyan Ministry of Health leaned forward and examined it.

It was a handheld video camera, covered in blood.

Hannah took a seat at the table. "They were here. The two Americans."

"Good work, Dr. Watson," Peyton said.

The young physician beamed.

Peyton pointed to a worn notebook on the table. "I've been reviewing Dr. Kibet's notes. He took a detailed history from Steven Collins before he died. He also spoke at length with Lucas Turner before we sent him back to Atlanta. Both men reported having a cough, headache, fever, and fatigue a week before Steven fell ill."

"My God," Jonas said.

"We're dealing with a completely new, unidentified pathogen here," Peyton said. "In the early days, it looks like the flu. A week or two later, it kills you."

"So where did it start?" Jonas asked.

"I see two possibilities," Peyton said. "Either it originated here in Kenya, or it was brought here by the Americans."

"The package from Desmond Hughes," Jonas said, looking suspicious.

Peyton was hesitant. "Possibly."

Around the table, the Kenyans, Hannah, and Millen glanced at each other, confused.

Peyton focused on the head of the Kenyan Ministry of Health team.

"You sent teams to the surrounding villages where the patients at Mandera Referral Hospital had come from, correct?"

"We did. It's nothing like this. Some dead. Everyone is sick though."

Peyton stood and put her hands on her waist. "Okay, let's think about what we know. Our index case is likely either Steven Collins, whose body is in the air on its way back to the CDC, or one of those dead villagers we just saw."

Millen, who was a veterinarian, spoke up for the first time. "If one of the villagers came into contact with a fruit bat or droppings, the reservoir hosts might be close by."

At the end of the table, a member of the Kenyan Ministry of

Health asked their local interpreter if there were caves in the area or other natural habitats for bats.

The man nodded. "A lot of caves."

Millen rose quickly from the table. "I'll get ready."

Peyton held up a hand. "Hold on, cowboy." She nodded toward the moon, which glowed yellow in the sky. "I want you to set out first thing in the morning—when your mind is fresh and the team supporting you is well rested. Besides, there's a lot we need to do here. The temperature will drop even more soon, and we'll be able to work a little longer in the suits. One thing the Ebola outbreak in West Africa reminded us of is that dead bodies carrying the pathogen can be just as dangerous as living hosts. Much of the Ebola transmission in West Africa happened at funerals, where African burial practices, such as kissing the dead, helped the virus explode beyond the villages."

Peyton surveyed a map on the wall, then circled the villages adjacent to their location and B9, the main road that led south.

"Jonas, I think we should deploy teams to these villages and follow our SOPs: isolation and quarantine. I think there's a good chance we've found ground zero."

"I agree," Jonas said. "I'll make the call to Mandera and assign personnel."

"Colonel, I think it's time for that checkpoint on B9," Peyton said.

The Kenyan officer nodded.

"And I'd like your men to dig a fire pit."

"How large?"

"Large enough to burn our suits from today and anything in this village that might be carrying the pathogen."

"Bodies?" the colonel asked.

"Not yet. We're going to put them in body bags in the next hour or two. We'll make the call later. Right now we need to stop any transmission. If they've been dead for at least a few days, bats, birds, rats, and any other hosts feeding on the bodies may already be infected."

"When would you want to burn the material?"

"At the end of each day."

"I'd recommend against it," Colonel Magoro said. "The al-Shabaab terrorists are likely already aware of your presence here in Kenya. A large fire would paint a target on us."

"What do you suggest?"

"We could dig the pit now, fill it, and place a tarp over it, sealing it as best we can. When we leave, I'll have two men stay behind and burn it after we're a few hours away."

Peyton glanced at Jonas, who nodded slightly. "That works for us."

The three hours just after sunset were physically and mentally grueling. When they were done, the pit was filled with suits and all manner of items from the village, everything from toothbrushes and toys to clothes and stored food. A patchwork of olive green tarps stretched across the crater, duct tape connecting the pieces together like silver stitching on a plastic quilt.

A stack of black body bags lay under a white tent nearby. With each passing hour, the smell of death and decaying flesh had faded, until finally, the night's winds that swept through the quiet village were fresh again.

In her tent, Peyton plopped down on her cot and began rubbing a topical analgesic over her legs and arms to soothe her sore muscles. She wore a white tank top and athletic shorts that stopped at her upper thigh; both were soaked with sweat.

Though her body ached, she felt more at home than she had in quite some time. Since her last deployment, she realized. That was the truth: this tent in the third world, not her condo in Atlanta, was home for her. She felt most at peace here—and filled with purpose.

Tracking outbreaks was her life's work, but it was also her way of life. Viruses were predictable: they could be tracked and understood. People were different. They were irrational and hurtful and never around when they should be. People were a blind spot for her. And a sore spot. Men in particular.

Peyton knew she was on the verge of making the biggest decision of her life: whether to settle down and have a family, or dedicate herself to her work. She still wasn't sure what she wanted, but she knew being here, in Africa, in the middle of this outbreak, felt right to her. But sometimes she felt an emptiness inside of her. Being here didn't fill it, but it did make her forget about it for a while.

Jonas threw the tent flap open and ducked to enter. He stopped and squinted as he inhaled the vapors from the rub. "Whoa, that stuff is strong."

"Sorry. I can do this outside."

"No. Stay. I want some myself. My back is killing me."

Without asking her, Jonas took the tube from her hand. "Here, let me." He squeezed some of the gel out. "What have you covered?"

"Legs and arms," Peyton said.

"Let's do your back." With his dry hand, he guided her to sit on the floor, positioning her back to him. Peyton sat cross-legged, her back arched, shoulders pushed back. Jonas's legs stretched out flat on the floor of the tent, the skin on his calves resting against her knees.

When his hand with the gel touched her back, Peyton inhaled sharply and arched her spine.

"Sorry," Jonas said.

"It's okay. Little warning next time."

Slowly, Jonas massaged the soothing gel into Peyton's lower back, working his fingers first into the soft tissue above her bottom. She could feel him pulling her shorts down, then tugging the drenched white tank top up as he moved higher.

"You'll never get the smell out of your clothes."

Without a word she slipped the shorts down her legs and tossed them aside. She pulled the tank top up over her head and laid it on the cot. It wasn't the first time Jonas had seen her in her underwear, but she still felt a tingle of nervousness.

His hands moved from her back to her stomach, massaging the gel into her abs. His hands pressed into her in large, rhythmic circles, lightly touching the underside of her breasts.

Peyton felt butterflies rise in her stomach.

"That was very smart work, finding the village," Jonas said quietly. "We might be close to solving this thing."

"It was just a guess." Peyton tried to keep her voice even, despite breathing faster.

"You guess right a lot, in my experience."

He massaged the analgesic into her sides, coating her ribs all the way up to just under her armpits. "You know, as long as we've worked together, you've never really talked about yourself. I know almost nothing about you—personally."

"Not much to tell."

"I don't believe that. Tell me something I don't know about you. What do you do for fun?"

"Not a lot. I work all the time."

"And when you're not?"

"I read. I run."

Peyton heard Jonas squeeze more of the gel from the tube, felt his hands moving up her back, applying pressure, slipping under her bra strap, pulling it tight against her chest.

"Can I ask you a personal question?"

"Sure," she whispered.

"I think you're an amazing person. Smart. Funny. You've got a wonderful heart. Why haven't you settled down?"

Peyton felt his hands stop at her shoulders, waiting for her to answer. For a moment, she thought about her brother. Then her father. And finally, about the man who had left all those years ago. "I've never met a man who was there when I really needed him."

"I've always been there when you needed me," Jonas said.

"That's true."

Jonas pulled his legs back and moved around in front of her. They sat in silence in the tent for a long moment. He searched her eyes, asking a question Peyton was completely unprepared for. When his lips moved toward hers, she felt a new type of fear.

In the next tent, Hannah Watson was busy applying an anti-inflammatory to her own skin. She had stripped down to her underwear for the task; her sweat-drenched clothes hung from a string she'd tied across the tent frame. She expected them to be dry soon. The rest of her items were unpacked, aligned neatly on her side of the tent. Her roommate's side was a sharp contrast: Millen's personal effects were strewn about like the aftermath of a raid by a family of bears.

She stood in the middle of the tent, bent over, her legs spread, using both hands to rub the white paste down her thighs and calves.

Behind her, she heard the tent flap open, and she peeked between her legs to find Millen, his face a mix of shock and fixation.

"Oh. Sorry," he said, his voice strained. He was turning to leave when Hannah straightened up.

"It's okay. Just... turn around for a sec."

She finished applying the last bit of gel and slid under the covers on her cot. "Okay."

He turned, and she held the tube out to him. "Want some? It helps."

"No. Thanks, though. I'm too tired." Millen opened a bottle of ibuprofen and took four.

"Me too," Hannah said. "I'm too tired to even read."

"Same here. But I feel like I can't go to sleep."

Hannah nodded. "Yeah."

"I'm too keyed up."

She stared up at the canvas tent. "I know. I'm completely drained, but I can't quit thinking about what's going to happen tomorrow."

Millen held up his phone, showing Hannah the Audible app with a book pulled up. "I was going to listen to *The Nightingale*. Haven't started yet."

Hannah propped herself up on an elbow, her eyebrows scrunched in surprise.

"What, have you read it?"

"No. But it's been on my TBR list for a while."

"What's a TBR list?"

"A to-be-read list."

"Oh. I don't have a list," Millen said. "I just pick a book and read it."

That didn't surprise Hannah one bit, but his choice of books did, and she must have been showing it.

"What?"

"I didn't, you know, think you would like *that* kind of book."

Millen glanced at his phone, scrutinizing the cover. "Wait, what kind of book is it?"

"It's a... literary-type book."

He reared back, feigning insult. "I'll have you know that I'm an extremely literary person. In fact, I'm uber-literarial."

"All right, Mr. Uber-Literarian, how does this work?"

"Like this." Millen plugged the white headset into the phone, put an earbud in his left ear, then crouched at the side of Hannah's cot and placed the other earbud in her right ear. He sat on the floor of the tent and leaned back against the side of her cot, ensuring his head was close enough to hers to allow her to move a bit. He hit a button on his phone, and Hannah heard the words that marked the beginning of so many good reads: *This is Audible.*

She pulled the earbud from his ear and said, "Don't be a hero. Come on."

She slid over in the cot, making room for him. He pulled off his shoes and lay down beside her.

At some point, she wasn't sure when, she turned away from him, onto her side, to make more room. Shortly after that, she felt his arm wrap around her stomach, pulling her close.

☣

When Jonas's lips were six inches from Peyton's face, she turned her head.

"I'm sorry," he said, looking away.

"No," she said quickly. "It's not that. I heard something."

"What?"

Peyton paused. "Helicopters."

She rose, pulled her clothes on, and dashed outside the tent. Two black helicopters were landing just beyond the village. Seconds later, soldiers armed with assault rifles were running toward her.

CHAPTER 29

AS THE HELICOPTERS landed, Colonel Magoro's soldiers fell back to the tent complex, forming a protective ring around Peyton, Jonas, and the other health workers. Magoro raced out of his tent, barking orders into his radio as he ran.

When the dust cleared, Peyton could just make out the insignia of the Kenyan air force on both helicopters.

"What's happened?" she asked Magoro.

"It's spread. They've asked for both of you. It's urgent."

Peyton headed back to her tent to pack.

"Take some food and water," Magoro said. "It may be a long trip."

☣

In the dark of night, the helicopter flew over the loosely populated region of eastern Kenya along the Somali border. Occasionally, thanks to the headlights from a truck or car, Peyton caught a glimpse of arid, rocky terrain and rolling hills below.

She was bone-tired, but she wanted to discuss what had happened—or had almost happened—with Jonas in the tent. Yet she just couldn't bring herself to do it. She didn't know where to start. She told herself it was because she was so tired and because of the low hum in the helicopter and because she didn't want to pull the headset on and allow the pilots in the front to hear them talking. But none of those were the actual reason.

Instead, she let her head fall back to rest on the back of the seat. The slight vibration in the helicopter slowly became soothing. Within minutes, she was asleep.

☣

When Peyton awoke, her head lay on Jonas's shoulder. A small pool of slobber spread out from her lips. She reached up and tried to wipe it away.

"Sorry."

"It's okay." His voice was barely audible over the helicopter's rotors.

They were losing altitude, descending toward a large, sprawling city.

Lights twinkled below. Dozens of fires burned, some quite large.

Peyton checked her watch. They had been in the air for hours. If the disease had spread this far—to a population center—everything had changed.

As the helicopter descended, Peyton saw that the streets of the city were laid out in a grid pattern. Very few cars moved about, only military trucks, but throngs of people had gathered in the streets, pushing at barriers and shouting.

The copilot turned to look back at them and pointed to his headset. Peyton and Jonas pulled their headsets on. "Where are we?" Peyton asked.

"Dadaab. At the refugee camps," the copilot answered.

Peyton remembered the Dadaab refugee camp from the State Department briefing. Located inside Kenya, just sixty miles from the Somali border, it was the largest refugee settlement in the world, home to more than three hundred thousand people, many barely surviving. Over eighty percent of the residents were women and children, and nearly all of them were Somali nationals who had fled the drought and wars in Somalia that had lasted for years. Recently, the Kenyan government had threatened to shut the camps down in response to al-Shabaab terror attacks in the area, which they believed might have been perpetrated by followers recruited from the camps. And in the last year, over one hundred thousand refugees had been sent back to Somalia.

"How many are infected?" Peyton asked.

Nia Okeke answered—she was in the other chopper. "Thousands. At least two thousand refugees are sick. A hundred have already died. There are cases in the Aid Agencies Camp as well, including workers from the Red Cross and UN."

Nia detailed the layout of the sprawling complex, which was composed of four camps: Ifo II, Dagahaley, Hagadera, and the Aid Agencies Camp.

In the distance, Peyton saw a transport plane landing on a single-strip runway.

"What are you bringing in?"

"Troops and supplies. We're quarantining Dadaab."

"How can we help?" Jonas asked.

"We'd need your advice. How would you handle the situation here?"

Peyton and Jonas asked a few more questions, then talked privately, their voices raised to be heard over the helicopter's rotors. Finally, they settled on a set of recommendations. They suggested that the Kenyans separate the camp into four separate sections: a quarantine area for suspected cases, an isolation zone for confirmed cases, and two support camps. The first support camp would house personnel who had come into contact with potentially infected individuals. The second support camp would be for workers with no contact with the pathogen. Workers from the safe camp would unload transports and conduct any interactions with people from outside the camps.

In their years fighting outbreaks, neither Peyton nor Jonas had dealt with a situation quite like the outbreak in Dadaab; they were largely improvising. They advised the Kenyans to quarantine Garissa, the nearest town, and to close the A3 and Habaswein-Dadaab Road, the two major routes in and out of the camps.

After some discussion of the details, the helicopter turned and began flying back to the village where Jonas and Peyton were camped.

Jonas pulled his headset off and leaned close to Peyton. "This is bad. This could be the worst refugee crisis since Rwanda."

"I agree." Peyton looked out the window. "It doesn't make sense. Dadaab is too far from Mandera and too far from the village. The American kids were never here—not according to their website or what they told Dr. Kibet."

"What're you thinking?"

"Something isn't right here."

"Like what?"

"I don't know. I need some rest. Time to think."

An idea was just out of reach, but in the vibrating helicopter, Peyton's sleep-deprived mind couldn't reach it. For some reason, she thought about her brother for the second time that night. He had died along the eastern border of Uganda, a few hundred miles from here, on another night in November, in 1991.

The sun was rising over the village when the Kenyan air force helicopters dropped Peyton and Jonas off. The white tent complex seemed to shimmer in the sun as the two walked toward it, their hair blowing in the wind the helicopters kicked up.

Peyton was exhausted, but she had to call Elliott—and the CDC's EOC. The situation had changed. The outbreak had spread much farther than she had imagined.

DAY 4

1,200,000 infected
500 dead

CHAPTER 30

WHEN HE AWOKE again, Desmond lay on his side, on hard-packed dirt, in a tiny open-air room. It had wooden walls on three sides and metal bars on the other. At first he thought he was in a shabby prison cell. Closer inspection revealed the truth: this was a stall in a barn.

His hands and feet were still tightly bound. His body was sore all over—even more than on that morning in Berlin. They had not been gentle when they moved him.

With some effort, he sat up and scooted forward. Through the bars, he could peer down the barn's central aisle. It was dark outside. How long had he been unconscious?

Whoever had converted the barn stall to a holding cell had been thorough. Though the floor was dirt, the wooden walls had been reinforced with vertical rebar that ran all the way into the ground. Given enough time, he might dig out, but he was quite sure he didn't have that kind of time.

The agony in his body and the feeling of being in a cell brought a memory to the surface. It replayed in his mind as clearly as if he was there.

☣

Desmond was five years old the morning it happened. He had awoken early, thrown on some dirty clothes, and bolted out of the homestead. His mother appeared on the porch as he reached the first gate.

"Be back for lunch, Des, or I'll tan your hide!"

He jumped the gate, pretending he hadn't heard her.

He ran through the brown field, his dog at his side. The kelpie's nose was often red from tearing into the game he chased down; for that reason, Desmond had named him Rudolph.

Desmond was certain that Rudolph was the fastest dog in Australia and the best herder in the world. Though he had not made a thorough survey of the country's other dogs, there was no doubt in his mind. Rudolph was also his father's star station hand, but his father had left the dog at home for Desmond today. Des was glad of it. His father could manage, and Rudolph loved their adventures more.

At the top of a hill, Desmond paused to look back at the homestead, the barn, and the painted fences running around both.

Atop a ridge, he saw his father, mounted on his horse. The flock of sheep before him looked like a dirty cloud. He took off his hat and waved it in the air, motioning for Desmond to come.

Pretending not to hear his mother was one thing; ignoring his father's summons was altogether different. Desmond's mother was quite a bit more forgiving.

Desmond set out at once, and when he was standing before his father's horse, his father said, "Don't go too far, Des. Come back and help your mother with lunch."

"Okay, Dad," Desmond muttered, as if merely hearing the words had attached shackles to his feet.

"And bring back whatever Rudolph kills." He pulled a sack from his saddlebag and tossed it down. "Well, go on. Have fun."

Desmond took off, sack in hand, Rudolph at his heels. He looked back once, and his father and the flock were nearly out of sight. The state of South Australia was experiencing its worst drought in years. His father had to drive the sheep farther and farther each week to find grazing land and water. The blistering sun and clear skies were killing their property.

Thirty minutes later, Desmond reached the thicket where he'd been building his fort. Without wasting a second, he set about the hard work of moving stones from the nearly dry creek bed and packing them with mud to form walls. He had left a small hatchet and a shovel in the bush to help with his work. If his father knew, he would be angry. Desmond made a note to bring them back with him that day.

He didn't have a watch, but he occasionally glanced up at the sky, dreading midday. In dutiful fashion, Rudolph kept guard while Desmond stacked stone after stone. He was covered from head to toe in mud when the sun told him his time was up.

He wished the creek still flowed, even a trickle to wash his hands with. It had dried up two weeks ago.

He headed back toward the homestead.

The second he cleared the trees, he smelled it: smoke.

Dark clouds rose in the east. A bushfire, moving in from the direction his dad had gone—moving toward their home.

Desmond dropped the hatchet and shovel and ran. He had to get home and warn his family. His father would be okay. He was the toughest man of all time; Desmond was sure of that.

Rudolph was at his heels, barking.

With each step, the wind seemed to gust harder. It whipped at his face. On the ridge to his right, the wind carried the fire, picking it up, tossing it about, slamming it into the land. The blaze danced like a dervish, swirling, jumping, wrapping around trees, turning them into smoke and soot.

At the ridge where he had stopped before, Desmond cried for help, hoping someone would hear him. Smoke surrounded him, a black curtain closing in. And when the wind parted the cloud for a second, Desmond froze, terrified by what he saw.

Flames rose from his home.

He screamed at the top of his lungs. Rudolph whimpered.

Desmond descended into the valley, charging toward the blaze. At the demarcation line where the fire was devouring the tall grass, he stopped and thought for a moment. Rudolph came to a skidding halt beside him, looking around. Quickly, Desmond took the sack from his belt, tore it in two, wrapped it around his forearms, and tied it with the string.

Then he pulled his shirt up to block the smoke and cover his face. He gathered up his courage and ran for his life—for his family's life—into the blaze.

The first few steps into the fire didn't faze him. Adrenaline fueled him. The flames singed the hair on his legs. Black ash and red coal kicked up in his wake, tiny specks stinging as they hit him.

When the bottom of his shoes melted, the pain took over. He screamed, almost fell. The fire was only waist high, and through a break in the smoke he saw his home's roof fall in, the flames devouring it. And with it, a little piece of him caved in too: an emotional wall, a hope he had held out. He screamed at the top of his lungs for the pain in his body—and in his heart.

He turned and ran out of the fire, not as fast as before, his legs shaking now. He screamed for help again, hoping, expecting his father to ride through the fire on his horse, throw him on the back, and charge out of the agonizing inferno.

But he never came.

Desmond's feet failed him. He wasn't going to make it. He could hear Rudolph barking. He pushed on toward the sound. He was lost in the smoke cloud. He felt dizzy, like he was going to pass out. Smoke filled his mouth, smothered him. He coughed, doubled over, but the heat of the flames near his waist propelled him back up. He couldn't think. His pace slowed. He was walking now.

Through a break in the flames, he saw Rudolph, dancing across the singed ground, barking. The sight gave Desmond a burst of energy. He pushed himself, dashed with the last bit of strength he had.

He fell the second he cleared the fire. The simmering coals on the burned ground were digging into his legs. He began crawling, the sack wrapped around his forearms sparing them the agony his legs endured. Rudolph whimpered, licked his blackened, soot-covered face, encouraging him.

Right before Desmond passed out, he thought, *I failed. I could have saved them. I should have saved them.*

☣

When he awoke, he still had the smell of smoke in his nose—and the taste in his mouth. His body ached, legs burned as if the fire were still roasting them. As he acclimated to the pain, he realized something was on his chest: a cold metal disc. He opened his eyes, which were watery and irritated from the smoke. A brown-haired woman, maybe in her early twenties, leaned over him, listening to a stethoscope. Desmond thought she was incredibly beautiful.

She smiled. "Hi."

Desmond looked around. He was in a large room with heavy blankets on the floor. White bedsheets hung from twine pulled tight, held with clothespins, loosely separating several makeshift beds from one another.

It was night; he could tell from the air. There was no power where they were. Gas lanterns lit the place.

At the end of the row of white sheets, he saw a blackboard with letters of the alphabet strung across the top.

A classroom. At the school where he would start soon. Or would have. Moans and cries rose from every corner, seeming to have no point of origin. Screams erupted every now and then. And the smell... it was like nothing Desmond had ever experienced. A barbecue came the closest, but this was different. And he knew why. When animals were slaughtered, the organs and fluid were discarded before the meat was cooked. But here... the fire was indiscriminate. The smells assaulted him. Charcoal. Sweet perfume. Burned fat. Copper. And rot, like a carcass shut up in the barn for a few days. When his eyes returned to the woman, she said. "You're going to be all right, Desmond. You were very lucky."

He didn't feel very lucky.

"Where's my family?"

Her smile disappeared. He knew before she told him. He closed his eyes and cried. He didn't care who saw him.

☣

She returned just before lunch the next day, performed an examination as she had the night before, and changed the bandages covering his legs and a few other places. He gritted his teeth through the pain, but never cried out. From the look on her face, he thought the episode might have caused her more anguish than him.

She told him her name was Charlotte and that she was a volunteer, one of many working in southeast Australia in the wake of the deadly bushfires.

"What will happen to me?"

"We'll be contacting your next-of-kin. They'll be around to collect you shortly."

"I don't have a next-of-kin."

Charlotte paused. "Well. Not to worry. We'll sort it out."

The other volunteers who had come through that morning had looked at him with sorrow in their eyes. They saw a broken, homeless orphan. Some averted their eyes as they distributed food and water and changed blankets and bedpans. It was as if seeing him could hurt them. Maybe it did. Maybe the more tragedy they saw, the more they felt, the more they hurt. Desmond didn't blame them. And he always thanked them. His mother was particular about his manners.

Charlotte was different. She looked at him the way people did before, like he was just a normal boy, like there was nothing wrong with him at all. That made him feel good.

Desmond lay there after she left, staring at the ceiling, listening to the news program that played on the radio owned by the elderly man across the aisle.

"Officials continue to assess the toll of the Ash Wednesday bushfires in southeastern Australia. At least seventy are dead, thousands are injured, and property losses are expected to reach into the hundreds of millions. In Victoria alone, over half a million acres burned yesterday. Over a million acres are expected to burn this season. Livestock losses are very high. More than three hundred thousand sheep have been lost, and nearly twenty thousand cattle. For the first time in its history, South Australia has declared a state of emergency.

"Fire crews are still battling the flames. They're getting a lot of help, too. Volunteers from around the country are pouring into the region. Over a hundred thousand are expected to join the effort, including military, relief workers, and others.

"The source of the fires is not known at this time, but the extreme drought conditions are no doubt a factor. Wind gusts and dust storms have also contributed. We've heard reports of road surfaces bubbling and catching fire, sand turning to glass, and steaks in a deep freezer turning up cooked well done..."

☣

That afternoon Charlotte returned with a gift. She had even wrapped it in newspaper.

"Sorry, best I could do."

Desmond tore into the gift, then tried to hide his disappointment as he turned the books over in his hands, gazing at the covers.

"What's the matter?" Charlotte asked.

"I can't read."

She was instantly embarrassed. "Oh. Oh, right. Of course."

"I'm only five."

"Is that so?" Her tone implied surprise. "I just assumed you were older." Desmond liked that very much.

"Well, I'll just have to read them to you." She paused. "If you can bear it, of course."

A few minutes later, Desmond was lost in the story world, the horror around him forgotten, the stench extinguished. Even the moans of the people sharing the room faded away—until a tall, black-haired man interrupted. He was roughly Charlotte's age, and he stood in the aisle gazing at her in a way that made Desmond want to get up and block his view.

"You coming, Charlotte?"

"No. You go ahead."

"You were off an hour ago, dear."

Desmond hated the way he said *dear*.

"I know. Gonna stay a bit longer."

"I'll wait for you."

"Don't."

The man exhaled deeply, the way Desmond's father always did when dealing with a stubborn horse.

When he was gone, Charlotte continued reading as if there had been no interruption.

They were halfway through the story when she closed the book. "Bedtime, Des."

She tucked him in and brushed his blond hair out of his face, then turned off the kerosene lantern. It was his first good night of sleep since the fire.

☣

The next morning he had hoped to continue the book, but Charlotte had another surprise. She brought around a wheelchair and asked if he'd like to get outside for some fresh air.

She didn't have to ask twice.

She pushed him out of the room, down the hall, and outside. The February sun felt good on Desmond's face. It had been a hot summer, one Australia would remember for a long time to come. He let the wind whip at his face and toss his hair about as he inhaled deeply, thankful to take a breath not tainted by the smell of death.

He propelled the wheelchair himself after that, glad for the freedom. His feet were still healing. The doctors had assured him he'd make a full recovery.

"You'll be walking around again in no time," they promised him. He couldn't wait. He'd had no idea how precious a gift walking was until then.

☣

Charlotte returned in the late afternoon and read to him until lights out. That became their pattern: a field trip in the morning, reading until bedtime.

A week later, Desmond again asked her what would happen to him.

"We're working on it, Des. Nothing for you to worry about."

Slowly, as the days went by, he got his feet under him again. He began to rove around the school without the wheelchair. He toured the cafeteria, the other classrooms, even the teachers' lounge, the idea of which thrilled him. In reality it was rather unimpressive.

He even volunteered, helping prepare the meals. The overweight cook had handed him a metal ladle and dubbed him the "souper scooper." The man let out a hacking laugh that turned into a cough every time he said it. Despite that, Desmond rather liked the bloke.

He was walking back to his bed when he heard Charlotte's voice coming from one of the offices they'd set up in another converted classroom. She was upset.

"You have to."

A pause.

"No, sir. You have to take him. We've tried—"

Another pause.

"Yes, that's correct. You're the only family he has."

He heard a phone placed on the receiver and her crying. He was about to go into the room when he heard the black-haired man's voice.

"You're getting too attached, Charlotte."

Desmond couldn't make out her muffled response, but the man did. And he didn't like it. His tone turned hard.

"I know what you're thinking."

"I doubt that," she shot back.

"You're thinking about adopting him."

A pause.

"You are. Have you lost your mind?"

"What would be so bad about that?"

"Oh, I don't know, where do I start? Are you going to put medical school on hold? How will you support him? Ask your parents for money? Will *I* have to support him? Were you even going to consult me?"

They argued after that, said terrible things to each other. Desmond could barely stand to listen, but he couldn't back away. The words burned like the flames that had seared his legs.

☣

Charlotte was different when she returned that afternoon. Sad. More reserved.

She read the books as if someone were forcing her to, not like before, when she had done the voices that made the stories come alive.

That made him sad all over again.

The next morning, she was at his bed when he woke up.

"We've sorted out your living situation."

She swallowed, collected herself, then told Desmond two things he already knew: that his father was originally from England, and that his father's parents, Desmond's grandparents, had passed away a long time ago.

Then she told him something he didn't know.

"Your father has a brother—Orville. They... weren't on the best of terms. However, he's agreed to take custody of you."

Desmond nodded, unsure what to say.

"Will I..." He wanted to ask whether he would see her again.

She shook her head slightly. A tear formed in the corner of her eye.

"I'll be taking you to Melbourne in two days to the airport. You'll fly to Oklahoma City. It's in America." She swallowed, forced a smile, and tried but failed to make her tone light. "Have you heard of it?"

Desmond shook his head.

He expected her to leave after that, but she stayed. She read to him again, and her passion had returned. She did the voices he liked, asked him what he thought was going to happen when the story was getting good, and read the chapter titles in a special voice.

She returned the next morning, and didn't leave until she turned the light out.

He never saw the black-haired man again, which didn't bother Desmond one bit. Good riddance.

Charlotte drove him to the airport, kissed him on his forehead, and handed him a bag that was filled with clothes. They were new, and he got the impression that Charlotte had picked them out.

"Something to send you on your way, Des."

He wanted to say something, but she was already starting to cry.

"Thank you," he said.

"Oh, now. It was no trouble." She was struggling to maintain her composure. She wiped away tears racing down her cheek and set a hand on his shoulder. "Better run along, Des. Don't want to miss your flight."

A woman from the airline took his hand and began escorting him through security. When Desmond looked back, Charlotte was still standing there, sobbing, waving to him.

The man who greeted Desmond in Oklahoma City was a sharp contrast to Charlotte. It made Desmond miss her even more.

CHAPTER 31

MILLEN THOMAS OPENED his eyes and squinted. Even muted through the tent's canvas, the morning sun was still blinding. Hannah lay on the cot right beside him, sleeping peacefully. Her breathing was barely audible. Her body was warm to the touch, and for a moment, he wondered how she could sleep in the heat. Then he remembered how exhausted they had been the night before.

He gently drew his arm from around her stomach, pausing twice, scared he had woken her. But she didn't move or wake. He rose from the cot and pulled the thin sheet over her. His body smelled of the heinous ointment she had applied so liberally the night before. It had rubbed off on him, and so had the stench. *Worth it*, he thought. *Totally worth it*.

Fifteen minutes later, he had eaten and prepared for the day. He stood at the old Toyota SUV with Kito, a local guide supplied by the Kenyan government. A map of the region was spread out on the hood.

Kito pointed. "I would start with the caves in this region, Dr. Thomas."

"Call me Millen. Why there?"

"Less likely to be lions."

That was a good enough reason for Millen. He still remembered the movie *The Ghost and the Darkness*, the story of two lions who killed dozens of people in Tsavo, Kenya, at the turn of the century.

"I like the less lions plan," Millen said.

He walked over to Dr. Shaw's tent, stuck his head in, and to his surprise, found her sleeping on her cot. Dr. Becker sat on the other cot staring at his open laptop. The German man raised a finger to his lips, urging Millen to remain quiet, then rose and led him away from the tent.

"What's up?"

"I'm heading out." Millen glanced back at the tent. "Is she all right?"

"She's just tired. Long night. You know where you're going?"

"Yeah. We've plotted the caves, should be back well before nightfall."

"Good. Make sure of it. Take your time inside; a fall could be deadly. If you have to go deep, the radios may not work. Once you have the samples, get out. There'll be time for sightseeing when this is all over."

"Will do."

"Good luck, Millen."

☣

The drive to the first cave took less than two hours, and the four men in the SUV mostly rode in silence. Millen and Kito discussed the map and the caves a little, but the two Kenyan army officers in the front seats merely gazed out the windows, scanning for any signs of trouble.

Millen was excited. To some degree, he had been training for this day his entire life. He was the son of Indian immigrants who moved to America, and they had encouraged him to explore all his affinities as a child. He had gone through a number of phases, everything from music to dance. But he had always come back to his first love: animals. He was awestruck with the diversity and complexity of the creatures that shared the world with humans. He loved how unpredictable they were, how each species seemed to have a special ability. Seeing a new animal, interacting with it, never got old.

He was especially interested in exotic animals and their habitats. He read everything he could about them and watched animal documentaries repeatedly. He considered a career at a zoo, but decided he wanted to work with animals in their natural environments. He also wanted to do something that made a big impact, not just on animals, but on humans as well.

When he graduated from veterinary school, his parents strongly urged him to become a practicing veterinarian—a career with a reliable income, a return on the considerable investment they had made in his education. But their strong-willed son won out. Instead of opening his own practice, he joined EIS, committing to a career in applied epidemiology. It was the perfect path for Millen. He would have the opportunity to travel the world, investigating outbreaks, seeking out animal hosts for infections that jumped to humans. He assured his parents that he could always go into veterinary practice if things didn't work out.

They had relented, and as he donned the PPE and looked into the mouth of the cave, he had never been more glad that they had. He was about to perform what might be one of the most important investigations of his career.

Kito wished Millen luck, and he began his march inside, a sample kit at his side. The dried, yellowing snake skins lying just beyond the mouth of the cave unnerved him, but he pushed on. The suit would provide good protection.

With each step, the dark cave swallowed him up. When the darkness was complete, he switched on his night vision goggles, bathing the scene before him in an eerie green glow. Kito pinged him with a comm check every minute, and Millen responded each time.

At the ten-minute mark, the transmission began breaking up. Millen had been dropping green chemlights each minute, but at the radio blackout point he sealed the bag of green sticks and began dropping orange markers. The tubes glowed in the dark cave, green and orange breadcrumbs tracing his path. They were military-grade, with a twelve-hour duration. He planned on collecting them on his way out, long before they went dark.

As he moved deeper into the cave, the ground became more rocky and damp. Ten seconds after dropping his twentieth orange marker, he spotted what he had come for: bat droppings.

He bent and took several samples, marking them with their depth within the cave, and placed a numbered blue marker and flag by the sample spot.

Excited to have collected his first sample, he stepped deeper into the cave, leaving the sample kit behind. He held a tranquilizer pistol in his right hand and a large net in his left. He felt his boots slipping on the wet rock, but he pushed forward. The bats had to be close by. If they were the carrier for the mysterious disease, it would be a huge breakthrough, possibly the key to finding the index patient, or even a cure. It would blow the entire investigation wide open, saving thousands, maybe millions of lives. He walked faster.

As he turned a corner, his left foot slipped on a wet rock, sending him tumbling. The gun and net flew from his hands as he slammed into the rocky floor. The fall frightened him, but he was unharmed. He rose and searched for the gun.

Bat screeches—a sound somewhere between the call of a crow and the yelping of a rodent—sounded from not far away, followed by the flapping of wings.

He turned in time to see a swarm of bats barreling toward him.

The creatures enveloped him. He threw his arms up, covering his faceplate, and stepped to the side, trying to move out of their flight path. He felt claws ripping at the PPE, the bony wings brushing past his arms and legs. He turned and ran, his head down. Rock crumbled beneath his feet. He slipped and fell, but there was no ground beneath him.

CHAPTER 32

A YELLOW SPOT burned through the white fabric tent above Peyton, like a heat lamp boring into her. She squinted, wondering what it could be. Then she realized: the midday sun, high in the sky. She sat up quickly, reached for her phone, and gasped when she saw the time. Eleven-thirty.

Jonas's cot was empty so she raced to the main tent.

Jonas and Hannah sat at a table, a large map pinned up on a board behind them. There was a lot more red on the map than there had been yesterday.

"Report," she said, trying to catch her breath.

"Want some breakfast?" Jonas asked, ignoring her order.

"I want to know what's happening."

Jonas glanced at Hannah, who got up and left. "I think you'd better sit down, Peyton."

"That bad?"

"Pretty bad."

Jonas brought Peyton up to speed on the reports from the teams in the field. Fifteen more villages were infected. Including the fatalities from the Dadaab refugee camps, the death toll had climbed to over six thousand.

Peyton shook her head. "It's impossible."

"What?"

"Let's assume Dr. Kibet was infected around the time the two Americans walked into his clinic."

"Okay."

"He broke with the disease within seventy-two hours."

"Right."

"But he never had the respiratory symptoms. His progression to the hemorrhagic stage of the disease was too fast—much faster than this village."

"True," Jonas said.

"Why?"

"Maybe because he contracted the disease from someone who was already in the hemorrhagic phase. Maybe he skipped the respiratory phase."

"Which means the disease has two separate courses, depending on whom you contract it from—and what stage they're in." Peyton thought for a moment. "There's something else: the Dadaab refugee camps were being infected at roughly the same time as this village."

Jonas nodded.

"The Americans couldn't have infected them," Peyton said. "From their travel log, they were pretty far north of Dadaab."

"Maybe they interacted with a trucker who was heading south?"

"Could be. But for the pathogen to amplify this much in such a short period of time strikes me as wrong." She pointed to the map. "It's like it's erupting everywhere in the region at the same time. How is that possible?"

Jonas stared at the map. "An index patient who infected a large group of travelers, maybe attendees at a funeral, or a meeting of representatives from dozens of villages? Could be infected food."

Peyton's mind flashed to Desmond Hughes. He had sent the package of food to the two Americans. What if the villagers had received similar packages? Desmond's call a few nights ago ran through her mind. It had ended with the words: *I think you're in danger.*

She looked around to be sure she and Jonas were alone in the tent. Her voice barely above a whisper, she said, "I know it sounds crazy, but I still think this is bioterror."

Jonas exhaled. "Okay, let's assume it is, and play it out. Al-Shabaab is the resident terror group in the area. If they could get a biological agent, it would certainly accomplish their goal of destabilizing Kenya. They want to take over the government and set up a fundamental Islamic state. The outbreak is a pretty drastic way to go about it, but it could set up an opportunity for them."

"So the motive is there."

"Yeah, but let's face it, this is way over their head."

"Maybe they had help," Peyton said.

"Maybe. But from whom, and why?" Jonas studied the map. "Look, I think it's within the realm of possibility, but I don't count it as likely. Maybe we're just looking for a group of five people who were infected at the same time. They could have set off the outbreaks at Dadaab, the airport, Mandera, and the surrounding villages. That seems more likely to me."

Hannah stepped inside the tent and handed Peyton a warm MRE and a bottle of water, both of which she badly needed. She thanked the young physician, who nodded and stepped back. While Peyton and Jonas studied the map, Hannah took out her satphone, dialed, and waited.

She spoke softly, then raised her voice. "How long?" She paused. "Hold the line."

Hannah put the phone to her shoulder. "Millen is in the first cave, but he hasn't checked in for over an hour."

"Who's on the line?" Peyton asked.

"Kito, the local guide."

"Put him on speaker."

Hannah hit a button on the phone. "Kito, I've got Doctors Shaw and Becker here."

"Hello, doctors."

"Kito, did Millen bring an extra hazmat suit?" Peyton asked.

"Yes, ma'am."

"Are you comfortable putting the suit on and going into the cave to see if you can make radio contact with him or find him?"

"Yes, ma'am," the man said instantly. "I will do my best."

"Good. We appreciate that very much. Millen should have left chemlights along his path. If the trail of lights stops, search the area for him. He may have been injured during a cave-in or accident."

"All right."

"Keep us posted, Kito. Thank you."

Hannah hung up, and Peyton looked into Hannah's worried eyes. "We'll find him."

The three physicians spent the early afternoon coordinating with teams in other villages and prepping the camp for disassembly. They planned to leave at dawn the next morning.

By two p.m., they still hadn't heard anything from Kito or Millen. Hannah had tried to call Kito's satphone, but had gotten no answer. Hannah was growing increasingly worried. So were Peyton and Jonas, though neither of the older epidemiologists voiced their fears. Peyton decided to send another SUV loaded with four of Colonel Magoro's men to the first cave Millen was supposed to search—just in case Kito found Millen injured and needed help transporting him out of the cave.

At two-thirty, Peyton called Elliott Shapiro's cell phone. Even after five years in the field without him, she had to admit that it calmed her to hear his voice. And going over the situation with him would help her get her head around what was happening.

She stood outside the large tent, out of earshot of Jonas and the staff.

"What are you thinking?" Elliott asked. "How could it have spread so quickly?"

"We've got a few theories. There could have been a group of four to ten people the index patient infected; they would have been traveling throughout the region and would have quickly spread the pathogen."

"Makes sense."

"However, I can't help thinking it could be another method of transmission."

"Like what? Infected blood? A burial?"

"Maybe. I don't know." Peyton watched the Kenyan soldiers patrolling the camp. "What's happening on your end?" She badly wanted to know how Lucas Turner was doing, but she resisted asking specifically.

"A lot," Elliott said. "The US has suspended all travel to Kenya, Ethiopia, and Somalia. We've also banned anyone from that region, and anyone who has recently traveled in that region, from entering the US. We're not alone: Europe has followed suit, Australia, most of Asia as well. They say it will be the death nail in the Kenyan economy."

"True. But I think it needs to be done."

"I agree. Also, there's been a new development here. We're tracking another outbreak."

Peyton began pacing. "Really? What are the symptoms?"

"It presents similar to the flu but with less initial intensity. It's intermittent, too. One day the symptoms are in full swing: headache, cough, fever, exhaustion, the next the patient feels almost fine. The mortality rate is exceptionally low—so far."

A chill ran through Peyton's body. He had just described exactly the symptoms the two Americans had experienced before developing the viral hemorrhagic fever.

She fought to keep her voice even. "How many cases?"

"Over a million in Asia, another million in Europe. Maybe two hundred thousand in South America so far. But we think there are a lot more. We've got half a million cases here in the US, but we're getting updated stats from state health departments so we expect that number to climb."

It was officially a pandemic. Peyton wanted to present her theory, but she needed to get all the facts first.

"How could it spread that far so fast? How did GPHIN miss it? How did we miss it?"

"The symptoms aren't differentiated enough from a cold or flu. When health departments realized that patients who had gotten the flu vaccine were still getting sick, they started tracking it more closely. The intermittent nature of the disease also made it hard to establish a pattern. But we've got a sample in the lab, and we'll have it sequenced soon. Whatever the virus is, we think it must be throwing off a lot of viral escape vectors. It's pretty tough. The good news is that out of the almost three million known cases, we've only seen a few dozen deaths. It's remarkably non-lethal."

"Interesting." Since Thanksgiving was tomorrow, Peyton asked the next logical question: "Is the director considering a travel advisory?"

"He is, but I count it as unlikely. The White House has already come out against it. Better to let a lot of people get the sniffles than kill the economy—that's the thinking on their end. If the mortality rate was higher, the calculus might be more complicated."

"Yeah. Figured. Listen, I know this is probably a long shot, but I want to mention it. The Kenyan physician who initially treated the Americans took a detailed history. Both of these guys had flu-like symptoms before they broke with the hemorrhagic fever."

A long pause, then Elliott said, "You think..."

"I think we should compare the genomes of both viruses to see if they're related—just to be safe."

The unspoken implication was that millions around the world were already infected with the deadly virus that was killing so many in Kenya.

Elliott's voice remained calm. "It's a good idea. I'll make it a priority."

Peyton exhaled and stopped pacing. "Great."

Curiosity finally overcame her. "How about the kid?"

Elliott's hesitation gave her the news before he spoke. "I'm really sorry, Peyton. He died in the air a few hours ago."

The words were a punch in the gut. Less than twenty-four hours ago, she had walked into Lucas Turner's hospital room and promised him she was going to do everything she could for him. She wondered if she had.

"So much for ZMapp," she said, trying to sound objective but failing to hide the emotion in her voice.

"You did everything you could, Peyton. And you sent us samples to work with. Let us do our part."

Peyton thought about the young man's note to his parents,

which Dr. Kibet had transcribed in the notebook. Lucas Turner had been brave. And selfless. And too young to die. Dr. Kibet had taken good care of him—the best he could. She hoped Kibet would fare better than Lucas Turner, but she wasn't optimistic.

She returned her focus to the phone call. "Right. Also, we've got another situation here: a missing EIS agent named Millen Thomas. He was exploring some nearby caves today, and we haven't heard anything from him for a couple of hours. I've sent out a search team."

"Understood. He'll turn up, Peyton. Probably lost his phone or batteries went dead."

"Yeah, I hope so."

"Anything I can do?"

"No, we're working on it here."

"All right. Call me if you need anything. And keep your head up, okay?"

☣

Back at the tent, Jonas was typing on his laptop.

"Lucas Turner passed away en route to Emory," Peyton said, trying to sound unemotional.

Jonas looked up, his big brown eyes focusing on Peyton. "I'm really sorry."

"Yeah. Me too."

☣

A few hours later, Hannah ducked through the tent flaps, the sat-phone held to her ear. "The second team is at the cave site. The SUV is gone. Kito hasn't made radio contact."

"Signs of a struggle?" Peyton asked.

"No," Hannah replied.

Peyton thought for a moment. "Maybe their phone is dead. They could be on their way back here, or they may have moved on to the second cave."

178

"Or they're trapped in the cave," Hannah said.

"It's certainly a possibility. Have two of the men suit up and go in. Tell them not to separate and to make radio contact on the minute. Call the Kenyan MOH. Request a medevac helicopter be sent to the location; we have reason to believe that one of our personnel and one or more of theirs is injured. If we don't find any signs of Millen, we'll move to the next location on their itinerary."

To Colonel Magoro, Peyton said, "Can you send more men?"

Magoro looked uneasy. "Yes, but we're spreading ourselves too thin."

"Do it," Peyton said. "And let's get reinforcements here asap."

"Understood."

☣

At six p.m. the team cleared some of the clutter off the long conference table and sat down to eat. They had still heard nothing from Colonel Magoro's second team. The third team would arrive within another hour.

The sunlight was fading fast, and the lights were on in the main tent. The army men were changing shifts, and about a dozen soldiers made their way into the tent, seeking their evening meal.

Outside, Peyton thought she heard a faint popping noise, like an air rifle. Jonas glanced at the flaps leading out of the tent. He had heard it too. Together, they walked to the opening. Just beyond the camp's perimeter, two helicopters kicked up dust from the dry terrain as they landed.

A moment later, a dozen figures emerged from the red dust cloud. They wore black body armor and carried assault rifles. Two of Colonel Magoro's men fell as bullets struck them.

Peyton heard Jonas yell, "Contact! Intruders!"

Around her, the camp erupted in chaos.

CHAPTER 33

THE FIRST SHOTS were deadly. The Kenyan troops dedicated to protecting Peyton, Jonas, and their team fell in waves as the invading soldiers advanced. In seconds, half of Colonel Magoro's men were dead. Bullets ripped through the white tent. Return fire shredded the thatched-roof huts of the village.

"Run!" Magoro yelled. "Get to the trucks and go!"

But instead of running away from the tent complex, Peyton ran back into it, to the biocontainment room where the three survivors from the Kenyan village were looking on with fear. She opened the room and pointed away from the camp.

"Go. Hide, like before. Don't come out until one of us comes for you."

Peyton felt a hand clamp around her bicep. She turned to see Jonas, panic in his eyes. "Peyton, we need to go."

Together, they ran toward the three Toyota SUVs parked on the outskirts of the camp. Hannah was ahead of them, already halfway there. She ran in the open, gunfire sounding all around her. Soft pops from the attackers' suppressed weapons interrupted the automatic rifle reports from Magoro's men. Bullets raked across the first two SUVs, carving a line of holes in their sides and shattering windows.

"Make for the last one!" Jonas called out.

Peyton put her head down and ran for her life. Her heart pounded in her chest, a bass drum out of tune with the symphony of death the rifles played.

A scream ahead—a woman's voice. Peyton looked up in time to see Hannah fall. Blood instantly flowed from the young physician. Peyton was at her side in seconds, kneeling, inspecting the gunshot wound in her shoulder. Tears filled Hannah's eyes, but she was already pushing back up, her teeth gritted. Peyton wrapped an arm around her, and they rushed to the SUV, where Jonas held the back door open.

He slammed it shut when they were inside and yelled, "Stay down!"

He got in the driver's seat, cranked the SUV, and floored it.

An explosion rocked the tent complex, sending white canvas and red dirt into the air. Remnants of the blast rained down on the SUV like hail.

Jonas was making for the main road away from the village, pushing the vehicle to its limits. It stormed along the rutted road, bouncing, each violent movement bringing a scream from Hannah. Peyton wrapped one arm around her neck, the other around her side, and pulled her student on top of her, trying to cushion her. Their faces were together now, and Peyton could feel Hannah's tears flowing down her own face, the salty taste touching her lips. Above them, a bullet shattered the back window, spraying tiny bits of glass. Peyton covered Hannah's face with her hands.

More bullets struck the side of the SUV, a few at first, then a full barrage.

"Hang on!" Jonas yelled.

The SUV turned sharply, bounced twice, then powered ahead, the engine screaming.

A deafening explosion rocked the vehicle, tossing it into the air. Peyton felt herself float for a second. The sensation was sickening, like the moment at the summit of a roller coaster, before it begins its rapid descent.

The SUV crashed to the ground on the driver's side, throwing Peyton and Hannah's intertwined bodies into the ceiling and then depositing them in a crumpled mass against the side wall. When the sound of twisting metal and breaking glass stopped, Peyton heard Hannah screaming at the top of her lungs.

Up front, Jonas unsnapped his seat belt and reached for the glovebox, which was now above him. He popped it open, took out a handgun, and pulled the slide back, chambering a round.

"No, Jonas!" Peyton cried out, but it was too late. He stood, his feet on the driver's-side door, his head and shoulders poking out through the window. He began firing, but only got three rounds out before automatic gunfire erupted, ripping into him, his red blood spattering the seats. He fell, and the gun dropped from his hand into the back seat.

Hannah cried and shook, the pain overwhelming her. Peyton wrapped her arms around her while she eyed the gun.

A second later, the SUV's back gate swung open. Hands reached inside and dragged the two women out.

CHAPTER 34

DESMOND STARED AT his legs. For the first time since he had woken up in that hotel room in Berlin, he knew how he had gotten the scars. The memory had left him wanting to know more. At the moment, however, he had a more pressing issue: escaping his makeshift cell.

He lay on his back and listened for a few minutes, hoping for any clues about where he was or who might be around. But the barn was completely quiet, the other stalls apparently empty.

He looked around for something he could use as a weapon. His best option was to pry one of the rebar rods free. He moved around the cell, studying the bases of the rods, searching for a weak link. He settled on a rod on the left wall, then swept his hands across the floor, searching for anything he could use to dig with. He found a rock that was almost two inches long, and went to work scraping the dirt aside.

When he'd moved enough dirt to allow the rebar to be wiggled, he planted his feet, grabbed the rebar with both hands, and pulled. His aching body sent waves of pain through him. He rhythmically pushed out and returned, hoping the change in pressure would crack the weld.

Ten minutes later, his head was drenched in sweat, his body spent, and the weld was just as solid as it had been when he'd started.

He sat down against the wall, panting. He picked up the rock and turned it in his fingers. Without thinking, he turned to the dark wood and scratched the words: *Desmond Hughes was here.*

He sat back on the dirt floor, studying his own name carved in jagged white letters. He leaned forward and added a second line: *I'm innocent.*

He had written the line without even really considering it. He wondered if it was true. In his memories, he had seen himself in a warehouse where people were being treated in makeshift hospital cells. But treated for what? He knew there was an outbreak in Africa—possibly of Ebola—and that Peyton Shaw was there. Peyton, the woman he, or someone else, had instructed him to warn.

Had he known this outbreak was coming?

Someone did. In another memory, he had seen a man with a badly scarred face, standing before a group, telling them the world would soon change.

Desmond lay on his back in the cell, his mind wandering. Wherever he was, it was hot and arid, easily seventy-five degrees in the dead of night. He was in the tropics in a very dry region: Africa, or maybe an island in the Caribbean. No, an island was unlikely—he didn't smell the salt of the sea. In fact, there was no breeze at all blowing through the barn.

He began assembling an escape plan. He knew his adversaries were pros. They had taken him alive for a reason. That meant they wanted to keep him alive.

The sweat covering his face might work in his favor. He spat on the jagged rock and wiped it on his pants, attempting to clean it. Then he lifted his shirt and scratched the rock against his side, just enough to break the skin and bring blood to the surface. He spread the blood around, then held his shirt to the wound, letting the dark red soak through.

The sound of boots marching down the corridor focused him. He lay on his bad side and slowed his breathing, trying to look more vulnerable. His best chance was to lure the visitor into his cell. If he couldn't do that, he'd have to attack the man through the bars and hope he could reach for the key. Perhaps he could throw the rock. With his hands bound together, it would be difficult to throw very hard, but if he could make the man stumble closer to the bars, Desmond might be able to reach through and get his hands on him.

The soldier stopped square in front of his stall. He wore full body armor, including a black helmet with a visor.

"I need a doctor," Desmond said, his voice weak. "Somebody ripped my side open dragging me in here."

The sweat on his face supported the lie, but the soldier made no movement or response.

"You hear me? I need a doctor."

The man's voice was gruff, hard. "This look like a hospital to you?"

"No. Apparently it's a home for idiot mercenaries. Incidentally, what do you think your employer will do to you when I die of sepsis shortly after delivery?" Desmond paused. "Gotta think your life expectancy plummets."

"Show me." Some of the bravado was gone from the man's voice.

"Doctor."

"You're lying."

Desmond turned and moved his right arm slightly, revealing part of his blood-soaked side. He made his words come out even more labored. "I figure they'll kill me anyway. Least I'll take you with me."

"Walk to me."

"Screw you," Desmond spat.

For a moment he thought the man was going to open the cell. Instead, he turned on his heel and walked out.

He returned ten minutes later, carrying a tray full of food and a small case. Hope filled Desmond until the man slid the tray through the bars. It was flimsy, Styrofoam—useless.

"Eat," the man said.

"Not hungry. Too busy dying." Desmond was incredibly hungry, but he knew what was in the food; he'd be unconscious shortly after his first bite. Then they would inspect his wound, discover his deception, and regard everything he said afterward with complete disbelief, ruining his chances of escape.

"You really want to do this the hard way?"

"I thought we already were."

The soldier set the case on the ground, opened it, and prepped something. Desmond rose, ready to throw the rock and charge the iron bars, but the soldier was quick: he drew a pistol from the case and fired once, striking Desmond in the chest.

CHAPTER 35

MILLEN CAME TO with a start. His torso ached, but it was a sensation at his leg that caught his attention: something slithering around his left calf. He lay still, waiting to see if whatever it was would move on. Instead, it closed tightly, squeezing like a vice. He thought it was no larger than an inch around, but it was strong, and with each passing second, it cut off more of his circulation.

He had fallen down a vertical shaft; he wasn't sure how far. He was surrounded by absolute darkness, except for a single point of light in the distance, like a penlight in a train tunnel.

The thing closed more tightly around his leg. To Millen's surprise, it pulled with incredible force, dragging him across the rock, into the wall.

The light shone brighter, raked across his body. He saw what had ensnared him: a rope, tied in a loop, lassoed around his leg.

"Stop!" he yelled.

The rope continued pulling at him, lifting him into the air. The pressure on his left ankle, where the rope had settled, was excruciating. His shoulders were still on the ground, but with each passing second, he rose.

They couldn't hear him. He still had his suit on, and it was muffling his voice.

He had no choice. He knew it might end his life, but he tore his helmet off and shouted as loud as he could, "Stop!"

The reaction, unfortunately, was instantaneous. He fell immediately back to the jagged rock floor. A shock of pain swept through his body. He rolled over, but it made the hurt even worse. He lay still, wishing it would end. For a moment, he thought he would throw up. The nausea passed, and slowly the voice calling down from above came into focus. "Dr. Thomas! Are you all right?"

"Not really," he mumbled.

"What?" It was Kito.

"Just... give me a minute," Millen yelled.

By degrees, he sat up and took stock. The fall had banged him up pretty badly. He had what felt like a bruised rib, and he doubted there was a single part of his body that wasn't either skinned up or bruised. On the whole, however, he was okay. He would live. He could hike out. He counted himself very, very lucky. The bulky suit had provided some padding.

But the shaft he had fallen into was at least twenty feet deep, and the bruised rib would make it difficult for him to climb.

Thankfully, Kito had called the camp for backup. He had four men with him, and together, they were able to pull Millen up—though the process was far from pain-free.

As soon as he caught his breath, Millen thanked the men at length. They had brought food and water into the cave, and Millen was glad. He hadn't realized how hungry he was until he took the first bite. When the MRE was half gone, an idea came to him. He placed his helmet back on and stood.

"Can you hike out?" Kito asked.

"I won't set any land speed records, but I can manage," Millen said. "But first, I'm going to finish what I came here for."

Twenty minutes later, Millen watched the bat land near the open MRE and begin nibbling at it. He took aim, pulled the trigger, and tranquilized the animal. It jerked for a moment or two, then fell limp. Millen scooped it up and placed it in the sack.

"Now we can go."

☣

When the six men reached the green chemlight, they made radio contact with two more Kenyan soldiers waiting by the SUVs at the entrance to the cave. Kito informed Millen that the two soldiers that had originally driven them here had gone missing—along with the SUV.

"Probably deserted," Kito said. "They have families too. They're no doubt worried about the virus reaching them."

The men at the SUVs relayed more troubling news: as soon as they had arrived at the caves, they had attempted to check in with the camp at the village, but no one had responded.

Millen's mind instantly went to Hannah, and the memory of her sleeping peacefully on the cot that morning. Despite the pain in his ribs and legs, he picked up his pace. The five Africans matched him easily, and less than fifteen minutes later, they cleared the cave.

Millen tore his helmet off. "Let's hurry," he said.

The drive back to the camp was a red-line, grueling affair. In the back seat, Millen held the handle on the roof and gritted his teeth.

When the SUV's headlights caught sight of the white tents, the vehicles screeched to a halt, sending a plume of dust forward like a ghost wandering from the car toward the camp. When the cloud cleared, Millen's worst fears were confirmed: there was no movement anywhere. He had hoped the communication blackout was only an equipment failure.

As the men exited the vehicles, Kito called the Ministry of Health to apprise them of the situation. One of the Kenyan army officers updated their command post at the Mandera airport. The remaining men, including Millen, approached the camp cautiously. The Kenyan soldiers held their semi-automatic rifles out, their fingers on the triggers.

The camp was a horror show. Dead bodies were everywhere: soldiers, WHO staff, CDC employees, and Kenyan Ministry of Health workers. Whoever had invaded the camp had left no survivors. There was no sign of Hannah—yet. If by some miracle she was still alive, she wasn't crying out.

The men spread out, searching the camp, but found only more death. Millen's fear mounted with every step. Still, he clung to the hope that she was alive, that Hannah had somehow escaped. He held his breath when he drew the flaps back on their tent.

Empty.

Quickly, Millen counted the SUVs. One was missing. There was still a chance she had gotten out.

One of the soldiers yelled from beyond the camp. Millen was at his side a minute later, staring in horror.

Dr. Jonas Becker's body lay in a crumpled heap at the bottom of an overturned SUV.

He died fighting, Millen thought. But whom had he been fighting? Al-Shabaab?

"Dr. Thomas," the soldier called from the back of the SUV.

The vehicle's rear door was open, and the ground behind it was covered in a massive pool of blood. Shattered glass was everywhere.

Millen got out his satphone and dialed a number in Atlanta. During the flight in, Dr. Shaw had been adamant that if the worst happened, the EIS members should bypass the EOC and call Elliott Shapiro directly.

It was five-thirty p.m. in Atlanta, and the call connected on the first ring.

"Shapiro."

"Dr. Shapiro, my name is Millen Thomas. I'm a first-year EIS agent deployed in Mandera."

"Sure," Elliott said. Millen could hear him walking in the background, a cacophony of voices and people typing on keyboards. "What can I do for you, Millen?"

"Sir, we have a problem."

CHAPTER 36

THE CALL HAD rattled Elliott. He had been doing his final rounds before leaving for the day, but now he sat at his desk, thinking through his next moves. What he did now could well determine whether his people in Kenya lived or died—including one young woman in particular who was very special to him.

Elliott and his wife, Rose, had been blessed with two sons. One had died at the age of three in their pool. They had filled it in and planted a garden in its place as a memorial. The other son was an anesthesiologist in Austin, and they saw him a few times a year. Peyton was a regular at their home, however, and over the years, both Elliott and Rose had begun to think of her—to treat her—as if she were the daughter they'd never had.

He knew that the hours immediately after her abduction were the most crucial to ensuring her safe return, that acting quickly and decisively was the only way to protect her, to prevent any truly evil act from occurring.

His first call was to the National Reconnaissance Office, where his request was met with immediate resistance.

"We need that sat telemetry right now, you understand?" he said. "I'm going to hang up now and call State and people way above your pay grade. I'm going to mention your name. If telemetry isn't available by the time I call you back, it will go badly for you."

He wasn't bluffing; he called the State Department next, and right after, his contact at the CIA.

The moment he hung up, his office phone rang. It was the

director of the CDC. Elliott had instructed Millen to call the EOC and update them immediately after their call; apparently word of the crisis had now reached the top of the food chain.

"Did you call State, Elliott?"

"Yeah." Elliott was typing on his computer, sending an email to Joe Ruto, head of CDC in Kenya, urging him to contact the Kenyans about any assets they had in the area.

"Did you threaten them, Elliott?"

"Uh, yeah. Maybe, I don't know. Why?"

Elliott shifted the phone to his other shoulder so he could type faster. "Because they just called me. They're not happy."

"Uh-huh. Is the White House going to approve the RDF?"

Elliott believed a Rapid Deployment Force scouring the area for Peyton and the other hostages was their best shot at getting them back; he had been working to make that exact scenario happen.

"They don't even have a target yet," the director said.

"Sure they do: the al-Shabaab camps in Somalia."

"Be realistic, Elliott."

"I am. *Realistically*, who do you think did this? There's one terror network in the region: al-Shabaab. They hate America. We've got extremely high-value targets in the area. It's them. They've got her."

"Her?"

"Our people."

The director exhaled. "Our people could be at any number of camps."

"I agree. We hit them all at the same time. It's the only way."

"Jesus, Elliott. You want to start a ground war in southern Somalia?"

"I want to raid known terrorist camps in search of American hostages. Since when did this become a tough sell?"

A pause, then the director said, "Hang on a second." Elliott heard mouse clicks. "All right, there's a White House conference call in fifteen minutes—"

"I want to be on the call—"

"No, Elliott. It's invite-only. The president and national security advisor are going to be there. Please don't make any more calls. I know you're worried. I am too. I'll call you as soon as the conference ends, okay?"

"Yeah. Okay."

Elliott slammed the phone down and sat, listening to his breathing for a long moment. A text popped up on his cell phone, which lay on his desk:

From: Rose
Message: Thinking of switching from Miller Union to Kyma. Okay with you?

Elliott tapped the phone and dialed his wife.

"We're going to have to cancel dinner."

Rose instantly read the tone of his voice. "What's happened?"

"It's Peyton."

"Oh my God."

Elliott avoided giving his wife all the details; he merely told her that Peyton and her team were out of contact, and they were trying to determine if it was a technical problem or something else. White lies had become a routine part of his job, especially during his time in the field, but they had been less common since his promotion and years at CDC HQ. He far preferred being honest with Rose, but now wasn't the time for it.

☣

Ten minutes later, an email appeared in Elliott's inbox. The NRO had made the sat footage available.

Elliott clicked the link and watched as black-suited soldiers attacked the camp at dusk. The footage ended with soldiers hauling two women out of the back of an overturned SUV. They placed black bags over their heads and dragged them to a clearing, before shoving them into a waiting helicopter.

Elliott grabbed his office phone and dialed the NRO analyst, defying the CDC director's order. "Where'd the helicopter go?"

"We don't know. The area's huge; we don't have coverage over the whole thing."

"Does the helicopter show up again—on another sat?"

"We don't know—"

"What the hell do you mean, you don't know?"

"It's an unmarked Sikorsky. We can't be sure it's the same helicopter."

"Do you have satellites over the al-Shabaab terror camps?"

The analyst hesitated.

"Do you?"

"That's... classified, sir."

"*Classified?* You're seriously not going to tell me if you can see a similar helicopter landing at a terrorist base?"

"I could lose my job, sir."

"*Lose your job?* Let me tell you something. Right now, some terrorist thug is torturing and possibly sexually assaulting American citizens—government employees serving our nation, just like you and me, men and women who put themselves in harm's way to protect our families and our friends so we can go home tonight and sleep in safety. If you care about that at all, I want you to pull that footage from all those terror bases, and if you see that helicopter or anything else going on, *please* make a call. Let the national security advisor know, or whoever the hell you guys call. Will you do that?"

"Yes, sir, I will."

At six p.m., Elliott's office phone rang. He snatched it up and listened, surprised at the voice on the other end: the head of watch at the EOC.

"Elliott, we just got a flood of signals in; this respiratory disease is amplifying. Millions more cases—"

"Uh-huh, uh-huh," Elliott said, interrupting. "Keep an eye on it. I'll call you back."

"But I think—"

"I'll call you back."

He hung up the phone and briefly considered calling the director to see if he had tried calling him.

He stood and paced across the room. His blood pressure had to be through the roof. He was glad Rose couldn't see him. He took a medicine bottle from his top desk drawer and swallowed a blood pressure pill.

☣

After what felt like hours, Elliott's phone rang again.

"All right," the CDC director said. "They're putting two RDFs on standby and dispatching an aircraft carrier in the Gulf of Aden. The CIA special ops teams at the Mogadishu airport are also on alert. As soon as they have reliable intel about the hostages' location, they'll move in."

"That's it?"

"It's all we can do until we know where they are."

"So, what, we're going to wait for these kidnappers to webcast their demands? Or maybe force our people to read a statement? Or are we just going to wait and hope somebody gets drunk in a Mogadishu dive bar and mentions some American hostages?"

"What do you want, Elliott?"

"I want special ops raiding those camps in Somalia. We ought to be turning that place upside down."

"What if they're not there? What if they're in Ethiopia, or still in Kenya? Raiding the camps could get American soldiers killed. And it could provoke the kidnappers to kill our people in retribution."

"First, those soldiers signed up for that," Elliott said. "Special operatives know the risk, they know they're putting themselves in harm's way to save American lives. That's their job. And when our people deploy, they go out there with a simple assumption: if they get in trouble, the United States of America will come for them. We're not keeping our promise. How are we going to ask the next class of EIS agents to put themselves in harm's way if we aren't willing to protect this class? Huh?"

"I'll keep you posted, Elliott. Go home. Try to relax."

The line went dead. Elliott threw the phone across the room. The gray Ethernet cord that connected it to the wall yanked it back like a yo-yo and slammed it into the desk.

His door flew open, and his assistant, Josh, peered in. The younger man always stayed until Elliott left for the day. He looked down at the broken IP phone. "I'll... call IT."

When the door closed, Elliott took out his cell phone and dialed an old friend.

"I've got a story for you."

"On the record?"

"Strictly off."

"Related to the Kenya outbreak, or this new thing?"

"Kenya. CDC employees have been abducted. The White House knows. They're not doing a damn thing."

CHAPTER 37

WHEN ELLIOTT GOT home, he poured himself a drink and downed it quickly. Then he had another, and sat in the large chair in the corner of his mahogany-paneled office, staring at nothing in particular. His eyes settled on a picture taken seven years ago in Haiti. He and Peyton were facing the camera, his arm around her. It had been taken the day they found out there were no new cases in the cholera outbreak. That had been a happy day—one of the few during that grueling deployment.

He picked up the remote and turned on the flat-screen TV.

CNN has learned that the abduction took place in eastern Kenya, near the border with Somalia...

Elliott watched the rest of the segment. It ended with: *The White House has issued a statement saying they are "following the situation and considering all options for the safe return of American and Kenyan personnel."*

He walked to the kitchen, looking for Rose, but instead found a whole, uncooked chicken in a glass dish on the center island, beside a few chopped vegetables. Rose had texted him to tell him she would cook, and he wondered if something had gone wrong.

Rose had retired from teaching when their first son was born. She had been a wonderful mother. After the death of their youngest son, she had dedicated much of her time to tending the garden they had created in its place—and to cooking the vegetables she grew there.

The oven was on. Elliott squatted down and hit the light. It was pre-heated but empty.

"Rose?" he called.

No response.

He walked to her office off the kitchen. The day's mail lay on her desk, unopened.

He found her in their bedroom, lying on top of the comforter, her clothes still on, the lights off. The curtains were open. The setting sun shone through the French doors that led to the patio.

"Rose?"

She didn't move.

Elliott sat on the edge of the bed and gripped her hand, feeling her pulse with his finger. She was burning up, her heartbeat rapid. He held the back of his hand to her forehead. Definitely running a fever.

She opened her eyes and, upon seeing Elliott, instantly grew worried. She glanced at the clock on the bedside table.

"Oh, no, I must've fallen asleep."

She pushed up on trembling arms, coughed, and fell back to the bed, reaching for the tissue box on the nightstand. Elliott heard the congestion in her chest as she coughed violently into a tissue. There were plenty more used tissues in the wastebasket beside the bed.

"When did you start feeling sick?" he asked.

"Shortly after you left this morning. It's nothing. I've got to get dinner ready."

Elliott felt her neck. Her lymph nodes were swollen; her body was fighting an infection.

She sneezed into the tissue, then sneezed again. Elliott brought the box closer, leaving it next to her in the bed.

"No, Rose. You're going to stay in bed, and *I'm* going to fix dinner."

She studied him skeptically.

"Okay. I'm going to *pick up* dinner."

She smiled and squeezed his hand.

He helped her out of her clothes and under the covers, then went into the bathroom to search the medicine cabinet. All the cold and flu tablets had long since expired. He found a bag of zinc lozenges and returned to the bedside.

"Stay in bed, honey. Try these—they'll help. I'll go get dinner and some cold medicine. Be back soon."

Elliott ate a small snack to soak up some of the alcohol, then turned the oven off and moved the uncooked food to the refrigerator. Completing Rose's cooking was above his pay grade; a few hot trays from Whole Foods were his usual fare when she was out of town. That would have to do for tonight.

☣

The drugstore parking lot was filled to capacity; Elliott actually had to wait for a spot. The scene inside took him aback. People filled the aisles and argued at the checkout line.

What's happening here?

He went to the aisle that held the cold and flu medicine, but the shelves were utterly bare. Every last box and bottle of medicine was gone.

There was a commotion at the back of the drugstore near the pharmacy desk.

"My kid is sick—"

"When will you get more—"

A pharmacy tech strode past the dropoff window and met Elliott's eyes.

"Excuse me," Elliott said. "Do you have any cold medicine left?"

The young woman shook her head as if she'd gotten that question a lot. "No, and we don't know when we'll get more."

If this was happening in Atlanta, it was likely happening across the country. Things were worse than the stats had revealed—much worse. Elliott needed to get back to work. They needed to get more aggressive, and fast. And it was now urgent that they get the virus sequenced so they could compare it with the samples from Mandera. If the viruses were the same... He didn't want to even think about the possibility. The US wasn't prepared for that. No country was.

He considered calling Rose, but that might wake her. She needed her rest, and she probably wouldn't have eaten much anyway. There were still leftovers from last night in the fridge if she did get hungry.

On the way to the CDC, Elliott dialed his son, Ryan, in Austin. Ryan and his wife and son were scheduled to fly to Atlanta that night to spend Thanksgiving at Elliott's home. He answered on the first ring.

"Hey, Dad."

"Hi. I was hoping to catch you before the flight." Elliott could hear cars honking in the background.

"Why? Is everything all right?"

"Yeah," Elliott lied. "Of course. Just checking on you. There's a bug going around here."

"Here, too. Feels like half the city is sick," Ryan said.

"Adam? Samantha?" Elliott asked.

"They're fine. We've all been lucky—dodged it so far. But Adam's day care sent all the kids home yesterday." He paused. "We're almost to the airport. You sure we should still come?"

Elliott had been pondering that very question. If things went south, he would rather have his family close. And he didn't want to worry them. "Definitely. We're looking forward to it."

"Okay. We'll see you later tonight."

"Be safe. I love you."

"Love you too, Dad."

At the front desk of the main CDC building on Clifton Road, Elliott swiped his access card. A red beep. He tried it again. The security guard at the desk walked over.

"I think something's wrong with my card," Elliott said.

"It's not your card, Dr. Shapiro. Your access to the campus has been revoked."

"What? By whose order?" In his peripheral vision, Elliott saw two more security guards walking to the turnstile.

"I'm sorry, sir, I don't know."

Elliott took a few steps back from the entrance, allowing other staff to make their way past. They glanced back at him. He took out his cell phone and dialed the director.

"Steven, I'm having a problem getting into the building."

"Get used to it. You won't ever get back in the building if I have anything to do with it."

Elliott considered playing dumb, but figured appealing to the director's sense of duty was the stronger play. "Look, whatever you think of what I did, it's done now. We've got a serious outbreak going on. We need all hands on deck—for the sake of the American people—"

"Save it, Elliott. We're well aware of the situation. Go home. And don't you dare say another word to the press."

DAY 5

50,000,000 infected
12,000 dead

CHAPTER 38

DESMOND AWOKE WITH a new, more intense pain. The welt covering the left side of his chest was like a bee sting—from a Volkswagen-sized bee.

While he had been unconscious, they had moved him from the barn. His new cell was quite different. He was indoors, in a very new and sophisticated facility. Metal walls painted white surrounded him on three sides, and a thick glass barrier looked out onto a wide corridor. He lay on a narrow bed with a simple mattress and no sheets. This was a proper prison—and a high-tech one at that. There was a speaker in the ceiling, and a pass-through slot on the wall opposite the glass for food.

The tranquilizer dart the soldier in the barn had shot him with had been powerful; Desmond sensed that he had been out for quite some time. They had taken his clothes, replaced them with green scrubs, and seen to all his wounds. He pulled up his shirt and inspected the cotton bandage on his side. It covered the shallow rut he had carved.

His hands and feet were unbound. It felt good to be at least that free again.

He wasn't certain, but he sensed that he might be on a ship. Perhaps it was the slight movement, or simply the proportions of the space and the fact that the walls, floor, and ceiling were all metal.

He sat on the bed and waited for how long he didn't know. The hum of the fluorescent lights slowly became annoying, then deafening.

Footsteps: boots on the metal floor, marching with purpose. A man stopped in front of the glass divider and stared for a moment. Desmond recognized him instantly: the scar-faced man from his memories. His hair was longer now. The blond locks hung across his face, partially obscuring the scars. The mottled, burned flesh stretched up from his chest, across his neck, chin and cheeks, and stopped at his forehead. He wore a scruffy sandy-blond beard that grew in uneven patches. It did little to hide the healed wounds, which must have once been excruciating. He looked almost inhuman.

Desmond rose and moved slowly over to the glass wall.

"Why?" His captor's question was laced with malice and, to Desmond's surprise, hurt. The man seemed enraged but also vulnerable somehow.

"Who are you?" Desmond asked.

The man sneered and spoke with a thick Australian accent. "Drop the charade, Desmond. I don't believe the whole amnesia bit."

"Look, I have absolutely no idea who you are. I woke up in a hotel room in Berlin a few days ago with no memories. I didn't even know who I was."

"We'll see about that." The man brought a handheld radio to his face and said, "Proceed."

Inside the cell, a soft hissing began. Desmond looked around, searching for the source: the slot in the wall, where he had assumed food was passed. He was unconscious within seconds.

☣

Awareness came in slow, fuzzy waves. Desmond's head felt heavy. He heard distorted voices, like people conversing quietly at the top of a well, with him deep inside.

The light overhead was blinding. He was strapped into what looked like a dentist's chair with his legs fully extended and his head strapped back. An IV was connected inside his elbow. A machine beeped somewhere beyond his vision.

"What have you done with Rendition?" It was the blond scar-faced man.

"He's conscious," another man's voice said.

"Dose him again!"

"You're giving him too much. You've got to let it wear off."

"Do it."

When Desmond awoke once more, he was back on the narrow mattress in the metal and glass cell. His mind was sluggish, still drug-addled.

Just beyond the glass, the blond man sat on a folding metal chair next to a small table, studying a tablet, his legs crossed. He set the device aside when Desmond stirred. His demeanor had changed: the hatred in his eyes was gone, replaced by a more serene, contemplative gaze.

Desmond sat up. "You believe me now?" he asked.

"Yes." The man stood and walked to the glass.

"Who are you?"

"My name is Conner McClain. Does that mean anything to you?"

Desmond shook his head.

Conner turned his back to the glass. "Right now, events are taking place that will forever alter the course of human history. Behind the scenes, *behind the headlines*, a war is raging. Very soon, it will explode around the world."

Headlines, Desmond thought. "The outbreak in Kenya."

"Yes."

"You're responsible. You started it."

"No, Desmond. *We* started it."

The words hit Desmond like a truck. He searched his feelings, wondering if it was true.

"We're running out of time," Conner said. "I need your help. I need you to tell me everything that happened to you. I need you to help me stop what's going to happen to all of us."

"Let me out."

"I can't."

"You can."

"Consider my position, Desmond. I don't know what happened to you."

"What do you *think* happened to me?"

"I see two possibilities. The first is that one of our enemies got to you. And they're using you to try to stop us."

"One of *our* enemies?"

"Yes. Until a few days ago, you and I were partners."

"Partners in what?"

"The greatest scientific endeavor in history."

"The Looking Glass."

"Yes."

"What is it?"

"I can't tell you that."

"Why?"

"Because of the second possible reason you might have lost your memories."

"Which is?"

"That you did this to yourself—that you betrayed us and our cause. That's actually the more frightening scenario. Either way, I'm not sure whose side you're on, Desmond. But *if* you recover your memories, you'll know the truth of what we're facing. You'll know that we're humanity's only hope—that *the Looking Glass* is our only hope."

"There are three pieces," Desmond said. "Rook, Rendition, and Rapture."

"You remember?"

"No. The journalist told me." Desmond's mind flashed to the man, the fear on his face when he'd said, *They have my fiancée.* "What happened to him?"

Conner averted his eyes.

"I asked you a question."

"We sent him on an all-expenses paid trip to Disneyland, Desmond. What do you think happened to him?"

"What do you want from me?"

"Rendition."

"What is it?"

"Your life's work. Your piece of the Looking Glass."

Sitting on the narrow bed, Desmond tried to remember anything about Rendition. Nothing came to him. The word evoked no memories—only a feeling: *it must be protected*. Instinctively, Desmond knew that if Conner gained possession of Rendition, an unimaginable catastrophe would occur, a loss of life on a scale never seen before.

He looked up. "What about the other components of the Looking Glass?"

"Rook is my project. It's almost complete."

"And Rapture?"

"Is safely secured by our partner. Listen, Des. It's imperative that you remember what you've done with Rendition. Lives are at stake; the very future of the human race."

The two men stared at one another, each trying to read the other.

The hatch to the corridor opened, and a man and woman marched in. They set a laptop and a flat-screen monitor on the table where Conner had been sitting. They turned the screen to face Desmond's cell.

"What's this?"

"We're going to try to help you remember."

The woman typed on the laptop, and a picture appeared on the screen. It showed a young, blond-haired boy, perhaps seven years old, standing next to a tall, ruddy-faced man in overalls. An oil rig towered behind them.

Desmond studied both faces. "It's me, isn't it?"

"Yes. Do you remember him?"

Desmond had seen the older man's face once before—in a memory. Out of pure instinct, Desmond lied.

"No."

To the woman, Conner said, "Keep at it. Call me if you make any breakthroughs."

CHAPTER 39

When Conner had slipped out of view, Desmond looked again at the picture on the screen. Seeing it *did* bring back a memory. An unpleasant one.

☣

Soon after arriving in Oklahoma, Desmond learned why Charlotte had been so hesitant to put him on the aeroplane. Despite being his next of kin, Orville Hughes had no use for Desmond, or any five-year-old boy for that matter. The man was tall and muscular, with a mean face, constantly arranged in a sneer.

He lived just south of Oklahoma City, in a small farmhouse outside Slaughterville. Orville worked on the oil rigs, usually on two- or three-week shifts, after which he'd be home for a few weeks. Desmond was largely left to fend for himself. He looked forward to the time alone.

When Orville was home, he drank whiskey late into the night and slept half the day. Sometimes he listened to music, mostly cowboy songs. The rest of the time he watched reruns of old Westerns. *Gunsmoke, Bonanza, and Have Gun—Will Travel* were his favorites. Desmond wasn't allowed to speak or make noise in any way when a movie with Charles Bronson, John Wayne, or Clint Eastwood was on. He was, however, required to cook and clean. His uncle meted out punishment only once for non-compliance. That was enough for Desmond.

He soon identified a pattern to his uncle's drinking. The first half of a bottle barely affected the man. The remainder was like a potion that changed him completely. He got meaner with every swallow. He talked more, sometimes to himself, sometimes at Desmond, his English accent growing thicker by the minute.

He talked about his childhood in London after the war. Everything was prefaced with *after the war*.

"You think your life is hard, boy? You don't know a thing about hard living. After the war, that was hard. You're soft, boy. Your daddy was soft too. He took over that sheep ranch from your mother's family, lived the soft life. Raised a soft little brat."

He talked about work on the rigs, how hard it was, how heroic he was. Late at night, when he was deep into the bottle, he talked about the accidents: men losing fingers, hands, entire limbs. Deaths. The stories were gruesome. When Desmond couldn't take it anymore, he got up to leave. That was a mistake. His uncle yelled at him not to walk away when he was talking to him. "You're so soft you can't even bear to hear about real men's work, can you?"

He took another swallow of whiskey.

"Can you?"

He studied Desmond.

"You watched them die, didn't you? Then you ran away. That's why you got them scars on your legs—from running."

He had argued then. That was his worst mistake of all. He learned after that. His uncle only wanted a verbal punching bag. It was like Orville was using his words to drain the poison out of himself. He didn't want that poison returned. Desmond learned to sit in silence.

A few weeks after he arrived in Oklahoma City, Desmond learned why the bitter man had taken him in. Orville was standing in the kitchen, the phone cord stretching from the wall, muttering about how much the call to Australia was costing him. When the line connected, he demanded to know when the money would arrive. Desmond sat in the living room, listening.

"I don't care if it's burned worse than the gates of Hell! You sell that bloody property and send the money. That was the deal."

A pause.

"Well send the money or I'll send the snot-nosed brat back, and you can deal with him."

Desmond felt the tears welling in his eyes. He couldn't bear to let that monster see him cry or to stay there another minute. He grabbed the rifle by the door and ran out of the house into the early March afternoon. He had decided: he was running away. He would live off the land, build another fort, live there until he could get a real job and get away.

An hour later, he sat in a tree, waiting. He missed the white-tailed doe with his first shot. The old rifle kicked like a mule, and Desmond nearly fell out of the tree—and the doe was gone before he could work the .30-30's lever and load another cartridge. But he held on and waited. Snow began falling, scattered flakes at first, then a steady downfall.

Desmond had never seen snow before. In Australia, his father had said that it only snowed in the mountains of the Victorian High Country, in the northeast.

He watched as the white flakes blew in the wind.

When the next doe emerged from the far tree line, he was more patient. It was smaller than the last, younger, less cautious. He waited as it meandered closer, sighted, held a breath as his father had taught him, and squeezed the trigger.

The animal fell and flailed on the ground.

Desmond was out of the tree in seconds, making tracks across the open field. He finished the poor doe quickly.

As he studied his kill, he realized the foolishness of his plan. He had no way to clean the animal, store the meat, even cook the portions his empty stomach cried out for.

But he could take it home, show his uncle that he could earn his keep. That he wouldn't be a burden. Seeing the doe would change his uncle's mind. Desmond was sure of it.

He took it by the legs, began dragging it through the snow. He didn't get far. Desmond was nearly four feet tall and strong for his age, but the animal weighed nearly twice what he did. He would have to run back and get his uncle's help.

He trudged through the snow, which was a few inches deep now. The cold wind whipped at his face and beat past the jacket Charlotte had sent with him.

With each step, the white wall became more complete. He didn't know it then, but he was marching through a rapidly forming blizzard. The winds tossed him from side to side, disorienting him.

It was like the fire in Australia: he was again caught in an inferno, only this one was made of ice.

He got turned around so much that he had no idea which way home was. He knew the bush and paddocks around his parents' station like the back of his hand. This land was foreign to him. There were no markers to guide him. He was completely lost.

He would die here, in the cold, alone. He was sure of it. He had survived the fire, had been brought back to life by an angel, only to die here, in the ice, left for dead by a devil.

His legs ached. He desperately wanted to sit down, to rest. But somehow, he knew if he did, he would never get back up.

He pushed forward, clutching the rifle. He knew dropping it— losing it—would be a death sentence. He tried to fire it in the air to call for help, but he couldn't get his fingers to work.

Through a break in the snow, he saw a column of smoke rising from his uncle's home in the distance. He made for it with every last bit of strength he had.

When he reached the porch, he expected the door to fly open. It stayed closed. A yellow glow from the fire inside shone through the windows. Salvation.

He threw the door open, leaned the rifle against the wall, and rushed inside. His uncle never looked at him, only shouted for him to close the door.

Desmond eyed the bottle. It was nearly empty. He would have to be careful to stay out of the man's way.

CHAPTER 40

OUTSIDE THE BRIG, Conner marched down the corridor, his footsteps echoing loudly. The entire crew of the *Kentaro Maru* was bustling, preparing for the next phase. They would have to work very quickly to assemble the Looking Glass. A delay could cost billions of lives, perhaps even *every* human life.

If he didn't find out what had happened to Desmond soon, their cause would be in trouble. Desmond held the key to the Looking Glass and to everything they had worked for.

Inside the infirmary's conference room, screens on the wall displayed x-rays, MRIs, and other scans Conner didn't even recognize.

"What did you find?" he asked the three researchers conversing at the end of the table.

A younger physician swiveled in his chair. "His body's a horror story. I've never seen so many fractures—"

"He had a rough childhood. Now tell me: *What. Did. You. Find?*"

Dr. Henry Anderson, an older scientist with white hair, spoke up. "An implant in his brain. It's located in the hippocampus."

"What kind of implant?"

"A Rapture Therapeutics model. It's been modified, though."

"Modified to do what?"

"That's not clear," Anderson said, "but the added component looks like a data receiver and transmitter."

"What would it link up with? A satellite?"

"Possibly. But I count that as unlikely. Not enough power. It's probably something shorter range. Bluetooth. Wifi, maybe."

The younger scientist spoke again. "Could be used to communicate with a smartphone, which could act as a bridge to the net. It could be downloading instructions that would unblock memories."

"Interesting," Conner whispered. Louder, he said, "How would it work?"

The older scientist shrugged. "Who knows? This is all pure speculation. I was never a Rapture employee and didn't work on the project; everything I know is from their published research. We know the original Rapture Therapeutics implants were used for depression, schizophrenia, bipolar, and other psych conditions. They monitored levels of key brain chemicals and stimulated the release of neurotransmitters. Basically, they helped balance the patient's neurochemistry.

"The later versions of the Rapture implant, like the one inside Hughes, focused on other areas of the brain. Their published trials focused on dissolving brain plaques. The implants targeted the plaques and released a protein called $GP3$, which dissolved them. The approach has the potential to cure a wide array of neurodegenerative diseases—Alzheimer's, Huntington's, Parkinson's, and more."

Conner held his hand up. "How does that apply here? You found plaques in his brain?"

"No. We checked. We found something else, though: an unknown substance throughout his hippocampus."

"What do you think it is?"

"I can only speculate—"

"Speculate away," Conner said, losing patience.

Dr. Anderson inhaled deeply. "A few years ago, researchers at MIT discovered a way to actually isolate the location in the brain of specific memories. It was a breakthrough—the revelation that individual memories were stored biochemically in specific groups of neurons in the hippocampus. I believe the substance in Hughes' hippocampus binds the neurons associated with specific memories, making them inaccessible—in a manner similar to the way that brain plaques affect memories in Alzheimer's and physical abilities in Parkinson's."

"And you think Rapture Therapeutics put that substance there. And that the implant in his hippocampus has a way to dissolve the substance, unblocking the memories—similar to the way GP3 dissolves brain plaques?"

"Yes, that's our hypothesis. We further hypothesize that the communication component that's been added to the implant is a triggering mechanism. A Bluetooth-enabled phone or wifi-connected computer could tell the implant to unlock the memories. Those triggering events could happen based on a set schedule, or when certain events occur. Or perhaps even when Hughes arrives at certain GPS locations. It's also possible that certain cues, emotions, images, or sensations could unlock memories. The implant could be keyed to determine which memories are safe to reveal."

Conner leaned his head back and stared at the ceiling. "Well, gentlemen, it seems there's a very simple way to confirm your plethora of suppositions. Call Rapture Therapeutics. Ask them. After all, we own the company."

"We just got through speaking with them," Dr. Anderson said. "Their chief science officer confirmed that they do have a team researching memory manipulation. And that project is still active. Or was, until very recently."

Conner sensed bad news coming.

"The project is called Rapture Aurora. They conducted their research following Looking Glass protocols: compartmental-ization, need-to-know access. The team working on the memory therapy was a completely independent cell, with its own budget and facilities. For the sake of the larger Looking Glass project, contact was limited. Rapture hasn't heard from the cell in three weeks."

"They must have had a case manager," Conner said. Realization dawned on him the moment he said the words. "Wait. Let me guess. The Aurora project was based in Germany. And the case manager was Gunter Thorne."

"Correct."

Conner shook his head. "What about Thorne's records? Protocol is for a secure backup in case he was compromised."

"Rapture has been looking since he turned up dead in Desmond Hughes' hotel room. They haven't found it. They're assuming Hughes hid the files or destroyed them."

Conner paced for a moment, then turned to the scientists. "Okay, let's back up, review what we know, and try to put together a working theory here. Fact: two weeks ago, Desmond Hughes hides Rendition. Every scientist working on the project goes missing. All the files are gone. Hughes turns up in Berlin, where he contacts a journalist at *Der Spiegel*—Garin Meyer. Hughes is going to expose us and the entire Looking Glass project."

Dr. Anderson spoke up. "Rapture Aurora—and his memory loss—must have been his backup plan."

"Right. Des would have known about Aurora. Icarus Capital was an investor in Rapture Therapeutics—in fact, we used Icarus to fund most of the Looking Glass projects operating out of Rapture."

"So," Anderson said, "Hughes contacts the Aurora project team, gets them to administer their memory alteration technology on him, then either kills or hides the team. He somehow figures out where Gunter Thorne is keeping the project files and destroys or hides those as well, wiping out any chance of us figuring out exactly how Aurora works."

"Very clever, Des," Conner mumbled.

"But somehow," Anderson continued, "Gunter Thorne figured out what Hughes was up to. Maybe he noticed the files were gone, or perhaps he has some intrusion detection system Hughes was unaware of. He tracks Hughes back to the Concord Hotel, confronts him. A struggle ensues. Desmond comes out on top. He assumes Thorne had already alerted us. He activates Aurora, wiping his memories."

Conner shook his head. "What a mess."

"In a sense, it's brilliant," Anderson said. "We can't torture the answers out of him—the memories are blocked no matter how much pain he endures. And without the Rapture Aurora research, we can't possibly unblock them."

Conner nodded. "He's brilliant, no question about it." Conner sat down and tapped his fingers on the table, thinking. "Is Aurora a core piece of the Rapture component? Could the loss of the Aurora research derail the Looking Glass?"

"No. Rapture is still intact. The memory piece was completed years ago. This additional Aurora research, using implants, seems to be a continuation beyond what was needed for Rapture."

"Okay. Options?"

"We see only one predictable path," the white-haired scientist said. "A brain biopsy."

Conner disliked the idea instantly. However, he simply asked, "How?"

"I wouldn't recommend we do it on board the *Kentaro Maru*. Our facilities are advanced, but given the risks, I would strongly advocate conducting it in a hospital that specializes in neurosurgery. Mayo Clinic and Johns Hopkins would be my top choices. New York-Presbyterian, Mass General, and Cleveland Clinic would also be appropriate. The problem is, very soon the pandemic will consume every hospital in the world, as well as the physicians we'd need for a biopsy."

"Assuming we could solve those problems, what would a biopsy tell us?"

"We could get a better look at the implant and sample the substance in his hippocampus. We try to identify the substance, run tests on it to see if we can dissolve it without harming the under-lying neurons."

"I'm guessing that's not a three-day turnaround."

"No, it's not."

"How long?"

"It's impossible—"

"Guess."

"Two months? Who knows. I should also add that any brain biopsy carries risk to the patient. In this particular case, there could be risks we don't appreciate."

"Such as?"

"A failsafe. If the implant and memory blockage are part of a purposeful plan on Hughes' part, or perhaps someone manipulating him, they might have programmed a failsafe. A foreign object entering his brain, in the region of the implant, might trigger some defense mechanism. Maybe it destroys the memories completely or even kills the subject. There's no way to know."

"It's all moot. We don't have two months." Conner rubbed his temple. He felt a headache coming on. "We have Rook and Rapture, but he has Rendition. Without it, we can't complete the Looking Glass. Two thousand years of work will go down the drain, and the entire human race with it."

The older scientist leaned back in his chair. "We could cut him loose and allow this to play out."

"Play out?"

Anderson nodded. "Hughes clearly has some sort of backup plan. It's tied to specific events or locations, or some signal that will activate his memories via the implant. So, what if we let him recover those memories? Then we collect him."

"That's a lot of assumptions, Doctor. The biggest being that we can simply 'collect' him when we're ready. Bagging him in the first place wasn't a walk in the park. When he recovers his memories—when he realizes what he's capable of—it'll be nearly impossible."

"Then I'm afraid that leaves us with no options."

"On the contrary. We have a very good option, gentlemen. And I'm going to take it."

CHAPTER 41

THE SOLDIERS WERE rough they jerked Peyton and Hannah out of the back of the SUV. Hannah's screams didn't slow them as they placed black bags over their heads, bound their hands, and marched them to a helicopter, where their feet were bound as well. In the darkness, the drone of the engines and rotors was deafening. The helicopter landed some time later, and they were dragged out, lifted up, and tossed onto the flat metal bed of a truck.

The drive was brutal. The truck bounced along ruts in the road, slamming them into the bed. And with their hands and feet bound, there was nothing they could do to protect themselves. It was like being blindfolded and left to tumble in a drying machine on an endless cycle. Hannah sobbed periodically.

Peyton lost all sense of time. The pain ebbed after a while; perhaps the nerves in her body simply stopped responding to the pounding. She wondered if any permanent damage was being done.

At last the truck came to a stop, and she heard canvas flapping. A ray of sunlight beamed across the black bag, only partially seeping through.

Someone gripped Peyton's feet, pulled her out of the truck, and caught her as she hit the ground. Her legs were weak, wobbly. Hands moved across her body, grabbing in places they had no right to. Peyton twisted, turned her shoulders quickly, trying in vain to fight them off. The action sparked loud voices, speaking in what she thought was Swahili. Laughs erupted.

She heard Hannah scream as they dragged her out.

"Don't touch her!" Peyton yelled. "She needs medical attention. A doctor."

A man responded in African-accented English. "She won't be needin' nothin' soon. Take them."

Hands reached under Peyton's arms, lifted at her armpits, and pulled her forward. Her bound feet dragged across the dry, rocky ground. To her surprise, her captors removed the bag before tossing her down. The light was blinding. She heard metal slamming into metal and the turn of a key.

When her eyes adjusted, Peyton took stock of her surroundings.

Her abductors had put her in a stall in a barn. Metal rods reinforced the slat wood walls. She turned—and froze.

Two sentences were carved into the nearby planks:

Desmond Hughes was here

I'm innocent

Peyton stared in shock. *Desmond was here? Why?*

She heard clothes ripping and Hannah's labored breaths. The young physician was close—perhaps in the next cell.

"Hannah," Peyton called.

"Yeah." Her voice was weak.

"How're you doing?"

Hannah spoke slowly, quietly. "Got the bleeding stopped." She paused to catch her breath. "Tied my shoulder up. Bullet went through. I think." She drew another breath. "Lost a lot of blood. Cold."

"Hang in there, Hannah. We're going to get out of here, okay? Some very brave Americans are going to come for us. Save your strength and be ready for anything. You understand?"

"Yes, ma'am."

At that moment something changed within Peyton Shaw. She had always lived a purpose-driven life, but it had been a life lived with a cold, clinical sort of passion. She never let her emotions master her. She was never out of control. She'd gotten that from her mother, she thought. Lin Shaw was always composed. And Peyton loved her for it. That same composure had served Peyton well during her professional life.

At work, keeping her emotions in check was imperative. Emotions clouded judgment, changed how a person looked at things. Becoming emotionally attached during an outbreak was a risk; she might be too focused on a particular patient or location, might miss the big picture, or a detail, a crucial contact or piece of information that could save lives. Her emotional detachment *had* saved lives, and had saved her a lot of grief over the years.

Now, however, as she lay on the dirt floor in this makeshift cell, the wall of detachment Peyton Shaw had carefully built up over so many years fell. Her emotions broke through in a wave. They took the form of raw, unbridled rage. Rage against the people who had killed Jonas—her friend, her colleague, and someone who might have been much more. Rage against the people who had started the outbreak in Kenya that had killed Lucas Turner and thousands of others. She would find these people. She would stop them. And she would make them pay—even if it was the last thing she did.

CHAPTER 42

MILLEN THOMAS HEARD the camp come alive outside his tent. Boots pounded the hard-packed Kenyan ground. Doors slammed. Body bags were tossed onto the bed of a truck.

He rose from his cot, threw the tent flap back, and walked out. The Kenyan army detail that had rescued him from the cave was scouring the village for their belongings—and for their fallen comrades who had died during the night raid on the camp.

Millen had known they would leave, but he hadn't expected it to be so soon. Last night, the CDC and WHO had evacuated all their personnel from Kenya. A flight with the field teams had left from Mandera; another from Nairobi evacuated the support personnel. Millen had been ordered to be on the flight that left Mandera, but he had refused. Evacuating meant leaving Hannah and Dr. Shaw behind. He had decided to disobey orders—to stay, wait, and hope there was something he could do here.

And now, when the troops left, he would be alone in the village. Kito approached him.

"We're pulling out, Dr. Thomas. Orders."

"Where?"

"Nairobi. The government has declared a nationwide state of emergency. Martial law. They're setting up containment camps in every major city."

Millen nodded.

"Come with us," Kito said.

"No. I need to wait for my people."

"If they're rescued, they won't return here."

Millen had been thinking the same thing.

"Where will they take them?" he asked.

"I'm not sure."

"What's common in kidnap and ransom—after the rescue?"

Kito considered the question a moment. "Depends on the rescuers. If they're operating from a ship, they'll be taken back there—somewhere in the Indian Ocean. Or perhaps to the closest airport. Mandera, likely."

Mandera—it was his best shot.

Kito read his reaction. "A word of advice, Doctor."

"What's that?"

"Set out at daybreak. It will be safer."

"Yeah, that's a good idea."

"We'll leave you a four-wheel drive, water, and rations." Kito paused. "And a gun."

"I won't need it."

"We'll leave it just in case. You have a solar charger for your phone?"

Millen nodded.

"Very good. Best of luck to you, Dr. Thomas."

"You too, Kito."

As the Kenyan was walking away, Millen yelled to him. "Kito!"

When he turned, Millen said, "Thanks again for getting me out of that cave."

"It was the least I could do. You came here to help us. We won't forget it."

When the cloud of red dust settled from the convoy's departure, Millen returned to his tent, ripped open an MRE, and ate in silence, surveying Hannah's neatly ordered side of their shared lodging.

He had met her six months ago during EIS orientation. At first, he had thought she was neurotic and uptight. But as he'd gotten to know her, he'd realized the truth: she cared. Being prepared and doing a good job were important to her. She had a kind heart, and it had led her to medicine. She cared about patients like he cared about animals. He had suggested they bunk together in camp during the deployment to compare notes from the medical and veterinary side of the investigation. *Who knows,* he had added, *in our off-hours we could find the breakthrough to stop the pandemic.* But he had been hoping for a different kind of breakthrough.

When the food was gone, he drew out his phone. The Audible app appeared with *The Nightingale*'s book cover, ready to resume the story where he and Hannah had left off. He needed a distraction, something to take his mind off the waiting and worrying. He wanted to press play, to listen to the story as he drifted off to sleep, but he decided what he wanted even more was to finish it with Hannah, when she returned, safe and unharmed.

He set the phone down and closed his eyes. Dr. Shaw was right: thinking was the enemy of sleep.

CHAPTER 43

ELIM KIBET DRIFTED in and out of consciousness. Day turned into night and back again, like a light being flipped on and off. The fever flowed like the tide, surging, overwhelming him, roasting his body from the inside, then withdrawing, leaving him to think it would never return.

His symptoms grew worse each day. He found it harder to think. His hope of recovery faded. Dread took its place. Only when he had lost that last bit of hope did he realize how much he had truly held on to.

The bonfire outside his window grew larger each night. At first they tossed only the suits and contaminated material onto the blaze. Then came the bodies.

And then the night arrived when no fire was lit—and Elim knew that he was not the only one in danger. The entire place was in trouble. He waited for the news he knew would soon come.

The door opened, and Nia Okeke entered. The official with the Kenyan Ministry of Health had given him ZMapp and insisted he take the room the American had stayed in. Now she wheeled in a cart piled high with bottles of ORS, clean buckets for bodily fluids, and boxes of antibiotics and painkillers. She parked the cart within his reach and sat on the bed, just beside his chest.

"We're leaving, Elim."

"You can't."

"We must."

He looked down, his fever-ridden mind searching for an argument to keep them here for the sake of his patients.

She seemed to read his mind. "There's nothing you can say. There simply aren't enough patients left here."

"How many?"

"Two, including you. The other young man will likely pass before we leave."

Elim exhaled and nodded. "Where will you go?"

"Dadaab. Then Nairobi. We're setting up camps with military and health workers."

In his mind, Elim could already see what would happen if they couldn't contain the outbreak. The government would fail. Warlords would emerge. A new civil war would start, sparking an endless fight over land and resources. Bandits would rule the roads. This plague would set Kenya back a hundred years. And it had started here, in Mandera, in this very room.

"Before you came," he said in labored breaths, "I was wondering how long I'd be able to keep this place open. I never imagined it would end this way. That I would be the last patient to die here. That it would die with me."

"Have faith, Elim. It's the best medicine. And you'll need it even more if the medicine doesn't work."

CHAPTER 44

IN HIS STUDY in Atlanta, Elliott Shapiro was growing increasingly frustrated.

"This is no time for politics. These are people's lives we're talking about here. Have you found them? Tell me. Please."

He listened, then interrupted. "I don't care what your orders are, listen to me—Hello? Hello?"

He set the phone down and rubbed his eyebrows. With each passing hour, he knew the possibility of recovering Peyton and her team was slipping away. It was like watching a family member die in slow motion. It was torture.

He hadn't slept a wink last night. Neither had Rose. He had sat in the den, scanning news channels and websites, waiting for any news while he listened to Rose sneezing and coughing. He had brought her water and food from the kitchen periodically, sat by the bed, and asked her how her book was. Her symptoms had stabilized, but he was still terrified that the virus she and so many others had contracted was in fact the same virus that had already killed thousands in Kenya.

They had created a sort of makeshift quarantine in the house: Elliott's son, daughter-in-law, and grandson had kept to the second floor, while Elliott and Rose occupied the first floor. His grandson was running around in the bonus room over the garage, having a great time, while his parents played with him. Each group was heating frozen food from the freezer and eating separately. It wasn't the ideal Thanksgiving, but it would keep the contagion from spreading.

In the family room, Elliott turned on the TV.

"Despite growing concerns about the flu-like virus spreading across the US, many families chose not to alter their Thanksgiving plans this year."

The video shifted to a middle-aged man standing in front of a brick colonial home.

"We figured everybody was sick, so, may as well be together. Tradition's important to us—"

Elliott flipped the channel, scanning for more news.

"The infection rate is now estimated at twenty million in the US alone. The virus, which authorities are calling X1, is intermittent in nature and causes symptoms similar to seasonal flu. Those infected report feeling under the weather for a few days, then well for a day or two before the symptoms return. Officials at the CDC and NIH have urged individuals to exercise vigilance throughout the flu season, including washing your hands and—"

Elliott changed the channel again.

"Triple-A reports that despite an uptick in flu activity, they expect a record number of travelers to take to the roads this Thanksgiving weekend. Air travel is also projected to set a new high. Retailers are banking on strong Black Friday sales with Wall Street analysts calling for a ten percent growth in sales over last year..."

It was a perfect biological storm. A highly contagious virus—amplifying at the precise moment when movement around the country was at its highest.

Elliott walked back into his office, closed the doors, and dialed a number at the CDC. To his surprise, voicemail picked up.

"Jacob, it's Elliott. Call me. Thanks."

He dialed the man's cell and was relieved when he answered.

"Jacob. Please tell me you've sequenced this respiratory virus and compared it with the Mandera samples."

Elliott sat up at Jacob's response. "What?... I know it's Thanksgiving—" He paused to listen. "Listen to me, Jacob, this is going to be the *last* Thanksgiving if those viruses are the same... No, Jacob. Monday is too late. You've gotta go back in, finish it. Call your team... What? Jacob—"

Elliott felt like screaming.

He called the EOC once again, hoping to get a different operator. The response was the same: the head of watch had instructed every operator not to give Elliott any status updates. He was officially locked out—at perhaps the most critical time in the agency's history.

DAY 6

300,000,000 infected
70,000 dead

CHAPTER 45

AT FIRST MILLEN thought it was the wind blowing through the camp, whipping against the empty tents, the flapping and howling only sounding like voices. As his sleepiness faded, he realized the sounds actually *were* voices—several people, arguing in hushed tones just outside his tent. He rolled over, careful not to make any noise.

The morning sun cast three figures in shadow against the tent's fabric, like shadow puppets creeping toward him. They paused, pointed, and continued past him, talking quickly. Millen heard them enter the main tent. Crates being opened, ransacked.

He rose and pulled on his shoes.

The SUV Kito had left him stood nearby at the edge of the camp. The main tent was on the opposite side of the camp, away from him, and Millen could see the shadows of three figures moving inside. They were turning the place upside down, looking for something.

They obviously thought they were alone now. They spoke more loudly, in a language Millen didn't recognize. Millen wanted to break for the SUV and get away, but what if they knew something? What if they had taken Hannah and Dr. Shaw?

He pulled on his flak jacket with the CDC logo and grabbed the rifle Kito had left him. It was semi-automatic with a banana-shaped magazine. Millen had fired exactly one gun in his life: a .22-caliber rifle during his stint in the Boy Scouts. The gun in his hand was a lot meaner looking. And deadlier.

He gripped the weapon, ensured the safety was off, and crept toward the main tent. The flaps were down, obscuring his approach. His fear gripped tighter around him with every step. His mouth watered. He swallowed, gathering up his courage. His heart was beating out of his chest. If he didn't charge or run at that moment, he figured he'd have a heart attack.

With the gun held out, he ducked and burst through the tent flaps. Three figures sat around the long table… gorging themselves. Opened MRE cartons lay strewn across the floor and table. Millen recognized them: the three Kenyan villagers they had found hiding when the team had arrived here. The villagers stared at him, eyes wide with fear, then jumped up and stumbled over the folding chairs, falling as they scrambled to escape.

Millen quickly set the gun on the ground and held his hands up. "Wait. Stop. I'm CDC." He pointed to the white letters on his jacket. "I was here before. American. Help." He spread his arms, blocking the entrance. A girl, maybe thirteen years old, stopped.

"I'm an American," Millen said again. "Here to help."

Millen finally got the three villagers settled down, and after a few minutes, he convinced them to resume their meal. The teenage girl, Halima, was the only one who spoke English. As they ate, she recounted the raid on the village. Hearing it firsthand was hard for Millen.

When the shooting began, the three villagers had hidden under their cots in the isolation tent. They fled after Peyton told them to. From the bushes at the village's outskirts, they watched the raid unfold.

"They ran, the dark-haired woman, a man, and the girl with reddish blonde hair. They shot her—"

"Who?"

"The red-haired woman."

Millen leaned back in the chair, unable to speak.

"I'm sorry," Halima said quietly.

Millen stared at the canvas swaying in the morning breeze. "What happened after that?" His voice was hollow.

"The dark-haired woman picked her up. They ran to a truck

and drove away. There was an explosion. The truck crashed. More shooting. I couldn't see what happened. I'm sorry."

Millen nodded. "Thank you for telling me."

When they were done eating, he asked them where they would go. The teenager simply shrugged.

"I'm going to Mandera," Millen said. "You three are welcome to come with me."

She hesitated.

"I'm sure the Kenyan government will be setting up survivor camps soon. There will be food, water. Probably work to do. Be a lot better than staying here."

The teenager conversed with her two companions. Finally, she turned to Millen. "Yes, we'll come with you."

During a deployment, standard operating procedure was to notify ops when changing a fixed position. But since the ops group had evacuated Nairobi, Millen called the EOC in Atlanta.

"You didn't evacuate?" the operator asked.

"No. I'm still here—"

"Hold the line."

Millen could hear shouting in the background. It sounded like a hundred voices talking at once, like the floor of the New York Stock Exchange had been transplanted to the CDC. He caught snippets:

"Fifty thousand cases in Kansas."

"Navy has confirmed cases on three aircraft carriers."

The operator came back on the line. "Stay where you are, Dr. Thomas. We've got a situation here. Someone will contact you."

"I can't stay here," Millen said, but the line was dead.

The call left Millen wondering what was going on in Atlanta— and the rest of America. *Fifty thousand cases in Kansas?* Had the virus they'd found in Kenya reached the US?

He desperately wanted to know what was happening—and to let someone know where he was going.

There was really only one more number he could call.

CHAPTER 46

ELLIOTT DIDN'T REMEMBER falling asleep in the chair, but he awoke in the middle of the night with a blanket drawn over him, the remote in his lap, the TV on.

He coughed several times, brought his hand to his neck, and felt his lymph nodes. They were swollen. Sweat covered his forehead. The fever was low-grade, but there was no mistake: he was infected.

On the TV, a reporter on a financial news network was speaking against a chart with a red trendline dropping sharply as it moved right.

"Asian stock markets shed more than forty percent of their value today following news that Singapore would close its borders and declare martial law, and claims that China would soon begin closing its ports to prevent further spread of the X1 virus. The WHO has stopped releasing infection estimates, sparking fears that infection rates may be far higher than has been reported. That fear seems to be spilling over into the markets. In America, the New York Stock Exchange and Nasdaq will close at one p.m. in observance of Black Friday, and losses are expected to be steep. Futures are trading off twenty percent..."

Elliott's phone rang, and he stared at the number, still groggy. He didn't recognize it.

"Shapiro."

"Sir, it's Millen Thomas. I called you day before yesterday. I was working with Dr. Shaw's team."

Elliott sat up. "I remember, Millen. What can I do for you?"

"The EOC in Atlanta is apparently overwhelmed. I'm here at our camp at the village where the raid occurred."

Elliott was shocked. "You're still in Kenya?"

"Yes, sir. I... decided to stay. I thought maybe I could help somehow."

Elliott nodded. "Okay. What's happening there?"

"The Kenyan military escort left yesterday; I'm thinking of going to Mandera, but I can't get any guidance on whether that's the right move."

"It's a better spot than the village, but it's hard for me to advise you. I don't know who's in Mandera or the status of any operations in Kenya. I'm sorry, Millen, I'm out of the loop here."

"Understood, sir. Well, I feel better knowing at least someone knows my location. I've got three survivors here—we found them in the village when we first arrived. I'm going to take them and head up to Mandera."

Survivors? Elliott felt a glimmer of hope. If they had survived the disease, then analyzing their antibodies could be the key to finding a treatment.

"Listen to me, Millen. We've got to get those survivors back to the CDC for analysis."

"How?"

"I'll arrange transport. Just get to Mandera and stay safe. I'll call you back. Keep your phone charged."

It took Elliott three calls before he reached someone who could transport Millen and the survivors back to Atlanta. It would be more than three days before they arrived in America—but better late than never.

Elliott napped in the family room until the morning sun blazed through the French doors. The house was still quiet, and he took the opportunity to do some work he dreaded, work he knew had to be done.

In his study, he turned on his computer and made a list of everyone he needed to warn. Then he made a list of his neighbors. He and Rose lived in an established, older neighborhood just outside Atlanta, close to the CDC. The homes weren't mansions, but they were authentic, well-built, and expensive. Doctors, lawyers, and business owners shared the street with them. Elliott wrote down the names of the neighbors he thought he could rely on, the ones he thought would have steady hands in a crisis.

And a crisis was coming; he was certain of that.

At seven a.m. he brought Rose, Ryan, and Sam into his office and told them his plan. By the time he was done, Rose was crying quietly. Ryan and Sam nodded solemnly and told Elliott he had their full support.

Next, he began making calls to the people he wanted to warn. By ten o'clock, five husbands and wives sat in his living room.

"I'm sorry to take you away from your families," Elliott said, "but I believe your families, and mine, will soon be in very real danger."

Surprised and confused expressions stared back at him.

"What are you—"

Elliott held up a hand. "Just... give me a minute, Bill. It'll all make sense.

"In 2004, Congress passed the Project BioShield Act. On the surface, it was a bill that called for five billion dollars to spend on stockpiling vaccines and other countermeasures against bioterror and pandemics. But what the public doesn't know is that there are secret provisions in the act—provisions that are only invoked in the event of a catastrophic biological event. I believe we are witnessing the beginning of such an event. I believe this respiratory virus—X1—may actually be the early stages of the Ebola-like hemorrhagic fever that is currently devastating Kenya. If they are one and the same virus, I believe that Project BioShield will soon be invoked to try to stop that outbreak.

"When that occurs, the America we know and love will change very drastically. What I'm about to tell you must never leave this room."

When Elliott was done speaking, one of the men leaned forward and said, "Let's say you're right. What do we do?"

"That's why you're here. I have a plan. And I need your help."

CHAPTER 47

IN THE METAL and glass cell, Desmond lay on the narrow bed, watching the never-ending slide show. A few of the photos were from his childhood, but the bulk of them depicted him at industry trade shows or at business meetings. They began in his early twenties and ran nearly up until the present. Either his captors didn't have pictures of his personal life, or none existed. The people who came and went outside his cell asked him a range of questions, careful to never reveal anything about their cause and goals, but here and there, he gathered small clues, which he cataloged, hoping they would help him escape.

After they left, Desmond felt his stomach growl. They had fed him very little, perhaps hoping to keep him weak and docile.

Instead, the sensation brought back another memory.

☣

For the first year that Desmond lived in Oklahoma, his uncle left him at a preschool when he was working on the rigs. The kids there were of varying ages, but at six years old Desmond was among the oldest. Several of the other oil workers left their children there too, and he made a few friends. But every time Orville returned to pick him up, he argued with the owners about the price, complaining that it was highway robbery.

One day, Orville announced that he was leaving Desmond at

home. He put some money on the counter and told Desmond that if he had to come home to tend to him, he'd make him sorry.

Desmond used the money to buy food at the small grocery store in town. The owner helped him count out the money and stretch it as best he could. His diet consisted of beans and canned meat. Still, he ran out of money a few days before his uncle returned. At the grocery store, he didn't ask for credit. He asked where he could find a job.

"For a six-year-old?" The skinny man with small glasses laughed. Desmond looked at his shoes.

"I'll give you some things on credit, Desmond. You can settle up when your uncle gets back."

"I'd rather not," he said quietly.

Thankfully, the grocer told him to sweep out the supply room and stock some of the shelves and sent him home with enough food to get him through a few more days.

When his uncle returned, the first thing he said was: "How much have you got left?"

"Nothing."

"Nothing? You spent it *all*? On what, boy? A new Barbie doll?"

He stormed off, muttering that Desmond would eat him out of house and home.

The man was obsessed with money. He would work on whatever rig paid him the most. He didn't care how dangerous it was or how bad the camp conditions were. He wanted the money. And he kept it all to himself. He deeply distrusted banks.

"They're all crooks," he said, one night when he was into the second half of the bottle. "Fools, too. They'll loan any Tom, Dick, or Harry money—*your* money, that is, the same dollars you put in the vault. The thrifts are the worst. They'll be busted soon, you watch."

Desmond was actually quite surprised when, a few years later, over a thousand savings and loans—thrifts, as they were known—collapsed, costing American taxpayers over one hundred and thirty billion dollars to bail them out. It was perhaps the only one of his uncle's predictions and conspiracy theories that came true.

His uncle continued to leave him home alone after that first time, and Desmond soon figured out how to make the money last: he supplemented it with meat from animals he killed. Some he took out of season, but he figured the game warden probably wouldn't fine a six-year-old boy slowly starving to death.

He made sure to have a few dollars left over, waiting on the counter when his uncle returned—and sometimes he managed to have a bit more, which he saved for himself.

When he'd saved enough, he visited the pawnshop at the edge of town. He had stood outside this shop at least two dozen times, gazing through the window at the bike, imagining himself riding it, all the places he would go.

Now he went inside, laid his money on the glass-top display case, and said, "I'll take the bike in the window."

The proprietor picked up the bills, counted them out, and said, "You're short ten dollars."

"That's all I've got."

The man said nothing.

Desmond reached for the bills. "Take it or leave it. I'm going to the hardware store next to make them an offer."

The man let out a ragged smoker's cough. "If you were a grown man, I'd tell you to piss off. But I like you, kid. Take it. Damn thing's been in the window a year now anyway."

It was Desmond's first taste of freedom, the first thing he had ever saved up for and bought on his own. He treasured it more than any gift he'd ever been given.

He also hid it from his uncle. That lasted six months. It was the best period of his entire childhood.

With the bike's added range, he was able to visit the next town over, Noble, which had shops along the main street, a post office, a small cinema, and a library. Inside the library, he wandered the stacks, searching for the books Charlotte had read to him. He just wanted to see the covers again to remind him of those weeks they'd spent together.

A woman with gray hair was taking books from a cart and placing them back on the shelves. "Can I help you find something?"

Desmond shook his head.

"You can check out anything you like," she said. She studied him for a long second. "It's free. You bring them back whenever you're done."

It wouldn't do him any good; he still couldn't read.

"Is there a… time when someone reads?"

The woman hesitated. "Uh, yes, there is."

"When?"

"There's… several times. When would be convenient?"

He told her, and she said that would be fine. Her name was Agnes. Desmond liked her voice. It was soothing and neutral, like other people in Oklahoma. It didn't carry the meanness his uncle's did.

As he was leaving, Desmond realized he hadn't asked about the book. It could be one he hated or one about people falling in love for all he knew.

Trying not to sound rude, he asked Agnes what book would be read. "There's several to choose from," she said. "What sort of books do you like?"

"Adventure books," he answered without hesitation. "Where the hero gets away."

"Then you won't be disappointed."

And he wasn't. The next day, he returned to find Agnes knitting behind the counter. She set down her work and held up a book.

"Are you ready?"

He nodded. As he had suspected, he was the only one at the storytelling session. That was fine by him.

He lost himself as the words she spoke became pictures in his mind, then characters that were as real as anyone he had ever met. The stories felt like another life he had only forgotten—a life much better than the one he was living.

Story time was his escape. The weeks when his uncle was home were a prison sentence.

Summer ended, and a letter arrived from the county school district, assigning him to an elementary school where he'd start kindergarten in the fall.

Orville tossed it in the fire with disgust.

"Kindergarten." He said the word as if it tasted like sour milk. "You don't need to get any softer than you already are."

That was fine by Desmond. He far preferred the library.

After Thanksgiving, Agnes began teaching him to read. He picked it up quickly. She used a good strategy: she read the first part of the book, enough to get him enthralled, then helped him read the rest. It was like learning to ride the bike: hard at first, but a breeze once you got the hang of it.

By Easter, he was reading to her.

And she was changing, little by little. She fell asleep during the stories. With growing frequency, she reached into her purse, took out a pill, and swallowed it.

One day that summer, he arrived to find the library closed. It stayed closed every day for a week. Desmond walked into the post office next door and asked the man behind the counter if he'd seen Agnes.

"She's at Norman."

"Who's Norman?"

The postman looked at Desmond like he was an idiot. "The hospital. Norman Municipal. Well, regional now, as if it matters."

"What's she doing there?"

"She's there with the cancer, why else?"

Desmond stood there, his world collapsing.

"Is she coming back?"

He could tell by the look on the man's face that she wasn't.

"How do I get there?"

"You better speak to your parents about that."

"What roads do I take?"

"Norman's ten miles away, young man. Your parents can take you. Now get on, I've got work to do."

At the gas station on the edge of town, Desmond bought a map. The hospital was marked with a large H.

The next morning, he plotted his course and packed food in a bag. Desmond never knew exactly what day Orville would be back from the rigs, but he usually arrived home by early afternoon, so Desmond waited until four p.m. before setting out, just to be sure he wasn't coming. He couldn't imagine what the man would do if he caught him riding home on a bike he had bought with Orville's money.

He figured the trip would take less than an hour, but he was wrong—it took him nearly three. The sun was setting when he reached the Norman city limits. The parking lot lights glowed in the clear night as he rode up, dropped his bike by the front door, and staggered in.

The woman at the reception desk gave Desmond Agnes's room number. For the first time in his life, he rode an elevator. On the fourth floor, he walked slowly toward Agnes's room, afraid of what he'd see.

The door was closed. He pushed the handle, let the thick wooden door creak open. The lights were dim inside. Agnes lay on her side, machines beeping softly around her.

She turned at the sound of the door and saw Desmond. A smile crossed her lips, and tears filled her eyes.

"You shouldn't be here, Desmond."

He couldn't think of anything to say. He just walked into the room, up to her bed, and held out his small hand, which she took.

"Why didn't you…" He didn't complete the sentence, because he had no idea what he intended to ask. He hadn't thought this part out. In his mind, he had never accepted what the postman had said. He'd expected to arrive and learn that it had all been a mistake.

She exhaled. "I was going to tell you I was moving away. I didn't want you to know I was sick, didn't want this to be your last memory of me."

Desmond studied his feet.

"Did your uncle bring you?" she asked.

He shook his head.

"Surely you didn't ride your bike."

She apparently took his silence for confirmation.

"Desmond," she said slowly. "That was very dangerous. Where's your uncle?"

"On the rigs. Won't be back for a few days."

A nurse appeared in the open doorway.

"Do you need anything, Miss Andrews?"

"Yes, dear. Some blankets for my nephew. He'll be spending the night. And, this may be a tall order, but I wonder if there are any children's books in the hospital?"

"Yes, ma'am. I'll bring some."

That night, Agnes read to Desmond for the last time. It was two a.m. when he drifted off to sleep in the reclining chair by the window.

In the morning, Agnes made him promise never to return, that it was too dangerous and that she would only grow sicker.

"Those are my wishes, Desmond. Will you respect them?"

"Yes, ma'am."

He pedaled his bike slower on the return, the wind no longer in his sails. Why did everyone he cared about die? And the people he hated live? Life was unfair. The world was cruel.

It was midday when Desmond got home. His mouth went dry when he saw his uncle drinking on the porch.

"Pretty bike, Des. Where'd you get it?"

Desmond tried to swallow, but it felt like he had a mouth full of sawdust. "Found it," he said with a cough.

"So you stole."

"No. I found it—"

"If you found it, then it belongs to someone—someone you stole it from. Put it on the back of the truck. I'll take it to town and return it to its rightful owner tomorrow."

"I own it," Desmond said, anger overtaking his fear. "I bought it."

"Bought it," his uncle said, acting impressed. "With what money?" he spat.

Desmond looked away.

"You answer me when I ask you a question, boy. What money?"

"The money I saved."

"Saved?" His uncle was mad now. "No. You bought it with money you *stole*—from me. I gave you that money to put food in your ungrateful little mouth. You were supposed to give me back whatever was left. You kept it for yourself and bought a little play toy."

Desmond grew quiet, let his uncle go on about how soft and useless he was. The tirade lasted nearly two weeks, until his uncle was set to go back to work. Instead of placing some money on the counter, he told Desmond to pack a bag.

"Time to show you the real world."

The real world Orville Hughes intended to show him was a camp outside a rig just north of the Oklahoma-Texas border. He put Desmond to work: cleaning outhouses, washing clothes, peeling potatoes, and doing anything the roughnecks didn't want to do. It was hard work, but it wasn't dangerous work. His uncle said he was too weak to be a real roughneck. He'd probably always be too soft, the man told him.

The workers were shaped like barrels, with muscular arms that hung at an angle, never straight down. They reminded him of the robot on *Lost in Space*, a program Desmond watched when his uncle was away. But unlike the robot, these men were constantly covered with oil. Every other word was an obscenity; the stories about prostitutes and their lewd jokes never ended. They worked twelve hours on, twelve hours off, constantly drank coffee when they were awake, and never smoked near the rigs. There was a small TV with bunny ears covered in foil, and they fought about it after every shift. Baseball was usually on, and there was always a card game in one of the tents.

Only one man out of the entire group read in his off-hours. Desmond befriended him, and he was nice enough to pass Desmond the book he had been reading.

Try as he might, Desmond couldn't get into the novel, which was about people hunting for a Russian submarine.

Strangely, spending time at the rigs actually helped his relationship with his uncle, such as it was. The man paid him less attention, even gave him some of the money he earned, and allowed him to keep the bike. Desmond had little desire to venture out, however. He was dead tired when they returned home from the camp.

Before they were to leave again, he did ride to the library. It had reopened, and a younger woman sat behind the desk, reading a textbook, scribbling notes. Desmond avoided her.

He checked out five books, which he read during the next tour.

A few days after they returned home again, a man wearing a clip-on tie and a short-sleeved button-up shirt drove out to the house, a wake of dust rising behind his Cutlass sedan.

"Mr. Hughes," he called from the porch.

Desmond watched as his uncle walked out, half-drunk, and argued with the man.

The visitor put up much more fight than Desmond had expected. Finally, he shook his head, walked down the steps, and turned one last time. "If that boy of yours isn't in school next month, you won't be seeing me again. Social services will come next. Then the sheriff. Good day, Mr. Hughes."

Desmond found first grade quite a bit less interesting than the rigs. He could already read, thanks to Agnes, and his math was far ahead, thanks to the grocery store owner who had prevented him from starving to death.

But he found it impossible to connect with the other kids. To him, they seemed like just that: kids, babies almost. They enjoyed playtime. Talked about childish things. He felt out of place, like he was several grades behind where he should be. The teacher noticed, tried to give him more advanced work, but she had her hands full. So Desmond was largely left alone. He sat in the corner and read while the class rotated stations around him.

The principal agreed to advance him to the second grade, but he felt disengaged there too.

Summer came, and he again joined his uncle on the rigs. The work got harder with every tour.

That became the routine of his life: the rigs each summer, school during the year, his uncle home only half the time.

He didn't know if it was because of his parents' death or Agnes's passing or because of the way his uncle had raised him, but he found it nearly impossible to get close to anyone. There was a wall inside of him. And the few times he brought friends over to his house, his uncle embarrassed him by berating him in front of them, so Desmond quickly learned not to invite anyone over. His uncle never gave him permission to stay over at anyone else's house either. Desmond was not stupid enough to disobey him.

When Desmond brought home the sign-up form for Little League, his uncle burned it. It was a waste of time and his money, he said.

Orville also refused to give consent for Desmond to join any of the clubs at school, Boy Scouts, or any extracurricular activities of any kind.

Desmond felt completely isolated. He had no connection with anyone or anything. He was happiest when he was reading, but by the time he was eight, he had read about everything that interested him at the local library.

The girl behind the desk noticed him wandering the stacks aimlessly. Her name was Julie, she was in her early twenties, and she seemed to have a new hairstyle each time Desmond saw her. It was in a bun on top of her head that day.

"If we don't have it, we can get it," she said.

"From where?"

"Another library."

She pulled the keyboard away from the computer. "We can request any book in the Pioneer Library System and they'll transfer it to us. What are you looking for?"

Desmond didn't know what he was looking for. He had no idea what was out there. "I'm... not sure."

"Well, what sort of books do you like to read?" Julie asked.

The last book Desmond had really enjoyed was a novel by Carl Sagan titled *Contact*. At the end, he had read that Sagan had a program on PBS. Desmond had wanted to watch it, but he knew Orville wouldn't allow it; he was far more interested in John Wayne than alien life and mankind's place in the universe. Desmond, however, was fascinated by the prospect of life beyond

Earth and other worlds. He thought anywhere had to be better than here. At the moment, books were his only escape.

"I can also search by author."

"Carl Sagan," he said instantly.

A whole new world opened up to Desmond after that. He read science books, history books, biographies. He was fascinated with how the world got to be how it was—and with the people who made it that way. To some degree, he was trying to learn why the world was so cruel and unfair.

A year later, Julie began bringing him books that weren't in the library system. She was a student at the University of Oklahoma, and their library was much more extensive. Desmond protected the tomes like treasures.

His life at home continued in the usual way. In the summers, he joined Orville on the rigs. He learned that his uncle had been taking contracts closer to Slaughterville for the past few years—safer jobs at sites close enough that he could get back home quickly if Desmond were hurt or got in any trouble. Before Desmond had come to live with him, Orville had worked on rigs farther away, some offshore. The pay was better there. Conditions were often worse—and more dangerous.

With each passing year, Desmond was given more responsibility, put more in harm's way. He broke his right arm outside Abilene when he was eleven, his leg near Galveston the following year. In May of '95, at a rig outside Nacogdoches, a roughneck who was high on cocaine dropped a swivel on Desmond's foot, crushing it. Orville beat the man to within an inch of his life. They never saw him again, on any job anywhere.

When Desmond got out of the hospital, his uncle welcomed him home with a pint of cheap whiskey. It was the only thing he had for the pain, and Desmond drank it down. It was disgusting at first, but no worse than the throbbing in his foot. It got easier to drink after a while.

To his surprise, his uncle didn't desert him. He brought food to his room and took him to his follow-up appointments. Their relationship changed even more after that.

At thirteen, Desmond started high school. Thanks to his time on the rigs, he was big and broad-shouldered, with arms like a thoroughbred's legs. He was still a loner at school. He didn't fit in with any of the groups, and he had stopped trying years ago. He was stronger than the farm boys and varsity football players and smarter than the kids who lived in town, whose parents owned the shops and had gone to college. Thanks to the library system, he knew more about history than most of his teachers. And there was a lot of math on the rigs. It wasn't calculus, but he picked that up quickly. He could attend half the year and pass all the tests. School became like visiting a prison camp on a foreign planet. People gossiped constantly. Football dominated everything. Everyone was always looking forward to the big game. Desmond only looked forward to his next book arriving—and his and Orville's next job. The locations fascinated him. Louisiana and South Texas were colorful worlds all to themselves.

He cut school more and more. When the teachers began complaining, Orville visited the principal and explained that he needed his nephew's help on the rigs and that the boy would pass all his tests. An agreement was made, and from then on, Desmond attended only enough to pass a few standard tests that would appease the school board if anyone came looking.

Desmond and Orville's relationship wasn't like father and son. They weren't exactly friends. They were more like drifters in the old westerns Orville watched, bound together by some shared need, on a quest, in search of something or someone, though whom or what they were searching for was never clear. They went from town to town, each one like an episode in the show, a new bad guy to best or a mystery to solve. The mystery was always how long it would take to drill the oil well, whether they'd hit oil, and whether they'd survive the days after the tour, what Orville called "blowing off steam."

For Orville, that usually entailed holing up in the nearest town for a week, drinking himself to sleep at the local bar, gambling, and running women. He fought a lot too. After a certain point, he would fight the first guy who said a cross word to him. Military veterans were the only ones he wouldn't take a swing at, and their wives were the only ones he wouldn't take home. He didn't like other men doing it either; that was always cause for a fight— fights that inevitably drew Desmond in, no matter how hard he tried to stay out of them. Eventually, he fell in beside his uncle the moment they started. The fights ended faster that way.

Desmond got pretty good at sizing a man up, knew who would be trouble, who would run, and when they should run. He developed a sort of sixth sense about whether he needed the beer bottle or the pool cue he was holding, or if his fists would do. He didn't like fighting with a knife, but he learned to take them from others. They had a few run-ins with the law, but Orville always had a good story and a few hundred dollars for the bar owner to cover the damage. Desmond nearly always had a bruised rib, a smashed finger, a broken knuckle, a black eye, or a healing cut; pain became commonplace to him, and so did their weird life, living by Orville's twisted code.

In the hotels, they drank and listened to songs by Robert Earl Keen, The Highwaymen, Jerry Jeff Walker, and Johnny Cash until dawn. They sobered up a few days before their next job, and didn't take a drink while they were working. It was too dangerous. That was part of the code too.

Desmond finally understood why his uncle had hated him so much when he'd first arrived. This was the life that Desmond had kept the man from, and Orville was finally getting back to it. That made him happy, and Desmond got some relief at home. They even went hunting together every now and then.

The weeks he worked became therapeutic. When they were on the rigs, it was non-stop action, some of it dangerous. It was hard work, the kind that kept you from thinking too much. When he was working, he didn't think about his family, or Charlotte, or Agnes, or anything else. When he was off work, the whiskey and beer made the thoughts go away. It was the only thing that worked—except for books. That became his life: the rigs, drinking, and reading.

His graduation in the spring of 1995 was a non-event for him.

His life changed very little—except now he no longer had to take the tests. Other kids were going off to college or to Oklahoma City to get a job, or they started working full-time with their family. Desmond wanted desperately to escape, to start fresh somewhere. But he needed money to do that, so he began saving every penny he could. By January 1996, the dented coffee can he kept in his mattress held $2,685. It was the sum total of every dollar to his name, and he was about to spend it on a device he hoped would change his life—and allow him to leave Oklahoma and the rigs behind for good.

CHAPTER 48

THERE WERE ALWAYS two people outside Desmond's cell: one working the laptop with the slide show, asking questions, another typing and filming him.

He had concluded that enlisting the help of one of the interrogators was his only chance of escape. The cell was well designed and constructed; brute force wouldn't free him. His first step was developing a profile of the captor he would turn. He had set about searching for any weaknesses or strongly held beliefs he could exploit, but thus far, his attempts to extract such information had fallen on deaf ears. He sensed Conner's hand in prohibiting the interrogators from speaking with him. None of them ever answered his personal questions. In fact, they became nervous when he addressed them personally—more nervous than they already were. And with each failed attempt, he felt his chances of escape slipping away.

He had taken note of several terms that had struck him as vaguely familiar:

"Do you remember the Zeno Society?" they had asked.

"No."

"The Order of Citium?"

He lied again. He did know the term, but he didn't know how or what it meant.

Meals were delivered periodically, and Desmond ate them with little concern. If his captors wanted to drug him, they could use the gas and then administer anything they wanted. And he needed to eat. He fell into a pattern: exercise, eat, answer questions, sleep, repeat. He lost all concept of time.

At some point, they began playing music, apparently hoping that would spur a memory. Desmond recognized the songs: "American Remains," "Highwayman," "Silver Stallion," "Desperados Waiting for a Train," "The Road Goes On Forever," "Angels Love Bad Men," and, playing currently, "The Last Cowboy Song." The songs were performed by a band called The Highwaymen, a quartet consisting of Johnny Cash, Waylon Jennings, Willie Nelson, and Kris Kristofferson. Desmond could see their faces on the cover of an old cassette tape, one that he had played many times. The songs reminded him of Orville, but he would never tell Conner that.

He knew one thing for certain: Conner had started the outbreak. And if he was capable of that, he was capable of anything. If Conner needed something, Desmond would deny him. He would resist—until the very end.

☣

The ship's server room was deep below deck, and the command center was adjacent. Four guards sat at a folding table playing cards just outside the main door. They rose as Conner approached, and opened the hatch for him.

Conner had never been in the server command center. It was impressive. Flat panel screens ran from the long desk to the ceiling. Charts and graphs updated in real time. A few showed temperature readings. Progress bars crept toward 100%. On one screen, a TV show played *Battlestar Galactica*. The high-tech command center certainly reminded him of a spaceship, although one flown by slobs. Crunched cans of Red Bull and Mountain Dew littered the floor. Empty wrappers from microwavable snacks curled up and stuck together like ticker tape after a parade. Piles of cracker crumbs ringed the keyboards.

Four faces turned in unison to stare at Conner: a skinny Asian woman with dark greasy hair hanging past her shoulders, two overweight white guys who could have been twins, and an Indian man, a little older and much skinnier.

The Indian man stood, a puzzled look on his face. "Sir?"

"I need a programmer."

"Ah." He hesitated, then pointed at a hatch at the back of the room. "They're in there, sir."

"You're not programmers?"

"No, sir. Sys and network admins."

Conner surveyed the pigsty again. *This pack of slobs is keeping all our information organized?*

He shook his head. "Right. Carry on."

"Sir... You might want to knock."

Conner wondered what that meant. But he took their advice, rapping loudly at the hatch three times. No response.

He glanced back at the Indian sys admin, who merely shrugged as if saying, *I guess you've got to go in.*

Conner opened the hatch and peered inside. The cramped space made the server monitoring room look like a biocontainment clean room. Papers, wrappers, cans, and porno magazines covered the floor. Three guys in their twenties sat hunched over their laptops, headphones on, typing furiously, lines of white text on black screens in front of them. Every few seconds one of them would curse and lean back or throw his hands up. It was like a weird human whack-a-mole exhibit.

"Hey!" Conner shouted.

Headphones came off. Annoyed faces turned to him.

The closest programmer, a kid with dark hair and an Eastern European accent, said, "What the hell, dude?"

"I need you to hack something for me."

"Can't. Working on CDC."

"Forget the CDC. I'll take care of it. This is a priority."

Another programmer spoke. "Look, talk to the bridge, man. They call the shots. And shut the door."

"Listen to me, *man*. I give the bridge their orders. *I* call the shots. Don't make me prove it."

All three paused, eyes wide. "Oh," the Eastern European guy said. "Uh, okay. What are we hacking?"

"Someone's brain."

In the situation room outside the ship's bridge, an analyst handed Conner a report; still warm from the printer.

"The infection has hit the tipping point."

"Good," Conner said, scanning the figures.

"There's something else. Alpha Site reports that southern Somalia is crawling with drone flyovers. They're concerned the US will find the farm soon."

"Fine. Transfer Shaw and the other woman here tonight."

"We've suggested that. They want more money."

Conner rolled his eyes. "Fine. Pay 'em."

It didn't matter. Money would be irrelevant in a matter of days.

CHAPTER 49

PEYTON'S MOST RECENT escape attempt had been her best, but it had also resulted in her jailers being more cautious with her. The black-clad soldier now used a wooden stick to push the Styrofoam tray across the ground, past the bars, and into her cell. A car battery sat just out of reach; its cables ran to the closest metal bar, which buzzed with electricity.

She was starving. She wanted to resist eating, but she couldn't hold out any longer. She crawled across the ground and devoured the food left out for her.

A few minutes later, Peyton slumped forward, out cold. The soldier disconnected the car battery, opened the cell, and hoisted the skinny woman up. She was a lot fiercer than she looked. They were glad to be getting rid of her.

CHAPTER 50

AFTER THE CALL with Elliott, Millen had presented his offer to the three villagers. Halima translated and talked mostly with the older woman, Dhamiria. They occasionally conversed with the six-year-old boy, Tian, as well.

Millen tried to imagine what the request was like for them. They had seen their family and friends die in a matter of days, and were left all alone. Now they were being asked to travel to a foreign land, where they'd be subjects in medical experiments—guinea pigs to find a cure. *It must be terrifying*, he thought.

Halima turned to Millen. "You are sure you'll find a cure?"

"No. I'm not sure. But there's a chance. I can't promise you anything, but you three may be the key to saving a lot of people's lives."

"We will be free to come back here—you will return us when you are done?"

"You have my word."

"We will come with you, Doctor."

"Call me Millen."

It was midday when Millen and the villagers arrived in Mandera. The Japanese SUV creaked on the dusty road, and the four of them stared at the deserted town in silence. Mandera was a chilling shell of the place Millen had seen just days before.

259

When the team had first arrived, kids had interrupted their soccer games as the convoy passed, or rushed to the streets to get a glimpse of the visitors. Villagers carting produce and herding livestock had clogged the thoroughfare. Now there was not a soul in sight. The buildings, both new and ramshackle, lay empty. To Millen, it felt like a ghost town from America's West—an African version of Dodge City. A boom town gone bust. But a different kind of boom had gone off in Mandera: a biological bomb, perhaps more deadly than any the world had ever witnessed before.

Millen expected the city's, and possibly the region's, last survivors to be concentrated at the hospital. But he found the tent complex empty and disheveled. Someone had raided every thing of use. The food, and every last medical supply box, was gone. Some water remained, likely because it was too heavy to carry.

"We'll run out of food before the transport gets here," Millen said. "The soldiers only left me a little."

"We'll search the town," Halima said. "We've become good at scavenging."

Millen got the PPE out of the back of the truck and began donning it. Halima pointed at the hospital. "You're going in there?"

"Yeah. It's my job."

The halls of the hospital were lined with empty buckets, bottles, and boxes that had once held medical supplies. The debris was stacked in tumbling heaps, with only a narrow walkway between them, like a mountain pass had been carved in the piles of used medical waste. Millen stepped carefully through the halls, mindful not to snag the suit or step on a needle. A mistake could be deadly.

In the large open room where Hannah had taken the samples, he found rows of dead bodies. Some held wooden crosses at their chests, their eyes closed. Others stared upward, glassy-eyed, at ceilings fans sitting idle. At the back of the room, body bags were stacked against the wall, a black plastic staircase of human death that led nowhere. Flies swarmed.

There were no unopened or unused medical supplies. No uneaten MREs. The room told the story of a medical mission slowly losing its battle against disease. They had bagged and burned the bodies for as long as they could, then had focused on the ones they hoped would survive. And then they had pulled out.

Millen was certain he would find no survivors here. Or food.

He wandered the halls after that, peering into the patient rooms, being thorough, looking for any clues or observations he could take back to Atlanta. He found only dead bodies, all with the same hemorrhaging, jaundiced eyes, and signs of severe dehydration.

Suddenly, he heard a rustling. Just down the hall from him, boxes fell to the floor. He raced toward the noise, moving as fast as he could in the bulky suit. At an open doorway, he peered in.

Empty.

Something darted from beneath a rolling cart. It dashed toward him, between his legs, and out into the hall.

Millen stepped back and turned quickly. A bat-eared fox. The sight of the animal filled him with excitement. He'd read about them before the deployment, but had never seen one. He would have loved to have seen it up close. The small fox fed mostly on termites and other insects—spiders, ants, and millipedes in particular—but also occasionally ate fungi or small animals. They hunted not by sight or smell, but sound, their large ears helping them locate even the smallest insects on the sprawling savannas of Africa. They were mostly monogamous, and the male, not the female, took the lead with caring for their young.

Another bat-eared fox emerged from the room, followed by another. That made sense; they were highly social animals that typically hunted in packs.

Behind him, Millen heard a door creak open. To his shock, an African man stood there, leaning against the door frame. He was weak, barely alive. But for the first time since Millen had entered the hospital, a living set of human eyes stared back at him.

The survivor tried to take a step, but his legs were unsteady. Millen was at his side, offering his hand to steady the man.

"I'm Millen Thomas. With the CDC."

The middle-aged African surveyed Millen's face through the suit's helmet. "Pleased to meet you. I'm Elim Kibet."

Millen knew the name. "You're the physician in charge here."

Elim smiled weakly. "*Was* the physician in charge here. I'm just a patient now."

"I think you might be the last one."

"I was afraid of that."

"Let's get you back to bed," Millen said.

"No. Thank you, but I need to walk. My fever broke this morning. And I've been in that room too long. In bed too long. I need to use my muscles before I lose them."

For the next thirty minutes, Millen helped Elim pace around the hospital. The older physician looked into the patient rooms as they passed. At the large open room, he paused for a long time, his bloodshot eyes filling with water.

Millen couldn't imagine what it was like for the physician—being trapped in the place where he had worked, where he had saved lives and done so much good. A prisoner inside his own failing body, barely able to walk, unable to escape from a deserted, post-apocalyptic realm. Millen wondered how he would react if he were trapped alone inside the CDC building in Atlanta, the outside world having fallen apart. It was a nightmare. But the horror of this place hadn't broken the Kenyan doctor's will to live. Millen was glad.

For the most part, they walked in silence. Elim gasped for breath as he put one staggering leg in front of the other. Millen held him as best he could. It was a furnace inside the suit, and sweat poured down Millen's face. He couldn't wait to take it off, but he wouldn't leave the man's side, not until he was finished.

When Elim was too weak to proceed, Millen helped him back to his room and into bed.

"It's amazing how quickly the muscles atrophy," Elim said. "If disease doesn't kill you, lying in bed will."

Millen nodded.

Elim motioned to the cart. "There's food there. Take some."

"Thank you, but some people with me are scouring the town. We'll be fine."

"The rest of your team is here as well?"

"No. They're gone. Our camp was raided while I was away. Most of my team was killed, along with the Kenyan soldiers assigned to protect us. Two of my team members were abducted."

Elim exhaled heavily. "I'm sorry. Disasters are an opportunity for the worst of humanity. And the best."

A pause, then Elim asked, "Were you close to your colleagues?"

Millen hesitated. "I've only been working with them for six months. But I was getting closer to one in particular. My..." he grasped for the right word and settled on, "roommate."

Elim smiled. "Does your *roommate* have a name?"

"Hannah Watson." Not knowing what else to say, Millen described her briefly. Talking about her actually helped; he didn't realize before then how hard it was to think about her—or to even say her name.

Elim thought for a moment. "Yes. I remember her. She took the samples when you were here last. Very thorough."

Millen smiled. "Yes. She's very thorough." He grew quiet. "They shot her when they invaded the camp. She was one of the ones who was abducted. I don't know if she's alive or dead."

Elim spoke slowly. "I've recently learned the value of something I've never had much use for: faith. Last night, I thought I would never leave this room. Have faith and patience, Dr. Thomas. Time works miracles. We must have the courage to wait for them."

They sat in silence for a few moments, sweat dripping from Millen's brow, soaking his face, the taste of salt touching his lips.

When Elim had caught his breath, he asked, "If your team is gone, who is searching the town?"

"Survivors. From a village nearby."

Elim looked surprised. "They were given ZMapp?"

"No. They survived the virus."

"That's good."

"I'm taking them back to Atlanta. Hopefully we can study the antibodies for clues about how to treat the infection."

"Have you told them?"

"I have. They know what they're signing up for. They've agreed."

"Good. It's a good plan."

"When will you be ready to move again?" Millen asked.

Elim peered out the window at the sun. "If you must, come again at sunset. It will be cooler."

Halima and the other two survivors returned pushing a cart filled to the brim with produce and packaged food. They joined Millen in the main tent and sat around the long table, sharing in a bizarre feast of junk food, MREs, fresh produce, and soft drinks.

When the sun began to set over the rocky hills in the distance, Millen donned the suit again. He was about to coat it with chlorine when Elim emerged from the hospital, pushing the cart full of supplies that had stood in his room.

"I didn't want to spend another night in there," Elim said, panting.

"I don't blame you," Millen said.

He introduced the Kenyan physician to the villagers, and the five of them made their way to the tent complex, which they set about transforming into a makeshift rehabilitation facility for Elim.

CHAPTER 51

IN ATLANTA, THE day had gone mostly as Elliott had expected. The stock market crash had rattled everyone. It was a cloud that hung over the euphoria of Black Friday.

The most difficult part of his plan had been convincing the other five families to pool their money with his for the purchases, which together added up to hundreds of thousands of dollars. They had begun by renting two twenty-six-foot U-Haul trucks. They drove them to Costco and filled them with survival necessities. It was mostly food; Elliott planned to be near a freshwater source if worst came to worst.

Next, they purchased two high-end RVs. The price was exorbitant, but they carried a thirty-day money-back guarantee, and they only had to make a down payment—the remainder was financed. Elliott had assured his neighbors that within thirty days, they would either be incredibly glad to have the two homes on wheels—or they'd have their money back.

Now he sat in his study, watching the news, waiting for the event he believed would come.

He hoped he was wrong.

DAY 7

900,000,000 infected
180,000 dead

CHAPTER 52

DESMOND'S CAPTORS WERE trying a new approach. Gone were the teams that showed him pictures and played music. Now three skinny white guys were camped out at a long folding table, typing on their laptops. Black cords snaked out of their computers, connecting to dozens of cell phones and tablets.

Periodically, the three stooges, as Desmond had nicknamed them, would erupt in an argument. They stood, shouted, paced, pointed, and threw their hands up. He couldn't hear them, though—they had turned off the speaker in his cell—so he could only watch the three guys argue like a silent slapstick comedy.

He had almost drifted off to sleep when a fourth figure entered the scene beyond the thick glass wall. She struck a sharp contrast with the greasy-haired guys. She was tall, blond, with piercing green eyes. When she glanced at Desmond, there was a glimmer of recognition in her eyes. The exchange was so brief that he instantly wondered if he had imagined it. She focused her attention on a tablet and tapped several times.

The speaker in his cell crackled to life. *Did she turn it on? Why?*

"Where are we?" she asked, her tone forceful.

"Grasping at straws," the closest programmer said.

"Grasp harder. We're running out of time."

Desmond wanted to turn toward them, but his instincts took over. He sensed that she—or whoever had turned the speaker on—wanted to keep that action a secret from the programmers or anyone watching the video feed. So he lay still in the bed, occasionally glancing over, showing only mild interest in the scene playing out.

"You know, telling us to work faster doesn't actually help us, Avery. It just wastes our time." The stooge grinned insincerely. "And I've heard we're running out of time."

"I see what you did there. That's cute." She raised her voice. "What *would* be helpful?"

"Oh, I don't know, maybe some actual clue about what we're looking for." The programmer held his skinny white arms in the air and shook his hands theatrically. "I know that sounds *super crazy*. Like, why would we even need to know what we're looking for?"

Avery turned away from them and once again fixed Desmond with a quick, fleeting glance. He thought this one said, *Pay attention*. Somehow he knew her. They were in sync, understood each other, like two friends who had known each other a very long time. Or lovers.

Avery's tone was more measured when she spoke to the programmers again. "Look, Byron, you have all the information you're going to get. Hughes has a Rapture Therapeutics implant in his brain. We think it's been adapted to release memories. We know he has a substance throughout his hippocampus—in the memory center of his brain. Something sends a signal to the implant to unblock the memories. And somewhere in those memories is the key to finding Rendition. Without Rendition, the Looking Glass will never work. It's very simple: you figure out how to trigger that implant, he remembers, we interrogate him, recover Rendition, and everyone lives happily ever after. You fail, the entire Looking Glass project goes down the tubes."

Byron shook his head in disgust and looked over at the guy sitting next to him. "You know, I wish some useless hot chick would tell me a bunch of stuff I already know and pretend like she's helping me."

Avery's tone betrayed no emotion. "I'm trying to help you see the big picture and anything you've overlooked. *And*, I'm trying to impress upon you the stakes of your task."

"You think I don't know?"

"I think you lack motivation."

"Are you kidding? McClain telling me I better get this done or else is all the motivation I need. That guy's like a walking *Nightmare on Elm Street*. Actually, Freddy Krueger's got nothing on him."

Avery smirked. "You know he's watching right now."

Byron went pale. The other two programmers slowly leaned away from him.

Avery broke into a grin. "Kidding."

"That's not funny."

"Sure it is. *That's* how scared you ought to be all the time—why you need to be working harder. Now—Hughes would have left himself a way to recover the memories. He may have already found it. Did you read the transcript from his interrogation?"

"Of course. He just found some prepaid credit cards and some dead ends. None of it worked."

Avery nodded.

"Look, even if it is an app, and even if we could hack it, it might not matter."

"What do you mean?"

"The implant could be set up to release the memories at certain times or certain locations. If so, until that time, or until he's at the programmed location, nothing will happen. Or, he could have loaded a set of memories to release no matter what, and reserved whatever he didn't want us to find for these locations or time points. Or—again, we have *no clue* how this thing works—memories could be keyed to sensations, images, sounds. Who knows?"

"Why do you think the memories might be triggered in different ways?"

Byron shrugged. "Simple logic. He wouldn't want himself to be in the dark, but he also wants to keep us from knowing any sensitive information. If he runs into something he needs to know about, the implant could release memories to help him out without compromising his goal."

Avery bit her lip. "Okay, fine. Just keep at it. Let me know what you find." She held the tablet up again and tapped it. The speaker in Desmond's cell fell silent, but Avery kept speaking to the programmers. Byron shrugged and gave an animated response, then Avery turned, glanced quickly again at Desmond, making eye contact for a fraction of a second, and left through the hatch.

The moment the hatch closed, Byron stood and began pacing and talking to the two other programmers. They pointed at the laptop screens and leaned back in their chairs.

Desmond wondered why she had let him hear the conversation. Was she an ally? Or was she trying to build trust? Was it part of their plan?

They were looking for an app. Could it be the Labyrinth Reality app? In Berlin it didn't seem to work. Maybe Byron was right— maybe the app was waiting for the right time or location. But *some* memories had come back to him—memories of his childhood. They wouldn't reveal what he had done with Rendition. Maybe that had been his plan: to hide the most sensitive memories until the right time. Or until he was ready.

He closed his eyes and rubbed his temples. He truly was in a labyrinth of his own making. He wondered if he would make it out alive. His breathing slowed, and another memory came.

☣

One Saturday, when Orville was waking up, sober for the first time in a while, Desmond said, "I need you to take me to Oklahoma City."

"What for?" the man grumbled.

"I need to buy something."

Orville shook his head, annoyed.

"I need to buy a computer."

The older man stared at him, an unreadable expression on his face. Desmond had rehearsed this conversation a dozen times in his mind, imagining what Orville would say. That Desmond had no use for a computer. That he needed it like he needed a hole in his head. That it was a waste of money.

Instead, Orville put a large pinch of Copenhagen snuff behind his lip and simply said, "All right then. Go get in the truck."

A minute later, Desmond sat in the Jeep pickup, waiting.

Orville walked past it to the shed behind the house. Desmond heard him open the hood of the broken-down Studebaker truck he had been threatening to fix up for years. He tossed some tools around, then slammed the hood shut, got in the Jeep, and drove to the city.

The CompUSA store was larger than Desmond expected, the choices much more numerous. He had considered ordering the computer by phone, from a vendor in a magazine called *Computer Shopper*, but he felt it was too risky; if the computer broke, he wanted to be able to take it somewhere and have it repaired under warranty.

He expected Orville to remain in the truck, or more likely, pony up at the nearest bar and drink until Desmond found him. Instead, he followed Desmond inside. They looked like the Beverly Hillbillies as they wandered the pristine aisles in their coveralls and dirty Carhartt coats, their tan faces and massive hands marking them as anything but computer geeks. Most of the clerks, who were young guys with glasses, glanced away and avoided them.

At the counter, Desmond described what he wanted in a computer and told them how much he had to spend.

"You're short."

"By how much?"

"Two hundred and fifty by the time you pay tax."

Desmond told the clerk that he could get the same specs from a number of places advertising in *Computer Shopper*. That set the guy off. He went on a tirade about the low quality of the computers they sold, compared small details, and insisted that having local service was worth something.

When the worked-up man finally finished, Desmond said, "Well, what do you suggest?"

"Drop the optional stuff. Modem. Downgrade the graphics card. Smaller monitor."

Before Desmond could speak, Orville stepped forward, pulled three one-hundred-dollar bills from his pocket, and slapped them on the counter. "Forget it. Build it just like he said."

The man raised his eyebrows. "What?"

"You heard me. Do it. We're in a hurry."

Orville wanted to put the two boxes on the back of the truck, but Desmond wouldn't hear of it. Between the cold and the wind, it was far too risky. So they placed the computer in between them in the cab, forming a barrier Desmond spoke over on the way back.

"Thanks."

His uncle grunted.

"I needed the modem to get on the internet."

"I know why you needed it."

"I'll be able to—"

"You don't need to explain. Buying that computer's the smartest thing you've done in a while."

Desmond had no idea what to say to that.

"I thought you were going to buy a truck with the money," Orville said.

Desmond had considered it. "I needed the computer more."

The machine and the internet access it granted were to Desmond at seventeen what the library had been to him at six: access to another world of seemingly endless knowledge. The web fed his mind and inspired his curiosity. It always led to more questions, more places to explore.

Every time he heard the noise of the Texas Instruments 28.8 modem, he came to life like never before.

In IRC chat rooms, he met like-minded people. Many were in San Francisco, Seattle, and New York, but plenty were in small towns across America, just like him. Most were young people in their basements or bedrooms typing away at night.

He downloaded several programming languages: C++, Python, Java, and Perl. He created a GeoCities page and began learning HTML and Javascript. He loved the logic of computer programming—it was a sharp contrast to the chaos and unpredictability of people on the rigs. Every day was a new puzzle to solve.

That summer, he busted three of his ribs on an offshore rig. He was home alone, recuperating, when two cars came barreling down the dirt driveway: a shiny Mercedes-Benz followed by a beat-up Ford pickup with two hunting rifles hanging in the back window.

Two men exited the Benz, both in suits. They were clean-shaven, their short hair combed to the side, and they were sweating like pigs. Desmond didn't know either of them. He did know the lanky man who stepped out of the truck and sauntered toward the run-down house like he owned the place. His name was Dale Epply. He was another roughneck, possibly the only man Desmond knew who was meaner than Orville.

The suits introduced themselves, said they were from the West Texas Energy Corporation, and asked if they could come inside. Desmond forgot their names as soon as he heard them. He already knew what this was about.

Inside, they sat down, took him up on his offer for some iced tea and water, and with words that sounded very practiced, told Desmond that his uncle had died in an accident on a rig in the gulf. They waited for his reaction.

"Thank you for telling me," Desmond said.

His eyes were dry. He couldn't wait for them to leave.

One of the suits pushed an envelope across the chipped coffee table. The man was wearing a tie. Desmond assumed he was a lawyer. What he said next confirmed it.

"Your uncle, like all WTE contractors, signed a contract..."

Desmond couldn't focus on the words. He heard only clips and phrases. Binding arbitration was part of the contract. Attorneys might contact Desmond about suing the company for wrongful death, but they were just opportunists and would be wasting his time. There was a standard death benefit, which was generous, they said, and, conveniently, it was contained in the envelope.

Desmond ripped it open. The check was for ten thousand dollars.

The two men watched him nervously. Dale looked bored. Desmond was pretty sure he knew why the man was there.

"Make it twenty-five thousand and you'll never hear from me."

The lawyer cut his eyes at the other man, who said, "I'm authorized to pay up to twenty thousand total."

"That's a deal," Desmond said flatly.

Dale smirked.

The oil executive drew a checkbook from the inside pocket of his suit, folded the alligator skin cover back, and wrote out a second check for ten thousand dollars.

The lawyer shuffled papers in his briefcase and presented Desmond with two copies of a four-page agreement.

"This explicitly waives your right to further litigation..."

Desmond signed them before the man could finish speaking.

The lawyer collected them from the table and took out an envelope.

"We've sent your uncle's body to the Seven Bridges Funeral Home in Noble. Due to the nature of his injuries, he's already been cremated. We will, of course, cover the expense."

The lawyer waited. When Desmond said nothing, the lawyer opened the envelope.

"Your uncle was required to file a will with us. We'll read that now."

He squinted at the page. Through the glare of the sun through the window, Desmond could tell there was only one line.

The sweating man in the suit cleared his throat.

"The last will and testament of Orville Hughes is as follows: To my nephew, Desmond Barlow Hughes, I leave everything. 39-21-8."

From the recliner, Dale let out a laugh. "Well, least we know Orville was sober when he wrote it."

All eyes went to him.

Dale shrugged. "He was a man of few words when he wasn't drinking."

No one responded.

The oil executive expressed his condolences again, this time without the forced sincerity. They were in a hurry to leave and were out the door within seconds.

Dale told them he wanted to stay, "in case Desmond needs anything," as if they were anything more than work acquaintances. When the oil men had left, Dale and Desmond sat across from each other in the shabby living room, Dale chatting about nothing in particular, seeming unbothered by Desmond's silence. He was working up to something. Or working up the courage to do what he'd come here to do.

"The thing is, Des, your uncle owed me some money."

"That right?"

Desmond had never seen his uncle borrow a dollar—or get up from a card table with a debt to his name.

"Sure did."

Desmond could see the outline of a small revolver in Dale's pants pocket. A .38 caliber snub-nose if he had to guess.

"Tell you what," Desmond said. "We'll head to the bank, I'll cash these checks, and we'll settle up."

Dale thought about it a moment. "Yeah, that's a good idea. Why don't you go ahead and sign the back of 'em checks right now."

His eyes bored holes into Desmond.

Slowly, the teenager turned the checks over and signed them.

"Old Orville wasn't much for banks, was 'e? Didn't trust 'em."

Desmond's eyes settled on the lever-action .30-30 leaned up against the door. Orville kept it there in case a deer wandered near the house. Dale saw him glance at it, tried to act like he hadn't, tried to make his tone casual.

"Heck of a will he left. Them numbers at the end—sounded like a combination to a safe to me. That what you think, Des?"

Desmond's mind raced. He needed to get out of this living room. He said nothing.

"Yeah, that's 'zactly what it is. Let's see if that combination works. I'll take what's owed me, and I'll be off."

He stood quickly, shuffled over next to the rifle. "Where's the safe, Des?"

Desmond didn't make eye contact. "Under his bed."

Dale smiled. "Nah, doubt that. Orville's too smart for that. Somebody robbing you is bound to search the house. Twister could get it too. Bad fire might burn it, melt the lock."

He stuck his hand in his pocket, the one with the gun. "Where is it? I ain't gonna ask again."

"Shed out back."

Dale stepped forward, snatched the will from the coffee table. "Show me."

He opened the door and stood with his back to the rifle, blocking Des from reaching it. The setting sun flooded into the shabby old farmhouse.

Desmond marched past Dale, onto the porch, and down the few steps. The grass was cut short. Brown dirt patches littered the ground like a coat that had been sewn back together countless times.

The shed was a hundred feet away. It stood there, placid in the fall wind, its oak walls and rusted tin roof silently waiting for an event that would change Desmond's life forever. The building had been just big enough for a tractor in the sixties. Now it held the broken-down Studebaker truck and a John Deere riding lawn-mower Orville had made Desmond cut the grass with.

"How'd he die, Dale?" Desmond walked quickly, trying to put distance between them.

Dale quickened his pace to keep up. "Blowout."

It was a lie. Desmond could tell by the way he said the word, knew the man would never tell him the truth.

At the door, Desmond paused, acting like he expected the other man to open it.

Behind him, he saw that Dale now held his right arm behind his back. His pocket was empty.

"Open it," Dale said, nodding to the door.

Desmond flipped the latch and pulled at the door, which caught on the grass around it. He slipped inside quickly.

Startled, Dale rushed forward, through the breach.

Desmond's eyes didn't have a chance to adjust, but it didn't matter; he knew what he needed and exactly where it was.

In the darkness, his hand reached from memory, gripped the

spare lawnmower blade hanging above the workbench, careful not to let the sharp side dig into his fingers. He swung it without even sighting his target.

It connected with deadly precision, cutting into Dale's neck. Blood painted the wall like oil gushing from an uncapped well. Dale's right arm fell limp at his side. The .38 revolver fell to the ground.

Dale reached for Desmond's throat with his left hand, grasped it, his fingers digging in. Desmond released his grip on the blade, put his shoulder into the man, and drove him out of the shack, into the light. Blood shot out of Dale's neck and onto the grass.

Dale's grip loosened. Desmond pushed him to the ground, stepped on his left hand. Within seconds, the color drained from the older man, the squirting blood slowed to a pour, then a trickle. He gurgled some words Desmond couldn't make out, then his eyes went still and glassy.

Desmond stood, stared at Dale Epply's dead body, lying there like a cowboy at the crossroads of a dusty western town—a gunslinger who'd been outdrawn.

What have I done?

The wind whipped Desmond's blond hair into his face. Blood dripped from the fingers of his right hand where he had held the lawnmower blade too tight. He had killed a man. In self-defense, but nevertheless, he had taken a life. It had happened so fast.

Desmond expected to feel remorse, but instead he felt nothing. *I did what I had to.* But he knew that his life was about to get more complicated.

The lawful thing was to call the sheriff's office and tell them what had happened. He figured they would believe his story: Dale probably had a rap sheet longer than the Missouri River. But Desmond's record wasn't clean, either; he'd been arrested in three states, mostly drunken brawls Orville had pulled him into. And Dale might have friends at the sheriff's office—or folks who might put pressure on the case. Desmond had nobody.

Calling the sheriff meant uncertainty, possibly being trapped in this place, maybe for a long time.

Inside the house, he washed his hands and got his uncle's truck keys. He backed the truck up, returned to the shed, and gathered what he needed: a tarp (which they used when the roof was leaking and they were too drunk to fix it), a shovel, a tank of gas they had used for the lawnmower, a bottle of Clorox bleach, and several unpainted oak planks they used to patch up the house.

He laid the tarp out next to Dale and took Orville's single-page will from the dead man's pocket. Desmond had seen men die on the rigs, knew how long it would take rigor mortis to set in. His body would be like a spaghetti noodle for a while. For that reason, he laid several oak planks next to the man, then rolled the man and the planks together into the tarp. With the stability of the boards, he hoisted the roll up, set the end on the tailgate, and pushed it onto the bed.

He scooped the blood-soaked dirt and grass into a five-gallon-bucket and capped it. With a handsaw, he cut away the blood-soaked portions of the shed's planks, stuffed them in a sack, and tossed them on the back of the truck too. He stripped off his bloody clothes and tucked them inside the tarp.

Naked save for his underwear, he returned to the house, washed up, put on a fresh set of clothes, and gathered his belongings, which barely filled the passenger side of the truck. The computer tower sat on the floorboard; the fifteen-inch CRT monitor lay facedown on the seat; and a bag with three changes of clothes buttressed the computer, making sure it didn't move. He put the .30-30 lever-action behind the seat.

He then went to Orville's bedroom; he knew his uncle kept a pistol by his bed, an old Smith & Wesson .357 Magnum. But when he opened the drawer on the bedside table, he stopped, surprised by what he saw. The pistol was there, but there was also something else: a slightly rumpled photograph. In it, an oil well towered behind a young boy of maybe eight—Desmond. Orville stood beside him. They were covered in dirt and oil. Neither smiled.

Without a thought, Desmond reached down, took the photo, and placed it in his pocket. Then he quickly drew it back out, as if it had burned him. He didn't want to wrinkle it.

He returned to the truck and placed the photo in the glovebox and the pistol under the front seat where it would be easier to reach.

Inside the shed, he popped the hood on the Studebaker and started taking the tools out. A few minutes later, he moved a straight pipe wrench, revealing some of the safe. He dug more quickly then, soon revealing the entire face of it. Had Orville welded the thing to the truck? He probably had, making it impossible for a robber to make off with it without a tow truck. Smart.

Desmond spun the safe's dial to the three numbers in the will and turned the handle. When it opened, Desmond was stunned. He had never seen so much money in all his life. Stacks of green bills, bound in ten-thousand-dollar bundles, sat there like a mirage. Desmond reached out, held one as if making sure it was real. The safe also held the deed to the house, the truck, and a set of US Army dog tags with Orville's name. Beneath those items lay a sealed envelope with a single word, written in rugged block letters: Desmond.

He stuffed the dog tags in his pocket and ripped the envelope open. It was a letter to him, written by Orville, dated a year ago. Unable to resist, he read the first line. He wanted to go on, to stand there and read it all, but he felt he should wait until he had time to process it. At the moment, all he could think about was getting rid of Dale's body and getting out of town.

He put the deeds and letter in the truck's glovebox and returned with a sack for the money. To his astonishment, he counted out thirty-two of the ten-thousand-dollar stacks.

Inside the truck, he pulled away from the home he had arrived at thirteen years before, after the tragic bushfire that had killed his family. He wasn't leaving healed, but he was changed.

He drove west on Slaughterville Road, turned off ten minutes later, and stopped at a gate to an abandoned ranch. He undid the wire holding it closed, pulled the truck through, and shut it behind him. He drove through a field, far away from the road and out of sight.

He dug a pit next. He was drenched with sweat by the time

he finished. He tossed Dale's body in, along with his clothes and the bloody boards. He doused them with gasoline from the tank, waited for the sun to slip past the horizon, and tossed a match in.

The smell of burning human flesh sickened him, reminded him of the elementary school where he had stayed with all those people burned by the bushfire. He thought of Charlotte as he walked away from the blaze, then he thought of Agnes, and finally Orville. The man had been mean as a snake. A hard man. But he was all the family Desmond had. Now he was gone.

With the fire burning in the pit a few feet away, Desmond took out the envelope and read Orville's letter.

Desmond,

Take the money. Don't be careless with it. Respect it, invest it, and take care of it, and it will take care of you. I've been saving it my whole life. After you came to live with me, I got a little more serious about not spending every last cent I earned. The rest is the proceeds from your family's ranch in Australia, which I have preserved in its entirety.

I hope you leave and go far away from this place. There's nothing here for a mind like yours.

People often say that what doesn't kill you makes you stronger. That's bullshit. Some events a person just can't recover from. They don't make you stronger, they make you weaker, no matter how hard you try to cover it up or how strong you try to act. That happened to me when I was twenty-five. It doesn't matter what it was. Don't go trying to find out. It's water under the bridge. When you came to live with me, I was well on my way to drinking myself to death. Probably would have been in the grave within a few years if the rigs didn't get me first. I told the woman on the phone that I was in no shape to care for you. I figured it was more dangerous here than wherever they would take you. But she wouldn't listen. She sent you on anyway. I'm glad she did. For my sake. Caring for you saved me. Changed me. After what happened to you, I thought you would do what I did, shrivel up and die inside. But you didn't. There's a fight inside you that's stronger than anyone I've ever met.

Not on a rig, or in the jungles of Vietnam and Cambodia, or on the streets of London when the bombs were falling.

This world broke me. I found my peace at the bottom of a bottle. Drinking was my crutch. Don't let it be yours. Don't take the road I took. Drinking and drugs only make you forget for a while, dig you deeper in the hole. Don't depend on them, Desmond. Get yourself clean. Leave the drinking behind. Quit the rigs for good. I don't know where in this world you belong, but it's not here. Live a life that makes you proud. As the years pass, it will be the wind in your sails. Regrets will sink you.

Orville

Desmond folded up the letter and watched the fire burn down until the flames receded into the pit. Sitting in that field in Oklahoma, he made a promise to himself: he would stop drinking for good. And he would do as Orville had suggested: he would leave this place and never come back. He knew where he had to go.

He took the shovel from the truck, stamped out the last glowing embers, scooped up the fire's remains, and deposited them in two five-gallon buckets. He filled the hole back in, drove the truck another half mile to the banks of the Canadian River, and slipped his waders on. He washed the blood off the tarp in the river, then cut it into small pieces and scattered them, along with the ashes from the buckets. For half an hour he dropped the remains in the river, watching them flow out of sight. Then he washed the truck bed out with bleach and cleaned his hands.

At a grocery store in Noble, he loaded up on supplies.

He camped in another field that night, though he didn't light a fire. First thing in the morning, he visited a lawyer. He brought his uncle's will and the deed to the house. The man was a professional, fair on his fees, and amenable to what Desmond suggested, though he said it was highly irregular.

Two hours later, Desmond signed a series of documents, which the receptionist notarized. The three of them walked to the courthouse for a brief meeting, which went as expected.

Desmond drove out of town that afternoon, heading for a place he'd never been but which would change his life forever: Silicon Valley.

CHAPTER 53

PEYTON OPENED HER eyes. Slowly, the room came into focus: metal walls, a narrow bed, and a glass partition. Her head throbbed. She felt hung over. She sat up, and a wave of nausea greeted her. After it passed, she still felt a slight motion, like a vibration. She recognized the feeling: she was on a ship.

A man with a badly scarred face and long blond hair was sitting in a metal chair beyond the glass partition, reading a tablet.

"Good morning," he said, an insincere cheeriness in his Australian accent.

"Who are you?"

"My name's Conner McClain."

Petyon studied him a moment. "What do you want?"

"Information."

Peyton wanted information too. She sensed that this man had it. "You started the outbreak in Kenya, didn't you?"

"We merely accelerated the inevitable."

"Pandemics aren't inevitable."

"You know they are, Peyton. You've said so yourself."

"I've said that pandemics *have* been inevitable—throughout human history. Not anymore. They can be a thing of the past. I've dedicated my life to that work. And you're destroying it."

Conner stared at her, a mildly amused expression on his face. "There's one person in this room who's going to make the human race safe from pandemics. And it isn't you. Your life's work is a drop in the ocean compared to our plan. We're implementing a real solution—one final pandemic to end all others."

One pandemic. "They're related, aren't they? The flu pandemic and the hemorrhagic fever in Kenya."

"You're smart enough to know the answer to that."

"Why?"

"Fear."

The pieces came together then. They had released the flu strain in isolated parts of Kenya a week before they had released it around the world. In the later stages of the virus, it presented like an Ebola-like hemorrhagic fever—an outbreak deadly enough to get every government's attention. They had wanted to demonstrate what would happen around the world in a week if the virus wasn't cured.

"You have a cure, don't you?"

He flashed her a condescending smile. "We're not monsters, Peyton. We have the means to stop the virus as soon as governments figure out their place in the new order." He turned away from her. "Now as much as I've enjoyed our talk, I have some questions I need you to answer."

"Screw you."

"Your friend Dr. Watson has lost a lot of blood. My people tell me she needs surgery, urgently."

Peyton stared at him, rage simmering. This man was responsible for Jonas's death and Lucas Turner's and so many others. He couldn't be trusted.

"Give me answers, and we'll help her," Conner said.

"I don't believe you."

He turned the tablet around, showing Peyton a video feed of Hannah on an operating room table, a tube running from her mouth, the wound at her shoulder exposed and prepped for surgery.

Three people in masks and surgical gowns stood around the table, gloved hands held in the air.

"How do I know you'll do it?"

"A show of good faith, Dr. Shaw." Conner touched his collarbone. "Proceed."

On the screen, the medical personnel sprang into action, converging on the wound. Others appeared from off-screen, pushing trays with instruments forward, within easy reach.

"You stop answering, or start lying, and we stop operating," Conner said.

Peyton nodded, still watching the screen, her eyes locked on the blood pressure readings.

"Have you had any contact with Desmond Hughes?"

Peyton looked up. *Desmond Hughes*—the words were like a cattle prod. "Yes," she said quietly.

"When?"

"Before I deployed."

"How?"

"He called me."

Conner looked confused. "You're lying."

"I'm not—"

"We tapped your mobile, Peyton."

"He called me at home. On the landline."

Conner spoke slowly, still suspicious. "What did he say?"

"Nothing—"

"Answer me," Conner said, his tone hard.

"He was confused. He didn't know who I was. He told me I was in danger. Then he hung up."

"In danger of what?"

"He didn't say."

Conner considered her words for a moment. "When did you last speak with your mother?"

"What?"

"Answer."

"When I landed in Nairobi."

"What did she say to you?"

Peyton recounted the conversation, as best she could remember.

"When was the last time you spoke with your father?"

"My father? The eighties. I was six—"

"You haven't spoken to him since then? No emails? No meetings?"

"Dead people don't send emails."

A smile curled at Conner's lips. He turned away from her.

"When was the last time you spoke with your brother?"

Peyton was shocked by the question. "My *brother*? He died in '91."

Peyton waited, but Conner only stared at her.

"He was a WHO employee working on an AIDS awareness campaign in Uganda. He died in a fire near Mount Elgon," she said.

"I know how, when, and where your brother died. Now answer my question."

Peyton stared at the monster's badly burned face, at the scars that ran down his cheeks, over his chin, and into his shirt collar. "Did you know him? Were you there in 1991?"

Conner touched his collarbone again. "Stop."

On the screen, Peyton saw the doctors remove their hands. But they didn't back away. They glanced at each other, seeming to weigh their decision, then resumed the operation. Another person wearing a surgical gown marched into the scene, raised a handgun, and pointed it at the closest medical worker. All three froze.

Peyton swallowed. "I haven't seen or talked to my brother since the Christmas of 1990 in Palo Alto."

"That wasn't so hard, was it? One last question. Your login and password to the CDC VPN."

"No."

Conner motioned to the tablet, where the medical workers were still standing at the table, waiting. Hannah's open wound oozed blood. "How long do you think she has? Another few minutes?"

Peyton considered his request. She had the highest level of security clearance: access to situation reports from the EOC, inventory levels at the strategic stockpiles, and notes from the labs investigating new pathogens. For these bioterrorists, her login was an all-access pass to the inside of the US response to their attack. It meant real-time intel they could exploit to kill more people.

"My login is pshaw@cdc.gov. Password: ashaw91#io."

Conner turned the tablet around and quickly typed.

"You know, the problem with lying about your password is

that it's easily discovered. Seriously, Peyton, I'm gonna need that password. Right now."

She swallowed and spoke with all the force she could muster. "You know, I'm a member of the Commissioned Corps of the US Public Health Service. We take an oath—to protect the public. So did Hannah. Telling you would violate that oath. I take my oaths very seriously."

"Dear God. Why does everyone around here have to do things the hard way?" Conner punched a few buttons on the tablet.

Seconds later, Peyton heard the hiss of gas seeping into her cell. She lost consciousness almost immediately.

Conner touched his collar. "Resume. We may need Watson for leverage. And prep an interrogation room for Shaw ASAP."

CHAPTER 54

IN THE OBSERVATION room on the *Kentaro Maru*, Conner watched the techs administer the drugs to Peyton Shaw. The questions began soon after, and within minutes, she had revealed her CDC login. He relayed it to the team in ops.

"We're in," the operator said over the radio.

"What do you see?" Conner asked. "Do they know yet?"

"No. The tests comparing the viruses have been delayed. Their infection models are way off."

"Good. Download everything and get out."

In his stateroom, he watched the video feeds. Desmond was in the middle of some push-ups. The three programmers were camped out beyond the glass, typing furiously. The area around them was starting to resemble the pigsty Conner had found them in: crushed Red Bull cans and microwave meal wrappers littered the floor.

Another feed showed the redheaded CDC physician. She was strapped to a bed in the medical wing. She'd been sleeping since the surgery.

Conner switched the feed to Peyton Shaw. She was just waking up. She staggered to the tiny bathroom in the cell and stood over the sink, bringing water to her face. She gagged once, then moved to the toilet, waiting, but nothing came up. She rested her back against the wall, staring at nothing for a long moment.

Slowly, she stood and stripped off her clothes. Water washed through her dark brown hair, over her curves, down her body.

Conner studied her for a long moment. She wasn't drop-dead gorgeous—not like the girls every guy went for—but he thought she had something even more attractive: an unassuming confidence. It drew people like a magnet, put them at ease, compelled them to want to be around her.

He was the opposite. He repelled people. Repulsed them. He had since childhood. Everyone who saw him instantly had the same reaction. Smiles disappeared. Eyes grew wide, raking over the scars on his face.

Soon, he would create a world where that didn't matter, where no child would have to grow up a monster, alone, rejected by every person who saw him.

☣

After her shower, Peyton lay on the narrow bed, her wet hair soaking into the mattress. She was scared. For her own safety, for Hannah's, and for everyone in Kenya and beyond. If the virus went global, it could claim millions of lives. Maybe more. It felt like her entire world had been turned upside down. She had felt that way only once, when she was six years old.

Her family had lived in London then, in a flat in Belgravia. She'd been asleep in her bedroom when the door flew open. Her mother rushed in and shook her awake.

"Wake up, darling. We're leaving."

Her mother made her dress and leave home with only the clothes on her back. She crowded Peyton, her sister Madison, and her brother Andrew into a black cab, and they sped to Heathrow. The four of them left London forever that night.

The first flight took them to Amsterdam, the second to Paris. A private car drove them through the night to Le Mans. At daybreak, they boarded a small plane that flew them to America.

For a few months, they lived in hotels, never staying in the same place for more than a few nights. Peyton's mother told her children it was an extended vacation and "tour of America." But Peyton sensed something was very wrong. Her sister and brother did too.

Periodically, Peyton asked her mother where her father was, why he couldn't join them.

"He's busy, dear."

Peyton tried to listen in on the calls her mother conducted in secret, often stretching the phone cord into the hotel bathroom and shutting the door with the shower running. Peyton could make out only bits and pieces. Someone had lost their dog. A beagle. Her mother was very worried about it. She was constantly asking about finding the beagle, which was strange, because she had never been one for dogs—or animals of any kind.

Finally, after four weeks, her mother sat the three children down and told them that their father wouldn't be joining them. With dry eyes, she said, "There was an accident. I'm very sorry, but your father has passed away."

The words destroyed Peyton instantly. Andrew met the news with disbelief that soon turned to skepticism. Then anger. He asked questions their mother refused to answer.

How did he die?

When was the funeral? Where?

The lack of answers only enraged Andrew more. He shouted and argued with their mother.

I want to see him. I can see my own father. I want to see his grave. You can't stop me.

I want to go back to London. It's our home.

Andrew became increasingly distant. Peyton was nearly catatonic. Her sister Madison was there for her, holding her as she cried each night for a week. Their mother was stoic, withdrawn. The calls continued. The secrecy only made them trust her less. Maybe it was simply because she had been the one who'd told them, but to varying degrees, all three of them blamed her for their father's death.

Despite Andrew's demands that they return to London, Peyton's mother refused to relent. They settled near San Francisco in Palo Alto. They changed their last name to Shaw, and Andrew completed his last two years of high school, then left for college, then medical school.

It took time for the family to come together again. In fact, it took more than time—it took Andrew's death to finally bring them all closer again. It was just the three of them after that—Peyton, Madison, and their mother, Lin—and they shared a strong bond.

Peyton hadn't thought about that night in London for a long time. As she drifted off to sleep, she wondered why she had thought of it now.

She awoke to the worst headache of her life. She returned to the sink and gulped down two mouthfuls of water. Bloodshot eyes stared back at her. She lifted up her shirt, afraid of what she would see. She swallowed hard when she saw it—a rash reaching up from her abdomen toward her chest.

She was infected.

DAY 8

2,000,000,000 infected
400,000 dead

CHAPTER 55

MILLEN SAT IN a folding chair, taking in the Sunday afternoon sun, watching Elim walk across the dusty field outside Mandera Referral Hospital. The older woman from the village, Dhamiria, helped him as he walked, encouraging him in Swahili. Halima recorded his progress, and Tian moved things around, providing a sort of obstacle course for Elim to walk around and step over. The six-year-old boy delighted in the task.

Millen played music from his phone, which all four Kenyans seemed to enjoy. He wouldn't have dared expend the phone's battery without the solar charger, but for the moment, sunlight and power were two things they had in abundance. The music and Elim's rehabilitation had been their routine for the past two days while they waited on the transport Elliott had arranged. Millen was eager to get home. On Friday night, a few hours after arriving in Mandera, he had slipped the satsleeve on his phone and opened Google News. The first article had shocked him:

US STOCK MARKETS TANK ON PANDEMIC FEARS

Growing concern over the scope and severity of the X1 outbreak has finally infected markets. Stock indices in the US declined over 25% today during the short session that ended at 1 p.m. in what is being called Red Friday. The decline is the largest stock market crash in history. The drop eclipsed

even Black Monday—October 19th, 1987—when the Dow
Jones Industrial Average shed over 22% of its value in a
single day. As with the crash in 1987, the rout began with
Asian markets and spread west to Europe and the US…

Millen had clicked the next headline.

WORLD GOES INTO LOCKDOWN AS TWO
SEPARATE OUTBREAKS SPREAD

Though the WHO has stopped providing estimates on the
number of X1 cases, experts project that at least 50 million,
and possibly many more, are already infected worldwide.
Nations around the world are resorting to drastic measures.

The UK announced this morning that it would close its borders. Germany, France, Italy, and Russia quickly followed suit.

Perhaps the most alarming and mysterious aspect of the
X1 outbreak is the virus's seemingly unlimited reach. Cases
have been reported aboard military vessels on long-term
deployment, in remote villages, and on cruise ships with little
outside contact.

The most deadly outbreak, centered around Kenya, has
also finally forced the world's hand. The Ebola-like disease,
currently called the Mandera virus, has killed thousands thus
far. Infection rates are not known. In hopes of containing
the epidemic, an unprecedented alliance of Western and
Eastern powers, including the US, UK, France, China, Japan,
Australia, and India, has announced a full-scale blockade of
all East African ports—from the Red Sea to South Africa.

Details of how the blockade would be carried out were not
immediately available.

Despite an hour of searching, Millen hadn't found the news he
was looking for: an update on the search for the missing CDC and
WHO workers, especially Dr. Shaw and Hannah. It seemed their
abduction had been forgotten in the chaos sweeping the world.

He had awoken Saturday morning to find Elim walking again around the tent complex, giving it his all. Dhamiria held his arm. They were both smiling and laughing. Their conversation was in Swahili, and although Millen couldn't understand it, their body language told him everything he needed to know.

He closed his eyes and pretended to be asleep. If the headlines from the previous night had told him anything, it was that tender moments and simple pleasures would be hard to come by in the days ahead.

☣

Later on Saturday, Millen had searched the headlines again:

KENYA BURNS AS EBOLA-LIKE VIRUS SPREADS

Rioting overnight gripped Kenya's largest cities as crowds demanded that the faltering government act to combat the mounting death toll from the Mandera virus. The death count from the fires and fighting in Nairobi, Mombasa, and Garissa is unavailable at this time, but sources within the Ministry of Health estimate that over 40 thousand have died from the virus, and many more are infected.

The crisis in Kenya's largest cities caused an exodus as residents...

Millen scrolled through the pictures. Bonfires at intersections. Overturned cars. Mobs pressing against police in riot gear. He decided not to show them to Elim or the villagers. They were having a good day—a day he didn't want to ruin. Elim was learning to walk again. The four Africans were living proof that the virus could be survived. It *almost* felt like the whole world wasn't falling apart.

Millen felt hope. And a reason for faith.

☣

Elim had grown stronger with each session of his makeshift rehabilitation program. His naps grew shorter, and he walked on legs more sure and firm. After dinner on Saturday, he took Millen aside for a conversation the younger man had been expecting.

"I'd like to talk with you about what happens when the plane arrives tomorrow," Elim said.

Millen wanted to spare the man from having to ask the question. "If she wants to stay, she should."

"She does," Elim replied. "However, she's made a commitment. An important one. Finding a cure is vital."

"I've been thinking about that," Millen said. "If we take enough samples from you and her, we should be fine." He paused. "Or, there is another option."

Elim raised his eyebrows.

"Come with us."

Elim shook his head. "My place is here. Now more than ever. My country needs me."

☣

Millen was packed and ready when the call came on Sunday.

"Dr. Thomas, we're on approach to the Mandera airport."

"We'll be there," Millen said.

At the airport, he led the two young villagers into the private plane, then returned to the SUV, where Elim sat behind the wheel, Dhamiria in the passenger seat.

"Where will you go?" Millen asked.

"Wherever we're needed," Elim said. "We'll head south and take it from there."

"Good luck."

"I hope your friends and colleagues are returned safely, Millen."

"Me too."

A few minutes later, the plane lifted off. Millen gazed out the window at the deserted airport. It had been bustling when he arrived last week. Now it was dead—like the charred remnants of a bomb test in the desert. He wondered what he'd find in America.

If the news was any indication, a lot of people were infected, and their fate might be the same as that of the residents of Mandera. He couldn't let that happen. He hoped he was bringing home the key to finding a treatment.

CHAPTER 56

ON SUNDAY MORNING in Atlanta, Elliott waited for the event he believed would change America forever. The news gave no clues of it. The people he called had heard nothing.

The first hints had leaked the day before across social media. All military personnel, including the National Guard, were called in to their nearest base or a designated rally point. Staff at hospitals, as well as police, fire, and EMT workers, were also called in.

Those without symptoms of the respiratory virus known as X1 were instructed to report first. Those who were sick were to arrive three hours later.

The first responders called and texted their family and friends to say that they were being deployed for an emergency preparedness drill and wouldn't be home for several days. Some noted that they wouldn't have phone or internet access during the drill.

Elliott had expected his phone to ring. He was not only a physician and an epidemiologist, but a rear admiral in the Public Health Service's Commissioned Corps. He was also a CDC employee—or he had been. His employment situation since he had leaked information about Peyton's abduction to the news hadn't been made clear. He was certain that he should be on the critical personnel list; perhaps multiple lists. But the call never came. His name had been deleted.

He didn't have to guess who had done it; he knew. And he had never been so angry in his entire life. For someone to play politics at a time like this, to pursue a vendetta against him when he could save lives, was unthinkable. But there was nothing he could do about it, and that bothered him even more.

The remainder of Saturday had passed without event. In the family room, Elliott sat in the recliner, Rose in a pull-up chair beside him. Her symptoms were worse today. The cough was nearly incessant, though she suppressed it, and she left the room when it wouldn't relent. Ryan and Sam were upstairs in the bonus room playing with their son, Adam. To all outward appearances it was the perfect Saturday after Thanksgiving: college football on TV (Elliott's alma mater, Michigan, was playing Ohio State), their grandson playing, the entire family together under one roof.

Elliott wondered how long the five-year-old's childhood would last. Would it be measured in days, weeks? He knew what was coming. He feared it—for himself and for Rose, but most of all for his son, his daughter-in-law, and his grandson.

Elliott watched the TV, wincing whenever news reports came on. Retailers were reporting record traffic at brick and mortar stores on Black Friday. Their stocks had taken a beating during the market's short session on Friday, and they were no doubt hoping to prop up investor confidence for the market opening on Monday.

Up and down Elliott's street, parcels sat on nearly every doorstep, thanks to Saturday and now Sunday delivery. Neighbors shuffled outside in pyjamas, coughing as they carried the boxes inside.

The event Elliott had been waiting for happened at noon on Sunday. Cell phones began issuing a shrill alarm, similar to an Amber Alert or Severe Weather Bulletin. But this message was neither of those. It instructed the phone's owner to click a link or turn on their TV.

A minute later, Elliott and his family sat in front of their TV, listening as the president spoke from his desk in the Oval Office.

"My fellow Americans, today our nation faces a new kind of threat. First, I want you to know that we are prepared for this threat. We have a plan, and we are executing that plan. I'm speaking to you now because that plan will impact you and your loved ones. We will need your help. Your fellow Americans will need your help.

"Departments at the state and federal level have been closely monitoring X1, the low-intensity flu-like virus currently affecting millions of Americans. We have decided that X1 cases have grown to the point that they represent a danger to our nation. Therefore, I have activated a program called BioShield. BioShield is meant to do one thing: protect you and your family during this time.

"Before I outline the steps we're taking, I want to first assure you that these measures are temporary. They are also born out of an abundance of caution, and a desire to ensure that every American receives adequate care."

Elliott listened as the president detailed the BioShield program. As he'd expected, a state of emergency was declared, including martial law and a nationwide curfew beginning daily at six p.m. Every citizen was instructed to go home and stay there immediately following the announcement. Homeless individuals were required to report to the nearest shelter or subway, where transportation would be arranged for them.

A combination of National Guard, military, and FEMA personnel cordoned off every major city. Checkpoints were established on every interstate and major road. Air, rail, and bus traffic ceased. Anyone outside a cordon zone would be directed to a series of shelters set up in rural areas at schools, sports arenas, and courthouses.

The federal government also temporarily nationalized every company in key industries: telecommunications, internet hosting, shipping and logistics, power and energy, and health care.

Around two p.m., school buses arrived on Elliott's street. Anyone with symptoms of the X1 virus was instructed to get on. It was a bizarre scene, the convoy of buses loading up coughing adults, teens, and children on a Sunday.

In his address, the president had warned that anyone who didn't get on the bus would not be registered for essential services. In the coming days, the National Guard and military would be distributing food and transporting sick individuals to care centers.

Anyone who refused to register would be denied food and medical care—and more, they would be detained and placed in a low-priority quarantine zone, a prison with only basic services. It could be a death sentence.

Elliott stood at the front door, peering through the glass. The half-empty bus stopped outside their home, and the doors swung open.

At his side, Rose held his arm. She whispered, keeping her voice too quiet for their son and grandson to hear.

"I don't want to go."

"We have to, darling."

Elliott turned to his son, who stood a safe distance away. He tried to sound casual, as if they were just going out for a movie. "We should be back in a few hours."

Ryan didn't buy it. "Don't go."

"They're just trying to get a head count. They need to figure out what they're dealing with. We'll be right back."

Standing in line to get on the bus, Elliott could smell the chlorine wafting through its open doors. He made eye contact with several of his neighbors—those he had enlisted in his plan. Their expressions said, *You were right.*

He was sorry that he was.

The bus driver stood at the top of the stairs yelling for everyone to bring their cell phones with them, that if they didn't bring their phones, they might not be able to get medical care and food in the future. Several people broke from the line and ran home for their phones.

The seats were still damp from the germ-killing chemical mix applied to them, but Elliott and Rose sat anyway. He put his arm around her, trying to keep her warm in the late November chill.

The roads were empty. They joined a convoy of other buses that barreled through Atlanta, past parked cars and empty sidewalks where bits of trash tumbled in the wind. Parked police cars with flashing lights blocked them from taking any other route. Police in riot gear lined the streets, yelling and pointing at anyone on foot. It was a bizarre tour of a city on lockdown, a city that a few hours ago had been free—and was now something very different.

After a few turns, Elliott knew where they were headed.

The FEMA tents outside the Georgia Dome confirmed his suspicion. The facility, home to the Atlanta Falcons football team, had been the largest domed stadium in the world when it first opened in 1992. It still ranked third.

It was also, however, no longer state-of-the-art. For that reason alone, the city was erecting a shiny new high-tech stadium right across the street—aptly dubbed the Mercedes-Benz Stadium. It was due to open in the next year.

Elliott would have expected the towering cranes to be still on a Sunday afternoon, but they were working feverishly, hoisting up parts of the stadium's retractable roof. It appeared they were trying to finish it, and quickly.

In so many ways, downtown Atlanta was the perfect place to conduct a quarantine. With Phillips Arena across the street, the authorities had three large stadiums in which to separate the population. Elliott imagined FEMA tents covering Centennial Olympic Park nearby, operations stations and administrative quarters set up in the Omni Hotel, and a command center at the CNN Center. The massive covered parking decks in the area were perfect for staging supplies. And if it was needed, the Georgia World Congress Center—the third largest convention center in the US, with nearly four million square feet of floor space—was also near, as were the Georgia Aquarium and the College Football Hall of Fame.

Ahead, a figure wearing a positive pressure personnel suit, or space suit, stood outside a FEMA tent directing traffic. It was unnerving to see someone wearing the suit in downtown Atlanta.

The line moved slowly as the buses ahead released their passengers in waves. When Elliott and Rose's bus came to a stop, along with six others, seven suited figures emerged from the tent and entered the buses. The man who entered Elliott's bus wore army fatigues under his suit—Elliott could see the top of his uniform inside the helmet.

In front of the FEMA tent, a man held up a red flag.

The man at the front of the bus spoke via a speaker, giving

his voice an unnerving, Darth Vader-like tone. "If you have been infected for seven days or more, please raise your hand."

A few hands went up slowly. The suited man's eyes darted across the bus, seeming to mark the people in his mind. He squinted as if something was wrong.

"Please, this is important. We need to know how long you've been infected to give you proper care. If you had a cough or were sneezing last Sunday, raise your hand now."

That's odd, Elliott thought. A few more hands went up. From his peripheral vision, he saw Rose raise her hand.

He was about to stop her, but the suited figure had already seen her hand go up.

Outside, the man by the tent lowered the red flag, as if calling for the start of a race.

"Okay, if your hand is raised, stand up and exit the bus. They'll direct you outside."

Elliott saw fear in Rose's eyes. The suited figure remained at the front of the bus, watching, making sure everyone who had raised their hand disembarked.

Elliott stood in his seat. "Can you tell us—"

"Sir, please sit down."

"I just want to know—"

"Sir, your questions will be answered inside. If you don't sit back down, I'll have you removed and placed in quarantine."

Elliott sank back down into his seat.

To Rose, the suited figure said, "Ma'am, please come forward."

She stared at Elliott.

He gave her his bravest face. "It's okay," he whispered. "Go ahead."

Outside the bus, the entire cohort was ushered into the Georgia Dome.

When the last person cleared the FEMA tent, the figure outside raised a yellow flag.

The suited soldier spoke again.

"If you are over sixty years of age, or if you are unable to walk without assistance, please raise your hand."

Elliott was sixty-three, and he didn't look especially young; his time at the CDC had been rough on his body. But he kept his hand down. For her sake.

The soldier eyed him with blatant suspicion. Elliott shrugged.

"I've got a stressful job. It ages you."

The man shook his head but let Elliott keep his seat.

When the over-sixty cohort had exited, the soldier left without another word. The suited figure outside held up a green flag, and to Elliott's surprise, the bus pulled away.

His head turned, and he stared past the white FEMA tents and the suited individuals milling around. His eyes were fixed on the entrance to the Georgia Dome, where Rose had disappeared. Where he feared she might never come out.

The bus stopped at a giant parking deck. The doors opened, and the driver yelled for everyone to get off.

The passengers filed out, bewildered looks on their faces.

A woman in a space suit directed everyone to take the stairwell to level five. The people walked past her in silence, but inside the stairwell, whispers erupted, frightened voices asking questions.

Why one week? Are those people going to die?

They're not going to let us go home. I knew it!

We should run now.

A booming voice from the landing above silenced the chorus.

"Keep moving."

A suited man leaned over the rail, his muscular, unsmiling face ominous behind the helmet.

"Keep moving. All your questions will be answered. Keep moving, people. Fall behind, you go to quarantine."

The horde surged forward in response with some pushing and shoving.

On level five, rows of booths were spread out. They reminded Elliott of voting booths on Election Day: each was just big enough for one person and stood on flimsy legs.

"Take a station. Any station. Spread out. You have five minutes to complete the questionnaire."

Inside a booth, Elliott found a tablet propped up, a large green start button glowing. He tapped it, and the screen showed a graphic with a cell phone and a prompt that read:

Place your cell phone in the box to your right.

The black box slid closed the moment Elliott dropped his phone inside. He heard the faint noise of electric motors.

On the screen, a questionnaire appeared. Many of the questions he had anticipated. It asked for his social security number, name, date of birth, home address, occupation, education, his current symptoms, when they began, his health history, especially any immuno-compromising drugs or conditions, and his travel outside the country, especially to Kenya, Somalia, Ethiopia, Uganda, and Tanzania. Elliott lied about his date of birth.

Some questions struck him as odd: Was he comfortable using a firearm? Had he ever been to prison? Had he ever been in the military or had military training?

What does it mean?

At the end of the questionnaire, a large thank-you box appeared. He didn't recognise the company logo: Rook Quantum Sciences. They must have developed the survey and database software the government was using.

The black box opened, and he took out his cell phone. The screen was now black except for the Rook Quantum Sciences logo.

He tapped the home button. Two dialogs appeared:

You have completed your questionnaire for the day.
You have no new messages.

So they had created an operating system for tracking the outbreak. Smart.

Around him, several suited figures were walking up and down the aisles. Occasionally they paused at booths and spoke into their radios, calling for tech support.

"Got an incompatible cell phone at 1291."

"Need a tablet reboot on 1305."

Seconds after Elliott stepped away from his booth, a suited figure wiped off the tablet he had used and directed him to the other side of the parking deck, where white curtains served as dividers between cubicles.

Inside one small cubicle, a woman swabbed the inside of his cheeks and took two vials of blood, then placed the samples in a bag labeled "Phaethon Genetics." She tore a label with a bar code off the sample bag and placed it on a bracelet, which she affixed to Elliott's right wrist.

"What's that for?"

"Sequencing your genome will help us find a cure."

She placed an identical bracelet on his other wrist.

"Don't take the ID bands off—you need them to get food rations and medical care."

He nodded. "My wife was taken—"

"Sorry, sir, they'll answer your questions at the next station. This is important, okay? Your phone will issue an alert each day. It will ask you questions about your symptoms. Answer the questions honestly. Your life may depend on it. Keep your phone charged."

He was about to ask a question when she raised her hand and yelled, "Next!"

"Exit to your right, please," she said to Elliot.

Ever since he had gotten off the bus, he had hoped to see someone he knew—a CDC official or Commissioned Corps officer. He hadn't. And his time was up.

It turned out there was no next station. After the blood draw, they herded everyone into a stairwell on the opposite side of the parking deck and back onto the bus they had arrived on. He waited for it to fill back up. It never did. Many of the people who had gone into the parking deck with Elliott didn't return. The bus was less than half full when it pulled away.

Elliott hoped it would return to the Georgia Dome. But instead it barreled down the road, retracing its route.

Before he left home, he had instructed his son not to get on the next batch of buses—the buses that would pick up anyone without symptoms. Ryan was an anesthesiologist, and Elliott assumed he would be identified as someone with essential skills, and would therefore be conscripted to help in the BioShield effort.

But now everything had changed. He needed to make sure his son *was* on that bus—and that they kept him. Ryan might be their only chance of getting to Rose.

He wondered how long he'd been gone. Had the buses for the well individuals already arrived? If so, that chance had already slipped away.

On his street, he bounded off the bus and dashed inside his home, ignoring his neighbors calling his name, yelling questions about the outbreak.

The house was quiet. The TV wasn't even on. He searched the first floor.

Empty.

The second floor. Empty.

He pounded down the unpainted wooden stairs to the basement. Stopping in the damp space, he searched for the light. He clicked it on.

Ryan, Sam, and Adam were seated on an old couch that Elliott had abandoned in the basement years ago. Adam was asleep in his mother's lap.

Ryan looked up. "Dad."

"Change of plans," Elliott said, panting.

"What?"

"You need to get on the bus when it comes."

"Why? What happened—"

"They have your mother. In the Georgia Dome. Find her. Get her out of there."

CHAPTER 57

DESMOND HAD LOST all sense of time. The only indicator of its passing was the growing trash pile that surrounded the three stooges—and even that was taken away when a janitor wheeled a cart in and cleaned the mess up.

He maintained his exercise routine, pushing himself for more repetitions each time, cycling the exercises, careful not to overexert himself. His ribs still ached, but he was learning his limits and tender points. He was preparing. It was all he could do.

Any break in the routine caught Desmond's attention. So when the tall blonde strode into the corridor beyond the cell again, he stopped in mid-pushup, turned, and watched.

She stood questioning the three slobs. The words that flowed from her mouth seemed to assault them like a swarm of bees. They shook their heads, threw up their hands, pointed at the screen, and argued back. Soon she was pointing too. Was she their boss? A messenger from their boss (Conner, Desmond presumed)?

Before she left, the blonde turned to him, for the briefest of moments, with a look that carried some meaning he couldn't read, like a language he had once learned but had forgotten.

And just as quickly, she was gone.

☣

Avery stood in Conner's stateroom giving a report. He held his hand up, stopping her.

"Just tell me if they can make it happen."

"They say it's like a needle in a haystack."

"What about the apps being developed by the companies Des invested in?"

"They've tried them. If it's there, it's in some kind of back door. They say the memories could be tied to a location or released at a certain time. Hacking it might not even work if the release is hardwired."

Conner looked up at the ceiling.

"What do you want to do?" she asked.

"We're running out of time. We have to try something new. Drastic."

"Such as?"

"Such as, *I'll let you know, Avery.*"

She averted her eyes. More quietly, she said, "Dr. Shaw is infected."

"I'm aware."

"With the Mandera strain—not the precursor flu virus."

"I said, I'm aware."

"Should we administer the cure?"

"No. Leaving her infected gives us more control."

DAY 9

3,800,000,000 infected
620,000 dead

CHAPTER 58

DESMOND LAY ON the bed, giving his muscles a few minutes to rest. He contemplated what the most recent developments meant.

The three stooges were gone. The folding table sat abandoned. Empty cans and food cartons lay where their computers had sat.

Were they giving up on him? He hoped so.

A crack shattered the silence. A seal breaking. Rubber brushing past steel. The glass wall of his cell slid to the right, into the bathroom wall.

His cell was opening.

Desmond rushed to the gap. His arm was through, then his torso. He wiggled, gaining inches each second, and then he was free, in the corridor, standing next to the card table.

A closed hatch lay at the end of the corridor, and its wheel was turning. *Someone's coming through.*

Desmond bounded toward it.

The hatch opened. A handgun emerged, then a skinny white arm. Desmond grabbed the wrist, snatched the gun away, and twisted the person's arm behind their back as he pushed through the hatch, the gun held out before him, sweeping the room, ready to fire.

The assailant was a woman with blond hair. He couldn't see her face, but he felt a hint of recognition. He focused, took in the scene. A long table with four flat screens and keyboards, computer towers below. Two uniformed soldiers on the ground, not moving. No blood.

The woman's elbow connected with his injured ribs, sending a wave of blinding pain through him. He lost his grip on her. A knee slammed into his forearm, and he dropped the gun. She spun him around and kicked him hard in the chest. The impact with the wall knocked the wind out of him. Gasping for air, he slid down, trying not to pass out.

She grabbed the gun, tucked it into a shoulder holster, and squatted down, her green, intense eyes level with his.

"Hey, genius, I'm the one rescuing you. You want to fight me, or you want to get out of here?"

Desmond glanced at the guards. They were out cold, but alive. Small darts protruded from their necks.

"What's it going to be, Des? I'm leaving, with or without you."

He remembered her name then—Avery. The woman who had allowed him to hear her conversation with the programmers. *Can I trust her? What choice do I have?*

"How?" he said, between shallow breaths.

Avery grabbed a semi-automatic rifle and a backpack from the corner of the room. From the backpack, she drew out a pile of clothes and night vision goggles.

"Put the uniform on. Hang on to the NVGs. Power goes out in twenty seconds. There's a helo seven decks above us. I figure we've got about three minutes to get there. If we're not there by then, we'll have to shoot our way out."

Desmond felt cornered, like the day Dale Epply had come to Orville's house. He had fought for his life that day, and he had killed a man for the first time.

He made his decision: he would fight his way out if he had to. He was going to stop these people, even if it killed him.

He took the clothes and began slipping them on.

Movement on one of the flat screens caught Desmond's eye. They showed four cells just like his. Three empty. One occupied. A woman, roughly his age, with dark hair. Her skin had the color and smoothness of porcelain.

"Peyton Shaw," he whispered.

So they had captured her too. Her phone number had been the

only clue he had left himself in Berlin. She had been investigating the outbreak in Kenya—the outbreak Conner had started, that the man swore Desmond had helped start. Somehow, she was connected to what was happening. She might even be the key to stopping it.

Desmond pointed to the screen. "We're taking her with us."

"No. No way."

"Listen to me, Avery. She's coming with us."

Avery exhaled.

"She's coming with us."

The blonde shook her head in frustration, but to Desmond's relief, she moved to the long table and typed on one of the computer keyboards. On the screen, the glass wall of Peyton's cell began sliding open. But it had slid only about seven inches when the power went out.

CHAPTER 59

PEYTON STARED IN disbelief as the glass wall started opening. Were they moving her? Or coming to kill her? That was it—they had gotten her CDC password when they drugged her. *Now they don't need me anymore.*

Fear rose inside her. But just as quickly, rage met it. The two emotions fought a battle as she watched the glass partition slide.

Rage won. If she was going to die here, she was going to die on her feet, kicking and screaming and punching. She wouldn't let it be easy for them.

The lights snapped out, plunging the cell into darkness and complete quiet. Peyton froze. A second of panic sparked. *Is this their plan, to kill me in the dark? I need to move.*

Peyton put her hands out, found the glass wall, and shuffled over to the opening. It hadn't moved far before the power went out. She slid her left arm and leg through, but her body caught at her chest. She placed her palm against the outer glass and pushed, trying to squeeze through. The exertion only made her breathe harder. Her chest heaved, expanding. Pain radiated from where the thick glass divider met her bones. It was no use. She'd never make it through.

A sound: metal creaking, then the loud boom of a hatch opening. Two white lights beamed into the corridor, moving back and forth like dueling lighthouses searching the darkness. The lights stilled, fixing on her.

Fear drove her then. She wiggled back into her cell. But there was nowhere to hide. Even the bathroom was too open. She would die in seconds, she was sure of it.

Two guards ran the length of the corridor. Bright LED lights shone from their helmets. She held a hand up, blotting out the beams so she could see the attackers. The first guard was a white woman with straight blond hair that spilled out of the helmet. Her face was slender, striking, her eyes intense. Night vision goggles sat atop the helmet. The second guard—

Peyton stopped cold at the man's face. *Desmond Hughes.* Seeing him in person brought on a conflicting mix of emotions that paralyzed her.

He moved to the opening.

"Peyton, my name is Desmond Hughes. I called to warn you."

He stared at her, not a hint of recognition on his face. *What's going on here? Why's he acting like he doesn't know me?* He had acted the same during the call before she learned of the outbreak—an outbreak he seemed to be connected to, according to Lucas Turner. His name had been scrawled on the barn wall in the cell. And now he was dressed as a guard, pretending he didn't know her. Why? Was it all part of some plan? Her instincts urged her to go along with him, to behave as though she didn't know him. She sensed that revealing any information to her captors would be bad for her.

"I remember. What do you want?"

"We're getting out of here. Thought you might want to come."

Peyton nodded toward the opening. "I tried. I won't fit."

The blonde leaned her head back, throwing the beam from her helmet at the ceiling. "We don't have time for this, Des."

He turned his head, bathing her in white light. She squinted, stared back at him a moment, then glanced away, signaling defeat.

Desmond moved the beam of light out of her eyes. "Can we shoot it, Avery?" he asked.

The woman shook her head.

He held his hand out to Peyton. "Then I'll pull you through."

Peyton hesitated. No way this was going to work. But Desmond waved her forward, confidence in his face.

What do I have to lose?

She moved to the opening, and Desmond gripped her arm, one hand on her bicep, the other on her forearm. "We have to go fast. It's the only way." More quietly, he added, "It's going to hurt."

She stared at him, trying to look brave. "I know. Let's get it over with." He planted his foot on the glass and leaned back, pulling.

Peyton closed her eyes as the pain took over. Pain in her chest as the glass raked past her ribs. Pain at her armpit as Desmond pulled until she was sure he was ripping her arm off.

And then she tumbled free and fell on top of Desmond. Her face connected with his, but he moved quickly, deflected the blow, and caught her before she hit the floor.

"You okay?"

"Yeah." Every breath through her bruised chest brought pain.

Avery led them away from the cell. "We need to hurry."

Footsteps sounded from beyond the hatch at the end of the corridor. Avery and Desmond quickly reached up to flip their night vision goggles down and switch off their helmet lights, leaving Peyton in darkness.

"Stay here," Desmond whispered, his voice close to her.

On instinct, Peyton crouched, making herself a smaller target, and moved to the wall. With each passing second, her eyes adjusted. Through the slightly open hatch, she could see beams of light crisscrossing the room beyond. Her chest ached as her heart beat faster, knowing these people were searching for her and would likely shoot her on sight.

Desmond and Avery rushed through the hatch. Five soft pops followed—silenced rifle reports. Avery's voice, barely over a whisper, called into the dark corridor: "We're clear. Come on."

Petyon moved forward and paused at the entryway. Desmond and Avery had switched on their helmet lights again. Beams from three more helmets pointed at the ceiling, wall, and floor, depending on how the fallen soldiers had landed. Blood flowed from head and chest wounds, slowly covering the floor, dark tendrils reaching toward her.

The gunshots reminded her of Hannah, of the blood that had flowed from her wound in the back of the SUV in Kenya.

Avery was crouched over a backpack in the corner. Her face was bathed in shadows, but Peyton could see her expression. There was no remorse, just cold concentration. She saw a woman who had taken lives before, and who wasn't troubled by the burden.

Avery reached inside the backpack, drew out a cell phone, and began tapping its screen.

"What're you doing?" Desmond asked, sounding alarmed.

"Backup plan," she mumbled. "I told you, we should have been out of here by now. We're out of time. We need a diversion."

Explosions rocked the ship.

"What was that?" Desmond asked.

"That was the sound of us getting five more minutes to get off this ship."

"How?"

"Hull breaches," Avery said. "She's sinking." She moved to another hatch. "Shoot anything that moves, Des. Don't hesitate."

"Wait," Peyton said. "They're holding my colleague, Hannah Watson."

Avery glanced at Desmond, silently saying, *Shut her up.*

"Is she still alive?" Peyton asked, looking from one to the other.

Desmond looked to Avery, who said nothing.

"Is she?" Peyton stepped closer to the blonde.

"I don't know. She's in the hospital wing."

So McClain hadn't followed through on his threat. They had finished the surgery. If the ship sank, they would leave her. Hannah would die for sure.

"We have to bring her with us," Peyton said.

"No way," Avery said quickly. "Absolutely not. I'm not even sure if *we* can get out."

Peyton fixed Desmond with a look that said one word: *Please.*

He turned to Avery and stared.

"We're dead if we do this, Des. I mean it."

"Then we'll die trying. We're not leaving anyone behind."

CHAPTER 60

DESMOND'S HEART POUNDED in his chest and in his ears, like the sound of a truck driving over train tracks. He gripped the rifle, trying to ready himself.

The night vision goggles bathed the cramped corridor in a green glow. Avery walked a step in front of him, to his right, giving him a clear shot if they encountered resistance.

Peyton's hand was tucked inside his waistband; he pulled her behind him through the darkness. She occasionally bumped into him and whispered, "Sorry," when they came to a stop or changed direction.

Boots pounded the floors above and below. Muffled voices echoed through the darkness like ghosts chanting, seeming to close in on them.

"What's happening?" Desmond asked.

"Chaos. Insubordination," Avery said. He knew she had an earpiece in, tuned to the ship's wireless comms. "Conner's ordered a search for us. But almost everyone is rushing to the lifeboats and tenders."

That was a break. Maybe they had a chance.

Avery crouched by a hatch. She raised her NVGs, so Desmond did the same.

"Inside," she said. "Stay along the perimeter. Move fast."

The hatch crept open. Light poured out. This section had power. A battery backup? Generator?

Avery stepped through the hatch and broke right, moving

quickly. But Desmond couldn't help but stop at the sight of the vast room. It was as long as a football field and almost half as wide. The ceiling hung thirty feet above. Rows of cubicles wrapped in sheet plastic covered the floor, with soft yellow lights glowing inside, like Japanese lanterns floating on a concrete sea.

Each cubicle held a hospital bed, most with a motionless patient. Quiet beeps chirped from within, an out-of-sync symphony of death echoing in the cavernous space. A cart with body bags stood in the central corridor, abandoned.

Desmond had seen this place before. This was the place that had come to him in a memory. He had thought it was a warehouse then; now he knew the truth.

The ship was a floating hospital, a laboratory where they conducted experiments. The setup was brilliant. The subjects had utterly no chance of escape. They were probably loaded on and off in cargo containers. Had they gathered vulnerable subjects from around the world? Used them up and discarded them? The idea was horrifying.

Peyton stood beside him, staring in shock.

Two barely audible clicks from his right drew Desmond's attention. Avery was motioning to him, her expression saying, *Come on, you idiot*. He seemed to be able to read her perfectly, and she him. He wondered how long he had known her. And *how* he had known her.

He caught up to her and grabbed her shoulder.

"Is there a cure on this ship?" he whispered.

"What?"

"To the outbreak in Africa."

Avery seemed annoyed. "No, Des. You don't remember?"

He stared, confused.

"They're testing something else here. It's... never mind. We have to hurry."

Testing something else. Desmond wondered what that meant.

He followed Avery around the outer row. At the far end of the room, she opened another hatch and burst through into a corridor, which was dimly lit with emergency lights. The entire medical section apparently had its own backup power system. Plate glass windows along one wall revealed operating rooms in disarray. Blood covered the tables and dripped onto the floor. Bloody sutures, clamps, forceps, and scalpels lay strewn about.

The opposite wall was solid except for a series of doors. Avery moved quickly, opening each one, her rifle held ready. Desmond covered her advance, sweeping his rifle forward and backward, Peyton tucked behind him.

"Found her," Avery called.

Hannah lay on a hospital bed, her eyes closed, her strawberry-blond hair spilling onto the white pillow. An IV line was connected to her hand, and a clear plastic bag hung beside her. A monitor displayed her vitals.

Peyton lifted the young woman's eyelids. "She's sedated." She began disconnecting the IV. "I'll carry her."

"You can't," Avery said, with force bordering on anger.

Peyton stopped. "I'm carrying her."

"We're going up seven flights of stairs—in a firefight. You can't carry that much dead weight."

"I'll—" Desmond began, but Avery flashed him a look.

"No you won't. You've got to fight. The stairwell will be crawling with people. So will the deck."

Desmond knew there was no negotiation this time. Avery was right.

To Peyton, Avery said, "Either wake her up so she can walk out, or leave her here. Your call."

Peyton glanced at Desmond. He nodded, silently insisting, *Make the call.*

Peyton studied the monitor a moment, then checked the end of the bed and began searching the drawers.

"What're you looking for?" Avery asked.

"A chart. I need to know what they've given her. And what dose."

"The charts are electronic," Avery said. She gripped Peyton by the shoulders. "Look, if you're going to wake her up, you've got to do it *right now*. Okay?"

Peyton exhaled heavily. Her hands and eyes were steady,

betraying no hint that she was nervous, but Desmond could sense her fear. Desmond wished he could take the weight off Peyton's shoulders, but he could only watch. Her next actions could save Hannah or end her life. If she brought Hannah out of sedation too quickly, it could be deadly.

Peyton pulled out drawers, read labels on vials, and tossed them back one by one until she found what she needed. She loaded up a syringe and stuck it into the IV. Slowly, she depressed the plunger, watching Hannah. She kept one hand on the young woman's wrist, monitoring her pulse.

Beyond the door, boots echoed in the corridor. Avery froze.

Desmond turned.

Hannah stirred, sucked in a breath, and let out a low moan.

The footsteps stopped.

Avery moved to the corner of the room, behind the door, and motioned for Desmond to join her. Peyton ducked down behind the bed.

Desmond heard men's voices in the corridor, speaking German. Something about gathering the samples.

Hannah's eyes opened. They went wide at the sight of Desmond and Avery, dressed like her captors, guns at the ready.

She opened her mouth to scream, but Peyton sprang up like a jack-in-the-box and covered Hannah's mouth with her hand. Peyton held her other index finger to her own lips.

The beeping of the pulse monitor was the only sound in the room. As the beeps got faster, Desmond felt his hands start to sweat.

The footsteps outside resumed. They were moving away— except for a single set, heading toward them.

Avery motioned for Hannah to get off the bed. Peyton reached up, disconnected the IV, and pulled Hannah down beside her.

Avery let her rifle slide out of her hands so that it hung by the shoulder strap. *What's she doing?* Desmond wondered.

At that moment, the leads connected to the monitor slipped off Hannah. The beeping machine changed to a droning flat line just as the door creaked wider and a semi-automatic rifle peeked through.

Avery drew a fixed-blade black combat knife from a sheath on her leg. It was about eight inches long with a rubber handle. As soon as the man's face cleared the door, she sprang up and stabbed the blade into the man's neck.

He gurgled as she guided him to the floor, his eyes wide in disbelief. Avery had severed his windpipe and spine in one lethal, precise blow.

Desmond stood in awe of her skill and poise. With barely a sound, she pulled the man clear of the door and readied her rifle.

The other footsteps continued moving away, their echo growing fainter by the second.

Avery withdrew the blade from the man's neck with a sickening sucking sound, wiped it on his chest, and re-sheathed it. Still crouched, she moved deeper into the room and whispered to Peyton and Hannah.

"Let's move." To Desmond, she said, "I'll lead. They follow, you bring up the rear. Keep them moving."

Avery was through the door a second later. Peyton wrapped Hannah's good arm over her shoulder and pulled her up. Both women stared, mouths open at the sight of the dead man, but kept moving.

Desmond stood guard while they raced down the corridor, following Avery to the stairwell lit with emergency lights.

Avery stopped on the landing, listening.

Voices echoed above and below, bouncing off the metal walls. Desmond didn't know if he was hearing twenty or a hundred voices, only that there were too many for them to slip past, and certainly too many for them to fight.

Avery set down her backpack, drew out a gas mask, and handed it to Desmond.

"Put this on. Stay here, then follow my lead."

She raced up the stairs. But no gas came. No shots were fired. He heard Avery's voice ring out, echoing through the stairwell with strength and authority.

"Corporal. I have the prisoners in my custody. I need your help securing them."

CHAPTER 61

PEYTON'S EXPRESSION SAID what Desmond feared: *She's betrayed us.* He had harbored that fear ever since Avery had freed him from the cell. Whom did she work for? What was her agenda? *Why* had she freed them?

More discussion above. Avery was arguing with another man now.

"These *are* McClain's orders. It's your funeral, gentlemen. Just stay out of the way."

More arguing, then Avery leaned over the rail and yelled down, "Johnson, bring 'em up."

She walked down a few stairs. "Johnson, get your ass up here with those women. We're ready."

Desmond finally understood her plan—her very brilliant plan. The look on Peyton's face told him she understood.

Still wearing the gas mask, he motioned for the two physicians to go ahead.

In the patient room, Desmond had been quite worried about whether Hannah could make the trek up the stairs. He was now relieved to see her keeping pace with Peyton. Her legs seemed to get steadier with each step, the sedation wearing off perhaps.

At the landing above, two young soldiers wearing uniforms similar to Avery's and Desmond's stood waiting.

"Where's Hughes?" one asked.

"Hughes is dead," Avery said flatly.

Their eyes went wide.

"Get going, or we will be too."

The two men took off up the stairs.

Avery went after them, then the two women, and once more Desmond brought up the rear.

One of the two soldiers was waiting for them at the next landing, pushing other soldiers and two civilians back to make a hole for them to pass.

"Stay back—McClain's orders," he barked.

The moment they cleared the landing, he took off up the stairs again, running past them.

The second guard was standing on the next landing, running similar interference.

It was working. They were going to make it out.

The next flight of stairs passed without event. And the next. The crowds were growing thicker though. The stairwell was clogged with people, civilians mostly, trying to get to the upper deck.

Avery was increasing her pace. Desmond had to urge Peyton and Hannah on. They trudged up the stairs, gripping the metal rails tightly, both women panting now. The bandage on Hannah's shoulder oozed blood. Tears streamed down her cheeks as she tried but failed to pull in a deep breath that Desmond knew must have been agonizing.

As they approached the next landing, a tall man entering the stairwell yelled, "Avery! Stop where you are."

She pointed at him and shouted back. "Traitor! Mutineer!"

The uniformed guards around him looked confused for a moment. The man raised his gun, but Avery was quicker. Her shot caught him center mass, right in the chest, propelling him back into the crowd. People scattered and ran out into the corridor or up the stairs—except for four soldiers, who must have been with the fallen man.

They raised their rifles, ready to fire on Avery. But the corporal she had enlisted stood in front of her, his own rifle raised at the four soldiers.

"Weapons down, right now," the corporal said.

"She's lying to you," one of the other soldiers said. "She's breaking them out."

The corporal hesitated, glanced back at Avery. It was a lethal mistake. One of the men shot him in his chest. He staggered back, went over the rail, and spun as he fell to the landing below.

Avery's rifle erupted.

Two soldiers dropped, then a third. The last man retreated out of the stairwell.

Avery moved even faster now, pumping her legs.

As she passed the bodies of the four fallen soldiers, she yelled up the stairs, "Cover us, Sergeant!"

The sergeant peered over the railing from above. He looked hesitant, but nodded.

The four of them barreled up the stairs, which were now empty. They were exposed.

He quickened his pace.

Avery reached the landing first. Sunlight poured through the open hatch. Freedom lay beyond the hatch. *Or death*, Desmond thought. They all hugged the wall, careful not to give anyone outside a shot at them.

"Good work, Sergeant," Avery said. "Take up position one flight down and cover our backs."

The man departed without a word. When he was out of sight, Avery unslung the backpack and drew out a round mirror with a long handle. She extended it into the hatchway just far enough to survey the scene outside.

Whatever she saw, she didn't like.

She pulled the mirror back and drew three grenades and two oblong objects from her pack.

"The helo's sitting on a pad at ten o'clock. It's well guarded. They're loading the tender and lifeboats on the other side of the ship." She paused, then looked at Desmond. "This is going to get messy. I'll need your help."

Desmond knew what she was asking of him. When he spoke, his voice sounded more confident than he felt. "I understand."

She tossed two of the grenades out, then the two oblong objects.

Explosions vibrated through the deck and sent a wave of heat through the cracked hatch.

"Let's go," Avery said, rushing out into the cloud of smoke with Peyton, Hannah and Desmond following close behind.

A firefight erupted instantly. Desmond could hear Avery firing, but he could see only her back, not her targets. The wind was whipping the smoke around, like a twister on the prairie, unsure which way to go.

A bullet whizzed past Desmond's head. He tried to follow the sound but failed. It was chaos. Through breaks in the smoke, he saw throngs of people screaming, running to the tender and lifeboats, most wearing life vests.

The wind swept the smoke aside for a moment, like a curtain being opened, and Desmond saw the helicopter ahead. Avery had pulled away from Hannah and Peyton, who were moving as fast as they could. The last two guards beside the chopper fell as Avery fired. She climbed into the cockpit, and a few seconds later Peyton hopped in and helped Hannah up.

Desmond spun around, his back to the helicopter, covering them while the engines started. After what felt like an eternity, the rotors spun to life, their wind whipping at his back, dispersing the smoke, revealing the carnage of wounded and dead soldiers.

Desmond swallowed, knowing what might come next. The rifle's stock rested against his shoulder, his finger around the trigger.

He desperately wanted Avery to yell for him to get on.

A figure burst through the hatchway from the stairwell. Desmond had a half second to scan him. Black body armor. Rifle held at the ready. The man was blinded momentarily by the sunlight.

Desmond squeezed the trigger.

His first shot went wide. His second caught the man in the shoulder. His third killed him.

Desmond waited, wondering, expecting a feeling that never came. He felt only cold focus as he held the weapon.

Over the roar of the rotors, he heard Avery's call for him. The moment his foot hit the helicopter's rail, it lifted off.

Peyton extended a hand, pulled him in. From the open door, he watched the sinking, smoking cargo ship as they flew away.

Quickly, he took stock of Peyton. She was okay. He couldn't say the same for the younger woman. The exertion and increase in blood pressure had been disastrous for Hannah. Her wound oozed dark blood. Sweat drenched her. She was pale. Too pale.

Peyton leaned close to him. Her lips brushed his ear as she spoke, just loud enough for him to hear over the rotors.

"Help me find a med kit. Hurry. She's bleeding out."

CHAPTER 62

FROM A TENDER floating in the Indian Ocean, Conner watched the *Kentaro Maru* sink. With each second, the sea swallowed more of the smoking heap. Unlike the *Beagle*, it would never be found. He was sure of that.

"Hughes had help," the captain said.

"Brilliant deduction," Conner muttered.

"Should we—"

"I'll handle it. I have this well in hand."

☣

Desmond had helped as best he could while Peyton sewed Hannah's shoulder wound closed. She had operated with focus and poise, not a single second wasted.

Desmond had no doubt that she had just saved the young woman's life. Hannah was extremely pale now, her face gaunt. Blood covered the floor of the helicopter. Gauze and boxes of medical supplies lay strewn about like volcanic islands rising from a blood-red sea.

Peyton sank back to her haunches. She exhaled deeply, and every bit of energy seemed to flow out of her. Desmond half-expected her to pass out herself. It must have been incredibly stressful, holding a friend and colleague's life in her hands, knowing every move she made could end the woman's life.

She looked at Desmond with what he thought was skepticism. Then she leaned close to him, her words impossible for Avery to hear in the pilot's seat. "What's going on here, Des?"

The tone was different from her words on the ship. It was somehow... tender, familiar.

"What do you mean?"

"Why are you acting like you don't know me?"

His eyes went wide. It was true. They did know each other. Quickly, he told her about waking up in Berlin with no memory of how he'd gotten there.

"We need to talk," she said. "There's something you need to know. But first..." She glanced around, found the headset hanging from the ceiling, and pulled it on.

Desmond grabbed another headset.

"Avery." Peyton's voice was once again firm, commanding almost. "Hannah needs a hospital. She's lost too much blood."

Avery glanced back at her.

Desmond sensed another Peyton–Avery argument coming on. Hoping to avoid it, he asked Avery where they were.

"Off the coast of Kenya, near the border with Tanzania."

"What's the plan?"

"Call for help," she said simply. Desmond sensed that she didn't want to elaborate—perhaps because her most recent plans had been so thoroughly questioned and amended by her passengers.

"Where're we headed?" Peyton asked.

"Mombasa."

Peyton squinted. "There's no American embassy in Mombasa. Or even a consulate. In fact, *no* Western nations have embassies or consulates in the city. It's too dangerous; they all pulled out years ago."

A pause, then Avery said, "At the bus depot, there's a locker with a field kit in it."

"How does that help us?" Desmond asked.

"There's a satphone inside. I'll call my handler. He'll arrange exfil."

Her handler? Desmond thought.

On Peyton's face, he saw scrutiny. She didn't trust the other woman.

"You didn't bring a satphone with you?" Peyton asked.

"I couldn't get my hands on one," Avery said. "We were under a comm blackout on the ship." She motioned to Desmond. "You saw the high security around even using a cell phone—they were under lock and key. Plus, they could have tracked any satphone I took off the ship."

"So assuming we get to the locker and make contact, how do we get out of Mombasa?" Desmond asked.

"There's a Kenyan naval base and a large airport."

"There are also several good hospitals," Peyton said. "The Aga Khan Hospital would be my first choice."

Avery shook her head. "Look, I disabled the *Kentaro Maru*'s other helo, but Conner McClain is very smart, and he knows we have an injured person on board. By now, he'll have hired every crooked cop, mercenary, and bounty hunter in Mombasa, and every other coastal town, to try to find us. And the first places they'll stake out will be the hospitals and airports."

Peyton was about to launch her rebuttal when smoke on the horizon caught their attention.

Mombasa was burning.

CHAPTER 63

THE SMOKE CLOUD over Mombasa was so thick they couldn't see the city. But after a few minutes of debate, Desmond, Peyton, and Avery agreed that it was still their best hope of reaching help and getting out of Kenya.

Desmond sat back against the helicopter's rear wall and closed his eyes. The sight of the city on the coast reminded him of another place, what seemed like another life to him. And somehow, it also reminded him of Peyton, though the memory of her was just a feeling. He sensed that seeing her—touching her on the helicopter and during the escape—had been a sort of key to unlocking another memory.

☣

The night Desmond disposed of Dale Epply's body outside Slaughterville, Oklahoma, he thought hard about where he would go. Thanks to countless IRC chat sessions, he had met people like himself from around the country and the world, but they were mostly concentrated in Silicon Valley, in cities like Menlo Park, Palo Alto, Mountain View, and Sunnyvale. He couldn't wait to get there and start over.

He drove all day and camped every night. He obeyed the speed limit and avoided hotels—he didn't want to leave a paper trail in case anyone from Oklahoma came looking for him. Thanks to Orville, money wasn't a problem.

It was morning when he drove past Fremont and Newark, onto the Dumbarton Bridge and over the San Francisco Bay, arriving in East Palo Alto. He found a small RV park off Bayshore Freeway, where he asked around to see if there was anything for sale. A few hours later, he was haggling over a well-used Airstream trailer with a bearded old man who was chewing tobacco and listening to talk radio. The man claimed he was in poor health and was headed, in his words, to the glue factory pretty soon.

"You'd rob a man on his deathbed?"

When Desmond finally got the price down to the high side of fair, he placed the hundred-dollar bills into the man's hand—slowly, one at a time, at the man's request, so he could count them out loud. The old man wished him luck and told him to take good care of the trailer. Then he walked across the street and moved in with another resident—a woman who the old man was romantically involved with.

Desmond hitched the Airstream trailer to his truck and towed it to the tiny site he had rented. Then he shaved, cleaned himself up, and stocked up at a local grocery store.

As soon as his computer was set up on the trailer's dining table, he connected to the internet and began chatting. Luckily the RV park offered telephone service as part of its base services, and there were a number of local AOL dial-in numbers available. Within the hour, he had three job interviews at promising web startups.

The next morning, he worried a bit about his appearance. He was about to turn nineteen and had worked outdoors most of his life. The wind and sun on his face had aged him some, but not enough: he still looked like a teenager. He was also built like an NFL linebacker, not a computer hacker. He expected to look totally out of place, and wondered if he'd get rejected on sight.

To compensate, he bought a dark suit, a white button-up dress shirt, and a tie. The clerk at Macy's tied it for him. He even bought a pair of dress shoes, which felt weird to him after a life spent in steel-toed boots. Shaved, showered, shampooed, and dressed in the crisp suit, he thought he looked like a roughneck dressed up for prom. He was still nervous.

He was also worried about his programming skills. He had been playing with all sorts of scripting languages on his free GeoCities page and a few other web hosts, but he wasn't completely sure what languages the startups would use.

His concerns about his appearance vanished at the first interview. They barely looked at him. Everyone was wearing T-shirts and Teva sandals.

In a cramped conference room, the company's CTO, Neil Ellison, slapped down a few sheets of paper with a programming problem on it. It was in PERL, a language he knew.

"If you don't know PERL, you can leave now."

Desmond picked up the pencil and began scribbling.

"Find me when you're done."

Desmond didn't look up. Fifteen minutes later, he approached Ellison.

"Problem?"

"I'm finished."

The man glanced at the page, started to discard it, then saw something that made him study it closer.

Another programmer peeked over his shoulder. "It's wrong," he said dismissively.

"No," Ellison said. "It's a better solution than ours." He looked up from the page.

"What did you say your name was?"

The next two interviews proceeded in a similar manner. Only the programming languages changed. Desmond solved problems in PHP, Javascript, and Python. At the end of the day, he had three job offers in writing. His first choice was an offer from a promising startup called xTV, but he needed help: he didn't understand half of what was in the contract.

He asked around about a good lawyer, and later that day, he was sitting in the office of Wallace Sinclair, Attorney at Law. The office was nice, which made Desmond worry about the man's rates.

The biggest disappointment with all the job offers was that he wouldn't automatically get stock in the company when he signed on. Instead, the companies had something called a vesting schedule: he would get the stock over time, as he stayed with the startup. And it wasn't even stock outright; he was granted options, which were contracts to purchase the stock at a set price.

"How does that do me any good?" Desmond asked.

"If the stock goes up, it does you a great deal of good," Wallace said. "Think about it. If you have an option to purchase the stock at one dollar and the stock is trading for fifteen dollars, your option is worth fourteen dollars per share."

Desmond understood that.

"Best of all, you don't have to pay tax on options when they're granted, assuming the strike price is near the stock value. They're worthless until the stock goes up and you exercise them."

There was more to the contract: a non-disclosure and a non-compete. Wallace walked him through it all.

"Sometimes we see clawback provisions or a buy-sell agreement," he said. "You don't have that here. This contract looks pretty good. I'd sign it."

Desmond thanked the man, and asked him to send him a bill. He wrote out his address at the RV park.

Wallace studied the address and said, "Forget it, Desmond. Just keep me in mind if you start a company or have more substantial legal work."

Desmond liked that. It meant the lawyer recognized his potential, was willing to bet that Desmond would one day be a bigger fish.

He called xTV back that night and said he could start the next day if they provided more stock and a lower salary. He wanted just enough to live on. They agreed.

☣

Desmond found startup life to his liking. It was strangely similar to working on the rigs: long hours, deadlines, stressed-out people keyed up on coffee and energy drinks, and wild parties at regular intervals. But where his and Orville's release had taken place in honky-tonk bars, strip clubs, and casinos, the startup parties were thrown at swanky restaurants and hotel ballrooms. Desmond couldn't imagine the cost. It was perhaps the only thing that worried him about the company.

He wasn't the only one concerned. The guys in finance were constantly obsessing about their burn rate—the amount of money the company spent every month. The CEO, however, seemed completely unconcerned.

At a hotel ballroom on a Friday night, their visionary founder stood before his employees and guests and announced that xTV had just registered its one millionth user.

Cheers went up.

He paced the stage, microphone in hand.

"We're democratizing TV. With the video cameras we provide, our users can capture what viewers really want to see: real life. And they can upload that footage directly to the xTV website, where they earn money from it."

The screen behind him began playing a montage of clips, all muted.

"We've got a farmer in South Dakota giving people a look at what that harsh life is like. A teen mom in Atlanta struggling to make ends meet. An artist in Brooklyn selling his paintings in the subway and coffee shops. A singer in Seattle. A fishing competition in Alabama. A drag strip in North Carolina. A firefighter in Chicago.

"This is real life. These are the stories we crave.

"As faster internet speeds become available, more viewers will flock to xTV and our groundbreaking content. Mark my words: one day, cable will be gone. So will satellite. You'll walk into Circuit City and you'll buy a TV that's internet-ready. And you'll be browsing xTV every night to see what's on.

"In a few years, we'll be bigger than Viacom and Time Warner combined. *We* are the future of TV. We enable real people to tell their stories. That is our mission."

Desmond believed every word he said. They all did. Cheers

went up again. The champagne flowed, and everyone seemed to be drunk except Desmond.

☣

A few months later, Desmond was invited to a Halloween party one of the programmers was throwing. He was tempted not to go, but the truth was he wanted to do something besides work and sleep for a change. He'd been told that there would be some people from work there, but that it would mostly be college students and recent graduates, like the host.

He considered two options. One, not dressing up; and two, going all out. Both had risks. He took the middle road. He donned the black suit he'd purchased for the job interview and only worn once, and bought a five-dollar dark-haired wig. At OfficeMax, he purchased a plastic ID badge holder with a metal clip. On a sheet of printer paper, he wrote "FBI," and below it, "FOX MULDER, SPECIAL AGENT." It looked pretty homemade, but it would get the job done.

The party was at a three-bedroom '70s ranch home in Palo Alto that four programmers rented. The owners hadn't done a ton of updates, and the place still had a Brady Bunch vibe: thick, worn carpet—which was orange—modern architecture, an open plan layout with a vaulted ceiling, and large windows and sliding doors that led out to a pool that hadn't been cleaned since Marcia's graduation party.

Desmond was glad he had dressed up. Everyone was decked out. The partygoers hadn't spent a fortune on their ensembles, but it was clear that they had put a lot of time and effort into them. *Star Wars* and *Star Trek* characters were well represented. Three sets of Princess Leia buns bobbed around the room. Two Darth Vaders stalked around, looming over small groups silently, their shiny outfits made mostly of black plastic trash bags. There were half a dozen Luke Skywalkers. Data and Worf from *Star Trek: The Next Generation* scored three outfits each. A lone Lieutenant Commander Geordi La Forge was drinking a Michelob Light.

His visor was a modified hairband, and he was telling a girl that she might as well take her top off, he could see through her clothes with his visor anyway. When he brought the bottle to his lips, she tipped it up and walked away, mumbling, "Bet you didn't see that coming."

At the island in the kitchen, a pale white kid wearing a bald cap and a red *Star Trek: The Next Generation* uniform stood by the blender, overseeing the contents being poured in. When the top went on the device, he pointed and said, "Engage." He tugged at the bottom of his tunic, turned, and nearly shouted, "You have the bridge, Number One."

It wasn't clear whom he was talking to.

One of the Darth Vaders called for a girl dressed as Marge Simpson to grab him a beer.

"I thought you were driving?" she said.

He grew still and made his voice deeper. "I am altering the deal. Pray I don't alter it any further."

Several drinking games were going on. Loud music played. Lines for both the home's bathrooms spilled down one hall.

Desmond was rather relieved to see no other Agent Fox Mulders, though there was one Scully. Her outfit was pretty good: a black pantsuit and a white button-up shirt with the collar laid over the lapels of the jacket. She'd printed her ID on a computer; it even had her own picture on it next to the large blue FBI letters. The red wig was the right color. She was about five foot six, slender, with dark brown eyebrows and fair skin. Her eyes were a little large for her face which Desmond found attractive.

She was standing with a group of five people, holding a red Solo cup she wasn't paying much attention to, when one of the Luke Skywalkers approached her. A Darth Vader was his wingman.

The guy's voice was nasal, rehearsed.

"Excuse me, am I to understand that you're a female body inspector?"

Scully smiled but didn't laugh.

"Nice try. Come back when you've got better material, Padawan."

Skywalker glanced at Vader. "The Force is strong with this one."

That did make Desmond laugh. Poor guy.

The two faded back into the crowd, leaving Scully staring directly at Desmond.

He had spent countless hours in bars, witnessed maybe ten thousand guys hit on girls. In that time, he had learned two things. One, if you see a girl you're interested in, don't hesitate. The moment you make eye contact, just go over there. Waiting hurts the cause. And two, pickup lines are useless. A woman is either interested or not; they pretty much know instantly. They don't pick a guy based on the pickup line. Confidence is the universal attractor, and nothing says confidence like *not* having a pickup line.

He held eye contact as he walked over.

"Hi."

"Hi."

"I'm Fox Mulder."

She extended her hand. It felt tiny in his.

"Dana Scully." Her face was stoic; Desmond thought it was a pretty good imitation of the character. She was definitely game for the role-playing.

"I know why you're here."

"Do you?"

"You've been sent to debunk my work."

"What can I say, Mulder? I'm a woman of science."

"So you don't want to believe?"

"With science, what I want is irrelevant. Proof of a hypothesis is all that matters."

She tucked a strand of red hair behind her ear. He could see her dark brown hair under the wig.

"What's your current case?" she asked.

He sighed theatrically. "Tough one. There've been reports of an aberrant human in the Palo Alto area."

"Aberrant?"

"An anomaly, Scully. A woman who doesn't conform to any of the known norms of the human species. Paranormal intelligence and attractiveness. Extreme wittiness. We could be looking at genetic engineering. Possible extraterrestrial involvement."

She finally broke character, smiled and laughed quickly, then returned to a straight face. "Extraordinary claims require extraordinary evidence."

"I've recently confirmed the evidence."

One of her friends, who was dressed like Uma Thurman from *Pulp Fiction*, grabbed her by the arm. "Hey, there you are. Let's go." The girl was very drunk.

"Yeah, just a minute," Scully said quickly.

"No, come on! Paul and Ross have already left. Come on." She was dragging her now.

Scully turned. "Sorry. Duty calls." A coy smile spread across her lips. "Good luck with your case."

She glanced back at him one last time before her friend dragged her out the front door.

In the kitchen, Desmond waited for the blender to stop mixing up a fresh pitcher of margaritas, then asked the host, "Who was the girl dressed as Scully?"

He concentrated on his pour. "Scully? That's... Oh yeah. Peyton Shaw."

Desmond opened his eyes and stared at Peyton, who was still holding Hannah's head in her lap.

A smile spread across his face. "Hi, Scully."

Peyton's eyes locked on to his. To Desmond's surprise, he saw shock, then what he thought was fear. A sad, remorseful smile crossed her lips.

"What?"

"How much do you remember?" she asked.

"We met in Palo Alto. At a Halloween party."

She nodded slowly but said nothing.

"Did I say something wrong?"

She shook her head.

"Hey," he said. "What happened between us?"

Before she could answer, Avery shouted from the pilot's seat. "Look alive back there. And put your headsets on."

Desmond's eyes grew wide when he saw the scene beyond the helicopter's windshield.

CHAPTER 64

AVERY PULLED BACK on the helicopter's stick, flying above
the smoke that spread out beyond Mombasa. A minute later
Peyton got their first glimpse of the carnage.

Mombasa was Kenya's second largest city and the largest
port in East Africa. At the center of the sprawling metropolis lay
Mombasa Island, which was connected by causeways to three
peninsulas from the Kenyan mainland. Right now those causeways were packed with cars and people trying to escape the
island. From above, they looked like ants marching over a bridge,
fleeing the chaos.

The Changamwe Oil Refinery, which lay just before one of the
bridges to the mainland, was ablaze, belching smoke into the air.
Its tanks and pipes would give the fire an endless source of fuel.

The fires were not the only problem. A dozen large cargo ships
lay scuttled at the mouth of the bay, their rectangular metal cargo
containers spilled into the water, the mountain of steel forming an
impassable barrier. "They've sealed the port," Avery called over the
headsets. "Could have been the Kenyans as an act of containment."

"Or another nation," Desmond said. "To protect themselves."
He peered out the window, his eyes narrowing. "They bombed
the airport's runway too."

Peyton stared in awe at the city. From their vantage point,
she could see one of the hospitals. A crowd was massed outside,
hundreds of people trying to get in. Bodies lay in the streets,
dying, trampled.

Mombasa was her worst nightmare: an uncontrolled outbreak in a major city, millions of people at the mercy of a pathogen with no cure and no treatment, all of them left to suffer and die. Peyton had dedicated her life to ensuring this very scene never became a reality. She had flown to Kenya to stop this. Yet now it was happening. She had failed. They—*Conner McClain*—had beaten her.

If this was happening in Mombasa, she wondered what Nairobi was like. What America was like.

In that moment, she set aside her fears about her own safety—and Hannah's.

She needed a place to start, needed to know how long she'd been in captivity, how long the virus had been loose.

"What day is it?" she asked.

"Monday," Avery replied.

That came as a shock. Peyton had flown to Nairobi the previous Sunday, a full week ago.

"What's the status of the outbreak in Kenya?" she asked urgently.

"I don't know," Avery said.

"What do you mean, you don't know?" Peyton didn't even try to hide her skepticism.

"*Again*, we were under a comms blackout. Any information about the outbreak was tightly guarded. People on that ship have families too. I've only heard rumors."

"Such as?" Peyton was almost certain she was lying—or at best, keeping information from them.

"Such as, there are two hundred thousand dead in Kenya from the Mandera strain. Another half a million around the world have died from the precursor flu virus."

Precursor. So what McClain had told her was true: the flu strain that Elliott had been tracking was the precursor for the Mandera virus; it mutated into the deadly hemorrhagic fever that had killed the two Americans. Some part of her had hoped McClain was bluffing, posturing, to scare her. She almost didn't want to know the answer to her next question.

"How many are infected?"

Avery was hesitant. "Hard to say. I've heard three billion. Maybe more."

Peyton's head swam. She swallowed. For a long moment she thought she might throw up, or even pass out. *Three billion* people infected. It was an unimaginable catastrophe. If what happened in Mandera occurred around the world, human civilization wouldn't recover for decades, possibly centuries. In fact, she had no idea what the world would look like after that. At the rate the virus was spreading, she wondered: Would there be only a few million survivors? A few thousand?

But Conner McClain had created a cure. Was he going to give it to his chosen few? Peyton had to find that cure, for her own sake, and the sake of so many others.

"McClain has a cure. He told me on the ship."

"It's true," Avery said. "They informed everyone on board that it had been administered recently in our routine vaccinations. All employees at Citium companies received it." She glanced back at Desmond. "Including you."

He only nodded and glanced out the window, staring at the horrific scene, a shadow of guilt on his face.

Avery moved the helicopter inland, away from the city. It was obvious that landing in Mombasa would likely be a death sentence. The helicopter would be mobbed, rushed by people hoping to get out or hoping for help to arrive. And once on the ground, they would find no way out of the city, and no help for Hannah within.

Avery reached under the seat, unfolded a map, and studied it.

"What're you doing?" Peyton asked.

Avery didn't look up. "Trying to figure out where to go, Princess."

"Don't call me Princess—"

Desmond held a hand up to Peyton. "Ladies. We're all on the same team here. Let's talk. What're you thinking, Avery?"

"I'm thinking we're screwed."

"Okay, so nothing new there. What do we need? A satphone and a plane, correct?"

"And a hospital," Peyton said quickly. She glanced at Hannah, asleep, helpless, taking shallow breaths as she lay in the floor of the helicopter. *I won't let her die.*

Desmond spoke before Avery could.

"Right. So, what, we fly along the coast, try to find a city still intact?"

"Dani Beach is close by," Peyton said. "They've got a great hospital and an airstrip. Lots of other coastal towns along the way. Once we cross the border with Tanzania there's Tanga and Dar es Salaam farther south. Plus the Tanzanian islands off the coast."

"They'll shoot us," Avery said flatly.

"Who?" Peyton asked.

"The Tanzanians. Think about it—you've got a raging outbreak to the north. Step one is to close your airspace, shoot anything flying in from Kenya. And the Kenyan coastal towns are no good either. They're probably in the same shape as Mombasa, and I'm sure Conner is enlisting search parties there too. The American government has no presence or assets in Dani Beach that I'm aware of. There's a CIA station in Dar es Salaam, and an embassy for that matter, but we'll never reach them."

"So we go inland," Desmond said. "Nairobi?"

"Suicide," Avery said. "If Mombasa looks like this, imagine Nairobi. And Conner will assume that's our only move. I think..."

"What?"

"I think we're trapped."

"We're not," Peyton said. She had an idea. It was a gamble, but it just might pay off.

Desmond studied her.

"I know where we can go," she said. "It's inland, in Kenya. It has an airstrip, satphones, and a hospital. My guess is the outbreak is contained at this location. And McClain will never think to look for us there."

After Peyton told them her plan, Avery studied the map.

"It's at the helo's max range. Fifty-fifty odds we have enough fuel to get there. If it's a bust, we're stranded for sure."

"Flight time?" Desmond asked.

"It's about three hundred and fifty miles away. Two hours, roughly."

Peyton looked down at Hannah. She didn't know if the young woman had two hours, but she felt like her plan was their only hope.

CHAPTER 65

DESMOND SAT AGAINST the back wall of the helicopter, side by side with Peyton. They glanced at each other for a moment, then stared forward, riding in silence. Out the window, the last rays of sunlight were receding behind the mountains in the distance.

The helicopter rhythmic drone was almost hypnotic, and before long, Desmond felt Peyton's head fall on his shoulder. The woman was worn out. He tried not to move; he wanted her to get some rest.

For him, sleep was elusive. Questions ran through his mind. What he had learned on the *Kentaro Maru* had shocked him. If what Conner had said was true, he was partially responsible for starting the outbreak. He wondered if somewhere buried in his memories was the key to stopping it. Or if it was buried in the Labyrinth Reality app he had found in Berlin. Or both. He closed his eyes and concentrated, trying to remember his past.

The morning after the Halloween party, Desmond stopped by xTV's accounting department. His investigative work had revealed that Peyton was a sophomore at Stanford, and that Andrea, an xTV intern who had graduated from Stanford in June, was a friend of hers.

Desmond found Andrea in her cubicle, staring at her computer screen, twirling a strand of sandy brown hair around her index finger.

"Hey, you know Peyton Shaw, right?"

"Uh-huh." She seemed to be tabulating figures on the screen. Finally, she turned. "What's up?"

He shrugged, trying to seem nonchalant. "Nothing. Just thinking it would be cool if you invited her to the company party on Thursday."

Andrea smiled. "Really? You do? You think it would be 'cool'?"

Desmond sighed. "Andie—"

Her tone was taunting now. "*Somebody's* got a crush."

"Oh, please. What grade are you in?"

"I could ask you the same thing, lover boy."

"Will you do it?"

"For a price."

Desmond stood there, dreading her next words.

She handed him some papers. "These are the time sheets for hourly employees and contractors. I have to type these in every week and verify them. I want a web form where they enter their hours and it automatically downloads to our payroll system."

Desmond opened his mouth to respond, but Andrea had more.

"*And*, I want error checking and validation. No non-numeric characters, verification on values outside expected ranges, the whole nine. And it better work in Netscape and IE."

"Is that all? Automate your entire internship?"

"It's a wicked world, Des. Even love has a price." She eyed him dramatically. "And it don't come cheap."

"You're a lunatic."

"Email me the link for testing."

He sent her the web form before lunch.

The xTV party was a celebration of a new round of funding, a new release of their software, and half a dozen milestones they had hit. They were barreling closer to their vision of taking over television forever.

Desmond found Peyton at a round table with Andrea. Two half-empty champagne glasses sat before them.

"Ladies," he said as he reached them. "Can I get you a refill?"

Andrea looked at him with a sadistic smile only a torturer would wear. "You waiting tables now, Desmond?"

"What can I say? Stock options don't buy groceries."

Peyton laughed.

Andrea rolled her eyes and grabbed her champagne glass. "I'm just gonna go smash this champagne glass and eat the sharpest pieces. You kids try not to kill anyone with those puppy love eyes."

Desmond sat down as she stalked off to the bar.

"She's very subtle," he said.

"Very."

"I think she may have a lot of pent-up aggression."

"Bad breakup last semester. And she sort of hates her internship." Peyton smiled. "Heard you helped her with that."

"Ah, well, all in the line of duty."

"Part of your *case*?"

"Yes, ma'am."

"Any new leads?"

"Working on something now."

"Promising?"

He studied her. "Too early to tell."

"I wouldn't be so sure."

She took another sip of the champagne.

"You like working at xTV?" she said.

"Yeah. I do."

"Why?"

"I like solving problems. Going home every day knowing I made some progress on something. Waking up every morning with a new set of problems to solve."

"What'd you do before?"

"Worked on an oil rig."

She smiled, about to laugh, then squinted at him. "You're serious, aren't you?"

"Yeah."

"Interesting."

He figured he might as well be up-front with her; no sense going down this road if it was a dead end. Better to get the deal-breakers out on the table.

"I didn't go to college. Just moved out here from Oklahoma."

He knew she was a biology major and wanted to become a doctor. Her pedigree was a little more sophisticated than an orphaned oil well driller who had recently killed a man.

"Why?"

The question caught him by surprise. "Why what?"

"What brought you out here?"

Since he'd been in the Valley, no one had actually asked him that. "The work." He thought a moment. "The people. I wanted to meet people like me."

"You want to meet some more of them?"

"Yeah. I do."

The coy smile returned to her lips. "Hold out your hand."

He extended his hand. She opened her handbag and drew out a pen, then scribbled an address on his palm.

"What's this?"

"Another clue for your case. There's a house party in Menlo Park Saturday night. With lots of people like you. I think you'd like it."

"Will you be there?"

"Yeah."

"Then so will I."

The house party in Menlo Park was quite different from the raging Halloween party where Desmond had met Peyton.

He was a little nervous walking up to the Mediterranean-style home, but that disappeared when Peyton opened the door and smiled at him. She wore a black dress, diamond earrings, and a light gray cardigan to ward off the chill in the November air.

She had been right about the partygoers. Desmond found the conversations incredibly interesting. It wasn't idle chat. No gossip.

No talk of what was on TV. They discussed big issues—everything from technology to science to politics to world history. Most of the attendees were Stanford students like Peyton, or recent graduates. About half had the next big idea for a startup that would change the world. Their certainty grew with each beer can opened, every bowl smoked. On the whole, it was an inside look at how founders thought about their startup ideas and shaped their vision. Some of the people there were just dreamers, big talkers; but he thought, maybe, some would actually start a company—and succeed. He just had no idea which ones they were.

Outside, on the porch, he found Peyton standing alone.

"Something wrong?" he asked.

She turned, a smile forming on her slender face. "Only so much hyperbole I can stand in one night."

He let out a laugh.

"You're loving it though, aren't you?" she said.

"I am."

"I knew you would."

He studied her a moment.

"This is what you're after, isn't it?" she said. "Starting your own company or being part of a hit startup."

"It's not the only thing I'm after."

They stared at each other.

"What about you, Peyton? What do you want?"

"Right now, all I want is to get out of here."

Desmond stood there, watching her walk closer to him.

"This is the point where any normal guy would offer to take me home, Desmond."

"I'm not exactly a normal guy."

"I know."

She took his hand and walked off the porch, leading him.

"My truck…"

"Is beyond scary. I saw you pull up in it."

She reached in her bag, tossed her keys in the air, and he caught them.

"We'll take my car."

☣

In her dorm's parking lot, he leaned over and kissed her. Her hand moved to his face, pulling him closer.

At the outer door, she swiped her card.

They were kissing again, her walking backwards as they stumbled into her dorm room. Desmond saw everything in flashes as they pulled off each other's shirts in-between kissing. Biology and chemistry books littered the floor. She tossed an IBM Thinkpad off her bed. He winced, hoping it would survive the fall. The place smelled of candles and something sweet he couldn't place.

He glanced back at the door. "Your roommate—"

"Is home in Seattle."

That night was like the first computer program he ever wrote: a series of run-time errors followed by a quick compilation.

He was thankful that it was too dark for her to see his scars.

In the morning, however, sunlight blazed through the window. He saw her eyeing the burns on his feet and legs, the knife wounds on his chest and abdomen, and a dozen other small scars.

She said nothing, only went to the bathroom, brushed her teeth, washed her face, and threw on some clothes. She was a lot less chatty than last night. Desmond wondered if she regretted it.

"I'm late," she said.

He sat up.

"I have lunch with my mom and sister every Sunday."

"I..."

"Relax, cowboy. Just pull the door shut when you leave."

She handed him a small slip of paper.

"What's this?"

"The last part of the *case* you're working."

He unfolded it. It was her phone number.

CHAPTER 66

AFTER THE NIGHT he spent with Peyton, Desmond's life settled into a pattern. He worked his heart out at xTV, saw Peyton in his off-hours, and read when he wasn't spending time with her. He found a new library and began requesting books on finance and investing. He read Benjamin Graham's *The Intelligent Investor* and *Security Analysis* and everything he could find on the subject. His inheritance, roughly $320,000, was still hidden in a sack in the Airstream trailer. His only real expenses had been the trailer, the suit, and the legal costs of settling Orville's estate. He became obsessed with how to invest the remaining money.

At lunch one day in the company break room, a solution of sorts presented itself. He overheard two of the company's early employees, a programmer and a database developer, discussing skyrocketing home prices and the outrageous cost of daycare. Their startup salaries were meager, and their wives were pressuring them to bail and get a job at a larger company like Oracle or Sun.

Desmond took a seat at the table.

"Gentlemen, I think I might have a solution for you."

That night, he told Peyton his plan.

"It's a bad idea, Des."

"Think about it: with the money I have, I could buy a huge chunk of options. They get the cash they need, I get more options. It's a great idea," he insisted.

"Okay. It's a good idea—"

358

"Exactly."

"But it's the wrong approach."

"What do you mean?"

"You need to diversify."

"No. xTV will be huge. I need to concentrate."

"And if xTV goes under?"

"It won't."

"You don't know that."

He sat there, wondering why she wasn't more supportive.

"Be prepared."

"What?"

"The Boy Scout motto. Surely that was big in Oklahoma."

He exhaled heavily through his nose. "My uncle wasn't keen on extracurriculars."

She looked away, sensing he didn't want to talk about it.

"I like the idea, Desmond. I just think if you buy options, you should do it in other companies. You already own plenty of xTV options. I've got a bunch of friends who work at other startups. I can ask around, see if anyone is interested."

The more he thought about it, the more he thought she was right. And he liked that she hadn't given up on her point. He needed someone like that in his life.

In the following weeks, Desmond met with dozens of startup employees in coffee shops and at their homes. His lawyer read their employment contracts to ensure that they were free to sell their options, and drew up a purchase contract that Desmond used to buy stakes in a few companies within a month. Those companies were happy to cooperate; they wanted to keep their employees happy, and the cash from Desmond allowed those employees to maintain their lifestyle while staying at the company.

A few months later, all of his money was invested. He owned stock options in fourteen companies. He was more selective after that. He used every penny left over from his salary to buy options in the most attractive companies. And he insisted this time Wallace send him a bill for the legal work.

Every morning, Desmond checked the website for the *Norman Transcript*, the local paper for Norman, Oklahoma, and the closest thing to a local paper for the Slaughterville area. He skipped the news, focused on the classifieds. As promised, the local lawyer ran a notification opening the estate of Orville Thompson Hughes. A few months later, a story ran under the local news section entitled *Library System Receives Surprise Donation*.

> Yesterday, the Pioneer Library System was pleasantly surprised to receive a donation for $32,000 in the name of Agnes Andrews, a longtime librarian who passed away ten years ago. Even more unexpected was the source of the donation: Orville T. Hughes, a recently deceased oil rig worker. Upon receiving the sum, the library found that Mr. Hughes had no library card, and as best anyone could remember, had never even visited one of the libraries in the system. Even more confounding, relatives of the deceased Ms. Andrews weren't aware that the woman had ever known Mr. Hughes.
>
> "It's a mystery," Edward Yancey, the Library System administrator said. "But we sure aren't trying to solve it. Lord knows we could use the money, and we're just thankful to have it."

Desmond smiled. He had expected the small farm to bring more, but it was done, and the money had made its way to the right place. Agnes and the library system had been there for him during one of the darkest chapters of his life. He hoped the money would ensure the library was there for the next person who needed it.

One Wednesday morning, Desmond arrived at work to find a group of xTV employees crowded around the front door. Nearly everyone was either on their cell phones or whispering to each other.

Desmond assumed there had been a fire or maybe an accident. It was none of those things.

The company had run out of money. The landlord had finally locked them out of their headquarters. The venture capitalists who had funded the venture were in control, and they were selling everything that wasn't nailed down: the servers, desks, routers. Even the xTV sweatshirts were donated to a local homeless shelter for a tax write-off.

Desmond's options were worthless. He couldn't even get inside to his desk to get his personal effects.

Things changed after that. Without a job—a purpose—Desmond felt lost. He watched three more of the companies he held options for fold. Each one was like a punch in the gut.

"It's not over yet, Des," Peyton told him.

He and Peyton began spending more time together. He helped her cram for her exams, and she helped him sort through a few job opportunities.

In May, when the school year was over, Peyton moved from her dorm room into a one-bedroom apartment in Menlo Park. Most undergrads at Stanford lived on campus and moved back home for the summer or got a short-term rental. She signed a one-year lease.

She got a summer internship at SRI doing genetics research, and she seemed to really enjoy it. That made him happy.

By July, he was sleeping at her place most of the time. It was comfortable. He liked being around her. But he felt a deep guilt about it. There was something wrong with him, and he couldn't figure out how to tell her.

Peyton had never asked him about the scars—or his past, for that matter. She rarely asked him for anything but that changed one Saturday night.

"Will you do something for me?"

"Anything," he answered.

"My mom and sister and my sister's husband are coming for lunch tomorrow. Join us."

He said nothing.

"They won't bite, Des."

☣

Her mother's name was Lin. She had an MD and a PhD and was the daughter of a German father and Chinese mother. He could see a strong resemblance between the two women. Peyton was Lin Shaw's younger daughter, Madison the older.

Lin was a researcher at Stanford and an adjunct professor. Madison worked for a nonprofit concerned with the preservation of wildlife. Desmond made a mental note not to mention how many deer, wild hogs, turkeys, and elk he had killed.

Madison's husband, Derrick, was an investment banker in San Francisco. He had an MBA from Wharton, a place Desmond had never heard of, and seemed to take himself rather seriously. He was also the principal interrogator at lunch. Desmond figured he was just being protective, trying to play the role of father figure since Peyton's own father had passed away.

"What's your alma mater, Desmond?" Derrick asked.

"Noble High School."

"You didn't go to college?"

"Didn't need to."

Derrick didn't like that answer, though Peyton smiled.

The man pressed on.

"What do your parents do?"

"They owned a ranch in Australia."

His eyes lit up.

"Before they died."

"You don't sound Australian, dear," Lin said.

"I moved here when I was young."

"To the Bay Area?"

"Oklahoma."

"Oklahoma..." Derrick turned the word over in his mouth like a bone he'd unexpectedly found in his soup.

Back at Peyton's apartment, Desmond stood in the kitchen. "They hated me."

"They loved you."

"I'm a country boy, but I'm not stupid. They don't think I'm good enough for you, Peyton."

"I'll be the judge of that."

"And so will your family."

"Maybe, but they don't make my decisions for me. I do. And I don't care if you don't have a college degree." Before he could speak, she added, "All I want is you, Desmond."

Desmond opened his eyes. The helicopter was vibrating even more. Avery was pushing it to its limits. Peyton's head still rested on his shoulder. She was out cold. He desperately wanted to wake her, to ask what had happened to them, how they had lost what he felt all those years ago. Somehow, he knew he was nearing the end of the memories he could access, like a faraway signpost he could just make out through a fog. He wondered if the programmer, Byron, had been right on the ship: had Desmond made these memories of his youth and his years with Peyton available via cues? The cold in Berlin. The cell in the barn. The picture of Orville. Seeing Peyton again, touching her skin. Each seemed to have opened the door to a chapter of his past.

But he sensed that his most crucial memories would not be so easily retrieved—especially the location of Rendition. That secret was the reason for his amnesia in the first place—the reason he had built this labyrinth.

That's it: the Labyrinth Reality app. It's the key.

His breadcrumbs had led him to the app; he was now more certain than ever that it would unlock the rest of his past. He needed to get a phone and re-download the app.

What he didn't know was whether he was ready to know exactly what he had done—and exactly what kind of man he was.

There was one memory left that he could reach now, and he closed his eyes, willing it to come.

CHAPTER 67

AFTER WHAT DESMOND considered to be a disastrous lunch with Peyton's family, he didn't see them much.

He interviewed at half a dozen startups, but he found himself with a new problem: he was gun-shy, afraid to commit. What if it was another xTV? He didn't want to make the same mistake.

Another startup he had options in failed that week. He would be out of money for the trailer park rent within a month. He needed to take one of the job offers soon.

Christmas was a week away. He was terrified Peyton was going to ask him to come home with her. She didn't. She seemed to instinctively know his boundaries.

"Just so you don't get carried away and buy me an island or something for Christmas, let's set some ground rules," she said.

"All right."

"We can each spend ten dollars on each other."

"Okay."

"And the gift has to reveal something about each of us."

That confused him.

"I want to know something about you, Desmond. It has to reveal something about your past. An experience that shaped you somehow. Understand?"

He did. And he had no idea what to give her. He obsessed in the weeks leading up to Christmas.

He also turned over the job offers. Yet another company he had options in failed. His stack of lottery tickets was slowly migrating to the trash can, as fate took the numbered balls out of the hopper and more startups closed.

He drove his truck to Portola Redwoods State Park one night, hiked in, and cut down a small redwood, then cut the limbs away.

He brought it home, whittled away at it for a few days, checked the local events calendar, and found what he needed.

Two days before Christmas, in her apartment, Peyton set her gift on the coffee table. It was wrapped immaculately. Desmond hadn't thought to wrap his and he felt nervous instantly.

He tore off the wrapping paper, revealing a cardboard box. He opened it and found a map lying on top of another box, also wrapped. He picked up the map and unfolded it. Cities were highlighted in yellow: London, England. Heidelberg, Germany. Hong Kong. Two small towns in Scotland, one in Ireland, and another in southern China.

"Yellow is where my family is from," Peyton said. "Parents. Grandparents."

Desmond studied the rest of the map. There were two dozen green marks.

"Green is all the places I'd like to go with you, Des. Someday."

He swallowed and fell silent, staring at it like he was reading a judge's death sentence. She had plans for them. And she'd been thinking about them for a while.

"Open the next one," she said, excited, oblivious to his anxiety.

The next box contained a miniature figure of a mermaid on a small spring. The base was emblazoned with the words "Palo Alto."

"Closest I could get," she said. She stared at him expectantly. "Any guesses?"

"Uh..."

"Come on."

"Your favorite movie is *The Little Mermaid*?"

She socked him hard in the shoulder.

"No. I was on the swim team. In high school."

"Oh. Of course. How could I have missed it? It's so obvious now."

Beneath the mermaid was a third box. She didn't encourage him to open this one. In fact, she seemed nervous about it, as if she had changed her mind. She looked away as Desmond tore the wrapping paper.

The object inside the last box was small. His fingers wrapped around it, lifted it out.

It was a glass object, heart-shaped, red.

"I love you, Des," she said.

He tucked it in his pocket, leaned forward, and kissed her.

"I've never felt this way about anyone before," he said.

She smiled quickly, clearly disappointed, but rolled her eyes, trying to seem playful, unbothered. "Jeez, what are you, a lawyer now?"

"I mean it." He held up the glass heart. "But I'm not like you. My heart isn't like yours."

"There's nothing wrong with your heart, Desmond." She stared at him. With increasing frequency, he had wondered if that was true.

"Okay, what did you get me?" she asked, eager.

He dug into this backpack, drew the item out, and handed it to her.

She held the carved wooden object, examining it. "It's... the Eiffel Tower? You're... you want to go to France?"

"No." He shook his head, frustrated. "I mean, maybe. I would. But it's an oil rig."

"Oh." She studied it again. "I thought they were shaped like hammers. You know, going up and down into the ground."

"You're talking about the walking beam and horse head. This is the rig. The thing that drills the well."

She nodded. "So..."

"It's what I used to work on."

"Oh."

"In Oklahoma. It's part of where I got the scars."

Her eyes widened. She held the carved wooden object with more care. "Thank you, Des. I love it. It's perfect."

"It's not all."

Her face lit up.

"The second part wouldn't fit in a box."

They loaded up in his truck, which she had gradually become less scared of, and drove up the 101 to 92 and over to Half Moon Bay.

They could see the roaring bonfire before they reached the beach. Desmond wrapped his coat around her, took a bundle from the back seat, and led her in silence toward the blaze. He laid the thick blanket out on the sand and unscrewed the cap on the cheap wine, and they sat together, the fire warming them, her in front of him, facing it, tipping the bottle up every few minutes. Desmond estimated there were only about fifty people there, mostly around their age, couples and some groups, talking, drinking, and laughing.

"You going to have some?" she asked.

"No."

"Why not?"

"A promise I made."

"To whom?"

"Myself."

She leaned against him, and they both stared at the fire and the water beyond. It was unseasonably warm for December, but there was still a chill in the air. Desmond wrapped the blanket around them, in case she was cold.

"You cheated," Peyton said.

"How?"

"Ten dollars was the limit."

"Then I'm under."

She turned, looked at him.

"The tree was free. So was the labor to carve it. The wine was $6.68. I figure three dollars in gas round trip is more than enough."

"You should have been an accountant."

The crowd thinned out, but the fire burned on. A few couples and stragglers remained, as well as the two park workers managing the event.

The bottle was half empty, and Desmond could tell she was

nursing it. She twisted around, kissed him on the mouth, a hungry, deep kiss that tasted of wine.

He stood, pulled her up, and led her away, past the dunes and the tall grass where the sand ended, to a depression where the moonlight was dim. He spread the blanket out again and lowered her onto it.

When he kissed her, she closed her eyes and let him lead.

☣

On the way home, she asked, "What did it mean?"

"What?"

"The fire. Each gift had to reveal something about its bearer."

The image of the heart, and her words—*I love you*—flashed in his mind.

"The fire is how my family died. In Australia."

He told her how it had happened then, the words spilling like water over a broken levee. He told her about Charlotte, how he had come to America, about living with Orville, Agnes's death, even Orville's passing and what happened after, when Dale Epply showed up at the house.

He never could have imagined the release it brought. Telling someone, telling the person he trusted most in the world, having no more secrets with her, it was like a weight was lifted, a weight he hadn't even known he was carrying. He felt freer and safer than he ever had before.

At her apartment, they made love again, slower this time.

They lay in bed after that, staring at the ceiling, listening to an MP3 playlist on her laptop with songs by Green Day, Weezer, Stone Temple Pilots and Smashing Pumpkins.

"I'm so sorry, Des. I had no idea."

"It got me here. That's all that matters."

"Come with me tomorrow."

His first meeting with her family had been enough for a lifetime, but a part of him wanted to go.

Despite that, he told her he couldn't, that he wanted to be

alone. It was a lie. He desperately wanted to be with her. He and Orville had never celebrated Christmas or birthdays.

He tried to imagine himself at her mother's house, sitting at the dinner table or by the fire with her at his side but he couldn't. It wasn't just because he was nervous about the prospect; it was because of something else. A problem far larger than he imagined.

He spent Christmas in the Airstream trailer, alone, a can of beans on the stove, an electric heater warming the tiny bedroom. He read library books and traded emails with Peyton. The tone in his replies never matched the warmth of her notes. That bothered him. He wrote and rewrote each message, like they were Egyptian hieroglyphics he couldn't seem to arrange just right.

Email wasn't his only problem. Money was still tight. His meals consisted of beans and canned meat, just like the early days when he'd gone to live with Orville. He couldn't help thinking about the grocer who had helped him ration his limited funds and made sure he had enough to eat. Knowing now that Orville had stashed a veritable mountain of cash in the safe inside the old truck out back actually brought a smile to Desmond's face. The old roughneck was miserly and mean as a snake, but in the end, he'd had a sort of logic to him. Desmond actually missed the man. He also worried that he had squandered every bit of money Orville had so carefully saved all those years.

After Christmas, four more of the companies he owned options in folded. They hadn't wanted to ruin their employees' holiday, but they also didn't want to start the year wasting any more investor money.

Each email made his stomach drop. He felt the prospect of financial security slipping away but it focused him and he dug in, trying to figure out why some companies survived and others went up in smoke. It seemed almost arbitrary. He spent hours thinking about it, reading articles, studying books on business history.

The week after Christmas, Peyton insisted that he stop eating canned food for every meal.

"You're going to get some weird digestive disease and die, Des. The obituary will say, 'Desmond Hughes, talented programmer and lover of books, died of pork and beans in an RV park outside Palo Alto.'"

He laughed and relented, letting her cook at least half his meals. They were a lot tastier. He also began staying at her place without exception; another one of her theories was that the electric heater was going to cut out in the night and he would freeze to death in the Airstream. Neither one of them really believed it, but in the days before New Year's Eve in 1997, they spent every night together, and neither of them was cold.

CHAPTER 68

IN THE HELICOPTER, Desmond watched the sun set over the mountains. Peyton was still asleep beside him, her head on his shoulder.

There were so many things he wanted to ask her. Why they hadn't ended up together—how they had lost what he had felt that night in Half Moon Bay. What had happened to *them*.

When Peyton stirred, he leaned forward and caught her eye. She seemed to sense the change in him. "What did you remember?"

"Us."

She looked away, down at Hannah, who lay still, her breathing shallow.

Desmond gripped her arm. "I remember the Halloween party, and xTV, and that mermaid ornament and the glass heart and Half Moon Bay and that badly carved oil rig I gave you." He smiled, but she didn't return it. To his surprise, she looked away.

Gently, he placed a hand on her chin, turned her to look into his eyes. "I remember us being happy. But not what came after. Tell me, please."

"No."

"What if it's related to what's happening right now?"

"It's not."

"Did I hurt you?"

Peyton closed her eyes. "It wasn't like that."

"What do you mean?"

"What happened... hurt both of us."

What does that mean? He was about to ask when Avery glanced back from the pilot's seat and pointed to the headset.

To Desmond's dismay, Peyton quickly pulled her headset on. He reluctantly followed suit.

"Let's talk about what happens when we land," Avery said.

Peyton methodically laid out her plan. Avery made a few suggestions. Demands, really, but they were all in agreement about the course of action.

With that out of the way, Desmond focused on Avery, asking the first question among so many he wanted answered.

"The people on the ship, in the hospital ward. What were they infected with?"

"I don't know. I was part of the IT group." She glanced back at him, a curious, unreadable expression on her face.

"What?"

"It was... It was your experiment, Des."

"*I* did that to them?" Desmond felt sick at the idea.

"It was part of the Rendition project."

"What is Rendition?"

"I don't know."

Peyton spoke up. "What *do* you know, Avery? Why did you rescue us?"

"I wasn't aware I needed a *formal invitation* to rescue you."

They started snapping at each other then, voices escalating. Desmond waited for an opening that never came. With forced calm in his voice, he interrupted.

"Let's just... back up here. Okay?"

A pause.

"Look, if we keep fighting each other, we have no chance of stopping what's happening."

He let another few seconds pass, hoping everyone's nerves would settle. Then he suggested that each of them share what they knew and see if the pieces fit together somehow.

Taking their silence as agreement, he went first.

The two women sat quietly while Desmond recounted his story, beginning with how he had woken up in a hotel room in

Berlin with a dead man on his floor—a security employee with Rapture Therapeutics. How he'd had no memories and no idea what had happened to him. How his only clue had been a cryptic code, a Caesar cipher that, when decoded, read, *Warn Her* and listed Peyton's phone number.

"Was the warning about the pandemic or warning me not to go to Kenya?"

"I've thought about that. I think the warning was meant to keep you from going to Kenya. I think I knew they would abduct you, that you were personally connected to this somehow. On the ship, did they ask you personal questions—not related to the outbreak?"

Peyton thought for a moment. "Conner asked me when was the last time I spoke with my father and brother."

"Why is that important?" Avery asked.

"They're both dead."

Avery glanced back at her, surprised.

Desmond turned the information over in his mind. There was definitely a larger picture here, a connection he couldn't quite make.

"Conner also asked about my mother. She's a genetics researcher at Stanford." Peyton paused. "They wanted my CDC password. They drugged me. I think they got it."

Peyton recounted the rest of her time on the ship, being thorough, which Desmond appreciated. When she was done, he continued his story, describing how the police had appeared at his door just as he had called Peyton. How he had spent the next few days evading Berlin's security forces while decrypting messages he believed he had left for himself. How the codes had led him to a reporter for *Der Spiegel* who had agreed to meet Desmond at a cafe on Unter den Linden.

"The reporter said I was an informant. I had told him that I was going to provide proof that would expose a network of corporations and scientists working on the largest experiment since the Manhattan Project. He said the project was called the Looking Glass, and that I had told him it would change humanity forever."

"Makes sense," Avery said.

"How?"

"You told me you were planning a major move to try to stop the completion of the Looking Glass."

Desmond studied her, wondering if she was telling him the truth. Was she really his ally?

He was about to question her, but Peyton asked, "What happened to the reporter?"

"Conner's men took his fiancée hostage to get to me," Desmond said. "It worked. They interrupted our meeting and captured me shortly after. I think it's safe to assume the reporter's out of play."

"What is the Looking Glass?" Peyton asked.

"I don't know. He didn't either." Desmond looked at Avery. "Do you know?"

She glanced back at him. "No. I never found out."

Desmond sensed she was holding back. Was it because Peyton was there? Or was there another reason?

"Did *I* know what it was?" Desmond asked.

"Definitely," Avery replied. "In fact, I believe your work was essential to completing the Looking Glass. Your piece was the last component they needed."

"Conner suggested as much when he questioned me on the ship," Desmond said. "Both he and the reporter told me that there were three components: Rook, Rendition, and Rapture. Conner said I had been in charge of Rendition, but I have no memory of it." He paused. "I have seen all of those names, though: they're companies my investment firm, Icarus Capital, funded."

"I think another one of your investments may be involved too," Peyton said. "The first cases of the outbreak in Mandera were Americans—two men who had recently graduated from college. They were in Kenya to launch a nonprofit startup called CityForge. Icarus Capital funded them. In fact, the two young men had dinner with you. They said it was very eye-opening."

"How so?"

"They were impressed, described you as larger than life."

Desmond saw a curious smile form on Avery's face, but she said nothing.

Peyton continued, unaware. "They said you were into some major next-generation projects and that you believed humanity was on the cusp of extinction."

"Why?"

"The absence of space junk."

"Space junk? As in..."

"Interstellar probes. Relics from alien civilizations before us, from around the universe. They said you told them the moon should be an interstellar junkyard, covered with crashed probes and satellites, yet we've found nothing."

"I don't understand," Desmond said.

"They didn't either. Neither do I."

Desmond leaned forward, silently asking Avery if she knew.

"Hey, space junk isn't really my department," she said, eliciting a quiet laugh from Desmond and an annoyed expression from Peyton.

"So what *is* your department, Avery?" Desmond asked. "How do we know each other?"

Avery hesitated. Desmond got the impression she was asking him whether it was okay for her to answer in front of Peyton.

"We're laying all our cards on the table here," he said.

Avery nodded. "Okay."

CHAPTER 69

AVERY BEGAN HER story with some background. She had been
raised in North Carolina and attended college there, majoring in
computer science and minoring in two foreign languages: German
and Chinese. During her senior year, she was invited to interview
with a new venture capital firm called Rubicon Ventures. It was
located just off I-40, in an older low-rise building in Research
Triangle Park. The office was small, the decorations spartan, most of
the walls bare. Her first impression was of a boiler room operation
set up overnight, not an established company. She pegged it as a
fledgling venture destined to fold, and she had already decided to
pass on the offer when the young woman at the reception desk
showed her into a conference room.

A middle-aged man with salt-and-pepper hair sat at the table,
a closed folder in front of him. He introduced himself as David
Ward, and said, "Don't mind the digs, we put all of our money
into our work."

To Avery's surprise, he asked no questions. He seemed to
already know everything about her. He told her that her unique
combination of skills—languages and computer science—would
be invaluable to their work. He added that her winning record on
UNC's tennis team was also a plus. That made her curious—just
curious enough to ask what sort of work she'd be doing.

"Due diligence," he replied.

She'd never heard the phrase, but he quickly elaborated. She'd
be researching the startup companies Rubicon Ventures was

considering investing in. He said they were high-tech companies with novel products, capable of changing the world.

"You'd be traveling a lot. Meeting with founders and executives to hear their pitches and gather information."

It sounded utterly boring to her. She wasn't sure what she wanted to do after college, but she now knew it wasn't "due diligence."

As if reading her mind, David said, "You wouldn't be doing it because you like the work."

"Why would I be doing it?"

"For the money."

That got her attention. Lately, she'd been doing a lot of things she didn't want to do—for the money.

He pushed a paper across the table. It was face down. She picked it up, read the job offer. A very strict non-disclosure. A non-compete. And a sum that raised her eyebrows.

"If you decide this isn't for you, Avery, you can quit at any time."

She had grown up on a farm that her family had lost to the bank three years before. Her father had always told her not to look a gift horse in the mouth. She was certain that the job offer she was staring at was exactly that. It was too much money—for work she wasn't really qualified to do. Something was wrong here.

Despite her father's advice, she looked up, and with three words, she looked the gift horse in the mouth. "What's the catch?"

Her host broke into a smile. "Very good, Miss Price. You've just passed our job interview."

"How's that?"

"In a word, guts. You've got guts." He focused on the pages in the folder. "You see, we do our due diligence too. We know you're an only child. That your mother died in a car accident about four years ago, right after you went to college. We know that your father has late-stage Alzheimer's, that his care is not cheap. That you've been paying for it, any way you can. You teach tennis. You work at a run-down ice cream parlor called," he peeked at the open folder, "The Yogurt Pump on Franklin Street, and though you're a straight-A student, you absolutely *hate* computer science. You chose the major for one reason only: money. You figure you can get a good job after college, earn enough to take care of your father, and one day, just maybe, live your life, which in your mind would involve a lot of traveling and doing something outside, something very exciting."

She stared at him, unsure what to say. Every word he'd said was true, but she couldn't imagine how he knew.

"One of the companies we're interested in is called Rapture Therapeutics. They've developed what may just be a cure for Alzheimer's and other neurodegenerative disorders."

He slipped another page across the desk: a research brief on Rapture's latest breakthrough.

"Does that interest you?"

She read while he waited, only half-understanding the science.

"So," he said. "What's your answer, Avery? I need to know right now. There's one position. You're the first in line, but not the last."

"You already know my answer," she said.

"Welcome aboard, then."

☣

She spent a year after that researching the companies Rubicon was interested in. And as the months went by, a sneaking suspicion grew in her mind. At home, she began to keep separate files from the ones she turned in. She thought about her theory during every waking hour: while visiting her father at the care facility, at the gym, during flights, and in the countless hotel rooms that all ran together. In every meeting, at every company she visited, she began looking for evidence, any clue that might confirm her suspicions—or confirm that she had officially gone crazy.

One morning, she walked into David's office, closed the door, and prepared to tell him what she thought. In her mind, she had imagined how he might react: laughing out loud, telling her to take a day off, telling her to stop watching so much TV.

She said the line she'd rehearsed a dozen times. "I think there's something going on at the companies you've asked me to research."

"Like what?" His voice was even.

"I think they're fronts."

He still betrayed no emotion. Not surprise; not even interest. "Fronts for what?"

She swallowed. "Terrorism."

He focused on his computer, began typing, acting as if she had told him their lunch meeting was canceled. "That's a very serious allegation."

"I'm aware of that," she said, unwavering.

"I'm going to a meeting in Virginia tomorrow. I'll be driving up. I'd like you to come with me. Are you free?"

Avery stood there, confused. It was as if he hadn't heard a word she'd said. "Yeah, I'm free—did you... hear what I just said?"

"I did. Let's meet here at nine. I'm sorry, Avery, I've got to run."

The next morning, they got on Highway 1 North, then I-85. At Petersburg, they took I-95 North. To Avery's surprise, they passed right through Richmond. After the exits for Fredericksburg, David turned off and drove through the country.

He parked in front of a large colonial-era home with a crushed stone driveway.

Inside, he ushered her into a wood-paneled library where several corkboards were covered with names and colored strings. She knew the names. Corporations. There were photos of the companies' officers and investors. Desmond Hughes. Conner McClain. They were all connected. These were the companies she had been investigating.

She walked up to the montage, her mouth open. It was all true.

"Congratulations, Avery. Rubicon has a lot of agents. You figured it out faster than anyone else."

She felt a moment of pride as she studied the photos and logos. "What is this?"

"A new kind of terrorism. These people aren't religious idealists. They're not zealots, foaming at the mouth, waving AK-47s in the air. They're scientists. Technologists. Rational people. Extremely intelligent. Working in the shadows, diligently planning."

"Planning what?"

"We don't know. It's big, Avery. Change-the-world-forever big. A device called the Looking Glass. The companies you've been investigating are creating the pieces—pieces that will be assembled at a later date."

"Like the Manhattan Project."

"Exactly."

"Who are they?"

"Technically, they're the modern incarnation of an ancient organization called the Order of Citium."

David walked to the bookshelf, took down a folder, and handed it to her.

"We know the organization was founded two thousand three hundred years ago in the Greek city of Citium by a philosopher named Zeno. History books cite him as Zeno of Citium. People came from all over the civilized world to debate with him. Those conversations grew into something more. A movement. That's what they were back then: a group of philosophers. Thinkers."

"What were they thinking about?"

"The meaning of the universe. The purpose of humanity. Why we exist."

"Pretty deep stuff for two thousand years ago."

"They were ahead of their time. They applied themselves to three disciplines: truth, ethics, and physics. And they were persecuted for their beliefs. They watched as polytheism, then monotheism, swept the world. They went underground. Stayed there. Waited for the world to catch up. It never did. Apparently, they're tired of waiting. They're going to do something about it."

"The Looking Glass."

"That's right."

"And what is the Looking Glass?"

"That's what we're trying to find out."

Avery frowned. "Okay. And when we find out, what are we going to do about it? What *is* Rubicon Ventures, really?"

"Rubicon *Ventures* is a front. One of several used by the Rubicon program. We're a covert organization—funded by the US government. Only a few people in government even know we exist. We have one mission: stopping Citium."

"People in government—like... what? CIA?"

"No, Rubicon isn't run out of any official government organization. We don't have ID cards with a three-letter acronym. No paper trail, no risk of leaks. But every month, seven very highly placed members of our government meet to discuss the Rubicon program. Only they know the truth of our activities. They provide funding and help when needed."

"So how do we stop the Citium?"

He smiled. "That is the question. I'll tell you the answer when you're ready."

"I'm ready now."

"No. You're not. Your real training begins today, Avery."

☣

That training took two years. Every Thursday night, she drove up to Northern Virginia to the colonial home in the country, where she learned things that had nothing to do with "due diligence." She learned to fire a handgun. She had gone hunting with her father since she was old enough to walk, but she'd had no experience with military firearms. She mastered hand-to-hand fighting. Close-quarters combat was foreign to her, but she picked it up quickly. On some level, it reminded her of tennis—quick reactions, fending off attacks from opponents, moving her feet, swinging with force.

With each passing week she grew and changed. Her focus became complete.

During that time, she continued her work at Rubicon Ventures. Rubicon was making real investments in the Citium companies, hoping that access would yield more information. Each month, Avery added more data points to the corkboard. Increasingly, those points connected.

The Citium were getting close to completing the Looking Glass. Finally, she and David sat down in the library and spread out the companies connected to Citium Holdings.

"Pick," he said.

"Pick what?"

"An insertion point. You're going to infiltrate the Citium."

"Hughes. He's the key."

"Why?"

"He's different from the rest," she said.

"How?"

"He's a true believer. He's convinced that the Looking Glass will save humanity. But I don't think he knows the truth about what they're doing. If I can get through to him, we'll have access to everything—and a shot at stopping them."

"And if you're wrong? If he does know? He'll kill you."

"I'll take that chance."

"Good. In the field, you'll have to trust your instincts. Make the right moves. Ask the right questions. Just like you have been. I won't be around to help you. If you think Hughes is the key, then he's the key."

☣

The next day, Avery applied for a job at Phaethon Genetics, one of Icarus Capital's portfolio companies. Her cover story was that while performing due diligence on Phaethon for her firm, she had been impressed with their product and technology. She told the interviewer that she believed in the work they were doing, and, if she was being completely honest, she thought the company would succeed and become worth a ton of money. She hoped to get in early, get stock options, and cash out when the company was acquired or went public.

They hired her a few days later. She was assigned to a programming team within the IT group. She hadn't done any coding since she'd completed her computer science major three years before, but she picked it back up quickly.

Phaethon was growing fast. The company was collecting genomic data and performing analysis, looking for insights that would help drug companies and healthcare providers make better decisions. They were taking a Big Data approach to medicine, and using a proprietary application that analyzed the genomic data. Their datacenter was struggling to keep up with the mountains of work the company was bringing in.

The company's root problem, however, was communication. The business side of the organization was constantly at war with the scientists, who were at war with programmers. The scientists didn't move fast enough for the business group, the programmers didn't move fast enough for the scientists, and the programmers were always complaining that they needed more computing capacity to run the simulations—simulations the business group refused to move to the grid for security purposes.

And that created the opportunity Avery needed to move up in the organization. Her background in due diligence, in analyzing hundreds of startup companies' science and business, had given her unique insight into problems like the ones Phaethon was facing. And with her communication skills, she quickly became the IT group's liaison with the scientists and business side. It didn't matter that half the programmers could code circles around her; they were a nightmare in meetings. When at last she was promoted, it was not because of the skills she had acquired in college, but rather because of what she'd learned in her time at Rubicon: how to read people, analyze a situation, and help everyone find a solution.

And as she had hoped, her new role increasingly brought her into contact with Desmond Hughes.

☣

"We got closer," Avery said over the helicopter's comm.

She paused. Desmond sensed that she was holding back. He wondered if Peyton was aware of it too.

"A month ago," Avery said, "you discovered that I was taking data off-site, leaving it at dead drops. You thought it was corporate espionage. You confronted me, and I took a chance. I told you the truth about the Rubicon program and what we believed the Citium were doing."

She glanced back at him. "It was news to you, Des. You had seen only pieces of the conspiracy. Two days later, you called me and told me that you had done your own investigation. You said it was true—the Citium was planning something unthinkable."

"The pandemic," Desmond said.

"I think so," Avery replied. "You told me that the Citium had begun with good intentions, that at their core, they had been a noble organization, focused on unraveling the greatest mystery of all time, one at the heart of our existence. In recent years, however, they had lost their way. Hard-liners had taken over, changed the agenda. They believed the human race was in danger. The experiments and steps they were willing to take had become more radical. You wanted to stop it.

"You got me reassigned to the *Kentaro Maru*. You said it would be the safest place—for both of us. You said if your plan failed, you would probably be taken there. I promised to help you if that happened. The next time I saw you was in that cell yesterday."

"So I failed," Desmond said.

"Maybe. I don't think we know enough to say yet. I think your first plan was to expose the Citium and cause a public uproar, focus media and government attention on them, and collapse the organization in one move. But they must have discovered you. You have one of the pieces of the Looking Glass. You hid it, or maybe destroyed it—that's why they were so intent on capturing you alive."

Desmond nodded. "Erasing my memories was a backup plan."

"I think so."

"Then it stands to reason that somewhere in my memories is the key to stopping the Citium and the pandemic."

"And the key to completing their work," Avery said. "You heard the conversation on the ship, Des. They scanned your body. You've got a specialized implant in your brain where memories are stored. Conner was convinced that implant could unblock memories and that you'd left a backdoor in a mobile application that would trigger the memories."

She glanced back at him. "In Berlin, did you find it? The application?"

Peyton turned to him and silently mouthed, *Don't tell her*. She obviously didn't trust Avery.

But Desmond had found Avery's story very convincing. It explained how she had come to be a Citium employee. How she had gotten on the *Kentaro Maru*. Why she had rescued them.

And yet, her story lacked something very important: it couldn't be verified. The Rubicon program was "strictly off-the-books" in her words. There was no doubt in his mind she was a special operative of some kind. What he didn't know was whose side she was truly on. What if her mission was to find the application that would unlock his memories? What if her story was just that—a story?

He made his decision.

"Yeah, I found it."

She stared at him, waiting, hanging on every word.

"In Berlin, I found some prepaid cards sewn into the label on a suit I left at a cleaner's. The card number led to a Google Voice line. One of the voicemail greetings referenced a web address, a hidden page on the CityForge website. There was a link to download an app called CityForge Tracker. It was location-aware, but I couldn't get it to do anything."

Desmond studied Avery, seeing if she bought the lie. It was a test. Revealing the Labyrinth Reality app would serve no purpose at the moment. Lying did. If she betrayed them now, they still wouldn't find the app.

"Good," she said. "We'll download it when we land, see if it works now."

☣

They flew in silence after that, through the night. Below them lay a blanket of darkness: no vehicle headlights on the roads, no twinkling cities in the distance. Stars shone above, brighter than Peyton had ever seen on any deployment.

She couldn't help thinking back to Desmond's riddle about the absence of space junk. What did it mean?

Beside her, Hannah stirred. Peyton leaned over. The young EIS agent had a fever. Was it from the gunshot wound? Peyton ran a hand over her lymph nodes. Swollen.

Hannah let out a cough, then another. Peyton pulled her shirt up, revealing a small, faint rash on her abdomen.

She's infected. Peyton's heart sank. She closed her eyes, felt them well up with tears, but she refused to let the tears break through.

A hand on her shoulder. Desmond staring at her, his eyes saying, *I will fix this.* She was usually the one who fixed things like this. But she needed help now.

From the pilot's seat, Avery spoke over the comm.

"Coming up on something."

Beyond the helicopter's windshield, Peyton saw a sprawling city dotted with several large bonfires. At first the fires confused her; these people wouldn't waste wood on bonfires. Firewood was too precious in this place. They weren't connected to the grid, had no electricity—they needed firewood to cook.

But a moment later, she understood. They were burning bodies. As they flew closer, she could see people piling them on the pyres by the dozens. No—hundreds. She felt sick.

In the swaths of darkness between the blazes, small lights glowed, their bearers moving about like fireflies swarming the arid ground. They were dry-cell battery torches, solar lanterns, and kerosene lamps, each giving off a slightly different hue—shades of white and yellow.

The helicopter hovered above the scene.

"You sure about this?" Avery asked.

"What's our fuel status?" Desmond replied, before Peyton could respond.

"Our fuel status is we're out."

Out the side window, Peyton saw crowds starting to gather, pointing up at the helicopter. Some held rifles.

"Find the main road and follow it north," she said. "There's an airstrip where it forks. The guards will be there. They'll keep us safe."

The helicopter banked, flew low over the dirt road, and found the airstrip, where a low-rise building glowed from the power of a generator. Peyton counted that as a good sign.

The moment they touched down, two dozen figures emerged from the building and ran toward them, rifles held at the ready.

Avery drew her sidearm.

Desmond saw it. "Let's stay cool here. I'd say we're outnumbered."

The men surrounded the helicopter, shouting as they closed in. Peyton scrutinized them, expected to see Kenyan army uniforms. She didn't. They were civilians dressed in dirty clothes.

One pulled the helicopter's door open. The smell of body odor rushed in with the warm night air. Above, the helicopter's main rotor roared and wind pushed down.

Hands grabbed Peyton. They were rough, gouging into the muscles of her arms. Voices shouted in Swahili and another language she didn't know—Somali, perhaps. Desmond kicked a man reaching for him, punched another. A rifle was pressed to his face, and he froze.

Peyton could hear Avery fighting too, screaming obscenities.

The men dragged Peyton out onto the ground, then held her up for a tall black man to inspect. Behind her, she heard them grabbing Hannah.

"Don't touch her!" she yelled, but the words were lost in the commotion.

CHAPTER 70

PEYTON FOUGHT THE men holding her as the helicopter's rotors thundered overhead. It took four large men to subdue Desmond, but they finally brought him down. They held him on the ground, twisting his arms behind him, but still, he refused to cry out—or to stop fighting back.

The crowd of rifle-carrying militia parted, and a middle-aged black man hurried through. Whoever he was, he was in charge.

Peyton had seen him exactly once before: in a large room in Mandera, filled with dying people. He had lain in a corner then, sweat covering his body, three buckets beside him.

That day, Peyton had given him a lifeline: a dose of ZMapp. She had hoped it might cure him.

It had.

Dr. Elim Kibet was vibrant now, his eyes full of life.

At the sight of Peyton, he yelled to one of the tall soldiers, who barked orders to his men.

Hands released Peyton as if she were a live electric wire. She fell forward, but Elim caught her and raised her up.

Over the dying roar of the rotors, he said, "Welcome to Dadaab, Dr. Shaw."

☣

On Elim's orders, two medical technicians brought a rolling stretcher from the building and ushered Hannah inside to an operating room. The facility wasn't high-tech, but it was clean and well supplied. Peyton and Elim operated on Hannah for over an hour. They removed dead tissue, disinfected the wound, and closed the gaping hole in her shoulder. When they were done, Peyton stood there for a long moment, staring at Hannah, hooked to the IV antibiotics and pain medication.

The woman was infected with the Mandera virus, but Peyton thought she had a fighting chance now. And she was in good hands—hands that were being washed just a few feet away.

Seconds later Elim slipped out of the OR, leaving Peyton alone with Hannah.

The redheaded woman was all Peyton had left of the EIS team she'd taken to the village. She imagined those young agents lying there in their tan service khakis, dead, left alone in the arid, barren land for the animals to pick over. She imagined them being found, hands running over glassy, staring eyes, bodies being zipped up in bags. It was a nightmare for her—to see someone she had deployed come home like that. She thought about them as if they were her own family, her own kids.

Hannah was her only chance to save one of them.

Peyton had done everything she could for her. That made her feel a bit better, a little more hopeful, for the first time since Conner McClain's men had raided the village.

The camps in Dadaab were sprawling settlements. There were several camps for refugees and a smaller camp for aid agencies. Peyton and Elim had performed the surgery in the aid agency camp.

During that time, there was not much for Desmond to do. With Avery at his side, he ventured out from the long, single-story building that housed the aid agencies, through a gate in a chain-link fence, and into the refugee camps.

It was good to stretch his legs. Over two hours in the vibrating helicopter hadn't done his bruised body any favors. Neither had the welcoming committee who had dragged him to the ground. Several of those men stood guard by the fence, and other armed men were scattered throughout the camp. They stood next to some of the larger buildings, which had been converted to hospitals. *"Hospital" isn't the right word*, Desmond thought. They were more like convalescent camps—places where those who were expected to survive were held. The patients who were not faring as well were kept in open camps, lying on blankets and wood platforms.

Screams and moans of agony sounded from every direction. Up ahead a fire burned, consuming the bodies piled high. Trucks crisscrossed the camp, collecting the dead and distributing food, water, and medicine. Desmond could see that the refugees were fighting as hard as they could against the virus; he could also see that they were losing. This place was a biological meat grinder, almost too hideous for him to watch.

I did this, he thought. In some way, he was responsible for what was happening here—what would soon be happening around the world.

In Berlin, he had been driven to discover who he was and what had happened to him. Now he had only one desire: to stop this. To save every life he could.

The look on Avery's face told him she knew exactly what he was thinking.

"It's not over yet, Des. We've got time to turn this around."

Behind them, a man carrying an AK-47 approached.

"The doctors are out of surgery. They've asked for you."

☣

Peyton was eating dinner with Elim, Desmond, and Avery in the building's cafeteria when an African woman approached them and sat beside Elim. Peyton recognized her instantly: she was one of the survivors from the village. Was it a coincidence that she was here? The village was hundreds of miles away; how did she get to Dadaab?

Elim looked exhausted, but his voice was strong. "Hannah is a very lucky young lady."

"Yes," Peyton said, taking a bite of the stew. She was glad there had been no label on the vat. "A few more hours in the air and she might not have made it."

"Perhaps. But she is lucky because she has you watching out for her."

Peyton had never been able to take a compliment; they seemed to wrap around her like a rope, constricting her, paralyzing her. She turned red.

"Just doing my job," she said quietly, taking another bite of mystery stew. "What happened here?"

"Biology," Elim said. "The virus got loose in the camps."

"How many are dead?"

Elim paused. "We'll be counting the survivors when it's over, Dr. Shaw."

"Any estimate would be helpful. I think this is perhaps the first large population center the virus struck. And please, call me Peyton."

He nodded. "There were about three hundred thousand people here when this began. I expect about ten thousand to survive."

Peyton sat in shock. "A three percent survival rate?"

"With better care, rehydration salts, the number might double —five or six percent."

The words hung there like a bell tolling. No one spoke for a long moment. Ebola Zaire killed ninety percent of those it infected. Mandera was even more deadly than that—and in its early days it was as contagious as the common cold. It was the perfect killer.

But why? How was the pandemic connected to the Looking Glass? What *was* the Looking Glass? What could possibly be worth killing 95% of the world's population? Or was there another plan?

Conner McClain had all but confessed to having a cure to the virus; finding that cure was the world's only chance. They needed to start putting the pieces together.

Peyton swallowed. "I really hate to ask. We came here for Hannah, but we were also hoping to find a couple of things."

Elim raised his eyebrows.

"We need a satphone."

He nodded.

"And a plane."

He broke into a smile Peyton couldn't read. She was reflecting on how outrageous the request was when he said, "I think I can help you."

☣

After they finished their meal, Elim led them through the building's main corridor. The facility was in complete disarray. Every room had been ransacked. To Peyton, it looked like a middle school with no teachers, trashed by students running wild. Half-empty boxes littered the hall; desks were overturned, drawers pulled out; supply closets stood open.

Elim opened a locked utility closet. The tiny room was overflowing with electronics—cell phones, tablets, and laptops—like a vault of plastic and silicon treasures.

"When containment broke and everyone started getting sick, the order of this place fell quickly. There were no refugees or aid workers any more. Only survivors and the dying. The aid workers stored their electronics here, hoping they would be of use to someone eventually."

"You can't use them?" Desmond asked, surprised.

"You'll see," Elim said, a hint of dread in his voice.

An African woman approached them and said, "Dr. Kibet, she's awake."

Hannah, Peyton thought.

Avery didn't wait another second. She grabbed a laptop and a solar charger, stacked a tablet on top, then began piling cell phones up like a Jenga tower, which wobbled after a few seconds.

Desmond eyed her curiously.

"Not sure where we're headed," the blonde said. "Satellites

393

might go out. We'll need phones from European, American, and Asian carriers on different networks."

The woman always seemed to be a step ahead.

Desmond collected a few phones as well.

Elim pointed to a shelf where a stack of smartphones lay. Attached were the CDC-issued satsleeves. The sight made Peyton's mouth run dry, like discovering a pile of dog tags from fallen comrades. She stared at the plastic and glass tombstones. How had they gotten here?

She took two of them. One for her, one for Hannah.

☣

Desmond watched Peyton follow Elim back to the OR. He found her compassion for Hannah incredibly endearing. Peyton cared with all her heart. She had poured everything she had into caring for her young colleague—had risked her own life to save her, to bring her this far. He knew one thing: any person on Earth would be lucky to have Peyton Shaw looking out for them.

He felt Avery's eyes on him, watching him stare as Peyton left. In a way, Desmond found her to be Peyton's mirror image. They were both headstrong and determined. They cared about their mission, and they didn't let anything get in their way. Maybe that was why they clashed so much—they were too much alike. But Avery took lives; Peyton saved them.

Desmond felt irresistibly drawn to both women, like a force of nature; he imagined himself as a piece of metal and they were magnets exerting strong pulls in opposite directions. Each was intriguing in different ways; each woman was a mystery he wanted to solve.

When Peyton slipped out of view, Avery retreated to a conference room and closed the door. The move surprised Desmond. She wanted to be alone. Why?

Ever since she'd shared her story on the helicopter—and even before that—he had questioned whether he could trust her.

She could be a plant, assigned to find out where he had hidden the Rendition device.

Or she could be telling the truth.

He pushed the door open. She had spread the phones out on the long table and was activating them.

"I need to check in with my handler," she said. She turned to him. "You need help?"

He paused, debating whether to stay and see who she called.

"No," he said, hesitating.

"You're downloading the CityForge app, right?" A small smile curled at her lips. He wondered if she knew he had lied on the helicopter.

He nodded, withdrew from the room, and closed the door behind him. But he stood just outside the door, waiting, hoping to hear her call. It never came. She must have been texting.

He activated a cell phone and downloaded the Labyrinth Reality app. He entered the code for the private Labyrinth he had created. He was once again asked whether he was the hero or the Minotaur.

He clicked *hero*. The dialog read:

Searching for an entrance to the Labyrinth...

In Berlin, the application had said there were no entrances near him. He waited. Finally, a message appeared:

1. Entrance Located.

He clicked the link. A map appeared with GPS coordinates and a glowing green dot.

The location was an island north of Scotland, which surprised him: it was much closer to Berlin than Dadaab. Why did the location not appear when he tried the app in Berlin? He decided the entrance must have been set to reveal on a timer, or perhaps only after some event had occurred. Or, perhaps, when a partner activated it. That possibility intrigued Desmond the most.

He zoomed in on the map dot. It was in the Shetland Islands. From the satellite photography, the place looked barely inhabited. There were some farms, a few roads, a seaport, and an airport.

The glowing dot itself lay in the middle of a forest. There was no building, no home, not even a road leading to it. But he knew something was there—waiting for him.

He hoped it held the key to finding a cure.

CHAPTER 71

HANNAH'S EYES WERE open when Peyton entered the office that had been converted to a patient room. The young woman tried to sit up in bed, but Peyton told her to lie back down.

Her voice came out hoarse, faint. "What happened?"

Peyton considered what to tell her. She decided that Hannah had been through enough. Details could wait for another day.

"We were rescued."

Hannah closed her eyes and breathed heavily.

"Are we going home?"

"Eventually. I need to make a few phone calls. You're in good hands here. I'll be back."

Outside the room, Peyton dialed Elliott's cell. The call connected without ringing.

"You've reached Operation BioShield. If you're calling from inside a cordon zone, press one. If you're calling from outside a cordon zone, press two."

After a brief pause, the recording repeated.

Why would Elliott's phone route to a call center? Peyton had never heard of Operation BioShield. She wondered if it was related to the congressional act, Project BioShield, that had called for stockpiling critical vaccines in the aftermath of 9/11.

Curious, she pressed one, indicating she was inside a cordon zone.

"If you or someone in your home is sick, press one. If you have training in an essential job role, press two. Essential jobs include anyone with military training, doctors, nurses, police, fire, EMT, and prison employees. If you are calling from an operations center, dial three. All other callers, press zero. Note: pressing zero will greatly delay your wait time. The current wait time is six hours and eighteen minutes."

Peyton hung up and dialed several of her CDC colleagues. She knew only a few of their numbers by heart. But all of her calls were routed to the same Operation BioShield hotline.

She dialed the CDC's Emergency Operations Center. A different recorded message played:

"You've reached the BioShield Command Center. If you are transporting supplies and need destination or route assistance, press one. If you work in an essential role and need an assignment, press two. If you have located unsorted individuals outside a cordon zone, press three."

The last option chilled Peyton. *Unsorted individuals.*

The recording repeated; there was no option for an operator.

Peyton pressed two. A man with a gruff voice said, "Name and social security number."

She gave him the information, and heard the man typing.

"Sir, I have critical information—"

He interrupted. "Location?"

"Dadaab, Kenya."

A long pause.

"Your ops facility is Phillips Arena. Report there immediately for assignment."

"What?"

"Phillips Arena is located at—"

"I know where Phillips Arena is. Listen to me, I led the CDC mission to Kenya, the one that first encountered the Mandera virus."

The line was silent. She had his attention.

"I have information regarding its origin and possibly the key to finding a cure. I need to speak with the CDC."

She heard furious typing in the background.

"Best number to reach you?"

"Did you hear what I just said? I know how this pandemic started—and possibly how to find a cure."

"I heard you, Dr. Shaw. We're getting about a hundred calls per hour now from scientists and physicians who are sure they have information regarding a cure. We have a queue that a research assistant is working through. They'll have to call you back."

"You're going to put my message in a queue and call me back?"

"Yes, ma'am."

"Are you serious?"

"Yes, ma'am."

"What's your name?"

"Corporal Travers, ma'am."

"When this is over, Corporal, the newspapers and TV shows are going to figure out why so many people died. They'll identify turning points, when people in critical roles made the wrong calls—moments when someone could have made a decision that would have changed the course of the outbreak and saved millions, possibly billions of lives. This is one of those moments. This is the moment when you can simply connect me to that research team or someone at the CDC. It will only take a few seconds. You can save a lot of people—right now."

"Sorry, ma'am, I don't even have their number."

Peyton paused, thinking.

"Ma'am?"

"I'm still here."

"Your number was blocked; I'm going to need a good callback number."

Peyton opened the phone's settings and read the number out. Travers thanked her, and Peyton said, "Corporal?"

"Yes, ma'am?"

"How many messages are in this... queue?"

"Three hundred and sixteen, ma'am."

She shook her head. "One last thing, Corporal. I'm the CDC's leading epidemiologist. I'm the one they sent to Kenya when we first found out about the outbreak. Maybe that's in your files, or maybe you can see my employment history. I'm *close* to this

399

investigation. Whoever is seeing these messages will know who I am. They'll call me first. You need to move my message to the top of the list. Do you understand?"

"Do you require further assistance, ma'am?"

She leaned her head back and groaned.

After she'd ended the call, she activated the phone's web browser. If she could get in touch with the WHO, maybe they could connect her to the CDC. But she didn't know the WHO's number. The thought reminded her of Jonas, and seeing his number pop up on her phone a week ago in her condo. If they had split up in Kenya, would he still be alive? Had being near her put him in harm's way? She tried to focus.

The WHO web address redirected to a site called EuroShield. The page prompted her to enter her information so she could receive the address of a local "EuroCordon center." The site asked questions nearly identical to those asked by the American operator. Europe apparently had a similar pandemic disaster protocol.

She tried navigating to several more web sites, but the only sites that ever came up were BioShield in America, EuroShield in Europe, and similar sites in Asia and Russia.

Clearly whatever had happened in America had also occurred around the world—almost simultaneously. Phones and internet had been routed, contained. Peyton wondered if it was the dawn of a new dark age, or perhaps something even worse.

☣

She found Desmond outside the cafeteria, staring at a smartphone, leaning against the wall.

"Did you find it?" she asked.

"Yeah," he said, lost in thought.

"Every web address redirects to emergency websites. Phone lines route to a call center."

"The app still works," he mumbled.

The news thrilled Peyton. This could be the break they needed.

"And?" she prompted eagerly.

"It gave me a location this time," Desmond said. "An island north of Scotland. It's barely inhabited."

She could see he was frustrated. Maybe he had expected something more substantial. Or maybe it was the time he had spent walking through the camp.

She told him about her call with the BioShield operator. They speculated on the state of things in America, Europe, and in particular Shetland, where the key to finding a cure could be waiting for them.

"If Great Britain is locked down, they might shoot us out of the sky the minute we enter British airspace."

"That's assuming," Peyton said, "we can enter British airspace. Can you fly a plane?"

An amused smile crossed Desmond's lips. "I don't know. Can't remember. There's really only one way to find out."

She studied him for a minute, unsure if he was serious.

Smiling, he said, "Kidding."

That left Avery. Neither spoke her name.

Peyton simply said, "I don't trust her."

"You don't like her."

"True. I also don't trust her. Her rescue was too convenient."

"Or timely."

"Do *you* trust her?"

Desmond exhaled. "I'm not sure. I want to. But... It's a weird thing, not knowing everything that happened to me, my true history with her. It's... impossible to explain."

He looked Peyton in the eye. "I'd also like to know the rest of *our* history."

She said nothing.

"Why won't you tell me?"

"It's in the past," she said quietly.

He was silent for a few seconds, then took the phone from his pocket. "I need someone I can trust. I lied to Avery on the helicopter. The app I found in Berlin is actually called Labyrinth Reality. I took two identical phones. I'll keep the one without the Labyrinth app; I want you to keep the one that has the app."

Peyton looked at the screen.

"It says downloading. Downloading what?"

"I don't know. The message popped up shortly after the entrance was located."

When Peyton looked up, Avery was standing in the hall. She hadn't heard the other woman walk up. She wondered how long Avery had been there—and how much she'd heard.

Desmond followed Peyton's gaze. To Avery, he said, "Did you get through?"

"Phones are down. Web, too. We're in the dark."

Peyton tucked Desmond's cell phone in her pocket. She saw Avery watching her.

"Did the app work?" Avery asked Desmond.

He recounted what he had learned, including the Labyrinth location in Shetland, though he still pretended as though the app was something associated with CityForge.

"Shetland's a long way away," Avery said. "Do we have a plane?"

Peyton started off down the hall. "Let's find out."

☣

Outside the operating room, Peyton found Elim talking quietly with the villager she had seen in the mess hall.

"About our other request," Peyton said.

Elim smiled. "Follow me."

He led them out of the building, across the aid camp, to a single-lane runway. At the end, Peyton could make out a large plane without many windows. A cargo plane. And as her eyes adjusted to the night, she saw the unmistakable emblem of a red cross on the side.

"They arrived with supplies just as the outbreak began. They didn't make it. It's yours if you can use it. Besides, there are no pilots here."

Without a word, Avery began walking across the runway.

Desmond shot Peyton a look that said, *I'll keep an eye on her and make sure she doesn't leave without us.*

Peyton thanked Elim, but the man waved it off.

"It's the least I could do for the woman who saved my life. I'm sure I would not have survived without ZMapp."

"You don't have me to thank for that," Peyton said. "A woman at the Kenyan Ministry of Health, Nia Okeke, was very convincing. She deserves the credit."

Elim nodded grimly, as if hearing the woman's name saddened him.

"I'm afraid we can't take Hannah with us," Peyton said.

"I expected as much. I assure you, I will give her the very best care I can."

Peyton could see that he meant it.

"I know you will. Thank you."

Back inside the building, Peyton took a deep breath before walking into Hannah's room. Elim and the woman from the village followed right behind her.

Hannah lay in the bed resting, her eyes closed. Monitors showed her vitals, which Peyton was glad to see were strong.

Peyton placed a hand on Hannah's shoulder.

"Hannah." She paused. "Can you hear me?"

Hannah opened her eyes slowly.

"I need to go. Elim is going to take good care of you."

Hannah nodded, thanked Elim, then looked at the woman beside him.

"You're from the village," she said.

Elim translated, and the woman nodded.

Elim then explained, "Your colleague, Millen Thomas, brought her to Mandera."

Millen is alive. Peyton was overjoyed at the news, but Hannah was even more relieved. A tear ran down her face.

"He found me in the hospital," Elim said. "I was alive, but just barely. Millen and Dhamiria rehabilitated me." He looked at the woman beside him. "Gave me a reason to live." To Hannah, he added, "I've recently learned how powerful that medicine can be."

There was a long pause.

Hannah reached out and took Peyton's hand. Hannah's tears were coming faster now, but she didn't cry out loud.

Peyton asked the question she knew the younger woman wanted to. "Where did Millen go?"

"Home. To Atlanta. He called someone—Elliott, I believe was his name. His colleague arranged transport. He departed several days ago, with the two children from the village. He was taking them to the CDC, in hopes they might find clues to a cure."

Peyton's mind raced. Millen taking the survivors to the CDC was a break.

To Hannah, Elim said, "Millen was quite worried about everyone he had traveled here with—but he was especially worried about you."

Peyton felt Hannah squeeze her hand.

☣

Elim gave Peyton some supplies for the trip: food, water, and—just in case, he said—medicine. Peyton had been coughing, and the physician had realized the inevitable: she was infected with the Mandera virus. The antibiotics he provided would treat any secondary infections.

As Elim led her down the corridor, he said, "There's something I've wanted to ask since you arrived."

She nodded. "Of course."

"The young American I cared for, Lucas Turner. Did he make it?"

Peyton shook her head. "No. I'm very sorry."

"So am I. He was a fine young man. And brave."

They were both silent for a moment.

"Well, thank you for everything," Peyton said at last.

"Good luck to you, Dr. Shaw."

"And to you."

☣

In the makeshift hospital room, Hannah dried the tears from her face and closed her eyes. She had never been so tired in all her life. She knew the fever was advancing, that the days ahead would determine whether she lived or died. She was ready. Because now she would face it with a very valuable thing, a thing she didn't have the day before.

Hope.

☣

In another patient room, Elim Kibet injected a vial of antibiotics into the IV.

"You're wasting that on me," the woman said.

Despite her deteriorating condition, her tone was firm, insistent. Elim had to agree with Dr. Shaw: Nia Okeke was a very convincing woman when she wanted to be.

"You know," he said, "for your sake, it's a good thing you are not the physician in charge here."

☣

The plane was similar to the Air Force transport Peyton had come to Kenya on, except a bit smaller. The crew cabin held six high-backed chairs and an open space where Peyton found Desmond stretched out on a sleeping bag. He wore only boxers and a T-shirt, which had sweat spots coming through.

He was still in great shape, with broad shoulders and the build of someone who did kickboxing or weight training. The burn scars covering his feet and stretching up his legs caught her eye, and she remembered the first time she saw them, almost twenty years ago, that morning in her dorm room. That felt like a lifetime ago, yet here and now, he was somehow more like that happy nineteen-year-old kid than he was like the troubled adult he had become after. Just like that night at the Halloween party, she felt herself irresistibly drawn to him, like a black hole pulling her in with no hope of escape.

She had felt the first spark when she heard his voice the previous Saturday night. And again when Lucas Turner had said his name. And when she had seen his name written on the wall of the barn stall. It had been Desmond who had rescued her from the ship and likely saved Hannah's life in the process. At each point, a little more of her had come alive, as though she was waking up from a long sleep. But she couldn't allow that to happen. They had work to do. Lives were at stake—things far more important than her and Desmond.

She settled into a sleeping bag beside him, and they lay in silence. She could feel him looking at her. She wondered what he was thinking, when he would remember—if he would remember. And what she would do then.

Five minutes later, the plane lifted off, en route to Shetland.

Despite the noise and turbulence, Desmond fell asleep quickly. *He must be exhausted,* Peyton thought. The temperature in the cabin dropped as the plane climbed. The engines roared; Avery was pushing the craft to its limits.

Peyton tucked a few pillows between Desmond and the wall, cushioning him in case they hit more turbulence. Then she slid back into her own sleeping bag and pulled in close beside his, trapping the heat between them.

Slowly, she became more aware of her fever. Perhaps it was the chill in the cabin or the solitude, but the heat engulfed her face. Her head ached. Her chest felt heavy. She really hoped they found some clue on the island. For her sake, and many others.

Desmond mumbled, but Peyton couldn't hear what he said over the roar of the engines.

She turned. His eyes were still closed. He spoke again.

She leaned in, her ear inches from his lips.

"I've figured it out." He paused, then mumbled, "The X factor."

Peyton remembered the memory. She had been there. And she knew what came next. She dreaded it for him.

She drew out the phone he had given her. A dialog read:

Download complete.

DAY 10

4,600,000,000 infected
1,000,000 dead

CHAPTER 72

BY THE TIME the Red Cross plane leveled out, sweat was pouring off Desmond. Peyton had unzipped his sleeping bag, but it was little help.

Every few seconds, he tossed his head from side to side.

Peyton tried to wake him for five minutes straight, but it was no use. It was as if he were in a coma.

She heard footsteps behind her, turned, and found Avery towering above her, squinting at Desmond wincing on the floor.

The slender woman squatted, wiped the sweat from his forehead, and cupped his face in her hands. She leaned close, listening to the words he mumbled.

It struck Peyton as a lover's embrace, not a clinical inspection. She wondered if it was an act—or something Avery had actually done before.

Without turning to Peyton, Avery said, "Should we land?"

"I don't know. Where are we?"

"Over Ethiopia."

"He's stable for now. I favor waiting until we reach Europe."

Avery left without another word. As soon as the door to the cockpit closed, Peyton wiped a new layer of sweat from Desmond's face and placed her hands where Avery's had been, feeling the stubble on his lean, glistening face.

All she could do now was wait.

☣

Two days after Christmas, in Peyton's apartment, Desmond presented his theory to her.

"I've figured it out."

"What? The meaning of life?"

"Better. Why companies fail."

"Oh." She was reading *People* magazine and watching reruns of *Friends*.

"It's the X factor."

"I don't follow."

"Think about it. First the company has to address a large market opportunity." He was pacing in the small apartment now, cutting off her view of Ross and Rachel. "xTV got that right. But success requires two components: operational proficiency and the X factor. For all these web startups, the operational part is actually the easiest. You make sure your code works and the product scales, you pay your rent, et cetera, et cetera. The X factor is the issue.

"For web companies, the X factor is consumer adoption. Every one of them is disrupting the world in some way—they're trying to change customer behavior. Think about it. Amazon wants to change the way we buy books. Instead of walking into a Barnes and Noble, you order it online and it arrives at your door. Who knows, maybe they'll deliver all kinds of stuff one day. Webvan wants to deliver groceries in the same way. No more driving to the store. WebCrawler wants to change the way we find information. Forget going to a library and looking it up— simply search for it on WebCrawler. Need to find a business? Don't dial four-one-one, forget the yellow pages, just search for it on WebCrawler. They're all trying to change the way we as consumers behave—and funnel attention and money to them."

"Makes sense."

"The mystery is how many consumers will change and when. That's what xTV got wrong. They overestimated consumer adoption. They ran out of money before the consumers adopted their product."

"Okay. I'll buy that." She was peeking around him. Monica had just inherited a dollhouse. How this show was so popular was a mystery to Desmond.

"It comes down to the founders," he said. "Companies that succeed have a founder or a leadership team that fundamentally understands their customers, sometimes even better than customers know themselves. They imagine what the customer wants before they know they want it, and they package it in a way that is irresistible. *And*, they manage well. xTV had the vision, but not the discipline. They didn't watch their bank account close enough."

"Uh-huh. So what are you going to do about this grand revelation?"

"Tomorrow, I'm going for three job interviews."

"Really?" She sat up, tossed the magazine aside. "Where?"

He told her, and she nodded.

"You going to wear the steel-toed boots?"

"Very funny. And yes. I am. Because I keep it real."

☣

On New Year's Eve, he accepted a job offer. When he told Peyton which company, she looked surprised.

"SciNet?"

"SciNet."

"I didn't see that coming."

The company was boring. It was early stage and developing an e-commerce platform to sell scientific equipment and products.

"It's a home run," Desmond said. "Low X factor. Very little waiting for consumer adoption. Their customers are scientists and office admins—very rational people, easy to target. *Very* easy to predict their behavior patterns."

"Don't be so sure. I was raised by a scientist."

"Well, you know what I mean. They'll hit it out of the park. Won't be a multi-billion-dollar company, but it'll succeed and do what I need it to do."

"Which is?"

"Provide financial security. The job offer is solid. Tons of options and a good salary. I can start buying options in other companies again."

"So you haven't given up on that?"

"Not by a long shot."

They went to a New Year's Eve house party that night. It was like no New Year's Desmond could remember. The whole world felt new again. He felt hopeful about everything: the new job, and his relationship with Peyton especially.

☣

The vibe at SciNet was very different from xTV. Where xTV had an almost Hollywood feel, SciNet felt like a university or a lab. Everyone was pretty uptight. Well, everyone except for a few of the developers, Desmond included. They couldn't help but make a few pranks to lighten the mood. Most were related to the movie *The Terminator*, in which an artificial intelligence called SkyNet becomes self-aware and tries to wipe out humanity with a robotic Arnold Schwarzenegger. Whenever the database or website was acting weird, someone would say, "Oh God, I think SciNet's becoming self-aware."

The site's error page featured a picture of Arnold Schwarzenegger wearing dark sunglasses and holding a shotgun, with a caption that read, *This page has been TERMINATED.*

The CEO finally sent an email banning all jokes related to *The Terminator*.

Desmond replied:

> Just to confirm, these jokes are terminated?

Despite their faux fears that SciNet would become self-aware, the platform did launch in the spring of 1998 and quickly became a hit. Across the country, labs and research facilities signed up, took inventory of the old equipment collecting dust, and posted it for sale. Some used the money to buy more equipment they actually needed—much of it from SciNet.

Desmond was the lead developer. He could have taken the role of Chief Technology Officer, but he'd rated that job as more risky. He would have had a higher salary with fewer technical responsibilities. If the company ran low on cash or needed to refocus, he figured managers with higher pay would be laid off more quickly than the programmers who would be needed to right the ship.

For the time being, however, the ship was sailing quite well. Their first clients were in the Bay Area: Lawrence Livermore National Laboratory, NASA's Ames Research Center, Stanford, and SRI International. Word spread among scientists and procurement departments. Signups and transactions soared.

Desmond periodically ran database reports for management, identifying their largest clients—organizations they should call on and keep happy. Some were companies he'd never heard of: Rapture Therapeutics, Rook Quantum Sciences, and Prometheus Technologies.

"These three companies are each buying more than Livermore. Stanford even," he said. "And it's all kinds of stuff. They're either just stocking up, or they're running the largest scale experiments in the world."

SciNet's CEO was in his early thirties, had an MBA from Harvard, and was all business.

"I fail to see a problem with any of that."

"Well," Desmond said, "the issue is that Rapture and Rook, in particular, aren't paying for their equipment. I can see the credit card transactions on the back end. They're using cards and bank accounts tied to two companies: Citium Holdings and Invisible Sun Securities."

The CEO was getting annoyed. "So?"

"So, we have two third-party companies buying massive amounts of scientific equipment and shipping it to these legitimate private research firms."

"Again, how is that a problem?"

"I'm not sure it is, but I think we ought to look into it. We've created something new here. What if someone's taking advantage of it? What if SciNet is being used to launder money somehow? Like Mexican drug cartels, the Mafia—"

"Okay, Desmond. I think you've been watching too much TV. We've got what we need here."

Management was in no hurry to question their best clients. The company needed the transaction volume, and Citium Holdings and Invisible Sun Securities were providing plenty of it.

But Desmond couldn't contain his curiosity. He looked the companies up. Both were dead ends. They didn't seem to exist beyond a few corporate records. There were no offices, no websites, not even phone numbers. They were like shells with seemingly endless amounts of cash.

Another mystery, closer to home, did get solved: Peyton was going to attend Stanford Medical School. She told him at her apartment one night, over dinner—lasagna she had cooked that was the best meal he had eaten in some time.

"That's great," he said. "It's nearly impossible to get in."

"I was worried, honestly."

"I'll do whatever I can to help you."

"I know you will. It's why I wanted to stay here in the area. I don't want us to be apart. We have to start thinking about the future."

The words *we* and *us* hung there in the air, present but unacknowledged.

Peyton used those words more often after that. She talked about the future more frequently. She asked whether he wanted to have kids. Where he wanted to live: in the city, a suburb, or the country, as he had done growing up. What sort of life he wanted his children to have. What he thought work-life balance should be for people with kids. Whether he wanted to travel if they had the chance.

Desmond found himself utterly unable to answer her questions. As the months went by, she began to apply more pressure, subtle at first, then more directly. Desmond's answer was always the same: that he was so focused on work at the moment that it was hard for him to imagine these scenarios.

"It's like a train in a tunnel. You don't know what's on the other side. How can you say what you'll do when you come out?"

That set her off. "You're not a train in a tunnel, Desmond! We're real people. It's not hard to imagine."

But for Desmond it was impossible. Throughout his entire life he'd always been at the mercy of someone, or something, else. The fire. Orville. Silicon Valley. And now he wanted independence. Freedom. That meant money, and once he had it he believed he could sort his life out. *Then* he could answer Peyton's questions, which haunted him more and more.

With each month, he saw the prospect of financial freedom slipping away. Four more companies he owned options in folded. SciNet's rate of growth slowed. The initial rush was over; those storage closets full of old equipment had been cleaned out, and now the users were spending less per month. Management came up with several ideas: expanding to Europe and using the platform to help industrial companies buy and sell equipment. Both presented new challenges.

Then, in the summer of '98, everything changed. A company Desmond owned options in went public. He only held 13,400 options, but they were worth $21 at the IPO price—which meant all told, they were worth a quarter of a million dollars.

He checked the stock price about a thousand times the day it debuted, fearing the worst—a crash or some freak accident. But just the opposite happened: the stock soared. By the end of the first day of trading, his options were worth $38.23 each. $512,282. The sum was nearly unimaginable to him. A fortune. Freedom.

He raced to Wallace's office. The attorney connected him with an investment bank that would help him unload the options, ensuring the profits were taxed at long-term capital gains rates.

"Are you sure you want to sell all of it, Desmond?"

"I'm sure."

Desmond had come up with a rubric for deciding whether to

keep or sell a stock: if he was willing to buy the stock at its current price, he would keep it. Otherwise, he would sell. He wanted the cash.

The transaction went through the next day, netting him just over four hundred thousand dollars after taxes and fees.

He again sat in Wallace's office.

"I need you to draw up some other agreements. Personal contracts."

He told the man exactly what he wanted.

"She'll have to sign them, Desmond."

"I know. It won't be a problem."

"You're a brilliant young man, but I think you've got a lot to learn about women."

Desmond's will was the easiest part. In classic Orville Hughes fashion, it read:

To Peyton Adelaide Shaw, I leave everything.

The other forms were a series of assignment agreements that gave Peyton ownership of half of all the options and securities he owned.

That night they celebrated the IPO with a dinner out. After dessert, Desmond showed her the will, which, to his surprise, sort of unsettled her.

"I just want you to be taken care of," he said. "What if I fell over dead? Got hit by a car?"

"Don't say that, Desmond."

"It's true. You're all I've got, Peyton. You're the only person in my life I'm really close to."

"Really close to? Is that how you'd describe us?" She chugged the rest of her wine.

This conversation hadn't gone the way he'd planned. He had thought she'd be relieved.

At her apartment, he showed her the assignment agreements that gave her half of all his stock and options.

"It's what's fair," he said. "You saved me, Peyton—when I

wanted to put it all in xTV. You introduced me to the first people I bought options from. You've been the only constant in my life since I've been in California. You practically supported me after xTV, kept me from starving. You've been my partner in this whole thing, and you should have half."

She exploded. "Your *partner*? Is that what we are? Business associates? Is that all this is?"

"No, Peyton—"

"Then what are we?"

"What do you want from me?"

"You know *exactly* what I want."

He did know. It wasn't stock options or any written agreement. It was three words he couldn't seem to say. After a few months she had stopped saying them, but he could tell when she wanted to. That hurt him too.

"Will you please sign them?" he said.

"Get out."

"Peyton."

"You heard me. And take all your... *legal documents* with you."

☣

Peyton didn't return his calls or emails for two weeks. They were the longest weeks of Desmond's life.

He also had problems at work. SciNet was nearly out of money. They arrived at a seemingly counterintuitive solution: go public. The IPO, if successful, would raise over fifty million dollars for the company. It would also make Desmond rich.

He watched in wonder as the finance department dressed up the books. Management asked him for endless reports, cutting and shuffling the data for the road show. There were all sorts of disclosures and disclaimers in the prospectus, verbiage about the risks to their business and things outside their control. But those dense sections weren't what investors saw. They stared at the graphs on the projection screen that showed rapid growth and read the parts that described a company with massive profit potential.

SciNet entered its quiet period and waited. Every person in the company was on edge. To Desmond it felt like being trapped in a submarine at war, knowing there were mines floating everywhere in the water around them, the entire crew holding its breath, waiting to see if they would hit one and sink or if they would make it out to freedom as heroes.

Every day, Desmond wrote another email to Peyton.

When she didn't reply, he camped out at her front door. He was nervous that the neighbors would call the police, but they must have had some sense of what was going on. They looked at him with sympathy as they passed. One guy said, "Good luck, buddy."

When Peyton opened the door that morning, she tried to slam it in his face, but he held it open.

"Please, just talk to me."

"You talk, I'll listen."

She stood in the living room, hands on her hips.

"I want you to try to imagine things from my perspective."

She was a statue.

"There is something broken inside me. Deep down inside. In a place I never knew existed before I met you. I never needed it before, because anyone who ever loved me was ripped out of my life before I could love them back.

"I watched my family burn to death. I was raised by one of the meanest guys I've ever known. He never loved me. I don't think he could, or maybe he couldn't show it. I never knew love as a child. I've never known it before. Until I met you. I don't know what to do or how to feel, because this is completely new to me. I care about you more than anything I've ever cared about in this world. You're my whole life, Peyton. But you need to know that I'm not a whole person. I'm not the person you want me to be."

The tears began streaming down her face. She put her arms around him, pulled him close, and pressed her body tightly into his. He could feel the tension drain out of his body. The release. The void filled with a desperate hunger. His body reacted.

So did hers. His hands moved across her body as they kissed. He walked her backwards into the bedroom as they kissed, sloppy, hungry kisses.

They lost track of time. She never mentioned class, and he didn't say a word about work. In the living room, he could hear his Nokia cell phone ringing. He wouldn't have answered it if the world was ending.

When they were spent, they lay in bed, staring at the ceiling the same way they had that first night.

Her voice was soft, barely over a whisper. "I thought you were pushing me away."

That confused him. He propped himself up on an elbow.

She continued, still staring at the ceiling. "I figured you had what you wanted—the money, the stock that would make you rich. You wanted to give me my share so you could walk away with a clear conscience that you had done the right thing."

The attorney had been right: Desmond really did have a lot to learn about women.

"That's the last thing I want," he said. "I want to take care of you no matter what, no matter what happens to us, or to me. I'm sorry I hurt you."

He was terrified that he would hurt her again. He feared that this was the first of what would be recurring missteps.

"I meant what I said: I'm not a whole person, Peyton. Your friends, the couples we go to dinner with—those guys are what you want. Someone normal."

"I'll be the judge of what I want. And it's not normal. Plus, I've got news, Des. Nobody on this earth is really normal. Everyone is faking it to some degree. Especially around here. Lot of freak flags flying on the inside."

As they got dressed, neither said a word, but there was a serenity in the air he'd never experienced.

Before he left for work, he asked her again if she'd sign the documents.

"I need to know you're taken care of. Please."

"Okay." She took his face in her hands. "If it's what you want."

She signed her name in beautiful cursive letters, and Desmond
kissed her before he left.

☣

She asked him again to come to Christmas at her mother's house
that year. This time, he accepted, but he wasn't looking forward
to it. He still didn't feel comfortable around her family. But things
had changed for him. He was a success now, with one IPO behind
him and another looming.

Her sister's husband treated him differently, though he
suspected he knew the series of events that had led to that:
Peyton had prevailed upon her sister, who had then spoken with
her husband. Derrick quizzed him about SciNet and his other
investments with the zeal of a kid trying to glean clues about his
gifts under the tree.

Their family was tight, Desmond could see that, and Peyton
had told him the reason: the death of their father had brought
them closer. Her brother's passing seven years before had also
strengthened their bond. Peyton said it had made them more
thankful for each other and every year they had together. The
tragedies were a reminder to them of what was truly important.

Her entire family couldn't have been nicer to him. He still
felt out of place, like an actor in a role that was wrong for him.
"Fraud" was the word that kept running through his mind. He
told himself that there was simply a wall inside of him, that the
emotions were there, behind it, waiting to come through. When it
came down, everything would be fine.

He would soon learn the truth.

CHAPTER 73

DESMOND FELT A hand on his shoulder, shaking him. He opened his eyes. Avery loomed over him, her pale skin and slender face like a ghost in the green glow of the plane's safety lights.

Peyton lay in a sleeping bag beside him, fast asleep. Avery hadn't woken her and apparently didn't want to. Her voice was barely over a whisper.

"You okay?"

He felt feverish and achy, he assumed from the memory, but he didn't want to give her any indication that he had recalled anything. "Of course. Why wouldn't I be?"

Avery studied him. "You were feverish earlier. Anyway, we have a problem."

"What kind of problem?"

"The life-or-death kind."

Avery informed him that they were about to leave Africa, cross over the Mediterranean, then into European airspace on their way to Scotland.

"And?"

"And," Avery said, stretching the word out, "if the Europeans have sealed their borders like the US, like they did in Kenya, they might shoot us down."

That *was* a problem.

"Can we go around?"

"Not enough fuel."

"Refueling—"

"Is a bad idea," Avery said. "Every time we land, we take a risk. If we land at an airport, the host nation will probably take the plane and throw us in a cordon zone. That's best case."

Avery motioned toward Peyton. "Want me to wake Sleeping Beauty?"

"No," Desmond said quickly. "And don't call her that. She's tougher than you think."

Avery seemed annoyed. "It's not her toughness I have a problem with."

"She was just protecting her people on the ship, same as you would have done."

Avery ignored him. "What do you want to do?"

"Who's the most likely to shoot us down?"

"What? I have no idea."

"Who has the biggest air force?"

"I don't know. The UK. Germany. France. Italy."

"What about Spain?"

Avery thought a moment. "They've got the planes but not enough money to repair them and keep them flight-ready. Their economy has been in crisis for years." She nodded. "So we fly over Spain, roll the dice, try to get to Shetland."

"Speaking of which, what happens then? Surely they'll shoot us down."

"I'm working on that."

Before he could ask, she stood and made her way back to the cockpit. Desmond adjusted the rolled-up blanket under Peyton's head and watched her sleep for a moment.

He closed his eyes and settled down, trying to remember more of his past.

The SciNet IPO was a turning point in Desmond's life, in ways he never anticipated. The stock soared. On paper, his stake, a little less than one percent of the company, was worth 3.29 million dollars. In reality, all of his options were subject to an employee lockup provision that prevented him from selling shares or exer-cising options for six months after the IPO. They were the longest six months of his life, and everyone else's at SciNet.

Going public changed the company. The management team now constantly obsessed over the stock price and investor relations. Quarterly earnings became the only events that really mattered. They issued press releases all the time, hoping to garner more media attention.

Where they had thought strategically before, taken risks, and tried to build the business for the long term, now they played it safe, trying to hit their growth and revenue numbers (there were still no profits to report). It was the beginning of the end, and Desmond knew it. When the lockup period expired in August, the stock had drifted higher. A rising tide in 1999 had lifted all boats, most of all shares of hot dot-com companies. His shares were worth $7,840,000. He sold every one of them and resigned. Including the proceeds from his stock options in two other companies that had gone public, and one that had been acquired, he had netted just over nine million dollars in the last year.

Peyton had insisted that whatever he did with his shares in the companies, she would do too. He sold everything and put the proceeds in two separate bank accounts.

Separate wasn't what she wanted—in banking or otherwise. She had recently asked him to move in with her. He was hesitant, still afraid he would hurt her. But saying no would hurt her too. They bought a small cottage-style home in Palo Alto Hills. For him, it was the easiest move ever. He simply hooked up the Airstream, backed it into the driveway, and carried his few belongings inside.

Despite their windfall, Peyton didn't change one bit. She kept going to med school, studied her heart out, and decorated the house in her free time. She painted every room and put wallpaper in the half bath. There was always a home improvement project for the weekend. Desmond was pretty good at them, but he figured half of her motivation was to give him something to focus on. In the months after he quit SciNet, he mostly lay on the couch and read. Or surfed the web. The last six months while

SciNet was public had been grueling. He'd worked long hours on endless deadlines. The year before hadn't been much better. Taken together, he felt like he'd crammed twenty years of work into eighteen months. He was burned out. But that wasn't the full extent of his problems.

He had believed that financial freedom would be a breakthrough for him. That he would feel differently. He'd thought that on the other side of that train tunnel he'd finally relax and open himself fully to life—and in particular, to love. Love without fear, love with Peyton. But the wall was still there. He felt like a greyhound that had run the racetrack his entire life, chasing a stuffed rabbit, and had finally caught it—only to discover that the thing he had been chasing was of no use to him, that it had all been a fool's errand. He now knew the truth: his true issue was far deeper, at a more fundamental level.

He read texts on psychology and researched it on the internet. Peyton became increasingly worried, and presented a myriad of solutions.

"You need to exercise more, Des. You've been physically active your whole life."

He got a gym membership and began running with her every morning. They swam every Saturday. It didn't help. Neither did getting outside.

"Maybe you need to actually interact with people," she said. "I mean, being here all day alone would be tough on anyone."

He joined a book club and began taking classes at Stanford on subjects that interested him: astrophysics and psychology. He went to lunch at least twice a week with old colleagues. But he felt no different.

Peyton begged him to see a doctor.

"I feel like I'm watching you slip away, Des. Please. Do it for me."

At the family physician's office, he filled out a questionnaire. Inside the exam room, the doctor sat across from him and said, "First, know that what you're experiencing is very common. Depression affects people of all ages, all races, and at every

426

socio-economic level. Sometimes it's temporary, sometimes it's a chronic medical condition that must be managed throughout a person's life. And it is that: a medical condition. I'm going to prescribe a medication: a selective serotonin reuptake inhibitor, or SSRI. Many patients improve on SSRIs. In your case, with the severity of your symptoms, I would also strongly encourage you to see a psychotherapist who can identify other underlying issues that could be at play and help you identify triggers in your life that you can manage. I've seen many patients improve on medicine alone, but many more benefit from a combination of medicine and therapy."

The recommended psychotherapist was named Thomas Janson. He was in his sixties, with short gray hair and a kind smile. He listened as Desmond recounted his childhood and every major event up until he had walked in Dr. Janson's door. The man took copious notes, and when Desmond had finished, Dr. Janson told him that he believed he could help him. He just needed a few days to consider what he'd said.

When Desmond returned, the man sat in a club chair, a notebook in his lap, and spoke slowly, his voice even.

"I believe you have a disorder we call post-traumatic stress disorder. Or PTSD."

The diagnosis surprised Desmond.

"I suspect you developed the condition after the bushfire that killed your family and very nearly you as well. I believe you never recovered from that event. You never came to grips with that severe trauma. In fact, you were placed in a new environment with its own dangers and hostility: your uncle's care. Those first years were spent in near-constant fear of starvation or verbal abuse from your uncle. In your work on the rigs, you were in physical danger; your injuries attest to how real that threat was. And in the days after, when you and your uncle were," he glanced at the notebook, "blowing off steam, that is, drinking and fighting, the danger and fear never went away.

"You also never got to mourn your uncle's death—or frankly to unpack your feelings about him at all. You were in danger the instant he passed, even having to fight for your life, to kill a man, which is in itself an *incredibly* traumatic event. The fact that you processed it with little emotion at all is evidence of the vast amount of pre-existing emotional scar tissue.

"Our brains are like a muscle, Desmond: they become conditioned to the strain they must endure. We are an exceptionally adaptive species. We change to survive in the environment in which we exist. For you, that environment has been one of near-constant danger. From the moment that fire took your parents, you have been in physical or emotional danger your entire life. Even after you came to California, you feared someone from Oklahoma would find you, arrest you. You feared you'd lose the money your uncle left you.

"But I believe perhaps the greatest issue affecting you is the people you've lost in your life. Your family. The librarian," he peeked at the notebook again, "Agnes. Your uncle. Everyone you've become emotionally invested in has been taken from you. Not just taken, but taken at a moment when you least expected it. Your mind, subconsciously, is now trying to protect you. It has seen this pattern before: you want to love, to care. But the moment you do, the object of your affection is ripped away. It won't let you. You are at war with your own mind."

Desmond sat for a moment, considering everything Dr. Janson had said. "Okay. Let's assume I agree with your diagnosis. How do I fix it?"

"Well, that's a tougher question. You didn't get this way overnight, Desmond. Nor will your condition resolve quickly. It will take time. And some faith on your part. Hope is also a powerful thing."

He encouraged Desmond to continue taking the medication and to establish a regular schedule of two visits per week.

The gloom Desmond felt was a sharp contrast to the euphoria around Silicon Valley. A new company seemed to go public every week, minting millionaires by the hundreds. Desmond was skeptical. Warren Buffett's adage, "When others are fearful, be greedy; when others are greedy, be fearful," seemed like good advice in the current environment. He invested his and Peyton's money in bonds. With a small portion of his funds, he placed bets against companies he thought were poised for a fall. Having been inside a dot-com startup, he could evaluate their technology and read through the BS in the earnings reports and press releases. He spent his days listening to quarterly investor conference calls and researching companies.

Desmond's bets failed at first. In the fall of 1999 and early 2000, he lost nearly half a million dollars. It seemed to him like the whole world had gone crazy. In 1999, there were 457 IPOs; most were tech companies. Of those, 117 saw their stock prices double on the first day of trading. And the euphoria wasn't limited to new companies. On November 25, 1998, Books-A-Million announced an update to their website. Their stock increased over one thousand percent that week.

Some companies were using their stock to snap up every hot startup they could. Yahoo bought Broadcast.com for $5.9 billion in stock and GeoCities for $3.57 billion in stock. A Spanish telecom company acquired Lycos for $12.5 billion (a few years later, they would unload it for less than $96 million—a loss of over 99% of their investment). In January 2000, AOL bought TimeWarner in the second largest merger in history. During the Super Bowl that month, sixteen dot-com companies ran ads. They cost two million dollars each.

The stock market soared. And crashed, in March 2000, with stocks falling as hard as they had risen. Over the next two and half years, stocks shed over five trillion dollars in value. People flocked to bonds, and Desmond's bearish wagers paid off. Their nine-million-dollar fortune was nineteen at the end of 2000, fifteen after taxes. He played it safe after that, diversifying and buying only a few high quality stocks.

Every week Desmond heard about another one of his friends who had lost their job or seen their company collapse. He felt for them. The memory of xTV's sudden collapse and his days of pork and beans in the months after were still fresh in his mind. He did the only thing he could: he took folks out to lunch, always picked up the tab, and tried to connect people with jobs when he heard about them. Their stories were horrifying.

The layoffs were nerve-wracking affairs. Large groups would be led into conference rooms and told they were being let go; consultants handed out packets with details. In some cases, the consultants even surprised the HR people conducting the layoffs by handing them a folder with their walking papers, right after the dismissals of everyone else.

The coffee shops that had teemed with bright-eyed entrepreneurs with the next big idea, written out on a napkin, were now packed with people working on their resumes, which they tweaked and proofread and scrutinized before printing them on thick paper stock so they would stand out. Startup execs who had been worth millions on paper found themselves broke, moving back in with their parents or in-laws. Many employees whose companies had gone public never made it past the lockup period to sell any of their shares before their companies folded.

Desmond watched it all in disbelief; it seemed the world had only two extremes: charging up the hill wide open, or free falling over a cliff.

He was in his own kind of free fall. Every month he grew less optimistic about his prognosis. The medication helped. So did the sessions with Dr. Jansen. But Desmond had plateaued. He wasn't making any real progress.

Peyton was. He watched as she changed, little by little. She took pride in her schoolwork and was near the top of her class. She was blossoming, becoming an incredible woman. She was ready for something more. That worried him. He wondered if he could ever be the man she deserved.

Christmas 2000 came and went; they had a little tree in the home in Palo Alto Hills and kept up their tradition of ten dollars or less in gifts. Peyton cheated though: hers was a box with a model aeroplane inside.

"It's great."

"The aeroplane's not the gift, Des." She grabbed his hand and squeezed it. "Let's go on a trip—back to Australia, to where you were born. Visit the remains of the home. Go to Oklahoma, where you grew up."

He knew what she wanted: for him to visit the places that had caused him so much pain and somehow come to grips with what had happened and move on.

He agreed. He was desperate enough to try anything.

In Australia, he walked across the paddocks where he'd once played. He visited the thicket where he'd built the fort that day, even straightened the overturned rocks he'd set down eighteen years ago. The house was still there, or at least its burned remains. He stood in the yard, inside the fence, where he'd rushed into the fire. There was no breakthrough. He didn't cry. He felt only sadness.

They stayed in a hotel in Adelaide for a week while he tried to find Charlotte. But since Desmond didn't know her last name, it was impossible to find her. Over a hundred thousand people had been part of the relief efforts in the wake of the 1983 bushfires. And it had been almost eighteen years; she might have left the area, or left Australia altogether.

In Oklahoma City, they rented a car and drove south, through Norman, then Noble, and finally onto Slaughterville Road.

He pulled off at the home where he'd grown up. Orville's home. It had been part of a farm once, but the farmland had been sold, maybe by Orville himself or someone who'd owned it before him.

The new owners had painted the home and put on a new roof. The asphalt shingles sparkled in the clear April day. A Chevy truck and a Ford sedan sat under a newly erected metal carport. A red Huffy bike sat on the front porch. It was about the size of the one Desmond had bought at the pawnshop—the bike Orville had threatened to take away.

The shed stood open. The old Studebaker was gone. Desmond's eyes lingered on the patch of ground where Dale Epply had bled to death all those years ago.

Peyton put an arm around him.

"You want to go in?"

"No. I've seen enough."

They drove past the grocery store that had sustained him, up Highway 77 into Noble. The small town hadn't changed much. They ate at a small cafe on Third Street and walked the three blocks to the library.

A girl a few years younger than Desmond sat behind the counter, a mechanical pencil in her hand, a large book open in front of her. Another University of Oklahoma student, if he had to guess.

"Help you?" she asked.

"Nah. Just looking."

He walked down the fiction aisle, Peyton close behind him. He spotted a few of the paperbacks he'd read as a kid: *Island of the Blue Dolphins, Hatchet, Hyperion.* He could even remember where he was when he read them.

The place had barely changed. The only addition was a wooden study carrel in one corner. It held a Gateway computer with a seventeen-inch monitor. A plaque on the top of the carrel read, *Pioneer Library System Technology Center Provided in Loving Memory of Agnes T. Andrews.*

It was the best thing he'd ever read in that library. He took Peyton's hand.

"Let's go home."

CHAPTER 74

IN THE PLANE'S cockpit, Avery stared in disbelief. Spain was dark except for a few glimmering lights in what she thought was Barcelona. They'd launched no fighters to pursue the Red Cross plane. Air traffic control hadn't even engaged her. She wondered what was going on down there and how many people were left.

On the navigation screen their destination loomed: the Shetland Islands, north of Scotland. She'd never heard of the place and found herself wondering what they'd find there. On the satellite map, there was only a forest. Was it a trap? Avery feared it might be. But she had no choice.

She engaged the autopilot, stood, stretched her legs, and walked back into the passenger compartment. Desmond and Peyton lay in sleeping bags, both facing forward, Peyton tucked into Desmond like a little spoon.

Avery leaned against the door frame and stared. She'd have to make a decision soon. A hard one.

☣

On September 11th, 2001, Desmond sat in the light-filled living room in Palo Alto, Peyton at his side, both staring in disbelief. The news channel showed a live view of Manhattan. The people in the buildings were burning alive, just as Desmond's family had in 1983. This tragedy, however, wasn't a natural disaster. It was

433

an act of humankind—the worst kind of evil. The sickening, cruel slaughter of innocents.

"Something is very wrong with this world," Desmond said. "I couldn't agree more."

The US stock market stayed closed until September 17th—the longest closing since 1933, during the Great Depression. When it reopened, stocks tanked. The market fell 684 points—the largest single day decline in history. By the end of the week, the Dow Jones Industrial Average was down over fourteen percent. The S&P lost almost twelve percent. Nearly 1.4 trillion dollars in market value was lost in that week alone.

While others were dumping American stocks, Desmond was buying. He returned to his criteria for identifying a successful company: a founder who instinctively knew what his customers wanted, and a tightly managed operation. He loaded up on stock in Amazon and Apple.

On the news every night, he watched sabers rattle and the world go to war. He was mad as hell too. He even considered applying at the NSA or CIA. But he barely had the energy to get out of bed. He seemed to get worse every month.

Peyton saw it and couldn't help but worry.

"What if you start your own company?"

"Doing what? Why? There's no point. I have no ideas. No drive to do it."

"You could start a nonprofit. Child welfare. Find something you care about."

He thought about it for a few weeks, researched it, and began volunteering at a group home in San Jose.

That helped him pass the time, but it wasn't enough. Deep down, he knew the truth: he was never going to change. He would never be able to love Peyton the way she loved him—with reckless abandon. It wasn't fair to her. She deserved more.

In the summer of 2002, he sat in Dr. Janson's office.

"This isn't working."

"It takes time, Desmond."

"I've given it time. I've been coming here for over two years now. I've tried medication, exercise, volunteering. Hell, we even retraced the tragic events of my childhood. I'm not getting better. I don't feel any better than I did the day I walked in here."

"Please realize that every person has emotional limits. Your... range may simply be very confined. It's also possible that two years isn't enough time."

"You want to know what I actually do feel?"

Janson raised his eyebrows.

"Guilt."

The man looked confused.

"I feel guilty because I know she'll never leave me. And I'll never make her as happy as she deserves to be."

That afternoon, Desmond packed his things. The gifts from Peyton he placed very carefully in a large trunk. He scanned all their pictures, printed copies of them, and returned them to their frames. He waited in the living room, and when she got home, they sat on the couch, feet from each other. She was nervous, clearly aware something was very wrong. He said the lines he'd rehearsed a dozen times.

"I have this vision of you in a few years. It's summer. You're sitting on your back porch, drinking a glass of wine while the kids play in the yard. Your husband is manning the grill. And he's playing in the back yard with the kids, and he knows exactly what to do, because he played in his back yard as a kid with his dad, who loved him. You all eat together, and he knows exactly how to treat you because he grew up with an actual mom and dad and they treated each other right. He reads a story to the kids before he puts them to bed, because his parents did that for him. When they act up, he knows what to do by instinct, not because he read it in a book, but because it's how he was raised, in a normal home. And he loves you. And them. Because he's able to love, because he hasn't drifted from one tragedy to the next in the years before he met you. Your life isn't perfect, but it has a real chance to be, because one of you isn't broken beyond repair."

"Desmond, I don't care—"

"I know you don't. I know that you will stay with me wherever our road leads."

"I will."

"But I won't let you."

"Desmond."

"I care too much about you, Peyton. You deserve to be happy."

"I am happy."

"Not as happy as you will be."

She hugged him and cried more than he'd ever seen her cry.

"I'm sorry. I'm so sorry."

"Please stay."

"I'll stay the night."

She looked him in the eye. "Stay until Monday. Please?"

He agreed. They were the most agonizing and joyous three days of his entire life. They made love every night and twice each day. It was a long goodbye. It was painful—even he felt it. He couldn't imagine what she was going through.

When he stepped out on the front porch Monday morning, she hugged him so hard he thought his ribs would collapse.

He pushed back just enough to look her in the eye. "Will you do something for me?"

"Anything."

"Don't wait for me. Live your life."

That set off a new bout of crying.

An hour later, he was driving south, the Airstream trailer in tow behind him.

He camped in Yosemite National Park, then Sequoia, and hiked through Death Valley. He read at night. And he thought long and hard about his next move. Each day, the solution became clearer. If he couldn't save himself, he would save others. That was a goal he could get excited about. That was worth living for. Before, his idea of setting up a nonprofit or focusing on child welfare had been the right idea—but on the wrong scale. He wanted to do something big. He wanted to change the world—to help create a world where no one grew up the way he had.

He set up shop on Sand Hill Road. Rents there had once been the most expensive in the world. Now the former offices of a dozen recently closed venture capital firms sat empty. They were all decorated lavishly. Desmond negotiated as hard as he had with the pawnbroker for the bike so many years ago. He moved in the following week and began making calls, putting the word out that he had a new investment firm with a different focus. Thanks to the soaring stock market, he had eighty million dollars to spend. Capital was in short supply in the Valley. His inbox filled. The phone rang off the hook. But nothing was quite what he was looking for.

He named his firm Icarus Capital. In Greek mythology, Icarus was the son of Daedalus, the craftsman who built the Labyrinth. In order to escape the island of Crete, Daedalus created wings of feathers and wax for his son. He warned Icarus: *If you fly too high, the sun will melt your wings. If you fly too low, the sea's dampness will weigh you down.* The story rang true to Desmond. The market's exuberance and implosion were in league with the allegory of Icarus, but so was life. People who flew too high—who lived beyond their means and ability—were bound for failure. As were those who never took a chance.

Despite his belief that his emotional growth had plateaued indefinitely, Desmond interviewed several psychotherapists. One suggested he talk to a firm that was developing a novel therapy. It was experimental, he said, but worth checking out. The company was called Rapture Therapeutics.

Desmond was stunned when he heard the name. He still remembered it from SciNet; it was one of the three mysterious companies that had been funded by Citium Holdings and Invisible Sun Securities.

A week later, he sat in Rapture's office in San Francisco. The company's chief scientist held up a pill.

"This is a fifty-milligram antidepressant. You and I could both take the same fifty-milligram pill, and you might have four times the physiological reaction that I do. What's the difference? It's the way your body metabolizes the drug. How it processes it. For doctors, and for patients, that's a problem."

"What's the solution?"

"Bypassing medicine altogether. At Rapture, we've built an implant that's placed inside the brain. It monitors brain chemistry and releases chemicals the brain needs—when it needs them. Imagine a world without schizophrenia, bipolar disorder, or depression—just to name a few. The market potential is nearly unlimited."

"I'm interested. I've tried medication, but it hasn't worked for me. What I'm most interested in is memory alteration."

The scientist scrutinized him. "What do you mean?"

"I'm interested in erasing painful memories. Starting over, if you will."

A pause.

"We don't currently have a technology or procedure to do that, Mr. Hughes."

"But you're working on something."

"Nothing we're ready to discuss at this time."

☣

Desmond underwent the implant procedure. He kept his expectations low but almost immediately he felt results. The depression lifted. He was more excited about work. He looked forward to things. And he feared that it would all go away if the implant failed or if Rapture as a company folded. He became obsessed with the organization. He made calls, requested company filings that weren't public. He got nowhere.

Finally, he requested a meeting with the CEO and CFO.

"I want to invest," he said.

The CEO's voice was flat. "We're very well funded."

"By whom?"

"Our investors prefer to remain anonymous."

"Citium Holdings? Invisible Sun Securities?"

He could have heard a pin drop in the room. Both executives excused themselves. They were scared.

Desmond researched Citium and Invisible Sun endlessly. Some of their corporate filings were public by necessity. They owned shares in a dozen companies—and they had donated millions to nonprofits and foundations he had never heard of. The nonprofits were funneling all that money into research at government and private organizations. They were funding projects in genetics and medical science, advanced energy technologies, and supercomputing. What did it mean? And why were they so secretive?

Increasingly, Desmond became consumed with unraveling the Citium mystery. But try as he might, he couldn't connect the dots. Every avenue led to a dead end.

For the most part, he lived a solitary life. He owned a small house in Menlo Park, rode his bike to work every day, and occasionally had lunch with an old colleague. He watched his investments grow and the seasons change like a time-lapse photograph, his own life in fast forward, slipping away.

He thought about Peyton almost every day. He had set up a web search alert for her name. He opened the emails instantly whenever something popped up. She graduated from medical school, began her residency and then was accepted to the CDC's EIS program. That made him happy. She had kept her promise to move on with her life.

Like Desmond, she had lost many of the people she had come to love: her father, brother, and now him. He hoped she wouldn't suffer his fate. He wanted to see her fall in love, get married, have children. He knew that was what she wanted, deep down, no matter what she said.

To him, the most terrifying possibility was that her time with him had made her unable to love; that by being with her, he had infected her with the fear of commitment that lay deep inside him.

On a cool November morning, a man pushed open the glass door to Desmond's office and strode inside. He was in his sixties or seventies, with short white hair and a pale face. His eyes were blank, unmoving, as if he were holding still for a medical procedure.

Desmond hadn't bothered to hire an assistant—there wasn't enough work for one.

He didn't have anything scheduled for that day.

"NextGen Capital is across the hall."

"I've come to see you, Mr. Hughes."

"What's this regarding?"

"Citium Holdings."

The words hung in the air, neither man moving for a moment. Desmond held out an arm. "Let's speak in the conference room, Mister…"

"Pachenko. Yuri Pachenko."

He walked past Desmond, seated himself, and declined an offer for water. He took his raincoat off, which was covered with a light film of water. Scars covered his forearms—burn scars, similar to the ones on Desmond's legs. Desmond immediately averted his eyes when he realized what they were.

In a slow, level voice, Yuri asked, "What are you trying to create here, Mr. Hughes?" His English was excellent, his accent slightly British.

"Please, call me Desmond. Ah, if you're asking about Icarus Capital, we invest in companies with the potential to shape the future. We—"

Yuri held a hand up, waited for Desmond to stop.

"You misunderstand me. I'd like to hear what you don't tell everyone who walks through your door. Tell me your true vision, the one you think might scare people, the one you fear is too grand."

Desmond leaned back in the chair. There was something about this man. His serenity, his directness. Desmond instantly felt a level of trust with Yuri. He let the words spill out. He was almost shocked to hear himself saying them.

"I want to create a world where no child has to watch their

family burn. Where no child is raised by someone who doesn't love them. A world where madmen don't fly planes into buildings and the economy's more than a worldwide casino."

"And what else?"

Desmond hesitated and glanced away.

"That's the world you want to create. What do *you* want, Desmond?"

"I want to create a world where any person can be repaired, no matter how broken their body, mind or heart."

A smiled curled the corners of Yuri's mouth. "You think that's possible?"

"I believe we're witnessing the beginning stages of a technology explosion that will someday make anything possible."

"What if I told you that the technology you're describing is already in development?"

"Is that what Citium is building?"

"Among other things."

"What sorts of other things?"

"Projects that would interest you. Projects that would give you what you so dearly desire: purpose, the potential to truly change this world. Are you interested, Desmond?"

"Yes."

They spoke for almost two hours. At the end of their meeting, Desmond committed to come to London, where more details would be revealed.

As he was walking Yuri to the door, he asked, "What's it called? The device you're building?"

"The Looking Glass."

DAY 11

5,200,000,000 infected
2,000,000 dead

CHAPTER 75

THE RED CROSS plane flew through the night over the Atlantic, toward the Shetland Islands.

Over Spain, Avery had made a tough decision: to fly around Great Britain and Ireland. They had been lucky that no planes had intercepted them while crossing Continental Europe; she was less optimistic about flying over the UK. But going around meant burning more fuel, so it was a costly gambit. As the southern tip of Shetland loomed, fifty miles away, the plane's engines began sputtering. She wiped her palms on her pants, depositing the nervous sweat. She gripped the yoke and disabled the autopilot.

As she began their descent, she realized fuel wasn't their only problem. Or their biggest.

☢

In the passenger compartment, the sound of the sputtering engines woke Peyton. She lay in a sleeping bag on the plane's floor facing Desmond.

He was looking back at her.

The engines sputtered again. The plane was descending rapidly.

Desmond realized it too; he stood, gripped the back of a chair, pulled himself toward the cockpit door, and threw it open.

Peyton followed close behind. In the pilot's seat, Avery was frantically twisting dials on the instrument panel.

In her headset, she said, "Scatsta ATC, do you copy?"

Through the plane's windshield, Peyton saw a wall of white. The cloud broke, and she got her first glimpse of the ground: dark green rolling hills, poking through a blanket of thick fog.

The night sky was streaked in shades of bright green and blue. She'd never seen anything like it. It took her breath away. She knew what she was seeing: the Aurora Borealis. It seemed to be pointing their way, fighting a losing battle with the fog.

A wind shear hit the plane. Peyton lost her balance and fell into Desmond, who steadied himself with one hand and caught her with the other. Instead of releasing her, he kept his arm around her, gripping her shoulder, pressing her body to his.

"How's it going, Avery?"

"Peachy." She didn't look back. She worked the yoke, trying to keep the plane level. "We're out of fuel. No visibility. Gale force winds. Air traffic control isn't responding."

The plane rocked again in the force of the wind.

"Oh, and I should also mention: this is *by far* the largest plane I've ever flown. Just saying."

Desmond took his arm away from Peyton, leaning forward to make eye contact with Avery. "Look, you can do this. We're not expecting a miracle, okay? Just slow it down and get us on the ground."

Avery said nothing, only nodded.

"How can we help?"

The sarcasm was absent from Avery's tone when she replied. "Just strap yourself in tight. Make sure there're no loose items. And put your helmet and body armor on."

In the passenger compartment, Desmond helped strap Avery's body armor onto Peyton. She inhaled sharply when he tightened the strap; her chest was still badly bruised from her escape from the *Kentaro Maru*.

"Too tight?" he asked.

She gritted her teeth. "It's fine."

They put helmets on and buckled themselves into seats along the aisle, away from the plane's sides. As the wind tossed the aircraft, Peyton stared at the aurora. Streaks of light green crossed the sky in curving forms, as if an artist had painted the black sky with phosphorescent paint.

They were dropping quickly now. The wind picked up with each passing second. Peyton put her hands on the seat in front of her and braced herself.

Outside the windows, the aurora disappeared, replaced by fog.

The tires barked as they caught pavement. The plane shuddered and barreled down the runway, then bounced and shook when it slipped off the pavement. Seconds later, it came to a halt.

Desmond unbuckled himself and sprang up. He opened the cockpit door and grabbed Avery by the shoulders.

"Good flying, A."

Peyton thought he was going to embrace Avery, but he held her at arm's length, staring at her.

Avery smiled.

"If anything had been on the runway, we'd be dead," she said.

"But it wasn't. You did great."

Avery looked exhausted. Peyton realized she hadn't seen the woman sleep since their escape. She looked like she might collapse right then and there.

Instead, she marched into the passenger compartment and stopped in front of Peyton.

"I need my body armor."

Peyton didn't like the woman's brusqueness, but with a nod she stripped the black garment off—a little self-consciously, as if she were on display. Avery donned it, grabbed her rifle and night vision goggles, and turned to Desmond.

"We need to secure the tower and refuel. If we get jammed up here, I want to be ready to leave."

☣

When Desmond and Avery were gone, Peyton finally relaxed. The plan called for her to wait in the plane for now—which was fine by her.

She felt the fever she had barely noticed before. Her mind's

447

eye flashed to the people at Mandera Hospital, suffering, dying. Without a cure, that would likely be her fate. She had traveled to Mandera almost a week ago. If she assumed she'd been infected for five to seven days...

She pushed the thought out of her mind. She had to focus.

She set about organizing their supplies and strained to hear any sound of gunfire or struggle. The fog was still thick on the runway and around the plane.

After what seemed like hours, she heard someone jogging on the paved runway. The sound stopped when the person or persons hit the grass near the plane. Instinctively, Peyton moved to the cockpit, ready to close the door and seal herself off if necessary.

Boots pounded the staircase, and Desmond appeared in the doorway.

"Miss me?"

Peyton exhaled.

"You scared me to death."

Outside, she heard the roar of a truck engine.

"What'd you find?"

"The airport is deserted. There's a fuel truck. We're going to fill up, get the plane back on the runway in case we need to leave in a hurry."

When they had the plane fueled and back on the runway, the three of them sat in the passenger compartment.

To Desmond, Avery said, "Any memories?"

"Nothing."

Peyton was amazed at how easily he lied. It scared her a little. Avery's reaction gave no hint as to whether she believed him.

They discussed what to do next, finally agreeing that Avery needed to sleep and that Desmond and Peyton would take one of the airport vehicles to the GPS coordinates. They would radio back if they needed help. Avery didn't like it, but she consented reluctantly. Not only did she need the sleep, but splitting up had one advantage: if something did go wrong at the site, she could potentially rescue them.

Desmond and Peyton found the keys to an old Citroen SUV in the airport's office, and pulled out onto a paved two-lane road that wound through the green, rolling landscape. The GPS location was about forty miles from the airport in an area of wooded hills. The fog hung heavy on the road; the headlights barely cut through it. The aurora loomed above, its green glow like a homing beacon. Peyton studied the aurora's curving lines; they were like the plasma contrails of a spaceship in a sci-fi movie.

As Desmond drove, he told Peyton what he had remembered. For a very long time, Peyton had wanted to know what had happened after he left her on the doorstep of their little bungalow in Palo Alto. She had thought about him for countless hours since that day. Hearing the full story was nearly surreal to her, a blank page of their life together now filled in.

Desmond's memories ended with Yuri Pachenko walking into his office in Menlo Park. The description of the man was vaguely familiar to Peyton. So was the name. But she couldn't place either one.

"Do you know where they're keeping the cure?" she asked.

"No." He glanced over at her. "Did you ever get married?"

Peyton shook her head.

"Because of me."

"Because of life, Desmond. It's not your fault. And it's in the past, okay?"

"Not for me."

They rode in silence a moment.

Peyton spoke first. "Do you remember Avery?"

"No."

"I still don't trust her."

"Same here. But she's given us no reason not to yet."

Peyton changed the subject. "How do you feel?"

"Like my head's going to split open." He studied her. "What about you?"

"I'm fine."

"Be honest. You're getting worse, aren't you?"

"Getting sick's an occupational hazard. I accepted the risks when I went to work at the CDC."

"Well, I don't accept it."

Peyton stared out the windshield.

"You're not going to die like this, Peyton."

She massaged her aching neck; the turbulent landing had done more damage than she'd realized. "I'm usually the one telling sick people I'm going to fix them."

"Well, I think you deserve a week off."

They drove in silence after that. Peyton didn't see a single building outside—no homes, no businesses. Except for the paved road that carved through the hills, this place was untouched by civilization.

"We're coming up on it," she said as she studied the Labyrinth Reality app. "A hundred yards to destination."

Desmond slowed the car. "Direction?"

"Roughly ten o'clock."

The road curved to the right. There was no driveway or path leading in the coordinates' direction. Desmond pulled the car off the road and parked.

"Stay here."

"No way."

"Peyton—"

"I'm coming with you."

"All right," he said, resigned. It was the reaction of someone who had been married twenty years and knew when an argument was futile.

Outside the car, they crept into the forest. The ground rose with every step; the road sat in a valley. Ancient evergreen trees surrounded them. Between their canopy and the fog, the light of the moon and the aurora faded away. Peyton could see less than twenty feet ahead of them.

She touched Desmond's shoulder, then pointed at the flashlight she held, silently asking if she should switch it on.

He shook his head no. His rifle was slung over his shoulder, a handgun in one hand. With his other hand, he reached back, took Peyton's hand, and led her through the dark forest.

It was utterly quiet. She heard no animals stirring, no birds calling. When she stepped on a branch and snapped it, the sound seemed deafening. Desmond froze.

"Sorry," she whispered.

He waited for any reaction, any sound. But the forest remained still.

"Distance?"

Peyton activated the phone. "Thirty yards. Straight ahead."

Desmond crept forward, the gun held out now.

Peyton held her breath as they walked the last ten yards. The fog seemed to close in on all sides.

The phone beeped. A message popped up:

Labyrinth Entrance Reached

Desmond took the flashlight from her hand, turned it on, and panned around the area, cutting through the fog. Suddenly he stopped.

Peyton saw it too. Her first thought was it's going to explode.

CHAPTER 76

DESMOND CREPT TOWARD the small metal box that lay on the ground. "Stay back," he whispered. "Could be booby trapped."

She retreated behind a tree ten yards away and watched him draw his combat knife. With the serrated edge, he sawed a limb off a nearby tree, cut the branches off, and used it to flip the box open.

To Peyton's relief, nothing happened.

Still cautious, Desmond stepped forward. He bent down, drew a small scrap of paper from the box, and exhaled.

"It's a new set of GPS coordinates," he said.

"Where?" Peyton asked.

He took the phone out and typed on it. "Still in Shetland. Maybe twenty or thirty miles from here, I think. We can drive."

An alert popped up on the phone's screen. It was a message from the Labyrinth Reality app:

1. Entrance Located.

She showed the message to Desmond.

He paused. "It's the same message as before, when I opened the app in Dadaab."

He took the phone and clicked the message. A map appeared. The location was in south Australia, near the coast. It was rural, and as Desmond zoomed in, Peyton saw a dark spot in a green and brown landscape. He zoomed in, and Peyton's mouth went dry.

Desmond was silent. They had gone there together, fifteen years ago—to Desmond's childhood home. The burned remains were more overgrown now, but the charred foundation of the old ranch house still rose above the weeds. There was no indication anything had changed, but Peyton didn't know how old the satellite images were. Someone or something could be there now. Or could have been hidden there, just like at this location.

"What do you think?" she asked.

He glanced at the phone, then at the scrap of paper with the nearby GPS coordinates. "I say we check out the coordinates here, then we can decide on going to Australia."

"Should we call Avery?" Peyton asked.

"No. Not until we know what's going on."

☣

A tree-mounted, motion-activated wireless camera came to life when Desmond entered the site. The individual who had been monitoring the feed woke and watched anxiously. It wouldn't be long now.

☣

Desmond and Peyton drove through the night. The fog was still heavy, but Peyton thought it was starting to lift. A constant breeze buffeted the car, as if they were driving through a giant wind tunnel. The road curved left and right as they went deeper into the mountains of Shetland.

At five hundred yards from the destination, a dirt road split off from the paved road. Desmond leaned over and saw on the phone that it led to the coordinates. He reached into his backpack and pulled the night vision goggles out. He cut the car's headlights as he pulled the goggles on and started down the dirt road.

Three hundred yards later, he killed the engine.

"We'll hike in."

They walked along the tree line of the dirt road that weaved through the forest. It ended in a clearing with a small cottage. There was no sign of life: no lights glowing through the windows, no smoke rising from the chimney. The rubble stone exterior was shades of gray, blue and purple; moss grew on the wooden roof. The place looked ancient, as if it had been built in the Middle Ages and abandoned.

In the dim light, Desmond gave Peyton a look that said, *Stay here.*

He didn't wait for her to respond, merely handed her the key to the car and ran toward the cottage, rifle held at the ready.

Peyton held her breath as he went around the right side of the house. Ten seconds passed. Then twenty. Lights came on, the front door opened, and Desmond walked out onto the porch. He waved her toward the house.

When she reached the steps, he said, "You've gotta see this."

She stepped inside and stared.

Cork covered the walls, and pictures, articles, and scribbled notes were tacked everywhere. Peyton recognized some of the names: Rapture Therapeutics, Phaethon Genetics, Rook Quantum Sciences, Rendition Games. There were pictures of Desmond and Conner. She scanned the scribbled notes:

> *Invisible Sun—person, organization, or project?*
> *What requires that much energy?*
> *Third world used as a testing ground?*

Some of the newspaper clippings went back as far as the eighties.

Whoever had lived here was obviously investigating the Citium. Had been for a long time. And they had only recently left. In the kitchen, dishes with food particles lay in the sink. On the kitchen island, a laptop sat closed.

"The place has power," Desmond said, turning on a small space heater. Peyton was glad for the warmth. "There's a solar array behind the house and likely on the back side of the roof. It's completely off-grid though."

Three filing cabinets lined one wall. Peyton was about to open the first when Desmond called out, "Over here."

He stood in the living room, tapping his foot on a floorboard. "You hear that?"

Peyton shook her head. *What's he doing?*

He grabbed a fire poker that hung beside the stone hearth, jammed it into the floor, and pried the board loose. A safe with a dial lock lay underneath. Desmond worked faster, ripping the adjacent boards free until it was completely uncovered. He gripped the dial and began spinning it.

Peyton crouched beside him. "You know the combination?"

"Maybe," he mumbled.

He tried the handle, but it didn't budge.

"What did you try?"

"The combination to Orville's safe."

Peyton instantly realized his theory: *He thinks he created all this—that it's his research.*

He glanced at her. "Ideas?"

When they had found the box in the woods, Peyton had wondered why someone would have hidden GPS coordinates there—why they were given two locations instead of just being directed straight here to the cottage. "The first location. It has to serve a purpose."

Desmond nodded. "Yes. Maybe it was to ensure the right people found this place—and that they had the key to finding whatever's hidden here."

He spun the dial again, using the GPS coordinates of the first location. The handle clicked this time, and he pulled the metal door open. A stack of pages lay inside.

The top sheet had a single line of handwritten text in large block letters.

HOW THE CITIUM LOST ITS WAY

Desmond flipped the page over, revealing a handwritten note below. He and Peyton read it together.

If you're reading this, the worst has occurred. The world will soon change. The enemy we face is more capable than any government or army the world has ever seen.

I believe, however, that they can be stopped. To do so, you must understand their origins, their history, and their true intentions. The pages included here reveal those things. It is the greatest and perhaps only weapon I can offer you.

First, you should know that the Order of Citium began with good intentions. They were a noble organization. A group of faith. They had rituals and beliefs, though they recognized no deities. They worshiped at the altar of science, and in science they believed they would find answers to our deepest questions—including one in particular that they called the great question: Why do we exist?

They went to great lengths to pursue that answer. But they lost their way. In a desert in New Mexico, on a July morning in 1945, an event occurred that changed the Citium forever. I know of that transformation because my father witnessed it; I have enclosed his story, which I have rewritten based on what he told me. The remainder of the pages contain my own story. I hope it will lead you to the key to stopping the Citium. Hurry.

—William

"William," Peyton said. "There's no last name. Do you remember him?"

"No." Desmond studied the pages under the letter, scanning them. "But I take it he was one of my allies. Maybe an informant."

"Makes sense. What do you want to do? Should we call Avery?"

"No," he said quickly. "Let's see what we've got here, read this, then search the rest of the house."

Peyton agreed, and they sat down on the worn couch in the living room. It was in the low forties outside, and it felt even colder inside. The small heater wasn't enough. She glanced at the fireplace, but decided the smoke it would generate would be too much of a risk. She opted instead to drape the thick quilt from the couch over her, and she slid closer to Desmond and spread it across him as well. The warmth of their body heat slowly filled the small space under the quilt.

He studied her face. She knew what he was thinking: this was just like Palo Alto, that small house they had shared fifteen years ago. She felt it too, them slipping back into that place they used to be. But there was too much going on for her to even think about that. She lifted the pages and began to read.

CHAPTER 77

MY FATHER'S NAME was Robert Moore. He was a scientist at perhaps the most important time and place for scientists—a moment when science ended a war and changed the world.

On that day, in July 1945, he slept only one hour, dressed in his best suit, and drove through the desert to the test site. At the gate, security made him step out of his car, so they could search it extensively.

The mood across the base was tense. Inside the control station, the project director was bordering on a breakdown. Several times, General Leslie Groves had to guide the man outside, where they walked in the darkness through the rain, the general assuring him all would go as planned.

Shortly before five-thirty a.m., the countdown began. The seconds were the longest of Robert's life.

The team had nicknamed the device the Gadget. It was the product of half a decade of work by some of the greatest scientific minds ever assembled. That morning, the Gadget sat atop a one-hundred-foot-tall steel tower. Desert stretched in every direction. The control station where the scientists waited was nearly six miles away. Even at that distance, Robert donned welder's goggles and focused through the tinted glass. He saw only darkness in the seconds before the countdown reached zero.

The flash of white light came first. It lasted for a few seconds, then a wave of heat passed through him, soaking his face and hands. When the wall of light faded, he could make out a column of fire rising from the site, expanding quickly.

The cloud broke through a temperature inversion at seventeen thousand feet—which most scientists had thought impossible. For minutes after the explosion, the cloud rose into the sky, reaching the substratosphere at over thirty-five thousand feet.

Forty seconds after the detonation, the shock wave reached the scientists in the control station. The sound of the blast followed shortly after. It had the quality of distant thunder, reverberating off the nearby hills for several seconds, giving the impression of a storm. The sound was heard up to a hundred miles away; the light from the explosion was seen from almost twice as far.

The blast instantly vaporized the steel tower that held the bomb, leaving a crater nearly half a mile wide in its place. An iron pipe set in concrete, four inches in diameter, sixteen feet tall, and fifteen hundred feet away from the detonation, was also vaporized. In the control station, there was silence. In place of the worry that had led up to the event, every person who had seen it now felt awe. And uncertainty.

As if coming out of a trance, the team members looked around, unsure what to do. Some shook hands, congratulating each other. A few people laughed. Several cried. All believed that in the New Mexico desert that morning, the world had changed forever.

The first atomic bomb had been detonated. They hoped it would be the last.

☣

Back at Los Alamos, a team member raised a glass. "To the dawn of the Atomic Age."

Many had feared the test would be a dud. Most of them now felt relief; for a few it was fear.

Robert spoke for the first time since the Trinity test. "Yes, a new age indeed. We have given the human race something it has never possessed before: the means with which to destroy itself."

When no one responded, he added, "How long will it be before a madman acquires our device and uses it? Five years? Ten? A hundred? I wonder which will be the last generation of humans? Our children, perhaps our grandchildren?"

When the group broke, Robert's supervisor followed him back to his office and closed the door behind him. Robert had come to respect and trust the older man, and so the words he said gave him great pause.

"Did you mean what you said?"

"Every word. We've opened Pandora's box."

His supervisor studied him a moment. "Be careful what you say, Robert. Some people here aren't what they seem."

☣

Less than a month later, the United States dropped an atomic bomb on Hiroshima.

Three days later, a second bomb fell on Nagasaki.

Death toll estimates ranged from 129,000 to 246,000.

☣

The depression Robert had fought his entire life finally overwhelmed him. When he stopped coming to work, his supervisor visited him at his home.

"Did you know?" Robert asked.

"Not the specifics. Only that the bombs would be used to end the war."

"We killed those people."

"The war would have dragged on for years."

Robert shook his head. "We should have dropped it just outside Tokyo, where the emperor and the residents could see it, then blanketed the city with leaflets demanding they surrender or overthrow their government."

"Toppling governments is a messy proposition—and unpredictable. Besides, Tokyo has been firebombed far worse than the damage that would have resulted from an atomic bomb outside the city. During two days in March alone, we burned sixteen square miles of it."

"What's your point?"

"My point is that the decision, no matter what you think of it, was not yours to make. You feel blame. You shouldn't. It was war. You did your job."

"Perhaps. But I can't help feeling as though nothing matters anymore. I know now that the project gave me something I needed: purpose—and belief in what I was creating. Yet having seen the horror of it, I know now that I was a fool. The die is cast. Our extinction is merely a matter of time."

The older man sat quietly for a moment.

"What if I told you there was a group of scientists and intellectuals, people like ourselves, from around the world, who believed as you do—that humanity has now become a danger to itself? What if I told you that this group was working on a sort of second Manhattan Project, a technology that might one day save the entire human race? This device would be controlled by the people who built it, intellectuals with only the common good in mind, not nationalism, or religion, or money."

"If... such a group existed, I would be very interested in hearing more."

☣

Several months later, the two men traveled to London. They were shocked at the state of the city. The war, and in particular the Blitz, had leveled entire sections; others lay in ruins. But the endless attacks had not broken the British. And now they were rebuilding.

At one a.m., a car took the men to a private club. They made their way up the grand staircase and into a ballroom, where a lectern stood before rows of chairs. Signs emblazoned with three words hung above the stage: Reason, Ethics, and Physics. The attendees filed in silently and faced forward. Robert estimated that there were sixty people in the room.

What that speaker said that night changed Robert's life forever.

�

A month later, Robert and his wife, Sarah, moved to London. The city had one of the largest concentrations of universities in the world, and he was offered several positions—all arranged by Citium members. He took a job at King's College, and published a paper from time to time—but his real work was done in secret. The protocols were largely copied from the Manhattan Project: independent teams working on components of a larger device. What that larger device was, he didn't know, only that it would save humanity from itself. Working on the Looking Glass was the solution to the depression he'd experienced after the atomic bombs had been dropped. He believed he was creating the antidote to the poison he'd injected into the world.

That gave him hope.

His wife also found solace in her work volunteering at one of the city's many orphanages. For years, she and Robert had tried to have a child, but without success. It was hard on her; being a mother was something she wanted more than anything.

One Saturday, she asked him to come with her to the orphanage. The facility was a converted hotel, and though it was a bit run-down, it was clean. He visited with several of the children, read stories, and gave out small toys and books his wife had brought with them that day. She asked him to join her again the following Saturday, and the next. Soon it became their ritual. He knew she was working up to something, and what it was.

She asked him on a Sunday afternoon, without preamble, as if she were confirming a decision they had already made. "I think we should adopt him."

"Yes, certainly," he replied, not even glancing up from the paper.

�

I was the boy they adopted, and to understand what that meant to me, you have to know what happened during the war.

CHAPTER 78

ON THE DAY Germany invaded Poland, they evacuated the children from London. There had been rumors of mass evacuations for months.

That night my parents fought about it. I didn't understand it at the time. Later, I learned the truth: my father had insisted my mother leave London too. She was now an assistant professor at the University of London's School of Oriental and African Studies, and spoke and taught courses in three foreign languages: Japanese, Arabic, and German. My mother's school was set to move to Christ Church in Cambridge—all of London's colleges and universities were being evacuated—but she wanted to stay and assist in the war effort. And she wasn't taking no for an answer.

My father was no pushover. He was a captain in the British Third Infantry, currently under the command of Bernard Montgomery. But he folded that night.

The next morning, she walked me to the train station. The line of children seemed endless. I would later learn that the mass evacuations were called Operation Pied Piper, and that over 3.5 million people were displaced. In the first three days of September, over 1.5 million people were moved, including over 800,000 children, over 500,000 mothers and young children, 13,000 pregnant mothers, and 70,000 disabled people. Another 100,000 teachers and support personnel were moved. The effort was massive; it seemed the entire city of London was focused on it.

They pinned a placard with my name on it to my coat and gave me a cardboard box that hung around my neck. A gas mask lay inside, a grim reminder that this was no field trip. Many kids took them out and put them on and played with them. I was a boy of five, and I must admit that I did too.

Older siblings held their younger brothers' and sisters' hands, ensuring they didn't get separated. My only brother had died two years before from tuberculosis; I would have given anything for him to be holding my hand that morning. I put on a brave face for my mother though. She hugged me so hard I thought my chest would collapse. As the train pulled away, she waved goodbye. She was crying; in fact I didn't see a single dry eye on that platform.

Eleven years later, C.S. Lewis wrote a novel titled *The Lion, the Witch and the Wardrobe*, in which four siblings are evacuated from London to a stately country manor with a dusty wardrobe that leads to another world. The evacuations weren't nearly as romantic as Lewis's tale, but they weren't as agonizing as *The Lord of the Flies* either.

On the whole, everyone in Britain was doing the best they could, and preparing for the worst: war with Germany.

My parents had arranged for me to stay with my mother's first cousin Edith and her husband, George. It was a few days before they could come around to collect me, and in that time, I got a glimpse of what the children without host families went through. Periodically they were brought out and made to line up while adults marched past.

"I'll take that one," a mother said.

"We'll take the third from the left," a father called out.

The first time it happened was sort of like not being picked for cricket—it wasn't the end of the world. But these rounds of selections had a cumulative effect on the children left behind. I felt for them and would have traded places with them. But there was nothing anyone could do. Most of those who remained were shuffled around, some assigned to the evacuation camps the government had built—in itself an act of great foresight.

Life became routine for a while. I went to school, did my chores as Edith bade me, just as my mother insisted I should in her letters.

Her notes to me arrived every few days. My father wrote less often, and shorter letters, but I was glad to hear from both of them.

In the den, Edith and I listened to the radio each night, hanging on every word of the BBC News report. George was in the Royal Air Force, and she was worried to death about him, though she tried quite hard to hide it.

In May 1940, Germany launched its offensive to the west. They took the Low Countries first. The Netherlands and Belgium fell quickly, providing the German army a route around the Maginot Line. They broke through in the Ardennes, separating the French and British armies. I knew my father had been deployed, but I didn't know where. I went cold when I heard that the Third Infantry had been one of the divisions evacuated at Dunkirk.

A letter arrived from my father two weeks later. I cried in my room that night because he was alive. Somewhere deep inside, I had convinced myself that he was dead, and that I was okay with it.

Four months later, in early September, a year after I left London, the Luftwaffe began their air raids on the city. Starting on September 7th 1940, they bombed London 56 out of the following 57 days. The attacks were relentless. And deadly. The bombings killed over forty thousand people, injured at least forty thousand more, and destroyed over a million homes. My mother was in one of those homes, and she was one of the forty thousand who lost her life.

I had been so concerned about my father's safety that her death caught me completely by surprise. I was filled with both hatred and sadness. At only six years old, the emotions overwhelmed me. I worried for my father, and then I tried not to care. But that was a lie I told myself.

On D-Day, the Third Infantry was the first to land at Sword Beach as part of the invasion of Normandy. I feared the worst when I heard that, but a letter arrived from my father three weeks later. Those letters continued to come for six months. I was hopeful. That was my mistake. The news that he had been killed in December destroyed whatever was left of my young heart. I was officially an orphan.

George returned home the following month. He had lost a leg and the better part of an arm, and the physical wounds were only half of his struggle. I helped Edith as best I could, but like me, she was overwhelmed.

I knew what was coming next, and I didn't blame her.

The orphanage in London was filled with other children who had lost their families in the war and had nowhere else to go. I shared a small room with three other boys. The youngest, Edgar Mayweather, was six. I was the oldest at eleven, and there were two brothers staying with us. Orville Hughes was nine, and his younger brother, Alistair, was seven.

The orphanage was in a run-down hotel on the outskirts of London; it had barely survived the bombings. Our days consisted of school and chores that were done under the threat of bodily punishment. We helped repair the old hotel, too. On the whole, things could have been a lot worse. We were fed, educated, and looked after. The hard work, at least for me, took my mind off what had happened and gave me a sense of purpose. Perhaps the only thing we didn't have was love.

No matter how much they hid it, every kid in the orphanage was out of sorts. Growing up with tragedy changes a person, trains them to expect still more tragedy around every corner. It's the mind's way of protecting you; and it is a very powerful defense. At night, many children cried endlessly in the dark. Some hid under their beds. Many were spooked at every loud sound. I didn't blame them. It was sort of like being in prison, in a way— and just like in a prison, none of us asked the other orphans questions about what they were in for. We'd seen enough of the war; no one wanted to talk about it.

We all handled it in our own way. Many of the kids fought. They'd fight you for a cross word or even the wrong look. They were mad about life and what had happened, and would take it out on anyone and anything. Though Orville was two years younger than me, he was bigger and as tough as a bucket of nails. I never saw him start a fight, but he ended more than his share. His fists and elbows saved me many broken bones and black eyes.

He guarded his younger brother Alistair like the queen's jewels. Me and Edgar too. Alistair was pretty tough himself, but less eager to fight; he was quiet, always had his nose in a book.

Turnover was high; kids were always being brought in or taken out. We knew some were moved to other orphanages as they opened. Most, however, were placed with families. I got another taste of what I'd seen during the evacuations: parents coming through, inspecting the kids, making their decisions—and then leaving the rest of us to wash up, comb our hair, and put on our best set of clothes for the next audition. Rejection eats at a person like a worm winding its way through an apple: sooner or later it reaches the core, and you become completely rotten.

I never got there, but I saw a lot of kids who did.

After my parents died, I told myself I didn't care what happened to me. But I did. I didn't want to grow up in an orphanage, with friends who came and went like ships in the night. I wanted a mother and a father and a home that only we lived in. I wasn't the only one.

One Sunday afternoon, a group called the Christian Brothers visited the orphanage. They described a better life: work outside in the fields, families ready to take us, a wonderful school in an exciting place called Australia. It sounded a lot better than this place, but I was skeptical. It sounded too good to me. But not to many of the others. Hands went up around the room. And as they did, the kids were called forward. One of those hands was Alistair Hughes. Orville reached for him to put it down, but it was too late; they were already ushering him into the crowd to leave. Orville joined them without a word. He nodded to me as he left.

I learned later that all was not as the Christian Brothers had promised. The program was actually the continuation of similar initiatives in the seventeenth century, when children were shipped to the Virginia colony as migrant labor. In the nineteenth and twentieth centuries, nearly 150,000 children were sent to Australia, New Zealand, Canada, and Rhodesia. They worked in harsh conditions, but the work was only part of their suffering. From the 1940s until 1967, about 10,000 children were shipped to Western

Australia to work in the fields and live in orphanages. Physical and sexual abuse was rampant and only discovered in later years. In 2009, Australia's prime minister formally apologized to those children who had suffered under the program, for what he called "the absolute tragedy of childhoods lost."

I, too, was watching my childhood slip away. I had started to grow pessimistic that I would ever find a home when a woman named Sarah Moore began volunteering at the orphanage. She was kind and very smart. She reminded me of my mother. She taught me French, which to her delight I picked up quickly. Her husband was more stoic, but I thought he liked me too.

One Sunday, the woman in charge of our ward told me to make ready to leave. I was scared to death as I stuffed my meager belongings in the sack they'd given me.

I was overjoyed when Sarah and her husband Robert came into the room and told me I was coming to live with them. Against my will, I cried, but that was okay with them. They simply hugged me and loaded my things into their shiny car and drove away.

I took their last name, but kept my original family surname as my middle name. In school the next year, I couldn't have been more proud when I signed my first paper: William Kensington Moore.

☣

Peyton stood and moved to the corkboard, scanning it again. Her eyes locked on a worn picture pinned near the floor. She pulled it from the board and studied it. Three children stood there: on the left was a girl, perhaps three years old; in the middle stood a girl of perhaps seven; and on the right was a boy of eleven, with only one arm.

"I know who wrote this," she said.

Desmond moved to her side and gazed at the picture. "You do?"

She pointed at the youngest girl in the picture. "That's me. Madison's in the middle; Andrew on the right. William Kensington Moore is my father."

CHAPTER 79

DESMOND TRIED TO process Peyton's words.

"I thought you said your father was dead?"

"I thought he was," she replied. "Maybe he is. We don't know when this letter was written."

She returned to the couch, sat down beside Desmond, and pulled the thick quilt back over her. Outside the stone cottage, the sunrise broke through the fog. She wondered how long they had before they'd need to make a decision. And what they'd find in the rest of the pages.

☣

What I remember about the first years after the war was that Britain was broke. We'd won the Second World War, but it had come at a fantastic cost—most of all in lives, but also in pounds and pence. America suddenly and unexpectedly ended the Lend-Lease program that had likely saved us. The Treasury was near bankruptcy. So began the Age of Austerity; it seemed we'd survived the Nazis only to starve to death. And we weren't the only ones. The entire world was freezing, starving, and still reeling from the greatest conflict in human history. In Britain, rationing and conscription continued. The winter of 1946–47 was one of the worst in recorded history. Coal and railway systems failed, factories closed, and people were very, very cold.

Things turned a little each year. The Americans loaned us 3.75

billion dollars at a low interest rate in July 1946. The Marshall Plan launched in 1948, further bolstering our financial situation. Everyone felt that the next war was right around the corner. I did too. It was hard not to. But the world was doing everything it could to stop it—and to get ready. The United Nations was formed in 1945, NATO in '49. Britain began giving its colonies independence: Jordan in '46, India and Pakistan in '47, Israel, Myanmar, and Sri Lanka in '48. Even more nations gained independence from the UK during the fifties and sixties: Sudan, Ghana, Malaysia, Nigeria, Kuwait, Sierra Leone, Tanzania, Jamaica, Uganda, and Kenya.

The country was back on its feet by 1950, but all eyes were now on the Soviet Union and the expanding Cold War. The UK joined the US in the Korean War that year, fighting the Chinese and the Soviet Union in what we all believed was a dress rehearsal for the next global war. It ended in a stalemate, and the country was split in two.

The US and Russia began mass-producing nuclear weapons, amassing thousands—enough to alter the Earth permanently, making it uninhabitable. Other nations developed their own nuclear weapons: the UK, France, Israel, India, China, and Pakistan.

Despite the whole world going crazy, life settled down for me at home. My teenage years were a sharp contrast to the turbulent first twelve years of my life. Mother and Father, as I had come to refer to Sarah and Robert, were loving to me, fair but firm, and never were there two parents who cared for a child more. They didn't dote on me, but they gave me every scrap of spare time and energy they had. Mother was adamant about keeping up with my chores and my schoolwork. Father always had a project he wanted us to do—usually science-related. I knew early on that he imagined me following in his footsteps. To him, science was the noblest endeavor, and physics towered above all other sciences.

But like every child becoming an adult, I learned the limits of my abilities. Where science and math were concerned, those boundaries didn't extend nearly far enough. I would never be a great scientist, or even a bad one. My mind just wasn't wired that way. I did excel at languages, however. Perhaps it was a gift from my biological mother. Picking up a foreign tongue was a piece of cake for me. And I loved history—military history in particular. I read everything I could about the Third Infantry, the division in which my biological father had served and died. I devoured histories of Germany and the British Empire.

University came and went, and my only notable accomplishments occurred in the boxing ring. I had no clue what I wanted to do with my life. Like so many others with the same problem, I joined the army. It seemed a noble pursuit and a good place to get my bearings and maybe see a little of the world.

It was the right decision. In the army I learned leadership and how to manage people. University had stuffed my head full of facts and knowledge and had taught me how to think and solve problems. But I had only ever managed myself. The army was a boon to me in that respect. It also gave me perhaps the greatest gift of my entire life: it revealed who I was. It tested me in ways school never had. And I found I was at my best during a crisis. In clutch situations, when I had to make fast decisions, I never faltered. And I lived for those moments, just as I had looked forward to the boxing ring. But more so—for in real life, there was no referee to pull you apart, no bell to ring.

To this day I believe a person's ideal first job is the one that reveals the most about them. Knowing who I was helped me avoid a lot of dead ends in life. A lot of opportunities look good, but I've found that sometimes success and happiness are about knowing when to say no.

I avoided routine. I liked moving around, doing something different every day. Maybe it was because of how I grew up during the war, being shuffled around, but it became my way of life. I moved from post to post, always the first to volunteer for a transfer. I never wanted my feet to go to sleep.

Just before my first tour of duty ended, a man came to see me. He asked if I was interested in a new type of opportunity, a way to serve Her Majesty's government in a far greater capacity than I currently was. They had me with the patriotic pitch. The job interview was a complex, bizarre process that would fill a book.

I imagine it was a little different for each of us who joined in those days. They vetted me, tested me some more, then began my real training. A year later, in 1959, I became an employee of the Gibraltar Trading Company.

On the surface, I was an antiques dealer. My job entailed a lot of travel, exchanging large sums of money with foreigners and foreign governments, recovering relics lost in the war. But in truth, I was an agent for Her Majesty's Secret Intelligence Service, or MI6, as it was predominantly known then. I had never been so filled with purpose. Or happier.

My mother had been worried about me when I joined the army. My position with Gibraltar Trading soothed her nerves considerably. My father's reaction was quite unexpected: a mixture of amusement and appreciation. He seemed to know exactly what I was up to. And our relationship actually improved. We began to have long conversations—philosophical in nature. I discovered a whole new side of him. In short, he opened up to me, taking an interest in me as he never had before—or at least, not since before university, when it became clear that I was never going to be a scientist. I knew that had disappointed him, though he never voiced it and never showed it. Like all parents, he just wanted me to value the things he valued. In some way, he wanted me to carry on his work.

When I visited home from my trips, I brought small trinkets, which my mother displayed in the parlor and my father placed on shelves in his study. He asked me about the trips with an amused look on his face, as if he knew what had truly taken place.

On Easter weekend in 1965, I learned just how much he knew.

I sat in his study, completely unprepared for what he was about to tell me.

"I'd like you to come with me to Hong Kong next week."

"Can't. I have a meeting with a new client in Warsaw."

He stood, walked to a shelf to the left of his desk, and moved a few items out of the way. He pushed the shelf's back panel; it clicked and sprang open, revealing a small safe. He drew a picture out and handed it to me.

"Twenty years ago, I helped create that device."

I had seen the image before, many times. This was a photo—an original, printed by someone who was there at the first atomic bomb test. I had never known Father was involved.

"I have regretted it every day since. Do you know how many nuclear warheads exist today?"

Still studying the picture, I said. "Thirty-seven thousand, seven hundred and forty-one. Give or take."

"And they're far more powerful than the ones dropped on Japan."

He paused, waiting for me to look at him.

"Communism isn't humanity's greatest enemy. Indeed, *we* are the greatest enemy we now face. For the first time in history, we have the means with which to destroy ourselves. I helped give that deadly weapon to the world. I've spent the years since trying to ensure it is never used again."

"How?"

"I'm part of an organization that's creating a new device, a device that will change the human race. Its reach will be unlimited. It will affect every person, of every nationality and race and religion. It will save us. It may well be our only chance of survival."

I was skeptical. In fact, I half wondered if the long hours in his lab had finally gotten to him.

"What sort of... device?" I asked.

"I'll tell you that in due time. You of all people know the importance of secrecy."

I was sure of it then: he knew I was a spy.

"The Looking Glass is the culmination of my life's work. It's in danger now. We're entering a phase of the project where our work will be more exposed. There's greater risk. I need someone to protect it. I think you might be that person."

He stared at me a moment. "Will you come with me to Hong Kong?"

I agreed instantly. I felt pride that day—that he had asked me, that I had grown into someone who could help him, after everything he had done for me.

☣

Hong Kong in 1965 was booming. The streets were clogged with people, and factories were springing up at every turn. More than half the population were young people about my age, in their mid-twenties and early thirties.

Walking the crowded sidewalks, with double-decker buses zooming by, belching heavy black smoke and releasing passengers every few blocks, I realized that Hong Kong in so many ways was an Asian facsimile of London: British-style government and capitalism, but with a fusion of culture from the East and West.

That night, my father and I strolled through the city, lit not by yellow streetlights like the London of my youth, but bathed in red and blue neon signs that stretched from street level to high above, featuring words written in Cantonese. Disco music wafted into the street as strongly as the scent of roasted pig and beef from the eateries. We'd had a drink at our hotel and another at dinner. I've forgotten the names of the hotel and the restaurant, but I remember how I felt about Hong Kong that night: as if I were seeing the future, as if every city would one day be like this blooming metropolis, a melting pot of human culture. Young people were flocking in from China and the rest of the world.

Hong Kong was the first trip I had taken with my father as an adult. Our relationship had changed, and that was evident now, as we embarked on this adventure together.

In the harbor lay the vessel that would change my life—and perhaps soon the world. It was a submarine, the largest non-military sub I had ever seen. It was nuclear-powered, with a diesel-electric backup. The tour of the vessel lasted an hour. I was shocked by what I saw: it was a massive laboratory capable of circling the globe. I paused at the nameplate, which read:

RSV *BEAGLE*
HONG KONG
1 MAY 1965
ORDO AB CHAO

I translated the Latin words in my head: *From chaos comes order.*

My line of work had taken me behind the Iron Curtain routinely. Order existed there, but the price was high: freedom. I wondered what this vessel's builders demanded for the order they sought. And what that order was.

Back in our hotel that night, my father told me the role I was to play.

"The *Beagle*'s mission will require it to travel to dangerous places. Some are hard to reach physically. Others are dangerous politically."

"The Soviet Union. China."

"Among others," he said.

"I was in the army, not the navy."

"Your role will be securing operations on the shore. That's where the true danger lies. The sub will dock at ports all over the world. You'll need to think fast, be ready for anything, negotiate with customs, get our people out of sticky situations."

He paused, letting me consider the words.

"I know your current work is very important. But so is this. If I'm right, it's the most important thing the human race has ever done. The world may well avoid a nuclear holocaust, but there will always be another device, another war. *We* are the enemy we face. The human race is on borrowed time. We are far too uncivilized to possess the weapons we do. We're racing the clock, just as we were during the Manhattan Project. Will you help us?"

I agreed there and then in that hotel room. I wondered what sort of device the Looking Glass was. I assumed the answer would be revealed in those first days aboard the *Beagle*. What I found was far more intriguing.

CHAPTER 80

IN THE SMALL cottage in Shetland, the sun had risen, driving the fog away. The wind still whipped across the stone, rattling the ancient windows every few minutes.

Desmond stood to stretch his legs. At the corkboard he scanned an article about the Invisible Sun Foundation donating ten million dollars to a genetics project at Stanford.

Peyton moved toward him, but he turned and motioned her back to the couch. "Let's keep going."

As he sat down, an object caught his eye. It was in the corner of the room, where the wall met the ceiling. It was well hidden by several trinkets at the top of a bookshelf, but there was no mistaking what it was: a camera. At the bottom, a small light glowed red.

Desmond hoped the camera was simply a left over security measure the cottage owner had installed. There wasn't much he could do about it at the moment except run, and that would tip off anyone watching. He focused on the pages of the story and began reading again.

☣

The *Beagle* was an incredible vessel, but most impressive to me were the people aboard. They were drawn from all over the world: American, British like myself, Germans, Chinese, Russians, Japanese. They were nearly all scientists, except for the staff who operated the submarine and me and my three security personnel. I must say, we non-scientists felt a bit out of place at first; on the mess deck, all the talk was of the experiments. I had expected there to be just one experiment. On that point, I was very wrong.

The *Beagle* was in some ways a floating university with multiple departments, each with specialists in the field, all of them conducting different research. We took ice core samples in Antarctica, collected soil samples from the ocean floor, and took on animals from all over the world. Human test subjects were common—people from all nations and races—and were taken to labs that were off-limits to non-essential personnel. All this activity baffled me. How could all of this be related to one project?

Of course, nothing inspires curiosity like a secret. Like the sailors, I did my share of speculating and prodding the scientists about what they were researching. I knew the vessel's namesake, the HMS *Beagle*, had carried a young Charles Darwin on the voyage around the world that helped him form his theory of natural selection. I wondered if the scientists on this vessel were testing a theory as groundbreaking.

I have never been claustrophobic, but my time on the *Beagle* tested my comfort level with confinement. The crew quarters were small and separated by gender. The bunks were stacked three tall, with twelve of us to a berth. We shared a shower the sailors called a *rain locker* (they called the bunks *racks* or *bunkies*). Indeed, the men who ran the sub seemed to have a language all their own, mostly comprised of curse words. Sailors not pulling their weight were called *bent shitcans*. Sailors who only looked out for themselves were *check valves*. Surface ships and sailors were *skimmers* (a derogatory term, apparently). Passageways were *p-ways*. Radiation was *zoomies*. Marine life spotted on sonar— dolphins and whales—were called *biologics*. *Clear your baffles* meant to look behind you. *Poking holes in the ocean* meant we were underway. There was a locker dedicated to holding porn, known as *the smut locker*.

On the whole, I felt more of a connection to the sailors than to the scientists. That changed when I got to know my bunkmate,

Yuri Pachenko. Yuri was thirty-three, about two years older than me, and smaller. But his size belied his strength, which lay mostly in his mind. He was the most intense person I'd ever met. His story revealed why.

He had been a child in Stalingrad when the German Sixth Army had arrived in August 1942. I had read about the battle, of course; it was one of the deadliest battles in the history of warfare, with millions of lives lost. Hearing his story firsthand made my experience during the war seem like a holiday in the country. The evacuations had largely spared Britain's children the horrors of the war, but in the Soviet Union, there had been nowhere to run. Yuri had fought for his land and scraped to survive.

And now, he wanted to create a world where Stalingrad never happened again. I have never seen anyone so focused on anything. His field was virology, and he was learning from the best in the world, who apparently were on board the *Beagle*.

In August 1967, we docked in Mombasa. Yuri and a team rushed to Uganda to investigate a viral outbreak. They brought samples back. Containment was instituted in the labs, and for good reason: I later learned the virus they'd brought on board was Marburg, a hemorrhagic fever close in nature to Ebola (which was discovered in Zaire about ten years later).

I found one scientist much more interesting than the others: Lin Keller. She was the child of a Chinese mother and a German father, and she had grown up in Hong Kong during the war. She described, in vivid detail, living through the fall of the island. On the same day the Japanese attacked Pearl Harbor, they also attacked the British colony of Hong Kong. Local troops, as well as British, Canadian, and Indian units, fought hard for the island but lost to the overwhelming Japanese forces. They surrendered on Christmas Day in 1941—what the locals would call "Black Christmas."

The Japanese occupation of Hong Kong followed. From the Peninsula Hotel in Kowloon, the Japanese ruled with an iron fist. Lin and her mother were separated from her father, who was in Germany, forced to work for the German government. Though he could have brought his family to Germany, he had felt his daughter was safer in Hong Kong, despite the conditions. They barely scraped by during the "three years and eight months," as the occupation came to be known.

The situation on mainland China was far worse. The Japanese had invaded in July 1937, beginning the Second Sino-Japanese War. The conflict was massive in scale and loss of human life; it would account for the majority of civilian and military casualties in the Pacific War and claim the lives of ten to twenty-five million Chinese civilians and over four million Chinese and Japanese military. The war in China exemplified a fact often forgotten about the Second World War: globally, more non-combatants perished than uniformed participants. Civilians in China and the Soviet Union suffered the most, but hunger and violence were a fact of life around the world in the early forties.

That was the world Yuri, Lin, and I had grown up in. It was a world we didn't want our children to grow up in. We were going to change it, no matter the cost. And in each other, we found kindred spirits, linked by a shared childhood across thousands of miles and two continents.

Lin's field was genetics, and the subject was an obsession for her. Her father was also conducting genetic research on the *Beagle*, which meant that her time here was a chance to reconnect with him. This was something Lin and I shared in common: the Citium was an opportunity to connect with our fathers, to share in their life's work, and perhaps even to fill in some of the years of our childhoods we had lost.

Genetics was a booming field. Watson and Crick had figured out that DNA was arranged in a double helix in 1953, and the discoveries had accelerated after that. When Lin talked about the promise of genetics, she lit up. She was unlike any woman I had ever met. Physically, she was an anomaly, the embodiment of Hong Kong itself: distinctly Asian features with a mixture of British mannerisms and behavior. She was unassuming, utterly without ego. Perhaps that was what attracted me the most. She was hardworking to a fault; often I found her in the cramped office outside her lab asleep with her head on her desk. I would lift her small body up and carry her through the p-ways. Sailors stood against the walls to make room for me to pass, never missing an opportunity to heckle me.

"Finally bagged her, eh, Willy?"

"What'd it take, Will, tranq dart or a shot of tequila?"

"Make way for Prince Charming, boys!"

I endured the jabs without a care in the world. I deposited her in her bunk, pulled the covers up, and turned the small noise-maker on—they were good for helping folks stay asleep; the berths weren't separated by shifts, and bunkmates were constantly coming and going. The hard surfaces throughout the vessel made for a noisy existence.

Reading people was part of my job. After a few weeks, I knew what Lin saw in genetics: the promise of a civilized human race. She believed that somewhere in the human genome lay the answer to why some people were evil. To her, the key to the Looking Glass was simply identifying the genetic basis for all the traits that ailed the world and getting rid of them.

Yuri, on the other hand, didn't believe that the threat of nuclear war was humanity's greatest enemy. Pandemics, he argued, had decimated the human population far more than any war. He believed that globalization and urbanization made an extinction-level pandemic inevitable.

It was then that I realized the truth: no one knew what the Looking Glass was—even the scientists working on the project. I would later learn that the entire project had begun as a mere hypothesis—a hypothesis that a device could be created that would secure the human race forever. The scientific experiments being conducted on the *Beagle* were simply gathering data to test that hypothesis, to figure out exactly what that device might be. To these scientists, the Looking Glass represented an abstract concept, like paradise. Something we all understood, but no one knew exactly where it was or precisely what it looked like. To some it was a sandy beach, to others a cabin in the woods or a penthouse in the city with unlimited wine and theater tickets.

Paradise was the product of one's life experiences and desires. In the same way, every scientist saw humanity's greatest threat through the lens of their field of expertise; they imagined themselves and their work in the starring role in the device's creation. If you put seven Citium members in a room and asked them to name the most likely extinction-level event in humanity's future, you might get seven different answers: robotics, artificial intelligence, pandemics, climate change, solar events, asteroid impacts, or alien invasion.

Creating one device that shielded humanity from *all* these threats seemed impossible to me. I would later learn that it was in fact possible, but it came at an unimaginable price.

Peyton stood from the couch and paced away from the pages laying beside Desmond. He sprang up and joined her, seeming to read her feelings.

"Just because your mother was in the Citium back then doesn't mean she's involved with what's happening now."

She stared into his eyes. *He still knows me so well.*

"And what if she is?"

"Then we'll deal with it."

"I can't—"

"*We* will. Together."

He pulled her into his arms and held her, neither speaking for a long moment.

With her mouth pressed into his shoulder, she whispered, "What does it mean, Des? All the connections. My mother and father were both in the Citium. So was Yuri—the man who recruited you. Your uncle met my father in an orphanage in London. It's like... we're all entangled."

"I don't know. But I think you're right: there's a larger picture here. I just can't figure out what it is."

He released her and stepped to the corkboard, as if he were searching it for the answer. He reached out and pulled a piece

of scrap paper from the pin that held it. It read, *Invisible Sun —
person, organization, or project?*

Peyton thought he was going to reveal what he was thinking,
but he merely slipped the note in his pocket and turned to her.
"Let's keep reading, see if we can figure out what's going on."

CHAPTER 81

THE *BEAGLE* PUT ashore at ports all over the world. I got to use my knack for foreign languages, but I didn't get to enjoy the scenery much. I was always on guard, planning for what might go wrong, and making contacts in case they did.

In Rio de Janeiro in 1967, I was glad I had made contingency plans. I was at the hotel one night when one of the researchers, a female biologist in her early thirties named Sylvia, threw open the lobby's glass door and ran in. Blood covered her face and matted her brown hair. One of her eyes was swollen shut. She barreled past the bar and the people checking in, yelling my name. I was sitting in the lobby reading a book. I rose, caught her by the arm, guided her to a phone booth, and closed the folding door. I finally got her calmed down enough to speak.

"They took them!"

"Who?"

"Yuri and Lin."

"Who took them?"

She was sobbing now. "I don't know. They wore masks." She shook her head as if she didn't want to remember. "They said they'd kill them if I didn't come back to the bus stop with twenty thousand dollars in two hours."

I took her up to my room after that, questioned her more, then called for two of my intelligence operatives. I sent one of them to the *Beagle* to get forty thousand dollars just in case. We kept a lot of money on hand for scientific provisions as well as kidnap and ransom operations. I sent my other operative to make inquiries with a few of my old MI6 contacts, to find a man I knew only by reputation, but who I was confident would ensure my operation's success.

When I was left alone with the trembling woman, I poured her a tall glass of brandy and sat her on the bed. She winced when the liquid hit her cut lip, but with a shaking hand, she finished it quickly.

"Listen to me, Sylvia."

She looked up at me with her good eye.

"Everything is going to be okay. I'm going to get them back, and I'm going to make the person who did this very sorry."

☣

Twenty minutes later, I was sitting in the back of a Portuguese restaurant, waiting for my host. He entered, sat without intro-ducing himself, and stared at me with blank eyes. He was a corpulent man, with long, greasy black hair plastered to his scalp. Two men stood by the door to the private dining room, hands stuffed in their pockets, fingers no doubt curled around the triggers of snub-nosed revolvers pointed in my direction.

I knew the man by his alias—O Mestre—but I didn't use the name to address him. I simply said, "We have a common enemy."

He raised his eyebrows.

"A wannabe gangster named Ernesto."

His accent was thick Portuguese, his English broken. "Never hear of this man."

"He's kidnapped two of my associates. He wants twenty thousand dollars for their return."

"Is police matter. I not police."

"I think you can help me more. I think you can guarantee my friends come home safe."

He looked away.

"There's forty thousand dollars in the bag."

"I am not bank."

"The money is for their safe return. And for protection in case this happens again. Here in Rio, and in São Paulo."

With his head, he motioned to the two men. One opened the bag and began counting the money. The other jerked me up from my chair, frisked me, then reached inside my shirt, making sure I wasn't wired. I wasn't stupid enough to carry a gun into a meeting like this.

The man who frisked me nodded at O Mestre, who rose and left the room. I had held back on the fact that I spoke Portuguese, hoping it would provide an advantage, but these men seemed to have a language all their own, communicating entirely with their eyes and slight motions of their heads.

The man holding the bag took twenty thousand dollars out of it.

His associate said to me in Portuguese, "The fee is twenty thousand dollars per year. You will return to this room next year on this day with payment."

I nodded. So they knew more about me than I suspected.

"Tonight, you will go to the bus stop. Here is what will happen."

☣

Exactly two hours after the thugs had taken Yuri and Lin off the street and assaulted Sylvia, I stood in the drizzling rain, wearing a fedora and a black trench coat. Rio was hot year-round, but in August it was cold, and rainy. The wind from the Atlantic carried a cold front from Antarctica into the city, past the cranes that were building skyscrapers by the dozen, erasing the old city, erecting a new one.

People from Brazil's countryside were pouring into Rio. Illegal immigrants came too, all in search of jobs and a better life. *Favelas* grew like ant colonies, seeming to spread overnight. In the glow of the streetlamp, I could see the shanties stretching up a green-forested mountainside, a pocket of poverty in the vast city. From my vantage point, they looked like tiny cardboard boxes stacked at the feet of the *Christ the Redeemer* statue, which towered over the people below.

The harsh quality of life in the favelas was a stark contrast to Copacabana Beach a few hundred yards away, where ritzy hotels, night clubs, bars, and restaurants glittered just off the Atlantic. Palm trees towered over the sandy beach and lined the promenade. Music thumped into the night, an out-of-tune anthem of the two worlds that existed here in Rio. I was about to descend into the other world, where desperate people took desperate actions to survive—and just maybe lift themselves out of poverty. The situation had forced me to do something I didn't like, but such was this world. My people were in danger. More than that: my friends were in danger. It was as simple as that.

The bus pulled away, puffing thick black smoke the rain couldn't force down.

Beside me, Sylvia started to tremble. I knew it wasn't because of the cold wind or the rain.

"It's all right, Sylvia."

I could tell she wanted to cry, but she resisted. One of my intelligence operatives was in the cafe behind us, the other in the adjacent alley.

A rattling Volkswagen pulled up, and a man wearing a bandanna over his mouth and a stained white tank top got out. In the back seat, another man pointed a handgun at Sylvia. Her cry broke forth then. I held my arm out, across her, and stepped in between the man and the trembling woman.

"The money!" he yelled.

"Give us our people first. Then we pay."

He shook his head. He was high on amphetamines of some sort. His eyes were wide, darting back and forth. "No! You pay now. If I not back in five minutes, we kill one."

I held my hands up. "All right. Fine. We'll pay. But I want to see them first. Show me they're alive, I make a call, and the money is delivered here."

Bandanna Man made eye contact with the driver, who nodded. He grabbed my arm and shoved me in the back of the tiny car, between him and the thug who had the gun. The thug pressed his old revolver in my side. His friend searched me quickly, found no weapon, then jerked my hat off and tied the bandanna from his face around my eyes. It stank of sweat and cigarettes, forcing me to cough.

They bounced me around in the back seat for ten minutes; the roar of the German car's engine was nearly deafening. I wondered if the divider between the back seat and engine compartment had been taken out.

Finally the car stopped, and they stood me up and perp-walked me down a cobblestone street. They were rough with me each time I tripped.

I heard a wooden door scrape open and slam closed behind us. They walked me slower, then pulled the bandanna off in a room with a single light bulb hanging from the ceiling.

Yuri and Lin were in wooden chairs. Electrical wire bound their hands together behind them, and more wire bound their ankles to the chair legs. They looked painfully uncomfortable. Yuri's nose was busted and covered in dried blood. More blood ran from his hair. One eye was closed, just like Sylvia.

My heart broke when I saw Lin. They had struck her in the cheek. It was swollen and bruised, like a jellyfish tattooed on her skin. Tears ran down her cheeks.

A man wearing a Che Guevara hat rose from behind a desk. The edges of his nose were red from snorting drugs. He fidgeted as he moved, stared at me, disgust plain on his face.

"You think you can play games with me?" He took a knife from his belt. "I'm going to show you how serious I am."

I made my voice even. "Before you do, I have a message for you. From O Mestre."

He stopped, stared, still enraged, but I could see hesitation now.

"He's a friend of mine. He wants you to call home."

He screamed obscenities at me, but he didn't move toward Lin or Yuri.

"Call home. Check on your family. Or O Mestre will make you sorry."

"I ought to kill you, you imperialist pig. And your capitalist whore!"

"That would displease O Mestre. I can't even imagine what he would do."

The kidnapper looked away from me. He took a step toward Yuri and Lin, then seemed to reconsider. At the desk, he picked up the phone, dialed, and listened. Whatever was said on the other end scared him to death. He sank into his seat and nodded, as if the person he was talking to could see him. "Of course. My mistake—"

He stopped; apparently the line had gone dead. He replaced the receiver and shouted to his men to cut Yuri and Lin loose, as if it was all a big misunderstanding.

Yuri stood on faltering legs, bracing himself on the chair. But when they cut Lin loose, she just tumbled toward the floor. I lunged forward and caught her. If not for the warmth of her skin, I might have thought her dead.

I hoisted her up and carried her out of the shack, holding her tightly. I don't think I really exhaled until the thugs let us out of the car at the bus stop. Lin could stand again, but she still held me tight.

Yuri hugged me too, an unusual show of affection for the man. "You saved us, William."

"Just doing my job," I mumbled.

"It was more than that."

"You would have done the same for me."

"Yes. I would have."

☣

Every three months or so, the *Beagle* docked at an island in the Pacific—the same island every time. I didn't know its location; no one except the bridge crew did. But I knew it was west of Hawaii, south of the equator, and that it had been uninhabited when it had first come into the Citium's possession. Everything was new here: the buildings, the port, the roads. There was no government save for the Citium, and no crime. No fear. Perhaps for that reason alone, the *Beagle* sailed for the island right after Rio. The entire crew was shaken, not just Sylvia, Lin, and Yuri.

Yuri and Lin had grown up in history's darkest hours but I think they hadn't experienced real life-threatening danger in twenty years—since their childhood. It scared them, though Yuri was stoic as usual. On the sub, Lin told me how he had fought them. He had been brave, but it was a useless fight. All the same, I liked him even more for it.

I don't know the island's official designation, but aboard the *Beagle* we called it the Isle of Citium, or simply the Isle. It had a deep-water harbor on its south side, with a massive seaport that was way too large for such a small landmass. Every time we docked, there was a cargo ship unloading supplies—building materials mostly, and some heavy equipment. The cost of building on the island was enormous, but I saw the logic in it. This place was completely off the grid and extremely hard to find. Most people don't realize how vast the Pacific is. Every continent and landmass on the planet could fit within the Pacific. It's larger than the Atlantic and Indian Oceans combined.

The Isle was the perfect place for the Citium to hide, and in August 1967, it was the perfect place for our crew to recuperate. We unloaded at the port, rode the electric golf carts to the residential building, and retired to our rooms. The place wasn't fancy, but it was clean and offered privacy: every bedroom had its own bathroom and a small living room. After three months on the *Beagle*, it felt like a vast penthouse apartment. Being able to shower in privacy was a luxury. Sleeping without a person above and below you, and three more across from you, was refreshing— and quiet.

In my time in the field, I have found that a brush with death always changes a person. Some not permanently, but everyone temporarily. That was true for Yuri and Lin. Yuri turned inward. On the Isle, he poured himself into his work. He was more convinced than ever of its importance.

Lin's change was the opposite to Yuri's. She *stopped* working herself to the bone. In the cafeteria, she laughed more, stayed longer at the lunch table.

At our post-tour bonfire on the beach, I saw her have a glass of wine for the first time. She glowed in her black dress. To me, that night, she was brighter than the moon, and the tiki torches, and the candles in the glass vases that lined the long table. I couldn't help staring at her. I tried to hide it less with every drink.

There were six people left at the table when she stood, said goodnight to the rest of the table, and looked me in the eye.

"Nice night for a walk."

I stood and held out my hand.

CHAPTER 82

IN SUMMER 1967, my life changed forever. I was three months into my second tour on the *Beagle* when I began noticing a change in Lin. She was more distant, avoiding me. We had been dating—such as it was on board a submarine—for about six months. I cornered her, wouldn't let her deny something was wrong, and finally got the answer out of her: she was pregnant.

I was overjoyed. And terrified. I believe people who had a difficult childhood are more averse to having children. That was certainly the case for Lin and for me. If biology hadn't intervened, who knows where life might have led us. But it did, and I will never regret that. We moved back to London into a flat in Belgravia that was owned by a member of the Citium (who rented it to us for a song). We got married in a small ceremony a month later. Yuri was my best man. Father and Mother were there, as were Lin's father and mother.

On a snowy night in March, our son, Andrew, was born. We both felt that our lives changed in an instant. From then on, nothing was more important than him. The doctors called his condition "amelia," a birth defect in which one or more limbs are missing. In Andrew's case, his left arm below the elbow was missing. Lin was crushed. No matter what I said, she felt responsible. She blamed her genes and her behavior: conceiving a child on a nuclear submarine where radiation may have caused the condition.

I could never bring myself to use the words "genetic defect," but to Lin, the answer clearly lay in genetics. After that, the Looking Glass took on a whole new meaning for her. Drive became obsession. She talked about a world where no mother would see her child born with a defect, where no child would have to face the world at a disadvantage or endure daily ridicule from his peers.

His condition most certainly didn't change our love for him. Andrew was a smart kid (which I believe he got from his mother) and adventurous to a fault (perhaps my contribution). He was brave, curious and never backed down.

Changes were afoot within the Citium. The experiments were growing in scale, and that required increasing amounts of money. So new members were recruited: billionaires, financiers, people with their hands on the levers of government research spending. They were all cut from the same cloth: people who believed the world was on the brink of catastrophe.

The influx of new members was a turning point for the organization, a Rubicon crossed unceremoniously. On the surface, things remained the same. Dozens of Citium cells were conducting Looking Glass research, and the members met every quarter at a conference we called our conclave. But behind the scenes, the organization was fraying. Each member increasingly thought that their own Looking Glass project was the sole solution for humanity's problems—and jockeyed for the funds they needed to make their vision a reality.

In 1972, I became head of Citium Security, a new organization dedicated to securing the cells and keeping our secrets. Only four of us, me and three of the Citium's oldest members, knew the full breadth of the Citium. We were creating a monster.

At home, life had settled into a pattern. I was gone a good while, but when I was home, I spent every spare minute with Lin and Andrew. He was growing up so quickly. We welcomed a daughter in 1973. We named her Madison—my mother's maiden name. Andrew was the most dedicated older brother I've ever seen; he may have been even more protective than Orville Hughes had been in that orphanage.

Lin worked herself to exhaustion. I worried about her, but the subject of how much she worked was a non-starter, so I gave up arguing about it. In marriage, as in war, some battles are unwinnable.

Our second daughter was born in 1977. We named her Peyton— Lin's paternal grandmother's maiden name. On the whole, she was more serious than Madison, and more inquisitive. She had the same curiosity and passion for adventure as Andrew.

I spent countless hours on planes and trains wondering what the three of them would be like when they grew up. And what sort of world they'd live in.

Then, at the Citium's Winter Conclave in Geneva in 1983, the unthinkable happened. A cell unveiled a plan for the Looking Glass—a functioning device that would accomplish our dream of securing humanity. The scale and cost of the project was incredible. Much of the science was still theoretical then (but has been proven since), but it was a working solution. War. Famine. Disease. Climate change. Meteor impacts. Cosmic events. Extraterrestrial interference. Artificial intelligence. The Looking Glass proposed that night at the lavish home overlooking Lake Geneva would protect us from all those threats—and many more. Even more impressive, it had the potential to unravel the great mystery the Citium had pursued since its founding: the purpose of humanity— the very nature of the universe and human existence itself. The scientists who proposed the Looking Glass saw it as the next step in the march of human experience, our inevitable destiny.

Not everyone was convinced.

The group of rational, even-tempered scientists I had come to know turned savage that night. The debate began as a spirited discussion and ended in screaming. I finally realized that we had been playing a zero-sum game. At the end of the Looking Glass project, there would be only one winner; only one device would be built. All other projects would be shuttered, the funds funneled to the winning project. And whoever controlled that device would have a power never before seen on Earth. Indeed, they would control the entire human race.

The night ended in a stalemate. Members made threats. Some said they would quit the organization and continue their research on their own, starting a new kind of arms race. Others threatened to expose the entire project; if their solution wasn't chosen, they would prevent anyone else from succeeding. Scientists, like all humans, can be very vindictive.

If I am guilty of anything, it's negligence. I didn't sense the ground moving beneath my feet. I took the words screamed that night for what they appeared to be: idle threats. Others did not.

A month later, I was flying from Cairo to London on a British Airways flight when it happened. Around the world, Citium scientists were assassinated. I had twelve Citium security agents in my employ; all were killed. I was unaware of this when I arrived at Heathrow. Indeed, in the cab on the way to the flat in Belgravia, my mind was only on Madison's birthday party, which was the following week.

The door to the flat was locked. When it swung open, I saw instantly that our home had been ransacked. I drew my sidearm, but I was too late. In my peripheral vision, I saw a figure, dressed in black, standing in my office off the foyer, the glass pocket doors closed, obscuring him. I spun, bringing my weapon up, but he was quicker. The bullet ripped through the glass, into my side, and blew me back against the console table and the antique mirror that hung above it. But I didn't lose my grip on the Sig Sauer P226. I squeezed the trigger, fired three rounds, and saw the man fall.

I spun and moved to the dining room. That action saved my life. The second man was in the kitchen. His shots into the foyer barely missed me. I fired through the wall, blind, then burst into the kitchen through the butler's pantry, catching him from behind. I had winged him. I didn't wait for him to turn; I shot him through the shoulder. He dropped the weapon.

I stood over him, held the gun in his face, listened for movement from my study, but heard none.

"Who sent you?"

Blood oozed from his mouth. He was European, with a close-cropped military haircut.

He gnashed his teeth, grunted. I grabbed his jaw, dug my fingers into his cheeks, separating his clenched teeth, but I was too late. He had cracked the tooth. The poison had already slid down his throat. I grabbed a ladle from the kitchen, forced the handle down his throat, and tried to gag him, but his body was already going limp.

Holding my side, I raced to the study. The other man was dead too. My files were gone. The safe lay open.

I grabbed the phone and dialed Lin's office at the university. No answer. I tried to stop the bleeding in my side. I'd need a doctor soon. I dialed my Citium assets in London. No answer. Berlin. No answer. Hong Kong, Tokyo, New York, San Francisco. They were all gone.

I raced to our master bedroom. Drawers lay open. Our luggage was gone. So was the children's. I counted that as a good sign.

I heard footsteps in the foyer. I peered out into the main hall, expecting to see a bobby, but instead saw two more black-clad former military men, guns drawn, sweeping the hall, moving toward me.

I squatted, took a spare magazine from my belt, thrust the Sig Sauer around the door frame, and squeezed off round after round. I wanted the men alive, but I wanted to live more.

I heard them collapse to the floor. I put a fresh magazine in, retreated to Madison's bathroom, found a hand mirror, and used it to peer into the hallway without revealing my position. They were down, unmoving.

I put on a black overcoat and fled into the night. Going to a hospital was a risk I couldn't take. A doctor we had used in my MI6 days patched me up.

In a cheap bed and breakfast near Tottenham, I made the rest of my calls. They confirmed my worst fears: an all-out purge of the Citium had occurred.

I still had several false identities; I used them to leave the country. I had no clue where Lin would have gone. Hong Kong was my first guess. I was wrong; she wasn't there. I tried everything to find her. I called her colleagues, but no one knew anything; she had given no warning about her departure. I placed ads with hidden meaning in the newspaper with no luck. I tried calling Citium members, but everyone was either dead or had gone underground.

So I did the same.

I waited, hoping the *Beagle* would make its scheduled docking at Nome, Alaska, but it never appeared. I saw three possibilities. My hope was that the vessel had been commandeered and the crew and researchers taken prisoner. Or that someone aboard had learned of the purge and that the *Beagle* and all souls on board had gone into hiding. I looked for proof of either scenario, but found none. That left the final option, my worst fear: they'd sunk her. The loss of the ship was tough. I had made a lot of friends on board during my time there. The research it carried was impossible to value—and essentially impossible to find.

I didn't try. I was entirely focused on locating Lin. She was a needle in a worldwide haystack, but I dug into it. I rented a small cottage in the country, a hundred miles from London, kept to myself, and spent every second investigating who had conducted the purge. There was no internet in 1983, no cell phones. People were much harder to find back then, but I made progress. Slowly, pieces began to emerge—Citium cells still operating. The names had changed, but there was a trail. A company called Invisible Sun Securities had absorbed much of Citium Security. I began putting the pieces together. I never stopped looking for Lin or the children.

The years went by, and my hope faded little by little. By 1991, I had designed an operation I hoped would reveal the truth about the purge. Everything was in place. But a week before I was to make my move, a package arrived at my door, delivered by an unmarked parcel van. No signature required. The house was like a fortress. I even had a bomb shelter built underneath.

With an extension arm, I cut the package open.

What I saw inside broke me.

It was a *San Francisco Chronicle* article about a medical student, Andrew Shaw, who had died in Uganda the previous week in a bushfire. He had been working for the WHO on an AIDS awareness campaign. I recognized my son's face, but I didn't want to believe it. Tears streamed down my face.

A handwritten note on a scrap of paper was also in the box.

Leave us alone, or the other two will be next.

Happiness and fear fought a war within me. Andrew was dead. Madison and Peyton were alive. But what of Lin?

I left that night, and I went deep underground. Off the grid. I never stopped researching the Citium, but I did it in a passive way now. I kept a folder on every known Citium cell, and year after year, I gathered more and more information. Several cells had survived the purge, and one of them was responsible for the slaughter. But I didn't know which.

I *had* gained one thing from Andrew's death: a last name. And with that single clue I discovered that Lin was alive in America. I debated for weeks whether to contact her, but finally decided against it. I followed her career at Stanford. I celebrated when Peyton was accepted to medical school. I cut out Madison's wedding announcement. And years later, I saw my children for the first time in twenty years: on YouTube. I watched videos of Peyton, sometimes for hours. She had grown into a fine woman, a wonderful doctor, with her mother's passion for her work. She reminded me so much of Andrew; I wondered if his death had influenced her career path.

I longed to reach out to her and Madison and Lin, but I knew it might put their lives at risk. Those years after 1991 were like prison for me. I dreaded the future. I saw the life I could have had slip away. I never got to be the father I wanted to be for my children, or a husband to Lin. My life was torture, but I held on to hope, and I prepared for a day when I could stop the Citium. Or, in the worst case, when they would find me—or force me to act.

Unfortunately, the worst case has indeed come to pass. As I write these words, our opportunity to stop them is slipping away.

Stop them. Don't give up. Use everything you know, take nothing for granted, and trust no one.

Desmond watched the words hit Peyton like punches in a boxing ring. She took them, her teeth gritted, for as long as she could— but eventually even this strong-willed woman he had met twenty years ago reeled under the weight of her emotions. She had seen her EIS team killed, had discovered she was infected with a deadly virus—and now she had learned that the Citium had destroyed her life and killed her brother—and that her parents had once been members of the group... It was too much for any person to take, no matter how strong.

A tear ran down Peyton's cheek. Then another. He pulled her into his arms. Her body heaved as she cried. He had never seen her cry so hard, even that day in California, when he had driven away pulling the Airstream trailer. He held her tight and made a promise to himself: he would save her life, and right the wrongs that had been done to her. He would do it, because in some way, he was responsible for what was happening.

And because he loved her. He couldn't say the words back then, and he didn't dare say them now, but at this moment, for the first time in his life, he knew them to be true. He loved her more than anything. He had loved her for a very long time.

He was so absorbed in holding her that he didn't hear the footsteps on the porch.

CHAPTER 83

THE DOOR TO the cottage flew open before Desmond could rise. The man moved quickly, closing the distance to the couch, a handgun pointed at Desmond. His eyes studied the back of Peyton's head resting on Desmond's shoulder.

She turned and froze, her eyes wide.

"Dad."

Peyton stood and threw her arms around her father, either unaware of or unconcerned about the gun in his hand. She hugged him with a force that made his eyes bulge. He was tall, with short white hair neatly combed over. His face was rugged, a few days' beard on cheeks that were red from the wind that swept the island. He was fighting back tears as Peyton held him.

But the events of this last week had confirmed to Desmond the wisdom of the advice in the pages on the table: *Trust no one.* With the blanket still covering his hands, he reached for his handgun.

William raised his own weapon.

"Don't, Desmond."

Peyton released her father, looking from him to Desmond.

"Hey, we're all on the same team here."

William's eyes never left Desmond. "We'll see about that. Take the gun, Peyton. Hand it to me."

Standing between the two men, Peyton hesitated. She reached over, threw the quilt off Desmond, and slid the gun out of his shoulder holster. She kept her body in front of his, shielding him, turned, and held out her free hand to her father, just inches from his gun.

"You too, Dad."

He scrutinized her, then seemed to read the *There's no negotiation* look Desmond had come to know so well. He smiled just a little as he handed her the gun.

"You've been watching us," Desmond said.

William moved out of the way of the windows and put his back against the stone wall. "Yes."

"Why?"

"You."

"I don't follow."

"I've been investigating the Citium for over thirty years—since the purge. I'm the only one with any chance of stopping them. And now, on the eve of the Looking Glass, they can't afford to leave me alive. It makes sense to me that they would send someone to kill me. Someone with a great story. Someone who could leverage perhaps the only thing in this world that could make it possible for anyone to get close to me." He looked at Peyton, indicating that she was that leverage—implying that Desmond had used her to get to him.

"I'm not here to kill you," Desmond said. "Just the opposite. I want to help you. To stop *them*. More than anything." His tone grew skeptical. "But I'm not the one who needs to explain. In '91, they sent you that box. They knew exactly where you were. Why didn't they just take you out?"

"I've thought about that a lot over the last twenty-five years."

"And?"

"And when I trust you, I'll tell you why I think they left me alive."

Peyton placed the guns on the kitchen table. "Let's start trusting each other right now. We don't have time to waste." She coughed, then inhaled deeply.

She's getting sicker, Desmond thought.

William studied her and seemed to realize it too. "Yes. Time is certainly of the essence."

Peyton motioned to the letter. "Let's start over. Dad, you wrote this letter to Desmond. Why?"

"Three weeks ago he contacted me online. I had developed a number of websites and identities related to the Citium and former projects. They were like breadcrumbs back to me in case someone ever surfaced. I expected maybe a scientist from before the purge." William motioned to Desmond. "Somehow, *he* found me. He said the Looking Glass was nearing completion. That he had been lied to, that what they were planning was very different from what he was promised."

He faced Desmond. "You told me you were going to stop them. Expose them. You wanted to meet. I refused. I told you to go public first. I didn't trust you. Again, I thought it might be an attempt to draw me out, eliminate me before the Looking Glass went live. I gave you the coordinates in the forest."

"Where we found the metal box."

"Correct. There were a hundred pounds of C4 under it. I would've blown you to tiny little bits if Peyton hadn't been with you."

Desmond looked over at her. "Well, thanks for that."

"I assumed you'd brought her along as leverage. But I needed to know for sure."

"You let us read your story to see my reaction."

"Yes." William walked closer to Peyton. "And to explain. I wrote most of it long ago, for you, Peyton, and for your sister. I wanted you to know what really happened. I thought about sending it to you a million times, but the risk was just too great. I decided it would be better for you to live not knowing, than to die for my peace of mind."

"Dad..." She began crying again, and William hugged her, held her tight.

Desmond nodded. It made sense. In fact, a lot of pieces were starting to fall into place.

William released Peyton and focused on Desmond. "What happened after you contacted me?"

Desmond sensed that the man was still testing him, trying to decide whether to believe him. He began telling his story, starting with waking up in the Concord Hotel a week ago.

"The message said, *Warn Her*, with Peyton's phone number."

"Warn her of what?" William asked.

"I think I just figured that out." But before explaining, Desmond wanted to get all the facts out there. He described his meeting with the journalist, being captured, and his time in confinement on the *Kentaro Maru*. He quickly summarized their escape with Avery, rescuing Hannah, and the Labyrinth Reality app, which he had re-downloaded in Dadaab.

"Before, in Berlin, the app didn't provide any entrances—no locations. But in Dadaab, it provided us with the coordinates you had given me."

"Interesting," William said.

"I must have programmed the app to release the location as a backup plan—probably after a set amount of time if I hadn't taken control of the situation. Coming here and joining forces with you would have been my last resort."

"Very clever."

"What about the second location—your childhood home?" Peyton asked. "It popped up after we reached the box in the woods."

"I believe that was a secondary backup plan," Desmond said, "in case this didn't pan out. Maybe I figured William might not show, or wouldn't be helpful."

"That was prudent." William motioned toward Peyton. "Let's go back to the message. *Warn Her*. Of what?"

"I believe I was supposed to warn her that she was in danger of being kidnapped, which is exactly what happened in Kenya. I think they wanted her to see the outbreak first, but mostly they wanted to take her so they could use her as a tool to get to you. For just the reason you stated: leverage. If you're right, and you hold the key to stopping them, Peyton becomes the key to stopping *you*—and thus ensuring their success."

Just then, Desmond wondered exactly how far the Citium would go to get to William. Would they have deliberately let himself and

Peyton go, so they would lead the Citium to William? Had the escape been a ruse?

He checked his radio. Avery should have checked in by now. Something was wrong.

Desmond stood, but he was too late. The door was already open. The rifle that breached the threshold pointed at him first, then moved to Peyton and William.

CHAPTER 84

AVERY DIDN'T TAKE her eyes off William. She pointed the rifle at the center of his chest. Her voice was commanding, devoid of emotion. "Step away from her."

William held his hands up and slowly moved away from Peyton.

Desmond saw a man ready to give his life for his daughter's without hesitation.

"He's on our side, Avery."

She sidestepped, moving between Desmond and William, as if ready to shoot either. She stole a glance at Desmond, then at the corkboards that were covered with articles, pictures, and names of Citium organizations and projects.

"What is this?"

"Thirty years of research," Desmond said. "The key to stopping the Citium."

"He's my father," Peyton said.

Avery cocked her head. "Okay... Didn't see that coming."

She lowered the rifle.

"How'd you find us?" Desmond asked.

"Tracking dot on your clothes." Avery smiled. "Not my first rodeo."

"Very clever."

"I figured if you were in trouble you wouldn't be able to radio me, and calling you would only reveal my presence."

They told Avery what they had learned, and she quickly

summarized her experience with Rubicon for William's benefit. He listened quietly, then asked her who ran the Rubicon program.

"I don't know. I was recruited by a man named David Ward."

"Are you in contact with him?"

"No. Phones are down. The websites I used for digital dead drops are too."

Desmond could read that William was skeptical. Time was running out—for Peyton and for so many others. They needed to make a plan, and quickly.

"Okay," Desmond said, "let's try to put it all together. We know the Citium released the virus. We know they have a cure. Let's assume they've manufactured a stockpile."

"Controlling the cure would effectively give them control of the world," Peyton said.

"Not if we find it first," Desmond said. "We find the cure, we stop them."

He walked to the corkboard. "Rapture Therapeutics. Rook Quantum Sciences. Rendition Games. Phaethon Genetics. Labyrinth Reality. CityForge. Charter Antarctica. Those are my companies. They were Citium projects for sure. The cure could be housed at one of these locations or at another Citium company."

"It's possible," William said, "but unlikely. I think the cure will have been developed and manufactured somewhere way off the beaten path. Outside an urban area, probably in the third world, where satellite coverage is minimal."

"The Isle of Citium," Peyton said. "In your journal, you said the *Beagle* stopped there periodically. It fits."

William nodded. "It's certainly a candidate, but not my first choice, for several reasons. One: whoever controls the Citium knows I'm still alive—and that I know about the Isle. Two: I've been monitoring it via publicly available satellite imagery. I haven't seen any activity."

Avery spoke up. "For locations that are considered uninhabited, those satellite images might only be updated every two or three years. Annually at best. The chance of spotting a supply ship arriving or leaving would be low."

"Perhaps," William said. "That's a reason to suspect the Isle. My final reason is more practical. The Isle is exceedingly hard for us to investigate. It's halfway around the world. Getting there will take us a long time, and will probably require refueling—and that's the easiest issue. If, in fact, the Isle is where the cure was developed and manufactured, it will be extremely well guarded." He motioned to the group. "We are four people. They'd know the moment we landed on the Isle, and we'd likely be facing a *very* large defensive contingent."

"We could make contact with the UK government," Peyton said.

"True," her father replied. "But convincing them to believe what we're saying might be a challenge—if they listen to us at all. They're likely struggling to survive. We need to act. We need proof before we go to any government for help."

"Let's back up," Desmond said. "Are there any Citium projects or companies that deal with infectious diseases or could be related to starting an outbreak?"

"Not during my time within the organization. If I had known any Citium members were doing anything even remotely like that, I would have turned them over to the authorities, and I'm not the only one. In fact, some of us were working specifically to *prevent* an outbreak or act of bioterror."

"How?" Peyton asked.

"It was Yuri Pachenko's project. I wasn't privy to the details, but I know he was designing what he called an adaptive antivirus: an agent that could be trained to recognize a virus and bind it, neutralizing it in the body. That might be the Citium cure."

"Yuri Pachenko," Desmond said. "He recruited me to the Citium."

William froze. "So he's alive."

"He was in 2002 anyway. That's the last I heard of him."

"All these years, I wondered if he had died in the purge."

"Is he an ally?" Peyton asked.

"Perhaps," William said. "Whoever controls the Citium now may have taken Yuri's research and completed it. Or perhaps the cure is something else entirely. Yuri may be dead by now."

Desmond noticed Avery eyeing him. Thanks to his comment

about Yuri, she now knew that he had recovered his memories—
and hadn't told her. Her expression was unreadable, somewhere
between nervousness and anger—or possibly betrayal.

He tried to steer the conversation back to the task at hand.
"What about Rapture Therapeutics? They were doing research
into bacteriophages with the potential to eliminate brain plaques
in Alzheimer's and Parkinson's. Could it be related?"

William thought for a moment. "I don't think we know enough
yet. The pandemic is certainly part of a larger end game—the
ultimate outcome being the Looking Glass. How Rapture ties in
isn't clear to me."

"Maybe there's a way to find out." Desmond held up his cell
phone. "There's the location from the Labyrinth Reality app. My
childhood home in Australia. What if the information we need is
in one of my memories located there?"

Avery spoke quickly, as if eager to shoot the idea down. "That's
a pretty big leap."

"I have to agree with Avery," William said. "And, the location
is a problem. It will take us a great deal of time to get there—
and it's remote. If the plane is low on fuel, we could be stranded.
I think it's too far away. And we have a better candidate."

William walked over to the laptop in the kitchen and opened it.

"Five years ago, I bribed an IT employee at an international
shipping company. I gave him the names of the Citium subsidiaries
and shell companies I knew about. He provided records of any
shipments paid for by the organizations or shipped to or from
their locations. At first, I thought it was a bust. But one location
intrigued me."

William opened an application Desmond wasn't familiar with.
On the left hand side of the screen was a series of satellite images,
each one dated; on the right was a world map with glowing
dots. William clicked a dot south of Russia, right at the border
of Uzbekistan and Kazakhstan. An overhead image appeared:
a small island on an inland sea.

"Several Citium-controlled companies were sending shipments
to this site: Vozrozhdeniya Island. The Russian doesn't translate

well, but it's roughly 'Rebirth Island' or 'Renaissance Island.' A fitting name. In 1948, the Soviet Union built a top-secret bio-weapons lab on the island. They expanded it in 1954, when it was renamed Aralsk-7. The Soviets' Microbiological Warfare Group operated there, testing some of the world's most lethal pathogens. In 1971, they accidentally released a weaponized form of smallpox. Ten people were infected; three died. Could have been a lot worse. People who worked at Aralsk-7 have admitted to working on anthrax spores and strains of bubonic plague— both of which were weaponized.

"The site was officially shut down in 1991. All the military and civilian personnel were evacuated. The town on the island, Kantubek, which had housed fifteen hundred people who worked at the facility, became a ghost town. That's why I was so surprised that the Citium was flying shipments into the island. Public satellite imagery showed no activity, but as Avery mentioned previously, for unpopulated areas, the images aren't updated frequently. I found a commercial satellite company that provided private imaging, and those images proved that the activity at the site has continued—until recently."

William clicked an image. "These are from the past month."

He hit the right arrow key, moving through the set. In the first image, the buildings on the island were lit. Desmond could just make out five figures at various points around the perimeter, wisps of smoke rising from what looked like cigarettes, dogs on leashes close beside them. In the next image, a convoy of trucks was backed up to a loading dock. Then the trucks were gone, but the guards were still there. In the final image, Desmond saw no signs of life, only darkened buildings.

"Does it show where the trucks went?" Avery asked.

"No," William replied. "The satellite contract was only for a limited coverage area. I assume they loaded the cargo onto a train in Uzbekistan."

That surprised Desmond. "I thought you said they were on an island?"

"It *was* an island—until 2001. The Aral Sea has been shrinking since the sixties. The Soviets diverted the rivers feeding the Aral Sea for irrigation projects. It's now about ten percent of its original size. In fact, it's just four large lakes at this point."

William turned to the group. "Overall, I think Aralsk-7 would be a perfect site to create the virus. The necessary infrastructure is already there. It's isolated. It can be defended. The land is split between the border of Uzbekistan and Kazakhstan. Either or both nations could have leased it to the Citium. And, the southern part of the island now has a land bridge to Uzbekistan, offering ground transport."

Desmond motioned toward the laptop. "But it looks like they're gone."

"Precisely," William said. "We know something's there—or was until recently. The evacuation of Aralsk-7 coincides with the outbreak—which means they no longer needed it at the exact moment the virus was released. And, with only four of us, it's a site we have a reasonable chance of infiltrating. Even if there's a small guard contingent remaining, we'll have the element of surprise."

"If they've evacuated the site," Peyton said, "what's our objective?"

"Information," William answered. "We're looking for a list of sites where they shipped the cure. We find that, we'll have something to send to governments around the world. And if we don't find that, maybe a sample of the cure. Perhaps it can be reverse engineered."

"Are there any other sites that could be potential candidates?" Desmond asked.

"No. Well, nothing this close. To me, Aralsk-7 is our best move." William scanned the room, prompting the others to weigh in.

"I like it better than the Isle. And a lot more than Des's childhood home," Avery said.

"Same here," Peyton said.

"Okay," Desmond said. He felt drawn to the Labyrinth location at his childhood home. He desperately wanted to know what was there—what he had left behind. But he knew William's plan was their best hope of stopping the pandemic. That was the priority. His own answers would have to wait. "So how do we get in?"

William pointed to what looked like a starburst carved in the brown terrain.

"What is that?" Avery asked.

"Four runways intersecting; only airport like it in Russia."

"Why would they intersect like that?"

"The weather on the island changes frequently. Wind direction shifts. Depending on the wind, you have to use a different runway. It's not exactly an easy landing."

Avery looked at the ceiling. "Wonderful."

DAY 12

5,600,000,000 infected
6,000,000 dead

CHAPTER 85

AT CDC HEADQUARTERS in Atlanta, Millen Thomas walked to the Biosafety Level Four laboratory deep inside the building. He stopped at the iris scan and held his head still. When the lock clicked, he pushed the door open.

The entire lab was a self-contained space with twelve-inch-thick concrete walls and a sixteen-inch-thick concrete floor with heavy steel reinforcement. The place was capable of withstanding an earthquake. By necessity, it also had its own air supply. Decontamination procedures involved flooding the space with vaporized hydrogen peroxide or formaldehyde.

In the clothing room, Millen grabbed a pair of surgical scrubs, socks, and underwear from the wire rack. He changed in the locker room, stowing every article of his own clothing. Glasses were the only personal item allowed inside the lab.

In the suit room, he taped his socks to the scrubs. He laid a positive pressure suit on the steel table, attached it to the air supply, and inflated it to check for any leaks. Even a small puncture could be deadly.

Upon landing in the US, the CDC had held him at the airport while they tested him for the virus. The CDC and health agencies worldwide were now calling it "X1-Mandera," as tests had confirmed that the flu and the hemorrhagic fever were in fact caused by the same virus, which mutated inside the body. Millen had breathed a sigh of relief when his results came back negative. He wasn't about to take any chances of getting infected now.

When he was sure the suit was airtight, he disconnected the hose, taped his inner gloves to his scrubs and checked them for punctures, then slid into the suit and donned the helmet. He braced himself on a steel table while pulling on a pair of rubber boots.

The entrance to the lab reminded him of the entrance to a spaceship. A door with a keypad loomed. He punched in his code and watched the red light turn green. The door opened with a pop, and Millen shuffled in and made his way across the room, past several researchers hunched over computers and microscopes. He connected his suit to a hose hanging down, then activated the speaker.

"How're you feeling today?"

Halima sat up on the bed, recognized Millen's face through the helmet, and smiled. "Good."

"Are they treating you okay?"

"Yes." She pointed to a portable DVD player lying on the bed. On the table behind her was a stack of DVD box sets including seasons of *Seinfeld*, *LOST*, *Alias*, *24*, and *The Big Bang Theory*. "They brought me some TV to watch. It's incredible."

The other villager, Tian, the young boy who didn't speak English, was asleep on the bed beside Halima's.

"How's the food?" Millen asked.

"Fine."

She glanced at the suited researchers behind Millen. "Are they close to finding a cure?"

He knew they had made little progress—and that the last few days had been pretty tough on the Kenyan teenager.

"They're very optimistic," he said. That was a bit of a stretch, but the truth seemed too harsh for what she was going through. "We appreciate what you're doing very much, Halima."

"I'm glad to do it." She held up the small DVD player. "Wanna watch *LOST*? I'm on season two. They just got in the hatch."

"Wish I could. My shift is about to start. I'll come back after though, okay?"

Outside the lab, with his suit still on, Millen waded into the chemical shower that lasted three minutes. After doffing the suit, he showered his body and changed back into his clothes in the locker room.

Many of the offices in the building had been converted to bedrooms where staffers like Millen now lived. He wondered how long they'd be there. Everyone at CDC headquarters was stressed and sleep deprived, but also incredibly focused. They all knew that the next few days would determine the fate of the world. For those like Millen, who had seen firsthand what the X1-Mandera virus could do, there was an added sense of urgency.

Everyone working and living in the building had tested negative for the virus. Some were CDC employees, but the vast majority had been assembled from the Department of Defense, Department of Health and Human Services, Homeland Security, and FEMA. There were a lot of new faces, and the place was chaos most of the time, but Millen was glad for the work. It kept his mind off Hannah—a little anyway. It was a losing battle though. He constantly came up with scenarios in which she was still alive. He imagined her escaping whoever had raided the village. Or that her captors had fallen sick, and now, being a physician, she was in charge; they needed her, couldn't kill her. Above all else, Millen wished he could turn back the clock and take her with him that morning when he went to the cave. Or at least say a proper goodbye.

He pushed the thoughts out of his mind as he entered the Emergency Operations Center. He needed to be focused for his shift. He signed in and walked past the giant screen that displayed all the cordon zones across the US. Real-time stats displayed requests for supplies and personnel.

Not a single operator sat idle; a hundred conversations were going at once. They all began with, "BioShield Ops."

A shift supervisor was rerouting a transfer truck full of medical supplies from the cordon in Durham, North Carolina to the one in Cary.

Riots had broken out in San Antonio; troops were being sent from Austin, and the CDC was routing additional medical staff with proper training.

Near Tulsa, a barge carrying oral rehydration salts had sunk.

In the conference room, the other shift supervisors were gathering for the mandatory meeting that took place an hour before their shift began. Millen braced himself for the updates; they were usually bad news. He sat down in one of the rolling leather chairs and waited.

Days ago, he'd watched Doctors Shaw and Shapiro attend a meeting in the same conference room. He had sat in the auditorium then, watching the people at the long conference table discuss decisions that would affect thousands, possibly millions, of lives. Now he was in the same position, literally. The weight of the responsibility was daunting, but there was nowhere he'd rather be.

The head of watch strode in and closed the door. His name was Phillip Stevens, and he was a senior epidemiologist at the CDC who had also been deployed to Kenya. Phil had led the contingent assigned to investigate the Mandera airport. His group had been evacuated after Millen's team was attacked. He was tall, with short blond hair, and didn't beat around the bush or mince words. Millen liked him.

"Okay, I've got some important updates. First, we're adding six new supervisors." He pointed to the video camera at the back of the room. "Like each of you, they'll have twelve operators. Their folks will work in the auditorium. IT has worked double-time to get it set up. That should ease some of the excess call volume.

"Last watch recorded a sharp increase in X1-Mandera fatalities." Stevens glanced at a page. "New York, Seattle, San Francisco, Chicago, and DC all report over four thousand deaths each. All told, at cordon sites nationwide, we saw over sixty thousand deaths in the past eight hours. There were only twelve thousand deaths during the shift before that. So we're looking at the start of a potentially rapidly increasing fatality rate."

Stevens paused. "That, in addition to what I'm about to show you, requires us to change our current approach. In thirty minutes, at your own pre-shift meetings, you're going to brief your staff on this decision. It may be the hardest conversation you'll ever have to have. Some may refuse to carry out our orders. There's a plan for that. The worst part is, you can't tell them the full truth about *why* we're doing what we're about to do.

"We have suspected for several days that the X1-Mandera pandemic was an act of bioterrorism. We know now that it was. We know who did it, and we know what they want."

CHAPTER 86

ELLIOTT STOOD IN his study, watching the BioShield convoy creep down the street. They usually came every afternoon and distributed food and medicine. Today they were early, and they weren't distributing food. They were taking people with them, loading them on yellow school buses as they had before. The National Guard, Army, Navy, Marine, and Air Force troops studied tablets outside the buses. They were apparently immune— they didn't wear space suits, and they displayed no caution as they herded the people onto the bus, often touching and shoving them. Their warm breath came out in clouds of white steam as they worked.

Methodically, they moved down the street. Families weren't taken together; they picked members seemingly at random. A father in his forties; a mother with gray-streaked dark hair who was slightly older than the man; a teenage girl; twin boys who were no older than twelve.

Elliott tried to see some pattern in it, but couldn't. Had the genome sequencing revealed something? Were these people potential carriers of antibodies that might fight the virus? He wanted to be hopeful about what was happening, but he was far too rational to believe it.

Sam and Adam were still in the basement. They had been rounded up along with Ryan after Elliott and Rose had been taken. Only Sam and Adam had come back. Adam had developed a fever yesterday. He was infected, and Elliott feared that soon Sam would be too.

They were all doing their best to maintain a quarantine in the home, but he doubted it would be enough to protect her.

The virus ebbed and flowed. For a few hours, Elliott would feel fine, or at least well enough to function, then it would hit him, overwhelming him and forcing him to lie down and rest until the fever and coughing passed. At the moment he felt pretty good—except for his nervousness.

He checked his cell phone. He had completed every one of the daily surveys on the Rook Quantum Sciences operating system. He'd had to: the phone beeped and buzzed incessantly until he filled them out. But there had been no survey today. What did it mean? And where were they taking everyone?

At the Dadaab refugee camp in Kenya, Elim Kibet sat in his office, listening to an official from the Ministry of Health. The man was sick. Elim thought he would probably die within five days. He coughed violently, and Elim stood, came around the desk, and offered him a bottle of ORS.

The man waved him off. "It's wasted on me." He stared with bloodshot eyes tinted yellow from the jaundice. "Will you do it, Elim?"

Elim leaned against the desk. "I will try. But it's their choice."

"That's all we ask."

"Will you stay?"

The sick man shook his head. "I must travel on."

"And die by the road?"

"If I must. I am dead either way. I will not lie here and wait for it."

Elim didn't blame him. He had felt the same way; it was why he had gotten up from his hospital bed in Mandera.

He showed the man out, watched him climb into his four-wheel drive and turn back onto Habaswein-Dadaab Road.

Elim made his way into the Ifo II camp, which held all the surviving refugees. Three fires burned, the flames smaller than they had been. This morning, the camp-wide count had revealed 14,289 survivors. When the outbreak began, 287,423 people had lived in the camps; he had found the earlier counts in the camps' records. The loss of life was staggering. And he was about to ask these people to see a lot more of it.

He asked one of the armed men to gather the camp's residents—at least, everyone able to rise from their beds—then he set about trying to find a bullhorn. It took almost an hour to get everyone assembled, but when they were ready, Elim climbed to the top of a box truck and stared out at the crowd that stretched across the rocky desert landscape.

"My name is Elim Kibet. I am a doctor, and a Kenyan citizen. I was born in this country and educated here. I've worked here all my life.

"Like many of you, I grew up in a small village. My parents were poor, and many nights we didn't have enough to eat. Thanks to this nation's generosity, I got an education. I served the people in my community as best I could. Fate led me here, to help you.

"I know many of you are not natives of Kenya. You are refugees from neighboring countries. This nation took you in when you were in need, fed you, kept you safe, and put a roof over your head. Now the people of our nation need your help. We are the ones who are starving and dying. We are in need, and *you* can help.

"Our government is not perfect. I have taken issue with much of what they have done in recent years. But its people—the people who paid the taxes that sent me to school, who fed and housed you and your family—those people are now depending on us. The government in Nairobi has collapsed. People are dying, not just from the virus, but from starvation and secondary infections.

"Right now, Kenya's survivors are scattered. That makes them vulnerable to armies large and small. War and famine may be the next enemies we face. To defeat them, we must come together.

"Tomorrow morning, at dawn, I will leave for Nairobi. I will stop at every village and town along the way, gathering survivors. In Nairobi, we will save as many lives as we can. I believe it is the best hope of survival for all of us. I ask you to join me. If you remain here, I will do my best to send help back, but I can't promise you anything. Together, I believe we have our best chance at survival. And we will save lives.

"Meet me here at dawn. I urge you. And I thank you."

Elim watched the crowd break. Many loitered to ask questions of the people who were effectively running the camp. There were no answers, no real plan other than to set out at dawn. He wondered how many would join him.

He instructed the men to travel to Garissa, the nearest city, and bring back trucks. They would stop there first. Garissa had had roughly 140,000 residents before the outbreak—roughly half the population of the refugee camps—but Elim hoped they would find many survivors there.

He returned to the aid agencies building, found Dhamiria, and took her by the hand. "I understand if you want to stay."

"You know me better than that, Elim. Wherever you go, I'll go too."

In Hannah's room, he inspected the young physician. She was stable, but the virus was advancing. Elim had been treating a secondary bacterial infection that he was quite worried about. The gunshot wound that had gone untreated for too long was likely to blame. She needed IV antibiotics, but Elim had none to give her. She was asleep now, and he was glad; the rest was good for her.

"Will we take her with us?" Dhamiria asked.

"Yes. It's her only chance."

☣

Elim barely slept that night. It seemed like there were a million things to do. He wrote endless notes to the nurses who would assume his duties when he departed (there were still thousands of people too sick to travel). He inventoried the supplies on hand, dividing up what would go and what would stay.

From the window in his small office, he watched the crowd gather at the trucks. They lined up, carrying sacks and backpacks and pushing carts with their belongings. Smoke from the fires rose into the sky, forming black clouds that hung over the camp and the mood of everyone within.

Dhamiria pushed the door open and walked to Elim's side. "They've loaded her up."

He nodded and rose. "Are you sure?"

She kissed him and squeezed his hand. "Let's go."

Outside, Elim surveyed the crowd. Over half the people who had gathered yesterday were here. Elim guessed there were four thousand people standing ready to join him.

To the nearest driver, he said, "We're going to need more trucks."

CHAPTER 87

IN THE CONFERENCE room at the CDC's Emergency Operations Center, Millen and the other shift supervisors listened as Phil Stevens stood before the large flat screen and briefed them.

"Two hours ago, the United States government, as well as governments around the world, were contacted by an organization that calls themselves 'the Citium.' The heads of watch were briefed an hour ago. We requested, and were granted, permission to play this message the White House received."

Stevens sat and worked the touchpad on his laptop. A recording began playing over the conference room's speakers.

"The Citium is a group of scientists and intellectuals dedicated to improving human existence through science. We have watched in horror as the X1-Mandera pandemic has decimated the world. We can stand by no longer. We have developed a cure for the virus—an antiviral that we have tested and used to cure thousands in our trials. We offer that cure to you and your citizens.

"In return, we ask only that steps are taken to ensure a similar global catastrophe never occurs again, and that other threats to humanity are removed. We seek a world with no militaries, no borders, no discrimination, and where every human is treated with decency and fairness. We are committed to this world; in fact, we demand it.

"In return for doses of X1-Mandera antivirals, we require that you take the following actions. Your congress or parliament will pass a law that places all government agencies and functions under the direction of an international oversight board called the Looking Glass Commission. The law will also place the power grid and internet under the commission's control. You will use the Rook Quantum Sciences application to allow your population to vote directly on the law, referendum, or constitutional amendment— whatever your system of government requires. It will be your job to persuade your population to approve and ratify the law.

"If you enact the Looking Glass laws, our first task will be to distribute the cure.

"Some governments may reject our help. Others will join us in creating the world humanity deserves. If you or your population deny our help, millions will die needlessly. We don't want that. We hope you join us. We look forward to working with you to create a better world for us all."

The recording ended, and Stevens stood. "This group, the Citium, doesn't explicitly take credit for releasing the virus, but we all know antivirals take longer than a week to develop—and even longer to mass-produce."

Millen spoke: "How did the White House respond?"

"They asked for a sample of the cure. That request was denied."

"They assume we might try to reverse engineer it."

"Correct," Stevens said. "The White House then insisted they wouldn't agree to the terms without a demonstration of the cure's effectiveness. I'm told that demonstration is to occur within the hour."

That shocked Millen. "So they're going to agree to the terms? Hand over the government, military, internet, power grid—everything to these terrorists?"

"No. We're going to fight. The White House is hoping to glean clues about the cure and possibly where it's being stored. The demonstration is an intelligence-gathering opportunity."

Another shift supervisor spoke—a slim black woman with graying hair who had worked in the EOC since before Millen joined EIS. "What are other governments doing?"

"The UK, Australia, Canada, Germany, Japan, and Russia have all committed to fight the Citium to the very end. France and

Greece have made no comment. We believe both nations have already surrendered."

The conference room fell silent. Millen felt that the entire situation had changed now. War? On top of the pandemic? It was unthinkable. He wondered what would be left of the human race when this was over. And what kind of world they would inherit.

Stevens took a deep breath. "The US is reaching out to China, India, Indonesia, Brazil, Pakistan, and Bangladesh. Roughly half the world's population lives in those six countries. If India or China join the Citium, or even if a few smaller nations join, the die will be cast. They'll have overwhelming numbers in a war."

"We have superior weaponry," a supervisor said.

"And very soon," Stevens said, "we'll have almost no one trained to use it."

Millen knew where this was going. The other supervisors seemed to sense it too. They waited for Stevens to continue.

"As such, the White House has ordered the CDC and all agencies under the BioShield command to begin preparing for the possibility of a conventional war here on American soil."

"Preparing how?" Millen asked.

"As we speak, BioShield forces are collecting individuals believed to have a high probability of surviving. Going forward, resources will be allocated only to these individuals."

Millen couldn't believe it. "And what about everyone else?"

Stevens stood staring at the shift supervisors. "This is the reality we face. If we can't field an army, the United States will soon cease to exist. If we accept the cure, the United States will effectively be conquered by the Citium."

Millen thought about his mother and father in Cleveland. He knew they were inside the cordon there. Neither was in a critical job role.

"What about our families?"

"They're on the list. Everyone's immediate family members—spouses and children, parents, siblings, and siblings' spouses and children—are on the list."

So they had thought of that too.

"What I just told you was very hard for me to hear an hour ago. I know it's just as hard for you to hear now—and it will be even harder for you to explain it to the operators working under you. If you don't think you can do that or carry out the orders that are about to be given to you, I need to know before you leave this room."

A supervisor next to Millen asked what would happen to their families if they refused.

"If you leave the BioShield command structure, their status will revert to whatever it would have been."

The supervisors sat in shock.

"I hope our intelligence agencies find where the Citium has stored the cure," Stevens said. "In the meantime, we all have our orders. Survival sometimes requires us to do things we don't want to do."

☣

When the meeting broke, Millen assembled his team of operators and began their pre-shift meeting. He didn't like what he was about to say, but he also didn't see any other alternative. He had to remain with BioShield—for his parents' sake, and for Halima and Tian.

"Okay, I hope everyone got some rest. I've got a very important update. There's been a change in strategic alignment. I can't tell you the specifics, only that we're facing a new threat. As of right now, BioShield is shifting its focus to saving high-probability survivors and preparing for an armed conflict."

CHAPTER 88

THE WIND TOSSED the Red Cross plane like a ship in a hurricane. William lined up with one of the four runways, then changed his vector and approached another. In the passenger compartment, Avery, Desmond, and Peyton buckled up and leaned forward, bracing against the headrests. Peyton was in the aisle seat, the safest place, with Desmond beside her, buffering her body from the plane's side. Avery was just across the aisle.

Peyton felt Desmond's hand touch her leg. He held it face up in her lap, waiting. She placed her hand in his. He squeezed. It seemed to drain the tension out of her. Touching him in that moment was like an electrical connection long dead and now activated. With it came a flood of emotions and memories.

Peyton stared forward. Out of the corner of her eye, she saw Avery watching them, staring daggers into Peyton's side.

The plane shook as the wheels hit the runway. On the whole it was a better landing than Avery's in Shetland.

Ten minutes later, the plane came to a stop at the end of the runway, and William stood in the passenger compartment.

"Desmond and I will sweep the tower."

Avery rose, ready to protest, but he cut her off with a raised hand.

"We'll need a pilot to leave if we're unsuccessful."

Peyton noted his syntax. He didn't say "killed." She thought that was for her benefit. She also saw wisdom in his plan: he didn't trust Avery either. Isolating her on the plane had that advantage. And it gave William a chance to speak with Desmond alone.

The two men suited up, descended the staircase, and disappeared into the night. Peyton stood by the door, watching as they slipped out of view. An awkward silence settled between her and Avery.

Finally, Avery spoke. "Did you know him?"

"What?"

"Before."

Peyton ignored her.

"You're the reason, aren't you?"

"What?"

Avery stepped closer to her, stopped two feet from Peyton's face. "You're the reason he joined the Citium. Why he wanted to build the Looking Glass."

Peyton wanted to swallow, but she resisted. She made her voice flat. "I couldn't say."

"Did you hurt him?"

"I'm not much for girl talk, Avery."

"We don't have to talk."

Boots pounded the ground outside, then up the ramp. Desmond appeared in the doorway to the passenger compartment and took in the tension in the room.

"If you two aren't going to kill each other, we could use some help."

☣

In preparation for the possibility of a hasty departure, they refueled and positioned the plane for takeoff. Desmond reported that the tower was empty, but that it looked to have been used recently.

William launched a drone he had brought with them. The device was small and nearly silent. They all crowded around a tablet in the passenger compartment, watching the images captured by the drone's night vision camera.

The town was deserted. The buildings were stone, two- and three-story, run-down mostly. They reminded Peyton of pictures of Germany after World War II. They almost looked bombed-out. Weeds and nature had retaken much of the landscape, and stone walls lay tumbled on the ground, the victims of time and gravity and perhaps the wind that whipped this strange island.

The drone flew on, toward the labs. A series of stone and brick buildings were arranged in a large horseshoe, forming a courtyard. A chain-link fence with barbed wire surrounded the complex; a metal gate with a curved sign hanging above it spelled out words in Russian that Peyton couldn't read. The motif was that of an American prison from the sixties—Shawshank, perhaps.

The drone made three passes, but found no sign of life.

William pointed to a house on the outskirts of the town. "We'll sweep the town, then stage here. Peyton, you'll monitor the drone feed from the house. Just keep flying over, and alert us if you see any movement. Desmond, Avery, and I will move on the complex."

☣

The town was creepy. Peyton thought it felt like an abandoned movie set: erected quickly, used and reused, then left to decay.

At the edge of town, closest to the labs, they found homes that showed signs of habitation. The windows were new, and the roofs had been repaired. But no lights burned, and they didn't hear a single sound except for the wind.

William and Avery took the right side of the road, Peyton and Desmond the left, systematically searching each house along the way to make sure it was uninhabited.

"Are you sure you're okay staying alone while we go to the labs?" Desmond asked.

"I'm not afraid of the dark," Peyton said.

"That makes one of us. This place creeps me out."

At the next house, Desmond ran through the rooms while Peyton waited in the living room. "It's clear," he said as he came back. But he didn't move to the door as she'd expected. Instead he said, "What was that about in the plane? With you and Avery."

Peyton glanced away. "Nothing."

"Didn't look like nothing."

"She's just trying to mark her territory."

Desmond bunched his eyebrows. "What territory?"

She smiled. "You know what territory."

Across the street, William and Avery entered another home and moved through it systematically, each calling clear as they swept another room.

Upstairs, William found a desk set into a dormer across from a single bed. Pinned to the wall was a wallet-sized photograph, faded and wrinkled, like colored wax paper. A picture of his three children. *Yes. This is the place.*

At the cabin in Shetland, William had held back on what he knew about Aralsk-7. He'd had to—for Peyton's sake. In truth, coming to this island had been a gamble. But now he was convinced: they'd find answers here.

CHAPTER 89

WHEN THEY'D FINISHED searching the town, the four of them regrouped at the house on the outskirts that would be their command post. It was empty and cold, but Peyton noted that there was very little dust on the furniture.

"Someone was living here very recently," Desmond said.

In the kitchen, Avery opened the refrigerator. "Within the last month."

Peyton got a whiff of the horrid smell before Avery slammed the door shut.

"Let's get set up," William said.

He placed a laptop on a coffee table in the living room and pulled up the drone footage for Peyton to monitor. He had pre-programmed a flight plan into the drone, and he took a few moments to show her how to alter it if needed. She waved his hands away from the laptop. "I got it. Go ahead. I'll be fine."

Peyton wanted to hug Desmond and her father before they left the small home, but figured it would be awkward with Avery left hanging. She settled for a nod, and the three departed.

Peyton watched them go from the window, then she sat on the cloth couch, pulled a thick cotton blanket over her, and watched the drone footage. Bathed in the green glow of night vision, Desmond, Avery, and William were now pushing past the complex's heavy iron gate. She let out a sigh and coughed— something she had avoided doing with the others around. The virus was gaining on her immune system.

☣

Desmond shivered as another gust of frigid wind hit him. He followed William, gun held at the ready, sweeping the man's left flank. The gravel crunching under their boots was the only sound in the night. Snow drifted down, then began falling harder. The wind caught the white flakes, tossing them around like the inside of a snow globe. The scene would have been beautiful if Desmond had had time to stop and observe it, and if he hadn't been so nervous.

William stopped at the complex's nearest building. The door was solid steel, with a hefty handle.

He nodded to Avery, positioned across from him, ready to sweep the room. All three pulled their night vision goggles down. Desmond stood behind William, who turned the handle, and then the three of them were rushing into the room, guns sweeping left and right, red laser pointers dancing over crates and plastic-wrapped pallets of supplies.

The building was a warehouse, and there didn't seem to be anyone inside.

Desmond moved across the concrete floor, to the first pallet, and peeled back the plastic. Cardboard boxes, flattened for shipping. There were dozens of pallets.

Avery called out in the darkness. "Packing tape over here, must be a thousand rolls."

William and Desmond joined her. Beyond, they saw pallets stacked with plastic jugs of water.

William stared at the pallets. "I think this is how they did it. Water. Boxes. Packing tape. It's a distribution system. I bet the cardboard contains the virus. It survives inside the closed cells. Any puncture lets it out. The tape, too. The infected water is likely highly concentrated; they mixed it with water bottles, maybe large jugs that go in offices or a city water supply. What's left here must be extras they didn't need. That assumes they manufactured the virus here. If we find it in the main lab complex, that will confirm it."

Desmond marveled at the genius of the plan. Parcels and water. A very simple yet effective way to distribute a contagion.

"But no cure," Desmond said.

William thought for a moment. "They may have shipped all of it off-site to test it elsewhere."

"Or manufactured it elsewhere," Avery said.

William nodded. "That's also a possibility. Let's keep moving."

In the next building, they found a manufacturing facility where the boxes and tape had been made and injected with viral particles. There was still no sign of anything that might treat the virus.

The main building, four stories high, held the labs. Desmond knew it the instant they crossed the threshold. The floor was white linoleum, recently cleaned. The walls were gray, with stainless steel handrails. It had the feel of a hospital in the sixties that had never been updated.

The three stood just inside the door, listening for any movement, hearing none.

William took a step deeper into the building, then another, cautious, as if the white square tiles might be mines that could explode at any moment.

He paused, turned his head.

Desmond heard it too: the whirring of a small electric motor.

William looked up to a black plastic bubble on the ceiling. Extending his rifle into the air, he used the barrel to bring the cover down, revealing a black security camera within. A red light glowed at its base. It panned to get Desmond and Avery into the scene.

William walked past them out the door, whispering for them to follow. The three stood outside in the falling snow, the yellow moon's faint light obscured, like a paper lantern behind a sheer white curtain.

"They're still monitoring the facility," William said. "Either someone on site or remotely."

Avery glanced around. "They could have a team in hiding or a rapid response force inbound right now."

William nodded. "We need to hurry. We're looking for shipping manifests." William motioned back to the warehouse. "They transported the tape, boxes, and water to their distribution centers. I'm willing to bet they shipped the cure there as well—whether it was manufactured here or somewhere else. We figure out where those facilities are, we find the cure. Let's move."

Back inside, the three of them split up and began racing through the four-story building. Desmond's boots pounded the white tiles. He found a surgical wing with bloody gurneys, scrubs left in piles, and ransacked medicine cabinets. These people had left in a hurry. On the second floor, he found a set of double doors that were locked. He activated his mic. "This is Desmond. I'm going to shoot a lock on level two. Have encountered no resistance."

Avery and William responded quickly, with the same word: "Copy."

Desmond shot the lock and pushed the steel doors open. The stench of rotting flesh overwhelmed him. He gagged, stepped back, bent over, and waited, fighting the urge to retch. The odor drifted past the doors, sweeping into the outer room like a ghost set free from its tomb.

By degrees, Desmond adjusted to the repulsive smell. He took a step into the vast room. It was a near copy of the *Kentaro Maru*'s cargo hold, with sheet plastic dividing cells that ran the length and width of the space. In the green glow of night vision, the scene was even more eerie.

At the first cell, Desmond drew back the milky-white plastic. An Asian male lay dead. Dried blood ran from his eyes and mouth. Had they just left these people here to die when they evacuated, locking them in here like animals in a slaughter pen? What kind of people could do this?

Fury erupted within Desmond, and the thought that he had once been part of this project repulsed him.

He activated his comm. "I've found bodies. They were testing something here."

"Copy," William said. "I've located the target."

He's found the shipping manifests. Desmond breathed a sigh of relief.

"Level three, front left corner," William said.

☣

William ducked in and out of the offices, searching quickly. In an office on the corner, with a couch and a long table, he found what he was looking for: the same picture he had seen in the home—his three children, holding hands on a street in London. It had been taken around 1982, William thought. This was the right office.

He moved to the filing cabinet, yanked it open, and began reading the folder names.

He paused at one that read, *Viral Candidates*. He pulled it out, scanned it. They had evaluated several pathogens for modification. He froze when he saw the notes in the margins. He was on the right track.

The rest of the drawer was filled with more research—documents of their trials. The drawer below that one had folders on distribution methods. They had tried air fresheners, hand soap, even cologne. All had proved either too expensive or ineffective.

The next drawer had folders marked with locations. Addis Ababa, Ethiopia. Dakar, Senegal. Harare, Zimbabwe. Lusaka, Zambia. Bamako, Mali. Conakry, Guinea. *This is it*, William thought.

He opened the first folder, read quickly. It was a study of the location's population, economy, transportation, and infrastructure. The page heading read, *Index Site Study*. These were places they had considered starting the outbreak. One of the files was marked *Mandera*.

William slammed the drawer shut, pulled open the last one.

A folder marked *Supply Shipments* sat in the very front. He pulled it out and let it fall open. Inside were shipping manifests— hundreds of them. Medical supplies. Water. Food. Were those words used as code for the virus, or the cure? They certainly wouldn't list "virus" or "cure" on the shipping manifests. No. This had to be it.

Into his mic, he said, "Desmond, Avery. I've located the target. Level three, front left corner."

He studied the folder, lost in thought.

Desmond's voice came over the comm. "William, I'm almost to you."

The explosion that ripped through the office threw William against the wall. The metal filing cabinet toppled over, trapping his leg.

☣

Back in the living room, Peyton heard the explosion. She leapt from the couch and raced into the street. The largest building in the complex was on fire. Another explosion went off, blasting brick and roof tiles from the facade like lava spewing from a volcano. She didn't hesitate. She began running toward the building, coughing as she went, her lungs already burning.

CHAPTER 90

THE BLAST KNOCKED Desmond off his feet. He rolled across the white tiled floor. Ceiling tiles rained down on him. He curled up, waiting for it to stop.

When the building fell quiet again, he caught his breath. He rose and ran toward the blast location. In the corridor, long fluorescent lights hung by wires from the ceiling. Doors stood open. Plate glass windows were shattered. Shards crunched under Desmond's boots.

In the stairwell, he felt warmth from above. He ascended, driving toward the blaze. When he pushed open the door to the office wing, a wave of heat blew past him.

A cubicle farm spread out before him; offices with exterior windows lay along its perimeter. Smoke and flames filled all of it. The fire was finding plenty to consume: papers, old wooden furniture, and most concerning, the wood studs in the walls.

"William, do you copy?"

William's voice was weak. "Copy, Desmond. I'm pinned. I found it. I'm going to read you the location where the supplies were sent—"

"Sit tight. Prep for evac."

Desmond studied the inferno churning through the office, trying to find a path to the corner office. Most of the cubicles and desks were burning, and the fire was moving quickly. For a moment, he was back in Australia at his childhood home, watching the blaze. Just like then, he gathered his courage as he prepared to wade into the flames.

But this time, a hand caught his shoulder.

Avery stood behind him. "Don't, Desmond." She grabbed his arm, but he threw her off.

"Come with me or stay," he said. "But don't get in my way."

Without another second's hesitation, he raced into the fire.

☣

Outside the building, the snow fell faster, sticking to the gravel courtyard. Peyton's footsteps left a track of prints in ash-coated snow, a trail that led directly to the front door.

☣

The heat of the fire was excruciating, but the asphyxiation was worse. Desmond held his breath as long as he could, then inhaled and coughed.

He was close to passing out when he reached the corner office. The blast had blown out the windows, and cool air rushed in, fueling the fire. Desmond inhaled for a few seconds, gathering his breath.

Ahead, he saw William squirming under a steel filing cabinet, looking for any means to work his way out from under it.

Desmond raced to him and gripped the steel cabinet. He was shocked when he heard steps behind him. Avery. She took hold of the filing cabinet, and together they pushed. The cabinet was not only heavy, it was buried under debris from the wall and ceiling. But it moved just enough for William to wriggle free. He stuffed a folder inside his body armor and tried to stand. One leg was fine, but he winced when the other touched the ground.

Desmond didn't wait for discussion. He leaned forward, pressed himself against William's abdomen, and lifted the man up onto his shoulder. Desmond estimated he weighed about 170 pounds, and Desmond's body protested under the added strain; his ribs still hadn't healed. But he pressed on, putting one foot in front of the other. Avery led the way, pushing desks and debris aside as they went.

Soon, Desmond let out the breath he had held, sucked in hard, got a mouth full of smoke, coughed, and stumbled—but he stayed upright. If he collapsed now, Avery would have to choose which one of them to drag from the flames.

He felt himself getting dizzy. His head swam, vision blurred. He was staggering. He felt Avery's hand grip his arm, pulling him forward.

Spots appeared in his vision. He was only vaguely aware of walking now. Waves of nausea washed over him.

The smoke was a wall of black. He thought he should have been clear by this point. The fire must have advanced since he entered the blaze. He had no hope of escape. His body was shaking, wobbling, as if he were being rolled in a washing machine, bounced around. His legs gave out. He fell to the floor, William on top of him. Everything went black.

☣

Peyton stopped just short of the burning cubicles. She panted, trying to catch her breath. Her chest heaved and ached. But she had to push on. She covered her mouth and drew the deepest breath she could, preparing to rush in.

At that moment, she saw a figure emerging from the smoke. Avery. Walking backwards. Dragging someone. Peyton peered around her, saw the short black hair. *Desmond.*

As soon as she was clear of the fire, Avery fell to the floor. Desmond's head rested in her lap. Avery's eyes rolled as she leaned back and coughed.

Peyton bent over Desmond, covering her mouth as she coughed. He wasn't breathing. The fire—the smoke inhalation—had asphyxiated him.

With every ounce of energy she had, Peyton dragged him from Avery's legs and ripped off his body armor.

Avery lay motionless, watching with watery eyes.

"My father?" Peyton asked urgently.

Avery closed her eyes and could barely move her head to shake it.

Peyton tried to focus.

She began chest compressions, counted to thirty, and started giving him rescue breaths.

Panting, she said, "Avery, I need you to find an AED."

The woman rolled onto her belly, pushed up with her elbows on shaking arms. Her head bobbed from side to side, like a boxer about to go down for the count. She collapsed again, rolled onto her back, and gasped for breath. She would pass out soon.

A scraping sound came from the wall of smoke.

Peyton looked up to find her father limping out of the fire, one arm covering his mouth.

She started another round of chest compressions.

William fell to his knees beside her and coughed. "Get out."

Peyton looked down at Desmond. She couldn't carry him. None of them could. But she wouldn't leave him. She had lost him once; she wouldn't again. She couldn't bear the thought of standing outside, watching the building burn, knowing he was inside.

In that moment, she finally understood, truly understood, what he had gone through as a child. It was unimaginable. The guilt. The remorse. And to go through it so young.

The flames and smoke were advancing. She placed her hands under Desmond's armpits and dragged him farther away. William crawled, collapsed beside Desmond, and panted, trying to get his breath. He unstrapped his own body armor, drew out a folder. His voice came out raspy and strained.

"Avery!"

The woman was ten feet from them, closer to the fire and smoke. She held her head up.

"The locations. Take it. Get out."

Avery's eyes flashed. The sight of the folder seemed to give her a burst of energy. She crawled across the floor, took the folder, drew a shallow breath, and coughed again.

William put a hand on her shoulder. "Go."

Peyton pressed her lips to Desmond's mouth again and restarted the rescue breaths.

From her peripheral vision, she saw William push Avery away. "Go. Before it's too late."

Avery stood on unsteady legs and staggered out of the office wing. Peyton rested on her haunches, gathering her own breath as she gave thirty more chest compressions. A tear ran down her face. Desmond was going to die, right here, in her arms.

Her father's eyes met hers.

"Please, Dad. Find an AED. He'll die without it."

CHAPTER 91

WILLIAM WAS PRETTY sure his ankle was sprained. Not broken, but it throbbed and spiked with pain every time he put weight on it. In the smoke-filled office wing, with Peyton leaning over Desmond, trying to save his life, he limped to a desk and found what he needed: an overturned table lamp and some clear packing tape. As quickly as he could, he disassembled the lamp and jammed the metal pole in his boot, parallel to his calf. He wanted to cry out from the pain, but he simply gritted his teeth, grabbed the tape, and wrapped his lower leg and ankle tight, ensuring it couldn't move.

He put weight on it, testing it. The pain was manageable.

He turned and began searching the walls for an AED, hopping along like a peg-leg pirate.

☣

With each step Avery took away from the fire, she could breathe easier. In the stairwell, she drew out the folder and scanned its contents.

☣

Past the cubicles, William hurried along the wall, searching. A minute later, he read the Russian letters for AED, pulled the device off the wall, and returned to where Peyton was still giving

Desmond mouth-to-mouth. She looked up when he approached. Her face was covered in tears. The sight was heartbreaking.

She took the device from his hand, tore Desmond's shirt open, and attached the patches to his chest. She made sure she wasn't touching him, then hit the large green button on the box.

It emitted a short squeal, then popped, causing Desmond to arch his back and inhale violently. His head thrashed about as he screamed—a ragged, raspy yell like that of a lifelong smoker.

Peyton took his face in her hands.

"Hey."

His chest heaved. His eyes were barely open. A tired smile formed on his lips. He said a single word. It sounded like "Scully." William didn't know what that meant, but Peyton laughed, and the tears flowed faster now. Tears of joy, William thought.

"We need to go," William said. "I can walk. Peyton, can you help him?"

She coughed, trying to clear her lungs and gather a breath. Then she helped Desmond stand, and the three of them limped out of the burning building.

Outside the front doors in the gravel courtyard, two sets of footprints were visible in the ash-coated snow: one from Peyton's arrival, and the other Avery's.

She had left them.

CHAPTER 92

CONNER SAT AT the conference table, listening to updates. France and Greece had become the first Looking Glass nations. On the large wall screen, he watched footage of doses of the cure being distributed in Paris.

"Stop right there. Take the five seconds preceding that and use it."

Someone behind him approached and handed him a note.

We have a situation. Hughes-related. Urgent.

Conner excused himself and made his way to his office, where an intelligence agent was waiting with a laptop. Though the government had taken control of the internet, the Citium's private network, connected by satellite links, was still functional. The agent opened a connection to the Citium net and pulled up a satellite video feed. It showed three figures opening the iron gate that enclosed Site 79.

"Zoom in."

Conner studied their faces. Desmond. Avery. William Moore. So Desmond had found the old man. Together, they could jeopardize everything he had worked for.

"How old is this footage?"

The agent checked the time stamp. "Fifteen minutes, sir."

"Do you have cameras inside?"

The man worked the laptop, brought up the internal views, and rotated through them. On three of the feeds, he saw them moving through the building, searching.

They've separated, Conner thought.

"Do we have charges in the building?"

"Yes. Standard Looking Glass precautions. In the labs and file areas." The young man paused. "Want us to blow them?"

"No." Conner held a hand up. "Let's wait."

They sat in silence for ten minutes. When William reached the corner office, he stopped at the desk and looked at a picture frame. The night vision camera revealed the change in his expression. Recognition. Realization. Then he rushed to the filing cabinet and began searching through the files.

"Whose office is that?" Conner asked.

"Unknown."

"Find out," Conner snapped.

On the screen, William paused at the last drawer, studied a file, and said into his mic, "I've located the target."

Conner stood. "Where's Hughes?"

The screen switched to one of the quarantine wards. Hughes was holding a plastic curtain back, disgust on his face.

"And the girl?"

The view switched to the mechanical room, where Avery was trying to crank a generator.

"Blow the charge in the office."

"Just the office?"

"Yes. And show me all the cameras."

The screen switched to a split-view of thirty night-vision cameras. They were motion-activated and could run for up to thirty hours without power.

Six cameras went black. Two more showed smoke billowing into the corridors. Another showed the office in flames.

Desmond and Avery raced through the hallways.

Conner leaned back, wondering what the man would do.

Desmond stopped at the fire. *He won't go into it*, Conner thought. He was sure of that. Avery gripped Desmond's shoulder, but he threw her off, and to Conner's shock and horror, he ran directly into the fire.

Conner stood and approached the door.

"Sir?"

He couldn't watch. "I'll be back. Don't leave," he said.

Conner made his way outside, wondering if he had made the right choice.

Ten minutes later, he returned to his office, where the agent was still watching the feeds.

Three figures stood outside the building: Peyton, William, and Desmond. So. He had made it out. And Peyton was with them. That further complicated things.

"What do you want to do, sir?"

"Let's make a new plan. One with no chance of failure."

CHAPTER 93

STANDING IN THE falling snow, Desmond, Peyton, and William watched the building burn. They were too tired and too injured to walk.

Desmond activated his mic. "Avery, do you copy?"

No response.

Peyton eyed him.

"Avery—"

The roar of an engine pierced the silence. The vehicle was moving toward them at high speed. Desmond couldn't make it out, but a cloud of dust rose from the road.

Headlights came into view, their yellow light fuzzy through the sheets of snow that blew in the wind. They crossed the threshold of the complex, past the iron gate, and into the courtyard, tires throwing gravel as they went, barreling directly for them.

The vehicle swung around and slid to a stop.

The driver door opened.

Avery stood and peered across the roof of the black Volga GAZ-21. The engine rattled like an ancient radiator on its last legs.

"Figured it wasn't the best night for a walk."

Desmond smiled as the three shivering passengers got in and the old Soviet-era sedan pulled away from the burning building.

They decided to take off immediately. If the explosions had been set off deliberately—instead of by an automated trigger—an incursion team might be inbound. They flew north initially, then banked east, then south, hoping to confuse anyone trying to track them across multiple satellites.

When they were at cruising altitude, William activated the autopilot and limped back to the passenger compartment. Peyton desperately wanted to examine his leg wound, but he waved her off. She had only just now recovered from the smoke inhalation. She was still getting sicker, and the physical exertion of the last hour hadn't helped her situation. Her body ached all over.

To Avery, William said, "We need to figure out where we're going. You have the folder?"

Avery handed it to him, and William threw open the manila cover and began rifling through the pages.

"I thought there was more here," he mumbled.

"What is it?" Peyton asked.

"Requisitions. Shipping manifests. Medical supplies. Water. Food. Tents. Antibiotics. Rehydration salts."

"Everything you'd need to test an outbreak," Desmond said. "But no shipments of cure or virus? We assumed they were using boxes, packing tape, and water."

"Water is on here," William said, deep in thought. "And the manifests would probably be faked—the actual cure or virus would be labeled as something else."

It was clear he thought something was wrong.

Desmond took out his satphone. "What's the nearest location?"

William looked up as if remembering they were all there. "Actually, they're all to a single location."

"Maybe that location was the distribution point to all the others. Aralsk-7 is landlocked and pretty out of the way."

"Maybe," William said, sounding unconvinced. "The address is in South Australia, near Adelaide. The destination is an organization called SARA: South Australia Relief Alliance." He read out the address, which Desmond typed into his phone.

Peyton, William, and Avery crowded around him.

A tent complex stretched out in a grid next to a single long metal building. It reminded Peyton of the Dadaab refugee camps. A dirt airstrip lay nearby.

Desmond panned the map right, then south. Peyton leaned in. *What's he looking for?*

He stopped on a black mark in a brown expanse. She realized then what it was: the remains of his childhood home. The second location the Labyrinth Reality app had provided. It was his second backup, and it lay less than seventy miles from the camp. *Why?* Was it connected? It had to be; the coincidence was too great.

"The backup Labyrinth location is here," Desmond said. "I *wanted* myself to go here, and now we know the Citium was shipping to this site. Even if, by some chance, those things are unrelated, we can follow two leads at once."

William rifled through the pages in the folder again, scanning the address on each manifest carefully.

Peyton said, "What's the matter, Dad?"

"This feels wrong. The location should be a port or a major shipping hub—not a relief organization."

Avery eyed him. "Some of the pages could have been lost during our escape."

William glanced away from the group. "True."

"Or maybe we got the wrong file," Desmond said.

"Well we can't exactly go back and search again," Avery said. "But we know they were shipping *something* to this site."

"At this point, I think going to this site is our only move," Desmond said.

Silence followed.

Peyton's met Desmond's eyes. She sensed that he wanted to see what was at his childhood home. She remembered going there with him, all those years ago, the pent-up emotions he had pretended weren't there back then. She agreed with him: this was their best option.

"I say we check it out," she said, staring at Desmond.

"Me too," Avery said.

William nodded. He was still distant, lost in thought. Finally he stood.

"Right. I'll set a course."

DAY 13

5,900,000,000 infected
9,000,000 dead

CHAPTER 94

MILLEN HAD BEEN asleep for two hours when the announcement came over the loudspeaker.

"EOC shift personnel, report to Auditorium A."

The tone was urgent.

Millen's bedroom was a small office in the interior of the building. It was dark and cold, but it was quiet.

He turned on the table lamp, rolled out of the cot, and staggered to the desk where his pants lay before hurrying downstairs.

The auditorium was filled to capacity. Phil stood at center stage, working a laptop.

"All right, listen up. The White House has received another message from the Citium—a video. I'm going to play it now, then we're going to discuss what we're going to do. Please keep quiet."

On the screen behind Stevens, the video played. Sick people stood in the streets of a city in a line that stretched for blocks. Many coughed as the video panned past them. Some were in wheelchairs. Toward the front of the line, people had rolled their sleeves up. A man in a white coat with a Red Cross logo held a jet injector. He pressed it to each person's shoulder, pulled the trigger, then changed out the single-use protector cap that covered the injector nozzle.

A woman seated at a table spoke to each person who'd been injected, typed something on a laptop—presumably the person's name—then handed them a sticker.

The camera zoomed in on one of the stickers.

X1 Guéri

The subtitle read *X1 Cured*.

The camera panned around and showed the Eiffel Tower in the distance. The scene changed. It was another city, with a similar line of people, their shirtsleeves rolled up as well. On a hill above them, crumbling stone ruins towered. The Acropolis. Millen recognized the Parthenon instantly. Athens.

A man's voice began to speak over the images. He had a slight British accent.

"Earlier today, the people of France and Greece received the life-saving cure for the X1-Mandera virus. We offered you the same cure. You declined. You sentenced your citizens to death so that you could stay in power. We are providing this video to give you one last chance.

"Do the right thing for your people. Save their lives.

"We ask very little. We seek a peaceful world, where no human can kill another, where science is the engine that turns the world, not greed, not war, not hate or selfishness.

"In the event that you require further proof, we have covertly deployed the cure inside your borders for you to confirm."

The video changed. On screen was a white woman in her mid-forties. A teenage girl and a younger boy sat with her, a black background behind them. The woman faced the camera and spoke with a southern drawl.

"My name is Amy Travis. I live in Johnson City with my daughter Brittney and son Jackson. I was sick. So were my children. A man came to my house. Said he was part of a group of researchers called the Citium. They were testing a potential cure. I agreed to try it. I'm making this video because I want others to know that it works. I'm proof. So are my children." The video changed again. This time a young black man spoke. A woman sat beside him, and in her lap was a boy only a few years old.

"My name is Roger Finney. This is my wife, Pamela, and our son, Brandon."

A voice off screen said something Millen couldn't make out.

"Oh, yeah, we live in upstate New York, just outside Rome.

We were given the cure. We signed the forms. Didn't have much to lose. It worked for us. Felt better that night. Headaches and fever were gone. Cough cleared up soon after that."

The screen faded to black, then began showing still photos from across America. Scenes of the cordon zones. Barbed wire across city streets. Buses loading and unloading people at the Astrodome in Houston and AT&T Park in San Francisco, canvas-backed trucks unloading supplies, National Guard troop carriers rolling through cities.

"This is your country right now. But it doesn't have to be."

More still photos appeared, but now of Paris and Athens, of lines of people receiving the cure, celebrating. Photos of the two American families followed.

"Accept our request. Pass the laws that welcome the Looking Glass Commission. If you do not do so within the next two hours, we will take our plea directly to your people. They will overthrow your government. The result will be the same—but there will be more bloodshed. Think carefully. Make the right decision—the responsible decision. Just as France and Greece have."

The video faded to black.

The auditorium erupted in questions. Synchronized shouts swept through the crowd like a beach ball being tossed around at a ball game. On stage, Phil whistled loudly.

"Enough!"

"Is it true?" a voice in the back yelled.

"Shut up and listen!" Stevens shouted. "Yes. What you saw is true."

The response was shock and whispers. A part of Millen thought maybe the video was faked.

Stevens continued. "Five hours ago, the French and Greek governments agreed to the Citium's terms. The Citium, as the terrorists have styled themselves, have taken control of both countries' military assets, power grids, and internet infrastructure. They have also distributed a cure that appears to be viable."

Murmurs went through the auditorium.

"The French and Greek governments have provided us with

samples of the cure. Military jets flew those samples here two hours ago. As we speak, researchers are studying it in this building."

Millen wondered if they were comparing it with the antibodies from Halima and the other villager, as well as the samples he'd brought back from Elim and Dhamiria.

"As you know, we've been preparing for the prospect of an armed conflict. Right now, survivors and likely survivors are staging here in Atlanta and other cordons. Here in this room, each of you needs to decide which side you're on: if you're going to help us secure this city, or if you want to join the Citium and attempt to overthrow the government."

For the first time, Millen noticed the Marines at the front and rear exits.

"Think hard. Your decision may cost you your life."

CHAPTER 95

ON BOARD THE Red Cross plane, Desmond, William, Peyton, and Avery were debating where to land. At Aralsk-7, they'd had no choice: the airstrip was the only access to the island, and it was far enough away from the town and labs to be reasonably safe. But the single dirt runway in Australia was directly adjacent to the camp.

Their other options weren't much more appealing in Peyton's opinion. Desmond wanted to land in a field, but was concerned that the struts supporting the landing gear might buckle, stranding them. Avery advocated landing on a road. They had consulted the map and identified several candidate sites, but William was wary: what if there were power lines, abandoned cars, mailboxes, and other items not on the satellite imagery?

Still, it seemed like the best option. They consulted the plane's manual, discovered the width of the wheel track, and did the math: the wheels would fit on the roadway—just barely. They picked a location, did a flyover, and were satisfied the path was clear of obstacles.

Peyton buckled herself in and braced for the worst as her father lined up the plane and began descending. The wheels screeched on the pavement, and the entire plane vibrated as it slowed on the straight stretch of blacktop, the morning sun blazing through the windows. The back wheels veered into the dirt shoulder, but William quickly brought the plane back and slowed to a stop.

Avery and Desmond left to scout the camp and report back.

From the plane's doorway, Peyton watched them hike across the brown terrain, their body armor on, semi-automatic rifles slung across their shoulders. She didn't like leaving Desmond alone with Avery—she still didn't trust the woman.

As if sensing Peyton watching him, Desmond stopped and turned. A small smile crossed his lips when he saw her in the doorway.

"Mic check," he said.

"Copy," she replied. "Be careful."

"Roger that."

Peyton reminded them again to keep their distance from anyone who might not be infected.

When Desmond and Avery disappeared over the next hill, Peyton turned to her father. She had rebandaged his leg as best she could and had inspected the other bruises and scrapes on his body, but he needed an X-ray—and a pain medication stronger than the ibuprofen she had given him. Those things would have to wait.

"I don't trust her," she said.

He was studying the folder from Aralsk-7, shuffling through the pages like he was counting a deck of playing cards.

"Neither do I."

☣

Two hundred yards from the camp, Desmond and Avery lay flat on their stomachs, taking turns using the binoculars.

What Desmond saw didn't make sense. Healthy individuals, moving about. Kids going to school. Breakfast cooking on an open pit grill just outside a building with a concrete floor, metal poles at each corner, and a corrugated metal roof. People sat at rows of tables eating. About half of them were aboriginals.

There was not a single sick person here. No personnel in PPE.

Was this the Citium's test site? Were these people the lucky ones—the test group who had gotten the viable cure?

Desmond focused the binoculars on the largest building, which was enclosed on all sides and had a small loading dock on the back. A sign above a roll-up door read: *SARA*. Below it were two lines of text: *South Australia Relief Alliance* and *A Hand Up, Not a Handout.*

The door was halfway up, and as Desmond watched, a woman with gray-streaked brown hair ducked under it and walked out onto the concrete loading dock. Spring was turning to summer here, and she was wearing a long-sleeved T-shirt that rippled in the early December wind.

Desmond focused the binoculars. His eyes went wide when he saw her face. She had aged some, but there was no mistaking who she was. He wracked his brain, trying to reason why and how she could be here—why the folder at the Citium lab would have led here.

He let the binoculars fall to the ground.

Avery sensed his unease. "What?" She took the binoculars, scanned the camp, searching for what had alarmed him. "What did you see, Des?"

He stood up.

She shifted to her side and stared up at him, aghast. "Get down."

"Come on. We're going to the camp."

"Are you crazy? You're just going to walk in there?"

"Yeah. This place isn't what we think it is."

CHAPTER 96

DESMOND HIKED ACROSS the field with Avery close behind him, making a beeline for the building to the right of the white tents.

Avery grabbed his arm. "Will you tell me what's going on?"

"Not sure myself."

"What does that mean?"

"It means there's something going on here that I don't understand. A piece is missing."

He stared straight at the loading dock where the woman stood. She had seen them, had raised a hand to shade her eyes. She was calling to someone inside.

☣

Back at the plane, William winced as Peyton taped the ankle again.

"Sorry," she whispered.

"It's okay. Just hurts a bit."

He held up a page and studied the handwriting in the margin. He was sure of it now.

He picked up the handheld radio.

"Bravo, Tango, report."

He released the button. But no response came.

☣

As Desmond and Avery approached, the woman stepped down from the loading dock and walked across the gravel drive. She stopped where the field began, squinting, trying to see who they were. Desmond wondered if she would recognize him.

A man walked out of the building, came to her side and asked her something. She shook her head.

Avery unslung her rifle.

"Don't do that," Desmond said.

"This is creeping me out, Des. Tell me what's going on."

"I told you, I don't know."

The people eating at the tables under the open-air building had noticed them. Some stood, trying to get a glimpse of the two armor-clad figures approaching.

When they were thirty yards away, the man waded into the field. Desmond guessed he was in his late thirties. His long brown hair blowing in the wind reminded Desmond of a surfer.

When he spoke, his accent was Australian, his tone suspicious.

"Can I help you?"

Avery cut her eyes to Desmond.

"No, I don't think so. But I think *she* can."

He kept marching forward past the man, who hurried back to the woman. She stood still, showing no hint of nervousness or fear, only curiosity.

When he was ten yards from her, Desmond stopped and studied her face.

"Hello, Charlotte."

☣

William tried the radio again and again, but there was no response. Peyton could tell he was getting more nervous by the second.

"What is it?" she asked.

"I'm not sure."

He began assembling his body armor, getting ready.

"Are you going out there?"

"Yes—"

They both heard it at the same time: a truck engine, barreling over the hills.

Peyton stood, was about to move to the door, but her father caught her arm. "This is important, Peyton. If you recognize anyone at the camp, don't say anything. Tell me first."

She nodded. "Okay."

She walked to the back of the plane to cough. The fever and chills were getting worse. She pulled her shirt up. The rash had advanced. She had coughed into the back of her hand, leaving tiny specks of blood. She wiped them on the underside of her shirt. She didn't want her father, or Desmond, to know how sick she was.

A few minutes later, Desmond appeared at the plane's door.

"It's safe."

"What did you find?" William asked.

"It's... not what we thought. Come see for yourself."

CHAPTER 97

THEY RODE IN an old Land Rover, Avery behind the wheel, Desmond beside her, explaining what they'd found.

"It's a relief camp. They take in anyone displaced by natural disasters: hurricanes, floods, drought, earthquakes. They take some folks who've just fallen on hard times, too. Their focus is getting people back on their feet."

"Do you think they tested the cure here?" Peyton asked.

"I doubt it. You'll see."

"Do you know anyone there?" William asked.

Desmond cocked his head, surprised by the question. "I do. The woman running it. Charlotte. In 1983, my family passed away during the Ash Wednesday bushfires. Charlotte was one of the relief workers who helped in the aftermath. She... took care of me, helped find my uncle and get me to America."

"Have you spoken with her since then?" William asked.

Desmond thought for a moment. "Not that I know of. But it's possible."

"Did she recognize you?"

"Yeah. She did."

William stared out the window, the wheels turning in his head. "Interesting."

The camp wasn't high-tech. It was optimized to stretch every dollar

563

to feed as many mouths and shelter as many lives as possible. The only advanced piece of medical equipment was an old X-ray machine, donated by the Royal Adelaide Hospital. Peyton insisted on using it on her father's leg. He protested as he limped to the corrugated iron building, wincing every time his foot hit the ground.

"This really isn't necessary, Peyton."

"It really is, Dad."

☣

Desmond and Avery found Charlotte in her office, tapping at her cell phone. They kept their distance and made no physical contact. Peyton had expressed serious reservations about entering the camp at all—she still didn't know how the virus was transmitted from person to person—but Desmond and William had argued that their need for information was more important than quarantine. They had to take some risks. Ultimately Peyton conceded, on the condition that the four of them remain in the building and avoid interacting with any camp residents other than Charlotte and her second-in-command.

Charlotte motioned them in, and Desmond and Avery sat across from her in a pair of '70s-style wood and cloth chairs that had probably been salvaged from an old government building.

"Any luck?" he asked.

"No. Internet still routes to the AussieCordon website. I check twice a day to be sure." She set the device aside. "Did you find your friends?"

Desmond nodded, told her about the X-ray.

"I'm glad we could help. It's about all we have around here. Broken bones are by far the most common injury we see." She paused. "And some burns."

Desmond nodded. Seeing her, and hearing her words, brought back a flurry of memories. He could vividly remember lying in that elementary school, in the makeshift cubicle, her reading to him by lantern light. She had been a lighthouse in the darkness. He wondered what she was now, how she was involved.

"Did you get my letters?" she asked.

He raised his eyebrows.

A remorseful smile crossed Charlotte's face, one that said a fear she had long held had just been confirmed. "After you left, I sent them every week. For maybe a year. Less frequently after that. Every month."

Desmond imagined Orville staggering out to the mailbox, half-drunk, tossing them in the trash and telling the mailman not to deliver anything with Desmond's name on it. "Boy don't need no bleeding-heart woman making him any softer than he already is," he would have said.

"My uncle was a complicated man. He wasn't much for keeping in touch with folks. Or allowing me to."

"I suspected you never got them. I thought about you a lot after you left, wondered how things turned out. Even thought about coming to America to visit."

"I wish you had."

"Was it terrible?"

"No. Not at all," Desmond lied.

Charlotte seemed to see through it. She grew quiet, stared down at her desk.

"What about you?" he asked.

"Not much to tell."

"I doubt that."

She shook her head. "The alliance is my life. This work. These people."

"You're good at it. You changed my life."

She smiled.

"Did you ever get married?"

"No," she said quietly. "I came close once."

"That guy who was at the school?"

Charlotte thought a moment. "Oh. Him. No. That was not a close call."

Avery was getting impatient. "I think we should talk about the reason we're here."

Desmond exhaled. "Right. Charlotte, we found this place

because of supplies shipped here. We want to ask you about that. But first, I think I should give you some background."

Peyton studied the X-ray of her father's ankle, which showed no fractures.

"It's just a sprain," she said to him.

"I'm telling you, I'm perfectly fine."

"Just try to stay off it and it'll heal up in a few weeks."

"The world doesn't have a few weeks." He made to stand up, but she blocked his path and put her hands on her hips. He exhaled and sank back down.

Despite his continued protests, she used some of the supplies in the medical closet to make a proper splint.

When she was done, they walked down the corridor toward Charlotte's office. Desmond's voice drifted out into the hall. He was describing what they'd found in Kazakhstan at Aralsk-7.

Peyton pushed the door open.

The woman sitting behind the desk looked to be in her early fifties, with a slightly lined face and trim physique.

Peyton did a double take. She turned quickly, trying to hide her shock. "Sorry, I forgot something. Be right back."

She grabbed her father's arm, guided him back down the hall to the medical exam room, and shut the door.

"Peyton, I really am fine—"

"I know her."

"What?"

"That woman. I recognize her. I can't believe it."

CHAPTER 98

WHEN PEYTON AND her father returned to Charlotte's office, Desmond was laying the folder on her desk.

"These are the shipping manifests we found in Kazakhstan."

Charlotte scanned the pages. "They look accurate."

"There was no sender name, just the shipping company."

Charlotte was still reading through the pages. "They were paid for by the Zeno Foundation."

The name caught Peyton's interest. According to Avery's story, Zeno was the Greek philosopher who had founded the Citium over two thousand years ago.

"What do you know about the foundation?" Desmond asked.

"Not much. They're very generous. They had a website where I could request supplies, food, water, even money."

"Who was your contact there?"

"Tanner Goodwyn."

The name meant nothing to Peyton.

"Did they ever ask you to do anything—to conduct trials on experimental vaccines or medicines?"

Charlotte looked disturbed by the idea. "No. And I would have refused, no matter how badly we needed the help."

The four of them questioned Charlotte at length, exploring a number of possible ways she might be tied to the outbreak, but found no common thread. As best they could tell, the Citium genuinely seemed interested in supporting her work.

"It's possible that *I* sent the supplies," Desmond said. "Though I don't know why I would have done it in secret."

"A good point," William said. "Charlotte, I wonder if you'd excuse us for a moment."

"Of course. I'll just wait outside."

When she closed the door behind her, William said, "We're getting nowhere here. And we're running out of time."

"There's still the location near here," Desmond said. "My childhood home. The second backup from the Labyrinth Reality app."

"I think it's our next move." William nodded to Avery. "The two of you should check it out. We'll continue questioning Charlotte."

☣

Ten minutes later, Peyton, William, and Charlotte stood on the loading dock watching the Land Rover drive down the dusty dirt road that led out of the camp.

"Charlotte, could we trouble you with a few more questions?" William asked.

"Of course." She held her arm out, motioning them back into her office. William closed the door. "Perhaps learning more about you might help us understand how you're connected."

She raised her eyebrows. "Oh. All right then."

"Desmond told us you were a relief worker in the early eighties."

"I was. Well, I was at university then, but I volunteered as much as I could."

"And after uni?"

"Med school."

"Specialty?"

"Family medicine. I got a masters in Public Health. That was really my passion."

"Where did you work?"

"After school? The WHO." Some of the cheeriness faded from her, as if it was something she didn't want to talk about.

"And you lost someone close to you there."

Her eyes grew wide. "Yes. In 1991."

That was the year Peyton had seen her. She had been thirteen years old then, standing at a gravesite in San Francisco. The cemetery was on a hill outside of town. Skyscrapers and the bay stretched out in the distance. A thick cloud of fog hung over the water and snaked into the city, its white tendrils flowing in and out of the red steel supports of the Golden Gate Bridge and the glittering silver buildings.

When the service ended, a woman in her early thirties had walked over, a sad smile on her lips. She spoke to Peyton's mother, then her sister Madison, and finally to Peyton.

Her accent was Australian, her voice kind.

"Your brother meant a great deal to me, Peyton. He told me you wanted to be a physician."

"Not anymore."

The woman took a small metal item from her coat pocket and held it out to Peyton.

"He was very proud of you. I believe he would have wanted you to have this."

She placed the small silver pin in Peyton's hand. The teenager examined it.

"I thought it burned."

"I had it cleaned and refinished." The woman smiled. "I wanted you to have it in the same condition it was in when your brother carried it. All things can be repaired, Peyton. Some simply require more time than others. Don't let tragedy take your dreams away."

The woman in the shabby office in Australia looked at Peyton now, twenty-five years later, with the same kindness in her eyes. And now, recognition.

"You're Andrew's youngest sister, aren't you?"

Peyton nodded.

"I still think about your brother a great deal—miss him a great deal."

"Me too," Peyton said quietly.

"Would you like to see him again?"

CHAPTER 99

DESMOND WALKED SLOWLY to the burned remains of the home where he'd spent the first five years of his life. Weeds had reclaimed some of the once-charred terrain. Only the masonry foundation and fireplace now stood, like a blackened tombstone.

He felt his cell phone buzz in his pocket. There was a message from the Labyrinth Reality app:

Download Complete

Download of what? Another memory?

Without warning, Desmond's vision blurred. His head swam. He staggered, lost his balance, and fell to his knees. *What's happening to me?* He braced himself on the ground with one hand. He felt nauseous. He tried to focus, but the memory came like a blow to the head, hitting hard, overwhelming him.

He stood in a bathroom at a long vanity with two sinks. In the mirror, he saw a bank of three empty urinals. He seemed to be alone. He couldn't place the location, but he felt like this wasn't long ago—probably shortly before he woke up in Berlin.

He stared into his own eyes in the mirror and spoke solemnly. "I hope you know what's going on by now. This location is a backup. I wasn't able to figure out where the Citium was manufacturing the cure, but I know they shipped it all around the world. There must be a storage site close by, maybe in Adelaide. Search for it. I'm also enclosing the rest of the memory that took place here. It may help you. But it could also hurt. It's leverage, but it goes both ways."

The bathroom disappeared, and Desmond was back in Australia, on that day in 1983 when the bushfires killed his family. Except this memory was from that morning, before the fire killed his mother. He didn't understand what he was seeing. His arms felt weak.

Then he felt Avery at his side.

He closed his eyes, thought he would throw up.

When he opened them again, he saw figures, clad in woodland camouflage, racing in from the tree line. A dozen of them. He reached back for his rifle, but it was gone. It lay on the ground twenty yards away. Who had thrown it over there?

He pushed up, but a boot hit his chest.

"Stay down, Des." Avery towered over him. Her rifle was pointed in his face.

"Avery—"

"I don't want to hurt you." She studied him. "You remember, don't you?"

"Yes."

CHAPTER 100

PEYTON WATCHED CHARLOTTE rummage through the old filing cabinets in the storage room.

"It's here somewhere... along with some other things of his I've kept."

Peyton's father cut his eyes at her, silently saying, *Where's this going?*

Charlotte pulled an old VHS tape from the bottom drawer.

In a room with a small, cathode ray tube TV, she popped the tape in a VCR and pressed play.

"This was taken the day Andrew died." Charlotte studied the picture, which was coming into focus. "He's in Uganda, on his way to Kapchorwa, his last stop."

Peyton saw her brother riding in the back of an SUV, which bounced on a dirt road with a trail of dust rising in its wake. It was so incredibly good to see his face again. His hair was dark, like Peyton's, but his features were less Asian than hers; he looked more British, like her father and her mother's father.

"Kapchorwa's a small town in East Uganda," Charlotte said, "roughly twenty-four miles from the border with Kenya. Only a few thousand people lived in the town then, but many more from the surrounding villages visited each month for the open-air market and hospital.

"This was 1991," she continued. "We were just realizing how bad HIV/AIDS was then. The virus had gone undetected for decades. It was spreading quickly in the late eighties and early nineties. Millions around the world were infected, most with no idea. They lived for years, often decades, without symptoms, spreading it unknowingly to their spouses and others. The virus was deadly for 99% of those who contracted it. The only available treatment merely slowed the virus's spread within the body.

"It was very brave what Andrew was doing. Visiting these towns and villages, standing in a room, telling the people assembled that their neighbors were dying of a deadly disease—and that they might also be infected. But we had to do it. It was the only hope of stopping the pandemic."

"You were part of the effort too?" Peyton asked.

Charlotte nodded. "I was in Kampala. Waiting for him to return."

The video switched to a scene inside a ramshackle building. Ugandans sat on worn wooden benches, painted white walls peeling behind them. Two ceiling fans buzzed overhead, and the audience fanned themselves as they waited. It reminded Peyton of a rural church in America's Deep South, Alabama or Mississippi perhaps. The analogy was apt; the assembled were disciples of a sort. These were community leaders—doctors, nurses, police officers, teachers, family planning association workers, resistance committee members, and village elders—gathered to hear a message that could determine whether the people who depended on them lived or died...

The Ugandan Ministry of Health had told the crowd only that they were to receive a critical announcement regarding public health and safety. Like other places Andrew had visited, the residents of Kapchorwa district had turned out en masse; over a hundred people filled the room. Those arriving late, after the benches had filled, stood at the back. Andrew waited at the front, where the collapsible lectern he carried around the country had been set up. It was his pulpit. To the credit of those assembled, not many had stared at him when they came in. Their eyes had lingered only a second or two on the tall white man, and many had averted their eyes when they saw his prosthetic left arm.

The congregation grew quiet when the district administrator cleared his throat and stepped up to the mic. His name was Akia, and he spoke in heavily accented English.

"Ladies and gentlemen," he said, then paused to make eye contact with as many of the assembled as he could. "Thank you for being here today. What you're about to hear may shock you. It may... change the way you see every person around you. It will likely frighten you. I, personally, am frightened. But I want you to know that the government of Uganda is committed to fighting this deadly epidemic. We will win, and you will be a part of this great victory, which will be remembered by your children and their children. With that, I welcome our guest, Andrew Shaw of the World Health Organization."

A few claps followed, but not many. Perhaps that was because so many held fans, or because they weren't sure whether they should clap after such a frightening introduction.

Andrew stepped forward and began the presentation he had given a dozen times before. He spoke with the British accent he had acquired growing up in London.

"In the early eighties, the CDC, the principal disease detection agency in the United States, began tracking a very deadly, very strange disorder. It attacks the immune system. When people contract this disease, they become unable to survive common infections. This immune deficiency develops over time, but it is lethal; a person who could normally fight off a cold or diarrhea or malaria might die from it. We call this condition Acquired Immune Deficiency Syndrome, or AIDS. It's the result of a virus called HIV.

"We've developed a test for this virus. We've tested blood at hospitals in Uganda as well as samples from the general population. Based on these tests, the Ugandan Ministry of Health estimates that roughly 14% of the people in this country are infected with HIV. That equates to one in every seven people—or about fifteen of the people in this room."

The people looked around, shifting uncomfortably. Spaces

were made between people in the pews. A few people held their breath. And questions erupted.

"Is there a cure?"

"A treatment?"

"A vaccine?"

Akia held up his hands, and the room again fell silent.

"There's currently no vaccine or cure," Andrew said, "but there is a treatment that prolongs the life of those infected. It's called AZT, and it will soon be available in Uganda and throughout Africa. In addition, the smartest researchers in the world are working on other similar drugs, vaccines, and even a cure as we speak. I hope they'll be available soon as well.

"But for now there's only one certain cure for a disease with no treatment or vaccine: isolation. We must isolate the virus so that it can't spread. If it has no place to replicate, the virus will die out. We have that power. The people in this room can stop the virus in this district. The solution is education and lifestyle changes. That's what I'm offering you today, and that's what we want you to teach to the people you serve."

Akia began passing out the information packets as Andrew continued.

"First, you should know that this disease cannot be spread by sitting or standing next to someone." The rows of worried attendees relaxed. "HIV is not an airborne infection. You also can't get it from shaking hands or hugging or touching someone. It's transmitted in four principal ways: birth, blood exchange, needle use, and unprotected sex. Blood and semen.

"There's nothing we can do about birth. A pregnant woman who is infected will pass the infection on to her newborn. But the other methods of transmission are all preventable.

"To combat the spread of HIV via blood exchange, the WHO and the Ugandan Ministry of Health are implementing testing procedures at hospitals and clinics throughout the country to detect the virus.

"That leaves needle use and unprotected sex. Sex is by far the most prevalent method of transmission, and the biggest concern.

"Those who are more sexually active are at far greater risk of contracting HIV. We believe, for example, that 86% of the sex workers in the country are HIV positive." Several of the men in the room grew still, their eyes wide. "About one in every three lorry drivers has the disease. IV drug users are also at high risk.

"However, as I said, there is a solution. Uganda has developed a simple method for stopping the spread. We call it ABCD. A for Abstinence. B for Be faithful. C for use a Condom. And D for die. If you're not married, choose abstinence. If you're married, be faithful. If you can't be faithful, use a condom. And if you don't use a condom, you die.

"There's one other thing I want you to take away from this meeting: compassion. The people with this virus deserve love and understanding and care—not discrimination. They don't mean you harm. They're just like any of us. Please don't stigmatize people with HIV. As I've said, many will be children who are simply born with the disease. We don't choose how we were born."

That last line drew every eye to his missing left arm. In the first town where he had said it, he had realized why he had been selected for this assignment.

The session lasted almost two hours. When it was over, the group filed out of the whitewashed room with their pamphlets in hand, and promises to contact Akia and others in the district office with any questions.

The two Ugandan soldiers assigned to escort and guard Andrew began breaking down the lectern. He gathered his papers and stashed them in his bag.

Akia reviewed the roster of attendees. "We did pretty well. Only two didn't attend."

"Do you know them?"

"Yes. They are from the same village—Kasesa."

"Where is it?" Andrew asked.

"In Mount Elgon National Park, near the Kenyan border. About twenty kilometers from here. I will go. It is important to me that everyone in my district knows of this disease."

Andrew slung his bag over his shoulder. "I'll go with you."

"No. It may be dangerous."

"I'm coming with you, Akia. If it's important to you, it's important to me. We're in this together."

The man smiled broadly. "Well then, let us go while we still have the light."

☣

The tape went black and the VCR clicked.

Charlotte stared at the old TV for a moment. "The camera crew went back to our regional command post at Mbale. That was the last anyone saw of Andrew. We found his burned remains, along with Akia and a hundred villagers, deep in Mount Elgon National Park.

"It was very brave what he was doing. HIV/AIDS is almost common knowledge now, but it was new and very scary back then. Uganda was a huge success in the fight against the AIDS epidemic. It was the first country where the WHO pioneered a single national plan and budget that all donors agreed to use and fund. The government got behind the effort. We synchronized the message and efforts, brought all the stakeholders to the table. It was all about changing lifestyle. It was our only weapon in the fight. And it worked. The US Census Bureau and UNAIDS program estimated that there was a 67% drop in HIV/AIDS infections in Uganda between 1991 and 2001. Millions of lives were saved. Children who would have been born with HIV, a death sentence then, were spared; they grew up healthy with a shot at a normal life.

"I think Andrew would have said that was a cause worth fighting... and dying for."

Charlotte grew quiet. "We had talked about getting married after our tours were up in Uganda. I've often wondered what my life would have been like if we had." She glanced at the old tape. "Seeing this again... it's tough. It brings back so many memories."

Peyton couldn't help wondering what could have been. Charlotte, this woman who seemed good-hearted and dedicated, could have been her sister-in-law. The thought made her miss her brother even more.

"Yes," William said. "It was bittersweet to watch. I think for all of us. Thank you for showing us the video, Charlotte. It means a great deal."

"Of course."

They walked back to Charlotte's office in silence. Ahead, Peyton heard papers rustling. Someone was waiting for them.

Charlotte pushed the door open. Standing inside her office were three men in woodland camo. Two pointed rifles at Charlotte and the others; another was looking through the folder from Aralsk-7.

Peyton turned and saw two more soldiers blocking the end of the hall.

"Don't do anything stupid," said the soldier looking through the file. "No one needs to die here."

CHAPTER 101

ELLIOTT HADN'T SEEN or heard anything from the authorities all day. The BioShield convoys that distributed food hadn't come. And just like yesterday, the Rook Quantum Sciences app hadn't prompted him to take the daily survey.

Rumors were going around. The most pervasive was that the government had developed a cure but was hoarding it. Another theory went that the government was preparing for a world war, conscripting survivors, and leaving the sick to die. With each passing hour, the absence of food and medicine made the rumors more believable.

Elliott sat in his study, thinking about what was happening. In his mind's eye, he saw Rose, sick and alone, lying on a blanket in the Georgia Dome, coughing, burning up with fever. The people who had cared for her were now gone; they were preparing to protect the downtown cordon headquarters from the mobs descending upon it. The city was tearing itself apart. He imagined Ryan, a physician, charged with caring for the wounded in the battle, trapped, his own life in danger. He thought about his grandson, Adam, whose cough was getting worse each day. Ibuprofen no longer controlled the fever. Sam was dedicating herself completely to caring for the boy now. She had given up on avoiding infection.

From his window, Elliott could see a convoy of trucks moving slowly down his street. Men and a few women sat on the backs of the trucks, rifles in their hands. They hopped out and walked to each door, talking with the neighbors.

When the knock at his door came, Elliott answered it, careful not to swing the door too wide.

A man in his thirties, with a weather-beaten face, long brown hair, and a beard, stood on his doorstep. He had left the rifle on the truck; his hands were held in front of him, slightly raised, showing that he meant no harm. He said his name was Shane, and that he and his wife had a daughter being held downtown.

"We're going after her. Lot of other folks are heading that way too. We ain't lookin' for a fight, just want to get our people and leave in peace. We're going out to the country to try to make it.

"Just letting you know. If you want to come along," Shane glanced at the RV, "maybe take some people with you. More numbers we got, more chance they'll just stand down."

Elliott considered this. "I've heard the roads are blocked—military checkpoints."

Shane glanced back at the truck. "Yeah, we got a plan for that." He stepped away from the door. "Hope you join us. Either way, good luck."

Back in his study, Elliott watched several neighbors raise their garage doors, get in their cars and trucks, and join the growing convoy.

When the procession had departed, the neighbors Elliott had convened at his home days earlier once again descended on his house. He gathered them in his study, where they sat and argued.

Finally, Elliott said, "Okay, stop. Raise your hand if someone in your family is being held in the downtown quarantine zone."

Four hands went up. "Raise a hand if you've got someone sick at home."

Three more hands went up.

He leaned back in his chair. "Here's what we're going to do."

At the CDC headquarters, Millen stood at a seventh-floor window. Below, his colleagues and other BioShield staff were filing out, loading onto the buses.

Phil walked up and stood beside him, but said nothing.

"Where will they take them?" Millen asked.

"Outside the cordon. Hopefully outside the battle lines."

Millen watched figures in FEMA jackets loading food into a box van.

Ten minutes ago, Millen had heard a rumor that the president had died from X1-Mandera. Or had been assassinated.

"Is it true? The president's dead?"

"Yeah."

"Who's in charge?"

"One way or another, I'd say the Citium is now in charge."

☣

Thirty minutes later, Millen was wearing a positive pressure suit. The door to the BSL-4 lab hissed open, and he walked in to find Halima lying on the bed, watching the portable DVD player. Tian was playing with a handheld game console.

Halima smiled at Millen and put the DVD player aside. "I was worried. Everyone left."

Millen set some food on the steel-topped table. "Are you hungry?"

"Starving. No one came this afternoon. All the researchers stormed out. We couldn't hear what they were saying."

Millen forced his voice to remain calm. "It's nothing. Just urgent meetings. I'll bring the food from now on. Is that okay?"

She nodded as she took a bite of the sandwich.

"Good. I'll come back in a few hours."

And he would. He had made a promise to take care of the two Kenyans, and it was a promise he intended to keep. His parents had taught him to take his commitments very seriously. He wondered where his parents were now, if they were safe. There wasn't much he could do for them. But he would do everything he could for the people of Atlanta and the two Kenyan villagers in his care.

Upstairs, he walked to the EOC, sat at his desk, and studied the satellite images. He pulled on his headset and typed:

MedSupply unit 227, be advised, combat units are assembling at Mitchell and Central Ave to meet hostiles inbound. Estimate two hundred, heavily armed en route with others arriving. Recommend you fall back to rally point Gamma-Bravo.

Elim Kibet rode in the passenger seat of the box truck that rolled through the littered streets of Nairobi. Buildings were burned. Cars lay in charred ruins. Children with blood on their faces watched the truck go by, the flames and smoke behind them a heartbreaking backdrop.

Elim could hardly look. His country's capital city had fallen.

He hoped that somewhere in the wreckage, he'd find survivors he could save—and IV antibiotics. Hannah was in the truck behind him. She would die soon without them.

The stoplights were dark and lifeless. At an intersection, the lead truck in the convoy paused as the driver checked the cross street. It was blocked off with two burned cars—roadblocks. Elim felt a tinge of nervousness.

Someone raised their head above one of the burned cars, peered at the truck, then ducked back down.

"Go!" Elim said.

The driver of the truck floored it, but it was too late. Ahead, two armored troop carriers pulled into the street, blocking their path. Armed men poured out, guns held at the ready. In the side mirror, Elim saw a similar force pull up behind the convoy.

They were trapped.

CHAPTER 102

DESMOND LAY ON the metal floor of the cargo container in near darkness.

At the burned ruins of his childhood home, the soldiers had zip-tied his hands and placed a black bag over his head. They hadn't pulled it off until they'd shoved him in the container.

His cell, such as it was, had six round holes about a foot off the floor, each about an inch in diameter. Desmond figured they were there to let air in, or perhaps for warehouse employees to verify the container's contents without opening it. He pressed an eye to one of them. Rows and stacks of cargo containers sat on a concrete floor.

After a few minutes of searching, he found a twisted edge on the corrugated metal wall. In the dim light, he carefully placed the zip-tie against the sharp metal, then sawed back and forth until his hands came free.

He heard tapping against the wall of another container. A pattern—Morse code, he thought. Someone in another container? Desmond didn't know Morse code. He tapped three times to acknowledge that he had heard the signal. Three taps responded from the original location. Then three more, and three more— both from different locations.

So, including himself, there were four of them. He was sure Avery would have captured William and Peyton. William was probably the one who'd started the Morse code tapping. Who was the fourth captive? Charlotte, because they'd told her too much?

Someone tapped a new pattern. This one wasn't Morse code, and it was familiar to Desmond. He squinted, listened, then grinned. The taps mimicked the theme song to *The X-Files*. It ended with a single large tap. He rolled to the metal wall, began tapping the same refrain back.

Twenty years ago, he had sat on a cloth couch in a living room in Palo Alto and watched the show every Friday night, Peyton beside him, a cup of tea in her hands, occasionally a glass of wine if she'd had a tough week at med school. Desmond would have given anything to go back there and start over. He wondered if it was too late for the two of them. He knew Peyton had been hiding how sick she was. How much time did she have? The thought filled Desmond with energy. He had to find a way out of the cell.

☣

Conner McClain sat at the head of the conference table, waiting for the call to connect. He was nervous. The Citium were on the cusp of completing their great experiment. In the following days, two thousand years of work would come to fruition. Or fail.

And now he had the last piece they needed: Desmond Hughes. If Avery had completed her mission, the man had recovered his memories—and the details of how to retrieve Rapture. Letting him go had been a risk, but one he'd felt he had to take.

The call connected, and the screen showed a view of an industrial office with cheap furniture. Plate glass windows looked down on a warehouse full of metal shipping containers. A man in woodland camo stood next to a solid wood desk covered in nicks and scratches, papers strewn across its surface. Avery stood beside the man, her arms crossed just below her breasts, her blond hair hanging down, her gray-blue eyes cold. Conner found her incredibly attractive. He wondered what might develop between them when this was over. She'd had no interest before—but soon he would be the second most powerful person in the world. That might change things.

The man spoke first. "We've got them."

"Why were they in Australia?"

"A woman," Avery said. "Charlotte Christensen."

Conner had never heard the name. "Who is she?"

"A relief worker who took care of Desmond after the Ash Wednesday fires."

"Interesting."

"We captured her as well, just in case she's connected somehow." Avery leaned off the desk. "We'll bring them to you."

"No."

"We need—"

"I'll come there when this is finished."

Avery's eyes flashed. Conner couldn't read the expression, but he thought it was anger.

"We had a deal," she said, her voice hard.

"We still have a deal."

"I want in."

"You'll get in. When I say so." Conner paused, letting his words hang in the air.

Avery exhaled, broke eye contact with him, and slouched back against the desk.

"I want him well guarded," Conner said. "As you know, he's a very resourceful man."

CHAPTER 103

ELIM OPENED THE truck door. The driver yelled at him to stay inside, but Elim knew his next move was his only choice, perhaps his convoy's only hope of surviving the ambush. Into his radio, he called for everyone to stay inside their vehicles. His white coat made him less likely to be gunned down than the rifle-carrying men in the canvas-backed trucks behind him.

He stepped down from the truck's cab, held his hands up, and marched forward. The troops exiting the armored personnel carriers came into focus. Elim exhaled when he saw their uniforms: Kenyan army. When he had seen the ambush, he had assumed the worst—that it was gang-related.

An officer strode forward. He was coughing. The lapels of his uniform were stained red, and his eyes were yellow and bloodshot.

His voice was much stronger than his appearance. "Who are you?"

"Dr. Elim Kibet. We're survivors. And we're here to help."

☣

Elim found the Kenyan Ministry of Health in shambles. The Emergency Operations Center wasn't staffed, and the phones were ringing constantly.

To Dhamiria, he said, "Get people in here, have them start answering these phones. Tell callers that we will send help when we can and to do their best until we get there. They need to hear that."

Kenyatta National Hospital was in even worse shape. Dead bodies lay on gurneys. People filled the waiting room. Blood covered the floor and walls. The staff had bags under their jaundiced eyes. Most were like walking zombies; they had been working so long they could hardly think. Elim insisted they take a break. He sent every one of the doctors and most of the nurses to the on-call rooms and a hotel nearby. They were too tired to argue with the newcomer.

Then he had his people set about cleaning up the hospital. Over the next four hours, Kenya's oldest and largest hospital went from a bloody, disheveled mess to at least some semblance of a functioning trauma and referral hospital.

He stood in Hannah's room now, gazing down at her. Even before the first mop had gone across the floors, before disinfectant was sprayed on the walls, Elim had made sure she was brought in, placed in a patient room, and hooked to IV antibiotics. She would survive the infection, but the virus was overtaking her body. Organ failure was beginning. She hadn't even woken up when they had brought her in. She would die within hours. The thought saddened him. It also reminded him of Lucas Turner, the other young American he had tried to save.

He stood for a long moment, then pulled the thin, white blanket up to her chin and walked to the window. A line had formed outside the hospital. That was good: there were still people healthy enough to get here.

He had work to do.

The CDC was in chaos. In the EOC, operators were ending their calls, getting up, and rushing out of the room. Millen stood at his desk. On the wall screen, scenes of the fall of Atlanta played without sound. The mobs were massing on the combined BioShield troops, which included Army, Navy, Marine, Air Force, and National Guard units. Many of those in uniform had lain down their arms and walked across the line to join the gathering crowd. They had taken an oath to defend the Constitution of the United States from all enemies, foreign and domestic—and for many of them that didn't extend to shooting their own mothers, fathers, brothers, sisters, and neighbors when they were simply sick and seeking help. Millen couldn't blame them. He wondered what he would do if he were on the line in riot gear.

Phil walked up behind him. Millen thought his supervisor was going to reprimand him for not answering the call beeping on his headset, but instead he told Millen to follow him.

At a floor-to-ceiling glass window on the seventh floor, they looked down Clifton Road. A crowd of people filled all five lanes, but a procession of three pickup trucks—each with men on the back holding semi-automatic rifles—weaved through the mob, toward the line of BioShield troops who formed a perimeter around the CDC complex. The trucks were like a fuse on a bomb; would the scene erupt when they reached the troops? Would the shooting start?

"This could get ugly," Millen said.

Stevens nodded. "Isn't there something you should be doing?"

Comprehension dawned on Millen. He turned on his heel and ran. At the kitchen off the cafeteria, he stuffed food into garbage bags. He needed non-perishable items, enough for at least four days.

The halls were filled with people, everyone arguing about what to do. They were scared. So was Millen.

He found the BSL-4 lab empty once again. He donned the suit, entered, and placed the food on one of the tables inside. Halima was asleep. He hated to wake her, but he had to.

After the third gentle nudge, she opened her eyes, rubbed them, and smiled.

She saw the fear on his face instantly.

"What's wrong?"

"I might be going away for a while. I need you to stay here. It's important. You understand?"

She nodded.

"If you run out of food before I'm back, you can leave. But be careful. Don't tell anyone you're from Kenya. Tell them you've lost your parents and they didn't want you to talk to strangers."

She looked confused, but agreed.

Outside the BSL-4, he changed quickly out of the suit. When he reached the ground floor, he heard gunshots.

CHAPTER 104

AUDITORIUM A at CDC headquarters was again packed to capacity. Millen stood with the other staff, listening to Phil outline the evacuation plan. It was ingenious. The train tracks that ran behind the CDC were free of the mobs that had massed outside demanding the cure—and within ten minutes, train cars would be whisking the staff to safety.

"The people at the back of the room will guide you to the exit," Phil said.

Millen fell in line, flowing with the crowd that rushed out of the room. In the distance, past the lobby, he heard more gunshots.

Instead of going outside, he broke from the crowd, made his way to the stairs, and descended to the lab level. He didn't don a protective suit this time. Pretty soon, he wouldn't need it—one way or another.

Inside the lab, he found Halima watching a DVD. She pulled one of the headphones out of her ear.

"No suit?"

He shook his head.

"Mind if I join you?"

He had made his decision: he would stay in the lab and try to protect the two children until the end. Leaving would mean saving only himself. And that wasn't good enough.

☣

The Atlanta streets were clogged with cars—some leaving the city, just as many going downtown to search for their loved ones in BioShield confinement. That's exactly what Elliott and his neighbors had done: split up.

One group had taken an RV and left the city, just in case it became a war zone between BioShield troops and citizens. Elliott sat behind the wheel of the other RV, driving toward downtown Atlanta. The massive vehicle was over thirty feet long. He had driven buses during deployments, some on muddy dirt roads in the third world, and none of them compared to this. He weaved the RV in and out of traffic, dodging stopped cars on I-75. Up ahead, the freeway was completely blocked with abandoned vehicles.

He veered to the side, taking the exit for Howell Mill Road. He wasn't sure if he was driving the massive RV or if it was driving him. It rocked like a fish being pulled from the water. His twelve passengers gripped the kitchenette table, the walls, and anything they could get their hands on.

"Sorry!" Elliott yelled back as the RV coasted to a stop at the top of the ramp.

He got as far as Marietta Street before the roads were completely blocked. He pulled the RV into an alley. About half the people on board rose and moved to the door. Sam and Adam were among those who were going to stay. If things went as planned, Elliott would be back soon and they'd all be leaving together.

He looked at his neighbors and their teenage children, wondering what they were about to confront. Were they ready? He had no idea, but he knew they had no choice.

"You have your sticks?"

The question was met with nods.

"Good. Let's try to stay together." He held up a can of orange spray paint. "Remember the breadcrumbs if we get separated."

After the others exited, he walked back to Sam and Adam. The boy was lying on the RV's bed with several other younger kids who were sick, all playing portable video games. Elliott put a hand on Sam's shoulder. "I'll be back soon. Don't worry."

Tears welled in her eyes. He pulled her into a tight hug, reached over and tousled Adam's hair, then made his way outside.

He and his neighbor Bill covered the monstrous vehicle with several tarps. Elliott's fever had been low-grade this morning, and to his relief, he was feeling pretty good at the moment. The adrenaline was likely helping.

Elliott gathered everyone around him. It was cold in the alley, and his breath came out in a puff of white steam.

"Remember, the knock is three raps, pause, then two, then one. Three-two-one. We're going to wait here until all of us report back. There's food in the RV, blankets too. Use the portable batteries and electric heater if you need them. Try not to crank it unless you have to."

Elliott looked each one of them in the eye. "Okay. Good luck."

On the buildings flanking the alley, he spray-painted a large E. As they walked, he put the same mark on every building they passed. It felt strange, painting graffiti all over downtown Atlanta, but he hoped it might get one or more of his people back. He expected some or all of them would be in a very bad mental state when they returned.

The streets were packed with people on foot, just like them, hiking toward downtown and the Georgia Dome, looking for their loved ones, or the cure, or both. Many carried guns and knives, while others simply jammed their hands in their coat pockets, trying to stay warm.

When Marietta Street met Northside Drive, Elliott heard the roar of heavy machinery. To his right, two bulldozers were pushing cars to the side, clearing a path. A front-end loader bounced along behind them. Two pickup trucks brought up the rear. Men in the beds held rifles.

One of the men called to the crowd.

"They surrendered! Come on, follow us!"

People broke from the crowd, began falling in line.

Elliott quickened his pace, jogging down Northside Drive. The heavy bulldozers had left track marks in the pavement, their own version of breadcrumbs leading to the Georgia Dome. People in orange vests were scattered along the road, making sure no cars blocked the cleared thoroughfare.

Elliott and his neighbors were forced back onto the sidewalk along with everyone else when two tractor-trailers powered down the road. The back doors to their empty trailers hung open, and men looked out, several of them smoking. It took Elliott a minute to realize why they needed the giant trucks: to hold all the guns they were rounding up. They were disarming the government troops.

A few minutes later, school buses emerged from downtown, heading away from the Georgia Dome. They were the same buses that had taken him and Rose, but now they were filled with uniformed people—National Guard, Army, and FEMA. The very people who had crowded Elliott and the rest of the population onto the buses days earlier.

Along the street, some people clapped and cheered; others, like Elliott, simply stared at the surreal scene. A few yelled out names and rushed toward the buses, but the orange-vested individuals held them back. That was something Elliott hadn't considered before—that some of the people making their way downtown were coming to help their friends and family in uniform.

When the buses passed, he waded back into the street and ran even faster. The cold early December air burned in his lungs. He was very out of shape, even for his age. His younger neighbors were pulling ahead; he was slowing them down.

"Go on," he said between breaths.

Bill smiled. "A wise man told me we should stay together."

Elliott just shook his head. But he was glad for the company.

Three blocks from the Georgia Dome, the crowd became too thick to run. Their group slowed to a walk, and Elliott caught his breath.

He drew out his long stick, which he had held to his body with his belt. Carefully, he unfolded the posterboard sign and taped it to the stick. Then he passed around the tape, and one by one, they all raised their signs. Elliott's read: *ROSE SHAPIRO*. It was one of thousands of posters waving in the air as the crowd pressed toward the Georgia Dome.

CHAPTER 105

DESMOND WAS CONTEMPLATING his escape from the cargo container when he heard a group of people marching across the concrete. The boots pounded in the vast space, drawing closer. It sounded like a stampede at first, then there was a screeching sound, and muffled voices. He recognized only one of them.

A single set of footsteps resumed.

The door to Desmond's container opened with another screech of metal on metal.

The dark space flooded with light. He squinted, held an arm up to shade his eyes.

Avery.

The blonde was shrouded in shadow, but Desmond could see that she was still clad in tight-fitting body armor. She looked like a superhero. She held a handgun at her side, ready, but not pointed at him. Her expression was remorseful, apologetic even.

"I had to," she said.

Desmond was stone-faced.

"We were getting nowhere at SARA. It was a dead end, Des."

She waited, but he still said nothing, only stared at her.

"This was my backup plan. We needed to get back inside the Citium. I knew the tactical team was at the house, waiting."

"You could have told me."

"I needed them to believe it."

"Like you needed us to believe the rescue was real."

Avery's silence confirmed his theory.

He had suspected that the escape from the *Kentaro Maru* was staged. Now he knew for sure. He wanted to know why. "They let me go because they wanted me to lead them—to lead *you*—to Rendition."

"Yes. It's the only thing they need for the Looking Glass." She stepped away from the container. "Look, I took a risk. I didn't want the group to debate it because I knew it was the only option we had. And we didn't have time for our little *committee* to vote. It worked out—better than I thought it would." She motioned away from Desmond's container. "Come on, I'll show you."

Across the aisle, another cargo container lay open, its heavy metal doors revealing cardboard boxes stacked on pallets. The closest box had been torn open. It held hundreds of oblong handheld devices roughly half the size of a cell phone and a bit thicker.

Avery handed him one. "It's a jet injector."

She pointed to another box, which held CO_2 cartridges. They were small and round, similar to the ones Desmond had used in his pellet gun as a child.

"They're CO_2-powered."

She pulled another open box closer. It was full of vials. She took a vial and a CO_2 cartridge and inserted both into the jet injector.

"This is the cure. I thought if they captured us here in Australia that they might take us to a warehouse like this one." She waited for him to respond, but Desmond said nothing. "It was the only way, Des. Our only option."

He took the device from her and stared at it. *We've done it.* He held in his hand the key to saving Peyton, and billions more. But it was her he thought of first. He realized then how worried he'd been about her. He didn't want to lose her—or the second chance he wanted so badly. Everything had happened so quickly in the last two weeks, he hadn't had time to process it. It all hit him now. They had found the cure—and they had a fighting chance of stopping the Citium. Erasing his memories had been a big risk, but the clues he'd left himself had worked. In a roundabout way, they had led him here, to this moment—to what he thought was a turning point. Now it was time to finish it.

Avery stepped closer. "I mean it, Des. This was the only way. Do you believe me?"

She needs me to forgive her. There was a deeper relationship between them, and he couldn't remember it. That was an unsettling feeling.

He looked at her, but he still didn't speak.

"It was the only way to get you off the ship," she said. "It was the only way to get us here, to the cure. I gambled. I did what I had to. I did it for you, and for the mission. Please tell me you understand."

A cough rang out in the silence; a congested, sick sound. Not a nagging, nuisance cough, but a deadly one. It was a bell tolling, reminding him that time was running out.

"Yeah, I understand, Avery."

She didn't smile. She only glanced away, as if his words of absolution had come up short.

He wasn't ready to forgive her; not until he trusted her completely. And right now, his only thoughts were for Peyton. He didn't want to wait another second to give her the cure.

"We've got some people who need this," he said.

He followed the cough to another metal shipping container, unlocked it, and pulled the screeching metal door open. Peyton was lying on the floor, squinting at the bright light. She barely sat up.

He handed Avery the jet injector, walked inside, and gathered Peyton in his arms. She felt like a rag doll as he lifted her and carried her into the light. She was no doubt worn out from the fitful sleep in the back of the plane, hungry, and exhausted from the sickness that had been slowly overtaking her.

In the glow of sunlight through the skylights, he sat her on the concrete floor of the warehouse and held her head in his hands. Her eyelids were droopy and her hair soaked with sweat from the fever.

Avery pulled Peyton's sleeve up and began to press the jet injector to her arm, but Desmond stopped her and took the device.

He wanted to administer the cure himself. He realized then how much it meant to him, and why. Twenty years ago, they had spent the most important years of his life together. Perhaps of hers too. He had discovered who he was. Before he met her, he had never known the true extent of the wounds from his childhood. He was broken. He had given up on waiting for his wounds to heal. He had left her because he thought that by leaving, he was saving her. He thought he was giving her the life she deserved. He knew now that he had been wrong.

He held the injector at her shoulder and pressed the button.

The pop of air and the pinch snapped Peyton to attention. She looked from Avery to Desmond, then at the jet injector in his hand.

"Hi," he said.

She smiled.

"Hi."

CHAPTER 106

EVERYWHERE ELLIOTT LOOKED, he saw death. The dead and dying lay on cots and blankets in rows on the infield of the Georgia Dome. The stench was overpowering. He gagged twice before he got used to it. He marched, his sign held high, searching for his wife's face or voice. His fear grew with each step. He tried in vain not to think about what he would do if he found her dead.

Elliott had spent decades of his career working in field hospitals. He had treated the victims of outbreaks, just like the living and dead lying all around him. But none of it had prepared him for being on the other side: being a family member of someone infected, whose life would be claimed by the pathogen. It was a feeling of complete helplessness. Tears ran down his face. Very soon, he would know whether X1-Mandera had claimed the love of his life. He dreaded that knowledge, and at the same time, he desperately wanted to know.

A voice he knew well called out. "Dad!"

Elliott turned to see his son weaving through the crowd.

When the thirty-year-old physician reached Elliott, the older man pulled him in, hugging him hard.

"Your mom?"

Ryan nodded. "She's alive."

Elliott saw in his son's face the words he didn't say: *But just barely.*

"Are Sam and Adam with you?"

"They're back at the RV. They're safe."

"Thank God. Are they...?"

"Sam's asymptomatic. Adam's infected, but it's still early stage. I'm so sorry, son—"

Ryan squeezed his dad's shoulders. "It's not your fault. We'll deal with it. Come on, let's get Mom and get out of here."

Elliott swallowed and steeled himself as Ryan led him into the Georgia Dome's offices. He was anxious and afraid but so eager to see her again.

Rose lay on a cot in a small office, her eyes closed, pulse weak. Elliott did a quick examination. The rash on her abdomen was dark red and had spread up to her neck. Her face was ashen; dark bags hung below her eyes. *But she's alive.* He was thankful to see her again, to hold her hand, still warm, if only to say goodbye.

Nearly an hour later, they reached the RV Elliott had parked off Marietta Street. He knocked three times, then two, then once, and waited. Three seconds. Then four. The door cracked, and he saw his neighbor's face.

Ryan took off the blankets piled upon Rose. He hoisted her out of the wheelchair and carried her into the massive motor home. The kids lounging on the bed sprang up at the sight, allowing Ryan to gently set his mother down on the bed. The instant he released her, Sam ran into his arms, and they were both crying and shaking as they hugged each other. Adam joined them, clinging to his parents, and Elliott was there too, wrapping his arms around the three of them for a few long seconds before crawling into the bed to lie beside Rose. They had brought medicine and oral rehydration salts, but for the most part, all they could do now was wait.

Elliott pulled her freezing body close to his. The tears flowed fast now.

"It's going to be okay, Rose. I'm here. We're going to fix this. Everything is going to be all right, you hear me?"

She said nothing, but he felt one of her tears touch his cheek. He held her tighter. "Don't give up. Please."

CHAPTER 107

AFTER DESMOND ADMINISTERED the cure to Peyton, he gave it to William, who they'd found in another container.

As Desmond had suspected, Charlotte was confined to a shipping container as well.

Avery read his question before he asked. "I ordered the team at SARA to capture her. It seems she's connected somehow."

"That was good thinking."

They freed Charlotte, and she thanked Desmond as he administered the cure.

The warehouse was huge, the size of a football field, stacked three tall with sea freight containers in rows. According to Avery, the building was in Port Adelaide, a suburb northwest of Adelaide, Australia. She led them to an office above the warehouse floor, where two camo-clad soldiers were laid out, glassy eyes staring at the ceiling, both with gunshots to the chest.

"Where are the rest of the soldiers?" Desmond asked.

"In a cargo container," Avery said. "They were more compliant."

Desmond still didn't know what to make of the woman, but he knew she was deadly efficient.

The five of them gathered around a large table the shipping company had likely used to plan routes and review manifests. Plate-glass windows looked down on the warehouse floor and the rows of cargo containers below. A window on an adjacent wall revealed a harbor where cargo ships were docked.

William focused on Desmond. "Did you reach the Labyrinth location before they captured you?"

In his peripheral vision, Desmond saw Avery cut her eyes to him.

"Yes." He paused, considering what to say.

"Well?" William said, eager. "What did you find?"

"A memory."

Peyton bunched up her eyebrows, studying him.

"It wasn't…" Desmond searched for the words. If he told them the truth, there would be an argument for sidelining him going forward. He couldn't let that happen. Stopping the Citium was more important to him than ever. "The memory was from the day of the fire. It was personal—not related to the Citium or the pandemic."

William eyed him. "Are you certain?"

"Yeah."

"In that case," said Avery, opening a laptop, "I've got something you all need to see."

Desmond couldn't read the expression on her face, but he was thankful for the change in subject.

She told them that the computer had belonged to one of the Citium soldiers, whom she had "persuaded" to provide the password. She played the two messages the Citium had sent to the US and other governments.

Charlotte and Peyton stood aghast. Desmond was deep in thought. William turned and stared at the rows of shipping containers, then spoke slowly in a reflective tone.

"That confirms it. They mass-produced the cure and shipped it to sites like this around the world—so they'd be ready to release it quickly." He turned to the group. "Governments need to begin searching ports and shipping terminals for the warehouses like this one."

Avery typed on the laptop. "That's going to be a problem."

Video feeds showed drone footage above the streets of major cities. Desmond recognized the Golden Gate Bridge. People were rioting, marching upon AT&T Park. Similar scenes played out in Chicago, New York, London, Moscow, and Shanghai.

Peyton crossed her arms. "It's a global civil war."

And the Citium's winning, Desmond thought. If the people who had started the pandemic got control of world governments, what would they do next? They were capable of anything. But what was their end game?

Desmond looked at William: "Why are they trying to take over world governments?"

"I'm not sure. All I have are theories. If they're still pursuing the Looking Glass device proposed in 1983, they need a massive amount of power and a large data communication network—the Internet, for example. Controlling world governments would provide them with both. The chaos serves another purpose. It keeps governments from conducting a search effective enough to find the cure distribution sites. They might find a few, but not all of them, not quickly enough."

"We need to help them. There has to be a list of the sites," Desmond said. He turned to Avery. "Can you do a search?"

Avery was already typing furiously. "No, this laptop only has information on what's happening at this facility. It's standard Citium policy—compartmentalization."

William walked across the room to a window that looked out onto the pier and the harbor beyond. "They wouldn't be that sloppy. These people are very, very smart. And efficient."

He pointed out the window to the harbor at a docked container ship. "But if we can find the ship that delivered the cure here, and see where it's been, we might be able to figure out where they manufactured it. And *that* location will likely have a list of all the destinations the cure was shipped to."

He turned to Avery. "Is there any navigational data from ships that docked?"

She worked the laptop. "It looks like the nav data downloads automatically when the ships make contact—but warehouse staff delete the records after review." She raised her eyebrows. "Hold on. They haven't deleted the records from the most recent ship, the MV *Ascension*." Her eyes scanned the screen. "It's still docked here."

Desmond felt a rush of hope. "Read the ports of call."

"Hong Kong. Singapore. Port Klang. Shenzen. Ho Chi Minh City.

Kaohsiung." Avery looked up. "This doesn't make sense. The ship's always full when it makes port, but it never takes on containers."

William stepped closer. "We're looking for a recurring location. It will occur after every port."

Avery worked the laptop. "There's nothing. Just an entry for Speculum."

"That's it."

"I've never heard of it," Desmond said.

"It's a Latin word. It translates to looking glass. On the *Beagle*, it was our code word for the Isle." William paused. "Yes, it makes sense."

"What makes sense?" Peyton asked.

"I think they created the virus at Aralsk-7," William said. He turned to Desmond. "You saw the subjects in the testing wing. But I don't think they manufactured the cure there."

"Why?"

"Simple logistics. Think about it. The virus is highly contagious. They wouldn't need a large amount to spread it. Maybe a few hundred or thousand doses strategically placed around the world. Aralsk-7 could easily manufacture and transport enough viral material to seed the outbreak. But manufacturing the cure, and shipping *it* around the world... that's a task on a completely different scale. We're talking about *billions* of doses. Sea freight is the only thing that makes sense. It's the cheapest way to transport bulk goods, and it allows them to reach any port in the world within a short amount of time." He nodded. "It's the Isle. This is their manufacturing center, I'm sure of it. It might even be their HQ."

"Wait," Charlotte said. "Why did they make all the shipments over the years to SARA? No one is sick there."

William shook his head. "I don't know. I still don't understand how you and SARA fit in. It's almost like the shipments were unrelated to the pandemic. Maybe we obtained the wrong file at Aralsk-7. I'm sorry we involved you in this, Charlotte."

"I'm not. If SARA is somehow connected to the Citium—if they used us somehow—I want to know why. And what they did to my people."

"I don't blame you." William turned to the group. "Look, we need to move quickly. I believe we should assume that somewhere on the Isle is a list of the warehouse locations."

"Okay," Desmond said. "But you said this place would be very well guarded. So what are you thinking? Can we contact the US military somehow and get them to send in Special Forces to raid the island?"

"We'll need to go with them." William motioned to Avery. "At least, Avery and I will need to. I know the island layout, and she has familiarity with the computer systems. We'll go in covertly; a head-on assault would be doomed."

Desmond spoke quickly. "No way I'm sitting this one out."

"That goes for me too," Peyton said.

"No, Peyton. You're too sick. I know you've been trying to hide it."

She stared into his eyes. "I'm not a hundred percent, but I'm close enough. They killed a lot of my people, and they're killing a lot more people I've dedicated my life to protecting."

William focused on Peyton. "It's too dangerous—"

"Dad, going into dangerous situations is part of my job. I'm all grown up now, and I make my own decisions." She glanced back and forth between Desmond and her father. "I'm going."

"And I'm going as well," Charlotte said.

Desmond shook his head. "Charlotte—"

"These... *terrorists* funded my work for some reason. Sent potentially dangerous material to my camp for years. I have to know why. *And* I might know something that we don't even realize—something that could help when we get there. If there's even a remote chance that I could help, I have to try. Billions of lives are at stake. I'm going. I know the risks. I accept them."

Desmond looked to William for help, but the older man just shrugged. Apparently he, too, sensed that they were fighting a losing battle. They weren't going to keep Peyton and Charlotte off the team, no matter how much they wanted to.

"Fine," Desmond said. "Let's assume that this island is our best shot at finding where the shipments of cure have been sent."

He looked around, watching the silent nods from the group. "So how do we even get there? We can't exactly fly there—landing on the island would end our little adventure pretty quickly. And by the time we get there by sea, the world as we know it will be over."

"I think I can help with that," Avery said. She drew a cell phone from her pocket and affixed a satellite sleeve. Desmond watched her activate an app called North Star. She shot him a sly smile. "It turns out I didn't trust you either."

The app beeped once, a long drone. Then a man's voice came over the speaker. "Ops."

Avery smiled. "We've found it."

CHAPTER 108

DESMOND WAS PUSHING the twenty-foot truck to its limits, trying to keep up with Avery ahead. She was barreling down the deserted streets of Port Adelaide with reckless abandon. They hadn't seen a soul, but Desmond was still concerned that they might hit a pedestrian. Peyton sat in the passenger seat, gripping the handle on the ceiling. She apparently was concerned too.

"I wish she'd slow down," Peyton yelled over the roaring engine.

Desmond nodded, but he had to admit: time was not on their side. Every minute that passed, people lost their lives.

William sat behind the wheel of the truck behind them, keeping up as best he could. In the rear-view, Desmond saw Charlotte in the passenger seat with an expression of terror similar to Peyton's.

At the Citium warehouse, Avery's North Star app had connected her to the Rubicon command center, who had quickly gotten in touch with the US and Australian militaries to coordinate the plan. They had directed Avery and the team to take as many doses of the cure as possible to the Royal Australian Air Force Base at Edinburgh, South Australia, and to expect details of additional arrangements by the time they got there.

At the base, the gates stood open. Planes sat on the runways with their glass canopies open. Avery was talking on the phone when she stepped down from her truck. As soon as she signed off, she walked over to the other four and said, "Okay, the US Navy has an aircraft carrier in range. We'll fly there, and get further orders. They're trying to organize a strike force now."

They ventured inside the barracks, which had been converted to a hospital of sorts. Nearly half the staff were caring for the other half. They seemed to all be sick.

A man with a captain's insignia, who introduced himself only as Mullins, was in charge. "My CO said to give you any plane you want and our best pilot."

After some discussion, they selected a small cargo transport with the range they needed. They loaded it with as many doses of the cure as it would hold and took off immediately. From a window on the plane, Desmond watched the Australian Air Force men unloading the box trucks, carrying the boxes of jet injectors and vials of the cure into the barracks.

We saved those lives.

And if they were successful, they would save many more.

☣

Peyton slept on the plane. Or at least, she tried. Her nerves wouldn't settle. Her mind raced with feelings and thoughts she could barely contain. Desmond Hughes was someone she had written off—had forced herself to forget about. Now he was back, and she knew her feelings for him were, too. They had never truly left her.

The same was true of her father. Knowing he had been alive all those years, unable to contact her, tore her apart.

And then there was the island. If her father was right, it held the key to stopping the pandemic. She wanted that more than anything—even more than her own happiness. She wondered if she would have to choose; if in the tangled web the Citium had spun, she would have to choose between saving many lives—or saving her father, or Desmond.

☣

In the cockpit, William stared down at the massive aircraft carrier. The USS *Nimitz* was America's oldest aircraft carrier in service, but the ship was still extremely formidable: over three football fields long and two hundred and fifty feet wide, with over four acres of flight deck and nearly five thousand crew on board. The sun was setting behind the RAAF cargo plane when the massive city on the sea came into view.

William activated the internal speaker. "On approach. Prepare for landing."

The Australian pilot nodded, activated the radio, and called to the carrier's tower. "Old Salt, this is Rescue Bird, request permission to land."

☣

The scene on the USS *Nimitz* resembled the airbase at Edinburgh, though on a much larger scale. A tall man stood on the flight deck, roughly twenty feet in front of about two hundred men and women in US Navy khakis standing at attention. The officer met Peyton and the other three as they were disembarking the plane, and informed them that the assembled group were members of the ship's crew who had volunteered for this mission. Each was either immune to the virus or wasn't incapacitated yet. They were ready to fight.

Minutes later, a fleet of helicopters lifted off, carrying Avery, Peyton, Desmond, William, Charlotte, and the two hundred US Navy volunteers. As they rose into the sky, Peyton looked down and saw crews moving the boxes of the cure out of the transport plane. They had brought five thousand doses—enough to save the entire crew of the *Nimitz*.

☣

They landed on the USS *Boxer*, which Peyton thought looked like a smaller version of the *Nimitz*. She soon learned that the *Boxer* was part of a US Navy Expeditionary Strike Group—a collection of ships capable of deploying quick reaction forces via land, sea, and air.

In a conference room just off the bridge, Colonel Nathan Jamison, the commander of the 11th Marine Expeditionary Unit, briefed the five of them on the reconnaissance his crew had gathered during the five hours since Avery's contact had begun coordinating with the United States Department of Defense.

An image of a harbor appeared on the screen. Massive canopies hung overhead.

Jamison's voice came out like a growl. "We haven't observed any vessels departing or arriving."

William stood beside him at the whiteboard. "You likely won't."

Through the windows, Peyton saw more helicopters arriving, unloading troops. The *Boxer* was gathering all able-bodied Marines and Navy personnel from ships scattered throughout the Pacific. The colonel had told them that his unit typically had twenty-two hundred active duty personnel, but the X1-Mandera virus had decimated their ranks. Peyton wondered how the Citium had gotten the virus onto so many ships. Had they used the water, packing tape, and boxes the team had discovered at Aralsk-7? Or was there another delivery method for the armed services and other isolated populations?

On the whiteboard, her father sketched a map of the island's buildings and roads. "This is how the island looked in the mid-sixties. That's the last time I was there." He paused for a moment, looking as though he remembered something.

He pointed at a building far inland, away from the main road. "This is the administrative building. It's the primary office complex on the island. I think the Citium leadership will be there. If so, the main server farm will be too. We get in there, get Avery logged in, and she'll be able to get direct access to the Citium's files including, hopefully, the list of warehouses around the world where the cure is stored."

Colonel Jamison began describing his plan, which involved paratroopers landing at the administrative building and amphibious vessels making landfall on a deserted beach a few miles from the harbor and immediately sweeping through with thousands of troops. Air support would begin as soon as the paratroopers hit the ground. Peyton and the others would follow once the site was secure.

When Colonel Jamison had finished, William spoke up, "It's a good plan. An attack with overwhelming force is the correct approach under normal circumstances."

Jamison stared at him.

"However, we have an advantage."

"Which is?" Jamison growled.

"Surprise. Knowledge of the terrain. And working against us, we have an enemy that is sublimely clever. They may well be prepared for a head-on assault—in ways we can't anticipate. Casualties will likely be high."

"The cost of failure is even higher," Jamison said.

"True enough. But I believe we should consider an amendment to your plan. A precursor, if you will. I suggest that the five of us land at your identified insertion point, reconnoiter the target zone, and make our way to the administrative building, where we will attempt to gain entry and obtain the objective."

Jamison shook his head. "Too risky. If you're discovered, we lose the element of surprise."

"I rate your plan as even more risky, Colonel. Landing in the harbor and on the beaches in force gives the Citium time to delete the very files we're after. No, it simply won't work."

The two men argued at length, with no one else able to get a word in. Finally, William raised his voice. "I'm not a civilian. I was previously in the employ of Her Majesty's Secret Intelligence Service. And we were *very, very good* at exactly this type of operation."

The assertion didn't dissuade Jamison; in fact, it enraged him. The two men did, however, come to a compromise: the five of them would land at the beach with a smaller strike force of Navy SEALs and Marine Force Recon. The main assault force and air support would be on standby, ready for rapid deployment.

Outside the briefing room, Peyton's father whispered in her ear, "I need to speak with you."

When they were alone, he said, "On the island, I want you to stay close to me."

"Okay."

"And keep Charlotte close."

"Is she…"

"Trust me, Peyton, okay?"

"All right."

"You may learn things that will… disturb you."

"Dad, what are you telling me?"

"I'm only telling you to be ready. And to stay focused on the objective: finding the list of sites holding the cure."

Desmond stood on the flight deck, the wind blowing on his face. Helicopters continued to land. Troops were massing for the assault. The sun was setting now; they would be wheels up within an hour.

Avery walked over, stood beside him silently for a few minutes.

"We need to talk about what you remembered at your childhood home," she said.

He spoke without looking at her. "No, we don't."

"Des, at least tell me what you're going to do about it."

"I have no idea."

CHAPTER 109

DESMOND FOUND PEYTON in one of the mess halls, sitting alone, a plate of untouched food on the table in front of her. He picked up a tray, loaded up on beef stew and cornbread, and sat down across from her.

"Not hungry?" he asked.

"Starving."

"I'm nervous too."

She pushed some green beans around her plate. "I'm used to going into dangerous situations. High stakes."

"But this is different."

She nodded. "And... there's something else."

"Such as?"

He wondered if she was talking about him. About *them*.

"Charlotte," she said.

He raised his eyebrows.

"She's connected to you. *And* me. Don't you think that's strange? And I can't think of a reason why someone was sending her supplies. It's just... Too many coincidences. We're missing something. A very big piece."

Desmond sat silently for a moment. This wasn't the conversation he wanted to have. But she was right, as usual.

"I don't know what it means, but I've figured something else out. It's taken me a very long time."

Peyton sat silently, searching his face.

"When I left you in Palo Alto, I thought I was doing the right thing. For both of us. I thought you would have a better life without me. Kids. Happiness. A normal husband."

She began to speak, but Desmond stopped her. "Just give me a minute. What I'm trying to say is that I thought time would heal me. It didn't. I wasn't better off alone. I wanted you to know because you were right. I wish I had never left."

"It's in the past, Des."

"I wanted to say it just in case…"

"In case we don't come back."

"Yeah."

"I tell you what. Let's make a deal. If we do make it back, we won't talk about the past. Only the future. And the present."

"Deal."

DAY 14

6,100,000,000 infected
18,000,000 dead

CHAPTER 110

ELIM WAS SEWING up a cut on a young girl's arm when the speaker in the exam room called out, "Dr. Kibet, dial the operator, you have an urgent call from the MOH."

The MOH was the Ministry of Health, or what was left of it.

The nurse assisting him glanced at him, but he continued sewing up the girl's arm.

"You're being very brave," he whispered to the young girl.

That made her smile. He didn't ask how she had gotten the cut, but he had instructed the nurse to ensure she had a safe place to stay before discharging her.

The voice over the speaker was calling him again as he walked to his office.

The operator connected him to the Ministry of Health. Dhamiria's voice on the line was music to his ears; they had both been working around the clock, and he desperately wanted to see her.

"Elim, the general's staff just called."

He sat up. The military was now the closest thing Kenya had to a functioning government.

"The UN has contacted them. They've made a deal with Greece. We're going to get seven doses of the cure within two hours— a Greek jet is flying them here."

"That's wonderful."

"The general wants all the doses, but we told him we needed at least one for research, in hopes of replicating it."

Elim smiled. "That was very smart."

The truth was, they didn't have the facilities to effectively research and manufacture a cure. But he did have use for a dose of the life-saving medicine. It would help him fulfill a promise he had made. And repay a debt.

☣

When the doses of the X1-Mandera cure arrived, Elim personally went to the military headquarters at the Ministry of State for Defence complex in Nairobi's Hurlingham area. One dose had already been used for the general currently leading Kenya's Defence Forces, and the general was using the other five doses to test the loyalty of those under his command and root out anyone who might challenge him. It was proving effective. Two other generals and three colonels had been assassinated that morning—all had been discontent with the current leadership. People were falling in line, and Elim could sense the change at the military complex.

As soon as he got the dose, he rushed back to Kenyatta National Hospital and raced through the corridors. He brought five of the survivors from Dadaab to protect him—and the cure. They were an intimidating presence in the hospital, but they were necessary.

Inside the patient room, he quickly administered the dose. He hoped he wasn't too late.

He tried not to think about the patient as he conducted his rounds. Hours went by without word. He wondered if the cure wasn't 100% effective.

He was diagnosing a middle-aged man with Hepatitis E when he heard that the patient was awake. That was a good sign.

He pushed open the door to the room. Hannah was sitting up in bed. Her eyes were sleepy and moving her limbs seemed to take immense effort. Elim remembered vividly the emaciation the deadly virus had brought with it. He had been forced to start over: to learn to walk again and to use his muscles. He knew she would have to travel the same road. But he saw strength in her eyes.

"They tell me I have you to thank for my recovery."

Elim shook his head. "I was just a delivery man."

"But you made the decision."

"I did. It's the hardest decision any person will ever make: whose life to save. It's especially difficult for physicians."

"And you chose me."

Elim answered the question she was really asking—*why*. He knew what she would go through next: survivor's guilt. Hannah was a physician and an epidemiologist; she had dedicated her life to saving others. Now Elim had put her before them at the front of the line.

"A couple of weeks ago, a group of very brave strangers came to help my people. We were dying. They put their lives at risk to help us. They brought what they believed was a life-saving cure for the virus. ZMapp. They brought it for their own people, but they agreed to give a single dose to my government, who gave it to me. That dose saved my life.

"I felt guilty about it at first, wondering if they had made the right decision. I asked why. They told me that mine was a life worth saving."

"And you think mine is?"

"I know it."

"Why?"

"You were one of those strangers who came here, risking your life to help us. But most of all, I know it because I know what you're thinking right now."

She looked away from him.

"Right now you want to get out of that bed, walk out into this hospital, and start helping people."

Her expression told him he was correct.

"The world needs people like you, Dr. Watson. It's a difficult choice, but sometimes we have to save the people who can help others. I realized the wisdom of my government's decision when I traveled to the refugee camp, and when I came here.

"A brush with death changes a person. For good people, it changes them for the better, makes them more thankful—and dedicated to the things that matter.

"Your recovery will take time. You've been bedridden for days. But it will happen. And when it does, we will welcome your help. Rest for now."

CHAPTER 111

THE MOON LIT their way. The boats were nearly silent, the passengers clad in black, their faces painted in jungle shades of green and brown.

The salt-laced wind blew through Peyton's hair, whipping it around when the boat bounced. Desmond sat beside her, eyes forward. On this early summer night in the South Pacific, with the wind on her face, Peyton was at peace. She marveled at the events of the last two weeks. Her father had returned, and so had Desmond. And she might be about to lose it all.

Avery sat across from her. The blond woman had stuffed her hair in the helmet and applied the facepaint liberally. Her eyes glowed, like a predator sitting silently in the jungle, examining its prey, contemplating whether to spring. She looked from Peyton to Desmond and back, her eyes saying, *So you're together again?*

Peyton wanted to kick the woman in the chest, send her over the boat's edge. But they needed her. And Avery would probably just catch Peyton's foot and snap it like a twig anyway.

Peyton's father seemed to read the exchange. He also glanced at Desmond and raised his eyebrows. Peyton felt herself turn red. It was so bizarre—all her teenage years squeezed into this moment.

Not to be left out, Charlotte eyed Desmond and Peyton. She smiled, apparently delighted at the prospect of her former boy-friend's sister and the orphan she had cared for getting together.

The beach ahead appeared deserted, but Peyton couldn't help but hold her breath as the small vessels crested wave after wave.

Their boat came to a crunching halt as sand dragged the bottom. The beach was littered with shells, driftwood, and fallen coconuts. It wasn't a pristine resort beach. It was an untouched land, the way nature had made it and kept it for all these years.

Soldiers were waving their arms forward, urging their five passengers out of the boat. Seconds later, Peyton took her first step onto the island.

CHAPTER 112

SEALS AND FORCE Recon operatives hoisted the two boats up and jogged into the lush forest. They hid the vessels under camouflage and led Peyton and the rest of the group deeper into the South Pacific island jungle.

The troops formed a ring around the five civilians. They crouched slightly as they crept through the jungle, over coconuts on the ground, with palm trees above and dense tree ferns in every direction. The air was humid, sticky almost. The heat was oppressive, but the breeze off the ocean beat it back every few seconds.

To Peyton, the jungle seemed alive, constantly in motion, like a single organism breathing in and out. The dense trees and plants swayed in the wind. Creatures she couldn't identify clicked and called and slithered all around her. The plants were so thick she could barely see ten feet in front of her.

Everyone was on edge. Several times they stopped, crouched, and waited, making sure they were alone in the jungle.

Peyton had had basic training in voice procedures for two-way radio communication, and it had come in handy on many of her deployments when interacting with armed forces, police, fire, and aviation personnel. The training had certainly come in handy of late.

Peyton's father spoke the first words over the comm, a whisper. "Target three hundred yards."

The group stopped, and three soldiers departed, moving quickly. When they returned, they motioned for the group to follow.

The forest gave way to a cleared area. From a hill in the trees,

Peyton made out rows of small houses in a Caribbean style: clapboard sides, metal roofs, hurricane shutters, and large front porches. A massive canopy hung over the homes, supported by metal poles set in concrete footings. An electric vehicle that reminded her of a golf cart with clear plastic sides zoomed away from one of the houses.

A Marine spoke over the comm. "Overwatch, units Bravo and Zulu. We are at location Tango. Proceeding."

"Bravo, Zulu, Overwatch. Copy that."

William and four soldiers departed from the group, made their way to the corner of the settlement, and sat for a moment, working their binoculars. The remaining troops spread out in the forest and took up sniper positions, most lying on their stomachs, peering through the scopes of their rifles, sweeping across the small settlement.

On the ship, Peyton's father had insisted on leading the advance recon teams. Colonel Jamison had argued against it, but William had insisted that he had the most first-hand information about the terrain and their adversary. In the ship's infirmary, he had made Peyton wrap up his ankle again, administer cortisone shots, and give him some oral painkillers. He had tucked the pills in his pocket, but hadn't taken one.

William and the four soldiers darted to the closest home and entered through the back door. The older man brought up the rear. His limp slowed him down some, but Peyton thought he was moving well considering.

She counted down the seconds, but nothing occurred. Minutes passed. Then two soldiers slipped out the back door, ran back into the tree line, and exited farther down, by the fourth house from the corner. They entered that house in a similar way.

A soldier spoke urgently on the radio. "Zulu leader, request backup at location two."

Orders then came quickly over the comm.

Six team members sprang up, raced along the tree line, and burst into the second home the troops had entered. Peyton was amazed at their speed. She swallowed. Her father was in the first house. *Is he okay?* The thought of losing him now terrified her; she only realized it in that moment.

Desmond looked at her and nodded slightly, a gesture only she could see, trying to reassure her.

Avery crept to the leader of Zulu team and whispered to him, too low for Peyton to hear. The man shook his head and pushed her back, seeming annoyed.

She didn't let it go. Seconds later, she rose and barreled down the hill. The man's voice was hard over the comm. "Medusa, return to rally point."

Avery didn't stop.

"Fox team, be advised, Medusa is inbound to your twenty."

Zulu leader looked back at Desmond, who just shrugged, letting the man know they'd been dealing with the same thing.

Another electric car emerged from the wooded path and parked at a house unoccupied by the soldiers. Two more cars drove to different houses. Along the perimeter, several of the black-clad troops began spreading closer to those houses.

Peyton desperately wanted to know what was going on, but she held her tongue and tried to stay calm.

A hushed voice came over the comm, a soldier; wounded, Peyton thought. "Zulu, Bravo teams. Move in. Hurry."

CHAPTER 113

INSIDE THE SECOND home, the blinds were closed. Blood spread across the wide-plank hardwood floor. Peyton stopped at the sight and walked slowly around it. The Marines and Navy SEALs moving through barely took notice. They went from room to room, calling "Clear!" before re-entering the central hallway.

Peyton relaxed when she heard her father's voice in the dining room. She found him standing with Avery and two other soldiers. They had taken a painting from the wall and had drawn a map of the island and its buildings on the back.

William activated the comm and laid out his plan, broadcasting to their forces and to the *Boxer*'s Combat Information Center.

He and the soldiers had interrogated several of the homes' residents and had learned a great deal. The map was an updated view of the island's layout, which had changed some since the sixties. About two hundred private security contractors were housed in barracks near the harbor. The island had also been upgraded with significant defensive capabilities, including advanced sonar and radar. The technology would likely have detected the larger amphibious landers long before they reached the beach. They were unsure whether the small boats they'd used to come ashore had been detected, but they were hopeful they'd gone unseen. The detection grid was focused on the harbor side of the island.

The most concerning fortifications were the island's surface-to-air and surface-to-sea defenses. The Citium was capable of fending off attacks from the *Boxer*'s air wing, and it had missiles with sufficient range to reach the ships of the expeditionary strike group.

William urged them not to move the vessels back; if the formation of ships was already under surveillance, withdrawing might raise suspicion and launch a search of the island.

William had flagged two buildings of interest: a lab complex, and an administrative building that housed the island's data center and communications equipment. According to the residents they'd interrogated, neither building was heavily guarded, and the current work shift would be ending within the hour.

Quickly, they made a well conceived plan to infiltrate the buildings. The SEALs and Force Recon troops would make their way to the barracks and defense complex. Their first priority would be disabling the island's radar and missile capabilities. Then they would rig explosives to the troop carriers; the logic was that if the island's infantry units were mobilized to repel a ground assault, they could be neutralized quickly. The plan was efficient and deadly, and perhaps the best they could do with their limited forces.

Their search of the homes had turned up an IT administrator named Carl and a senior biomedical engineer named Gretchen. Their shifts were about to start, and they would provide a cover for the infiltration teams. Desmond, William, and Avery would enter the administrative building with Carl, who would tell anyone who asked that they were new consultants who needed access to the database. Charlotte and Peyton would enter the lab complex with Gretchen, and search for any information related to the cure. Two Navy SEALs would go with the second team. Each team member had brought along civilian clothes for exactly this type of infiltration.

In the bathroom, Peyton began washing off the facepaint. When she looked in the mirror, she saw Desmond standing in the doorway.

"Be careful."

She stared at him in the mirror. "You too."

"I'll see you on the other side."

"I'll be there." And she hoped he would too.

CHAPTER 114

PEYTON RODE IN the back of the electric car with Gretchen and Charlotte. The two Navy SEALs sat in the front, both silent, eyes forward, occasionally glancing around for any signs of trouble along the dirt road that wound through the island. The car's tiny lamps barely cut the darkness; Peyton assumed that was to avoid being spotted from above. The roads weren't covered with large canopies; instead, large trees lined both sides, their massive limbs stretching overhead.

Peyton glanced over at Gretchen. The woman was in her mid forties, fit, with blond hair and an annoyed expression. Peyton wondered what had happened in the house to convince her to take them into the lab building. She assumed some sort of coercion was involved. Most of all, she wondered how a person with a PhD in biomedical engineering, who seemed rational enough, would ever cooperate with the Citium.

"Why did you do it?" she asked.

Gretchen replied without looking at Peyton. Her accent was German, or perhaps Dutch. "I dispute the premise."

Peyton bunched her eyebrows.

"You assume we have acted against humanity's best interest." Gretchen looked at Peyton now. "I assure you that is not the case. Our actions will save lives. It is you whom I should ask why."

"I think distributing a deadly pathogen is just slightly against the human race's best interest."

"Your perspective is myopic."

"You have killed millions of people in the last week."

Gretchen looked away. "Something we regret. Many of the deaths were due to decisions by your government and others. But the end result will be the same. An outcome easily worth the price."

"Which is—"

The Navy SEAL driving interrupted. "Look alive, ladies."

The car exited the dirt road and moved onto a heavily wooded promenade with covered walkways, no doubt with camouflage images on top. A large covered parking area loomed to the left.

"Take any space," Gretchen said.

As they parked, the SEAL in the passenger seat turned and said to her, "I want to remind you of our arrangement—and the consequences of deviating from it."

"I require no reminder."

LED lights on the dome of the canopy lit their way toward the lab complex. They walked in silence as other staffers joined them on the path.

Inside, a guard at a desk barely glanced at them. Gretchen led them to an elevator and pressed a button that read B4. At the house, Peyton had considered where to go first. The others had the primary mission: finding the warehouses where the existing cure was housed. But as a backup plan, Peyton's job was to find where the cure was being created, and gather any information on its mechanism of action. If the others failed, and governments around the world were forced to try to manufacture the cure themselves, that information would be critical.

Gretchen led them to an office with plate-glass windows that looked down on the floor of a vast manufacturing plant. The facility was clearly underground, but it was the machinery that shocked Peyton the most.

"What is this?"

"What you requested."

"This is where you manufacture the cure? Impossible."

An amused smile crossed Gretchen's lips. "Again, your premises are incorrect, Dr. Shaw."

Peyton activated her comm. "Something's wrong here."

There was no response.
"Desmond? Avery?"
She waited.
"Dad, come in."
No reply came.

CHAPTER 115

ON ANOTHER LIGHTED path, Desmond and Avery walked in silence. William and Carl were roughly ten feet ahead of them.

At the island bungalow, Desmond had changed clothes, wiped the paint off his face, and donned a wig with brown wavy hair. He wore a mustache that itched constantly. The polo shirt was a size too small, the shorts too big. Avery kept glancing over at him.

"What?" he whispered.

"Nothing."

"Seriously."

She smiled. "You look like a seventies porn star."

He couldn't help but laugh. "Thanks."

"Looked like you were putting the moves on Peyton back at the house."

Desmond studied her a moment, but the young woman wouldn't look at him.

"Hey."

She turned toward him.

"Before..." he said. "What was our relationship?"

"Does it matter?"

"It matters to me."

"Yeah, well, I'm not sure it matters to me anymore."

Before Desmond could say another word, William stopped in the path and whispered for them to be quiet. The administrative building loomed.

☣

In the building's lobby, they each swiped their magnetic access cards; Carl swiped his own, and Desmond, William, and Avery used cards they had taken from residents of the bungalows—people they had verified had access to the building and critical areas. The people attached to the access cards looked vaguely similar to each of them in their disguises, but they certainly wouldn't fool anyone who actually knew those residents. Desmond just hoped they could get by the guard at the desk—and not be noticed by the staff manning the security cameras.

To his relief, the front desk guard barely looked up. In seconds, they were past the lobby, at the elevator bank, and Desmond finally exhaled.

The building was four stories. Carl led them to the server room on the second floor. It was expansive, at least a hundred feet long and seventy feet wide, and extended to the two floors above.

The place buzzed with the sound of countless servers. Rows of metal cabinets and cages stretched out. Some enclosures lay open, cords spilling out like the entrails of a mechanical monster that had been gutted by a tech. Some of those techs were in the room. They stood at carts piled high with server parts, worked on laptops, and typed on keyboards below fold-up flat screens that extended from the racks themselves. The room was windowless, lit by fluorescent lights, and cool from the air conditioning blowing down on them from above. Plastic tiles formed a raised floor in a gridded metal framework, and the space underneath the floor allowed conduits and wiring to reach all areas of the data center. Their feet thumped as they walked across the tiles.

The scale of the data center was far beyond what Desmond had expected. *What are they doing with this much computing power?*

At various points, Avery attached a small camera to the end of a row of servers. The cameras had magnetic bases and snapped right onto the metal frames.

Carl stopped at a rack and punched in some numbers on a keypad next to a small door. The door opened with a click, and

Carl pulled out a laptop. He attached an Ethernet cord to a port on a switch above the servers.

"This terminal has administrative privileges on the network."

He stepped aside, and Avery took his place. She set a tablet next to the laptop and brought up a view of all the security cameras she had placed. Thus far, no one was following them.

She typed furiously on the laptop. A second later, the logo for Rook Quantum Sciences appeared.

"I'm in."

CHAPTER 116

PEYTON TRIED THE comm again.

"Desmond. Dad. Avery."

She waited.

"Please respond."

To Gretchen she said, "Why are the radios down?"

"I have no idea."

"Don't lie to me."

"It's not really my department."

"Meaning?"

Gretchen sighed. "Industrial espionage was one of the biggest risks we faced."

"What does that mean?"

A humorless smile formed on the woman's lips.

Peyton thought a moment. Yes, they would have done anything to prevent anyone from taking information off-site—including blocking electronic transmissions. "The building's shielded, isn't it? Comms won't work inside."

Gretchen's silence confirmed her theory. If the administrative building was shielded as well, Avery wouldn't be able to upload the location list via the satellite internet link. She needed to know—quickly.

Even more concerning was what Peyton saw below—the massive machines manufacturing the cure. They were all wrong. Peyton had toured dozens of facilities that manufactured vaccines, antivirals, and monoclonal antibodies. And they all had one thing in common: they were based on biological material.

Most vaccines were simply a form of the actual virus they provided immunity for. The vaccines for measles, mumps, rubella, oral polio, chicken pox, and shingles were weakened forms of the target viruses. The weakened forms reproduced poorly inside the body, allowing the immune system time to study and attack them. The body eventually manufactured antibodies, then committed the formula for those effective antibodies to memory— so that when the real virus appeared, the immune system could neutralize it quickly.

Another set of vaccines worked via a chemical process that inactivated the virus so it couldn't replicate inside the body. The vaccines for polio, hepatitis A, influenza, and rabies worked that way. Inactivated vaccines had no chance of causing even a mild form of the disease they were inoculating against, making them ideal for anyone with a weakened immune system.

Vaccines, however, were mostly ineffective in treating patients already infected with a virus, especially if the pathogen was prone to mutation—as was the case with influenza and HIV. For patients already infected, antivirals were the key.

Like vaccines, many antivirals were grown from living matter. Monoclonal antibodies, for example, were predominantly grown in cell cultures that fused myeloma cells with mouse spleen cells that had been immunized with an antigen. Other antivirals were chemical in nature and targeted a virus's protein layer or enzymes.

But whether vaccine or antiviral, the bottom line was that all known solutions to fighting a viral outbreak required a manufacturing process with a biological or chemical component. And here, Peyton saw no evidence of that. Was the cure a fake? Were the videos of Paris and Athens staged? Or was the Citium cure something else entirely? And if so, what would distributing it do?

Peyton pulled Charlotte close and whispered, "We need to get out of here and warn the others."

A shot rang out, then three more. The Navy SEALs who had

accompanied Charlotte and Peyton spun. Blood spilled onto the white floor. They never even had a chance to draw their weapons.

The three men who advanced through the doorway wore security uniforms similar to the one worn by the man at the front desk. They swept the office, then walked over to Peyton and Charlotte and began patting them down.

The tall man reached under Peyton's armpits and ran his hands down and over, across her chest. She pushed him back, but he grabbed her arms.

"Don't touch her!"

The voice was like a lightning strike.

When Peyton saw the face of the speaker, her jaw dropped. It was impossible.

CHAPTER 117

DESMOND STARED AT the tablet that showed the cameras they had placed throughout the data center. Thus far, there had been no movement except the technicians who walked between the rows and occasionally opened an enclosure to service the equipment inside. Lights blinked throughout the room, flashing green as data packets were exchanged on the network and hard drives served up data. There were blinks of yellow and red when packets collided or hardware failed.

Desmond leaned close to Avery. "How much longer?"

"Almost there."

From his peripheral vision, Desmond saw movement on the screen, someone running fast. He stopped, studied the tablet. No—it was just another technician, rushing to a cabinet to work on a server.

Over the next sixty seconds, the server room filled with more technicians. Two or three entered at a time and broke off from each other, veering to different server enclosures and opening them. The scene bothered Desmond, but he didn't know why. It was off somehow.

"Got it!"

Avery pulled a flash drive from the laptop and inserted it into her cell phone, which had a satellite sleeve attached.

Desmond continued to study the camera feeds.

What's wrong here?

Were the men moving too quickly? No—that wasn't it. It was their shoes. Boots—all the same. Soldiers' boots.

"We've got a problem here."

Avery squinted at the phone. "I know. It's not connecting."

William took Carl by the arm. "Why?"

The man shrugged. "Phones are banned in the entire building. I—"

"We need to get outside."

Desmond nodded at the tablet. "That's going to be a problem."

They were surrounded.

☣

The figure who had reprimanded the troops walked closer, never breaking eye contact with Peyton. There was no smile, only a hard stare that Peyton thought said: *I'm sorry.*

The person spoke to Charlotte first.

"It's nice to see you again, Charlotte."

The Australian doctor looked as surprised as Peyton felt. She merely nodded.

There were a million questions Peyton wanted to ask. She had no clue where to start. Most of all, she wanted to know *why.* Why this person she loved so much, this person who meant so much to her, was involved with this.

The newcomer stopped just a few feet from Peyton, and with a sharp head motion, dismissed Gretchen. The soldiers who had cut down the Navy SEAL and attempted to frisk Peyton departed as well.

"Hello, darling."

Peyton swallowed. "Hi, Mom."

CHAPTER 118

DESMOND PUSHED CARL against the wire mesh wall. "How many exits are there from this room?"

"Two," the nervous man said.

"They'll be covered," William said.

Desmond knew he was right. But Peyton's father always seemed to be a step ahead. William was already reaching into his bag. He took out three round green cylinders, ran to the end of the row of server racks, and tossed the canisters in different directions. Smoke poured out as they rolled across the floor. The canisters thumped as they crossed the joints where the tiles fitted together; they sounded like the beat of a drum before the start of a battle.

William returned and handed Avery a grenade.

"Go. You'll have to make your own exit. I'll buy you some time."

Before either Desmond or Avery could speak, the man slipped into the smoke. Gunfire followed a second later.

Bullets ripped through the cages around them. Sparks flew. A dozen electrical explosions and pops went off. Shards of metal and plastic issued from the cages like a lethal mix of confetti.

"Stay down, Carl!" Desmond shouted as he and Avery left the man behind and sprinted away.

Overhead, fire suppression nozzles hissed, pumping the room full of gas—argon, or perhaps nitrogen, to reduce the oxygen level and choke off the fire.

Avery ran ahead of Desmond, tossed the grenade at the end of the row, then drew her handgun from inside her waistband and squeezed off two rounds.

Desmond had counted to three by the time he reached her. Most US-made grenades went off at four or five and a half seconds.

He wrapped an arm around Avery's midsection and pulled her behind the metal cage just before the grenade went off, blowing them to the floor, him on top of her.

For a moment, all went silent—then the quiet was replaced by ringing. Lights overhead went dark. The constantly blowing air conditioning and fire suppression gas ceased. Debris fell onto the raised floor like heavy raindrops on a metal roof.

Avery rolled Desmond off her and stood, gun drawn. She looked left then right, then extended a hand to help Desmond up. He marveled at her. *She's unstoppable.*

His body ached when she pulled him up.

Seconds later, they stepped through the opening the grenade had created in the wall of the server room, into a corridor lined with offices. Soldiers in body armor stood at both ends of the hall. They dashed across the hall into the closest office, and Desmond ran to the floor-to-ceiling window.

They were on the second floor; Desmond estimated about a fifteen-foot drop. Doable, but it would hurt—and probably break a few things. He raised his gun, fired two rounds into the glass.

"Are you crazy?" Avery snapped.

"Yes. He is."

They turned to find Conner McClain in the doorway.

"You disappoint me, Avery."

Desmond moved in front of the woman. He knew Conner wouldn't harm him. And he knew why.

CHAPTER 119

WILLIAM CREPT THROUGH the room, peering around the servers, moving as quickly as he dared. It reminded him of playing hide-and-seek as a child. But this game was more deadly.

The smoke was thick now. He could see only a few feet in front of him. The aftermath of the explosion had brought calm. He desperately hoped Desmond and Avery were outside the building by now. He had picked off two soldiers advancing on their opening, and that had driven the rest back into the smoke.

He moved around another cage, listened, heard nothing except for the scattered debris falling and the pop of electrical circuits blowing. Gas issued from the overhead nozzles across the room.

If memory served him, he was close to the exit—three rows away.

He moved to another row and paused. Then another. He was almost out. He desperately wanted to activate his comms—to tell the Marine and Navy SEAL forces to execute a diversion and for Jamison to move in, but the comms still didn't work.

Too late, he heard footsteps behind him. He turned, but the man was already on top of him, knocking him to the ground. Another soldier joined him, and in seconds they had bound William's hands.

They raised him roughly to his feet, then walked him out of the server room, through the halls, and onto the elevator. It reminded William of that night in Rio, when the thugs had hauled him out of the taxi and marched him through the favela. He had saved Yuri's and Lin's lives that night; they had been captives of a madman, kept confined in a dirty back room of a shanty house. Now *he* was the captive.

They exited the elevator on the fourth floor and marched him to a room with a piece of equipment that reminded William of an MRI machine, except far larger.

It's true. They've done it, he thought.

A voice William knew well came over the speaker. "Scan him and bring him to me. Quickly."

The soldiers forced William onto an exam table, unbound his hands, and strapped his arms and legs in. A woman wearing blue-green scrubs walked in and injected something into his shoulder. The soldiers stood back while he lost consciousness.

☣

When William opened his eyes, he lay on a couch, his hands bound once again.

Through blurred vision that slowly cleared, he took in the room around him. It was a corner office, with floor-to-ceiling windows on two sides that looked out on the island landscape. He stood, uneasily, and shook his head, trying to clear it.

A man rose from behind the desk, walked over, and grasped his upper arm.

"Here, old friend. Have a seat. Relax. Everything will be fine very soon."

The man deposited William in a chair in front of the desk. Sitting up helped.

When the man's face finally came into focus. William was unsure if he was saved or truly trapped.

Yuri stood across from him.

CHAPTER 120

THE HURT PEYTON felt in that moment nearly overwhelmed her. It was like the pain that night in London, when her mother had taken Peyton and her siblings away and told them that their father was dead. And like the dark chapter of her life she had shared with Desmond. She had felt the same then: alone, confused.

But this was worse. Seeing her mother here—apparently in charge—involved in the slaughter of millions, complicit in releasing a pathogen upon a defenseless world, perpetrating an event Peyton had dedicated her life to stopping... It was the ultimate betrayal.

Peyton tried but failed to keep the emotion out of her voice.

"Mom, how could you do this?"

Lin Shaw glanced away from Peyton. "There's more going on here than you understand."

"Then explain it. I'm not a little girl anymore."

"We don't have time—"

"Explain to me how killing *millions* of helpless people serves a purpose."

"Peyton."

"And what's the cure? I know it's not a vaccine and it's not an antiviral—not like anything in use today."

Lin exhaled but remained silent.

"What is it, Mom? What does the cure really do? I know you're not growing a virus or biological material down there. It's not a chemical agent. Tell me. What are you all planning?"

Lin stepped closer to Peyton. "I'll explain, but right now, we need to go."

"No. I'm not going anywhere with you. Not until you tell me why you're doing this."

"I'm *not* doing this. There are two factions within the Citium. We're at war."

The words shocked Peyton—and infused her with hope. She desperately wanted to believe that her mother was innocent. "Prove it."

"Peyton—"

"She's telling the truth."

All eyes turned to the man in the doorway. He wore a white coat; his hair was short, tinged gray at the temples. Peyton's brother Andrew stood there, alive and well. She wanted to cry at the sight of him, to rush to him and hug him. But the words he said next crushed her, shattered her heart.

"She didn't do it, Peyton. I did."

CHAPTER 121

TIME SEEMED TO stand still. With Avery tucked safely behind him, Desmond studied Conner's badly burned face. A gust of wind caught the tall man's long blond hair, pulling it back like a curtain, revealing more of the mottled flesh. Desmond now knew how Conner had gotten the hideous injuries.

At the remains of Desmond's childhood home, he had recalled the full memory of that day in 1983.

That morning when he awoke, he had rushed into the kitchen, where his mother sat in a chair, holding Desmond's infant brother: Conner. The baby was smiling—in fact, Conner always seemed to be smiling or laughing. Their father had often remarked that the boy cried a great deal less than Desmond, and because of that, they might be getting another sibling. Desmond had hoped so. He was as taken with his younger brother as his parents were. But that morning, he had paid the infant no attention at all. He had stuffed his face full of eggs and toast spread with Vegemite and beaten a path out the door.

Later that day, when the flames were devouring the home, he had screamed Conner's name before running into the blaze. The desire to get his mother and his baby brother out of the home drove him on as the fire burned his legs and the smoke strangled him until he could go no farther. He had failed both of them that day, and that failure had haunted Desmond his entire life.

In April 2003, he had gone to Australia to visit his family's grave, to lay a wreath there on the twentieth anniversary of the bushfires. He had expected to see a grave marker for Conner, but there wasn't one. That sparked Desmond's curiosity—and hope. He spent weeks in Adelaide, tracking down old records. He hired the best private investigator in the country, and the second best. The cost was exorbitant. He paid for endless travel, record requests, and attorney fees for court proceedings when records were withheld. Finally, he learned the truth: their mother had saved Conner in an act of breathtaking bravery and sacrifice. She had cleared the wood and ashes out of the fireplace, then set Conner inside it. She had rolled the refrigerator close, then tipped it over to cover the fireplace's opening.

The initial search party who found Desmond saw only their mother's burned remains. She had stayed in the house, clearing as much of the flammable material as she could away from the fireplace.

But a second group of relief workers searching the area for survivors found Conner badly burned, dehydrated, and malnourished. He was at death's door. They flew him to Adelaide, where he spent months in an intensive care unit.

Desmond cried when he read the doctor's notes. They had expected the infant to die, but at each turn, he had defied the odds. By the time Conner was well enough to leave, Desmond had long since gone to Oklahoma to live with Orville. The doctors called the boy's uncle, but Orville refused to take Conner. Desmond had no doubt that part of the report was true: the roughneck had been in no shape to take Desmond, even at age five; he couldn't have cared for an infant.

Conner was remanded to the foster system. Desmond couldn't imagine what it had been like for Conner growing up, so badly injured—physically and mentally. He imagined the would-be parents touring the facility, gazing upon the young boys and girls they might take home, averting their eyes when they came to Conner.

Desmond was surprised to learn that the boy had been placed with adoptive parents in 1995 at the age of twelve. The records stopped there. Both McClain parents were deceased by 2003.

Conner had dropped out of school at seventeen and was unmarried and lived alone.

There was only one thing left for Desmond to do.

On an overcast day in June 2003, he parked outside Conner's apartment building and waited, rehearsing what he would say. That morning, he saw his brother for the first time in twenty years. The sight broke his heart. Not with joy, but with sorrow. Conner McClain had long, grungy hair and wore baggy, dirty clothes. Track marks ran down his right arm. He lit a cigarette and set off on foot for his back-breaking job on the docks.

Sitting in the rental car, watching his younger brother, Desmond's life changed. From that point forward, he dedicated himself to helping Conner turn his life around. He bought a company in Australia and directed the HR department to hire Conner. He found out the young man's strengths and weaknesses, and insisted Conner's supervisor challenge him. He watched him grow over the course of a few years. Conner moved out of the run-down apartment and left drugs behind, but he could never chase away the demons inside of him. He was the shell of the person he wanted to be. Desmond knew that feeling all too well; more than anyone else, he understood exactly how his younger brother felt.

The night when he revealed to Conner who he truly was— that they were brothers—the two of them hugged and promised to never keep another secret from each other. Desmond told him the full truth then, about the Citium, and the Looking Glass, a device that would change the world and allow both of them to be healed, to start over, to literally rewrite the past if they wanted. He saw what he had hoped to see since the moment Conner had walked out of that run-down apartment: true transformation. Hope. Faith. Belief that a happy life was possible for him.

Peyton had been right: Desmond did need someone to save. Helping Conner gave purpose to his life. The Looking Glass took on a whole new meaning for him. It became their project, their obsession. The two brothers, along with Yuri, became the trinity guiding the project, each with their own component: Desmond oversaw the creation of Rendition, Yuri created Rapture, and Conner completed Rook.

And then everything changed. Desmond learned the truth about what Yuri intended to do. He learned about the pandemic, and he was horrified.

But Conner wasn't; he insisted that it was the only way. He was willing to do anything for the Looking Glass; Desmond wasn't.

In the conference room on the *Kentaro Maru*, they fought over it, said things they both regretted. A bridge officer opened the door and informed them that an American expedition had found the *Beagle,* the Citium research submarine that had conducted advanced research in the early years of the Looking Glass. It was a tomb at the bottom of the ocean that held secrets they wanted to keep buried—secrets that might compromise everything they were doing.

Conner ordered a strike on the American ship. Desmond pleaded for him not to, but it was no use. Conner and Yuri were going forward with the pandemic, and there was nothing Desmond could say to convince them otherwise. So he created a plan to stop them.

Desmond contacted Garin Meyer, an investigative journalist in Berlin who had unknowingly stumbled upon the Citium conspiracy. Desmond tried and failed to expose the Citium before the pandemic began, but Conner and Yuri acted too quickly.

Desmond had created a backup plan: hiding Rendition and erasing his own memories. In doing so, he prevented Conner and Yuri from completing the Looking Glass *and* ensured they couldn't kill him. He hid clues to himself in the hotel room in Berlin and in the Labyrinth Reality app. His backup plan had led him to Peyton; to William; and now here, to the Isle. Behind him, Avery held the tablet with the list of sites with the cure. If they could transmit the data to Rubicon, the information could save countless lives.

Desmond saw the same thing on Conner's face that he had seen there a week ago in the holding cell on the *Kentaro Maru*: hurt. Desmond understood now. His betrayal had wounded Conner in a way the man had never thought possible.

Desmond expected Conner to threaten him, but his tone was soft, pleading.

"Please, Des. End this. We'll forget about it."

"You know we can't."

"We've won, brother. The world is ours. The Looking Glass will be completed within days. We've done it. The hard part's over. Please, Desmond. Please."

His little brother needed him. In some ways, the fire that had almost claimed Conner's life had never stopped hurting him. But now his pain could end. The Looking Glass could save him. And Desmond alone held the key to the final piece: Rendition. With it, he held the power to heal his brother.

Soldiers peered around the door frame behind Conner and trained rifles on Desmond and Avery, the red dots moving over their bodies like crawling insects.

Avery leaned forward, hiding her head behind Desmond.

Her voice was a very nervous whisper. "What are you thinking here, Des?"

CHAPTER 122

WILLIAM WATCHED YURI pace across the office. The small Russian man dismissed the guards but left William's hands bound.

William knew he had to buy time. It was his only chance of escape, and the team's only chance to complete their mission. If he could stall long enough, maybe Desmond and Avery could get out of the building and upload the list to the US government servers. Or maybe Peyton and Charlotte could find something they could use.

And if he was really lucky, the Marines would arrive to save them all. In the years William had known Yuri, the smaller man had always been stoic, his face made of stone. William had wondered if that was a result of his growing up in Stalingrad during World War II. Day and night, the Nazis had pounded the city to rubble and slaughtered its people, including Yuri's parents and two brothers.

But now, in the fourth-floor corner office, William saw a softer, more reflective expression on his old friend's face. He hoped he could use that.

"There's still time to stop this, Yuri."

"There isn't. We both know it."

"It was you, wasn't it? The purge."

Yuri sat on the end of the desk. "Yes."

"They were our friends, Yuri. And you slaughtered them."

"You didn't know them the way I did. You protected them, but you weren't one of them—you weren't a scientist. You never saw some of the things they were working on. Or what they were really like. Obsessive. Vindictive. Ruthless. I knew a long time ago—long before anyone else—that there could be only one Looking Glass device. The other cells wouldn't have stopped. We would have created a completely new type of warfare. A techno-war. Looking Glass projects competing, consuming resources, pitting nations against each other. It would have ripped the world apart. I saved us. I don't regret that."

"Do you regret sending those men to my home to kill me?"

Yuri looked away.

"Why didn't you finish the job? You found me years later—when I was close to finding you and stopping you."

As he said the words, William realized the truth—why Yuri couldn't do it back then. The man had killed every one of his friends—except for William. He was his last true friend. Perhaps Yuri had realized that after the purge.

"I owed you. You saved my life in Rio. I pay my debts."

"Yet you took my son's life."

"I did no such thing."

A relief beyond words swept over William. It was true—the theory he had harbored for so many years: his only son was alive. His suspicions had grown when he found the old picture in Kazakhstan—it could have belonged to Lin or Andrew, William didn't know which. But what had happened during the last twenty-five years?

He took his best guess.

"Andrew has been your prisoner?"

"For a time."

"And then?"

"My partner."

William shook his head. "Impossible."

"You would have been proud of him. He resisted far longer than we expected. His re-education took years. But we broke him, showed him the truth. He found in the Looking Glass what we all see: a way to fix our broken world. And himself. The bargain we presented was simple: one last pandemic to end them all. An end to disease. And for himself, a world where he has two arms, where he is just like everyone else, a world where no other boy will have to sit on the sidelines while the others play ball, where no person is born with a disability."

Rage built within William. "You brainwashed him. Chose him—to get me out of the way."

Yuri seemed unconcerned by William's anger. "And to complete my own work. I'm not as young as I used to be."

William strained against the plastic zip ties, causing them to cut into his wrists. A trickle of blood rolled down his hand. He desperately wanted to rush the monster who stood before him, but he maintained his composure. Yuri had one commodity he desperately needed: information.

He considered what Yuri had done: enlisting Andrew, Desmond, and Conner to complete the Looking Glass. They were all broken in a way, all completely dedicated to the cause. They were all perfect examples of the type of person who could be radicalized, made to do terrible things in the name of a brighter future. In a way, they were mirrors of Yuri, William, and Lin. They had all grown up in a desperate and broken world, had come to the Citium seeking a balm for their pain, as well as for the world.

William wondered if the cycle would ever be broken.

Another question had always bothered him, and Yuri was the only person who could answer it.

"The night of the purge. Lin was tipped off. She left while I was in the air en route to London. She was on a flight to France when I landed. It was you, wasn't it? You told her to get out."

Yuri raised his eyebrows. He was impressed. "Yes."

"You couldn't kill her either."

"I needed her to complete my work."

"And she went along?"

"To a point. Taking Andrew as a hostage helped."

"She didn't know, did she? About the pandemic."

Yuri's reaction told him it was true.

William pressed on, hoping for more answers. "And Hughes didn't either. That's why he went off the reservation when he found out. Why he contacted me."

"A minor setback."

"You underestimated his morality. That's how he's different from you."

"We're a team for a reason. He lacks the fortitude to do what must be done. I do not. I did those things in Stalingrad. And during the purge. And now."

"What's happening now isn't courage, Yuri. It's mass murder. You made the world sick."

"The world was already sick. It just didn't know it. I've seen that sickness in a way few have. During the war, you were spared the horror; they evacuated you to the English countryside for tea and playtime. Death and misery were on every doorstep where I grew up. I'm saving future generations from that. Soon, our solution will be distributed."

The words struck fear into William: *Our solution* will be *distributed*. "The pandemic..."

"Was a means to an end."

"The cure. It's your true end game. That's why you started the out-break in Africa."

Yuri smiled.

"Yes. To show the world what the pathogen was capable of—on a small scale in a place where people would take notice but not alter their patterns. Not cancel flights. Or their shopping trips." Yuri paused. "And when that horrific pathogen reached their shores, they would do anything for the cure."

"Including giving up their freedom."

"Don't pretend like you don't know the true nature of freedom."

"Who knew? About the cure?"

"Only Andrew and myself."

Yuri had turned his son into a monster.

"It's over, William. Whether we release the cure or the government does makes no difference."

"What's in the cure?"

Yuri was silent.

"It's one of the Looking Glass components, isn't it?"

"Yes."

CHAPTER 123

PEYTON WATCHED HER brother walk closer. She could see that he had changed. The Andrew Shaw she had known was a kindhearted person, dedicated to helping people. Now his face was hard, almost possessed. *What's happened to him?*

Her heart broke at seeing her brother—her hero—involved in this.

He looked her in the eyes and spoke without emotion. "She's right, Peyton. There is more going on here than you realize. I'll explain everything to you—"

"You'll never explain this to me."

"Don't judge the method until you know the reason. This is a pandemic to end all others. The final pandemic. The world will be safe soon. It's a small price to pay."

At that moment, Andrew saw Charlotte. The sight of her took him aback. His voice changed, softened.

"What are you doing here?"

Charlotte swallowed. "Peyton and Desmond came to my relief camp in Australia looking for answers."

Andrew looked concerned now. "You shouldn't be here."

"What have you done, Andrew?"

"What had to be done."

"You sent me the supplies, didn't you?"

He nodded.

"It was you I was writing to. You were writing back all those years." Charlotte's voice cracked. "I never forgot about you. Or stopped caring."

Andrew stood still for a moment. Peyton could see a struggle within him.

"I knew your work was important to you," he said. "I wanted to see you happy."

Charlotte stepped closer to him. "If you still do, you'll stop whatever's happening here."

"The Looking Glass—"

"Can't be worth what you've done."

Andrew took a step back, as if withdrawing from the pull the woman was exerting on him. "None of you understand." He stared at Peyton. "The Looking Glass is the only hope. For all of us."

CHAPTER 124

THE SMOKE FROM the server room drifted through the hole in the wall, through the corridor, and snaked into the office, its wisps wrapping around Desmond, Conner, and Avery like a preternatural demon trying to wrench their souls from their bodies. The wind pulled the smoke through the room out the broken windows.

Conner held his arms out to block the soldiers stepping forward on each side of him. His eyes locked on his older brother, the man who had rescued him from an impoverished, drug-addled life and given him purpose—and hope. Now Desmond threatened to take it all away, as if it had been a prize dangled before him only to be ripped away.

"Please, Des. Don't do this. Just give me the tablet Avery's holding—I *promise* I won't harm her."

When Desmond said nothing, Conner's voice hardened. "You promised me, brother. You swore we'd finish this together."

Desmond exhaled. The smoke was slowly filling the room, clouding his vision, the wind losing the battle to suck it away completely. On the way to the island, he had thought he saw things so clearly. He hesitated now.

In Dadaab, he had seen the evil the Citium had unleashed upon the world: hordes of helpless people dying, bodies being tossed upon bonfires, orphans who would grow up never knowing love—just like him. Even if the Looking Glass offered a panacea for humanity's problems, Desmond would never ask the world's people to pay that price, much less force it on them against their will.

He looked Conner in the eye. "I'm going to help you, brother. I mean that. Do you believe me?"

Conner nodded. "Yes. Good."

Desmond turned his head quickly and whispered to Avery. "Go. Do it now."

She didn't need to be told twice. She spun on her heel, crouched to make herself a smaller target, and dove out the window as the room erupted in gunfire.

CHAPTER 125

THE THICK BRUSH below the building broke Avery's fall, but the landing from the fifteen-foot drop was still agonizing. She groaned, rolled, and fought to catch her breath. Bullets ripped through the tree canopy and raked across the ground just inches away.

She pushed up and ran. Her left leg screamed in pain, but she didn't stop. She activated her mic.

"Overwatch, Medusa, our cover is blown. Request immediate backup, air support, and exfil. Bravo, Zulu, Medusa. Any hell you could unleash would be greatly appreciated."

Seconds later, explosions rocked the island. A fire rose from the harbor. In a thick clump of trees, Avery slumped to the ground, got the sat-phone out, connected it to the tablet, and began the upload. After a moment, the screen flashed:

Upload Complete

She activated the North Star app, which initialized a voice-over-IP phone connection. David Ward's voice came on the line.

"We just saw the upload."

Avery was still breathing hard. "What happens now?"

"Leave that to us. Just get out of there in one piece."

Bullets ripped into the tree trunk at her back and across the dense ferns around her. She rolled, pulled the handgun from her holster, and emptied the magazine. She saw three soldiers fall.

There were at least ten more behind them. She slid her last magazine in and began limping away.

They were gaining on her, moving slower now, taking their time, hiding behind the palm trees that swayed in the wind. The smoke issuing from the window descended into the jungle and streaked across the glowing moon above. The darkness aided her retreat, but it wasn't enough. Her time was short.

Explosions lit up the night sky above her—missiles from the expeditionary strike group, being intercepted by a missile defense system on the island. It was breathtaking, some of the world's most advanced weapons of war fighting a duel over this placid island in the South Pacific. The strike group was winning. Their missiles began reaching the ground, which shook with every impact.

Avery hoped the soldiers would desist in the face of the air power, but they kept coming, closing in. She slid behind a tree and caught her breath. She was cornered. There was only one thing left to do.

"Overwatch, Medusa. Request tactical strike against hostiles near my location."

The CIC responded immediately. "Medusa, Overwatch. Negative. Hostiles are too close—"

"Do it or I'm dead, Overwatch."

Bullets tore through the tree beside her. Splinters sprayed across her side as she dove to the ground. In the air, she saw a flash—a missile launch from a drone. A second later it landed at the feet of the soldiers, annihilating them. The ground below Avery erupted. She could feel the heat. For a split second, it felt as if she were in the grasp of a hurricane. The blast tossed her through the forest. A tree trunk broke her fall. But she didn't get up this time. Her limp body lay there as burned debris fell, burying her.

CHAPTER 126

IN THE OFFICE above, Desmond rushed the troops who had fired at Avery. He leaped, colliding with Conner and one of the men. A fist connected with his face. He nearly blacked out from the impact. They pulled him to the ground and kicked him in his already injured ribs. He gasped for breath, but a knee landed on his chest, suffocating him. The last thing he saw was the butt of a rifle coming down and connecting with his forehead.

☣

Yuri eyed William. "Who did you bring with you, William?"

William stood silently, his hands still bound.

"Surely you didn't bring your daughter here. That would be very dangerous." Yuri studied him. "Then again, you were never afraid to push all-in, especially when the stakes were high." He paused. "You did, didn't you? Where is she?"

William didn't answer.

"She's not in the building," Yuri said. "We would have seen her on the cameras." Realization dawned on him. "But we don't have cameras in the labs. The risk of espionage is too great. She's there, isn't she?"

When William still said nothing, Yuri snatched the handheld radio off the desk. "Major Reeves, Pachenko. Send a unit to the labs—right now. Secure Rapture access control. You're also to apprehend Pey—"

William jumped up and rushed forward. His sprained ankle protested, but he closed the distance between him and Yuri. His hands were still bound behind his back, but he threw his head forward, connecting with his captor's. He had to stop the man— to give Peyton and Charlotte a chance of escape.

Yuri slammed into the wall, William the floor. Yuri was out cold. William got to his feet just as the office door flew open and two guards ran in, assault rifles raised. They fired as William desperately tried to lunge behind the desk.

☣

In the situation room at the White House, the recently sworn-in president of the United States watched Chinook helicopters lifting off from air bases across the country. Drone footage showed BioShield reserve troops raiding the locations Rubicon had provided. Every single one of them had held doses of the cure so far. Those doses would be distributed within minutes.

The UK, Germany, Australia, China, Russia, and Canada had also confirmed dozens of Citium sites. They had done it. The United States would survive, but the president couldn't help wondering what the nation he loved so much would look like in the aftermath of the pandemic.

☣

The lab complex shook when the first blasts went off. Ceiling tiles dropped to the floor. Glass cabinets rattled. Vials fell and broke.

"We need to get out of here," Lin said.

Peyton shook her head. "No. I'm not leaving until I get some answers."

Charlotte matched her tone. "Neither am I."

Peyton faced her brother. "Tell me what the cure is."

He studied her but said nothing.

"Are you willing to risk our lives to keep your secrets?" She paused. "Explain it, and then we'll leave." It was a bluff, but she needed to know.

Andrew swallowed, then spoke quietly. "It's something new. A nano-tech device."

Peyton knew very little about nanomedicine. It was a growing field with incredible potential. Doctors were experimenting with nanorobots to do a number of things: treating cancer, delivering drugs to hard-to-reach parts of the body, and identifying pathogens. It was conceivable that it could be used to neutralize a virus or bacteria.

Her brother confirmed her theory with his next words. "The nanorobots find and inactivate the virus. They're also programmed to do limited tissue repair in critical areas, reducing mortality." His tone changed, grew bitter. "If more of the world's governments had complied, the death rate would be a fraction of what it is."

Peyton studied him. "What *else* does it do?"

Andrew said nothing.

"That's what this is about, isn't it? The pandemic was for this moment. The nanorobots you're distributing within the cure— *that's* the Looking Glass."

He shook his head. "No. Only a part."

"One of three," Peyton whispered, almost to herself.

"Yes. The cure is Rapture."

"How does it work?"

Another explosion rocked the building, this one stronger.

Those were missiles from the sea. They're firing on the island.

Lin grabbed her daughter by the arm. "Peyton, it's time."

She pulled away. She wouldn't leave. Everything she'd gone through in the past two weeks had been for this exact moment. It all led here to this turning point.

Peyton had finally realized the entire truth. Desmond had discovered what Rapture was. He had called her to warn her. And though he didn't know then *why* he was warning her, it was clear to her now: he had known that Yuri and Conner would try to capture her—to use her as leverage. She alone connected all the critical players who could stop the pandemic: Lin, Desmond,

William, and Andrew. She alone could be used to *control* all
of them.

"They're going to use Rapture for some sort of alteration, aren't
they? They're going to change human biology."

Andrew and Lin both stared at Peyton in disbelief—or perhaps
with admiration that she had put it together so quickly.

Andrew gazed down at the manufacturing floor as he spoke.
"The nanorobots are designed to take additional instructions after
they neutralize the virus. Their size limits their memory capacity."

Peyton marveled at the plan. Research was already ongoing that
used nanorobots to insert genes into a host, altering its genome.
The nanoparticles could cross the blood-brain barrier, allowing
them to alter pathways in the brain and the biochemical balance.
That must be what happened to Desmond. He used Rapture
Therapeutics' core Rapture device—the nanorobots—to block
his memories. Rapture would give the Citium an unimaginable
control over the human race, the power to alter every person at
a cellular level. All the Citium had to do was send additional
instructions to their nanorobots after the virus was eliminated.

Which meant that was the key to stopping them: preventing
the Rapture nanorobots from getting further instructions. That
would take away the Citium's power.

She looked at her brother a long moment. They had radicalized
him. Peyton wasn't sure if she could make him see the truth, but she
had to try. "Andrew, think about what they've done—how many
people the Citium has killed. If they control Rapture, imagine
what they'll do."

He shook his head. "You don't understand—"

"I do. I've seen it. The stacks of dead bodies. Andrew, Dad's
alive."

The words shocked him. "Impossible."

To Peyton's surprise, her mother spoke up. "It's true, Andrew.
Yuri tried to kill him, but he survived."

He stepped back, away from them, wincing as he tried to come
to grips with the information.

Peyton sensed that this was the moment to make her move.

"Andrew, can you disable the remote access? Prevent the Rapture nanorobots from taking additional instructions?"

Andrew said nothing, but Peyton still knew him well enough to read him. She could see that she was right: he could stop this.

"Do it. Please. It's the only way to stop them. I'm not leaving until you do."

His eyes flashed to her. "I'll have you dragged out of here."

Another explosion rocked the building. All four of them crouched as more ceiling tiles rained down.

"You'll have to drag me out too then," Charlotte said.

Lin walked over and stood next to Peyton and Charlotte, showing her willingness to stay as well.

"Listen to what we're saying," Peyton said. "They've brainwashed you, Andrew. We're telling you the truth. Please, do it. Even if you drag me out of here, I'll never forgive you if you don't stop them right now."

Andrew stared at Peyton, then Charlotte, then his mother, and finally out at the factory floor.

"Trust us," Peyton said. "Nobody cares about you more than the three of us. Believe what we're telling you." She waited a moment. "I'm willing to die to try to stop the Citium. They've killed people I cared about. Tried to kill Dad. They took you from me, Andrew. This isn't who you are."

"I don't care what the Looking Glass is," Charlotte added. "This world isn't perfect, and that makes it worth having. Just like you."

Another explosion shook the building, much closer this time, with far greater force. The glass walls overlooking the massive manufacturing machines exploded outward, raining glass down. A tall cabinet over-turned, barely missing Charlotte.

Andrew was quickly at her side, pulling her away.

"You okay?"

She nodded.

Charlotte gripped Andrew's shoulders. "Please." She pulled him closer to her. "Please, Andrew."

Like a wall crumbling, his hard expression dissolved. He smiled a remorseful, yet kind smile. Peyton saw then the older brother she had grown up with, the brother who had helped take care of her in the years after their father was gone.

Slowly, he nodded. "Okay." He moved to a raised table with a computer terminal. "I can disable the remote access to the Rapture nanorobots from here and remove the backup program from the Rook servers."

He twisted the hand portion of his prosthetic and removed it. He stuck it in a pocket, then took out another attachment that was affixed to his belt. It resembled a hand, but with yellow-white plastic fingers that barely hid the wires below. He twisted it onto the end of his prosthetic forearm. Peyton watched in wonder as the fingers twitched. The stump must have given tiny impulses to the prosthetic, which electronically controlled the hand and fingers. For the first time in her life, Peyton saw her brother use a real left hand. She wondered if the Citium had leveraged this gift to gain control over him. She couldn't imagine what he had been through, or what his road back would be like. He was a classic victim of Stockholm Syndrome—when captives come to trust and, in some cases, join their captors.

Another series of explosions rocked the building. The lights flickered, and everyone froze. If the power went out, it was over— and if the building was hit, they'd be trapped down here.

"Keep working," Peyton said. "I'm going above to radio them, tell them to not hit the building."

"I'll go with you," Lin said. "If there are Citium troops, I'll be able to help."

All eyes turned to Charlotte. She moved to stand beside Andrew. "I'm not staying here."

CHAPTER 127

THE LIGHTS FLICKERED in the stairwell as Peyton pounded up the stairs. The elevators were either broken or had been shut down.

Her mother lagged behind her. The woman had always been in excellent health, but she was now in her late seventies.

Another explosion rattled the metal staircase, nearly throwing Peyton off her feet. Lin grabbed the handrail and braced herself on the wall. "Go on, darling, I'm right behind you."

"No, you're not. We're staying together, Mom."

She wrapped her arm around the lithe woman, and they climbed the stairs together, the bombs exploding outside as they marched.

At the ground floor landing, Peyton paused when she saw a thin film of smoke issuing forth from the crack beneath the door. She placed her hand on the door, felt warmth, then pulled the bottom of her shirt around her hand and lightly touched the handle. It was too hot for her to touch.

We're trapped.

Conner crouched over his brother's limp body. Desmond's face was bloodied and bruised. He took his brother in his arms and hugged him tight.

"Des," he whispered.

Right after Desmond had been knocked out, the air raids had

struck the building. It sounded as though a large portion of it had collapsed, and fire was consuming the rest. The flames were closing in, marching down the hallway toward them. The soldiers had left. Rats fleeing a sinking ship—or more precisely, a burning island.

Conner had been too young to remember the fire that had permanently scarred him, but the burns had left him terrified of fire. He didn't even like eating in restaurants with a fireplace, wouldn't set foot inside a home with one. The sight of a large open flame paralyzed him. He watched the blaze clawing away at the building, consuming more of it each second.

He was alone now with his brother, in much the same way their lives had started: in the face of an unstoppable fire. All those years ago, it had been Conner who had lain helplessly as the fire advanced. Desmond hadn't saved him. There was something fitting about leaving him, completing the cycle. But Conner was ashamed of the thought. Those dark impulses were exactly the thing Desmond had tried to help him control. Tried and failed. He was what he was.

The fire was closer now. Conner felt himself start to shiver, as if he were naked in the Arctic. The force rattling his body, however, was not cold, but fear—an overwhelming, petrifying force.

He heard footsteps behind him, but Conner barely turned his head. Yuri squatted down in front of him. His face was bloody, one eye swollen shut.

He examined Conner, searching for a wound, confusion clouding his face when he found none.

His voice was hoarse, perhaps from the smoke inhalation. "What's happened?"

"I can't," Conner whispered.

Yuri glanced at the flames closing on them and seemed to understand.

"You must, Conner. Every man faces his demons. Yours is here. Will you cower and let it best you? Now is your chance. Show me what you really are."

CHAPTER 128

ON THE LANDING of the smoke-filled stairwell in the glow of the emergency lights, Peyton ripped her clothes off. First the body armor, then the breathable mesh Kevlar undershirt.

She knelt over the garments, clad only in her bra and khaki pants, and drew the knife from a sheath on her belt. She cut two long strips of mesh from the short-sleeved shirt, wrapped one around her mouth, and handed the other to her mother. The older woman followed Peyton's lead.

Peyton pulled the shirt back on, and wrapped the body armor around her left arm, prepping it to use as an insulated shield against the fire. She made sure her comm unit was still affixed.

She crouched down and turned her back to her mother. "Climb on."

"Honey."

"Mom, do it. We don't have time to argue."

Lin exhaled as she stepped closer to her daughter. Her voice seemed to slip deeper into her British accent as she muttered, "Well, there's no need to be rude."

With her mother's arms around her neck, Peyton rose, hit the door handle with her armor-wrapped hand, and rushed into the hall.

The smoke was thick, but the flames were mostly confined to studs in the walls and the furniture burning in the offices. She turned a corner and saw the lobby. The wooden reception desk blazed like a bonfire. The wind rushed in, feeding the fire endless amounts of the oxygen it needed to burn. Waves of heat pushed deeper into the structure, past Peyton, like the tide lapping at a beach. But beyond the desk, beyond the shattered glass windows, the darkness of night loomed. Freedom. She could make it.

Peyton pressed on, putting one foot in front of the other. Her lungs burned. Her head swam. She felt a new admiration for Desmond: days ago, he had carried her father out of a burning building at Aralsk-7. Now it was Peyton's turn, and she pushed with every ounce of energy she had.

Her legs didn't give out until she crossed the threshold of the front doors. She felt herself collapse then, but she didn't hit the ground. Her mother wrapped her arms around her and dragged her from the blaze.

Through watering eyes, she saw dark hair streaked with gray hanging down in front of her, a curtain across her face. It was drawn back, and Peyton saw her mother staring down, tears in her eyes. She ripped the mesh Kevlar from Peyton's mouth, turned her head, and held her ear to Peyton's mouth. Lin let out a cry of joy when she realized her daughter was breathing. She pulled her closer into her lap. "It's going to be okay, honey."

Slowly, Peyton's senses focused. Automatic gunfire rang out in the distance. *They're fighting for the harbor. The Marines must have landed.*

Engines roared. High-caliber artillery guns pounded. Overhead, she saw more missile strikes that found their targets, churning earth and trees and bodies in massive explosions of fire and smoke. The entire island seemed to be erupting.

She brought a shaking hand to her collarbone, activated her comm, and spoke with a scratchy, strained voice. "Overwatch, Artemis. Cease fire at my location. We have friendlies in the adjacent building. Confirm."

"Artemis, Overwatch, confirmed, ceasing air strikes at your location."

A second later, the CIC operator opened the comm line again. "Artemis, Overwatch. Be advised, there are hostiles inbound to your twenty. Estimate a force of twelve, heavily armed. Reinforcements are two clicks out. Advise you take cover or retreat."

CHAPTER 129

IN HER PERIPHERAL vision, Peyton saw the soldiers closing on them.

Carefully, Lin placed Peyton's head on the ground and stood tall, her posture rigid, facing the oncoming troops—a proud mother ready to defend her child with her own life. Peyton desperately wanted to stand with her, but she couldn't. She didn't have the strength. Every breath burned.

The soldiers halted their sprint when they saw Lin.

The nearly eighty-year-old woman's voice was strong as it called into the smoke-filled night. "Major, we have friendlies in this building. They are mission-critical to our cause. Rescue them. Do it now."

The man hesitated, then touched his collarbone. "Dr. Pachenko, Major Reeves."

The man paused, listening.

Peyton was shocked. *Yuri Pachenko is here.* The man had taken so much from her. Her hatred boiled as the mercenary activated his comm again.

"Dr. Pachenko?"

Lin took a step toward him. "Send your men in, Major. Do it now or there will be consequences."

Reeves motioned for four of his men to enter the building.

To the soldiers entering, Lin said, "Basement level four. A man and a woman. They'll be together."

Major Reeves scowled at Lin. "My last orders were to secure the Rapture Control program."

"The situation has changed, Major. And so have your orders."

"Dr. Pachenko—"

"Is no longer in charge here. I am. Tell your men at the harbor and elsewhere to stand down."

Reeves was shocked. "Ma'am?"

"Those are your orders. We face an overwhelming force. The battle here can't be won. We must surrender for the greater good. We are prepared for this contingency, I assure you, Major."

The soldier nodded slowly, activated his comm, and ordered a full surrender.

Peyton sat up, seeing her mother with a whole new appreciation. *She did it.* This was an entirely new side of the mild-mannered woman who had raised her.

Peyton activated her own comm. "Overwatch, Artemis, be advised, hostiles have been ordered to stand down."

The gunfire in the distance stopped. Seconds later, so did the missile fire coming in from the sea.

For a moment, the dense island jungle was quiet. The towering palm trees swayed in the wind, bristling with each gust. The fire blazing behind her crackled. Here and there, pieces of the building collapsed.

With each passing second, Peyton was able to catch her breath.

"Artemis, Overwatch, cease-fire confirmed. Commencing search and rescue operations. First wave of helos inbound. ETA thirty minutes."

"Copy, Overwatch."

"Ground teams are en route to your location."

"Copy that. Thank you."

Peyton sat up and stared at the building. Andrew was in there, trapped beyond the fire. In the years after she was told he'd died in a fire, she'd dreamt about it a thousand times. Nightmares with Andrew trapped, and her unable to help. But this time it was real. The building was collapsing in on itself.

She lay on her back again. She couldn't bear to watch. She wanted to go back in the building, but she was too weak.

She activated her comm again. "Dad. Desmond. Avery." She

had forgotten their call signs, but it didn't matter now. She just wanted to hear their voices. But no one responded. She called again. And a third time. Nothing.

She closed her eyes, willing it not to be true. Desmond. Her father. Andrew. In the past four days, all three had been returned to her. Now they might be taken away again. And somewhere deep inside her, she knew she would never recover this time.

CHAPTER 130

IT HAD BEEN ten minutes since the soldiers entered the burning lab complex. Peyton was on her feet now, able to breathe better, but not one hundred percent. She peered into the flames, looking for any signs of figures emerging. The pulsing heat warmed her face and body. A breeze pushed the blaze back every few seconds.

A gruff voice came over Peyton's comm. "Artemis, Zulu leader, we've got a live one. Request medical assistance. We're at the admin building."

Major Reeves had been coordinating his troops' surrender, which was finally complete.

Peyton interrupted a string of orders he was calling out. "Can one of your men take me to the admin building?"

Reeves glanced at Lin, who nodded. He instructed one of his soldiers to accompany Peyton, and they set off down a stone path, walking as quickly as she could manage. Her lungs still ached, but hope drove her on.

The administrative building was a charred ruin. The entire top two floors had burned down. Trails of smoke rose from orange embers crackling in the night. A half dozen of the camo-clad special forces waded through the wreckage, turning over the blackened pieces of wreckage with the barrels of their rifles.

Ahead, a Navy SEAL motioned for Peyton to come quickly. She swallowed, dreading what she would see. She repeated the words over the comm in her mind: *We've got a live one.* Alive, but in what condition? And who?

She knew who she wanted it to be. In the moment, she was completely honest with herself. She wanted to see Desmond's face. She wanted to leave the island with him more than anything in the world. In the *Boxer*'s mess, he had said the things he needed to say, but she hadn't. She knew that had been a mistake—one she might live to regret.

Beyond the Navy SEAL lay a burned-out crater, nearly smooth in the center. A ring of bodies circled it. In hot zones around the world, Peyton had seen pathogens rip through a population, leaving death behind. This was an altogether different form of carnage. Men lay in pieces. Dead eyes stared up at her, or out into the forest. Severed limbs lay alone, remnants of the slaughter strewn about without care or mercy. Rivulets of blood flowed into the crater like the veins on the back of a dark earthen monster. Steam rose from the hole as Peyton descended.

The Navy SEAL told her that he was a corpsman. He had stopped the bleeding, but the patient needed an infusion quickly. A medevac was inbound with blood, but it would be close. The *Boxer* had a capable operating room; unfortunately, it would be almost an hour before the patient reached the table.

As the SEAL shifted to the side, Peyton held her breath.

Avery lay on the ground, dirt plastered across her pale face and in her blond hair. Her breathing was shallow. Peyton knelt at her side. A six-inch gash ran across her abdomen. The corpsman had done a good job; the wound was packed tight. Splinters from shattered trees dotted her body. Avery murmured a phrase Peyton couldn't make out. The corpsman had loaded her up with a painkiller. That was good. There wasn't much else Peyton could do. In truth, the Navy medical officer was better trained to treat battlefield injuries than Peyton was. There was only one thing she could give the young woman, and for that reason, she sat silently, waiting.

Avery cracked her eyes, mumbled again. Peyton gripped her hand. "You're going to be okay, Avery. Medevac is on the way. Surgeons are already prepped and waiting on you."

An amused grin formed on Avery's lips. "You taking care of me now?"

Peyton smiled back at her. "Yeah. I am. You know how I am about that. About my people."

"Then I know I'm going to make it. You're a real pain in the ass."

Peyton laughed—a nervous, cathartic laugh, like a pressure valve releasing the tension from her body. "Look who's talking," she shot back.

More seriously, Peyton asked, "Did you get it?"

Avery nodded. "Yeah, we got it."

We. The word filled Peyton with hope.

Avery's smile faded. "What did you find in the labs?"

Peyton considered what to say. "Nothing that'll be a problem."

A soldier searching the building called out, "Got another one."

Instinctively Peyton's head snapped around, seeking out the caller. She desperately wanted to rush over, but she returned her focus to Avery. The blond woman released Peyton's hand. "Go. That's one of *our* people. They need you too."

"I'll see you on the *Boxer*, Avery."

Peyton stumbled over the bombed-out ground, weaving around bodies and into the ruined building. Up a stairwell littered with debris, she found soldiers pulling wreckage away, revealing more of a body. It was limp. The torso came into view. The chest was caved in. Not breathing.

The moment Peyton saw her father's face, she closed her eyes. Tears flowed. Her legs gave way. She sank to her knees, letting them dig into the ash-covered floor. Her eyes settled on a half-burned picture frame. The picture was of a short, white-haired man with a cold, blank expression. He matched Desmond and her father's description of Yuri Pachenko—and Peyton had no doubt that was exactly who it was. This was Yuri's office. *He killed my father.*

Her entire life, she had blamed fate and bad luck for the loss of her father. Now she had a name to put with the rage that consumed her: Yuri Pachenko. He had taken her father from her. She would make him pay. Yuri had wanted to change the world—and he had certainly succeeded in changing *her*.

She would be the end of him. In the burned remains of the building, with her father lying dead ten feet away, she swore it.

Another soldier's voice called into the night. "Got another one."

CHAPTER 131

ELLIOTT HELD HIS wife's head in his lap. The RV sitting in an alley off Marietta Street was warm from the small heaters and the people crammed inside. Ryan was with them, as well as Sam and Adam, and a dozen of Elliott's neighbors and their loved ones. At the table, a mother was reading *Charlotte's Web* to four children packed in around her. The kids were leaning in, gazing at the pictures. Two teenagers were stretched out on opposite ends of a couch, playing games on tablets, headphones in their ears. Three adult couples snacked on protein bars and sipped bottled water while they tuned a handheld radio, searching for any signal on the AM band.

The chorus of coughing never ceased. The X1-Mandera virus was ravaging all of them, some to a greater degree than others. It was only a matter of time before their bodies began surrendering to the pathogen. Elliott feared Rose would be the first casualty.

A series of beeps sounded from the radio—the prelude to an emergency message. One of Elliott's neighbors tuned the dial. The static cleared, and the beeps came into focus, then stopped. Every eye turned to the radio. Even the teenagers jerked their earbuds out and sat up. A man's voice spoke slowly in a solemn, deliberate tone.

"My fellow Americans, wherever you are, whatever you're doing, please stop and hear this message. It may save your life, or the lives of your loved ones. My name is James Marshall. Many of you know me as the Speaker of the House. Two days ago,

I was sworn in as President of the United States. I'm speaking to you now because we face a threat unlike any in the history of our great nation. First, know that I bring you good news: the X1-Mandera pandemic that has ravaged our great nation and others around the world will soon come to an end. The United States, working with scientists in the international community, has developed a viable cure for the virus. The treatment also functions as a vaccine for anyone not infected."

Inside the RV, cheers went up. Some stared in disbelief. Elliott was instantly suspicious.

"However, the best news I bring you today is that the cure we've developed is available right now in your city. As we speak, the combined BioShield forces have established treatment check-points throughout your cordon zone. It's important that you receive the X1-Mandera cure as soon as possible, but I also urge you to remain calm and proceed in an orderly fashion. Those committing acts of violence and disorder will be sent to the back of the line. There will be a zero tolerance policy for rioters and anyone cutting in line or preventing others from getting treatment.

"This broadcast will now switch to a local announcement that will list the X1-Mandera treatment centers in your area. The announcement will repeat.

"I wish you good luck, wherever you are. May God bless you and your family, and may God bless the United States of America."

The RV erupted in shouting and questions. One of the neighbors pounded an empty can of beans on the counter, like a gavel in a courtroom, demanding silence. The voice on the radio was already reading the locations in the Atlanta cordon. At the words "Centennial Olympic Park," everyone began pulling on their overcoats and moving toward the RV's door.

Ryan approached Elliott. "What do you think?"

Elliott didn't say what he thought: that something was very wrong. Treatments for novel pathogens weren't created overnight, or in a week. They certainly weren't mass-produced that fast, with doses in the hundreds of millions, and distributed all over the country.

On the other hand, his wife was dying. The love of his life would be gone in hours. *What do I have to lose?*

"I think we need to hurry," he said.

He lifted Rose up and staggered out of the RV, into the cold late afternoon. Ryan carried the wheelchair out, unfolded it, and held it while Elliott set Rose down. Sam was at Elliott's side, holding Adam, whose fever had been running high. Ryan took the boy into his arms and followed closely behind Elliott.

They exited the alley and jogged down Marietta Street. The chill in the wind was merciless on Elliott's face. An endless flow of people poured out of buildings and adjoining streets. Soon the crowd was as thick as a Christmas Day parade, marching, pushing toward the tents that loomed in Centennial Park. Metal fencing funneled everyone to canopies where soldiers stood watch beside individuals wearing flak jackets printed with the letters FEMA.

When Elliott reached a FEMA official, she took one look at Rose, said, "Line One!" and handed him a red card. The soldiers motioned him onward. There were five lines prioritized based on need. Line One was for the most critical patients. It was also the only line moving. Elliott glanced back at Ryan, who was still holding Adam. Ryan simply nodded, urging his parents to go on ahead.

Another FEMA staffer directed the people in Line One to cubicles where medical staff were holding jet injectors. Vials were spread out beside them, as well as silver oblong objects: CO_2 cartridges.

Elliott tried to get a look at any labeling on the vials or injector, but there wasn't any. He wondered if he would ever know the full truth of how this life-saving cure—the cure that had just been injected into his wife—had arrived in the nick of time. For some reason, he thought of Peyton. He hoped she was safe.

On the other side of the treatment cubicle, another FEMA staffer was directing them out of the park.

Someone asked, "What do we do now?"

"Stay warm and keep hydrated. Now move on, make room for the people behind you."

Back at the RV, Elliott curled into the bed with Rose again. He had something he didn't have an hour ago: hope. For the first time in two days, he fell asleep.

CHAPTER 132

PEYTON WAS STILL numb from seeing her father's dead body. But she still walked across the charred ruins of the building, toward the body the soldiers were pulling from the wreckage.

She stopped when she saw the wig with wavy brown hair—the wig Desmond had worn into the building. It was half burned away and matted with blood.

A hulking Navy SEAL pulled a wooden beam off the body. It didn't move. It was limp, the left arm severed, the legs burned. Dead—with no hope of coming back.

Peyton's hands began to shake. She clasped them together and continued to march forward.

The Citium security operatives conducting the search parted when she reached them.

She exhaled. *It's not him.*

Peyton studied the face closer. He wasn't one of the SEALs or Force Recon members who had been part of their team. "It's not one of ours."

Another tear, this one of joy, rolled down her face.

She walked away from the building then, back to Avery, and held the woman's hand while they waited for the medevac. The slender woman drifted in and out of consciousness while Peyton monitored her pulse.

A Citium security contractor tentatively made his way over to them.

"We've finished the search," he said. "We didn't find any... non-Citium personnel."

Peyton nodded. "Thank you for telling me."

The man unclipped his radio and earpiece and handed them to Peyton.

"Your mother's on the comm."

The moment she slipped the earpiece in, Peyton heard her mother's voice giving rapid-fire orders to the soldiers around her.

"Mom?"

"Peyton. Your brother and Charlotte got out."

"Are they—"

"We've stabilized them, but they need medical assistance."

"Will they..."

"Yes. I think they'll make it, darling, but we need to hurry."

"I'm coming. I'll be there with a medevac as soon as I can."

When the medevac landed to pick up Avery, Peyton helped hoist her onto the stretcher and load her aboard. Then she hopped into the helicopter as well and directed them to the labs.

When they landed again, she raced to her brother. His prosthetic was badly burned. He must have used it as a shield. That could be replaced, but his good arm was taped to his body, and a large gash ran across his forehead. He and Charlotte were both unconscious. Charlotte had a bandage across her upper chest.

Peyton stood aside as soldiers loaded both of them onto the medevac. She had lost her father for a second time that night. She was terrified that she was going to lose her brother too.

When the medevac slipped out of sight, Lin began walking away. "Come on, Peyton; we need to talk. Your brother's life depends on what we do next."

CHAPTER 133

MILLEN WAS SITTING on a cot, opening an MRE, when the door to the lab unsealed.

He stood quickly, ready to defend the Kenyan villagers, then relaxed when he realized it was Phil.

"It's over, Millen."

"We—"

"A cure. Come on, get upstairs. We've got work to do."

Millen joined the line in the auditorium, rolled up his shirt sleeve, and got his injection. The room was as lively as the New York Stock Exchange in the days before electronic trading; everyone was shouting questions about the mysterious cure. There seemed to be no answers.

Millen returned to his desk in the EOC after his dose and studied the new SOPs. Dr. Stevens had written them hastily; Millen had to re-read several passages twice. When he finished, he pulled on his headset.

"Centennial Park Checkpoint, BioShield Ops. We need an updated vial and head count."

Near the end of Millen's shift, an operator notified him that he had a call on a CDC landline.

The voice on the other end belonged to someone Millen had thought he might never hear again: Elim Kibet.

His tone was serious. "I've got news, Millen."

When Elim finished speaking, Millen simply said, "I'll be there as soon as I can."

⚕

Millen waited outside Phil's office door for him to finish his phone call, then stepped inside.

The senior CDC employee didn't look up from his laptop. "What can I do for you, Millen?"

"I need a favor. A big one."

⚕

Millen didn't know who was called or what favors were traded, but he got word a few hours later that a deal had been made.

In the BSL-4 lab, he found Halima and Tian, both watching TV.

"Get your stuff together."

Halima raised her eyebrows, fearful.

"You're going home."

They ran to him, and Millen hugged both of them.

"I didn't know—" Halima began.

"When you agreed to come with me, I promised you I'd take you home when this was over. I honor my promises."

⚕

They flew to DC first, then to Ramstein Air Base in Germany. The plane was filled with personnel who weren't very chatty, which made Millen curious. About half the tight-lipped operatives disembarked at Ramstein, and were replaced by people boarding from the base and from Landstuhl Medical Center. From there, they flew through the night to Incirlik Air Base in Turkey, and a smaller plane took Millen and the villagers to Kenyatta National Airport.

Elim and Dhamiria were waiting for them. They had brought

presents for the two villagers: a soccer ball for the boy and a beaded Maasai necklace for the girl. The two seemed overjoyed by the gifts—and that Elim and Dhamiria had been thinking about them while they were gone.

Millen had a feeling they would adopt the two children and the thought made him very happy. He believed the four of them would be a wonderful family, despite the tragedy that had brought them together.

At the hospital, Millen walked the halls with Elim. The place was packed, a madhouse, but things were getting done; Elim was seeing to that. The Kenyan seemed to know everyone by name, and what they were doing. This was Elim's passion. In Mandera, when he was recuperating, Elim had told Millen that his own hospital was on life support; its decline had taken the wind out of the Kenyan's sails. Now the man's energy was back. In a way, the pandemic that had almost taken his life had actually restored his purpose and vitality. Millen thought it was a strange twist of fate, but he couldn't be happier for the man.

Elim slowed as they approached the hospital room where Hannah lay. Her strawberry-blond hair spilled over the pillow. The machines by her bedside had been turned off.

Millen stepped into the room. Behind him, he heard Elim pace away, already giving more orders.

He reached out, took the white sheet, and pulled it up, covering more of Hannah's body, then sat in the chair by the window. He was asleep within minutes.

Millen awoke to the sound of sheets rustling. He looked toward the bed with bloodshot eyes.

"Millen." Hannah was sitting up, gazing in amazement at him.

"Hi."

"Hi yourself. How did you get here?"

"I was in the neighborhood."

"Seriously."

"I told the CDC we had left somebody behind—close to where it all started."

His response drained some of the excitement from her. "Oh."

"And, we never finished our book."

She raised her eyebrows.

"You know how I am about my TBR list."

She laughed. "You don't have a TBR list."

"True. I have a To-Be-Listened-To list. So, I guess a TBLT list." He feigned being deep in thought. "Just doesn't have the same ring to it."

"No. No, it doesn't."

"Anyway." He held up the cell phone with the Audible app. "Shall we?"

"We shall." She scooted over in the bed, making room for him. "I believe you know the drill."

As he had done before, he lay beside Hannah, plugged one earbud in one of his ears and the other in hers, and wrapped an arm around her. The last time he had clicked play, the pandemic was still a brush fire in a remote corner of the world. The two of them had been only a couple of weeks younger, but it felt almost like a lifetime ago. Millen had grown up a lot in that short amount of time. He taken risks, handled new responsibilities, and learned what was really important. He wasn't going to let her out of his sight. Not for a while.

"You know," he said in a mock boastful tone. "I actually oversaw the first-ever patient recovery from X1-Mandera."

Hannah turned to him. "Oh really?"

"Really. That patient turned out quite well. He saved you, after all."

"Uh-huh," Hannah said. She could obviously tell he was working up to something.

"I could extend those same services to you."

"Oh, you could?"

"I could." In a serious tone, he added, "Would you like that? Do you want me to stay?"

"More than anything."

CHAPTER 134

THE SUN WAS rising over the island by the time Lin and Peyton reached the burned remains of the administrative building. The Citium search teams had brought out their fallen comrades and laid them out in rows of body bags with clear openings at the face.

Peyton and Lin marched down the row, peering at the windows into the body bags. Near the end of the row, Peyton saw her father's face. They had closed his eyes.

Lin Shaw knelt, unzipped the bag, and touched her husband's cheek.

Peyton couldn't remember ever seeing her mother cry. But in that tropical island forest, with the first rays of sunrise beaming through the tree canopy, Lin sobbed. Peyton realized it then: in some way, her mother had always expected her father to return. Lin Shaw had had one great love in her life, and she had never given up hope of being reunited with him.

Peyton understood that. Desmond was the only man she had ever truly fallen in love with. For the first time, she realized that she had always been waiting for Desmond to return. That's why she had never moved on with her life. Just like her mother had never dated after her father was taken from them.

With her hands still on William's face, Lin said, "A long time ago, we bought burial plots in London. I'd like to bury him there. And I'd like for you, your sister, and brother to be there."

Peyton nodded. She found it fitting. She knew now that her

parents hadn't fallen in love in London. That had occurred on the *Beagle*. But they had become a family in London. It was also where her father had been adopted, taken in, and helped to become the person he was.

Lin zipped up the body bag, composed herself, and turned to Peyton. "This crisis will soon be over. When that occurs, anger will replace fear. People won't be focused on how to survive. They'll want someone to blame—criminals to hang."

Peyton realized what her mother was telling her: Andrew was in danger. She felt conflicting emotions. Her brother had created the pathogen that had killed millions. But he had been brainwashed to do it.

"I know what you're thinking," her mother said. "You should know this: Yuri Pachenko is a survivor. He was a young boy in Stalingrad when the Germans came. He survived by the strength of his mind. When everyone was dying around him, he learned how to manipulate people to his will. Every person has a breaking point, weaknesses—levers that can be turned."

"What was Andrew's?"

"Yuri threatened you."

Peyton exhaled.

"And yours?"

"Andrew—and you. And Madison." Lin paused. "If we give Andrew to the world, they will try him and kill him. Or imprison him. He isn't completely innocent, but he's not entirely guilty either. When he realizes what he's done, that weight will be a punishment more cruel than any the world could put upon him. What he needs now is to find his way back, to learn to live and love again."

Charlotte, Peyton thought. Lin detailed her idea to Peyton, then looked her daughter in the eye, waiting for her response.

Peyton nodded. "All right. I'll do it."

They rose and began walking away from the bodies. Lin spoke quietly.

"There's something else. A month ago, someone located the *Beagle*. I don't know how; I can only assume the location was somewhere in the most classified Citium files. Perhaps Desmond found it and told Avery. Or maybe she found it herself."

"How do you know?"

"Rubicon sent a US Coast Guard icebreaker, the *Healy*, to find it. Conner sank the ship. I still don't know where it is. I need you to ask Avery for the location."

"Why?"

"Because of what's on it."

"Which is?"

"A conversation for another time, Peyton."

They walked in silence again, Peyton deep in thought. Like a compass returning to true north, her mind always drifted back to Desmond. She feared the answer to her next question, but she had to know.

"Desmond's not here, is he?"

"As I said, Yuri's a survivor. He wouldn't set foot on this island without an escape plan. And he wouldn't leave without Desmond and Conner. They possess Rendition and Rook, both of which he needs."

"What will they do to Desmond?"

"They'll try to help him regain his memories."

The thought terrified Peyton. "I'm going after him."

Lin turned to her daughter. "There are greater forces at work here."

"Not for me, there's not. You want the coordinates of the *Beagle*? I want Desmond back. You're going to help me. And you're going to tell me exactly what's going on."

Her mother smiled. "Now that's the young lady I raised."

CHAPTER 135

WHEN DESMOND WOKE up, Conner was sitting on the bunk across from him. He realized that he was on a ship. A submarine, he would have guessed.

Conner cocked his head, but didn't speak.

Desmond's arm and leg hair were singed. Minor burns dotted his body, but he was okay. He looked his brother in the eyes.

"You pulled me out, didn't you?"

"I did what you wouldn't do for me."

"I tried, Conner. I was five."

"I was three months."

Desmond sat silently, hoping some of the anger would drain away. "Where are we going?"

Conner smiled. The scars contorted on his face. "We're going to finish this. You're going to help us." He stood and walked to the hatch. "Get some rest. You'll need it."

☣

In the passageway, Yuri was waiting.

"Don't worry, we'll reach him. Thirteen years ago, I helped him rehabilitate you. You had lost your way, just as he has lost his. Together, we'll save him. And we'll complete the Looking Glass."

CHAPTER 136

PEYTON WAS SITTING in Avery's tiny hospital room when she awoke.

She rose and walked to the bed. "Hi."

"Hi."

For the first time since the two women had met, there wasn't an undercurrent of tension in their voices.

Peyton still felt like clearing the air. "Listen, I know you and I haven't always... seen eye to eye."

"I applaud your skill at understatement."

Peyton laughed. "Thank you." She sat on the edge of the bed. "I guess what I'm trying to say is that I want to start over."

Avery nodded, but said nothing.

"How're you feeling?"

Avery glanced at the ceiling and opened her mouth, but quickly shut it, biting off a snide remark, Peyton thought. Maybe they really were starting over. Without making eye contact, she mumbled, "I'm okay." A pause, then she stared at Peyton. "Desmond?"

"We're searching the island. Haven't found him yet."

"You won't," Avery said flatly.

"We're working on the assumption that Yuri and Conner escaped with him in custody."

"You're going to go after them."

"Yes. My mother knows the Citium—and Yuri—better than anyone alive. She's going to help me. And I'd like your help. No. I want—"

"You want us to be partners?"

"I think there's no two people in this world who will work harder to find him."

"You got that right."

"So what's it going to be, Avery?"

"Yeah. Count me in, Doc."

Peyton smiled. "Call me Peyton. There's one more thing. I need you to make a call for me."

"What kind of call?"

"An important one. We need the coordinates of the *Beagle*'s wreckage."

☣

Ten minutes later, Peyton opened the hatch to her mother's stateroom.

Lin Shaw looked up from her notebook. "Did you get it?"

Peyton placed the scrap of paper on the desk.

Lin studied the handwritten GPS coordinates as if they were an ancient treasure, thought forever lost.

"You've been looking for it for a very long time," Peyton said.

"Yes."

"Why?"

Her mother exhaled. Peyton knew the reaction well. She was digging in.

"Mom."

Lin still said nothing.

"We made a deal."

"Very well. If you want to know, I'll have to show you."

DAY 20

Final death toll: 31,000,000

CHAPTER 137

ON THE DECK of the US Coast Guard icebreaker, Peyton breathed in the cool morning air. She heard footsteps behind her, and turned to find her mother approaching.

"It's time."

Minutes later, they were in a submersible with two research assistants, drifting toward the bottom of the Arctic Ocean. The four of them donned protective suits, docked with the wreckage of the *Beagle*, and disembarked.

The dark, frigid tomb gave Peyton the creeps. There was so much history here. This was where her parents had met and fallen in love, and, according to her father's account, where her brother had been conceived.

The LED lamps on their helmets cut through the dark vessel, revealing it in swaths. Frozen, dead bodies lay on the deck. Others had died in their bunks, a book by their side, covers pulled over them.

In the labs, they found some more recently deceased bodies: members of the Rubicon team that had found the *Beagle*. They had starved. Conner had sunk the *Healy*, stranding the team here to preserve Citium secrets. Peyton wanted to know what was so valuable that it was worth taking the lives of these brave souls.

Rows of doors lined the wall of the lab. They reminded Peyton of cold chambers in a morgue, except these doors each had a small peephole that could be uncovered.

Peyton's mother moved to a safe on the wall and turned the

dial. It clicked open, and she withdrew a set of keys. She turned to the two research assistants, who had brought with them several airtight containers.

"When I place the specimens inside, seal them quickly."

They acknowledged her orders, and Lin moved to the closest door, opened it, and slid the drawer out, revealing a set of bones. They were human. No—the skull was different, and so was the pelvis.

Lin gently took hold of the skull and placed it in the first container. To the two team members, she said, "Quickly now."

When the drawer was empty, Lin closed it and used the key to open another.

More bones. Human, but not that of a *Homo sapiens*. A prehistoric ancestor, forgotten until now.

The team Lin had brought with her made trip after trip, returning with empty containers, filling them, then leaving to return the specimens to the ship waiting at the surface. Peyton watched in amazement as the chambers were emptied. She counted five different human species in total. The other chambers held other animal species: a large feline, a seal, a porpoise, and many more.

Peyton activated her comm. "Mom, what is this?"

"Let's speak when we're done. We have to preserve the samples."

When the last cold chamber was empty, Lin told the research assistants to wait at the submersible. Then she gestured for Peyton to follow.

They snaked through the dark passageways to a series of cramped offices. Lin pulled open a drawer and rifled through the files. She opened one that was scribbled with German handwriting, then began to read the pages to herself.

"Mom."

Lin looked up as if she had forgotten her daughter was still there. She seemed almost possessed.

"Whose research is this?" Peyton asked.

Lin said nothing.

"It's yours, isn't it? You collected those bones. Why?"

Lin took the folders out of the drawer and piled them on the desk. Finally, she faced Peyton. "Switch to channel seven."

When they were alone on the comm channel, Lin spoke again.

"Our Citium cell was the original. Committed to the core belief. The founding question, we called it."

"What question?"

"The question every sentient mind asks itself at one point or another: Why do I exist?"

"The answer's here on the *Beagle*?"

"Yes and no. We named the sub the *Beagle* in honor of another famous ship of the same name."

"The ship that carried Charles Darwin around the world—when he formed his early beliefs, what became the theory of evolution."

"That's right. We believed that Darwin's theory was only half of the true picture of the nature of humanity—that the full truth was even more shocking."

"And you found evidence of your theory?"

"Yes. We called our work the Extinction Files. We believed that by studying the genomes of extinct and living species, we could finally unravel the greatest secrets of the human race. What we found was... it was something none of us would ever have imagined." Lin paused, as if considering what to say next. "But we needed more data to confirm our theory."

More data, Peyton thought. "In the cordons, they took DNA samples from every patient."

"I was only told that the data would be collected, not how. Nevertheless, right now, somewhere in a Citium lab, those billions of genetic samples are being sequenced. If we can obtain that data, and combine it with the samples down here, we'll finally know the truth."

"What are you telling me, Mom?"

"There's a code—buried in the human genome. And if our theory is correct, what it leads to will change our very understanding of human existence."

EPILOGUE

In the days after the X1-Mandera pandemic ended, the South Australia Relief Alliance was inundated with refugees seeking help. Luckily, they had a new staff member.

Andrew was thankful for the work. It kept him from thinking about what had happened and what he had done. He would never forgive himself, no matter how many patients he treated, how many lives he saved. For the rest of his life, he would carry a debt that could never be repaid.

Charlotte had tried to get him to move on, but he couldn't. She insisted that time heals all wounds. He wasn't sure he believed that. But he wanted to.

He stepped into a patient room and closed the door. His prosthetic arm held a simple attachment, his other hand a clipboard with the patient's name. His own name had been something of a dilemma. Andrew Shaw was technically dead. And if anyone ever came looking, he didn't want to be found. In that sense, the remote, outback aid camp was the perfect place for him. All there was to do here was work and spend time with Charlotte. They had a lifetime to catch up on.

"Hi," he said. "My name's William Moore. I'm the attending physician today. How are you feeling?"

Avery sat in the conference room in the low-rise building in

Research Triangle Park, the same room where she had interviewed with Rubicon Ventures so many years before. The same man who had interviewed her back then, David Ward, sat across from her.

"I'm proud of you," he said.

"I'm proud of me too."

"Seriously, Avery. Listen for a second. What you did was beyond the call of duty. There's no award this nation confers that even begins to recognize the type of risk you took or the skill you displayed. What I'm trying to tell you is, I know what you did, and everyone up the Rubicon chain of command knows. And we appreciate you."

Avery fidgeted in her seat, unsure what to say. After a moment, she asked what she'd come here to ask. "My father?"

David nodded. "Was very well taken care of. We had him transferred to the Dean Dome. He's still there. I'll call and let them know you're coming."

"Thanks."

David leaned back in his chair. "Can we trust them?"

Avery knew he was asking about Peyton and Lin Shaw. She didn't know what to say. "Time will tell."

"It would be *nice* to know ahead of time."

"I don't see what option we have."

David let the chair ease forward. "Lots of people are unhappy about Lin Shaw's immunity agreement."

"I don't blame them. But they'll have to get over it. We need her."

"You're sure?"

"This isn't over. We don't know what's next. It could be worse than the pandemic. We need to start dismantling the Citium. We need somebody who's been on the inside to do that. We can sort everything else out once we've finished this."

"All right. I can live with that."

Avery stood, and David walked her out. At the door, his tone softened, "Don't worry, okay?"

"About what?"

"You know what, Avery. We're going to do everything we can to find him. Every resource we have is at your disposal. I know what Desmond means to you."

☣

At the Dean Dome, Avery weaved through the rows of makeshift cubicles. She had waited until she was well enough to pretend she wasn't in any pain. She didn't want her father to know—just in case he recognized her.

At his cubicle, she waited at the opening for him to see her. His reaction to her always told her what sort of day he was having. The Alzheimer's had progressed a lot in the last few years. Good days were becoming more and more rare.

"Can I help you?" he asked.

"No," she said quietly. "I was just coming by to visit. See if you needed anything."

He glanced around. "No. Think I'm all set." He scrutinized her face. "You look... Do I know you?"

She walked into the cubicle, scanned it, and found what she was looking for. She pulled out the folding metal chair, sat at the small table, and moved the deck of cards to the middle. "How about a game of Gin Rummy?"

He raised his eyebrows as he sat across from her. "Sure. Why not? It's my favorite game, actually."

After the second game, he asked, "So what did you do during the pandemic?"

"Oh, nothing important."

☣

Peyton sat in the car outside the stately home, waiting for the line to connect.

Millen Thomas was laughing when he answered. "Yeah, hello?" He was distracted and amused by something.

"Millen. It's Peyton Shaw."

700

She could hear him walking away, exiting a room where people were talking. "Dr. Shaw. How are you?"

"Just fine, Millen. Listen, I'm short on time, so I'll get right to it. I'm putting together a team for a new type of investigation. It's not CDC. It's a cross-sectional group. Are you interested?"

"Uh. Maybe. I don't know. What kind of investigation?"

"A scientific one. With far-reaching implications." Peyton waited, but Millen made no response. "It involves animals."

"What kind of animals?" he asked slowly.

"Extinct ones."

Peyton could hear a pin drop.

"Millen, are you there?"

"Yeah—yeah, I'm definitely here. When would you need me?"

"Tomorrow."

Silence again. He exhaled deeply. "Look, I'd like to, but there's something—there's someone I need to take care of."

Peyton smiled. "I understand, Millen. It's a good choice. A really good choice. Tell Hannah I said hi."

Peyton got out of the car and walked up to the house. When Elliott opened the door, he didn't say a word. He merely stepped outside and hugged her. Fifteen minutes later, she sat at the dinner table with Elliott, Rose, Ryan, Sam, and Adam.

Elliott looked at each one of them, then said, "Well, I thought since Thanksgiving got just a little interrupted, a do-over was in order."

He looked at Peyton. "One with *all* of our family. If this year has shown us anything, it's how much we have to be thankful for."

READY FOR BOOK TWO?

Don't miss *GENOME,*
the second book in
THE EXTINCTION FILES.

A code hidden in the human genome...
will reveal the ultimate secret of human existence.
And could hold humanity's only hope of survival.

Visit www.agriddle.com/genome for details.

AUTHOR'S NOTE

Thank you for reading.

Pandemic is the longest book I've ever written, and it was a challenge far greater than I ever expected. The complexity and amount of research for *The Extinction Files* series actually exceed the work I did for the Atlantis novels. And it occurred during the busiest time in my personal life. I began working on *Pandemic* about two and half years ago. Somewhere in between researching, drafting, and editing the novel, Anna and I moved from Florida back to North Carolina, welcomed our first child, a daughter, and finalized plans on a new home. I can't remember the last time I slept through the night. But I'll tell you, I wouldn't trade it for the world. Getting up at two a.m. to change a poopy diaper, prep a bottle, edit a chapter, unpack a box, or review a new floor plan was a fact of life while I wrote *Pandemic*. Each was a labor of love, and that kept me sane (coffee kept me awake).

I've heard from so many of you that you'd love for me to publish more frequently. I've tried to balance that request with delivering the highest quality product I can. I have mostly erred on the side of quality. I hope the wait was worth it.

If you'd like to know how much of the novel is fact vs fiction, please visit my web site: agriddle.com/pandemic.

So many of you were kind enough to write a review of my past novels, and I will be forever grateful. Those reviews helped shine a light on my work, and I've tried very hard to deserve the attention. I've also learned a great deal from those reviews, and the many words of encouragement were certainly a source of inspiration while writing this novel.

If you have time to leave a review, I would truly appreciate it. Since *Pandemic* is the first book in a new series, reviews really help other readers find the book.

Thanks again for reading and take care,

GERRY
A.G. RIDDLE

PS: Feel free to email me (ag@agriddle.com) with any feedback. Or questions. Sometimes it takes me a few days, but I answer every single email.

ACKNOWLEDGEMENTS

I had a lot of help with this one, so I've got lots of debts to pay.

Anna: thanks first and foremost for being a wonderful mother to our daughter. And for helping me weather everything life throws our way.

David Gatewood: thanks for the incredible job editing. Your suggestions made the novel so much better and your eye for detail saved me from a lynching on the internet (or at least reduced the number of lashes). Visit www.lonetrout.com to learn more about David's work.

Several early readers and subject matter experts made suggestions and provided guidance that signicantly improved *Pandemic*. They are: Sylvie Delézay, Carole Duebbert, Kathleen Harvey, Fran Mason, and Lisa Weinberg.

I am grateful to Hannah Siebern, a friend and fantastic German author, who advised me on the German language passages.

I am indebted to my fantastic group of beta readers, who caught things I never would have seen. They are: Lee Ames, Judy Angsten, Jeff Baker, Jen Bengtson, Kari Biermann, Paul Bowen, Jacob Bulicek, Robin Collins, Sue Davis, Michelle Duff, Skip Folden, Kay Forbes, Marnie Gelbart, Lisa Gulli Popkins, Mike Gullion, Aimee Hess, Justin Irick, Ajit Iyer, Kris Kelly, Karin Kostyzak, Matt Lacey, Cameron Lewis, Kelly Mahoney, Nick Mathews, Kristen Miller, Kim Myers, Amber O'Connor, Cindy Prendergast, Katie Regan, Dave Renison, Teodora Retegan, Lionel Riem, Chris Rowson, Andy Royl, John Schmiedt, Andrea

Sinclair, Christine Smith, Duane Spellecacy, Phillip Stevens, Paula Thomas, Gareth Thurston, Tom Vogel, Ron Watts, Sylvia Webb, and Lew Wuest.

I am continually inspired by the intellect and curiousity of these readers: Michael Alaniz, Shannon Barker, Roe Benjamin, Matthew Blaquiere, Emily Bristol, Tom Buckner, James Burge, Jim Burns, Sarah Cartwright, Stephania Cheng, Jim Critchfield, Dan Davis, Kevin Davis, Robert Defibaugh, Norma Fritz, Tim Gallagher, Kelley Green, Corey Guidry, Michael "mooP" Haymore, Jonathan Henson, Brandon Holt, Rodney Keith Impey, Alex Jones, Josh Kling, Louis Laeger, Mark Lalumondier, Logan Lykins, Timothy Mak, Stephen Maxwell, Carrie McNair, Steve McNaull, Henry A. Mitchell III, Elias Nasser, Najar Ramsada, Joshua Ramsdell, Gabriele Ratto, Ryan D. Reid, Ignaty Romanov-Chernigovsky, Mandie Russell Clem, Alfred Sadaka III, John Schulz, Nicolò Sgnaolin, Jack Silverstein, Vojtěch Šimonka, Antonio Sonzini, Josh Sutton, Matt Tobin, Joshlyne Villano, Maegan Washburn, Ryan White, and Raymond Yep, Jr.